To Tracy—

SEEK ME

Nyla K

BFF's 4 Lyfeee !!

Nyla K
xoxo

Copyright © 2020 Nyla K
All rights reserved.

Cover design by Jada D'Lee Designs.
Photography by FX Quadro & Eugene Partyzan.
Formatting by Evenstar Books.

Seek Me is the intellectual property of Nyla K.

Except permitted under the U.S. Copyright Act of 1976, no part of this publication may be reproduced, distributed, or transmitted in any form or by any means, or stored in a database or retrieval system without prior written permission of the author.

Paperback ISBN: 978-0-578-65002-9

This book is a work of fiction. Any references to historical events, popular culture, corporations, real people, or real places are used fictitiously. Other names, characters, places, and events are products of the author's imagination, and any resemblance to actual events or places or persons living or dead is entirely coincidental.

From the author of *The Midnight City Series* and *PUSH* **comes an all-new standalone contemporary friends-to-lovers romance that will make you laugh, cry, and swoon through this Flipping Hot Fiction!**

When she was seventeen, Alex Mackenzie fell madly in love with a white knight, who turned out to be the devil in a Versace suit.

Through years of torture, she lies awake at night dreaming of an escape. Her heart is painted black and blue, battered and barely surviving her destructive marriage.

Until one fateful night, when she meets an unlikely ally on a rooftop in Manhattan. A dark prince, glazed with ink and dripping in sin, hiding behind an easy smile and classic Ray Bans. Noah Richards has a reputation. His bedroom is a revolving door of one-night-stands, heart remaining forever off-limits... Until this twisted fairy.

Bruised and flighty, Alex captivates him, and despite his aversion to feelings, he wants more. But his fairy needs a friend, so a friend he aims to be. Brushing over wrong places and wrong times, their hearts never stop seeking solace in one another.

Happily ever after isn't usually granted to friends with benefits...

But this fairy tale has only just begun.

Foreword

Seek Me is a standalone in *The Midnight City Series,* and can be read and fully understood on its own. It is a spinoff from *TMCS*, where its characters and their story were first introduced.

To those who have read Andrew and Tessa's trilogy, get ready! There are a few parts of this book that will bring you back, with nods to the first three books, and many visits from the characters you know and love.

If you haven't read the first three books in the series, worry not! You can read *Seek Me* without any prior knowledge of the *Midnight City* world. But I will warn you, there are some spoilers to Andrew and Tessa's story in this book, so bear that in mind, should you choose to read their books after this one.

Since Seek Me spans over an almost five-year time period (even before that at times), we do get to see events from *Midnight City, Never Let Me Go,* and *Always Yours,* but from Alex and Noah's points of view. If you have read the other books, you'll recognize these scenes, but will find that it's all much different through the eyes of Alex and Noah. And if you haven't read the other books, these certain scenes may not feel as significant to you, though it's all still important to the overall arc of the story.

All I ask when reading any of my books is that you go in with an open mind, and an open heart. My novels are meant to push some boundaries and make you think. But I promise, my characters will always get the happily ever after they deserve. So get ready to laugh, cry, and swoon right along with them!

To my Mom,

Strength comes in all shapes and sizes; saviors in many forms. Sometimes the fight can last forever and a day. But no matter what, it's up to us…
To *win*.

Alex & Noah's Playlist

Dancing With A Stranger - Sam Smith & Normani
Sex On Fire - Kings of Leon
I Caught Fire - The Used
Who Do You Love - The Chainsmokers
It Ain't Me - Kygo feat. Selena Gomez
Eyes Closed - Halsey
Yellow - Coldplay
Rebel Rebel - Lena Hall
The End of Heartache - Killswitch Engage
Grind With Me - Pretty Ricky
Hey Look Ma, I Made It - Panic! At The Disco
Trampoline - SHAED
Light My Fire - The Doors
I've Been Waiting (feat. Fall Out Boy) - Lil Peep
No Sleep Till Brooklyn – Beastie Boys
Say Something - A Great Big World feat. Christina Aguilera
Break Free (Acoustic Ballad) - Sam Tsui
Basket Case - Green Day
Me vs. Maradona vs. Elvis - Brand New
Everyday (feat. Future) - Ariana Grande
Lunchbox - Marilyn Manson
Broken (feat. Amy Lee) - Seether
Someone You Loved - Lewis Capaldi
Just Like Heaven - Katie Melua
SOS (feat. Aloe Blacc) - Avicii
I Want To Know What Love Is - Foreigner
Wake Me Up When September Ends - Green Day
Ghost - Halsey
Fell In Love With A Girl - Lena Hall
All Or Nothing - O-Town
Power Trip (feat. Miguel) - J. Cole
Love Hurts - Joan Jett
Dancing On My Own - Robyn
Let Me Know - A R I Z O N A
Circles - Post Malone
All These Things That I've Done - The Killers
Everlong (Acoustic Version) - Foo Fighters
Powerful (BOXINBOX & Lionsize Remix feat. Ellie Goulding & Tarrus Riley) - Major Lazer

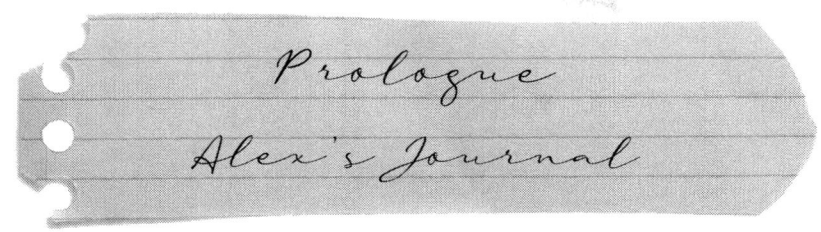

Prologue
Alex's Journal

I NEVER CARED MUCH FOR THE NUMBER THREE.

It isn't a number I consider *lucky*, nor has it held any significance in my life before.

I mean, it's a prime number, but other than that who cares?

The Holy Trinity. The Three Musketeers. Alvin, Simon and Theodore. Snap, Crackle, and Pop. The original Star Wars. Hmm... That's a good one.

Three was *never* a big deal in my world.

Until today.

Today is March 3rd, 2003. Three three oh-three.

And today I met the man of my dreams.

I know what you're thinking, Barnaby. *Alex, you're seventeen. How could you have possibly met the man of your dreams?? All the dudes you know spend their free time smoking pot out of various carved-fruits and pantsing freshmen.*

Well, you'd be right. But today, on three three three, I met a *man*.

I was at the hospital for my volunteer job. Candy-striping is barely even a thing anymore, but Mom was insistent that I spend my after-school hours doing something completely lame and ridiculous. She's convinced if I'm not constantly preoccupied with performing mundane tasks I'll turn into a drug-addict. So it was either this or walking the neighborhood dogs. And you know how I feel about dogs...

Anyway, I was at the hospital in my stupid uniform, heading down to Mr. Preston's room to read him the next couple chapters of *Misery*, when I bumped into *him*.

And I mean literally bumped into. I ran right into the guy. Smack into his chest.

He's so tall I was momentarily frightened that I had stumbled upon a secret wing of the hospital that housed giants. I'm short, as you know, but this guy is like six-four.

He steadied me with his hands on my arms as I nervously gazed up at

1

his face. Blue eyes brighter than the sky shone down at me, stealing every last breath from inside my lungs. I couldn't move or speak. I just stood there, dumbfounded, while this *man* held onto me and looked me over.

He's *really* gorgeous. Did I mention that?

Probably the most beautiful person I've ever seen in real life. Like a mixture of Justin Timberlake and Luke Wilson. His nose slightly crooked - not as bad as the other Wilson brother - but clearly from some kind of impact at one point in his life. But I like it. It gives his face character.

He smiled down at me and finally released my arms, slowly, as if his fingers didn't want to stop touching.

"That's quite the outfit, young lady," he said, grinning to reveal the straightest, whitest teeth I've ever seen. "Where are you off to in such a hurry looking like that?"

"I'm um… a candy-striper…" I murmured, struggling to find my voice. He was just so tall and hot as hell. It was very intimidating.

"Hmm… And what exactly does a *candy-striper* do?" He lifted an interested brow.

I shrugged as my cheeks burned a flush under his intense gaze. "I just help out the nurses. I was going to read to Mr. Preston downstairs… He has early onset dementia, so sometimes he gets scared. My reading seems to keep him calm."

Tall guy regarded me with an intrigued look, blinking a few times. I had no idea why he was even talking to me, but I really liked that I had his attention. I found myself craving it already, and I didn't even know him. Like if *I*, Alex Mackenzie, the shy, awkward artist girl from Bay Ridge could manage to captivate someone like *him*, it gave me purpose.

"That's very selfless, little one." His voice was deep and rough. I wasn't a huge fan of the nickname, but anything to keep him looking at me the way he was.

I chose not to tell him my mom is forcing me to do this *selfless* thing, and nodded along.

"I'm Alex," I spoke softly, reaching out to shake his hand.

"Roger." His giant hand engulfed mine and as soon as it did, sparks sprinkled across my body.

I've never felt anything like that before with a boy. I never knew I *could* feel something like that…

"Are you visiting someone here?" I asked, prying; desperate for more

Seek Me

information and more of his words.

"Yes, a patient of mine." He cocked his head to the side, regarding me with a curious look. It sent a surprising shiver below my waist.

He was a doctor. But I had never seen him there before…

So I asked, "Who's your patient?"

"Kamal James," he told me. "He sprained his ankle today at practice."

The basketball player? Everyone had been all excited, and nervous, about his presence in the hospital today. He's a pretty famous NBA star, though I wouldn't know. I'm not the biggest sports fan.

"I'm in sports medicine," Roger filled in the blanks from what must have been a confused look on my face.

"Oh…"

I really didn't know how to respond or what I was doing standing around talking to this sexy doctor. He was obviously much older than me, and I had two more hours of work to do. No good could come from continuing this conversation.

But I didn't want to leave yet…

"Well, I should probably let you get back to your duties, Miss Alex," he said, somehow reading my thoughts. "Maybe I'll see you around sometime."

He winked at me and then turned to leave.

I watched him walk away until he was out of sight, and even then, I couldn't bring myself to move. My feet were glued to the floor.

All sorts of new feelings rushed through me, and I didn't have the time to identify or obsess about them. So I forced myself to get going, and went downstairs to read to Mr. Preston.

If you're feeling like this story is anti-climactic, Barnaby, let me tell you now… It's not over.

Two hours later, my shift ended. I got changed into my regular clothes and left the hospital, walking toward the bus stop. But before I could get there, a black Mercedes pulled up right in front of me. I stopped abruptly, ready to dive out of the way in case this rich asshole was trying to run me over. And then the window rolled down.

"Need a ride, candy girl?"

It was Doctor Roger.

My jaw went slack as I considered myself. Getting into a car with this strange man was certainly not the best decision. Mom watches *Dateline* all the time, and a lot of the scary missing person episodes start just like this.

Nyla K

But then again my toes were already curling just from looking at him.

Dad often calls me reckless and too adventurous for my own good. And he's absolutely right.

"Fine, but I'm texting my mom to let her know I'm in a black Mercedes just in case you decide to abduct me," I quipped as I rounded the vehicle and hopped into the passenger side.

Roger chuckled and I internally cheered for my wittiness. And of course I didn't text Mom because what would that get me? Other than a thirty-minute lecture when I got home about how irresponsible I am.

His car was so nice and comfortable, and the interior smelled like wealth and masculinity. I felt insanely cool sitting in this fancy car with him, though I was becoming more fidgety than I could stand. I had to keep pinching my thigh to remember to keep calm.

I told Roger where I lived, which again probably wasn't the smartest of ideas. But for some reason I trusted him. He seemed like a nice guy, and he's super sexy, a factor that was certainly clouding my judgement just a tad.

"So how old are you anyway?" I blurted out, then immediately regretted being so brazen.

He chuckled some more and I swooned. "I'm thirty-one. How about you, Miss Alex?"

I had an overwhelming urge to lie, but decided there was no point and whispered, "Seventeen."

Roger's pouty lips curved into a subtle frown, drawing my attention to his mouth. He has this Cupid's bow that I just want to lick. And that rugged-looking stubble men have, a feature that only serves to remind me how little interest I have in the boys at school.

And one that prompted me to add in a hushed and eager tone, "I'll be eighteen in four months."

Roger's head tilted in my direction and the frown twisted into a devilish smirk.

Fifteen-minutes of chitchat later, and we were parked in front of my house.

"Well, this is me," I uttered stupidly. I really wish I was smoother.

"I was thinking that maybe I could call you sometime," he turned his torso toward me. He was almost too big for his own car. His presence seemed monumental compared to teeny little me. "On official business, that is. In case my patients ever need some… candy striping."

An uncontrollable smile swept over my face and I could feel my cheeks warming under the heat of his bright blue stare.

"You can get my number from the hospital," my voice crawled out of my throat. "Or you could pick me up there tomorrow. Same time?"

I was afraid to look at his face. My belly was suddenly overcome with a rampant warmth and butterflies running amuck. When I finally summoned the courage to slide my eyes up to his, he wasn't looking at me like a dumb, impulsive girl, or some timid art-nerd.

On his face, I saw the picture of a man who had somehow stumbled upon something he'd been searching for his whole life.

And in my gut, surrounded by fluttering, I felt the exact same thing.

Fate.

Roger, the thirty-one-year-old sports doctor, leaned in closer to me and hummed, "It's a date, little one."

Chapter One

Noah

I'M ON CLOUD TEN. NINE CLOUDS JUST AIN'T ENOUGH FOR TODAY.

    For the most part, happiness is a fleeting concept. When triggered, your mind often has a tendency to - unintentionally, of course - smother it pretty damn quick.

    That's why when something happens to send the endorphins bounding through our nervous systems, making up the emotion we call *happiness*, we should cherish it while we can. And that's exactly what I plan on doing tonight.

    Because I'm so freaking over the top, all-around joyous at the moment, dammit, I deserve that extra cloud.

    My boys and I just sat down at the rooftop bar at Maxwell's, my favorite local watering hole. Well, less of a *hole* and more of an infinity pool with a waterfall and dual tiki-bars.

    Maxwell's is a great place for us to grab a few for happy hour on a Monday to celebrate. Their security is tight; they don't let any Joe-Shmo in off the street. The bartenders all know me and have the uncanny ability to make my drinks appear in front of me like David Copperfield. And even more captivating are the luscious ladies that frequent the establishment.

    The girls at Maxwell's are perfect. Beautiful, low-key and available. Exactly what a guy like me is in endless market for. I think that's the main reason why I wanted to stop in here. Otherwise we could have celebrated at my place. But I'm in the mood for some soft company, and this is the absolute best place to find it.

    Since I stepped through the door, I've had many sets of wide eyes on me, which is to be expected. But the crowd is more sparse than usual, being that it's Monday and still light out. And I like it. I'd prefer to remain on the low tonight. Casual is my middle name, and while I'm happy-freaking-pappy and ready to get a little rowdy in honor of my spectacular career moves being made, I don't necessarily feel like being drooled over.

    All of that said, I plan on chasing my drink with some flirting. I have a strong desire to share my stellar spirits with a special lady tonight. Now, it's just a matter of locating her...

My head pivots to the right and I pause.

There she is.

I'm surprised I didn't see that girl when I walked in. She's a drop-dead stunner, and sitting only a few feet away from me. *Maybe she just came in?* Either way, she's mine. I already decided. Just now. *It really happens that fast.*

My assistant, Brant, slides a shot of tequila over, distracting me from the raven-haired beauty planted on the bar stool to my right. I slurp my tongue back into my mouth long enough to rip my shot and suck the lime. The booze primes my throat, and now I'm ready.

"Don't wait up," I grunt in his direction and my friends hoot.

But I'm not paying attention. I set my sights on this girl as I saunter to her, eyes traveling slowly from her studded leather boots all the way up.

A short little thing in skin-tight black jeans and a *'Burbs* t-shirt that it looks like she cut into a crop-top. I've already spotted a nose piercing and at least a dozen visible tats.

My kind of girl.

I'm now standing right next to her, but she still hasn't noticed me, and it's thrilling. Everyone else in this place has been studying my every move for each of the fifteen minutes I've been here. But not her. She's just sitting there all small and quiet, scowling at her glass of brown liquor, worrying her lower lip, the sight of which is giving my dick a beat. I lean up on the bar and wait. Let's see how long it takes her to spot her new companion.

Watching her allows me to take in some details. Her hands are dainty and I instantly observe the dried paint around her cuticles. *A painter maybe... Hmm. Interesting...*

I like artsy girls. Well, to be fair, I like *most* girls. And they like me back. But if I were to pick any one type out of the lot, it would be a sexy art freak nerd, which is one-hundred percent the vibe I'm getting from this girl, even though I haven't even spoken to her yet. For all I know, she could be a total poser. *Let's air on the side of optimism.*

I blink and keep waiting. *Man, she's really focused on whatever's in her head right now.*

Maybe she won't be into me. Or anyone, for that matter, because she looks pretty bummed. And now I've officially decided it's my new mission to make her smile. I've gotta cheer this girl up. I'm in *way* too good a headspace not to pay it forward and spread the wealth.

I'm going to rub myself off on this girl. And not in a creepy way. Well, maybe... If she lets me.

Take it one step at a time, homie.

I finally get tired of waiting and decide to make myself known, clearing my throat.

That does it. The dark-haired goddess startles and gapes up at me with wide, emerald green eyes. They're big and beautiful, surrounded by thick, dark lashes that fan over her cheeks as she blinks at my face. I'm momentarily taken aback by how good it feels to look into them. It's like a shot of dopamine.

"Hi," my voice comes out more gravelly than I expected.

"Hi..." she squeaks, but says nothing else.

She's just staring at me, and it's interesting that she isn't commenting on who I am, or asking me what I want. She's not saying anything at all, just looking at my face. But to be fair, I'm doing the exact same thing.

"How are you?" I ask, then purse my lips at myself. Do I know this girl? Have we met? *No*, we haven't. So why am I talking to her like we're old acquaintances?

"I'm... alright," she answers, and her gaze breaks away from mine as she glances gloomily back down at the drink in front of her.

Wow, we just met and she's already lying to me. I don't know how to feel about that...

"That's a load of bullshit," I grin, taking a seat next to her, putting our faces level. Well, *almost*, since she's much smaller than me. She quirks an eyebrow. "You're over here sulking. Something must be wrong."

"I don't know..." she mumbles, giving me a guilty look. She's already the most complex person I know and we've said basically nothing to each other. "I should be happy. I just booked the space across the street for an art exhibit."

"You're an artist?" *I knew it.*

"Yea. Painter, mostly," she nods. "I have a collection I'm debuting in a few weeks. It'll be my first one..."

"So... then why do you look like you're here to drown your sorrows?" I invite, picking up the glass the bartender just sat in front of me.

"It's complicated," she mutters, then takes a big gulp to kill her drink.

"I love complicated stuff," I flick my hand and the same bartender pours her another round. Scotch. I won't acknowledge my intrigue. "Remember K'nex? That was like my favorite thing when I was a kid."

She giggles and her face lights right up. It's fascinating. She has a wonderful complexion; skin dark golden like wildflower honey, and some freckles dusting her cheeks, which are now subtly flushing. I like it, a *lot*.

Seek Me

I raise my drink and she lifts hers.

"To a great day for both of our crafts." We clink and sip.

"What's your craft?" Her head tilts to the side while she gives me her undivided attention. It pleases me so much more than when other people pretend to pay attention to my answers, like in interviews, or when fake assholes mock giving a shit about what I have to say.

Must be her eyes. They're very inquisitive.

"I'm an actor," I tell her, settling into my seat. "I just signed a new job today on a potential series. Pilot season that could lead to a contract."

Her lips curve into a smile, and I'm drawn in hungrily to how good her mouth looks. Full, naturally pink lips that almost take the shape of a heart when pressed together. I tighten my fist around my glass to stop my train of thought before my dick can respond. Besides, I've already achieved my goal of making her smile, and we've been talking for five seconds. *Mission accomplished.*

"Wow! Congratulations!" She chirps with animation. "That's amazing!"

I chuckle and bite my lip. This is getting a little ridiculous.

I'm a bachelor. Flirting is my side-game, and I bed more girls than a Tempurpedic store. *How* is this chick siphoning my edge when I don't even know her name?

"I'm sorry, but I'm really trying to put a name to your face," she cringes, shooting me a timid look that sends a tremor through a certain organ that's not supposed to be getting involved right now. "I know I've seen you in stuff before, but…"

"Oh my God, please," I lift my hands and laugh. "I don't expect everyone to know who I am."

It's the truth. I've been a professional, working actor since my twenties, but I don't play lead roles. I stay in my lane as a supporting actor because it's what I'm good at, and I'm more than fine with it. I've been nominated for awards before, I have fan pages dedicated to me on Facebook and I make enough money to fill massive spaces with it and swim around, a la Scrooge McDuck. I'm more than happy with my acting career, and I don't need the validation of everyone I meet recognizing me to feel successful.

"Well, I'll spare you the awkwardness of pretending you don't know who *I* am," she teases and extends her hand. "I'm Alexandra Mackenzie. But non-fanboys call me Alex."

I laugh out loud. *Cute, witty, sexy… Really feelin it.*

"It's an honor to finally meet you, *Alexandra*," I smirk and she giggles while we shake hands. Hers are surprisingly warm, and my heart raps a few significant times. "Noah Richards."

"So, Noah Richards... What is this part we're celebrating?" A look of pleased contentment settles on her face, accentuating how truly gorgeous she is.

Her features are exquisitely symmetrical. Pointed slope of a nose between those round, brilliant green eyes; high cheekbones, perfect mouth and jaw... Even her chin is somehow cute. If I was a total loser, I would ask if she's ever modeled before. I mean sure, she's short, but that face... It's the kind of inspiration artists like herself search for their whole lives.

I zone back in on the conversation. "It's freaking amazing. The role of a lifetime. I can't tell you all the details, but basically it's an apocalypse survivor drama, and I'll be supporting the lead... Let's just say you definitely know this guy. If all goes along schedule, I'll meet him soon. Hopefully he's not a total dickwad. He's British, so you never know." We both laugh.

I'm surprised at how much I enjoy talking to this girl. She's easy to converse with. *And even easier on the eyes.*

"Well, I'm sure you'll rock it," she flips her hair, and I can't help but grin wide as we clink glasses again.

The next thing I know, two hours have gone by, and we've killed a whole bunch more drinks.

In short, Alex Mackenzie is my new favorite person.

She's smart and funny, and is exactly the artsy nerd I guessed she was when I started staring at her.

And clearly she's vibing on me, too.

I don't want to get my hopes up for anything, but she's already touched my leg a few times, and I'm more than pleased that the sullen, sad girl I noticed earlier is long gone. She's been laughing and smiling up a blizzard, telling me all about her art, her interests and how excited she is to finally exhibit her work at a real, apparently *hip* gallery.

She's also been asking a lot of questions about me, but not obnoxious stuff. She's as interested in my career as I'd want her to be, but she seems more amped to hear about my favorite music and recent shows I've gone to. We have the exact same taste in music, which is usually a make-or-break for whether I can stand to be in a girl's presence, when talking is involved, that is.

Now we're comparing tattoos. She's showing me her identical lilies on her wrists, and I've slipped my arm inside my shirt so I can show her the shoulder piece I finished last week.

Seek Me

"Oh my God!" She gasps, trailing her finger along the muscles in my blade. It leaves electric tingles in its wake, which is startling, though it feels too good for me to panic over. "This is the Mad Hatter?"

I nod, keeping quiet while she touches me gently. I shift subtly in an attempt to keep the movement below my waist in check. Those soft little caresses from her fingers are winding me up for reasons I really can't fathom.

"This is incredible, Noah." Her voice is melodious; sweet and slightly raspy. And did I mention awfully close to my ear...

I swallow hard. *Maybe I've had too much to drink...*

But I'm not drunk. I'm more buzzed on *her*.

"Wanna go dancing?" I blurt out, and she glances at me, appearing mildly shocked by my sudden invitation. "I mean, Sensay is pretty cool. The music is decent..."

I don't understand why this is all falling from my mouth, but it seems based on a deep craving I have to go somewhere darker, where maybe I can return the favor and touch her a little... To my dismay, she looks like she's waging an internal war. Her face is even more flushed now, possibly from all the drinks. But she's gawking at me like I'm insane. I hope I didn't scare her off...

Oh fuck... Maybe she has a boyfriend. Shit... I didn't even think of that.

But surely she would have mentioned something... We've been flirting for hours.

"Um... I don't know if I should..." She chews on her lip. "I didn't really plan on staying out late..."

"It's not late at all," I grin, giving her my signature *bad influence* look I've perfected over the years. "Come on, Alex. Let's go have some fun. Celebrate our world domination."

An uncontrollable smile overtakes her mouth, and she nods slowly. "Okay... We can go dance. Just a little."

"Little dancing," I bob my head in agreement. "No Swayze moves, I promise."

She cackles out loud and I have to bite my lip to keep my enthrall under wraps. I enjoy making her laugh *way* more than I should at this juncture.

I grab her by the hand and we leave, nodding a brief goodbye at my assistant and my friends who are still gathered around the bar, chatting up another group of acquaintances.

My driver, Jimmy, is waiting outside at the curb. I open the door to his Navigator for Alex, sneaking a peek at her butt while she hops in. For a small, relatively petite girl, she definitely has a nice perky ass going on. I haven't really been able to peep her tit situation yet, because her crop-tee is sort of baggy, but I'm internally desperate to find out what she looks like naked.

Though if I'm being honest, I don't really get the one-night-stand vibe from Alex. She's a very cool girl, and as much as I'm itching for her body pressed up against mine, I've enjoyed talking to her more than I have with any other girl in as long as I can remember. She fun, interesting, quirky and wildly alluring. The ultimate combo.

I'm having a great time, let's just leave it at that for now.

Once I'm settled in the backseat adjacent to Alex, I tell Jimmy to bring us to Sensay, the club near my place, and he speeds off into the night, cruising the Manhattan streets toward our destination.

I peek at Alex. She doesn't look wasted or anything which is a relief, but she's gone quiet on me, staring vacantly out the window. I make a snap decision to reach out and hold her hand, but she flinches, which has me pulling back. *Shit. I shouldn't have done that. Hands to yourself, Richards.*

"Sorry..." she whispers with an awkward chuckle. "You scared me."

She slides her hand back to mine and touches me, hesitant, as if she's testing the waters.

"I don't want to scare you..." I hum, tracing the flower on her wrist with my thumb.

"You don't," she jumps in, reassuringly, though her eyes are wide.

I don't know what to think about this girl. She seems a little flighty. It's probably not a good idea to get my hopes up for anything, since she clearly has something going on...

But I wouldn't be able to end the night yet if I tried.

"We don't have to go out if you don't want to," I mutter, contradicting my own desires to give her an out. If it's what *she* wants... "I can bring you home right now."

Alex regards me with a look of awe, then takes a visibly deep breath. "Noah, I'm having fun with you. I want to go out. I haven't been dancing in as long as I can remember." She smiles, showing me her straight, pearly white teeth.

I can't ignore the bubbling excitement popping inside me like Pop Rocks. Her fingers slide through mine as she stares down at our hands. It's like she's examining mine and I'm not sure why, but I like it.

Ten minutes later, we arrive at Sensay. Jimmy gets the doors for us, and we walk to the entrance, separate but close, assessing our surroundings. I'm glad it's Monday, and getting cooler out, because in the summer this place is always

Seek Me

jam-packed, even more so on weekends. Tonight is pretty mellow, which I have to appreciate. Alex seems like she might startle easy, and I don't need paparazzi snapping pictures of us, or fans approaching when I'm just trying to get closer to her without accidentally crossing some line and frightening her away.

Inside I buy us drinks at the bar. We both sip Macallan on the rocks as the loud music thumps around us, enveloping our bodies in a pocket of pop-dubstep mixes. We wander the perimeter of the club until we find a slightly secluded area, where we kill our drinks while staring at each other.

It's a little too loud to talk when we're this far apart, but I'm alright with it because I'm not exactly sure what I would say right now, anyway. An overwhelming urge ripples through my limbs, a strong want to get next to her... To close the gap. Despite how unexpected it is, I'm captivated by this gorgeous, enigmatic little woman. Just being near her is making me several degrees warmer than usual.

She sets her glass down on a nearby table and steps up to my front, and I'm momentarily frozen in bemused anticipation. My breath shallows as her hand runs up my arm, and now I can do nothing more than follow her lead, dropping off my glass and reaching for her waist. I move slow and easy, so as not to scare her off as she gazes up at me, watching my face closely, for what I'm not sure.

Then she glides both hands up my frame, touching my chest and shoulders before draping her arms around my neck. I pull her flush against me by her hips and she gasps, then giggles; a quiet vibration that gives me chills. I grin down at her gorgeous face, holding onto her tight.

And we start to dance.

I'm not a big dancer, but I have to say I'm *obsessed* with the feeling of her tits on my chest, squishing into me while we grind our bodies together slow and steady. The rhythm of the music is quixotic, the bass beating through the speakers mirroring the drumming of my heart; hard, out of me and into Alex.

The way her small body fits with my much bigger one is encouraging. I have a full head on her, so it's even more of a move when I lean down to tuck my face into the crook of her neck. I inhale her scent and I'm already coming undone, which is just so bizarre I don't know what to make of it. She smells incredible, like strawberries and vanilla and gardenia. *God*, I'm dying here.

She writhes against me, her fingernails tenderly scratching the nape of my neck, in my hair. I couldn't help the groan that escapes me if I tried, my breath hot on her warmed skin. I feel her shudder, and my hand slips onto the top of her ass.

This is *too* good. I'm already sporting a semi, and it's active *work* trying not to let myself fully harden. I get the inexplicable sense that our bodies were made to be pressed together like this, which is alarming. I've never experienced this before with someone I just met, and I do this with lots of girls, a fact that now has me feeling guilty for some reason.

I never feel guilty.

What is happening to me?

Where did this girl come from??

"Noah..." she breathes my name onto my clavicle and even that sends a rush of blood straight to my cock.

I can't help myself. My hips push forward to rub it on her. Just a little... I'm not trying to be a huge creep but, *my God*, this friction feels better than all the dry-hump sessions of my teenage years.

At this point, we're practically fucking through our clothes on the dance floor of a not-so-crowded club. Her thighs part just enough to let me in between and I'm aching; straining against my jeans that shield my erection just enough for me not to look like a fucking psycho. But I'm definitely hard. She can absolutely feel it. And she *absolutely* likes it.

No. Nope, I'm done. I'm kissing her, like now.

I tear myself away from her neck which I may or may not have kissing a bit, and move my face in front of hers. We lock eyes for moment and I'm trapped; held hostage by those effervescent green irises. In the low light I can see specks of gold in them, like sunshine on a field of clovers.

My heart is jumping against my ribs as I watch, ensnared, while she licks her lips.

"Alex..." I pant her name, so close the ends of our noses are touching. "I want... *Fuck*, you feel good like this..."

I have no idea what I'm saying. I don't know why I'm talking at all right now, but I just have some mystifying need to voice to her what's happening inside me. Because it feels foreign. And insanely good.

She whimpers, squirming in seemingly similar frustrations, her curious fingers grazing all over my neck, shoulders, jaw, chest... Her touch ignites a fire of need inside me.

What is this feeling?

"I..." Her voice trails off into a little gasp when I think she feels my cock throbbing against her exposed stomach.

"You're driving me crazy..." I growl, pawing at her butt, squeezing gently and pulling her harder. "God, you're so sexy." She purrs by my mouth and I can already taste her; like scotch and honey.

"Noah…" she moans on my lips, and my dick pulses.

"Mmm… I love how you say my name." Bodies, moving; slow and deep.

I *need* her in my bed tonight. I need her legs wrapped around my waist. I need to feel her warmth coating me while she scratches my back and says my fucking name the way she keeps saying it. I'm so wound up for this girl, lost in a haze of lust and hopeful fantasies.

"No, I… uh, I have to tell you something…" Her voice is meek and nervous.

Am I coming on too strong?

No way. I can feel her nipples on my chest through separate layers of clothing. She wants me, I know it.

"Please don't tell me *anything* unless it's that you're coming home with me," I tell her, salivating over her sweet, soft, shivering pink lips. Like two delicious pieces of candy, waiting for me to devour them.

Alex shakes her head subtly and I gaze down at her face, observing something uncertain flash in her eyes.

I run my fingers through her silky hair. "What's wrong, beautiful? Am I moving too fast?"

My tone is nothing but sympathetic and gentle. I barely even recognize myself, and it's worrying. This girl has me wrapped around her slender little finger, and I'm suddenly uneasy, as she also seems to be. She's obviously overthinking something.

"No. Well, I mean, not really…" she huffs, blinking those wide eyes at me.

"You can tell me anything, Alex," I assure her.

She freezes. We're no longer humping, but we're still melded together, unable to let go as I take a deep breath and wait.

"I'm married."

The words fall out of her mouth like a bomb, exploding all the way down to the floor.

I'm stunned still. My face inches back as I stare, fully bewildered and ill-equipped to respond.

She's married.

That's a hard limit for me. As much as I tend to sleep around with all sorts of women, I draw the line at married chicks. I don't want that kind of involvement. But my first gut reaction is to feel crushed. Disappointed and, wait for it… Jealous. Another thing I *never* feel.

So why on Earth am I feeling it now for this girl I just met, and the fact that she has a husband?

She has a fucking husband…? Really?? Who? Why? I don't get it.

"Jesus," I grunt, squeezing my eyes shut tight while I process this. "You weren't wearing a ring…"

"I'm sorry," Alex squeaks, and my eyes spring open to catch the look of remorse covering her perfectly lovely face. Her eyes shine up at mine with guilt swimming the edges. *Well, I don't want her to feel bad…*

"No, *I'm* sorry," I shake my head. "You must be dealing with something… rough and I sort of just… maneuvered myself into your situation…"

"Noah, you did not," she says. "You're so sweet and charming, and of course I wanted to hang out with you but…"

"You're married."

We're no longer tangled and I briefly register how much colder I am without the warmth of her hot body draped around me.

Her hot married body…

Fuck. What the hell, man?!

I'm super bummed. I really like her. This blows.

"This is so embarrassing." Her brows push together and she steps back. "I'm sorry I wasted your time…"

Before I can process what's happening, she's turned and is darting off, toward the back door.

What the fuck…? Don't let her go.

So I sprint after her, dodging and weaving through people to catch up. She's running away from me. And I'm chasing her.

This is not at all how I thought tonight would go.

Alex pushes open the door to the rear of the club and jumps outside into the alley. Stammering up to the back of her, I grab her arm and she winces, so I immediately let go. *Shit, I didn't grab her hard, did I?*

"Whoa, whoa. What are you doing?" I gasp, stepping in front of her. "Where are you going?"

"Noah, let me go…"

"Alex, it's okay. I'm sorry, I didn't mean to come off judgy. Your marriage is your business -"

"That's not what this is about!" She shouts, her nostrils flaring as she glares at me with hardened eyes.

I gulp. "Okay. I'm sorry. Look, I don't care that you're married. I still want

to hang out with you." *What the hell am I saying right now?* "We can be friends."
Friends? Have you lost your mind?? Since when are you friends with married girls?!

"Friends?" She scoffs, crossing her arms over her chest, embodying my internal thought process. "Really?"

"It's not my usual MO, I'll be honest," I grin. "But I like you."

"Exactly why we can't be friends."

"Are you saying you like me too?" I dip my head to catch a smile she's clearly trying to cover up.

"Noah," she scolds me with her eyes and I can't help but smirk.

How come when she says my name it feels familiar? Like we've known each other for years?

"You want to get something to eat?" I ask, hoping a subject change will keep her from bolting for a little while longer. I can't put my finger on why, but leaving her in this moment doesn't feel right.

She sighs and shrugs. "Sure."

My dread retreats, and I breathe out slowly with relief. This girl seems so easy to please, which fascinates me because she looks like such a badass. But she obviously has something going on… Some insecurities, demons, or something causing her wayward behavior. *And she's married…*

But rather than heading for the hills, I find myself wondering all about her. *What does she like? What has she seen?*

Who is this dipshit husband who lets a masterpiece like her out of his sight?

I smile and take her by the arm, catching another pained wince. Puzzled by all her recoiling, I glance down at her bicep and that's when I see them…

The bruises.

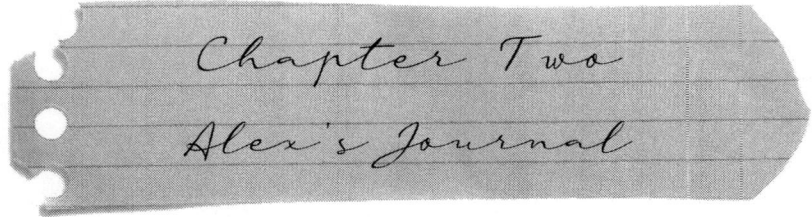

Chapter Two
Alex's Journal

LET ME START OUT BY APOLOGIZING, BARNABY.

I know I used to write in you almost every day, and now it's been six months. I'm really sorry... But I've been busy as hell!

Busy being in love.

Busy being a new wife.

Yes, that's right, Barn. You heard it here first. Your little Al got hitched!

Let's take it from the top.

So I told you about how I met the man of my dreams, right? Well Dr. Roger Glines is all that and then some.

True to his promise, he took me out after that first day. And we started seeing each other.

I know what you're thinking... A thirty-one-year-old doctor dating a seventeen-year-old high school student isn't normal. Well guess what? I don't care about being normal. I don't care about anything other than the fact that I met my soulmate and I'm so in love with him it sometimes hurts my heart. I actually get palpitations in my chest thinking about him, that's how deep I'm in it.

Roger and I snuck around for four months until my eighteenth birthday. I didn't tell anyone about him. Not my parents, not my friends. It was sort of isolating I guess, but I really didn't care. I didn't need anyone else because I had Roger. And he was perfect. He *is*.

Shortly after my birthday, and graduation, Roger started hinting that I should tell my parents about us. I wasn't sure why he was suddenly harping on it. I told him I've never had a good relationship with them. That they just don't get me, and they probably never will. But he was still insistent, and I was curious.

Well, that curiosity got killed real quick when we were taking a walk around his neighborhood one night (he lives on the Upper East Side in a *ginormous* coop. Seriously, his place is so big and fancy I wouldn't dare touch anything, even though he keeps assuring me I can touch whatever I want.)

Seek Me

But back to the walk. We were strolling around after dinner when he pulled me into him and gave me one of his staggering kisses. The ones that leave me so breathless I feel the need to reach for an inhaler I don't have. Then when he was done tonguing me down good, he dropped onto one knee and took out a massive diamond ring.

Yes, a ring. No, I'm not lying.

He proposed. Proposed frickin *marriage*!

I was so stunned I couldn't function. I began shaking violently and crying like such a girl. It was the first time I'd ever cried in front of him, which would have been super embarrassing if he weren't laughing that soft, adorable chuckle.

And finally when I got it together enough to speak, I said yes.

I said yes because even though in my mind I knew it was fast, in my *heart* I knew I loved him.

I know he's my soulmate, and my forever. I trust him, and I can see a life with him. A future.

So I said *yes*, and he slipped the ring on my finger, and we were engaged.

For all of two weeks.

After twelve days of engagement, neither of us could wait anymore. We were both just too excited, and we wanted to tie ourselves to one another for eternity.

So he flew us to Vegas and we got married.

I did it, Barnaby. I got married in Vegas! Remember how I told you I always wanted to? Well, I did.

It was so much fun. We held the quick ceremony at the Little Chapel, and spent the rest of our four-day trip in the honeymoon suite at the Bellagio. And I don't mean that as a teasing newlywed joke. We literally didn't leave the bedroom for days. I think the hotel staff was getting nervous.

But it was the best time of my entire life, Barn. My husband is so damn sexy, I can't get enough.

I know I don't have all that much experience to compare him with. But as you'll recall, losing my virginity to Billy Hunters was two-minutes of my life I'll never get back, and the four times that Keith and I did it weren't much better. It was to be expected with *boys* like that. Selfish, immature high school boys don't know what they're doing. They don't know how to treat a lady, and they most certainly don't know how to give one an orgasm.

But Roger - my *husband*, cue the girly squeal - is like a professor. He's taught me things about my body that I never would have learned with those twerps. He knows exactly where my clit is, doesn't need help finding my G-spot, and at one point, he made me come so hard I had actual tears coming out of my eyes. His tongue works wonders, and his dick... Well, let's just say my first time meeting it was significantly more painful than it was with Billy and Keith. But I didn't mind. The pain was welcomed, maybe even appreciated. It made me feel *alive*.

I never used to feel alive. Not before Roger.

When we got home, I prepared myself to talk to Mom and Dad. I was going to tell them about Roger, about the wedding, and let them down easy about me not going to college. Over the course of our whirlwind romance, I decided not to go to SUNY. I was never excited about it anyway, and I just couldn't stand the thought of being away from my man.

I'm an artist. I want to paint and draw, and take photographs for a living. I don't need some silly degree to do that. Mom and Dad never understood these things.

But they would get it, because I would finally break it down in a way that they could hopefully accept.

To say that it didn't go well would be more of an understatement than saying Superman is only *meh* about Kryptonite.

Here's the rundown of the convo with the parental units. Or should I say, *former* parental units. Yes, it was *that* bad.

"So I'm in love, and we're married, and I'm moving into his place on the Upper East Side where I'll spend my days painting and living and loving, so you don't need to be scared, or upset or angry, because I'm happy. And as my parents, you should want me to be happy... right?"

I held my breath, praying that they could find it in their hearts to accept what I was saying, and finally support me for the first time in eighteen years with more than food and a roof over my head.

The silence in the room was suffocating.

Dad spoke first. "I always knew she'd pull some bullshit like this."

"She got it from you, Dan!" Mom shrieked. "You're the starving artist who set the bar so low, she had nowhere to go but down." She covered her face with a shaky hand.

"Mom, I'm not -"

"Alexandra, we wanted a better life for you!" Dad shouted at me. "That's why we wanted you to go to college and get a decent education. So you could make a real career for yourself and learn from our mistakes!"

"I don't want a *career!*" I shouted, flinging my hands up. "I don't want to be

Seek Me

like every normal, nine-to-five shmuck out there! I want to live and breathe art."

Mom scoffed, shooting Dad an evil look.

"Alex, following a career in the arts is virtually impossible," Dad went on, glaring at me like the errant child they always thought I was. "You'll never make enough money to support yourself."

"Well, she doesn't need to support herself, Dan. She's already found a Sugar Daddy! Jesus Christ, I'm going to be sick."

"Roger is not like that!" I cried. "He's a good man! And he loves me."

"He doesn't love you, Alex," Dad grunted. "He's thirteen years older than you. He's a rich creep, and he'll eventually get bored and leave you to fend for yourself. And then what will you have? Nothing."

I gulped down the pain and hurt filling my throat like bile. Their words were like daggers, cutting me all over my trembling body.

"So you don't think I'm talented enough to make something of myself?" I seethed, directly at my father. He was such a fucking hypocrite I was sick to my stomach. "*You* don't love art down to your marrow?"

He momentarily faltered. His face flashed with the slightest remorse and shame, burying it only seconds later in a mask of anger and disgust.

"It won't work out, Alex. And when it doesn't, you will not crawl back to us." My father stared into my eyes, and not once did he plead with me to reconsider, or tell me he loved me and that he was worried. Instead, he gave me a weak excuse and an ultimatum. "You have to choose right now. Him, or us."

And without a single hesitation, I stood up, went to my room, and began packing.

I packed all my Earthly belongings that meant anything to me and waited outside on the curb for Roger. When he got there, I collapsed into him, inhaling his sweet scent and using it like a Band-Aid for my bruised and scraped up heart.

My parents came out of the house, and I took my things to the car. I had no desire to hear any more of their negativity. If they wanted to let me go, they would get their wish.

I didn't need them, anyway. I never had.

I sat in the passenger's seat, watching as Mom and Dad talked to Roger. They weren't doing anything of significance, but I was still just the tiniest bit curious. After a couple minutes, they turned and went back inside. And Roger got into the car with me.

And that was it.

As he drove us home, to my new home, with my husband, I began to

Nyla K

silently fume.

What kinds of parents could just write their only child off like that? What kinds of people could disown a child just for wanting to live her own life? Technically, I'm not a *child* at all. I'm eighteen-years-old. I have every right to live my life how I see fit, especially if I'm not under their roof or expecting them to pay for anything.

All I ever asked was for them to love and trust me. And they couldn't do either. I was so shaken I felt numb inside.

"What did they say to you?" I finally spat out, peering at Roger to my left. "My parents…"

He was quiet for a moment, just staring ahead at the FDR. Finally he took a breath and released it quickly.

"They just told me you're my responsibility now," he shrugged. "And that they don't think very highly of me, not that I really fucking care about that."

His tone of voice was very blasé and unaffected. For some reason it rubbed me wrong. Of course he didn't need to worry about what my parents thought of him. They didn't even *know* him. I certainly didn't care.

I guess I just thought maybe he'd feel a little more sympathetic to his wife, and the fact that she'd just chose him over her own flesh and blood. But he really seemed like he didn't care about anything that had just happened.

An uncomfortable feeling began crawling inside me, urging me in some way I couldn't understand. But I chose to ignore it. I was just upset about the drama of the day.

You know me, Barn. I've always been independent. There was nothing that Dan or Cara Mackenzie could give me that they hadn't already. Food and clothing and a bed to sleep in. They loved me because they had to, because I was *theirs*, but they never showed me any affection. Dad is a bitter artist who was never dedicated enough to make anything of himself, and Mom is an ex-junkie who never wanted kids. They were a match made in parental hell, and I was just the unfortunate burden.

Well, no more. I'm done feeling sorry for them. I taught myself how to be an adult when they didn't. I learned every single thing I know about the world on my own, and I'll keep learning.

Accept that I no longer need to feel alone, because I have Roger. And he's my world.

I reached over the console and ran my fingers up his shoulder, rubbing him in a comforting way. Letting him know that it's just us against the world, and

Seek Me

I'm fine with that. We're like Bonnie and Clyde, only without the misery and the painful ending. Ours will be happy, I just know it.

He turned his head and gave me a small smile which I returned. I loved being the one to make him smile. And I know I'll keep loving it until the end of time.

"I can't wait to get you home," he crooned. And I swooned.

He's all I need.

Chapter Three
Alex

This is sufficiently awkward. But believe it or not, it isn't because we were dry-humping each other in public five minutes ago.

I saw Noah looking at the bruises on my arm.

I knew I shouldn't have worn a t-shirt today.

Hiding my shame slipped my mind tonight, merely because I didn't think I would be hanging out with someone. I never hang out with anyone.

I hadn't even planned on stopping for a drink, but I was just so excited about how everything went at the gallery, I figured I'd earned a scotch. Little did I know, the universe had some hilarious plans, and now I'm having a seat in a booth at a quaint diner with *Noah Richards*.

And he's looking at me like he wants to ask a million and five questions, none of which he'll ask, because we barely know each other.

Even though... dry-humping. *Yea, that happened.*

I still can't fathom it.

I can't believe I spent all evening getting faced with Noah Richards, and we almost started hooking up in public. Jesus, that was idiotic. Imagine if someone there recognized me and told Roger... Holy moron, Bat Girl.

I'm such a fucking dumbass.

But I mean, it did feel *amazingly* good to dance with him like that...

He's just so drop-dead, stone-cold beautiful, it's almost hard to believe he's a real human person.

Of course I've seen Noah Richards in movies and TV shows before. Everyone knows his face, even if he's not necessarily an A-list actor. He's a well-known dude, especially in NYC.

And he just so happens to be a bazillion times hotter in real life. That was part of the reason I didn't recognize him. On the screen for some reason he doesn't look as tall. He's at least six-feet, maybe more. And his hair is a bit lighter, his eyes much more brilliant.

And his body... Well. Let's just say having him pressed up against me,

Seek Me

grinding with that tall, muscular frame, was satisfying on a level I can barely understand. I almost had an orgasm just from dancing and rubbing into his boner. And I think he was kissing my neck a little… I can still feel his lips there as I hesitantly trace the scorches he left on my skin with my fingertips.

It's now midnight, but my body is wired from all the excitement. And I *am* starving.

"What would you like to eat?" Noah asks, flipping his menu pages back and forth, though he's not looking at them. His eyes are stuck on me. "Order whatever you want."

"Thanks…" I murmur, feeling very unsure of myself.

I'm sitting here with a guy I barely know; a guy who also happens to be rich and famous, and who I was two hot seconds away from climbing like a sexy tree a few minutes ago. And he's asking me what diner food I want to eat, aiming that gorgeous, celebrity face directly at me.

"The waffles are good here," he chirps, his pillowed lips curled into that easy smirk he wears so much. I'm secretly obsessed with how he always seems to be smiling. I'm over guys who scowl all the livelong day.

"I like waffles," I tell him with a small smile, because his is contagious. I don't think I've smiled as much in *years* as I have tonight, being with him.

He nods, apparently pleased with my acceptance of his suggestion, then flags the waiter and orders waffles for both of us. I nestle into the booth and keep my arms tucked securely under the table. He's watching me again, and his forehead creases.

I can tell he's thinking about the bruises. It's a look I'm slightly familiar with at this point. People always look at my bruises like that, especially when they're on my face, though I try not to go out as much if that's the case.

But why would Noah need to think my bruises are from anything bad? Maybe I just bumped into something. I am sort of clumsy sometimes. And he doesn't know me. It's fully plausible that I was doing something normal to bruise my arms. No one should be jumping to any conclusions…

Or it could be a vibe I'm giving off. I'm not the best at hiding stuff, and I've had to get good at it, which I don't enjoy. I know I must look like a downtrodden little lump of emotions, but I just can't help it.

I hate my life.

Accept right now, because I'm sitting with the coolest guy I've ever met, and his dark eyes are locked on *me*. This is the best feeling I've had in a while… And I want to hang onto it for dear life. I want to grab it and smother it and absorb everything it has to give until I'm replete.

God, I'm so messed up.

Don't get used to having him around, Alex.

"So, how long have you been married?" Noah asks, rubbing his hands together.

He seems uneasy. I can't say that I blame him. He probably thought he would get laid tonight, before I dropped the *husband* bomb. And because he seems to have manners, he offered to hang out with me so I didn't feel like the dick-tease I so obviously am.

I almost wish I *had* asked him to take me home…

"A little over seven years…" I tell him honestly because lying seems like so much work, and I'm already mentally exhausted.

He makes a face I can't read, and I witness his Adam's apple bob in his throat, sheeted in sexy stubble that makes my insides shiver.

"Wow…" he breathes. The tension surrounding us is palpable. "Long time…"

I really have no desire to talk about my marriage or my husband right now, especially with Noah Richards, of all people. Quite frankly, it's unnecessary. There's no way we'll ever see or speak to each other again after tonight, so what's the point in bringing up all this marital nonsense?

I nod slowly, my eyes locking on my silverware. If I'm going to say anything else, I should do it now, and change the subject before he can continue with this line of questioning.

"So when are you going to meet your new costar?" I peer up at him, unable to help the vulnerable look that's likely possessing my face. It's abundantly clear that I'm attempting to redirect the conversation off of me and my problems.

Noah's quiet for a beat while continuing to watch me. All I can see right now are his eyes, and how shockingly dark they are. They must be brown, but they look almost black, like coal or obsidian. It's mesmerizing. I've never seen irises that deep. I wonder how many secrets they hold…

"Well, we just signed the contracts for the pilot, so probably not for a few weeks," he answers my question, his face instantly sweeping into the excitement he was wearing earlier at the bar when he was telling me about his good news.

Obviously he's ecstatic about this job. For hours he's been bouncing around, giddy every time he mentions it. It's pretty adorable to witness, and to my own surprise, I'm oozing pride for him and his accomplishments, a strange way to feel for someone you barely know. I can just tell he's happy and uber-dedicated to his craft. It's a very endearing quality, something he seems to have a lot of.

"I just have a feeling this job is going to change my life, you know?" His head tilts to the right. "I mean, I've played some pretty awesome parts, but this one sounds like a dream come true. And the producers asked for me, which is always flattering."

I smile wide. "That's sick."

"Right?" He chuckles. "I totally nailed the audition though. Just saying."

I laugh out loud, which makes him beam. He's so freaking cute. *Honestly...*

The waiter drops off two plates of waffles and we eat and talk. Noah was right, the waffles are fantastic. Fluffy with just the right amount of crispiness on the outside. I slather mine in butter and drench them in syrup, which has Noah chuckling at me.

"Sweet tooth," he murmurs, forking waffle into his mouth. Even *that* is sexy when he does it.

His mouth is very alluring, with lips that are curved and temptingly full, a contrast to how sharp and angled the lines of his face are. I've just decided his mouth is my favorite part of him, paired with the adorable things that come out of it.

"That's an accurate assessment," I quip, then groan out loud over the exploding flavors on my tongue. Sweet mapley goodness and probably too much butter. I can't remember the last time I had waffles, which sucks because I love them. Especially now, being enjoyed in the company of this even sweeter man.

Noah laughs softly at watching me enjoy my food, and I peek up at him, wondering if he's just being nice to me because he knows we'll never see each other again. I don't know much about Noah Richards: *celebrity*. But from what I've seen in the occasional blog post or gossip article, he's a chronic bachelor. A womanizer extraordinaire, just like his Hollywood brethren. They're all the same, after all.

And as charming and kind as Noah Richards seems, the fact of the matter is that there's no way he hangs out with women as *friends*. He beds them, fucks them - probably really well - and then sends them on their merry way.

Well, that's not what's happening here. *So again, don't get used to him.*

I pout to myself because I'm not ready to give him back yet.

"I have a question..." he asks, and my stomach instinctively tightens.

"I hate questions," I grumble which just makes him chuckle again. He does that a lot. He's a smiley, chuckley kind of person, which is so foreign to me, I barely know how to react around it.

He's just staring at me so I raise my brows at him in a *well? What is it?* kind of way.

"Why don't you wear a wedding ring?"

Believe it or not, his tone is soft and inquisitive; curious and welcoming. He's not accusatory or butt-hurt over having wasted his night on a girl who's not putting out. It's unexpected, but I'm beginning to think he actually is a good guy, despite his penchants for sleeping around.

I use my chewing as an opportunity to stall while I think of how to respond. I know the answer in my head, but I don't think it's something I can say to him right now. *Or ever.*

I took my ring off years ago, because I couldn't stand the constant reminder of what a joke my entire marriage is. And I only put it back on when he's around, as a preventative measure.

I finally swallow and tug my lower lip between my teeth. It's the only thing that seems to break his unwavering gaze long enough for his dark eyes to drop to my mouth. I squirm in my seat. *I bet he's a great kisser…*

"I lost it," the words jump out of my mouth, then I return to chewing on my lip. I don't like lying to him for some reason. His presence is like a truth serum. I just want to open up to him, but I can't.

He stares at me still, dark brows stitched together in skepticism and concern. I think he knows I'm lying and again, I'm not sure how, but I'm guessing his manners won't allow him to grill me any further.

"Your husband must have been mad," he grumbles, and one of the brows lifts. "Does he have insurance on it?"

I shrug because I physically can't say anything. I have no words. The sounds of Kings of Leon *Sex On Fire* playing over the speakers is enough for right now.

My silence must give him a hint that I don't want to talk about this, because he graciously changes the subject.

"When did you start painting?"

I release a shaky breath and smile softly, thankful for the out he's given me. And I launch into a story about my fifth grade art class, when my teacher, Mrs. Henley, told me I had some real talent. It was the first compliment I'd ever gotten on my art, and it lit a fire inside me. After that, I knew I had an artistic gift, and it was my responsibility to utilize it.

"Being creative is like growing a plant," I tell him. "You have to care for it constantly. Water it, give it sunlight… Be constantly working at it. You can't just sit back and expect it to grow on its own. It takes patience and dedication. A lot of people think that if they have talent, things will just come to them, but it's the opposite. You have to make it happen. I'm sure you know all about this..."

Noah smiles, his eyes rounded and bold. "No, I just get stuff." I laugh at his teasing and roll my eyes, to which he leans back and says, "You're pretty smart, huh?"

An awkward giggle slips out as I shrug through my humility. "You should tell my parents that. They think I'm an idiot because I never went to *college*."

"Fuck college," he scoffs. "I didn't go either. It's not for everyone. I never understood this whole *American dream* concept of putting yourself in suffocating debt just to have a college degree. Sure maybe if you want to be a doctor or a lawyer. But for people like us, it's a waste of time."

I grin at him, nodding along. He's just voiced my exact feelings toward secondary education. My parents never got it, and I know it's because their small minds can't accept that there's more to life than money, worthless degrees and boring jobs. You'd think they would understand, being that neither of them went to college. But they think *that* was the reason for their lack of success, when really it's the opposite. They have no motivation.

Having a degree won't change your life if you don't hunger for something more.

Our plates are empty, and our bellies full by the time I check the clock on the wall. It's two in the morning. I'm not worried, since Roger's out of town on business until tomorrow. Still my stomach turns at the thought of him being home unexpectedly when I get there. My muscles instinctively stiffen.

Noah catches me checking the time and rests his elbows on the table.

"Can I have your number?" He asks, giving me a look that I can now say with certainty is exclusive to him. It's like these cute puppy dog eyes mixed with a playful peer pressure. I bet he was the guy in high school who got everyone to go skinny dipping in the neighbor's pool or break into the zoo after hours. "Strictly for friendly purposes, of course."

I shoot him a scolding glare, but he's so damn charming I find it hard to deny him of anything. It's like I want to just do whatever he says, without a second thought. *Damn, the look really does work.*

I say nothing and simply hold out my hand for his phone, to which he laughs and forks it over instantly. No hiding or *hold on while I delete all these naked pictures*, which shocks me.

During the one-minute process of entering my number into his contact list, his phone buzzes eight-million times with incoming text messages, all of which are likely from girls he's done this exact same thing to. Well, maybe not this *exact* thing. But definitely girls he's bought drinks for, danced with, and requested phone numbers from.

Each buzz in my palm serves as a reminder to my gullible mind.

This. Is. A. Mistake.

Only difference here is that I'm not going home with him tonight. Because I'm married. And he's a famous actor who doesn't chase. *It's not happening.*

As soon as I'm done, I hand his phone back.

He stuffs it into his pocket and grins at me. "Did you give me a fake number?"

"No. Aren't you going to answer all those texts?" I raise my brow.

"No. Standard etiquette is to call yourself from my phone so you'll have my number in return. Thus confirming that the number is legit."

"I'm still not even sure why you'd want my number in the first place…" I murmur, rubbing the back of my neck.

"We had fun tonight, right?" He asks casually.

"Yes…" *More fun than I've had in years…*

"Then why wouldn't we want to do it again?" He's so nonchalant, it's equal parts refreshing and infuriating.

I squint at him. "Because."

"Because why?"

"Because you're *you*," I huff. "You're Noah Richards."

"And you're Alex Mackenzie. What's your point?"

I laugh softly to myself, shaking my head. *Okay, you wanna play this game? Fine. Let's pretend you're going to call me, Noah Richards.*

We'll see what happens.

"Alright, fine. Whatever." I sigh.

"I like your enthusiasm. It does wonders for my ego," he smirks, and I can't help but laugh. It just bursts out of me like a reflex.

Damn him and his charm and nice hair and strong tattooed body.

Noah pays for the food and we leave the diner. This time there's no big SUV waiting for us at the curb, because we walked here from Sensay. Apparently, Noah lives a couple blocks away, further proof that this is definitely his pick-up game routine.

I still feel slightly guilty for getting his hopes up. I don't like stringing people along… But the night is still young. He could easily go back to the club and find a girl to bring home tonight. *Or just respond to one of his thousand text messages, most of which are probably booty calls anyway.*

The thought turns my stomach and my mood sour.

"Well, I'd better get home…" I mutter. *To my lonely Upper East Side mansion.*

"Where do you live?"

I contemplate lying again, but decide against it and tell him.

"Let me call you a car," he insists.

"No thanks, Richie Rich. I'll take a regular cab like everyone else." *He doesn't need to know that I'm also rich, and have my own driver at my disposal if I need him, though I never do.*

Initially Noah looks like he wants to protest, but his casual mask recovers for him and he shrugs, stepping out to wave down a passing yellow cab. I join him by the car and he opens the door for me.

I can't help the gloom that's bumming me out, since I'll never see him again. He helped me celebrate something so pivotal in my career tonight, an achievement I would have otherwise been observing alone. He made tonight one to remember, and in all honestly, I know *I* won't forget this, whereas I'm sure he'll wake up tomorrow with no recollection of the sad little girl he took for waffles.

"I had lots of fun tonight, Alex," he says, his voice laced with lust, though I might just be imagining it that way. I have to actively stop myself from reaching up to grab that sharp, masculine jawline of his. "I'll call you."

My eyes lock on those dark irises, which seem to say so many words his mouth would never speak.

"Whatever you say," I whisper and he laughs a soft, grumbly thing that's so hot I need to step into the car before I do something I'll regret.

"Goodnight, Alexandra," he winks.

"Goodbye, Noah…"

He closes the door and I give the cabbie my address so he'll drive. I refuse to turn and look out the window until I'm sure Noah's fully out of sight, releasing a stiff breath as I flop against the seat.

Well, this sucks.

I count the avenues between me and Noah as we drive across town. *Ten Avenues. That's practically a world away.*

When the cab stops in front of my building, the fog swirling inside my head clears abruptly as my mouth goes dry. I get out slowly, stiffening in preparation for an attack. If my husband is home, this will only go one way.

I enter the lobby and Javi, the night doorman, is there watching his iPad behind the desk. He looks up when he hears me and gives me a smile and a wink.

My shoulders drop, tension leaving me while I breathe out hard, a smile of relief tugging at my lips. I wave goodnight to him and step inside the elevator. *Roger's not here. Thank God.*

I have a very good relationship with the employees of this building. They're basically my only friends. And all of them have seen me in pretty rough condition, but since my husband pays them each handsomely, and because of the obvious confidentiality, they don't speak a word of what they've seen or heard to anyone. I'm grateful, and not, at the same time.

I appreciate them, though. And because I try to make the best of everything, and always remain polite and friendly despite how much my own life is in shambles, they refrain from giving me looks of sympathy and pity when they see me. I appreciate that the most.

I unlock the door to our massive co-op on the penthouse floor of the building, waltzing inside and setting the alarm behind me. I meander through the supercilious palace into the wide-open silence; the endless darkness.

Our home is like a museum; cold, sterile and filled with art. I like the art aspect of it, but I would much rather live in a place that was warm and homey. I tried decorating when I first moved in, but Roger hates clutter. So I quickly abandoned the idea of adding my personality to anywhere other than our bedroom, and my studio.

In the bedroom, I strip out of my clothes and get into the shower. I need to wash Noah's scent off myself, even though I don't want to. I can still smell him on my skin and in my hair, surrounding me and giving me comfort. I'm surprised how much of him rubbed off on me from just a few minutes of grinding.

My mind drifts back to the club… to the feeling of his hard body, strapping and strong, holding me close, his breath on my neck, chasing the chills his lips left. I squeeze my thighs together at the memory of them parted, his erection dragging in rocking motions along their apex. *Fuck.*

I'm slippery wet, my thoughts sending arousal pulsing out of me. I lean my back against the tiles and close my eyes, remembering…

His dark eyes watching me like I was the most fascinating thing he'd ever seen. His strong hands, long shapely fingers, searing the skin of my exposed lower back. Those hands have the potential to do so many amazing things to me. They're perfect.

Forget him, Alex. Nothing will ever come of this little crush. Shut it down.

I take my brain's advice and shake the memories away, washing my hair. I'm alone, and it's fine. I'm used to it. I have no one at all, not even my abusive, adulterous husband.

I'm basically a ghost. Why Noah Richards would ever want to call me is beyond any rationality.

Don't worry. He won't.

I'm in my studio, putting the finishing touches on a piece I've been working on for weeks. The canvas is covered in bright yellows and oranges, a swirling black and brown mass in the middle with eyes. Before today, the eyes were sort of shapeless and plain. But now they're deep, dark and curious.

They have a touch of desire in them, and some visible humor. They're alive as I'm looking at them.

They're calling to me.

Life isn't as awful as you've made it for yourself. There's still hope out there.

I bite my lip, touching the oil paint with my finger.

My phone rings, jolting me out of my reverie. I huff and dunk my brush into the jar of mineral spirits, spinning over to the table to grab my phone. When I pick it up, my eyes narrow at the screen in confusion.

It's a number I don't recognize. My heart leaps in my chest as hope blooms around it like a wildflower. But I quickly smother it and swipe to decline.

Nope.

I toss the phone down and return to my station, grabbing the container of gesso for my blank canvas. I open it up and sniff; not up close or anything, but I just love the smell.

My phone chirps behind me and I roll my eyes. *Distractions. I should have turned it off.*

I stomp back over to the table and pick it up again. This time there's a text, from the same number that just called me.

Unknown number: Hey it's Noah! I just tried calling you but it occurred to me you don't have my number saved & you might screen. Anyway hi! :) I hope your day is going well

I gulp, staring vacuously at the message in my hand. Another one pops in before my eyes.

> **Unknown number:** I had fun last night... I know I said that already but I just wanted to remind you. Maybe we could hang out again...

Is this really happening?

I'm beyond confused right now. Why in the world would he be texting me? What is he getting out of this?

I desperately want to respond and ask him just that, but I force myself not to. I can't give in to the false hope. Noah Richards is not a friend, nor will he ever be anything more. The sooner I get that through my head, the better.

I put my phone down and slowly walk away, glancing over my shoulder at it to pout. I really want to talk to him, and it's bafflingly stupid. *What the hell is wrong with me?*

I go back to my gesso, brushing it over the fresh canvas, smoothing it around to erase the knit. By the time I'm done, it's all over my hands, which is pretty standard. I'm a messy artist, but I like it that way. It's just my process.

I blow a strand of hair out of my face, wiping my hands on my oversized flannel shirt. I don't like wearing smocks when I'm working, so I usually just buy men's shirts from thrift shops and ruin those with paint stains and turpentine.

My phone ringing distracts me from my sticky hands. I'm already shaking my head as I pick it up again and see that same number from before. *Noah's* number.

He's calling me again. *What kind of fresh hell is this??*

I don't want to be rude, so I don't decline the call, but I also know I *can't* answer him. It's not an option.

I leave my phone on the table before I can change my mind and shrug out of my big shirt. I leave the studio in my sports bra and leggings, heading downstairs to the kitchen. I'm starving from painting up an appetite, and it's time for lunch, so I make myself a salad and eat at the breakfast bar, in front of the TV we have in there. I flip through channels while munching away, then stop in giddiness. Beetlejuice is on. *Score!*

I watch the whole movie, following my salad with a side of pineapple and cottage cheese. And by the time it's over, I'm stuffed and happy. I love how relaxed I can be when Roger's not around. I wish my contentment didn't have a timer on it...

Break time is over, so I head back up to the studio. But when I get there,

Seek Me

curiosity begins prickling at me inside and I pick up my phone.
Ten missed calls. All from Noah. *Jesus.*
And eighteen more texts. *Da fuq?!*

Unknown number: Are you busy? I'm sorry I don't want to interrupt your day...

Unknown number: Or you're ignoring me.

Unknown number: Shit

Unknown number: Are you busy with your husband? Fuck I'm so sorry. I'm stupid.

Unknown number: My bad. Call me back if you want...

Unknown number: Wait...

Unknown number: If you were worried about your husband seeing me calling you would've blocked me right? Or turned off your phone...

Unknown number: So you're just ignoring me then

Unknown number: Alex

Unknown number: Alex

Unknown number: Alex

Unknown number: A

Unknown number: L

Unknown number: E

Unknown number: X

Unknown number: Wow... FINE! I get it. You HATE me. I'll leave you alone.

Unknown number: Never mind. I can't do that.

Unknown number: *correction. I CAN but I don't want to

Hysterical giggles are flouncing from my throat at how completely ridiculous this dude is when my phone starts ringing in my hand. And you'll *never* guess who it is...

"My God, what do you need?!" I answer the call with attitude and forced annoyance in my voice. I'm secretly more pleased than I want to admit that he's stalking me like a total weirdo.

"Oh so it *is* your number!" Noah growls through a humorous tone. "I was starting to think you had given me a fake one."

"No, I was just ignoring you," I bite my lip, relieved that he can't see me at the moment. And how big I'm trying not to smile.

"Now, why would you want to do that?" He asks, his deep, raspy voice sounding incredibly sexy in my ear.

His voice is *very* hot. He sounds a little like Christian Bale doing the Batman voice, only not in an annoying way. He has this hoarse whisper tone that rumbles into my brain and commands it to make my nipples hard.

"Because I don't know what you want, therefore I see no point in encouraging you," I tell him, wandering over to the far side of the room where my couch is against the wall.

"I already said what I want," he whispers as I plop down, lying on my back, staring up at the ceiling. "Let's hang out."

I laugh, drawn to how damn charming he is, his persistence oozing that *Noah Richards* confidence and swagger. He's practically begging me to hang out with him, but he doesn't sound affected by my ultimate decision in the slightest. It's very interesting how he's able to do that... Remain captivating yet aloof, even over the phone.

"Why?" I ask, lifting my legs up and watching my toes wiggle.

"Because I think you're cool," he answers casually. My internal response is anything but. His words, said in that voice, make my heart jump in my chest and warmth spread over my whole body.

I can't understand why he likes me so much, or what's different about me than the other girls he knows. I mean, other than that I'm not biting yet. Maybe he *does* like the chase...

But I'm still not entirely convinced I wouldn't let him catch me.

"I think you're cool too," I hum in a small, timid voice.

"Then come over," he rasps, and my lip is about to bleed from how hard I'm chomping on it. "We don't *have* to have sex. We could just make out." I snort out a laugh. "I wouldn't say no to a blowjob, but that's totally up to you."

I'm still laughing as he chuckles, and I can picture him blessing me with

Seek Me

that devilish smile. I'm surprised he can use that thing to seem so unassuming, because really it makes him look purely wicked. In a good way.

"You're completely ridiculous," I sigh, toying with barbell in my navel.

"Hmm… and yet you're swooning, Alexandra Mackenzie." There's an audible grin in his voice. And I've never been gladder I kept my own name, because hearing him say it is life-affirming. "I can hear it through the phone. Don't worry, I won't tell anyone."

I giggle again, wiggling around at how flirtatious he is and how fucking *good* it feels. I haven't felt anything like this in seven years, and I immediately capture it, desperate to keep this warm intoxication for as long as I can manage.

"Me? What about *you?*" I tease, grabbing my ankle with my free hand and doing a cheerleader's high-V with my legs. "Pretty sure you're stalking me. Are you outside, like the creepy murderer from *Scream?*"

"What's your favorite scary movie, Sydney?" He does the voice and I'm chortling so hard my stomach muscles are beginning to cramp.

I hear sudden heavy footsteps ascending the stairs, and I freeze. The hairs stand up all over my body and fear squeezes my windpipe, making it hard to breathe.

"Gotta go," I whisper and hang up immediately.

I power my phone off as fast as technologically possible, stuffing it between the couch cushions just as my husband appears in the doorway across the room. My heart is thudding against my chest as I sit up, taking a deep breath and holding it, willing myself to calm down before he accuses me of something.

Roger crosses the room in his expensive suit, looking just as striking; just as cold and suffering as always.

"Hi, little one," he rumbles, taking a seat next to me.

I force a smile that neither one of us believes and scramble to my knees, leaning over to kiss his cheek. He strokes my hair gently, and it's all so choreographed. Noah Richards may be my new actor friend, but my husband and I have years of practice in pretend under our belts.

"How was the trip?" I ask in my docile voice. *Robot wife at your service, sir.*

"Good," he replies, and says nothing more. Even if I wanted to know what he did on his trip, he would never tell me. His index finger grazes what's left of a purplish-yellow mark on my arm. "Let me take you to dinner tonight."

I ache to scream *no* at the top of my lungs, because the last thing I want to endure is one of our forced tense dinners wherein we portray the rich power couple, out for a night on the town.

39

But of course I have no choice. There's a reason he doesn't *ask*, after all…

I nod slowly and pull a fake smile of excitement. "What dress should I wear?"

"The black Dolce and Gabbana," he murmurs, tugging my chin and pressing a chaste kiss on my lips. "We'll go to Jean-Georges."

He stands up and saunters away, calling over his shoulder, "Be ready by eight-thirty."

Yes, your highness, I roll my eyes to myself. My gaze slips to the crevice in my couch where my phone hides. I hope Noah's not upset. I didn't want to do that to him, but there's no way Roger can find out I'm talking to anyone, let alone a *man*, who's famous and sexy, and makes my heart and vagina shudder.

Roger isn't all that possessive, which actually makes me angrier than if he were. He just knows I'm not going anywhere, and it's infuriating. It's also scary.

Because who knows what he'll do when I eventually work up the nerve to leave…

Because who knows *when that will be*.

I swallow down all of those thoughts and leave my phone where it is, heading downstairs to shower and get ready for *dinner* with my *husband*.

Chapter Four
Alex's Journal

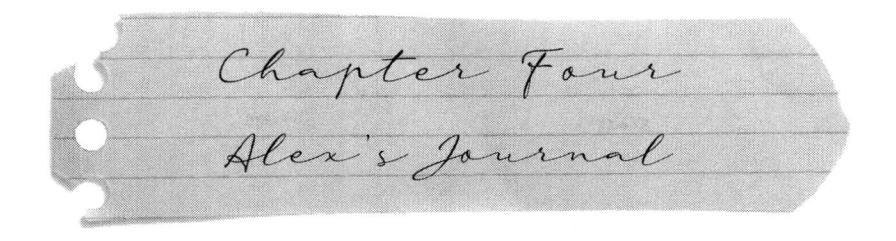

ALRIGHT, BARN. Let's just accept that my life is far too hectic for me to write in you as much as I used to. I hope you're not mad, because I'm not.

Far from it, actually.

I've been living life to the fullest. So full that my cup runneth over.

Here's some more proof that Roger is my Prince Charming: He treats me like his princess and whisks me away at every opportunity.

It's been three years since we got married and moved in together. And in those three years, we've traveled more than I had in my eighteen years of life before him. More than I ever *dreamed* I would travel.

Six months after our wedding, he took me to Istanbul. It was a spur-of-the-moment vacation, and just the most beautiful, perfect place for us to explore as newlyweds.

For our one-year anniversary, he brought me to Paris. We kissed in front of the Eiffel Tower, and yes, it was corny as hell. But I guess things that may seem corny on the outside are spectacular and magical when you're madly in love, and in freaking *Paris*. I bought a beret, and I wear it when I'm painting in my studio. My husband did indeed build me my own *studio* in our Upper East Side mansion. I'm so spoiled, but he loves me and wants me to develop my skills. I think it's sweet how much he gives.

Two months ago we went to Milan. It was yet another breathtaking and gorgeous land filled with endless sceneries for me to capture. I spent the whole time sketching everything my eyes could gaze upon and brought them all home to paint.

Milan was a vacation, but Roger had to work a bit while we were there. Apparently, he has international patients as well, though I would have no idea how or why because he never really talks to me about his work. He tells me he doesn't want to burden my broad, artistic mind with his *boring job*, as he always refers to it. I try telling him we're man and wife, and I'm happy to share his burden in sickness and in health, in good times and bad, for richer and for poorer, all that.

But he still won't hear it. The extent of our conversations about his work is me asking him how his day was when he gets home, and him saying, "Fine." Then he proceeds to make me naked and fuck me up against whatever furniture is nearby.

I'm not complaining. I love making love to my husband. Even when it doesn't necessarily feel like *love*.

At this point, I'm perfectly content. Roger and I are inseparable, our sex-life is on fire, and I have everything my heart could want. I'm learning a lot about my art every day I keep at it, and I know that soon enough, with Roger's connections, I'll paint something that will grab the attention of the galleries.

I have more money than I could ever spend in this life or the next. I'm happy. Centered, even.

But something still feels off.

It's not much more than a feeling I have; a feeling which seems to tug at me late at night when I lie awake, with Roger sleeping soundly beside me. Or when he's at work all day, hours often stretching into the evening, and I'm at home in our giant co-op, wrestling restlessness. Even outside of painting, I have so much free time on my hands. Time that could surely be spent on something, or some*one* else.

Barnaby, I know it sounds selfish to cry loneliness when I have the man of my dreams and enough money to do whatever I want to fulfill myself. But honestly, I don't think money can by the kind of attention and grounding I crave. It's something deeper than that… Something missing in a hollow place, somewhere outside the reach of any materialistic possession. A thirst that neither my love for painting, nor a sexy as hell husband can seem to quench.

I haven't admitted this to Roger yet, and I think the reason is because I know, in my heart, exactly what would fill this emptiness inside me.

A baby.

CHAPTER FIVE
Noah

THE FRESH AIR FEELS GOOD ON MY SKIN. It was way too hot in there. But the girl is complaining that she's cold, and I didn't bring a coat, so now I have to listen to her whining. Maybe I could fill her mouth with something so she'll stop talking...

"Look! Insomnia cookies!" I interrupt her inane rambling and point across the street at the popular cookie shop.

"Do you know how many calories are in one of those?" She scoffs, flipping her platinum blonde hair over her shoulder.

I shrug. "I don't know. Eight-thousand?"

I yank her with me as we make our way over, Drunk Girl hobbling in her high-as-fuck Louboutins. I don't understand why girls insist on wearing heels like that if they can't even walk in them. Do they have magical powers or something? Do they pump youth serum into you through your feet? Do they possess some miracle orthopedic weight loss technique?

We huddle together inside Insomnia to escape the chill I was rather enjoying, but my companion wasn't, and I'm immediately eyeing the display case to decide which cookies I want. *Peanut butter... white chocolate macadamia... chocolate chunk...*

"Is there anything fat free?" Kelsey, or Kasey, or whatever the fuck her name is, asks the guy at the counter, and I gape down at her like she's just asked why everyone loves The Beatles so much.

This girl is lame. But she's also hot, which is the *only* reason I picked her up at the club I was at and asked if she wanted to come back to my place.

Actually, I asked if she *wanted*, and then she squealed an enthusiastic *YES* before I could even finish my invitation. How she knew I wasn't about to ask if she'd like to partake some Helter Skelter, I have no idea. My guess is she would've said yes to that too, as long as I promised to kiss her a few times first.

The truth of the matter is that there's only one girl I actively can't stop thinking about, and it's not little Karlie in her way-too-short dress and way-too-high heels.

Alex Mackenzie is ducking me. I blame myself, really. I knew she was a flight-risk, and I called her fifty-million times, then texted her seventy-billion times. I obviously came on too strong, which is the more startling and befuddling thing here, because I *don't* do stuff like that.

I'm Noah Richards. Mr. Cucumber, first name: Cool As A.

I *don't* obsessively call girls. I barely even call them at all. Usually they call me. My phone is the one blowing up, not the one doing the blowing.

So what the fuck is going on?

How the hell has Alex managed to wedge herself into my brain like this? Because she's there right now… Sitting snugly between my hypothalamus and my amygdala.

I *do* like the chase. All of my recent experiences with women feel less like a hunt and more like a drive-thru window. That could be why I'm so drawn to Alex. Because she didn't give in the second I said *hello*.

Or maybe it's because of her.

Sigh. *Alex*… With her big green eyes, long, dark hair and all those tattoos; her cute little nose ring and sexy pillowed lips; her timid looks and witty responses, and her laugh so refreshing it made me feel like I stuck my head out the window of a moving vehicle when I got to hear it.

Her smell… Like ripe fruit and sweet baked goods. Equally mouthwatering as the smell of cookies in this shop. I can almost smell her right now…

Actually, I *can* smell her right now. *That's weird.*

My mind springs back into focus from the sound of the bell on the door that just dinged, the cool air bursting in from outside, signaling that someone else has walked in.

What's her face is still preoccupied, blabbing at the guy behind the counter about gluten-free something when I hear a hopefully familiar voice mutter a curse behind me.

I turn fast and my heart jolts. *Alex!*

Oh my God, calm the fuck down.

"Hey," I chirp, grinning way too big.

Not that I ever could have forgotten how gorgeous she is, but it's been almost a week since I saw her perfect face, and now that she's here, standing in front of me, I'm practically breathless. On a scale of one to ten, she's a crisp Benjamin.

"Noah… Hi…" she squeaks, not at all looking or sounding as excited as I am that we've been reunited. She's tilting her face away from me, unable to look

Seek Me

me in the eye.

"I haven't heard from you..." I snake my neck around to catch her gaze, but she's going through a lot of trouble to turn away from me. Actually, she looks like she's about to run out the door. And I'm fully prepared to chase her again. *Based on recent events, I think that much is clear.*

Kelsey, having forfeited her pointless conversation with the cookie guy and is now paying more attention to me, grabs me by the arm and smooshes herself up to my side, running her fingers up my chest in an obnoxious display of forced affection.

"Oh, hi," she drawls with a fake smile on her injected lips. "Noah, who's this?"

Her jealousy is off-putting. We're not a couple... I just met her an hour ago.

The benefit of her trying to mark her territory is that it causes Alex's head to pop up, her gaze locking on me and the blonde girl. Her eyes are wide, and she looks slightly crushed that I'm here with someone.

But I can't enjoy it. Not one bit.

Because now I have a full view of Alex's face. And I see something that makes every fiber of my insides burn with anger and confusion.

There's a pretty significant bruise beneath her left eye.

It's on her cheekbone; a black and blue mark, painted with some cover-up, but still visible. A bruise on her perfect face... A symbol of hurt on the girl I like.

I feel fucking murderous.

It's not actually that big. But it's big enough for me to see it, and obviously for her to feel the need to hide it from me.

"Noah, baby..." the ditz who's feeling me up speaks again, but I'm not listening at all.

I'm just staring down at Alex with a ringing in my ears.

My mouth drops open, but I can't formulate words. I lock my wide eyes on Alex, conveying the hurt that I'm feeling for her. And the hurt I'm going to inflict on someone else...

Alex picks up on what I'm seeing and that, mixed with what I think is some light jealousy over seeing me with this girl, though I can't be sure, prompts her to turn fast and whip the door open even faster. She stumbles outside, and of course, I go after her, ignoring what's-her-face who's shrilling behind me.

Alex is almost running to get away from me, but I jog up to her. Just as I'm about to grab her by the arm, I remember the bruises from the other day, paired with her pained expression, and I stop myself, blood rushing in my ears from how fucking enraged I am.

These are too many bruises for regular slip-n-fall accidents. I don't care how clumsy she is.

I'm not a fucking idiot. Someone's hitting her. And I'm willing to bet who that someone is.

Someone's going to be very dead, very soon.

I dive in front of Alex and she's forced to stop short, though she crashes into my chest a little, her face aimed straight down. I hold onto her back gently to stop her from leaving again.

"Alex, what the fuck?" I pant, out of breath, but not from running. From being so angry I can barely see straight.

She says nothing, nor does she pull away from me. She just breathes heavy, huffing with her fists balled and resting on my chest. Unaware I'm even doing it, my fingers trail softly up her back and I run them through the ends of her smooth hair, like dark silk in my hands.

"What happened?" I beg, just wanting her to talk to me. I put my murder-plans aside and focus on her, because I need her to be okay. "Tell me, Alex. Talk to me, beautiful."

She sniffles and my heart shatters like a pane of glass as she rests her head gently over where it's thudding in my chest, collapsing into me. Her arms wrap tightly around my waist as her body breaks into trembles. I think she's crying, but she's doing it silently, likely trying to hold herself together. I don't know her that well, but I can already tell that her strength could move mountains.

Why the fuck is she letting someone hurt her?

I can't even pretend to understand something like this. I've never known anyone who's suffered from domestic abuse. All I know is what I've seen on TV, like on Dr. Phil. The victims often say leaving isn't as easy as people make it seem, and now that I'm just about positive Alex is being abused by her husband, I don't doubt that one bit. Because she's so smart and awesome; a badass, sweet, funny artist girl, who must be in over her head.

My heart is breaking so hard for her. Not even just my heart… My whole body. I'm being reduced to a pile of rubble on the sidewalk.

I swallow hard over the growing lump of helplessness in my throat and hold her small frame against me, rocking her slowly, kissing her hair while she shakes in my arms.

"Okay," I whisper, my palm cradling the back of her head while my other hand strokes her back. "I'm here. I have you."

We stand on the sidewalk like this for a while. I just comfort her while she has her little break-down moment, a thousand questions scrambling my brain, though I won't ask any of them. If Alex wants to tell me what's going on, I think she knows she can. I'll make sure to let her know, in case she doesn't. But that's all I'll do for right now.

I won't accuse her. I won't bombard her with all the shit that's pile driving my mind. I won't look at her with sympathy or pity. Because I don't pity her.

I like her. I like her and I want her to be alright.

So I'll just keep comforting her for as long as she'll let me.

When I feel her shiver in more of a cold way than a sadness way, I pull back to look down at her, keeping my arms securely around petite shoulders, shielding her from the cold. I'm happy to do this for her, unlike with the girl I just ditched. Why, I'm not entirely sure. But I'm thinking maybe it's because Alex is different to me.

She's more important, and again, I don't know why, or how it is that a girl I only hung out with once for a few hours is suddenly bringing out these new behaviors, but I can't think about that right now.

She finally raises her head to gaze up at me, no longer attempting to hide her face, because the jig is up. I saw the bruise, and she knows I see it. Her wide eyes set on mine and they twinkle with guilt and shame, two things I absolutely do *not* want her feeling when she's with me.

"We should get out of the cold," I tell her, lifting my hand to brush her hair away from her face. She's so blindingly gorgeous, I'm surprised I can even speak when she's looking at me.

"Noah, you really don't have to do this," she creaks, sniffling and trying to hide it. "Go back to your date. I'm fine."

"My *date* wasn't a date, and it doesn't matter," I explain, keeping my voice easy. "I want to hang out with you. In case I didn't make that clear the other day."

A breathy laugh escapes her as she tugs her lower lip between her teeth. This sight always seems to make my dick pop up to say hi, but I internally remind him to back off. She's mine right now.

"Well, I came here because I had a hankering for the white chocolate macadamia..." she grins, nodding her head down to block to the cookie shop we just bolted from.

"Funny, I had the same idea," I chuckle, then finally release her, taking her hand in mine. "Come on. Let's satisfy that sweet tooth of yours."

She laughs softly again, shaking her head up at me while giving me a look I can't read. But I think I see a hint of gratefulness in her eyes. I wink at her, and we walk, hand-in-hand, back to Insomnia for some cookie action.

"More milk, Mrs. Mackenzie?"

"Please, Mr. Richards."

I pour milk into a champagne glass and hand it to Alex. She accepts it graciously, chomping off another huge bite of delicious cookie. She's chewing with purpose, and it's totally adorable.

"Oh, and it's actually *Ms.* Mackenize," she murmurs, lapping at some chocolate on her lip. "Mackenzie is my name. I kept it."

I swallow and use extreme effort not to gape at her like I want to. I'm trying not to make her feel any type of way that will have her itching to leave, so instead I just peer at her casually, watching as she sips her milk.

She kept her name?? There are so many questions I want to ask right now. God, I'm so curious. But let's just remain quietly grateful, because I like her name. I'm really glad it doesn't belong to her abusive fuckwad of a husband.

"Good to know," I mutter, and finish off the last of the peanut butter.

We're sitting in the backseat of the Navigator eating our cookies and drinking our milk, and this is definitely the strangest, most amazing date I've ever been on in my life.

"This isn't a date, Noah," Alex grumbles to my right and my head pivots in her direction. *What the hell?? I didn't say that out loud, did I?* "I'm just making that clear." Her eyes flick toward me and she glares, cocking her sexy little eyebrow with a warning.

"No, no. Of course not," I hum, grinning nonchalantly at her, though still internally shaken that she can actively read my mind. *My thoughts aren't safe. Quick! Stop thinking about her tits!*

"We're just friends," she adds.

She sets her glass down in the cupholder, leaning back against the seat, and I can't help but watch. Each new small factoid I learn about her is fascinating, and I'm itching for more glimpses into the world of Alex Mackenzie. She's tossing me scraps, and like the dog I am, I keep snatching them up faster than

Seek Me

she can dole them out.

I can do friends. It's not something I've explored before, but I feel confident I could at least attempt to swing it. *Naked friends* is probably something I'm more equipped to handle, but I'm fully aware that's not going to happen. So I'll take what I can get.

After all, if the alternative is not having her around, then I'll get myself on board with the friend thing stat.

"Well then, as your friend, I feel obligated to tell you that you can talk to me about anything," I speak cautiously. "You don't *have* to. Of course you know that. But if there *is* anything you need to talk about, I'm here. As your friend."

Her neck rolls and she aims her gaze at me once again. I'm waiting for her to scoff at me, but she doesn't. Instead she just stares, the contours of her face shadowed from the dim interior lights of the vehicle. Her eyes are giving off some serious emotions, and I keep my face even, so as not to show her how much I really *want* her to talk to me about what's going on.

Finally she breathes out slowly and says, "Thanks, Noah. I appreciate it."

I nod definitively. "Don't mention it."

Then I lift my champagne glass filled with ice cold milk, signaling for her to do the same. She grins and picks hers up.

"Here for you, girl," I rasp, then clink my glass on hers.

"You rock," she says before taking a sip.

We sit in silence for a few more minutes before either of us speaks again. She does first.

"You know, you didn't *have* to end your night to hang out with me..." her voice trails. "I was just going to grab some of my favorite cookies and go home. I bet your original plans would have been much more satisfying."

I give her a look. "Alex, there is *nothing* more satisfying than having cookies and milk in the backseat of a vehicle."

She giggles. "Yea, but you were going to take that girl home. You're forcing me to be a cock-block, which is not something I want to be, especially to my friends."

Wow, she really has no idea how much I'd rather be hanging out with her doing anything than banging some annoying girl who only wants to sleep with me so she can say she did.

"You're not blocking my cock, Alex," I crumple a napkin in my fist. "He's just fine. I mean, he appreciates the attention, but let's not encourage him. He's got a big enough head as it is." I wink at her and she bursts out laughing.

"Oh my God!" She squeals, covering her face with her hands. I register the sight of Jimmy, my driver/security friend, chuckling in the rearview mirror.

I sigh out my laughter. "Plus, that girl was annoying. You saved me from having to listen to her blather on about trans fats."

"Well, you probably take home a lot of girls like her," she cocks her brow. "You must be used to it."

"What are you insinuating?"

"Noah, everyone knows you're a manslut. It's fine. You don't have to pretend you were interested in that girl for her glowing *personality*."

My face morphs into one of faux-appall at her audacity, but clearly no one's buying it. I guess my reputation proceeds me.

I huff and fold my arms across my chest. "Alright, yes. I do enjoy the company of women sometimes… But I'm more than just a gifted package, Alex. I have feelings too, you know."

She laughs softly then turns her whole body in her seat to face me, resting her head against the back.

"Oh yea?" She sneers, grinning wickedly.

"Uh-huh," I nod, mirroring her body language.

"What kinds of feelings do you have in here?" She asks, reaching out to tap her finger on my chest.

I instinctively tense from being put on the spot, and definitely *not* because she touched me. Honestly, I'm not used to talking about my feelings with anyone. It's not something I do, ever. So her asking me about them makes me all fidgety.

"I feel… stuff…" I mumble, swallowing hard over my increasingly dry throat.

"Like what?"

"Nervousness," I whisper.

Her eyes go round, the smile slipping from her lips. "What are you nervous about?"

"My new job," I go on, and she visibly relaxes. "I'm excited about it, sure, but I'm also nervous. It's really… big. What if I fuck it up?"

"You won't," she says with certainty that makes me laugh.

"How do you know?"

"Because, I barely know you and I can see how amped you are about it. This means a lot to you. You'll rock the shit out of that role and make it your bitch."

My lips curl into a giant smile. She's so sweet. Sweeter than the cookies we just devoured.

"I also feel worried…" I whisper, my eyes stuck on the purple on her left cheek.

"You don't need to worry, Noah," her head shakes back and forth. "You're a talented actor. You'll be -"

"Not about that," I cut her off, my brows pushing together.

She clams up when she catches what I'm focused on. Her eyes fall away, and I witness her gulping. I hope I haven't upset her by bringing this up. But she asked what I was feeling. This is it.

"Leave it alone," she breathes. Then her eyes come back up to mine, and they're filled with angst. "Please?"

I nod slowly, because I have to. If she doesn't want to talk about it, what can I do? I won't push her. She's the one dealing with the worst situation ever, and she doesn't need any more grief, especially from her new friend.

I want her to tell me what *she* feels, because her feelings are much more important than mine. But she's probably in her head constantly, obsessing over the negative. I should help her focus on the good in her life. That's what friends do.

"Tell me what you feel about your upcoming art show," I nudge her.

She smiles, relaxed again. "I'm nervous about that, too. But I'm also excited. Almost antsy. I can't wait to have my pieces up in a successful gallery. I feel pride, for my work. I know I put everything I have into it."

I grin. "What else?"

"These two contradict each other," she huffs a modest laugh. "But I feel both inadequacy and victory at the same time. I'm sort of devastated that my parents don't love me enough to check up and see how I'm doing... But I'm also vindicated because I proved them wrong. I'm showing pieces in a *gallery*. I made my dream come true when they never believed in me. Part of me wants to rub it in their faces. But then the other part knows they'd never show up, so it doesn't matter."

I can't believe what I'm hearing. Her parents sound like assholes.

What kinds of parents wouldn't support their child in her journey to following her dreams? Mine did.

Sure, there were a lot of times when my parents thought I was insane for trying to be an actor. And they often questioned my decisions, but they always stuck by me, and supported me through all the failed auditions and rejection. Because that's their job.

"When's the last time you spoke to them?" I ask, my voice deep and hoarse with disdain for the morons she calls parents.

"When I was eighteen," she answers, her tone and face not giving off the same repugnance I'm feeling. Clearly she's made her peace with it, which is commendable. "They didn't agree with how I was... living my life. So they basically disowned me."

My heart lurches. This girl is so strong, it fills me with pride, while also making me want to ring so many necks for her.

Hmm... She said she's been married for seven years... And she's twenty-five. So it would seem her parents disowned her right around the time she got married to Captain Ass-Face. Makes some sense, I guess.

Still, they seem like giant pieces of shit.

"Alex," I murmur her name in a confident tone and take her face in my hands so she's forced to look at me, those green eyes large and coated in anticipation. "Fuck them."

She laughs softly and bites her lip. But I'm not done.

"Seriously. Parents are supposed to support you no matter what. And if they don't agree with something you're doing, they don't just write you off. They talk to you and tell you how much they love you. And they stand by your side, even if they're right and you fail. They don't say *I told you so*, or give up on you. I'm sorry that your parents are assholes, but you don't need them. Clearly, because you've made yourself into a badass, dedicated, strong woman. It's their loss."

Alex blinks at me a few times, stunned by my words. She's completely silent, just staring at me in awe.

"Now, if you want to give me their address, I will gladly have someone go over there and bust their kneecaps. But only if *you* want me to."

She laughs out loud, and I grin. I really love making her laugh. It's such a great look on her, and the sound is like a new favorite song I just discovered and want to play on repeat.

"You're the best friend ever," she whispers, chewing on her bottom lip.

My dick twitches, but I ignore it, releasing her face, but not before she can take my hand and squeeze it. More twitching. *This is getting inconvenient...*

"So is that a yes, or...?"

She cackles again and grabs the brim of my hat, yanking it down over my face. I reach over the armrest and poke her exposed stomach, tickling her while she squeals and giggles hysterically. It was a playful, friendly move, but now that I've felt it, I realize how toned her abs are beneath her soft skin, and it's my new mission to touch her there as much as secretly possible.

Seek Me

After a few more minutes of play fighting, my hat is off my head and on Alex's, and she's punching me over and over again in the chest. It's fully ridiculous that this is what we're doing right now, but it feels great to mess around with her.

As much as we apparently love talking, the flirting is quickly becoming my new favorite thing. I don't think I've teased or played with a girl like this since high school. All my *teasing* with women now is done naked and in a more compromising fashion. And while it's encouraging how much Alex touches me, I can't deny that it feels platonic, and I have to keep reminding myself it's never going to happen in the other way.

You're her friend. Regular friends, too. She's married to a piece of shit. You need to turn off these feelings you're coming down with like a bad case of crabs.

"I should probably go home," Alex sighs, kicking me in the butt once more for good measure with her bare foot. "It's getting late."

She's lying down next to me in the backseat of the SUV, having already lost her Uggs she was rocking. And I'm lying sort of next to her, but still trying to keep my distance. Because I really want to lie *on top* of her, but I'm guessing that would be considered *forward*.

I can't help wondering how she's able to stay out late like this with a husband like hers… It seems like something she could get in trouble for, and I'm dying to ask, but she told me to leave it alone, and I need to respect her wishes. Even though the questions are burning on my tongue like a mozzarella stick fresh out the deep fryer.

"Are you sure?" I ask, flicking her dangly little belly button ring that has two tiny dice hanging off the end. "You could stay at my place." She shoots me a warning look. "Just as friends, I mean, obviously. I have a really nice guest room."

"I'm sure you do," she grins as I sit up, draping her legs over my lap. "But no, it's fine. I'm alone this week, anyway. Thanks, though. For the offer."

She's alone this week…? What does that mean?

God, this friendship is like waterboarding. I need more answers, and she gives them to me with the gusto of someone picking lint off their clothes.

"So maybe we could hang out again, then…" I murmur, tracing the shooting stars on her foot. "Like tomorrow?"

She laughs and wiggles her toes. "I'm not sure…"

"Come *on*, Alex. Tonight was super fun. You have to give me that."

She huffs out a breath as if I'm annoying her, but I can tell she's having a gay old time, Flintstone's style.

"Yes, tonight was fun," she says quietly. "You're very fun to hang out with, Noah. Despite your whoring ways."

"I'm offended. I'm not as much of a womanizer as you seem to think I am."

Cough* Lies *Cough

"So you're saying the media portrays you in a negative light?" She gasps. "Why would they ever do that?" Her sarcasm is cute as hell.

"I do sleep around a little, but obviously everything they show in the tabloids will look a million times worse than it really is."

"Well, I don't really pay attention to that stuff," she tells me, slinking her foot underneath the fabric of my shirt, her toes tickling my abs. I'm not a foot guy, but hers are really nice. I'd let her touch me anywhere with these sexy little feet. "I know you're a good guy, even if you have a whole slew of skanky girls ready to drop their panties the second you walk into a room."

She's saying this as if she's watched it happen herself, and now I'm wondering if she was possibly paying more attention to what was going on around us at Maxwell's and Sensay than I was. I wouldn't be surprised. I was *really* focused on her that night.

"I appreciate that, Alex McMuffin," I take the foot in my hand and lift it up, pretending to bite her toes. She shrieks and kicks it around, laughing like a lunatic.

"That's a good way to get kicked in the face!" She barks through her fit.

"Jimmy, let's take Ms. Mackenzie here home, please," I instruct, and Jimmy drives away without another word.

He heads uptown, since we're already on the East Side. I can't believe I actually ventured East tonight… I'm a West Side playa, since it's where I reside, so I do most of my slumming around my hood. But tonight for some reason I breached the divide. Maybe I was subconsciously hoping I would run into my new friend…

It's a likely possibility.

We arrive at Alex's block and she has Jimmy stop before we get to her building, though I'm not sure why. If her husband is really away this week, then it shouldn't matter if she gets dropped off directly in front of her building, right?

Who knows. This girl's entire persona is shrouded in mystery. Her name might not even be Alex.

Seek Me

"Talk to you later, boss," she rasps and we high-five.

"Have a wonderful night, Alexandra, and by all means, don't be afraid to think about me." I wink.

She laughs as she opens the door to the vehicle, peering over her shoulder to admonish me with her eyes. Then she pauses and removes my hat from where it's sitting atop her wild black mane. She goes to hand it back to me, but I shake my head.

"You keep it. It looks better on you, anyway."

Her smile is shy and just the sweetest damn thing. "Doubtful. Night, Noah."

She hops out of the car and wanders toward her building, with my Supreme hat on her head. I physically can't stop grinning.

Without me even asking, Jimmy waits until Alex is securely inside her building before he drives me back home to the West Side.

I'm silent for the entire ride, which isn't unusual. But this time the silence feels different. It's a heavy silence, overburdened with my unspoken thoughts and missing something. Or rather, *someone*.

"I think she likes you," Jimmy says, his gruff voice pulling me out of my head from the front of the car.

"As a friend? Sure," I mutter, gazing out the window at all the lights of the city.

"No. More than that," he interjects. My eyes flit to the mirror where his meet mine for a moment so he can give me the *I'm serious* look.

Jimmy is more than just a driver. He's a friend and head of my security team. I was set up with him last year, and I instantly realized that he's fucking awesome. I trust him with my safety, which isn't something I take lightly. Also, he knows me pretty well, being that he carts me everywhere, and has definitely dragged my drunk ass into my apartment more times than I'd care to admit.

So if he says he thinks Alex likes me, I have to listen, even though I'm not exactly sure what it would mean if he's right.

We pull up in front of my building and I pause before hopping out.

"Jim, you think you could maybe… watch out for Alex for me?" I ask with slight hesitation. "I mean, just if you have time, like keep an eye on her. I'm worried -"

"Say no more," he cuts me off with a curt smile aimed over his shoulder. "We'll make sure she's alright."

I smile and pat him on the back. "Thanks, homes. See you tomorrow."

Once I'm inside my place, I kick my shoes off and meander about. My apartment is a brownstone, and it's massive. I decorated it myself, which is sort of obvious when you look around. It has a real bohemian vibe that I love, and I have it stocked with just about everything I could ever want or need in a dwelling.

I'm not really tired so I grab myself a drink and plop down onto my leather sofa, ready to watch a movie. I'm reminded that my phone is on silent, so I pull it out of my pocket and check the notifications. Missed calls, voicemails, and texts galore. My phone is always going off, and I only answer it about ten percent of the time.

Texts are still coming in before my eyes.

Becky: Hey boo! Miss you tons. Let's hang out again soon k? xoxo

Charlene: Noah! OMG my bff just told me she's never seen Royal before so we're watching it right now and she's swooning! Maybe you should come over ;)

Kelly blonde: Where have you been all my life?????? Call me! :-*

Kelly brunette: I see you're still ignoring me. Noah come on... I'm not saying we need to get married or anything but you could at least call me back.

Kelly red: Remember when I told you I was gonna get my clit pierced? Well I JUST DID! Here's a pic

Random1: The other night was awesome babe. Call me so we can have a repeat ;)

Girl from Gramercy: Noah I'm naked in bed thinking about you... You have my address but in case you forgot it's...

I slap my phone face down on the couch next to me.

The amount of trim that's currently available to me is almost mind-boggling. Having potential orgasms waiting at just the touch of a button is something I always found titillating. I'm not a relationship guy, so these women serve their purpose. We have fun together and then it ends. No muss, no fuss.

Well, sometimes there's a little fuss. Girls always have this idea that they can *change* me. They hold out hope that they're the one who will tame my wild ways and mold me into boyfriend, or dare I say, *husband* material.

Seek Me

But that's just not me.

Honestly, I can barely remember the last time I had a *girlfriend*. I think I was in my early twenties... It was definitely before I started acting.

There are a few girls who stand out in my mind; ones I'd dated exclusively. But it never worked out. We always found some reason to part. And I'm sure they're all happily married with kids by now, or at least working towards it.

But not me. I'm the bachelor. The one who picks women up casually for some fun and then takes off. Sometimes I feel a little bad, when they get attached, but I'm always straight forward about not wanting a commitment, and recently my reputation serves as an unspoken disclaimer for what they can expect.

Everyone knows Noah Richards doesn't do relationships.

Everyone except Noah Richards, apparently.

Because right now, with my phone sitting on the couch next to me, the only person out of my endless contacts who I actually *want* to talk to is Alex. *My married friend.*

I shake my head and flip on the TV. It's for the best. Relationships always end badly anyway. I've seen it happen all too often.

Not to my own parents, which is lucky, but with almost all my friends. My assistant, Brant, has been divorced twice. My best friend, Tucker, is going through a really rough custody thing right now. And my other friend, Keith, just found out his wife of three years has been cheating on him with his brother.

And that's just the tip of the iceberg.

It could be because I'm the biggest bachelor any of my friends know, but they're always quick to turn to me when their love lives go in the shitter. I'm the guy they want to hang out with when they just got dumped and need a solid wingman to help them forget the one who broke their heart. And I'm pretty good at it, if we're being honest.

I like to party; I throw killer ones. I know all the best spots in the city to pick up girls, and I clearly have zillions of them on speed-dial. I'm the best lone-wolf any of my pack could ever ask for.

Which is exactly why I *can't* settle down. Ever.

No matter what crazy things are going through my head, I just keep reminding myself that it's all in good fun.

My bachelor lifestyle will remain intact.

Don't worry, guys. I'll be right here when you inevitably need me.

Chapter Six
Alex's Journal

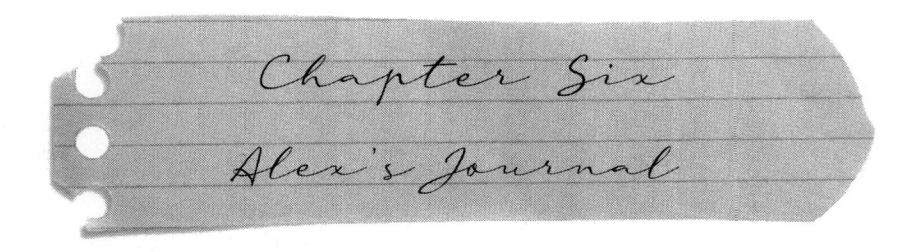

THINGS HAVEN'T BEEN GOING GREAT since we last chatted, Barnaby. And I only have myself to blame.

I talked to Roger about kids. In hindsight, I guess I shouldn't have. But there's no way I could have known how he'd react. After all, we've been married for four years. He's thirty-five. Don't guys usually want kids around that time?

Apparently not my husband.

The conversation went a little something like this…

"Sweetie, I was thinking…" I murmured nervously while Roger and I sat, cuddled up on the living room couch watching some movie I wasn't at all invested in. "About our relationship… The two of us…"

Roger tensed by my side. I decided to keep going before he could freak out and think I was divorcing him or something.

"I love how much freedom we have, you know that. And I love spending time with you more than anything. But when you're not here sometimes I get… well… sort of lonely."

I almost choked on how pathetic I sounded.

"Alex, you told me you spend all your free time painting," he grumbled, tilting his chin in my direction. "This was the dream you had for yourself."

"No, I know that," I backpedaled. "I do paint a lot. And I love doing it. I mean, it's necessary for me to stay focused at this stage, you're right about that."

"Then what's the problem?"

"There's no *problem*…" I mumbled, unease gripping my throat, making it hard to speak. I was always afraid to talk to him about anything serious. For some reason I felt like he would be angry with me. "It's just that, um, it would be nice to have something else to do here in this big, giant house."

He gaped down at me like I was an alien who had just landed in his living room and was asking him for directions back to the Milky Way.

"Do you… um… ever think about… wanting kids?" I tried to breathe out as quietly as possible, but I was shaking so hard my teeth were chattering.

Seek Me

Roger's eyes were uncharacteristically wide. After what felt like hours, he finally blinked, then shifted next to me, slowly sliding his arm out from where it had been resting around my shoulder. He turned his body to face mine fully, and I braced myself for whatever his answer might be.

"Alex, I…" He paused once more to regroup. "I'm not sure if now is the time."

My heart sank. "Oh… um…"

"I just mean that we have a good thing going on here," he added, and my lip trembled. "I'm working really long hours all the time, and when I come home, I relish the quiet. I like having you here, all to myself. No worries, no screaming babies or dirty diapers. Our life is perfect the way it is."

The back of my neck began to heat up and I felt an odd scratchiness in my throat.

"But Roger, I have no one but you," my voice cracked. "You go out with your colleagues all the time, and I have no one. I barely have any friends, none that I ever see, anyway. I'm not allowed to go out with you anywhere…"

"Alex, don't be ridiculous," he grunted, raking his long fingers through his hair. "It isn't that you're not *allowed* to. I go out to doctor's benefits and things like that. They're completely boring for someone like you."

I gasped as if I'd been slapped in the face. "Someone *like me*? What does that even mean?"

A sneaking insecurity crept into my brain, one that I was always struggling to smother.

He's ashamed of me.

Of course I know how it looks. I'm a twenty-two-year-old artist with tattoos and piercings. Sure, I know how to dress up as well as the next girl, but if we're being stereotypical, I don't *look* like a doctor's wife.

I've always found it strange that he goes stag to all his charity things and benefits. I can count on one hand how many times I've accompanied him to an event, and they're always small, low-key ones. He's a successful, well-known doctor in Manhattan. He gets invited to a lot of stuff, and normally I never cared if I was invited or not, because I know what we mean to each other. But deep down, I'm hurt that he never even *asks*…

"I just mean that you're real and honest and special," he tried using the patronizing, sugar-coated voice, which was only pissing me off more. "You don't belong with all those phonies. You belong here with me."

"I *want* to be with you, Roger. Don't you get that?" I barked. "I want to be with you *everywhere*. I don't care where it is. But you keep your work life and your home life completely separate. Do you know how that makes me feel?"

He stared down at me, his bright eyes giving away the wheels turning in his mind as he concocted plans to diffuse the bomb that was his young wife.

"Alex, you're my wife, and you mean the whole world to me," he rasped, taking my chin in his fingers. "I just don't feel it necessary to involve you in work stuff. We have the perfect thing going on here, darling. Don't ruin it."

And with a kiss on the nose, he was affectively shutting down the conversation.

"So you don't want to have a baby with me?" I wasn't done. Not yet. Not until I heard him say the words.

"Never say never," he grumbled, and turned back to the movie. His tone was firm and definitive.

It was a warning without the warning. His tone was telling me to drop it now, so his words didn't have to.

That was three months ago.

We haven't spoken a word about the baby thing since, and I'm anything but pacified.

It's not that I necessarily *want* kids right now. But I need something.

When Roger isn't home, which is all the time, even more, it seems, since we had that mind-fuck of a conversation, all I have is my art. But I've been finding it increasingly difficult to paint anything decent when I'm this unsettled.

I spend most of my time wondering where he is, and what he's doing. He's just so vague all the time. He rarely talks to me about anything going on in his life.

The things we talk about are superficial, surface topics. Movies, TV, books, my art, the fucking weather. We're like coworkers or acquaintances. And the less we talk about anything real, the less I feel like I actually *know* him at all.

I talk to him about everything. I tell him details about my life all the time, because I'm always itching to get him to open up. So I share things in hopes that he'll reciprocate, but he never does. It's next-level frustrating.

I recently tried to reconnect with some old friends via social media, thinking that maybe if I had a girlfriend to talk to, it would make me feel less hopeless.

I went out to lunch yesterday with my best friend from high school, Lindsay. It was a mediocre visit. We didn't mesh as well as we used to, but it felt good to talk to someone who wasn't Roger, or the people I see every day, like our doorman or the barista at the coffee shop next door.

Seek Me

And then later when I told Roger about it, he had the nerve to act upset. As if he really didn't want me seeing anyone who wasn't him.

As if he doesn't want me to have friends.

As if he wants me all alone.

The confusion and anxiety were building inside me, bubbling to the surface. All these negative emotions are what prompted tonight's disaster.

Roger came home later than usual. I had dinner ready and waiting for him, so I was already annoyed that it was cold and I had to heat it up.

I was on edge. Not the best time to have serious conversations.

But I threw caution to the wind and said, "Roger, I really want to try for a baby."

His eyebrows pushed together in a way I'd never really seen on him before, and his bright blue eyes turned dark.

He took a step toward me, and I instinctively backed up.

"Alexandra, where is this coming from?" His voice was so eerily quiet, goosebumps sheeted across my skin.

I gulped down a knot of heightened tension in my throat. "N-nowhere, I just want -"

"Who is telling you that we need to have a baby?" He asked, creeping even closer to me. "Who has been planting these ideas in your head? Was it that bitch you were with yesterday?"

I froze. Completely still, like a statue.

I had never heard him use that tone before, much less call anyone - especially my *friend* - a bitch. My mind rushed to convince myself it was nothing, but my body was still so terrified it wouldn't move, my mouth clamped shut so hard my jaw grew sore.

"Answer me!" He snapped, and I jumped, his voice echoing loud throughout the kitchen.

"No one! No one, I promise," I answered him quickly, meek and fearful, trying desperately to pacify him. "It was me. I wanted to talk to you about it. I just thought -"

"Alex, when I told you it's not the time, I was very fucking serious," he moved in closer, trapping me between his large body and the wall. His eyes bore down into me and I wanted to look away so badly, but I physically couldn't. I still couldn't move. "We're not having a baby right now, do you understand? Have a made myself clear?"

He was towering over me. My heart was slamming against my chest so hard he could probably feel it on his ribs. All the hairs on my body were standing straight up as fear held onto my breath and my voice.

But I was terrified he would yell at me again, so I knew I had to answer him. My body finally reacted and allowed me to nod.

I kept on nodding, my shivering lips finally parting enough for me to squeak, "Yes."

He narrowed his gaze at me, and I saw his jaw clench. I began to cower.

I wasn't sure why, and even thinking back on it now, I don't understand it. But my body seemed to understand it was in danger and was bracing itself for something my mind still couldn't comprehend. Something my heart refused to believe.

After another few silent moments of tension where nothing could be heard other than my pulse rapping and my blood rushing in my ears, Roger backed up and left me glued to the wall in our kitchen.

He stammered off, and I flinched when the front door slammed hard.

That was four hours ago.

It's now two in the morning and my husband hasn't come home. I have no idea where he is.

He hasn't called. And every time I've called his phone, it's gone straight to voicemail.

I refuse to believe all the awful things running through my mind. I don't want to believe what happened tonight...

That my White Knight is gone. Flame puffed out on my fairy tale, leaving me alone again.

In the dark.

Chapter Seven
Alex

Brush brush brush.
Swirl swirl swirl.
"There she goes, just a'walkin down the street..."
I keep swirling, keep brushing, keep pushing.
"Singing do-a-ditty-ditty-dum-ditty-do..."
Singing and painting. Painting and singing.
Mind racing through memories.
Pain. Torment.
Anger. Sadness.
Brush... brush...
Roger's hand around my throat, his thumb pressing into my windpipe.
"Do... a... ditty!"
Grinding the brush into the canvas.
"Ditty... Dum..."
His eyes, blue flames of raw force and power, blazing into me as he slams me against the wall. My back still hurts from where I connected with the drywall.
"Ditty..."
Say you love me, wife. He growls, the smell of Jack on his breath so strong I can taste it. I cower and he laughs, smacking me with his left hand.
The wedding ring connects with my cheek. *That's convenient.*
Fitting, really.
"DO!" I shout, mashing black paint into the middle of a giant face. I'm panting so hard, I can barely stand up anymore.
I need to relax. I need to sit for a minute.
I wipe the sweat from my brow and reach behind me, pulling out the stool I know is right there to plop down on it. I take a few deep breaths, in and out, my heart rate steadily returning to normal.
I got swept up in my zone when I couldn't stop thinking about my husband's

reckless violence the other day. He usually refrains from bruising my face, just because if it happens all the time people might start to intervene. *Jesus, I hope they would.*

But the night before he left for his weeklong *business trip* to wherever the fuck, he was in a mood. *Maybe he was going to miss me and figured a bruised cheekbone was a nice gift. Everyone gets flowers and candy...*

And then of course, to make matters worse, I had to run into Noah when my husband's *gift* was still noticeable. I really shouldn't have left the house, but I was in such a glum mood, and the only things that cheer me up in such circumstances are sweets. I guess it worked out for the best though, being that Noah ditched the skank he was with to hang out with me and eat cookies in the car.

My original plan was to never see or speak to Noah Richards again. Of course not for lack of want, but because I'm a fucking train wreck and I think it would be wise to keep other people, sexy tattooed TV stars in particular, out of my problems. But when I saw him at Insomnia, it really looked like he was excited to see me. And the rage I witnessed on his beautiful, chiseled face at the state of my cheek made my heart soar so hard and so rapidly, I had no choice but to run away in tears.

And then he chased me... Which caught me completely off-guard.

I'm still very wary of how wonderful it felt to be comforted by Noah Richards; having him hold onto me and whisper sweet words in my hair... It felt like I was in a dream I never wanted to wake up from. I haven't been held like that in longer than I can even remember. It's a high I'm still riding now, days later.

So I ditched my original plan and let my buzzing heart guide me to hang out with Noah as a friend, which ended up being even more fun than the waffle night. At first, I was worried he was doing it out of pity, because he felt bad that I'm a pathetic doormat who's getting beaten by her gorgeous psychopathic husband.

But I kicked that idea when he was tickling me in the backseat in a way that felt reminiscent of the dry-humping at Sensay. Either he was rocking some kind of semi just from being next to me, or he was smuggling produce in his pants... I'm going with the former, which I must say, is immensely satisfying. And if we're getting into the nitty gritty, he did rub it on me just a little, the memory of this subtle action moistening my panties even now.

I haven't dry-humped so much since I was seventeen, and yet for some

Seek Me

reason with Noah it's all I want to do.

Well, not *all*. There are *many* things I'd like to do with him, and only some of them include humping through our clothes. Most of the rest include humping *without* our clothes...

Why does he have to be such a damn manwhore? He's so sweet and kind, and funny as all hell. Why ruin it by being a fucking *cliche*, screwing every girl who crosses his path?

I sigh out of frustration and kick my easel. I'm sick of guys who fuck around everywhere. Or maybe I'm just sick of it because I have to sit here like an afterthought while they get to be out having all the fun.

I've only slept with three guys in my life, and the first two barely count because we were teenagers and they almost couldn't find where to put it at first. Who's to say I don't want to be out sleeping around with no strings attached? It doesn't seem complicated. I'm sure I could get the hang of it if I tried real hard...

Though at the moment, the only person I want to grind into the mattress is my new *friend*, the chronic bachelor. *It's never smart to develop feelings for someone who's relationship-stunted. Remember that forever, Al.*

Noah may not do the relationship thing, but apparently he does the friend thing, and does it damn well, at that. He was such a doll that night, asking me about my feelings and threatening to inflict violence on my scumbag parents. It totally wiped away the yuckiness of seeing him with that gross bimbo at Insomnia.

I smirk when I recall that I'm still wearing his hat. I've been wearing it since he dropped me off two nights ago, with the brief exceptions of taking it off to sleep and shower. I really like that it smells like him, but I know I'll have to get rid of it before Roger gets home. So I'm getting in all my time while I still can, thus my reason for painting with a hat on.

My smile widens and I pull the brim down over my face. Then I freeze and gasp, remembering that my hands are covered in black paint.

Fuck!

I remove it carefully, and whimper to myself at the black fingerprints on my bright red hat.

"Waa... you dumbass," I say to myself, pouting at the smudges. But then an idea pops into my head.

Maybe I should give it back to him. I mean, I'll have to ditch it anyway in a couple days. And knowing Noah, he'll totally love to rock this hat with my paint marks all over it.

And I'm back to beaming stupidly again. He's just the sweetest thing ever, and mind-numbingly sexy. I don't know how he does it... How he manages to be easy-going and funny, while also being so hot his clothes would burst into flames if they weren't clearly made of some flame-retardant material.

My phone starts ringing on the table, and I think *there's no way.*

I pick it up and see his name with the incoming call. Or rather *Norma*. Because not that I think Roger checks my phone, but to play it safe, he'll have to be *Norma* for now.

Anyway, he's calling me. And I may or may not be squealing like a child.

"Hello, Norma," I answer, already giggling like the stupid schoolgirl he turns me into.

"Hello... Myrtle? Are we giving each other old lady nicknames now?" Noah's tone is confused, but still bathed in humor and casual wittiness, which I adore to the fullest.

"You bet," I grin, getting up to clean my brushes. "What's up, home skillet?"

"Not a whole hell of a lot, except that I just found out when I'll be meeting my new costars!" His voice is rippling with excitement and unbridled optimism, and it's so enchanting to hear I almost burst into tears. I love how happy he is all the time. It's the polar opposite of everything else that happens in my life outside of our friendship.

"Oh, so cool! When?" I ask, giddy with anticipation for him.

"I meet the star on Saturday, and then I think they're planning a dinner thing sometime in the upcoming weeks for most of the cast," he tells me, and it sounds like he's walking. "But I'm totally amped to meet Andrew. He lives in London, so I guess he's flying out for -" He stops speaking abruptly. "Shit! I totally wasn't supposed to say his name."

"Why not?"

"Because it hasn't been officially announced yet, so no one's supposed to know... Ah, screw it. I trust you. It's Andrew James! Cool, right?"

My smile is out-of-control. I might need someone to come reel me in, because I think I'm losing it.

The fact that Noah trusts me is a wonder all on its own, but hearing him talk about his new costar makes me melt everywhere. He's obviously beyond thrilled to be working with a star like Andrew James. *Everyone* knows who that guy is.

I'm so proud of Noah. I can't wait for him to show off his skills among other gifted actors.

Seek Me

I've watched things that Noah's been in before, but it's a different story now that I know him personally. I always remember thinking, *Wow. Who's that hottie with the dark eyes and the bad boy smirk?*

But now, I look back on watching him act in TV and movies and think, *My friend Noah is so talented. He could easily be starring in box-office movies and graciously accepting awards. Maybe giving a quick thanks to his good friend Alex who always believed in him...*

"That's very cool, Noah. And of course you know I won't say anything to anyone. I just hope you get along with him."

"Me too. Ugh, imagine if he's, like, a huge douchebag?" He chuckles. "That would suck."

"I'm sure it'll work out."

"Um, okay, so the real reason I called..." he changes the subject, and my heart raps quickly in my chest. "I want to see you. Let's hang out."

My initial response is an emphatic *yes*. But I can't allow myself to fall into his web like this.

We're friends, and that's fine, but if I spend all my free time hanging out with him I just know I'll start crushing on him eventually.

Eventually?? Who are you kidding? You're two seconds away from hanging up his poster in your room and kissing it goodnight.

"I don't know..." I whisper, grasping for the will to say no to something I desperately want to do. "I'm painting and stuff..." I can't help but sound completely lame.

"*Please*, Alex," he whines into the phone with an audible pout that makes my insides swell. "I miss you *so* much..."

"Noah, it's been like two days since we last saw each other," I giggle, twirling my hair around my finger. *Dammit! I got paint on that now too!*

"Yea, two excruciating days without my bestie," he huffs. "Come on over. Come on over, baybaayyy!" He sings this in an awful Christina Aguilera voice that has me in stitches.

"Come over... to your place?" I ask in reluctance. Going over to Noah's could derail my attempts at *not* dry-humping him.

"Yea!" He shouts in my ear, overly excited. "It'll be so fun! You've never been to my place."

"That's because we've known each other for all of five seconds," I grumble. I don't know why I'm still playing this game. I'm already deciding what to wear in my mind.

Nyla K

"Five awesome seconds," he adds, and I think I hear him clap. "I'll text you my address. Just bring a couple pizzas and some chips and dip, and a molten chocolate lava cake. I'll do everything else. Like sit here and wait for you."

I can't stop laughing. I'm going to bust a gut if we continue on with this friendship.

"Okay, fine! Jeez…" I sigh out my remaining giggles and get up. "I'll be there in an hour."

"Yay," he whispers. My stomach must not have gotten the *friend* memo, because it's twisting up like a pretzel. "Can't wait. Oh, and Alex?"

"Yes, Noah?" My voice almost cracks.

"I was kidding. Don't bring anything but your gorgeous self."

This friend *will be the death of me.*

An hour later, I'm dressed in my super-tight ripped up black jeans, combat boots and my favorite sheer Nirvana shirt. The one that hangs off my shoulder, showing the pretty lace fabric of my new bra. My hair is styled the way it always is, straight and hanging well past my shoulder blades, and topped by Noah's red Supreme hat with the black paint smudges on it.

I'm standing in front of his building, looking over how incredible it is. It's a brownstone on 83rd, right across from the park. The perfect place for a celebrity to live, and yet I still can't believe he lives here. I know these buildings are probably brimming with richies, but Noah isn't just rich. He's rich *and* famous. The fact that he lives amongst the people is very cool.

Although walking up to the door, I see that it does have some very elaborate security. There are a few different cameras, motion sensors, and some weird little touchpad with numbers all over it.

I press the button for his place and stand there feeling insecure. I think one of the cameras is moving.

Someone's watching me. I squint up at it.

"Big Pete's taxidermy emporium. You snuff it, we stuff it. How can I help you tonight?" Noah's voice of amusement and snickering filters through the intercom thing, and I press my lips and thighs together before I pee myself.

"Let me in, you ridiculous idiot!" I shout at the screen, laughing through every word.

Seek Me

"Is that Alexandra Mackenzie? *The* Alexandra Mackenzie? World famous painter?? Oh my God, oh my God, okay. Hold on."

I sigh out hard, shaking my head as his door buzzes and I push it open. There's only one way to go, straight down a very long hallway, so I follow it toward the door at the end, and sure enough, it opens before I get there.

Noah is standing at the threshold of his home wearing only some very fitted black jeans, which are sitting far too low on his hips. He leans up against the doorframe and crosses his arms over his chest, face decorated with that signature smirk.

Now, this is my first time ever seeing Noah with no shirt on. I've certainly felt his muscles before when we were grinding in the club, and the other night when he was hugging me. So I knew they were there for sure.

What I didn't know, and what life had unfortunately not prepared me for, was how they would look.

Noah Richards is *cut*.

He's not overly huge, but his body seems to be perfectly defined in all the right places. His shoulders and chest are broad, with those lovely trap muscles that are like handles, and curved pecs with no chest hair, which appears to be natural. He has a very precise eight-pack of abs - that's two more than the normal amount, I might add - clustered on his stomach, leading down to a nice little happy trail and, wait for it... The *V*.

Oh, the glorious V. How we love you so...

And of course, because this is Noah we're talking about, he's made his drool-worthy body into his own canvas with a hefty collection of tattoos all over, and a silver barbell through his left nipple.

Good God, someone should have warned me. I'm not in the right headspace to be standing next to a man this fucking fine.

My mouth is actually watering. I need to stop staring, but I just *can't*. He looks like every girl's bad boy wet dream.

As I slowly step closer to him, I observe some of the tats he didn't show me the night we met., like the ones on his chest and pelvis. Yes, he has tattoos on his pelvis, and *yes*, they're outstanding.

He has matching tribal suns on either side of his happy trail, disappearing into his pants. And his Mad Hatter tattoo from his shoulder and back continues onto his front in a very elaborate way that has me drawn to the art of it as much as how dang good it looks on him.

He also has the word *Seek* written in some very beautiful script above his left pectoral. And a whole slew of others I would need days to explore and gush over. *In more ways than one...*

"Are you done studying me?" He finally speaks, and I realize I've been staring at his body for quite some time.

But it's really a work of art. He looks so good in every single way, and the tattoos just make him that much more unique. *His look definitely matches his personality, that's for sure.*

"For now," I say with a smile, gleaming up at him, because as much as I gave him crap for it on the phone before, I did miss his crazy ass the last two days.

"Good," he chirps then bends down and scoops me up into a giant hug that forces me to wrap my arms around his neck and my legs around his naked waist.

He burrows his face in my neck, and I think he's sniffing me. *Well, if he can do it...*

I smoosh my face into the crook and breathe in his *Noah* smell. He smells appetizing, like I'm meant to eat him or something. It's his natural scent that's sort of sweet and super manly. Add to that whatever soap he uses and the faintest hint of hemp. It's very nice, and again, exclusive to Noah. *Jeez, even his smell is different than everyone else in the world.*

He continues to hold me tight, and then I notice him moving, walking inside his apartment with me in his arms, kicking the door shut with his foot. He walks through a massive foyer, and into another wide-open room. My head bobs all around as I take in the scenery.

His place is fantastic. I've never seen anything like it. It's the most gigantic apartment I've ever been inside, with the highest ceilings *and* what looks to be a spiral staircase heading to an upstairs.

He steps up to a table and picks up a bottle of water with his left hand while he holds me onto him with his right. He takes a sip and makes an *ah* noise when he's done.

"Are you ever going to put me down?" I ask with a laugh. I'm barely even holding onto his shoulders, and my legs are now dangling off the ground.

He's very strong. *So that's what all those elaborate muscles in his arms and shoulders are for...*

"Nope," he mutters and I laugh again. "*My* Alex."

I squirm around in his grasp, wiggling until he chuckles and finally sets me on my feet, but not without first pressing a soft kiss on my cheek. And I mean *very* soft. His lips are like marshmallows.

I compose myself now that I'm walking on my own again, and continue to gaze about his kingdom. My attention is immediately stolen by giant wall-length windows that look like they open up onto some kind of terrace. He has a huge living room filled with gorgeous leather furniture, plants everywhere, a fireplace, and the biggest damn flat screen I've ever seen.

The decor in his place is everything I love in home decorating sitting in one space. It's all warm, mahogany and Cherrywood, with sprinkles of Noah all over the place in the forms of collector's items, cool accents and what appears to be some kind of medieval sword hanging on the wall.

"Okay, so first thing's first. It appears you've decorated my hat," his voice pulls me back to him and I look up to catch his raised brows.

"Oh… yea. It was an accident," I stutter, remorseful. "I was wearing it while I was painting and -"

"Alex, I gave it to you," he chuckles, tilting his head to the side. "You can fill it with fish guts if you want. Although I would ask why you were doing that if you did…"

I giggle and bite my lip, removing his hat from my head. "Actually, I wanted to give it back to you. Now that I left my mark on it, I think you should wear it again."

His face lights up, which is such a wonderful thing to witness. "You want me to *wear* an original Alex Mackenzie?!" I laugh and nod, handing it over. He snatches it from my fingers. "Yes, please!"

He tucks the hat onto his head, covering the top of his shaggy light brown hair. It's *his* look, and he's really pulling it off.

"So… What do you have planned?" I ask sauntering around him, continuing to check out his awesome pad.

"Well, I think I should be a polite host and give you the grand tour," he murmurs, then locks my arm with his.

He proceeds to guide me all over his place, showing me his giant kitchen, massive dining room, huge living room and the terrace, which is another synonym of *big*. Then he shows me the guest room he was talking about, which is super nice, the downstairs bathrooms - plural - his office, library, and a home-gym. After that, we ascend the insanely cool staircase and he shows me the upstairs, which houses another bathroom, a slightly smaller office, and lastly, his bedroom.

"This is where the magic happens," he teases and I elbow him in the side. "Sorry. I just love using tired clichés."

"This place, Noah… Jesus, it's phenomenal."

I can't even comprehend how amazing his entire home is. But his bedroom is a baby-maker if I've ever seen one. It's just as large as every other room in the house, but decorated more… sensually, I guess would be the word. The color scheme is dark, and he has black and white photography on the walls of the erotic nature. I'm obsessed with it.

His stuff is everywhere, and it totally smells like him in here, giving me the secret chills. He has his own master bath, naturally, and all kinds of big oak furniture that's so beautiful I can't help but run my fingers over it.

When I take a closer look at his huge, very comfy-looking California King bed, I realize that we're not alone.

"Oh my God! Who is this?" I squeal, trying to be quiet as I step closer.

"Alexandra, meets Boots," Noah croons, walking over and picking up the cat who was previously curled up like a fluffy ball in the middle of his bed. He hugs the animal to his chest and kisses it' head over and over. My ovaries are exploding. "Boots, this is Alex. We like her a lot, so be nice."

I whimper and pout, huddling up to Noah and petting his cat's head over and over. He's the softest, sweetest orange and white tabby ever. I'm instantly in love.

"You're not allergic, are you?" Noah asks, turning away in a moment of apparent panic.

I chuckle and shake my head. "No! I love cats!" I return to my place, kissing Boots all over. He seems perfectly content to just lie in Noah's arms and receive the love, though I don't blame him one bit. "He's such a good boy! Boy?"

Noah nods with a grin. "I've had him for seven years. I rescued him when he was just a kitten. He was a total alley cat, all mangy and malnourished. But I took him in, fixed him up, got rid of his balls - sorry, buddy - and he's been my little homie ever since."

I have to say, seeing this big, muscled-up, tattooed hottie snuggling an adorable, fuzzy little cat is making my vagina weep. I don't think I've ever been as attracted to someone as I am right now, and I need to physically step away before I kiss him.

Noah, not the cat.

My cheeks redden as I turn and clear my throat. "Do you have anything to drink?"

"No. I don't believe in liquids," Noah smirks. "Yes, Alex, I have something to drink. Come on." He sets Boots down on the bed, who curls back up in his spot from before, closing his yellow eyes. "Later, Boots. Don't cause a ruckus or

Seek Me

anything. We'll be right downstairs."

Boots is already asleep.

Noah brings me back downstairs to the kitchen, then spins in place.

"So do you want booze, or something with actual hydration properties? I have everything. I mean it. *Everything.*"

"Okay, you're making me want to name odd drinks now to see if you have them," I tease.

"Try me," he grins.

I pause for a moment in thought. "Cranberry juice?"

He cocks his head. "You're gonna have to do better than that, sweetheart. I've got regular, concentrate, cran-apple, cran-raspberry, and cran-grape - in normal *and* juice box forms."

"Jeez, okay. Clearly I don't know who I'm dealing with…" I giggle as he shakes his head slowly. "Okay, alright… uh… buttermilk?"

"A whole half-gallon. I use it for pancakes and biscuits. Well, my chef does. Next."

"Prune juice?"

"Yes, and let's move on from that one, please."

I laugh out loud. "God! Um… Pabst?"

"Alex… come *on*. I'm a red-blooded American man. Sheesh, I thought you came to dance!"

"Alright, alright!" I gasp, my brain sifting through every obscure liquid I can think of. "Oh shit! Okay, I have a great one. And if you have this, I'm going to need some of it right freaking now."

"Show me what you got, hot stuff," he rubs his palms together.

I pause, building the suspense before whispering, "Surge."

Noah's grin widens to an almost Cheshire-cat-like size. He says nothing, simply walks over to his refrigerator, yanks open one of the giant doors, and crouches down. He opens a drawer and rummages around for a few seconds before pulling out a green and red can.

I'm. In. Fucking. Awe.

He turns to face me and hands it over, wiggling his brows. I'm now holding a can of Surge Cola, and I've been transported back to 1999.

It's nostalgically uncanny. I'm suddenly standing in my best friend Alicia's basement drinking Surge because my parents wouldn't buy it since it's like cancer in a can, and apparently Alicia's parents didn't care about stuff like that.

"Oh… my… God!"

I'm shocked. I gawk at the can in my hand with my jaw hanging agape, like I'm looking a missing relic from Blackbeard's ship. My head jumps back up to Noah, who looks awfully pleased with himself.

"Where the *fuck* did you get this?! It's been discontinued since 2003!"

"I ordered it online a few years ago from some weird Russian website that sells things that have basically been outlawed in the States," he chuckles. "So… I mean… you *can* drink it if you really want to. But to be honest, it's mostly for show at this point."

I peek back at the can again. My mouth is watering.

I really want to drink it, but I am sort of afraid I might get sick. Not only because it's so old, but also because Surge had a tendency to make people sick. Hence why it was discontinued.

"I'll drink some if you do," I whisper, raising my brows at Noah.

He smiles big and nods enthusiastically. "Okay, deal. But hold on. There's something we gotta do first, to make the experience just right."

He opens a drawer next to me and as soon as it's ajar there's an unmistakable smell filling our general vicinity.

Noah pulls out an already-rolled joint and holds it up in front of me.

"Are you cool, man?" He purses his lips.

Ohhh duuuude! I so want to smoke that!

I haven't smoked weed in years. It was only ever something I did recreationally, once in a while. But Roger *hates* it. I mean despises it. *Doctors really are buzzkills sometimes.*

"Bad influence…" I whisper, lusting after the joint between his fingers.

"That's my name, don't wear it out," he smirks. "No, but in all seriousness, are you down? If not, it's totally fine. I just don't think I've ever drank Surge without being stoned." He chuckles.

"Really? I have…" I tell him. "But then again, I was like thirteen when I was drinking this stuff. Man, I wonder if it had any long-term affects…"

"Thirteen? Oh crap, I forgot. You're young," he scoffs and I giggle, then bite my lip.

"Why, how old are you? Thirty?" I ask. I'm surprised I don't know how old he is.

"I like you," his lips twist. "You're twenty-five, yes?" I nod slowly. "Welp, looks like I'm a decade older than you, youngin."

"Wow, I wasn't far off!" I grin with pride. "You're thirty-five?"

"Mhm," he hums.

Seek Me

"Okay, so you're like, a grown-up," I tease.

"Any day now."

I laugh, then lick my lips. Because he just got like a thousand times hotter. *Jeez, what is it with you and older guys? Can we say daddy-issues?*

"Anyway, are we gonna smoke this shit or what?" He asks, running the joint beneath his nose and sniffing it.

"I can't... Roger can always tell," I pout in disappointment.

"I thought you said he was gone for days..." he mutters. "That's at least a few showers from now."

"He'll still know. He's got the nose of a damn bloodhound."

"Well, I might have a solution," Noah says, and nods for me to follow him, which I do, into his living room.

He saunters over to the coffee table where there appears to be a big bowl of wrapped candies, of all different shapes, sizes and colors.

"We've got it in other forms," he picks up a gummy bear in clear plastic.

"You have a whole bowl of these on your coffee table? What if children come over?"

"My apartment is an eighteen-plus attraction," he sneers. "I would obviously put it away if kids were stopping by. You want one?"

"Yea!" My eyes light up and it makes him laugh. "What other edible stuff do you have here?"

"Girlfriend, I've got it all. You name it, I have it," he rasps. "Cookies, muffins, butter, oils... fuckin pasta sauce. Whatever."

So Noah Richards is a pothead? *Why am I not surprised?*

"What about brownies?" I ask, lifting a brow.

"I don't have any made right now, but we could always bake some."

"Oh my God! Yes! We should totally do that!" I squeal, jumping up and down.

Noah chuckles, watching me in amusement. "You want to bake pot brownies?"

"Only hell yes! Come on, Noah! It'll be so fun!"

"Alright, you're the boss," he shrugs.

I'm jittering with excitement. I'll be combining all my favorite things. Sweets, Noah and getting high.

We head back into the kitchen and Noah begins pulling things out of cabinets and cupboards. Then he slips an apron over his head, tying it behind his back. It has a rooster on it, and it says *Kiss The Cock*. I laugh and poke him in the rooster. He swats my hand away, giving me an evil smirk that has me clenching my thighs together.

Noah wearing that apron over his beautiful bare chest will be haunting my dreams for a while, I'm sure of it.

We float around his kitchen, making a mess while we cook, and I really love how well we seem to get along. The teasing flirtations are quite possibly my favorite part of our entire friendship. He's a touchy feely kind of guy, and I can't get enough because it's not something I ever experience at home.

When Roger touches me, it's calculated; alarming. And then there are the times when it's painful and bruising…

But when Noah touches me, it's soft and playful; sometimes even hesitant. As if he wants it really bad, but fears crossing some line that will upset me. I wish he knew that I've been craving his touch every day since we met… But then he *can't* know that.

Once the brownie batter is all mixed together, Noah opens the jar of oil and takes out a measuring spoon.

"How much do we add?" I ask, peering over his shoulder while he works. He looks like part sexy chef, part mad scientist. I'm getting some *Breaking Bad* vibes, for real.

"Not too much," he adds a few spoons of the oil to our brownie mixture. "I don't want you going all *Fear and Loathing* on me."

He gives me a side-wink and I bite my lip like an instinct.

"Hey, that's a great movie. We should watch it later."

"I can't watch that movie when I'm high. It gives me anxiety." He chuckles nervously and I cackle.

We stir in the good stuff, then pour the batter into a pan, placing it immediately into the oven.

"Would you like some wine while we wait for our creation?" Noah asks.

I nod. "Sure. Red would be nice."

"Coming right up."

He pours us each a glass while I stand in his giant, fancy kitchen, reveling in how at home I feel here. My kitchen is nice, and equally big, but it feels like it was set up for someone else. To be honest, the whole place does.

I've always felt like a guest in my own home, which is an uncomfortable way to live. The fact that everything is so neat and clean just makes me nervous that I'll mess it up.

But Noah's place is nice and homey without feeling like you're in a display of some kind. You're allowed to dirty up the kitchen while cooking brownies and it doesn't make a lick of difference.

Noah hands me a glass of wine and we clink like we always do, then take our sips, eyeing each other over the rims of our glasses. It's interesting, the eye contact. As if we're both trying to read the other's mind at the same time.

"So..." I speak softly, wondering what happens now.

"So," his deep voice grumbles in my direction.

There's some serious heat in the air, and I don't think it's the oven. *Need a distraction.*

"Can we go out on the terrace while we wait?" I ask him, requiring fresh air soon, before I spontaneously combust.

He nods slowly and walks away, leaving me following behind him like a puppy. He whips the stupid apron off and tosses it somewhere, going for the big glass door to his terrace, which could easily be mistaken for a window. We step outside into the cool night air, which feels nice on my heated skin.

We both take a seat in adjacent chairs, and I admire the view of this intricate, private little spot. There are even more plants out here. Potted trees, flowers, all kinds of vegetation. It feels like we're in a jungle.

"Do you take care of all these?" I ask, looking around.

"Nah, I wish I was that good," he chuckles. "I have two cleaning ladies, one of whom does the plants."

"They're really pretty," I tell him and he smiles.

We both go quiet again for a moment, just watching each other, enjoying one another's company without having to fill the silence with words. It's nice; peaceful. I can't remember a time when I was this at ease.

"Thanks for coming over, Al," he finally breaks the silence with a soft voice. "I like having you here."

"I like it here," I respond, then take another sip of my delicious wine. "Your place is great. The perfect home. It really fits you."

He says nothing, just continues to stare at me. I can't tell what he's thinking one bit, and I'm not sure if it makes me nervous or enlivened. *Maybe both.*

Noah glances down at a watch on his wrist I didn't notice until right now. "Time to get those brownies out. You can stay here if you want."

He gets up and meanders back inside while I take his advice and stay seated. I look around some more, fascinated that I'm still in the city. This little terrace is so secluded, you can barely hear the noise, although it's still there. The city noises are *always* there, and it's oddly comforting.

I grew up here, in Brooklyn. The city is a part of me. I can't imagine living anywhere else in the world. Don't get me wrong, I love to travel, and I definitely want to see a lot more places in my lifetime. But I'll always come back to New York.

The concrete jungle is my home.

A few minutes later, Noah comes traipsing back outside with a plate in his hand. He sets it down on the table and there's actual steam billowing off the brownies. They smell so good, my mouth is filling with saliva.

"Dig in, lovely," he nods at the plate and I squeal with excitement that makes him laugh.

I grab one of the warm, gooey confections and take a bite, instantly launching into a moan because it's like chocolate heaven in my mouth.

"God, these are *good*," I drawl in between scarfing the thing down like a beast.

"Right?" Noah agrees with a mouthful of brownie. "You didn't see my secret ingredient."

"Uh yes I did," I scoff. "Weed oil, remember? I was standing right there. Are you already high?"

He huffs a chuckle and shakes his head. "No, silly ass. I added butterscotch chips. See?"

He holds up his half-eaten brownie and points at the blondish chunks scattered inside.

"Oh man! That's what that flavor is!" I gasp. I would look at mine, but it's already gone. So I go in for another.

"Um, Alex... Maybe you should only have one," Noah murmurs in slight hesitation. "This shit's pretty potent."

"I'm fine, *Mom*," I snort, chomping down the sweet, moist goodness.

"You weigh like a hundred pounds soaking wet," he says, eyeing me speculatively.

"Well, that's not accurate," I mutter. "But thanks."

He laughs at me and shrugs while we finish our treats. Once we're done with the wine too, we head back inside, and Noah turns on the fireplace. It gives the whole open space a nice ambience, what with the warmth, and the glow, and the crackling noises that might be fake, but still make it seem like we're in a cabin in the woods.

"Okay, so... Movie? TV?" Noah begins suggesting things. "Or we could put on some R&B and you could dance for me."

Seek Me

I giggle and tug my lip between my teeth. "Genuine *Pony*?"

Noah throws his head back in a booming laugh that makes my chest tight and my panties wet. *God,* he's just so hot. And he still hasn't put a shirt on, which is dandy. Now that the fire is going, I imagine he won't have an excuse to. *Maybe I could take something off...*

Oh boy. I don't like where my mind is going. We're alone in his place, drinking wine in front of a fire. And soon the weed will make me even more relaxed and giggly than I already am, which will make me want to cuddle up on him. I can already tell that's where I'll end up. I can only deny myself for so long...

"Let's just um... watch a movie," I stutter, likely sounding just as nervous as I feel.

I plop down on the hella comfy couch and watch as Noah glides gracefully around his living room, so assured in who he is, it's a wondrous thing to witness. All long, toned limbs, silky hair and easy smiles. Such a magical creature to be around. Like a unicorn.

He turns on his gargantuan TV and *Fear and Loathing in Las Vegas* starts playing.

"I thought you didn't want to watch this high?" I ask him with a grin.

"You can hold me if I get scared," he winks. And I freeze like a deer in headlights because I totally would.

The movie plays for a bit, and we just sit next to each other, watching. We laugh and point things out, reciting our favorite lines as they happen. For me, Noah is the most fun person to be around, and I think part of it is because we're so similar. I get along better with him than anyone I've ever known. We just mesh.

The next thing I know, the movie is over. It's a long movie, so I'm surprised it seems to have gone by in the blink of an eye. The credits are rolling, and I'm lying on my back with a fuzzy pillow behind my head, legs draped over Noah's lap. He's playing with my toes and I'm giggling because it tickles.

Actually, I think I've been giggling for several minutes now. I can tell because my abs hurt.

And Noah's giggling, too.

Oh, shit. I'm fucking high.

I'm high as a fucking kite!

I laugh even harder.

"This little piggy went to the market," Noah chuckles, fingering each of my toes. "This little piggy stayed home. This little piggy wears lipstick. This little piggy says, *Bill, why are you wearing lipstick, bro? That's for girls!* And this little piggy fell in love with the wolf who was blowing their houses down, even though they're from different worlds, but he didn't care that their love was forbidden because that was part of the excitement."

I'm laughing so hard I'm snorting and there are tears pooling in my eyes.

"What?" Noah snickers at me, his head tilting to the side in that way he does, and it's just so cute I want to pinch his cheeks. His butt cheeks.

Jesus, what?!

"You're the most insane person I've ever met. Did you know that?" I sigh through my never-ending giggle-fit.

"I believe it," he shrugs. "I'm pretty weird."

"I love it." My smile is out of control.

But Noah seems to like it because he suddenly grabs me by both calves and drags the rest of my body closer to him, until my butt is almost on his lap. Then he crawls over me slowly, planting his palms by my shoulders, holding himself hovering, with his face right smack in front of mine.

That does it. The smile has been wiped clean off my mouth, which is very dry right now.

I try to swallow but it barely works. My heart is pounding in my chest because he's so damn close to me. The ends of our noses are practically touching.

"Alex," he whispers. All I can do is blink up at him. "You wanna know what we should do?"

"W-what's that?" My voice sticks in my throat.

"Let's play…"

My pulse thrums inside me as my body tingles all over, especially below my waist. *Play? Play what?*

His breath is warm on my lips, and despite everything I've been thinking since I met him, about keeping my distance and not letting this go too far, I'm about to close my eyes and let him kiss the shit out of me because it's what I want.

I want Noah's lips. Noah's lips are what I want.

"Mario Kart 64," he finishes his sentence and my eyes snap back open. "I have it. Wanna play? It's only like, the most fun game ever. And I don't want to toot my own horn, but… toot toot. Because I'm really freaking good."

He grins wide with excitement and presses a chaste kiss on my forehead before diving off me and stumbling away. And I'm left panting on his couch,

Seek Me

recovering from whatever the hell that just was, and the fact that I almost came from it.

Ok, so we're both high, and we're going to play video games, and I'm acknowledging that I'm crazy attracted to him and all I want is to be close enough to feel his warmth and his soft skin because it's amazing, and he's amazing, and being next to him is the best high in the world, weed be damned.

Wow. That was a lot.

I rub my head and sit up slowly, blinking back my fluffiness. Despite being on edge about my attraction to Noah, which seems to be magnified now that I'm baked goods, I must admit I feel pretty nice right now. His cozy apartment is going to be my happy place from now on. The place I think about when I'm depressed.

Noah is ransacking through all kinds of things, and he reminds me of the Tasmanian Devil cartoon character. I'm not sure how he's moving so fast, because I feel like I'm in slow motion.

He finally stops spinning and sets up a Nintendo 64 console. Another shot of nostalgia. I haven't seen one of these things since I was a kid.

Oh, shit! The Surge!

"Noah!" I gasp, darting over to him and tugging on the waist of his pants over and over, because they're the only things he's wearing. "We have to open the Surge!"

"Oh shit, you're right!" His face turns adventurous, and he sprints out of the room, then returns one-second later with the can. "Okay. Here we go. You do the honors."

He hands it to me, and I gaze over it one last time.

Wow, this is crazy. I'm about to drink Surge! I hope I don't puke. That would be embarrassing.

I take a breath, and Noah stands before me, eyes wide with mischief. I pop open the top and we both squeal. This is fully ridiculous.

"Here goes nothing," I whisper, and bring the can to my lips, taking a small sip.

It's still bubbly, though probably not as much as it once was. And it's disgustingly sweet on my tongue. *Jesus,* it tastes like diabetes in a can.

"Well!?" Noah lifts his brows. "How is it? Is it the same?"

I pause and cluck my tongue a few times. "It's exactly how I remember it."

He breathes out hard then claps. And we both cheer for the nineties. The best damn decade to be a kid.

Nyla K

Noah takes a few sips, and I take one more before we decide that's enough. Surge kind of lost its appeal over the years, but I will say, it's a very cool thing to have after all this time. *Definitely brings me back.*

After that, we sit on the floor in front of the TV and fire up the N64. Mario Kart was and always will be the great game of my adolescence. It's an effortless kind of fun, and playing it now makes me feel like a kid again. I love this feeling.

I got married very young. I dove headfirst into adulthood without once looking back and now, given the events of the last couple years, I'm like a fifty-year-old in a twenty-five-year-old's body.

I'll be forever grateful to Noah Richards for bringing me back to simpler times.

We pick our players and get ready to race. Noah picks Mario and I choose Toad - naturally. And then we're off.

"Ohhh shit! Lookie who's got the red shells, baby!" I squeal, nailing the crap out of Noah and sending him flying.

"Dammit, Alex! Not cool," he grumbles, rushing to speed back up to my commanding lead.

He gets a few blasters, but it's still no match for my Toad-like agility, and I beat his ass, first game.

"You cheated," he pouts, grabbing my shirt and tugging me until I fall into his side.

"Did not! Toad just rules. There's no way around it," I shrug, shoving him playfully, though now that I'm even closer to him, I'm not moving away to save my life.

Our thighs are pressed up against each other's as we start our second game. Koopa Troopa Beach. *Homeboy's goin down.*

I'm in the lead out the gate, but then Noah starts shooting things at me and I fall behind. Still, I'm determined. I can't let him beat me at Koopa Troopa. It's my bread and butter.

I summon all my Toad powers, and use the best advances I can get, blasting in all the right places; a hop here, a swerve there. Noah's laughing like the cocky bastard he is when, with the finish line in my sights, I release the Bowser shell I've been holding onto and shoot him right in his smug Mario back.

He goes spinning off to the side, leaving the win open for yours truly as I speed to victory.

"What what!" I cheer, raising my arms in the air and dancing around in place. "You were saying, tough guy? I'm pretty sure you were supposed to be unbeatable!"

Noah gasps in outrage, his jaw hanging open while he tries not to laugh.

"Alexandra! I can't believe you just did that to me!" He growls and grabs my waist, pulling me onto his lap.

I'm breathless and giggling feverishly, holding onto his shoulders, the warm skin feeling like silk under my hands.

"Don't be a sore loser," I smirk down at him, victorious. "Just admit it… You got beat by a toad."

I stick my tongue out at him and his lips part, eyes darting to my mouth. I swallow hard because I'm suddenly aware that I'm still sitting on his lap. And he's gazing at my mouth with some obvious hunger in his shiny dark eyes.

My chest moves up and down with forceful breaths and for reasons unknown I feel empowered. It probably has nothing to do with winning that stupid video game, and everything to do with the sexy celebrity who's holding onto me and lusting after my lips and tongue.

My body reacts on its own and pushes him until he reclines onto his back on the floor. I'm sitting in a strange position, with my butt pressed against his crotch and my legs off to the side. But my hands are holding his shoulders, so I have no choice but to let gravity take over and sink down until our chests are touching.

As soon as my tits touch his firm pectorals, he lets out a quick breath, still staring up at me with wide eyes, like he has absolutely no idea what I'm doing, but he's afraid I might stop at the slightest provocation. My eyes stay with his as my hands slide over his skin, down his arms which are resting by his sides, touching his hands briefly before they land on his waist.

I see him swallow, slowly, and it reminds me of how much I like his neck, and throat. And that sexy stubble that looks like it smells good and tastes even better. Whatever is happening right now is so bizarre and jacked up, but it already feels amazing.

Just go with it.

I shift my hips subtly, rubbing my butt on his crotch, and his eyes flutter shut, a soft moan escaping his slightly parted lips. *God, that sounds so fucking hot. And looks fantastic.*

I move in slow, circular motions, rotating between his parted thighs as I press my ass up against his growing hard-on. I can totally feel it. It's inflating right beneath me, getting bigger and bigger with every flick of my booty. Noah makes a strangled noise, and I glance down to see his fingers digging into the carpet. I'm not sure why he's not touching me, but it seems like he's enjoying letting me torture him, so I'll keep going.

I'm writhing against him, and he's squirming beneath me, lifting his hips to build the friction between our bodies. It's so fucking hot around us, like we're on the sun; the lust stirring up even more heat than the burning fire across the room. I press my tits harder on his chest, begging for some sensation on my sensitive nipples, and the barbells in them.

Noah has one, too. I wonder if his feels as good as mine do right now...

I make sure to give the right side a bit more pressure on his left, and since he's shirtless and my clothes are very sheer, it almost feels as satisfying as doing it naked. *I said* almost...

Could I take my shirt off? Would that seem slutty? Jesus, that ship has sailed, sweetheart. You're grinding all over a guy who's not your husband.

I push those thoughts out of my mind and keep moving, Noah moving with me, so painfully slow it's like we're barely doing anything, but somehow it's divine. My fingers slip into the waist of his jeans, desperate to take in the feeling of his soft, warm skin in that sensitive place.

"Alex..." he grunts, and I hum, inching my face even closer to his neck. "Fuck..."

Suddenly his hands grab my hips and he pulls me down even harder, groaning at what I'm guessing feels really good for him. This is confirmed by the giant firm object throbbing through both of our jeans.

His dick feels very big... Dammit, I want to feel it without clothes in the way. Why are we always dry-humping each other?

He lifts my hips and turns me a bit, forcing me to spread my legs and wrap them around his waist, as much as I can while we're lying down. My knees are now on the floor, and our crotches are together, and I agree with this move. Very much.

Noah grinds hard in between my thighs, and I can feel the shape of his length dragging along my pussy. I whimper into the crook of his neck, which makes him gasp. He holds my butt even harder in his big hands, palming it, squeezing while I grate my entire body on his. I'm so small and he's so big, but we fit together perfectly and it feels phenomenal.

My hands travel all over his torso, in between us so I can touch his abs, scratch his happy trail, cup his pecs and tease the silver in his nipple.

"Uhh..." he breathes, the long, hard shape between my thighs resembling a metal pole.

Seek Me

His scent is driving me nuts, and his skin is so hot it's practically burning my lips, because they're right there, itching to kiss him somewhere.

What I really want are his lips. The desire to kiss those soft, delicious-looking things is taking over my mind. But I know that once we start kissing then it's a whole different ballgame. Then we're making out, and getting naked, and kissing other places, and doing stuff with our mouths and our hands, and he's taking me upstairs to his giant bed, which is exactly where I want to be, but I don't know if I can do that right now.

I'm nervous. I can't sleep with Noah Richards. That will change my entire life.

So for right now, I'll just kiss the part of him that's readily available, and seemingly less complicated.

I press my lips softly to his neck. Actually, it's more like the spot between his jaw and his neck, which isn't a spot I ever thought about before until this moment, but Noah's is really nice. It smells like heaven, and it's rough and stubbly, but in a good way. So I kiss it gently and I immediately know I made the right decision.

His whole body tremors under me, the sounds coming out of him more like vibrations. He's so growly, he's become a giant vibrator built just for me. His strong hands are still holding my ass, moving it up and down with his hips while he thrusts in steady, tender motions. I imagine this is how he fucks without clothes, too. And it's utterly fucking flawless.

My lips go again, using the motivation from the euphoric friction of his rock-solid cock sliding up and down on my clit through our jeans, and I kiss. And I kiss again. And the next time my tongue peeks out a little.

"Fuck..." he groans out the absolute hottest thing I've ever heard. His voice is rough and hoarse and shaking with desire. Noah's sexy-time voice is my new obsession.

Nope... Wrong. This is.

His dick is so fucking engorged it's trying to fight its way out of his pants. Honestly, he must be a little uncomfortable. *Maybe I should unzip them...*

I can't decide that right now so I suck harder on his juicy neck.

"Alex..." he whispers, breathless, his wide chest moving rapidly as his heart pounds into me. "God... what... Mmm..."

I don't know what he's trying to say, but I think I'm about to expire. I'm grinding my pussy so slow, yet so hard on his dick that I really think I could explode into orgasm at any minute.

"Noah," I purr and he groans out a little louder. I trail my tongue over his throat and give that spot a little suction, too. "Why do you feel so good...?"

"I... God fucking dammit..."

I leave my right hand on his chest, subtly toying with his nipple ring, while the other slinks up into his hair. I can't help but tug on it just a little. Okay, maybe I do that to the nipple, too...

"Alex... we..." Noah's struggling to say something, but everything around me is all echoey and dark.

I've slipped into a wormhole, where it's just me and him, and nothing else matters. He just makes me feel so *fucking* good, in every possible way.

I'm whimpering and panting and moaning quietly in between kissing and sucking his neck. And he's helping me ride him so hard and deep it's almost as if our clothes *aren't* there. Maybe they're not. They could have disintegrated by now.

"Noah..." I gasp as I'm swept up into a fluffy cloud. I can feel us falling away from reality as we hold on to each other for dear life. "Fuck... me..."

"Baby..." he rumbles and does the unthinkable. He reaches one of his hands up to my tit and squeezes.

I am so fucking done for.

I erupt. Suddenly I'm plummeting into an abyss, clutching Noah as hard as humanly possible while my insides quake.

I'm coming.

I'm coming...?

"I'm fucking coming..." I gasp in disbelief, crying out all kinds of nonsense into his neck.

He holds me so hard against him; I swear we're the same person right now. One body. One soul. One life.

I've never felt such bliss in ever.

"Shit shit shit..." Noah rumbles, his thumb skimming the steel in my nipple through my clothes, causing another tremor inside my pussy. "What the fuck... are you doing... to... me?"

His chest is hauling like crazy as his whole body trembles everywhere, and I register in the midst of my own internal contractions that he's throbbing between my thighs. His dick is pulsing so hard I can actually feel it.

Holy fuck, he's coming too.

"Alex!" He croaks and squeezes the life out of me, rocking us together, making me come even harder because he's coming. He's having an orgasm right beneath *me*, and it's fucking incredible.

Amazing. Stupendous. Magnificent.

Jesus Christ, what the fuck are we doing?!

The two of us are strangling each other's bodies for what feels like an eternity, breathing so heavy it's as if we just swam for miles. The noises he's making will be forever etched in my mind. He sounds like I've stolen every single bit of edge he's ever had. And I kind of love it way too much.

Once we come to, I swear to God hours went by. Maybe even days. I'm so dazed and stupefied, I wouldn't know what to say or do if I was given a lifetime to prepare.

Noah's arms eventually release me, and slowly we unwind from each other. He's sprawled on the floor under me as I lift my head, neck, then my torso, enough to roll off of him. I feel light as air, and yet it's hard to move. I flop down on my back beside him and stare up at the ceiling. We stay like this for a few more minutes, wondering what in the *fuck* just happened and what on Earth we're supposed to do now.

Noah grunts himself into a sitting position and despite how completely awkward I feel at the moment, I glance up at him. His hair is all over the place, cheeks flushed, and he has little love bites all over his throat.

My heart seizes in my chest and my stomach clenches. He looks so unbearably beautiful like that, I don't know how to react.

His dark eyes dart down to me and he bites his lip. It looks like his arms are shaking as he holds himself up. The urge to grab him and kiss the adorable expression off his sweet, sexy face is so overwhelming I could burst into tears.

Actually, I *am* going to burst into tears. It's happening and I can't control it.

I need to get the fuck out of here.

Now I'm panicking. I'm freaking the fuck out. *Oh God, oh Jesus. What the hell did I just do? I basically attacked him!*

I jumped him and dry-humped him until we both came our pants?! What are we seventeen?!

Which is exactly what I'd been thinking since the night we met, when we humped each other at Sensay. I really don't understand what our fascination is with humping one another, but it's very unorthodox.

Shit... The weed... Surge... Mario Kart... dry-humping on the floor. We *are* fucking teenagers!

Damn you, nineties!

I sit up fast. So fast my hair flings around my face. Noah looks at me like he's concerned and wants to say something, but can't. He's still stunned into silence and I get it. There's nothing I can say right now either, other than…

"I have to go."

I stand up on shaky legs, between my thighs drenched from the orgasm. I hurry to compose myself and before I know what I'm doing, I dart toward the door.

"Alex…" Noah's voice calls from behind me, and he sounds so worried and sweet that all I want to do in the whole world is turn around, but I *can't*.

I just fucked up everything, and now I have to leave.

I whip open his door and jump through it, slamming it shut a little too hard behind me. I race through the hall fast in case he chases me like he always does, but when I reach the front door, I realize that he's not.

I leave his building and thank my lucky stars there happens to be a cab driving by. I almost dive in front of it, then clamber inside. I'm breathless and on the verge of tears as I give the driver my address, all the while watching Noah's front door. He doesn't come out in the time it takes for my cab to drive up his block. And I know he didn't come out at all.

He's not chasing me this time. Because this time, I ruined it all. I ruined what we had, and I did something awful and stupid in the process.

The sensational high is already gone and now I'm numb. I squeezed it too hard, and it died.

I manage to hold the tears in until I'm home, securely tucked inside the bedroom of my quiet prison.

And then I crawl into bed and cry myself to sleep.

Chapter Eight
Noah

THE BAND OF US WALK, through the hall and out to the lobby, turning heads all along the way. There are ten people, maybe more, walking in a huddled group, talking and conversing and shaking hands. So many publicists and agents and assistants, it feels like an episode of *Entourage*.

At last we make it into the massive marble lobby, and everyone sections off. Today went well. Actually, better than I could have hoped, and I'm ecstatic.

We just had our first official meeting for what will hopefully be the first of many seasons of our brand new project they've dubbed *Hell Storm*.

I like the name. It sounds like something right up my alley, as does the entire plot for the show. I think it may just be the job I've been waiting my whole life for. This is it.

The role of a lifetime.

"Hey Noah," a deep voice with a British accent calls from my right, and I turn. "Would you like to grab a drink?"

I nod with enthusiasm. "You read my mind."

Andrew and I say a few quick goodbyes to our people, shake some hands, and then leave together, rounding the corner from the giant studio office building and sauntering down the sidewalk.

"There's a chill spot on the next block," I tell him and he nods, following my lead.

I just met Andrew James, my new costar, a couple hours ago at the start of the meeting, and I already like him. He's quiet and uber-professional; serious yet obviously just as amped as I am over our new gig. Not to mention he's a pretty famous guy - crazy talented - but he manages to remain low key and casual, which I like a lot. In my business, you meet an abundance of people who think they're God's gift to the screen, and have egos so inflated you're tempted to shoot them up with Benadryl.

But I can already tell Andrew's not like that. He barely even seems to register how famous he is. He just loves acting, and apparently the entire process of production. *He'll be a great front-man for our show.*

We step into a quaint little pub I've been to a few times and make our ways to the far end of the bar, so as to remain inconspicuous. Since I spend ninety percent of my life wearing a hat and sunglasses, it's sort of hard for me to disguise my appearance in New York City. But Andrew's pulling the same game, rocking a worn-out red baseball cap pulled down over his face.

The place isn't crowded by any means, but it is Saturday. Still, it's barely pushing four in the afternoon. Not exactly the pub-crawling time of day. Hopefully, we can enjoy a few minutes of uninterrupted conversation and alcohol ingestion. I'm not really in the best mood, despite how awesome the meeting just went.

But I'm trying hard not to think about what's bothering me right now…

Andrew orders a Macallan and I follow his lead, drumming my fingers repeatedly on the bar out of all the jitteriness I'm currently feeling.

"I think that went well, yes?" He lifts his brow at me. "They're making some moves already. I'd love to start filming in April."

"You think the schedule will stick?" I ask as the bartender sets our drinks down.

"I don't see why not," he shrugs. "They seem to have everything in order."

We pick up our glasses and raise them, both of us wearing excited smirks.

"To summer in Georgia," he says and I laugh softly as we each take our sips.

The scotch goes down smooth, calming my overstimulated mind. Maybe getting crunk at four in the afternoon isn't what some people call *normal*, but I need it today, to distract me from the chaos happening inside.

"It's gonna be hot as balls," I mutter, gulping more of my drink. "But Savannah should have some pretty boss houses. Southern McMansions and all that."

Andrew makes a face, his lips twisting down as his eyes fall to the drink in his hands. He's staring at his wedding band, then spins it methodically on his finger, like a nervous tick.

"You're married?" I ask, wondering why he's clammed up all of a sudden.

"Yea…" he sighs, pursing his lips. "My wife's not exactly thrilled about the prospect of leaving London for months at a time." He picks up his drink and kills it, nodding at the bartender for a refill.

"Really?" My forehead creases in perplexity. "Why the hell not? I mean sure, being on location can be stressful. But Georgia is nice."

"I don't even think it's just Georgia…" he murmurs, visibly biting the inside of his cheek. "Last time I was on location we fought more than we ever have before... I knew she didn't want me to take this job, but how could I say no? It's the role of a lifetime!"

"Right?" I agree with his sentiments of my exact thoughts on the subject. "Do you have kids?"

He nods. "Michael is five and Luciana, the baby, just turned two." His face instantly lights up as he tugs his phone out of his pocket, swiping furiously. "I'm going to show you pictures, I hope that's cool." He peeks at me.

I laugh. "Yea, it's cool. I don't have any myself, but kids are pretty dope."

He's beaming as he shows me a few pictures on his phone of his kids, who are, by all definitions, completely adorable. I peep his wife in one of them and my eyes dart back up to his face.

"So... the fighting? That's gotta suck, huh?"

"It's bloody awful," he blinks hard. "I don't understand what the problem is. I was acting when she met me. She knew this was where I saw myself going. And she was always fine with it when they were local jobs... You know, around Europe. But as soon as I began filming in the States suddenly it was a problem. I don't know... Sometimes I think we're..." He pauses and gulps. "Never mind. Sorry..."

"No, it's all right. Tell me," I insist, having no reservations at all about lending him my ear. I'm used to it, after all.

This is what I do for all my friends. I listen to their marital issues. And sure, Andrew and I aren't exactly *friends*. We just met. But I like him. I think we'll definitely get along working together.

He breathes out hard and takes another big sip of his booze. "Sometimes I think maybe we're not meant for one another. I was a bachelor for a while... It was rather crazy." He laughs to himself, mentally reminiscing at something that makes him shake his head, to which I chuckle.

"Yea, trust me, I know the game," I murmur, though the confidence I usually possess when talking about my female companions suddenly feels forced. And I definitely know *why*...

"You don't say!" Andrew scoffs, quirking a brow at me. "Even if I hadn't heard of your gallivanting all over the city with a new woman every night, those hickeys on your neck would be a dead-giveaway." He laughs out loud and points at the horrified look on my face.

Yes, I still have hickeys on my damn neck and throat. They won't go away, though it's only been two days since they were given to me by the little raven-haired culprit.

Part of me loves that Alex left marks on me. It's as if she actually *wants* me, more than a friend, and used her lips to claim her territory. She practically peed all over me.

Ew. No thanks, R. Kelly.

But the potential sweetness of the whole thing is tainted because she took off after we... did what we did... And I haven't heard from her since. I've tried calling her dozens of times and have gotten nothing but voicemail.

After the initial shock wore off from the fact that we dry-humped each other to orgasm on my living room floor while playing Mario Kart like a couple of fucking children, I was able to compose myself enough to go after her. I sprinted out of my building, hoping that maybe I could catch up with her on the street. But no such luck. She was already gone.

I called her phone over and over until I finally got it through my thick skull that it was off, and obviously for a reason. She was clearly upset.

And I felt like a giant pile of garbage.

Still do.

"I don't think I've had a hickey since I was seventeen," Andrew sighs nostalgically and I give him the side-eye. "But then, I've been married for six years."

"Yea, well I'd hold off before you envy me," I huff, swallowing a mouthful of scotch. "My love life isn't exactly all tits and rainbows."

"Why, what happened?" He turns in his seat to give me a very concerned blue-eyed stare. "Some little totty steal your edge and make you question whether you still *want* to be a bachelor?"

I gape at him. "You sound like you have some experience in this..." I try to shift the attention off of me.

"Well, a bit, I suppose," he runs his fingers along his chin. "Vivian settled me down. But I'm unsure if it was about her, or simply that I was done whoring around. You have to admit, it *does* get old after a while..."

Ain't that the truth...

"I think life is too short to spend it flitting around forever," he goes on. "But I think settling down for the sake of settling is a mistake, as well..." His voice trails off as he considers his own words.

"It doesn't seem like either of us are in a position to be giving anyone advice," I scoff, to which he laughs.

"Cheers to that, mate," he grins and we clink glasses again. "I like you,

Seek Me

Noah. I think we'll get along quite well."

"I think we'll have a lot of fun, and get into a *lot* of trouble," I show him an evil grin and he laughs again.

"Oh, I don't doubt it. And add Johnny to the mix... Jesus. Watch out, world."

We both laugh together. "It's gonna be a hell storm."

The music is pumping loud around me.

It's comforting; the way the bass beats into my chest, covering up the rapping of my own heart.

I'm out at Sensay, because it's been a long day and I just want to keep drowning myself in liquor so I'm not tempted to think about my feelings or check my phone for the hundredth time in forty-five minutes.

Naturally my phone is blowing up the way it always is, but I still keep praying for a call or text from Alex, and it's starting to feel like that might never happen.

I just can't believe I blew it. I can't believe I ruined our friendship by letting us slip into this awkward, tense bizarro realm of mistakes and regrets.

I don't really regret what happened with Alex, because it felt amazing. She came in my arms. Jesus, all the cold showers in the world can't erase the memory of how fucking sexy that was.

What I do regret is that I wasn't supposed to push her, and that's exactly what I did. I should have stopped it the moment she started grinding that tight, taut little body on me. I should have took a fucking second to be a good guy, not the degenerate I so clearly am, and thought about what it would do to our friendship. And more importantly than that, what it could mean for her.

She's married.

M.A.R.R.I.E.D.

So what if her husband is an abusive waste of human life? He's still her husband, and it's up to her to leave him, and deal things in her own way. But I fucked with her head. I stole her ability to process things properly by teasing her and touching her and wanting her so fucking bad it clouded both of our judgements.

Man, I am a piece of shit. Maybe it's a good thing she's not calling me. She should probably stay away from the relationship enema. Turning all relationships into explosive shit.

I really hate feeling like this. I don't do depressed. I don't do insecurity, or vulnerability or regret. I don't do *feelings*, which is exactly why I avoid falling in love. Because this is what love gets you... Perilous self-doubt, jealousy, and desperation. Being in love sucks big hairy balls.

Wait, why are we talking about love?

My chest tightens and sweat appears Houdini-style on my brow and in my palms. My heart is suddenly racing.

I'm not in love... Am I?

No no no no... This can't happen. Not me. Not casual, unassuming Noah Richards, King of the Bachelors.

Love's not in my vocabulary.

Fuck.

Well, that's it. I need to move the fuck on, right now. I need to prove to myself that Alex is better off without me... Even if she is in danger, and I still feel really fucking bad about that.

But I'm sure if she needed help she would seek it out... Right?

I'm so all over the place I can't barely think. All I know is that I'm out, I'm sort of drunk, and there's a blonde girl over by the bar who's eyeing me like she just found her next snack.

Good. Great. This is perfect.

I can use this. Let's go over and talk to the blonde girl in the shockingly tight dress, flirt and maybe bang, and forget all about the mess I've made.

I stammer up to the girl and we just stare at each other for a few minutes, because it's too loud in here to converse. Which is fine. I don't want to talk *at all*. If I can manage to get her naked and wrapped around my dick without having to speak *any* words, or listen to any of hers, then tonight will be considered a victory.

The blonde leans in close to me, her fingers dancing along my abdomen. I rest my hand casually on her lower back, basically the top of her butt, and pull her so she's flush against me, then twirl my fingers around in her bleach-blonde hair.

It's not as soft as someone else's hair I know. Those silky smooth dark strands...

No. Stop it right now. Focus.

We're doing this, not that.

I lean into her ear and whisper, "A girl's who's coming home with me says what?"

"What?" She huffs in a soft giggle.

It's showtime.

The girl and I down our drinks, all the while touching each other teasingly, then we leave the club hand-in-hand, stepping out onto the street, into the cool, fresh air of Saturday night in Manhattan.

"Should we get a cab?" She asks, slurring a little as she sways on her feet.

I grab her hips to steady her and almost fall over myself, the both of us giggling like drunk children.

"I live like three blocks away," I hiccup. "We can walk it."

"Really?" She whines, pulling some unenthused face that serves as a buzzkill and a turnoff at the same time. "These shoes kill my feet. Let's just get a cab. Please..." She presses her boobs into my chest and nibbles on my earlobe.

Ugh. Fucking fine.

"No problem, love," I rasp with an easy smirk to cover up my annoyance, then tug my phone out of my pocket to call Jimmy.

Just as I'm about to press call, my phone starts ringing in my hand. I focus my blurred vision on the screen, because I must be imagining this.

There's no way it's her... Is it?

It is. It fucking is! Alex is calling me right now.

My heart surges behind my ribs and I frantically swipe to answer the call.

"Hello? Al?" I'm out of breath from literally nothing.

"Noah..." she whimpers and it's immediately clear she's crying. Her voice is small and meek in my ear and she sounds scared.

"What is it, baby? What's wrong?" I ask, fast and panicked. *She better be okay.*

I've completely forgotten about my mantra from a few minutes ago; surrounding the what happened the other day. And I'm fully ignoring the girl standing next to me, who's tugging on my shirt to reclaim my attention. But it's not working. The only things I'm focused on are the soft, breathy little sobs coming out of Alex, slinking right into my brain.

"I'm here, Alex. What's going on? Do you need me to come get you?"

"N-no... No-ah..." she sputters, sniffling over and over. "I can't..." Then she stops abruptly, going fully silent.

I check the screen to make sure the call is still connected.

"Al? Alex?! Talk to me, baby. What's going on?" The blonde girl stomps away from me in a huff.

"Noah, I'm scared," Alex whispers and my heart cracks down the middle, whilst my blood simultaneously rushes in my ears.

I'm going to kill him. I'm going to fucking *kill him.*

My fist clenches at my side, every muscle in my body constricting with the need to hurt someone. One someone in particular.

"I'm coming over there. Right now," I growl into the phone, gritting my teeth like a madman. I think my eye is twitching.

"No! No, Noah you can't," she shrieks as quietly as possible.

The thought that she's hiding from her psychotic monster of a husband has me walking. I'm not sure where I'm going. I can't very well walk across town. *Maybe to a cab? Yea, that's good. I'll get in a cab. I'll ride to her house and somehow get inside her building and murder her fucking husband with a... knife? Yea, a knife. That'll do.*

"Noah... Please promise me you're not coming here," she pleads, her soft, uneasy tone slithering inside me and forcing my feet to stop moving.

I squeeze my eyes shut tight and release a steady breath.

"Noah, promise me."

I bite the inside of my cheek so hard I taste blood.

"I *promise*," the word crawls out of my throat, against my will, contradicting the rage burning me from the inside out.

"Thank you," she sniffs as I swallow hard.

"You're leaving that house right now though, Alex. Do you understand?" I hiss, struggling to keep my anger in check for her. "Right now. I'll send Jimmy."

She's quiet again.

I check the screen. "Alex?"

"Yea, okay," she whimpers, and I can see her nodding in my mind. It's so cute and sad I just want to curl her up in my arms and protect her from everything that wishes to cause her harm.

"Okay. I'll hang up and call Jimmy," I tell her, possessed by determination. This is good. We have a plan. We can fix this. "Give me one minute and then call me right back, okay?"

"Mhm..." she breathes and falls into more quiet crying.

"Alex, baby, please... Sixty seconds and you call me right back, alright?" I beg her. "I'll stay on the phone with you until Jimmy gets there. One minute, Alex, or I'm coming over there."

"Okay, yes. I'll call you right back in one minute," she sighs through a raspy voice that's barely existent. She sounds like a ghost. This fucking asshole is killing her.

And I'm going to kill him.

Seek Me

"Good. Alright. Hang tight, beautiful."

"Thank you, Noah."

Everything inside me is falling apart.

"Don't thank me, babe. We're gonna fix this."

She murmurs a quick *okay* and I hang up to call Jimmy. I bark at him to go to Alex's right the fuck now and not to leave until she's securely inside the vehicle, then bring her straight to my house. He agrees and tells me he's less than ten minutes from her place.

I disconnect with Jimmy and wait only about twenty seconds before Alex is calling me right back. I pick up fast.

"Hey, love. He's on his way. You think you can get downstairs?" I ask, hurriedly stomping up the block toward my apartment.

"Yea, I think so," she sounds a little less terrified now, like she's up moving around. "I think he left."

"Good," I breathe out in relief. "What the hell even happened?"

"I don't want to talk about it right now, Noah, please," she squeaks in exasperation and I frown.

This whole thing is actively killing me inside. I hate that she's going through this. I hate that she feels scared and alone and that some walking piece of human shit is actually *hitting her*, and yet she doesn't want to talk to me about it. She's got me up against a wall. There's nothing I can do but try to be here for her as much as humanly possible until she decides she's ready to leave the scumbag.

And maybe then she'll let me help her.

I arrive at my place, phone still plastered to my ear while I listen to Alex breathing and whimpering on the other end of the line. I'm not sure what she's doing, but she won't let me ask any questions other than *Are you alright?* So I guess just sitting in silence is fine.

"I just got home," I tell her as I walk into my apartment.

I immediately turn on the fireplace to get it nice and warm in here, then I run to the guest room to make sure the bed has fresh linens and there are enough towels in the guest bath.

As I'm making my way into the kitchen to ransack the cupboards for snacks that might make her feel better, she asks, "Where were you?"

"At Sensay," I tell her while pulling out three different kinds of Oreos, Doritos, an unnecessarily large bag of Sour Patch Kids, and a couple packs of Ho-Ho's.

"Oh... Were you... with someone?" Her timid voice chirps at me, and I freeze in place, squinting at nothing. Because why is she allowed to ask me if I was with someone tonight if I can't ask her anything about her nightmare of a marriage?

Not at all the same, Noah. Remain calm. You're going to be here for your friend. That's it.

"I was talking to a girl, yes..." I mutter, deciding that lying is the wrong way to go. I don't lie to girls about other girls.

Because I'm single.

"But nothing happened!" I add at the last second, the words flying right out of my mouth.

Totally single...

"Oh. Alright..." she whispers. I have no clue what any of this means, so I just stay quiet. "I'm gonna head downstairs now."

"Okay," I breathe.

She stays on the phone as she leaves her apartment. She loses service in the elevator, but calls me right back before I can freak out to let me know she's with Jimmy.

A wave of relief comes over me, and I finally let her go, because she'll be here in a few minutes, and we'll sort all of this out when she gets here...

Right?

God, who knows. Honestly, I'm so completely twisted up, I don't have the slightest inkling as to what's going on. All I know is that the second Alex was in trouble, I swooped into action, because she's my friend and I care a great deal about her.

I also know that I seriously want to kiss her when she gets here, and that muddies things up just a tad.

What have I gotten myself into??

I pace around my apartment for another ten minutes or so before the door buzzes and I practically jump out of my skin.

I rush over to the intercom. "Alex?"

"It's me," her small voice squeaks through the speaker and I press the button fast to buzz her in, then rush to my door.

I open it as she's making her way up the hall, and my heart has already smashed into my stomach. As she grows nearer, I can see what that monster has done to her, and it makes me feel things I've never felt in my entire life.

Scary things.

Things that terrify me, because if I were ever to happen upon her husband out in the world somewhere, I know I wouldn't be able to control what I did to him. And that's scarier than all the other feelings I have for Alex combined.

She stops in front of me and I gaze down at her; my beautiful broken girl.

Her face doesn't look so bad. The bruise on her left cheek from the other day is basically gone, with just a yellowish dot in its wake. But now her bottom lip is busted open and swollen. And even worse are the obvious thumbprint bruises developing on her throat. They're sort of dark and blotchy. They look painful.

It's fucking insane. I'm standing here with little purple love bites on my neck and throat from Alex just two nights ago in the heat of our lust-filled grind-fest on the living room floor, and now she's back with her own neck-bruises of a less playful variety.

I'm so angry I can barely see straight. And it's mostly because I'm totally helpless. There's nothing at all I can do to take this pain away from her. I can't make her leave her husband. And despite what I keep scheming in my head, I can't *actually* kill him.

I'm powerless here. My friend is hurting and there's nothing I can do to stop it.

I snap out of it when I realize we've been standing in the doorway for a while, just staring at each other in silence. I swallow hard and step aside, but rather than walk into the apartment, her puffed up lower lip quivers, and she crashes into me.

I catch her, holding her against my body while she sobs and cries in my arms. My heart feels like someone tossed it into a shredder. The noises she's making are so soft and sweet and vulnerable, sending shivers of remorse throughout me.

I step inside the foyer with Alex still clutching me for dear life, and shut the door to my apartment, setting the alarm. Then I just stand there, rocking her gently, giving her hair the occasional kiss.

"Shh... It's okay, baby," I whisper. "I have you. You're safe now."

"N-Noah, I'm s-so s-sorry to d-do this to y-you." She's shaking and trembling. I need to get her into the living room where it's warm.

"Alex, what are you saying? You didn't do anything to me," I keep my tone easy, though I'm confused as to what she thinks she did to me. "You're my friend, and I care about you so much. I will always be here when you need me, you know that."

"You're amazing..." she whimpers, tears soaking through my shirt. "How did I get s-so lucky as to meet y-you?"

My chest tightens and my stomach twists. *I can't believe she's saying that about me... Wow.*

"I think you're amazing," I croak, fighting not to give away how much of a sack she's turning me into. She scoffs. "No, seriously. It's true. Alex, you're smart, and funny, and the coolest damn girl I've ever met who looks like you do." She snorts a shaky laugh onto my chest, which allows me to crack a small smile.

"You're talented, and you're kind... And you're strong, Alex. You are. Never doubt that. You're going through something awful, and it's not your fault whatsoever. But you still manage to be awesome at every turn, despite the shitty things that are happening to you."

I pause and she makes this tiny noise that prompts me to kiss her head again.

"To me, that means you're the most amazing person in the world."

I expect her to turn and look up at me with those shimmery emerald eyes and give me a look, but instead she just squeezes her arms around me tighter and kisses my chest, right over my heart. Right where my tattoo is.

Seek.

My mom used to quote some Bible verse to me.

Seek and ye shall find.

I'm not religious, but I liked the sound of it. It seemed so easy. Look for something and you'll find it. Nothing complex about that.

But as I grew up and learned things, while I was pursuing my dreams, I realized that it's about having faith. *Seek and ye shall find.*

Believe and it will be yours.

Even if you weren't sure it was something you wanted... Until you found it.

I swallow hard. My stomach is fluttering like crazy, and I'm becoming increasingly warm.

"Thank you, Noah," Alex murmurs, her lips still moving on the word.

Seek.

"You're one-of-a-kind, you know that?" She finally tilts her gaze up at me and I fall so deep into my own panicked mind, I'm not sure if any of this is really happening.

There she is.

"Are you sore anywhere else?" I ask her, because I have to say something fast, or I'll do something I *can't* do right now.

Seek Me

She looks momentarily baffled by my question, but eventually she shakes her head. "No."

"Good," I whisper then bend down fast and scoop her up into my arms, carrying her through the foyer, into the living room while she holds onto my neck.

I plop down onto the couch and keep her on my lap, hugging her close to me to keep her warm. She's giving me a very intense look, but I choose to ignore it. I can't keep making this about me, when she feels like shit and needs a friend. She needs comfort, not stress.

"Tell me what you need right now," I rumble, taking her small hand in mine. "Are you hungry?" She shakes her head. "Thirsty?" Another shake. "Do you… want me to draw you a bath?"

Our eyes connect and hers shine right into me. I summon all my telepathic powers in an attempt to read her mind. I want so badly to know what happened to her tonight, but she doesn't want to tell me.

Her husband… Did he… touch her? Did he do things that she didn't want…? Why did he hurt her like this? What reason could there ever be to put your hands on someone…?

I know there aren't any black and white answers. Nothing that will ease my mind, or help me understand. Guys who hit women are just psychos, and there's probably no rhyme or reason to it at all, which is such a bullshit empty notion.

"No, thank you," she whispers, responding to my bath suggestion. "I just want to decompress for a few, if that's okay."

"Whatever you want, Alex," I say with certainty. "Just tell me what you want and it's yours. You can stay here as long as you like. The guest room is set up, and you can -"

"I appreciate that, Noah, but I'll probably just stay the night. He just needs to cool down and then -"

I beg my body not to do it, but it's no use. The words come up like projectile vomit.

"Cool *down*?" I bark and her eyes widen. "Alex, there's no *cooling down*. He's fucking beating you! He'll *never* cool down. You need to leave him!"

As soon as I pause my angry outburst long enough to take a breath, I'm instantly swept up in a giant cloud of guilt. *Are you serious?! You're yelling at her?? She just got attacked by her husband and you yell at her… What the hell is wrong with you??*

"Alex, I'm so sorry," I start backpedaling, fast. "I didn't mean to get angry or involve myself. I don't know anything about what's going on and obviously I could never put myself in your shoes… It's just that I care about you so much.

It's killing me to see you like this."

I watch her face closely to make sure I haven't terrified her. And surprisingly she doesn't look scared or upset at all. She's just gaping at me with wide, unblinking eyes. Her tongue sweeps over the cut on her lip and it catches my attention. Even with the pain, her lips are so tempting...

My eyes slide back up to hers from that perfect mouth and I swallow hard. I hadn't even noticed that our fingers had laced together.

"I just wish you'd talk to me," my voice is barely audible.

She nods slowly and sucks in a long breath, letting it out steadily.

"Okay."

My brows spring up. "Okay?"

"Okay, I'll talk to you. I'd like that, actually. To talk... to you." Her face is very still, but everything I saw on it when she first arrived dissipated, replaced by a brilliant wonder. I have to say, it's a marvelous look on her, though I don't quite know why she's giving it to me.

"You can tell me anything, Alex," I reiterate what I've told her before.

Her head bobs again in acceptance. "Alright. But I'm really tired. Could we maybe... lay down? While we talk...?"

Her eyes are so inquisitive, bordering almost on excited. I think this could be, quite possibly, the first time she's ever talked to *anyone* about her situation. I feel honored that she's chosen to do so with me, even if I did kind of beg her for it.

Still... Progress.

"You want to go lie down in the guest room?" I ask quietly. Her head shakes slowly while she traces my fingers with hers. "You want to... go up to my room?"

I'm barely breathing at all, which is strange. We're just going to talk. Nothing is happening. But having her in my bed... lying down... Even with all these terrible circumstances surrounding us, I can't help but succumb to the budding anticipation.

Alex nods with zeal at the suggestion of coming to my room.

Fuck me...

"I mean, if that's okay..." she mumbles, her other fingers now caressing the base of my neck.

I breathe out a shaky one, trying not to be obvious. "Of course it's okay. Ready?" She nods and the smallest smile breaks through, which has my heart soaring.

Seek Me

No, really though. What *am I getting myself into...?*

I stand up, with Alex still in my arms, and walk to the stairs, carrying her up them slowly. She's incredibly light, which doesn't necessarily mean anything. Her body is luscious as all hell, and I've seen her stuff her face before. She's small and petite, but with a fine-as-fuck booty and plump tits that fit in my palm like a handful. I just think maybe she would eat more if she wasn't so stressed out and afraid.

And now I'm remembering the other night, when I squeezed her tit while she was coming and it immediately made me come in my jeans, like a damn loser.

Like I haven't touched hundreds of breasts in my life, and now for some reason touching these ones has my dick decorating the inside of my Calvin Kleins.

She has her nipple pierced though. I felt it through her bra... That's fully hot. I liked when she was touching mine. Mmmm... yes...

Wait! Stop it. You're not doing that again, remember?? You're just going to talk. As friends.

Absolutely no humping tonight whatsoever. Do you understand me??

I'm mentally scolding my dick. That's what it's come to.

I lay Alex down in my bed, where Boots is already napping. That's essentially all he does, but Alex seems pleased with it, and she moves to cuddle up with him, kissing his soft head all over. I grin to myself and crawl into bed beside them.

Attempting to make this whole thing more comfortable for both of us, I grab the remote to my stereo system and turn it on, queuing up a playlist of relatively smooth songs. As smooth as I go, anyway.

The End of Heartache starts playing and Alex perks up.

"I love this song," she croons, lying down on her side, propping up on her elbow.

"Me too."

I mirror her position, the both of us parallel to one another in my massive bed, with Boots in the middle.

I stay quiet, figuring that she'll start speaking when she's ready, and nothing I say now will be of any use to her, so shutting up is key. We stare at each other for a while, just breathing; no other sounds outside of Killswitch Engage.

It's interesting to have her in my bed with me like this. No woman has ever been here unless we'd already had sex and passed out from being exhausted, or drunk. Typically, if I can avoid it, I don't let women sleep in my bed with me. It's too intimate. Cuddling is what you do with someone who means something to you.

Hence why Alex is here. She *fits* in my bed, and it feels good to have her here, no sex involved. Not that I would say *no* to it, if it were offered… But it will not happen, so I might as well kick that thought out and lock the door.

Alex flops down onto the pillow and rolls onto her back. She's stares up at the ceiling deep in some intense thoughts.

"I met Roger when I was seventeen," her raspy voice starts, and I barely even notice that I'm holding my breath. "He was a doctor. Sports medicine. Still is. He's thirteen years older than me, which definitely seemed odd to some people. But I was young and in love… and I didn't see the many red flags when we started dating."

My heart thuds against my ribcage while I listen, watching her closely.

"We snuck around until I was eighteen and then we got married in Vegas. I never really thought about him not having many friends before… So because of that, he didn't want a big wedding. And I liked the notion of running off and eloping in Vegas because I was a young, rebellious teenager. So that's what we did.

"Shortly after is when I told my parents and they disowned me. It wasn't just about Roger, though. They never understood me, and they never tried. They saw me as a failure because I didn't want to follow *their* ideas of what would make me successful. The day I moved out of my home and into Roger's was the last day I saw or spoke to them. And with everything in me, I believe I'll never hear from them again. Not until they're dead and someone calls me to let me know…"

I've always known I was fortunate to have two loving parents who would do anything for me. But it's not until right now, listening to Alex talk about her worthless, dipshit fuckface parents, that I feel like I might've taken mine for granted from time to time.

I'll call them tomorrow and maybe go out there.

This is crazy. Alex doesn't deserve that… No one does.

"So after that, it was just me and him," she continues, lifting her legs up and kicking them slowly in the air. Then she abruptly stops and rolls back onto her side to face me. Her eyes are wide and locked on mine. I wouldn't be able to look away if I tried. "I don't know if you've ever been in love, Noah. Like, *really* been in love… Where it consumes your world and makes you go completely crazy.

Seek Me

You consider doing things you've never done before... Acting in ways that the old you never would. You feel so strongly toward another person it pains you inside sometimes... To think about anything ever taking that person away from you is like slicing yourself open and letting all your guts spill out."

I gulp over my scratchy throat. *Fuck...*

"It probably sounds mental to someone who's never experienced it before. And that's because it is. People in love are total lunatics. But in the best possible way, because it teaches you how to be truly selfless. When you fall in love, you're not *you* anymore. You're this magnified version of you. It's like a high that you never come down from. And that's how I felt about Roger."

I refuse to register the stinging prickliness all over my body like pins and needles, or the burning lump that's traveling from my gut all the way up my esophagus.

"For the longest time, it worked with us. I was busy learning about my art, so it didn't bother me that I had no friends, and that Roger had another life outside of me - his work. Because art was my life outside of him. So it was fine. It was... good. But after a while I wanted more. Subconsciously I felt him slipping away from me, and I wanted something that would tie us together more than just a piece of paper. So I started asking him about a baby."

I blink slowly. *A baby?* My head wants to shake *no* over and over, but I force myself to remain still.

"Roger didn't want a baby, and for reasons I didn't understand at the time, he didn't want me wanting one either. So he started going out more and more to get away from me, staying out all hours, drinking too much. And then I found out he... was cheating on me."

She pauses to bite her lip, chin dropping in despair.

"I still remember the first time it happened. I think about that night all the time, replaying it in my mind over and over, wondering if there was something I could have done to change the outcome..."

That's it. I can't stay quiet any longer.

"Alex, there is *nothing* you could have done, or could ever do, to warrant someone -"

"Noah, I know," she cuts me off, remaining calm; almost sedated. "I know that now. But honestly, before I met you, I had no one. I had no friends or family... nothing but time to think... To sit and stew in my cold Upper East Side cage. I painted, yes. I painted my fucking heart out, which is the only silver lining I can take from this whole thing. And I'm keeping that. I'm holding onto it for dear life, because I can't possibly fathom that I wasted seven years of my life and got *nothing* in return but bruises and a broken heart."

Her voice cracks and tears pool in her eyes in a split second. Never in my life have I hurt so badly for someone else. It feels like my own heart is crumbling to tiny, jagged pieces.

"Alex... baby..." I have to put an end to this. I can't stand to see her in pain.

I reach out and grab her, as gently as I can manage, pulling her into my arms. Boots gets sort of kicked out of the way, so he's a little annoyed, but he'll get over it.

I hug her against my chest, burying her face in my throat while she shivers. And she's not openly weeping or wailing out her distress. She simply shakes and mewls out these noises that drive me to cuddle her more.

We lay like this for the longest time. Just breathing and existing, together with her pain on the outside. I have to believe she feels better for letting it out. I need to feel like I'm helping her in some way.

Eventually, Alex's breaths regulate and her heart beat becomes a faint murmur, tapping on my chest. I'm lying on my back with her small frame on top of me, nestled up and calm. For a moment I think she might've fallen asleep. But then she breaks the quiet.

"I will get out, Noah," she whispers through a hoarse voice. Her cheek is resting over my heart, and I can't see her face, but I just know she looks determined. "It's been a while... of me feeling sorry for myself and hating myself for letting him keep this grip on me. But I'm not too far gone. I will leave him, and when I do, I'll always remember the strength you lent me."

"I didn't lend you anything but a shoulder and an ear, Alex," I murmur. "You've had this strength in you all along. The strength to keep going. To endure. The fight isn't the part when you leave... It's the part you've already been living for years."

Slowly she lifts her head, bright eyes shining in the darkness of my room. I swipe at a tear rolling down her cheek, catching it with my thumb.

"Leaving is how you *win*."

Chapter Nine
Alex's Journal

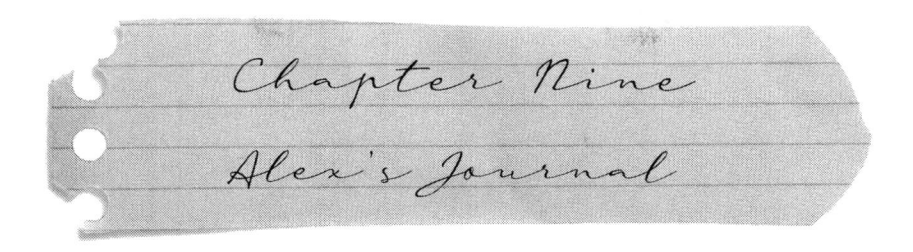

Oh, Barnaby. Where do I even begin?

My body feels drained, yet somehow weighted down. My hands are almost too heavy to write this.

But nothing is as heavy as my heart.

My husband hit me.

Even writing the words feels like a sick joke. Like something dirty and torrid and oh-so *wrong*.

My husband hit me once, and then he did it again. Because that's how it goes, right? Once the floodgates open, there's no closing them.

He cheated on me. I confronted him, and he hit me.

Whose life is this??

I'll tell you what happened, Barn, but only because I know you won't tell anyone. You're not here, or alive or anything like that, so I know you can't judge me, or look at me with those sad, sympathetic eyes. I can't have that… I don't want anyone to look at me like that.

It was about six months ago… After the whole baby conversation fiasco.

I was smart enough not to bring up the baby thing again. But something had changed in Roger after that. He was distant. Quiet - well quieter than usual - and tense. He seemed to be pushing me away, and because I'm still hopelessly, pathetically in love with him, I kept trying to pull him back to me. And with every pull I tugged, he yanked himself further and further away.

He was working even longer days, staying out until all hours. He would come home smelling like booze, which seemed unlike him, but then how would I know? I was realizing I didn't know him at all. Not even slightly.

I'm not stupid. I know once I tell you about all of this, you might think I am, but I promise you, I'm no fool. When your husband stays out all night getting drunk, it can only mean a handful of things.

I was wrecked with despair. I could barely paint or draw. I didn't answer any of my so-called friends on social media, because I was too sullen to speak to anyone. But also because I was afraid Roger would react like he did last time.

One night, after calling his phone for the umpteenth time and getting his voicemail, he stumbled through the door, reeking of gin.

And perfume.

So there it was. My suspicions were confirmed. And I absolutely hated myself for being right.

But I was just so angry. The rage inside me was burning wild like an inferno. I couldn't believe he had done this to me…

I jumped out of bed and followed him as he made a beeline for the bathroom, trying to get straight into the shower. As if that's not the most obvious thing in the entire world.

"Are you fucking kidding me?!" I shrilled, loathing myself for letting him turn me into this woman.

The woman in her billion-dollar Upper East Side mansion, whose husband comes home after fucking some skank, and forces her to yell at him like a desperate nag. He had made me someone I never *ever* wanted to be, and I was disgusted. All because I fell in love with his lying, cheating ass.

I stomped over the bathroom as he was shrugging out of his dress shirt. He tried to shut the door in my face but I pushed it open, storming in after him.

"Roger, look at me!" I snarled. "The least you could do is look into your wife's eyes after fucking someone else."

His head pivoted in my direction and he raised his brow in this lazy, unenthused way that stunned me for a moment. *My husband is a fucking sociopath.* Then he continued tossing his clothes, removing his belt, and going for his pants.

That he was trying to ignore me only served to enrage me further. I was seeing red. Hurt and angry and impotent… fucking devastated.

I wedged myself in front of him. My eyes widened and shot flames of hatred directly into his.

"You're a fucking coward," I hissed, projecting my voice. "You're not even a man."

I wished I could spit on him.

Unfortunately, I didn't have time to think about that any further, because he back-handed me across the face so hard my body slammed against the vanity.

My hands flew to my face, holding my stinging cheek, which was already pounding in pain. Though my back felt raw and scraped, it didn't stop me from throwing myself against the opposite wall behind me, in an effort to get away from him in case he wanted to do more.

My gaze stayed on my husband, who was watching me closely, after what he'd just done. I expected to see at least a little remorse. Maybe fifteen percent. But it just wasn't there, and that hurt more than my aching face, or my bruised spine.

His eyes remained wide as he stood, stock-still, his broad chest heaving up and down. And then he took a small step toward me. And that was my cue to leave the room.

In that moment wanted nothing more than to get the fuck out of there and never look back. But realistically I knew I was stuck. I had nowhere to go.

I had no one, and nothing. Nothing but my cheating husband who had just hit me.

I darted into the bedroom and snuck into the walk-in closet. I curled up into a ball on the floor and began sobbing, rocking back and forth while I held my cheek, which was burning so hot I felt it might melt right off my face.

When I heard the shower turn on, I cried even harder.

My mind was flashing over everything that had led me to that moment. The fact that Roger was my whole world. That I had no friends or family outside of him, and he knew that. He had me right where he wanted me.

It was all so textbook, I wanted to retch. And then I did.

I gagged over and over, but nothing came up. I was gasping for air, struggling to breathe. The only solace I could find at the moment was him being preoccupied in the shower, likely scrubbing some other woman's pussy off his dick.

I gagged again.

That body… It's mine. *He* belongs to me. He's *my* husband.

This wasn't supposed to happen. It wasn't supposed to go down like this.

My anger turned to sadness, turned to regret, turned to fear, then circled back to anger again.

I got up and began pacing around the closet, my mind unkempt and racing. I needed to do *something*. I couldn't stay there with him. Not after that.

It was only a matter of time before he did it again. Either he would apologize; beg and plead for my forgiveness. Promise it would never happen again, and then some day down the road something would happen to trigger him and I'd get hit. Again.

Or maybe he wouldn't apologize. Maybe he would just go on fucking women and beating me with no remorse. And what could I do?

I could divorce him. My cheek was already swelling up. I could go to the police and press charges. Stay in a hotel until I could get the divorce in order.

But my money is his money. He would always be able to find me. Plus, he's a rich, powerful, respected member of Manhattan's elite circle. He has connections I can't even fathom. He knows the Police Commissioner. They golf together.

Fuck.

It didn't matter. I just needed to leave. I could figure it all out. I'm resourceful, always have been.

I grabbed my suitcase and started whipping clothes into it as fast as possible. Then I heard the shower stop running and fear shot through every muscle in my body.

I rushed to pack everything else I could find, then snuck into the bedroom to get my purse. Roger crept around the corner from the bathroom and our eyes locked, but mine quickly fell away. I raced over to the dresser and got my purse, averting my gaze as I went back to my suitcase in the closet. He appeared in the doorway, leaning against the frame with only a towel wrapped around his waist.

"Where are you going?" He asked, his voice calm and collected.

Really?! I shouted in my mind. *That's the first fucking thing you have to say, you fucking piece of pure evil?!?!*

I thought carefully about my words. "I'm going to stay in a hotel tonight."

"Why?" His tone was so soft and inquisitive I couldn't help but look up at him.

"Are you fucking serious?" I muttered, and then immediately cringed. I hadn't thought that one out before I said it. I needed to try not to get him angry again. To stall him long enough to get the hell out of there.

"Alexandra, please don't go," he whispered.

I blinked. I was in some warped other dimension. None of this was making any sense.

"Roger…" My vocal chords gave out, and I cleared my throat. I could only imagine what I must have looked like at that moment. "I can't be here. Not after what just happened. I'm just going for tonight…" I was lying through my teeth, but I needed to be smart about this. He was so much bigger than me. He could easily kill me right now if he wanted to.

He didn't speak, but he was walking toward me, and I was trapped. My eyes darted around looking for anything sharp.

He backed me up into the corner of the closet and I whimpered out loud, closing my eyes as tears streamed down my face.

Why... Why is this happening to me?

"You were right," he breathed, so gentle that I couldn't believe it had come from his mouth.

I peeled my eyes open and slid up to him.

"I did cheat on you..." he croaked, his forehead creasing. "I'm sorry..."

He reached out slowly, hesitantly, and brushed my throbbing cheek. I couldn't help the involuntary noise that escaped me from the pain on my face, and in my heart.

How could you do this to me? To us??

"It didn't mean anything, Alexandra. It was just sex... But I know I hurt you. And then this..." He swallowed visibly. "I don't know what to say other than I'm sorry. But I know you won't believe me..."

I sniffled, suddenly more exhausted than I ever had been in my entire life. My limbs felt like they were filled with sand.

"I-I'm just going to go..." I squeaked in between unsteady breaths as tears flowed down my face. "I have to go..."

He nodded slowly, his hand trailing down my neck as he played with the strands of my messy dark hair.

"Just stay tonight... please?" He begged with his eyes and his tone. He was confusing every fiber of me. My brain was so tired it wanted to shut down. "You can leave me tomorrow. I promise you can, if that's what you want. And I won't try to stop you. But just... tonight. Stay."

My brain was screaming at me as it powered down.

Get. Out.

Leave!

Don't stay, you moron!

And then it went dark. And I nodded. And I went limp in his arms as he lifted me up and carried me to our bed, where he laid me down softly. He turned off the lights and crawled in next to me, holding me against his body. His warmth and his comforting scent lulled me to sleep.

I wanted to hate him. I really did.

But that didn't change the fact that I loved him.

That was the first time my knight broke my spirit. And he wouldn't stop until he broke the rest of me with it.

Chapter Ten
Alex

My eyes slide open, and they're scratchy. My whole head weighs a hundred pounds, and I'm much groggier than normal. I feel hungover.

And hot. Very hot. It's stiflingly warm for some reason. And dark.

What the hell? Where am I?

I struggle to move any part of me, but the more I wake up, the more I realize I can't. Because I have a giant body wrapped around me like a cocoon.

I shift my head and tattoos come into focus. And skin. Smooth, very warm skin.

I can't help but grin stupidly to myself because Noah is all the fuck over me right now, and it has to be the most endearing thing I've ever experienced.

My head is being squished between his arm and his chest. Sort of his armpit, I guess. But I like it. That might be embarrassing to admit, but I like having my face in Noah Richards' armpit. He smells good.

The rest of me is flush against his torso, and he's sort of on top of me a little so I can't move my arms. Also his legs are wrapped around my legs. He's essentially got me in some kind of wrestling hold, and he's knocked out cold, breathing peacefully.

I giggle under my breath. His bed is huge. There's probably enough room to sleep five people comfortably in this bed, and yet Noah sleeps on me like a tarp.

Oh, and did I mention he's wearing only his boxers? No?

Well, that's because I just realized it myself. That's why I can feel his warm skin all over me... He's rocking nothing more than some fitted Calvin Klein boxer briefs, like the ones David Beckham models. And I think Noah's giving him a run for his money...

He could totally be in one of those ads. His body looks like it's photoshopped already, so they'd save themselves a step.

Now I'm wondering when he stripped out of his clothes. The last thing I remember, we were talking. We talked all night, for hours and hours, until I eventually passed out on his chest, with his big arms wrapped around me, sort of like they are now. I've never felt safer in my entire life. Nothing can get to me here. I'm protected.

He's my protector.

I'm amazed at how spectacularly freeing it felt to get all that stuff off my chest. To open up and tell someone, other than my journal, what's going on in my life; about my past, and all my insecurities. It didn't make me feel weak or pathetic, telling Noah. He makes me feel strong, because he sees me as a fierce, badass chick. And I guess I kind of am.

A smile tugs at my lips. I *never* thought of myself as badass, even before I met Roger. I dressed the part, with the tattoos, dark hair and ripped clothes. But really, that's just my style. My hair is naturally dark, and I happen to love body art. I snuck off to get my first tat when I was sixteen. I think that was the official day my parents gave up on me. They took one look at my tattoo - the shooting stars on my foot - and thought, *she'll never amount to anything*. Which is a complete overreaction, by the way. It's on my *foot*, not my face. And my parents are true hypocrites because they were exactly like me at that age. Which is why I find it so mind-boggling that they can judge me.

I huff to myself and close my eyes. *Forget all this nonsense. It's like Noah said... Fuck them. They don't deserve to know me.*

Thoughts of Noah and his sweet-as-pie words bring me back to the present, where he's still holding me while he sleeps, humming out adorable little noises. As much as I'd love to stay like this forever, I sort of have to pee, and my arm is numb.

I wiggle until my arms and head are free, though my legs are still trapped by his, which are big, long and heavy. So I choose to give up my attempts at breaking out and sigh, melting against him, acknowledging that if I'm going to die of starvation or strangulation, this seems like the best possible way to go.

With my right arm and hand free, I take the opportunity to touch him in secret. Since he's asleep, I don't have to worry about us defining what we are to each other every time we share a look, or a touch. He's passed out like a drunk sorority girl and my fingers are itching to do some exploring.

First, I go for his shoulder, the one that's not buried in his immensely comfy pillow-top mattress with the eight-million thread count sheets. But I have to stop to admire the love bites I left on his neck and throat. I saw them last night when I first got here, and I was momentarily taken aback. I honestly didn't mean to do it so hard, obviously caught up in the moment. But now that I'm looking at them up close, with Noah asleep and cuddling me, they fill me with pride.

They make it seem like he's *mine*.

I glide my fingertips over his shoulder blade and down his back, tracing the Mad Hatter, which earns me a soft grumble. I briefly wonder if he's awake, but he's breathing deep, in and out, and it's clear he's still sleeping.

Next stop is his arm, the one that's draped over my waist. I roll away a bit so I can touch all down his ripped bicep and forearm, and onto his hand. I have to take a second to appreciate the hand. It's perfect. A large, wide palm with long, shapely fingers and nails that are not so nice they *look* manicured, though they probably are. And this is the hand that has a big, dark skull tatted on the back of it. It's a great piece; another one to add to the collection of my favorite Noah Richards tattoos.

I'm feeling exceptionally steamy all of a sudden as my fingers brush over the curves of his pectoral and down, tapping on all four of his abdominal muscles that I can reach on his right side. He shifts his hips and groans quietly. I have to refrain from giggling, because I think I'm tickling him in his sleep, which is amusing to me.

Down we go, and I'm about to check out the pelvis tats when I gasp out loud and slam my eyes shut. I chomp down on my lip hard by accident then wince when I remember that it's split open from my husband's hand.

But I can't even be concerned with that because Noah's dick it out.

His dick is out! I repeat, dick is out! This is not a drill, people! Code pink!

I'm squeezing my eyes closed hard, afraid to look again. Because it's not right. I shouldn't look. *Should I?*

No. It's rude. I can't peep on someone's morning wood while they're asleep.

But I mean… It might be ruder *not* to look. I should at least maybe try to tuck it back in for him…

Why the heck is his dick out, anyway? Did he pull it out last night to rub it on me while I was sleeping? Did I pull it out while he was sleeping??

My eyelids crack open and I slowly tilt my head back down below his waist.

"Holy fuck…" I whisper, eyes widening in a moment of sheer disbelief.

It's not that anyone took his dick out of his boxers. The thing is as hard as stone, and so *long* that it's peeking out on its *own*.

Jesus Fucking Christ. You mean to tell me this dude's cock is so big it physically doesn't fit in his boxers when it's aimed up??

That's… incredible.

Now I can't stop looking. The head is fat and smooth; a round curve that's staring up at me. And the rest of it is almost as thick, and obviously long. I'm not great with eyeballing measurements, but that thing must be *at least* nine inches. It *has* to be.

I'm staring so hard my eyes want to bug out of my skull. My tongue is practically hanging out of my mouth and I'm now ten degrees warmer. I want to look at the rest of it. I *need* to see where this thing ends. It's medically fascinating.

Mischief getting the best of me, I reach out slowly and pinch the waist of his Calvins between my fingers, tugging them away from his skin and peering down.

"Mmm... Al..."

"What? I wasn't doing anything!" I huff, releasing his clothes and playing dumb. But when I peek up at his face, ready to defend my actions, his eyes are still closed, his face smashed into his pillow.

Is he talking in his sleep?

Curious, I gently curl my fingers around his hipbone, caressing his warm, silky skin with my hand.

"Alex..." his voice rumbles, and now I'm convinced he's having a dream about me.

I've never been happier in my entire existence.

"Noah..." I whisper his name, sliding my hand onto his butt, which is so damn nice my vagina's crying tears of joy. It's round and firm, with those muscle dips that look luscious. *God, how is his butt so perfect?*

"Alex..." he pants into the pillow. "Don't... leave..."

I pout while my heart melts in my chest like a snow cone in a sauna.

"I'm not leaving, Noah," I breathe, my heart racing. "I promise I'll stay... if you do."

"Always... baby..." He hums and pulls me closer with his arm around me, smooshing his fully erect length against my stomach.

I smile like a total loon, mildly obsessed with him calling me *baby*, especially when he's unconscious and rubbing his man meat all over me.

And for a moment I close my eyes and allow myself to wonder what it would be like if he was my *boyfriend*...

If we woke up like this every Sunday, in this giant, warm bed; him draped around me, and me playing with his perfect dick.

We'd get up and wander around his insanely nice apartment, which has more than enough space for two people to reside together comfortably. I could make him breakfast - waffles - and serve them to him wearing only his t-shirt from the night before. And we'd spend hours fucking all over the apartment, making each other feel good, because that's what lovers do. They make each other feel bliss, not pain.

We could go out and do things together... Go to museums or shopping for art supplies or books. Then come back here and watch TV or play Mario Kart.

We would laugh and tease one another, smile at each other and kiss, often.

The images in my head are making me so happy, so confused, I could cry. Or throw up.

Noah Richards is *not* my boyfriend. He will never be my boyfriend, because he doesn't do relationships. He's a womanizer for a reason; because he can't commit. It's not in his DNA.

Sure he's sweet, and kind and he treats me differently, but that's just because we're friends. I *can't* think of him that way. It'll break my heart wide open.

Because putting aside the fact that I have a husband, who I'm definitely leaving soon, I swear to God... Noah Richards will *never* be mine. It won't happen. *Ever.*

Speak of the devil, he begins to shift, tossing a bit, his body moving in slow motion like mine was when I first woke up. His large hand runs up my back and into my hair, his fingers combing through the messy strands, playing with them.

"Mmmm..." His voice rumbles into me, setting my loins ablaze.

He pulls back just enough to look down at me, his sleepy eyes a bit lazy and squinted, which makes him look boyish and cuter than ever. I stare up at him, praying that I don't have mascara all over my face.

"Hi," he whispers. Just that one word, and the way it sounds coming out of his mouth, makes my heart leap.

"Hi," I respond, unable to scrape together enough voice to say anything else.

"Did you sleep well?" He asks, making no move whatsoever to separate our tangled bodies. In fact, he's now running his foot painfully slow, up and down my leg. It nudges my foot, and we're playing footsie. In bed, with his dick touching me and his beautiful dark eyes searing me over.

"Uh-huh," I nod as my hand trails his abs, and up to his chest.

He breathes out a soft huff, clearly enjoying the way I'm touching him. For once, he's not smirking. He's fully serious, the coal in his irises burning for me. He shifts more and grabs my hips with both hands, scooting me in line with his face. I gasp, quietly, unable to look away from those illustrious eyes.

"I'm glad you're here," he breathes, his face awfully close to mine.

Seek Me

Normally I would feel insecure about morning breath or something meaningless and stupidly vain like that, but my panic train is derailed because Noah's breath smells minty. Like toothpaste.

"Did you brush your teeth?" I ask, and he smiles; a big, giant heartthrob thing that has me swooning so hard my panties go up like kindling.

"After you passed out, I got up to brush my teeth and get undressed," he tells me, tilting his head. "You know, like I normally would if there wasn't some snoring cover hog taking up my bed."

I giggle, because he's obviously teasing me. I'm the smallest of tiny people in his massive bed.

"Do you like?" He's still grinning, his eyes dropping to my lips while his hand explores my butt casually; not grabbing or squeezing. Just a soft innocent touch laced with curious hunger.

"I like..." My tongue skims my lip for show, and he growls in the back of his throat, like a sexy animal.

Somehow we've begun writhing together, so slow it's like we're barely doing anything. Except that his leg is still wrapped around me, his erection cradled between our bodies.

The smile slips off Noah's pouty lips, and I witness him swallow. Whatever is happening in this bed has my pulse hammering in my neck as I brim with nerves so significantly that if he weren't holding me close, I think I'd be shaking uncontrollably.

"Alex?" From his mouth, my name sounds like lust and trepidation. I *really* like it, but I'm just as scared of what's going down between us.

"Yes..." I can't help that the word comes out like a moan. It just happens because of what he's doing to me. Everything feels so *ever-loving* good.

"I'm... tired..." he sighs, defeated and yet somehow determined; ready. "Tired of not having you."

I press my lips together because they're trembling.

"I *want* you..." he murmurs, his face now so close to mine that I can feel his lips shivering too. "So fucking bad..."

My eyes flutter shut, and the last thing I see are his doing the same.

"Do you... want me?" Minty breath warms my lips.

And before I can even fully utter the word *yes*, he kisses me.

He kissed me. He's *kissing* me!

My brain is scrambled. I can't believe this is happening. Noah Richards has his soft yet oddly powerful lips pressing up to mine, and I'm in shock.

Shock and awe. It feels *stupefyingly* good.

He sucks my bottom lip and I whimper into his mouth, partly because it's marvelous, but also because this time we both forgot about my split lip.

"Oh, shit! Fuck, I'm sorry," he breathes out heavy, with obvious concern on his gorgeous face.

"It's okay, I don't care," I grunt, grabbing his jaw and pulling his lips back to mine.

I catch him smiling, but as soon as we get going again, he's back to business.

Noah's lips are made for kissing. Cushioned and curved, parting so he can suck, a little softer this time. Then he slides his tongue gracefully into my mouth and flicks it on mine. As soon as our tongues touch, I moan quietly into his mouth and he returns it with his own deeper, hungrier sound.

He's claiming my mouth for himself, and I can't even think. My mind is all fuzz. I'm a mass of sensations and pleasures. From head to toe, he's got me coming undone.

With every second that passes between us, his kisses grow deeper, more sensual; heavily passionate. He holds my face and neck with both of his hands, one resting on my jaw, the other gripping my nape, in my hair. Then he aligns me right where he wants me as he licks and sucks my lips, panting into my mouth and slowly straining every inch of his body on mine.

My right hand stays planted on his chest, his heart pounding aggressively on my palm, while my left scratches his back with my nails, then drifts down to his ample butt, squeezing and yanking him closer to me.

"Mmm," he grunts with a fistful of my hair, tracing my top lip with his tongue before nipping the bottom between his teeth, as gently as he can, minding the cut. But I really don't care at all if it hurts.

Noah Richards is kissing me right now. I can't feel anything other than unrelenting gratification.

"Why are you so good at that?" I squeak, breathless in between licking his tongue, then lips then tongue again, in rapid succession.

"Good at what?" He asks, then growls when I tug his juicy lower lip with my teeth. Every time I do it, his cock flinches on my belly.

"Everything," I moan, and suddenly I'm beneath him.

He just rolled me under him, pushing my legs apart forcefully so he could wedge his big body in between. I gasp at the feeling of his length, engorged and stroking the slit of my pussy through my thin leggings.

"Alex," he hums, kissing me harder and deeper and so mind-numbingly fantastic I'm seeing stars behind my eyes.

"Noah," I purr his name, rubbing up on his chest and abs, cherishing the feel of silken skin covering solid masses of muscle while daring myself to go lower and chickening out.

I can't help it, I'm scared. This is Noah we're talking about. He's my friend…

If I touch his dick, then I won't stop touching it until I'm making him feel really good, and then he'll make me feel really good, and even though it seems all good, this is the stuff we're not supposed to be doing.

"Baby, you're so perfect," he whimpers, dragging the exposed head of his cock through the wetness that's now soaked through my pants.

My face and neck are flushed pink and so warm my skin is glistening. I'm crazy nervous, because I can't stop thinking about what I was thinking about earlier… That little fantasy wherein Noah was my boyfriend.

Kissing him feels *right*. It feels insanely right. It feels *so* right, in fact, that I'm afraid nothing else will ever feel right again after this.

"I want inside your gorgeous body," he rumbles, and my walls contract so hard, it spreads tightness all the way up to my chest.

He's so fucking hot. Everything he says and does it like hotness overload.

From his candy lips, sweet and supple, to his strong hands, touching me everywhere, searing my flesh like a soldering iron; to his god-like body, hard everywhere and covered in lustrous, warm, creamy skin.

He's everything I've ever found attractive in a man, and he's here, kissing me. Pinning me to his mattress with his hips, while his mouth explores my neck.

Noah slides his hot, wet mouth down my throat, placing a gentle kiss on one spot.

"Do you know…" his tongue peeks out before he presses another small kiss there, "How beautiful you are?"

Breathing for me is uncontrolled, my hands gripping his broad shoulders as my chest lifts and sinks. The feeling of his mouth on the sensitive skin of my neck is threatening to give me an orgasm already. It's still pretty sore from last night…

Oh… That's what he's kissing.

Noah's mouth glides a few inches and stops, kissing the new spot, just as tender and slow.

"You're *gorgeous*, Alexandra," he speaks in a breath, kissing and tracing my bruises with his tongue. "A work of art. A masterpiece."

It's euphoric, what he's doing, and his words… That he's kissing the pain away from my body makes me want to cry and come at the same time.

He's perfect. There's never been anyone like him.

I'm suddenly still, and Noah picks up on it right away, bringing his face in front of mine.

"You okay?" He asks, breathlessly.

His lips are swollen now from ferociously kissing me, a few strands of messy golden hair falling in his face. He has never looked better.

But if I'm being honest, I'm not okay.

"Noah, we can't do this..." I speak, regretting my words; hating them with every fiber of myself.

He regards me warily for a moment, cocking his head to the side before he nods and says, "I know."

"You're so fucking sexy..." I tell him, grabbing his face and kissing his lips one more time, committing them to memory in case this never happens again.

Fuck me... The thought of never feeling this again makes me want to drink bleach. I finally found the perfect high and I'm stomping it out before I can get it all.

Noah groans on my lips, urging himself back. He seems pained.

"I'm sorry I pushed..." he whispers, and even that is almost enough for me to climax.

"You didn't," I tell him with sincerity. "Trust me, I want you just as much, Noah..."

"But it's not a good time," he nods, and I don't think he realizes that he's pouting.

We're both quiet for a few minutes, trying to compose ourselves and rein it in a little. I'm telling him we can't, but we're still in his bed, panting and touching.

"You have to stop first..." I plead, unable to remove my hands from his chest... And that god-forsaken nipple ring.

"Yea right!" He gasps. "There's no way I can stop first..." His hips are still thrusting slowly in between my thighs.

"Maybe we shouldn't then..."

I'm giving myself mental whiplash, but seriously... How am I supposed to convince myself to stop doing something that feels like this?

"I don't want to," his hands glide up my waist. "But we probably should."

I nod and release a small whine of reluctance. Noah takes my hand in his and brings it to his lips, kissing my knuckles in such a romantic display that I'm ready to throw all caution to the wind. But then he pulls away, sitting back on his knees. His eyes travel all over my body, wearing a look of torment. Then they

Seek Me

fall below his own waist and he frowns.

"How long has my dick been out?"

I burst out laughing. I can't even help it. I laugh so hard I'm snorting, and Noah beams at me, tugging his swollen lower lip between his teeth to stifle his own humor. I watch him in amusement as he tucks his erection into his boxers, trying to stuff it down by his thigh, though it's not really working. Now he's just tenting the material, which makes me laugh even harder.

"What's it like walking around with the Loch Ness Monster in your pants all day?" I ask, giggling as I lean on my elbows.

Noah crawls away on the bed, chuckling with humility. His cheeks are actually flushed a bit, likely from what we were just doing, as well as the reference to his blessings. But I'm smitten with how humble he is. He jokes around with his cockiness, but when it comes down to it, he's not a smug asshole, even though he easily could be.

He's like a big, tattooed teddy bear. And I just want to hug him forever.

Which is precisely why I need to leave right away. The longer I stay here, the more I'll be tempted to keep thinking of him as a boyfriend, and not my friend Noah, the chronic bachelor.

He stands up at the edge of his bed, eyes locked on me while I get up, adjusting my shirt.

"You can stay in here and rest some more if you want," he offers, swaying in place. "I'm sure you're still pretty exhausted. I mean… Does your neck hurt? Maybe we should go see a doctor?"

I gawk up at him with wide eyes. *See? It's already weird. Now every time he says "we" I'm getting those butterflies…*

He doesn't want to be your boyfriend, dumbass. Wipe that thought clean out of your head.

"I'm fine," I grumble, taking his hand that's extended and letting him help me up. "I just need a hot shower and some coffee."

"We can get you both of those," he smiles sweetly and I cringe. *Stop saying we.* "Shower's right through there. Clean towels in the closet, whatever you need. I'll have coffee waiting for you when you're ready."

He kisses the top of my head softly, fingering the strands of my hair. "Al, I know I complicated things… But we're good. I'm still here for you, no matter what. And you don't need to worry about anything with me. I'll never push you into something you don't want."

I curl my face to gaze in his direction, studying the ardent look in his eyes.

I know he means what he's saying.

This is the world's most complicated scenario. But I trust him emphatically, and it feels like an awakening to have someone on my side, finally. I can't give that up, no matter what happens.

"I'm so happy I met you," I tell him, because it's true, and wrap my arms around his waist, hugging him tight.

He surrounds me with his arms and holds me the way I need. I don't want to ruin this heartfelt moment by upsetting him, but I do have to say…

"You know I have to go back, right?"

He stills, but surprisingly he doesn't pull away and give me a scathing look of disdain. Instead, he squeezes me tighter and I can feel him nodding before he rests his chin on top of my head.

"I know."

"But it'll be okay," I add, throwing in some optimistic words to pacify us both. "I just have to get everything ready for my show. That's the most important thing right now."

"When is it again?" He asks in a pensive voice.

"Wednesday at seven. I'll text you the flyer."

"I'm really proud of you, baby," he whispers and my throat constricts.

"I know. You're the best."

"No, you are."

"No… You."

"Don't start this game, sweetheart," he grins down at me. "You won't win." He finally releases me with a pat on the butt. "Now, go take your shower. Coffee and breakfast coming right up."

I begrudgingly let go of him, and make my way into the master bathroom, marveling at how big and fancy it is. The shower is giant, with dual massive shower heads, and there's a separate clawfoot tub across the room that looks quite luxurious. I can picture myself bathing in it, but I'm not in the right mood for a bath. I need to just shower and figure out what the hell I'm going to say to my bastard of a husband when I get home.

I'm not too worried about Roger for today. His pattern is that he never attacks me two nights in a row. Usually after a particularly brutal event, like last night, he'll take off for a day, sometimes even two, I'm guessing to give me space and sort out whatever psycho shit is going through his head. He might not even be home when I get there…

Here's hoping.

Seek Me

I strip out of my leggings and tunic then turn on the shower, getting the water to a nice warm temperature. I step under the waterfall and let it cascade over me, washing away the bad memories. I find some body wash and lather it up in my hands, scrubbing at my throat to erase Roger's harmful touch.

But then I remember Noah's lips there and my movements slow, fingertips grazing the skin where he kissed and licked, gently and revering. The steam surrounds me and I'm sufficiently warmed, my insides churning a small, glowing fire.

My lips still burn from Noah's searing kisses, the bottom feeling a bit bruised, and now I can't tell if it's from Roger's backhand or Noah's sensual little nips. I press them together to stifle a moan that wants to escape me. Thinking about his tongue in my mouth, exploring, tracing, tasting and devouring… It's making me gush.

My walls constrict, eyes sealed shut as I picture Noah right in front of me. His tall, muscular body, the ink that covers his glowing skin giving him that wicked look. Dark eyes and soft shaggy hair, sharp nose and jaw… *He's* the work of art here.

I remember his long, thick cock… Hard and throbbing between my legs as he pushed it into my clothes, rocking his hips into me while he growled out noises of burning lust into my mouth.

In my mind, I can see him standing before me, dripping wet; water and soap sliding over all those defined, hardened ridges. I imagine that he steps into me, holding my ass in his powerful grip, while the other hand cups my breast. I whimper, touching myself the same way, washing my breasts the way I imagine Noah would if he was in here.

His thumb flicks the barbell in my nipple and I moan quietly, pleasure shooting straight between my thighs. He does it again, squeezing and tugging, torturing me in the best possible way.

Then he uses his mouth… That hot, wet mouth, sucking my nipples… Kissing them, swirling his tongue around the peaks before suckling with force. I gasp, yanking his wet hair by the roots while he owns me with that perfect mouth.

In my head he drops to his knees, gazing up at me with voracity shimmering in his dark eyes, before kissing and nipping a path down my stomach then my hip bone, wasting no time using his mouth on my pussy, so sweet I'm already falling apart.

"Noah…" I whisper, eyes rolling back as he holds my ass hard and licks my slit slowly, back and forth, slipping his tongue inside my opening. I cry out as soft as possible. It feels like heaven.

"Baby, you are beautiful..." he groans, the vibrations rumbling on my clit.

Flattening his tongue, he licks me over and over again until my knees buckle. He tugs my clit with his teeth then greedily sucks, alternating between kissing and swirling his tongue so damn fucking good I'm about to explode.

"Come for me, Alex," he demands and I'm aggressively panting, muscles stiffening all over my body. "I know you want to..."

"I want you so bad..." I hum, holding myself up on his shoulders as I succumb to the sensations and fall back against the shower wall.

I force myself quiet as I erupt into a staggering orgasm that leaves me breathless and tingling everywhere. My legs are like jelly as my insides finally stop pulsing and I open my eyes. I take a deep breath in, blinking myself back to reality.

Noah's not here.

He's downstairs, making me breakfast while I'm touching myself in his shower, thinking about him. Imagining him...

He's my friend. The only one I have.

Then why do I seem so hard-pressed to ruin it?

I step inside my home and look around. Every time I come back here from being somewhere else, I expect to be walking into a war zone.

I'm not exactly sure why. It's never happened before, so there's no reason it would start now. But still it's this fear I have, that eventually the calm, rational way my husband behaves when he's not lost in the few minutes of chaos that causes him to attack me will expire; will run out.

After all, when you have the kinds of demons he has, there's nowhere else to go but down. Sooner or later, he'll completely unravel and become the monster that only *I* know, for good. And then he'll be unstoppable.

My plan has always been to leave before he gets to that point. But I worry that I'm running out of time.

He's been hitting my face more often lately. I don't know if it necessarily means anything - God, I hope not. But it could very well mean he's done being cautious.

I need to get the fuck out of this terrible, awful relationship.

I walk through the foyer and the sitting room, making my way to the bedroom. I need to get changed into fresh clothes and go up to the studio to start packing all my pieces and put the finishing touches on my catalog.

As soon as I set foot through the door to our bedroom, I gasp out loud.

Roger is sitting on the bed, with his back resting against the headboard, reading a book. He's dressed casually, in jeans and a white t-shirt, which is odd. He rarely ever dresses like that. It's always suits, or at the very least slacks and a polo or something preppy.

Jesus, this guy has never been my type. What the hell was I thinking?

His head pops up when he sees me and he closes the book fast, crawling to the edge of the bed.

"Hi, sweetie. God, I was worried about you," he breathes, his tone eager and maybe a little desperate. I've never heard him sound like that. Not once in our seven years together.

My brow furrows as I stare at him, wondering what the hell I'm supposed to say. It's then that I notice what's on the nightstand beside him.

Flowers. A huge bouquet of red roses, colored so vibrant, they look like they're dipped in fresh blood. They smell incredible, but roses have never really been my thing. *Maybe if they were spray-painted black…*

"Are you alright?" Roger asks, bringing my attention back to him.

He stands up and walks to me slowly, stopping when he's towering over me and taking my chin in his fingers. His bright eyes study my face, the cut on my lip that's still visibly dark, despite Noah's attempts to clean it up with bacitracin. Then his eyes slide down to my throat and he squints. He looks confused; as if he's seeing the marks for the first time and he doesn't understand where they could have possibly come from.

Oh my God, he's insane. He's completely lost it. I need to get out of here…

"I'm fine, Roger," I whisper, struggling to project my voice while keeping it as passive as possible. "I just needed some *me* time. You know it's important."

I cock my head slightly, giving him one of my looks I've perfected over the years. The *I'm a silly woman and you're in charge* look. It works well when we're pretending he didn't almost strangle me to death last night.

"Alex, you left," he breathes, eyes soft and shimmering with concern. I'm so baffled by how he's looking at me, and the tone in his voice, I'm almost taken aback. *Who is this man?*

He must be taking on a new tactic. It'll give him more jollies or something to get me thinking he actually cares about my well-being. He's a freaking headcase, so I'm not really surprised by anything he does after the initial shock wears off.

"Roger, *you* left," I lift my brows.

"Yes, but I came right back," he murmurs, taking my hand in his. "You were gone all night…"

I gulp, fear clawing at the inside of my bruised throat as I tremble suddenly with terror. *He's going to accuse me of fucking someone. And he's going to beat me… Hard. And he may kill me.*

Fuck, I don't want to die.

The first thing that pops into my panicked mind is Noah. He'd be crushed if I let Roger kill me. And *I'd* be crushed if I let Roger kill me, because I want to stay alive. I was to stay here on Earth… with Noah.

I used to care very little whether I lived or died. Sure, I was minutely afraid of no longer existing. The thought of blank nothingness… Lights out. That's pretty scary. I mean, I try clinging to the idea of an afterlife, but really there's no physical evidence to support that. And even if it's true… How would I know that I'd be going to *heaven*? I'm not as evil as my husband, but I have a lot of issues, clearly. What if I go to *hell*? That's also scary, though maybe not as scary as the *lights out* thing. Who knows…

But back to reality, it's alarming that Noah is quickly becoming the center of my universe. He's the first person I think of when I'm about to be attacked by my psycho husband. That being said, it feels good to have someone to care about. It's always nice to have a reason to live, even though I'm not sure how Noah would feel about him being mine… That's rather intense.

Either way, I'm still bracing myself for Roger's rage. I know it's coming… Any second now.

I swallow and grit my teeth, preparing for a blow.

"Alex, sweetie, please come sit down. We need to have a talk," Roger says and tugs me gently by my hand, over to the bed. He has a seat, so I hesitantly sit next to him.

He's still squeezing my hand in his, over his lap, and I watch as he runs his thumb across my knuckles. Tension radiates through my body. I hate this. I hate sitting around waiting to be hit. It's incredibly stressful.

"I want to talk to you about something," he starts, his tone even and attempting to convey sincerity. I wouldn't buy this act if it was on sale, two for one. "I know you think every time I leave this house, I'm going to the home of

Seek Me

some mistress... That any time spent not working, I'm screwing miscellaneous women all over the city."

That's not true, Roger. I wouldn't put it past you to go to Jersey, too.

"And well, at one time, I suppose you would have been right," he keeps going, staring down at our joined hands.

I witness him swallow hard, his throat adjusting as he does, something I used to find so attractive on him. But now, all I can think of is how his neck would look bruised and battered the way mine is.

"But Alexandra, I promise I'm done with that," he turns his head and finally looks at me, catching me off-guard with those gem-like blue eyes, wide in some emotion I can't determine, because I didn't think he possessed *any* emotions outside of anger, hostility, and disdain. "I can never take back what I've done to you... To *us*. And my... infidelities..." His voice trails and he huffs, shaking his head. "Well, let's just say I learned my lesson. I only want you, Alex. You're my forever."

I gape at him in silence, my mouth hanging open like it's waiting for someone to reach in and pull out whatever words I'm supposed to say right now. I'm completely confused.

What in the name of all that is holy is he TALKING ABOUT?!

This man's been cheating on me for *years*, not to mention simultaneously beating the crap out of me, which just adds insult to literal injury. And now he thinks he can give me some weak apology and tell me I'm his *forever*?!

He's been my forever! The whole time, up until two years ago! Where was this guy then??

My blood is boiling, muscles stiffening all over my body in blinding rage. I need to keep my cool and not freak out. I can't give him a reason to go on the defensive and slap me just to shut me up, but I really want to say so many things. I'm not sure I can keep my mouth shut this time...

"Roger..." I grind his name, closing my eyes.

"And I know, you're not just going to *forgive* me," he goes on. "I know, Alex. I fucked up so many times... Just a few apologies won't cut it. Even me changing my behavior won't... I know that. But I want you to know that I will keep trying. I will fix this relationship, you'll see. I'm going to be the husband you deserve."

He stops to breathe out slowly, grasping my face in his hands. I don't mean to, but I flinch. He notices, but it just makes his eyes wider.

"I don't want to give you any more excuses to leave me."

I'm unable to move my eyes from his. They're so blue; so bright and effervescent. I've never seen anything like that color before. I remember how special they used to make me feel when he was looking at only me.

But then things changed. He became the person I'm assuming he always was; the evil he was hiding. And now when he looks at me with those eyes, all I feel is regret.

Regret for what we could have been, if he wasn't a monster. Regret for the years; the time wasted. Regret for all the tears I've cried, all the excuses I've made, and all the things I've missed out on doing because I was too busy chaining myself to a man who would never be what I needed.

Even if I wanted to believe his little speech, which I don't, I wouldn't allow myself to. It's been too long. Too much has happened...

But I can't let him know that.

This is actually the perfect opportunity for me to get my life together enough to leave him. While he's sitting around, pretending to be a good husband - which I imagine will last all of two weeks before he gets bored and angry and decides to smack me around again - I'll be planning my escape.

It shouldn't take me too long... I've been mentally preparing for two years. The only problem before was that I had no confidence in myself. I had no one to turn to for love and support... and courage. I was all alone.

But now I have a friend. I have Noah. He believes in me and wants to help me get the hell away from my abusive husband. And for the first time ever, I think I'm ready.

I can do this.

So I summon all of my internal bad-bitch - trust and believe, she's been cowering for far too long - and I pull the fakest smile I can manage, leaning my head into my husband's touch.

"It will be really hard to trust you again..." My tone is on-point. I've had two years of practice, after all.

He blinks, brows zipping together. "I know, darling. But I swear to you, I'll make this right. I'll make it up to you and make you proud to be my wife again."

Barf.

"I hope so, baby," I nod. "It's all I've wanted."

"I love you so much, Alex," he leans in and kisses my lips softly.

I hate you. "I love you, too."

Chapter Eleven
Alex's Journal

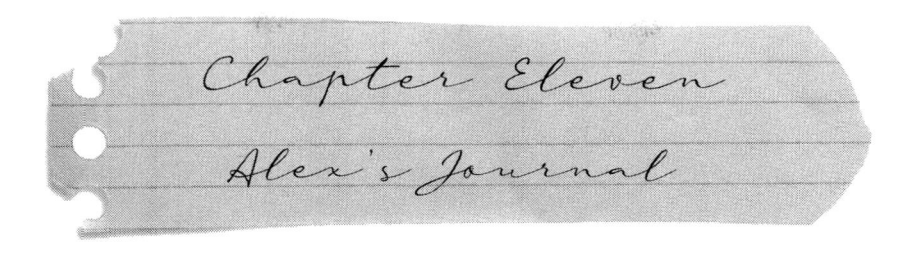

Barnaby, let me tell you about something good that happened.

I just sold a piece to a local gallery. And I did it all on my own. No help from anyone.

I've never been more proud of myself than I am right now. But unfortunately my pride comes coated in shame and misery these days.

In the past year, I've painted more than ever. And every single piece is magnificent. They're dark, and edgy, and provocative. Everything I've ever wanted to be as a painter.

The pain in my life serves as my motivation, the emotional, and the physical...

Roger, my husband, is also like my captor. My home feels like a prison, but really I'm free to leave whenever I want.

It's my heart that keeps me locked up in chains.

He still hits me. And he cheats on me. And I let him because I'm afraid. Not even of him so much as I am afraid of *me*.

Who would I be without Roger? I don't know any life without him.

I know there was an Alex before Roger Glines, but for some reason I can't picture her. Everything about me is so tangled up in him I can no longer tell where he ends and I begin.

He's a real piece of shit, of the lowest caliber. And I know he loves that I stay with him, despite how awful he is to me.

I hate him. I loathe him with a fiery fury deep in my gut.

But the truth is I hate me even more.

I hate myself for staying. I hate myself for the small glimmer of hope inside every time he apologizes, and says it's *the last time*. I hate myself for being a cliché, and for letting a man break me.

I hate myself, and yet there's a voice in my brain that speaks up every now and then. Not often, and barely loud enough for me to hear it. But when it does, I want to grab onto it and squeeze.

Nyla K

I can get myself out of this. It's not too late.

Roger taunts me about not having kids. It's his new obsession. His new kink.

He has a doctor friend of his come over to the house so he can watch me get my birth control shots. He says that in any other form I could neglect it. Pills can be flushed down the toilet, IUD's can be taken out. Condoms can break, I guess. Not that he uses them with me. The birth control is almost one-hundred percent effective, so I suppose there's no need.

Roger wants to control me. It turns him on. And I let him, which makes me even more ridiculous than he is.

I fantasize about screaming in his face that I never want to get pregnant with his child anyway, but I can't actually tell him that, because I fear that it would make him knock me up out of spite. He grows more and more evil every day, Barn. He's Lucifer in a Versace suit.

And I'm his little Mrs.

His Princess of Darkness.

To think we're celebrating our seven-year wedding anniversary next month makes me want to vomit. I'm just numb most days, coasting through my life like a zombie, locking onto any passing joy that I find and strangling the life out of it with need. I'm so desperate, I chase fleeting highs wherever I can find them.

I drink too much. Not enough to get sloppy or develop a problem, because my husband would never allow it. Nor would he tolerate the use of any actual drugs, which I would love to get my hands on for that reason.

When I have a truly great day painting, sometimes I just burst into tears. I want to savor that feeling, for as long as possible, but it always passes.

Roger has been traveling more and more for work, which is a bonus. Any time I have away from him is a victory, though - and it pains me to admit this - I do miss the sex. I should probably start masturbating more or something, because while I cling to the high of orgasms with my piece of shit husband, I hate that I still give him this part of myself.

He fucks other women, of this I'm sure. But when he's with me I know it's different, because I'm the only one he owns completely. Body, mind, and heart. He thrives on that power.

I hate that I'm still turned on by him. I'm so sick of finding him attractive, it pisses me off. I want to find another man who turns me on more than Roger does.

Lately I've been craving the look and feel, smell and taste of a new man.

Seek Me

Someone who isn't Roger Glines.

You'd think because of what I've been going through, I'd be afraid of men... But the opposite seems true. I find myself looking at them when I'm out of the house, silently pleading with my eyes for them to recognize my distress and save me.

It's ridiculous. Only *I* can save myself. But it doesn't mean I don't need a little help, or at the very least a hot guy to be my muse.

I just want to meet someone who isn't a liar and a mind-fucker of the highest degree, like my husband. Someone just as gorgeous, but also sweet. Someone who laughs and smiles often. Someone with kind eyes and strong hands that touch me softly and sensually; not rough and threatening.

I miss having fun. Even in the beginning, the fun Roger and I had was usually based on our surroundings. Now that we've been together for so long, and I've spent the last seven years studying him silently, I finally see how fraudulent our happiness was. How it was all for show; hollow and empty. We were lying to ourselves, and worst of all, I believed it.

Sometimes after we have sex, I go into the bathroom and draw myself a hot bath. I don't mean *hot*, like relaxing. I'm talking *scalding*. And then I dunk my body into it and let the water burn any trace of him off me. It makes me feel better for all of two minutes.

I might have to cool it soon, though. I burnt my leg the other day, and he got pretty pissed off. I still have the bruises from that *reprimanding*.

I've tried scarring my body in ways that would hopefully turn him off, but it hasn't worked yet. I pray for the day he'll leave me because he's sick of the mess I've become, but so far no such luck. He likes me this way. All the new tattoos... He loves them. My pierced nipples and nose... They make his eyes light up with part ferocious lust and part dangerous depravity.

I just keep telling myself to hold on. To keep going, keep breathing.

Soon I'll build up the courage to leave. Soon something will happen to give me that final shove in the right direction.

I can only hope I don't wind up dead waiting.

Chapter Twelve
Noah

WHITE OR BLACK?
I'm choosing a hat. The white one, or the black one? Or maybe I should go bareback? I can't decide.

Already I'm fussing over my outfit tonight more than I have since I was eighteen. But I need to look good. Not like I'm trying too hard... Just casually sexy and awesome, which is how I always look, though tonight it feels like more of an effort than usual. And I need to hurry up. I should leave in twenty minutes if I want to get to the gallery on time.

I'm going to Alex's show. *Duh.* Like there was ever any question of whether I would.

I've been to many an art show in my day. Gallery openings, exhibits, stuff like that... I get invited to them all the time. It's something rich New Yorkers love to do in their spare time, and they love it even more when famous people, such as yours truly, show up.

So since this ain't my first rodeo, I know what to expect. Shows for a newbie like Alex will be roughly three hours long, and a majority of the RSVP's won't show up until about halfway through.

I, however, will not be doing that. I'm getting there the second they open the doors, and I'm staying until they close them. If anyone were to ask me why I'm staying the whole time, I'd say it's because I care about Alex greatly, I'm proud of her, and I want to support her as a friend.

The unknown reason, which I won't admit out loud and if anyone accuses me, I'll lie through my teeth, is that I want to catch a glimpse of Dr. Wife-Beater.

I have to assume Alex's asshole husband will be there tonight. I mean, why wouldn't he? Even if he's an abusive fucktard, his wife is hosting her *first ever* gallery show tonight. It's his obligatory husbandly duty to show up and support her, even if it's just to save face and keep up the facade of the fancy-pants Doctor with the stunning, bohemian artist wife.

From what Alex told me the other night when we stayed up until the wee

Seek Me

hours talking about everything under the sun, despite his general awfulness, Dr. Husband has been very supportive of her art career. Building her a studio, paying for art classes, introducing her to other bougie people in his circle who could help get her name out there. Apparently, his love of inflicting physical violence on her doesn't affect his ability to be an encouraging spouse.

Who knew…

Regardless of his occasional benevolence, she's leaving him. We already talked about it. I'll be damned if I enable her to get sucked back into the web of lies and deceit he's been spinning her in for years. I assured her I wouldn't push, and I meant it. But that doesn't mean I'll just stand by and watch her fade away either.

I'm going to check this asshole out tonight. And since murdering him in cold blood in public could be deemed *inappropriate*, I might end up peeing in his drink a little.

We'll see where the night takes us.

I settle on the black hat, because it fits better with the black tailored dress shirt with matching skinny tie and black jeans I'm wearing. I'll jazz the ensemble up with some bright red snake-print Vans or something. And my classic Bans. Naturally.

As I'm finishing up getting ready, my phone buzzes in my pocket. Brant's texting me about the realtor. Season one of *Hell Storm* was confirmed to film on location in Georgia for four months, starting in April of next year. That's a little over six months away, but I guess Brant's itching to lock me down a house out there, since my agent and publicist both feel rather confident that this series will pick up. And if that's the case, I'll be living somewhere outside of Savannah every summer for the foreseeable future.

I'm brimming with excitement. I've never worked on something so big before. The hype is real already, which riddles me with the desire to bounce off my walls.

Looks like I'll be flying out to Georgia to look at houses soon!

I reply to Brant quick then pull up a text to my new costar, just to check in. Andrew and I have been texting regularly since that meeting the other day, and I smell a brand new bestie in the works.

Me: Georgia here we comeeeee!

He writes back almost instantly, though I'm not sure what time it is in

Nyla K

London.

> **Andrew:** OMG please get me hyped right now! Viv is giving me so much grief already and it's rather cocking up my mood

I laugh at his odd British terminology, then frown because I feel bad. He's such a cool guy. I don't understand what his wife's problem is.

> **Me:** That sucks bro. It's gonna be killer tho! All of us living out there!

> **Andrew:** I know! Johnny's excited as ever to meet you. He's a hellraiser so prepare your liver now lol

> **Me:** LOL dude I'm so game! The 3 of us out and about could be nothing but trouble ;)

> **Andrew:** Make sure to clear it w your girlfriend :-P

Okay, so I may have told him about Alex.

I couldn't help it! I needed to talk to someone, and I couldn't tell my usual friends that I'm vibing on a girl. I can't even tell them I have a friend who's a girl, let alone one who I am not actually banging. They'd have me committed.

So Andrew knows that me and Alex made out a little… in my bed… with my dick out.

Ball-busting is to be expected.

> **Me:** Haha you're HILARIOUS. Speaking of, I'm going to her art show right now so I'll ttyl. Ignore your wife. Georgia's gonna rock!

> **Andrew:** Thanks man. Have fun… and don't do anything the old me wouldn't do ;)

I'm still laughing as I tuck my phone into my pocket and head out the door.

Jimmy's waiting for me outside with the Nav, and I hop into the backseat quick, signaling without words to get this show on the road. He speeds off, and we make our way downtown to the gallery.

It takes us only twenty minutes to get there, and as we pull up in front, I'm shocked to see a line. I squint out the window in disbelief. There's an actual *line* in front of the gallery for my friend's first art show. That's unheard of for an unknown artist. The gallery must have one hell of a PR team.

Or Alex is that good, which I don't doubt in the slightest.

Jimmy gets the door for me and as soon as I step out of the vehicle, lights start flashing in my face. I'm thrown off for a second because I didn't even see any paparazzi, but it turns out the guest list includes more celebs than just little ol' me. I recognize some fellow actor friends being ushered inside another entrance, along with a couple famous musicians and socialites I've seen out and about at parties.

This event is *poppin* already and it just freaking started!

I ignore the questions being shouted at me by the paps as Jimmy guides me to the side door the others were being led into. There's a man wearing a headset and holding a clipboard standing there, but he obviously doesn't ask me for my name, he just moves aside. I nod a silent *thank you* to Jimmy, and I'm in.

The place is nice inside. It's freezing, like galleries always are, and the lighting is dim, which I'm guessing is done on purpose to showcase Alex's work. There aren't many people in here just yet, since most of the RSVP's are still waiting on line. But I'm already receiving nods, waves and pats on the back from some people I know, and some I don't remember, which isn't me being a dick. I just meet a fuck-ton of people.

I say hello to everyone I see because I'm polite like that, but I'm not stopping to talk to anyone until I greet the star of the show. I need to give my friend a hug because damn... I'm *proud* as hell and I haven't even inspected any of the pieces yet.

That being said, I can't help but sneak a few peeks as I'm walking through the place in search of Alex. Many of them catch my eye right off the bat. Her style is very gothic-chic, some echoing her weirdness, some showcasing her pain. But all of them scream *Alex*.

They're gorgeous.

I finally spot her, standing with a tall woman and a short man, a glass of champagne in her right hand while she motions about something with her left.

And I'm stopped dead in my tracks by how much of a goddamned *smokeshow* she is.

Donning a black leather dress that's one-shouldered and so fitted I can see every intricate curve of her delicious body from where I'm standing, she is by far the most beautiful woman in this place, and even the whole damn city. She has on these chunky black platform booties that are exactly her style, since she doesn't rock Louboutins like every other basic girl in NYC. She's Alex, and she's different. Her clothes are expensive, but she doesn't *look* like she's trying... at all. That's not to say she doesn't look put-together. In fact, the opposite is true. Her style and beauty are effortless.

That dark, illustrious hair is long and straight, swept over to one side, and I can see she has some big earrings and bracelets going on. She just looks so cool. She's the most captivating woman in the room, no matter where she goes.

I urge myself to move so I'm not standing around gawking like a weirdo, and saunter over to my *friend* whom I kissed the other day for several leisurely minutes, all the while checking out her legs and ass, and even the scrumptious skin on her neck. Now I know just how good it tastes; how warm and creamy it feels on my lips.

I need to calm the hell down before I lose space in the crotch of my already very fitted jeans.

"It's definitely reflective of the relationship between God and man, you're right about that," Alex speaks, sounding sophisticated and worldly, while also managing to come off cuter than those baby otter videos everyone shares on Facebook. "But I don't know, when I look at it, I see the humor, as well. I found it to be voicing that God had a secret, and was more than willing to hold it over the man's head... If that makes any sense."

Alex lets out a breathy giggle, flipping her hair while her guests laugh and clap, their faces lighting up over her words, and her description of the piece they're all standing before. It's a deep blue background, heavily scraped across the canvas, with a large formless being of mostly eyes looking down at a crumbled mass of limbs beneath it.

Wow... It's intoxicating to look at. I'll have to check each one of these out very closely. *And decide which ones I want to buy.*

I came here with blank checks, prepared to drop some serious coin.

"There she is," I whisper as I step up to *my* Alex, wasting no time slinking my arm around her waist.

She doesn't startle in the slightest. Instead, she leans into me before turning her luminous face upward, smiling at me with ease and appreciation. Her eyes are so green and glowing, like dewy leaves on forest trees.

Thankfully, the cut on her lip is basically healed, covered in shimmery pink gloss, and the remaining bruises on her throat have been fully hidden, likely by some strategic cover-up.

Seek Me

"Hi," she chirps up at me and I lean in to kiss her cheeks. She whispers as I do, "I'm so happy to see you."

"Likewise. You have a fucking *line* outside," I give her eyes wide with mutual excitement. "Are you sure this is your first show?"

She laughs and takes me by the arm. "Excuse me," she says politely to the other two people who nod, immediately going back to her painting on the wall. "Have you checked anything out yet?"

"Not yet. I just walked in and I needed to see you first," I tell her as we wander slowly through the space. "This is incredible, Al. You have no idea how proud I am of you."

"I know, Noah, oh my God! Can you believe how many people are already here?" She squeals and tugs my arm which has me chuckling. "It just freaking started! The director thinks we'll sell out! Isn't that insane?!"

"No," I shake my head vigorously. "I could've told you that. I mean, I don't know about all these buffoons, but I came to shop."

She huffs a laugh, and her face is gleaming. I can't believe how happy she is, and how damn good she looks like this. *Mental note: make Alex this happy all the time.*

"Noah, you don't have to buy anything," she admonishes me, though she's still smiling her face off. "You're my best friend. I'll paint you whatever you want for free."

"First of all, yea you will. Second of all, it's not about that. I just want to support you. And third of all..." my voice trails for a moment as I watch her head bobbing all around with zeal. "Am I really your *best* friend?"

She pauses her giddy movements and peers up at me. "Yes. I told you that, remember?"

Yes, she told me she didn't have any other friends... Or family. So I guess that leaves me. Her best and only friend.

God, that makes me feel really guilty about how obsessively attracted to her I am.

But again, she needs a friend tonight, and that's what I am. Her best friend.

"I remember," I rumble, brushing her hair behind her ear, noting that there's an adorable braid on one side. "You're my best friend, too."

She giggles and taps me in the stomach. "Uh false. You have plenty of friends you've known way longer than me."

"Yea, but you're prettier than all of them combined, so they don't count," I smirk as she laughs out loud, and I manage to pry my eyes away from her long enough to briefly scope the vicinity for Dr. Dickwad.

Alex reaches up to straighten my tie. "You look sexy."

"You wanna ditch this thing and go make out somewhere?" I tease and she hits me again.

My eager gaze continues to dart around. *Where are you, fuckface? Show yourself!*

"What are you looking for?" She asks, giving me some eyes.

"Nothing. A drink," I recover, grabbing a glass of champagne off the tray of a passing waiter. "Can I get you a refill?"

"No, thank you. I can't get tipsy, I have to speak in a few minutes. I'm nervous."

"Don't be. You'll knock 'em dead," I wink.

"Alexandra, darling!" A loud female voice booms from behind us.

A white-haired woman with giant black-rimmed glasses floats over and grasps Alex by the shoulders, kissing both of her cheeks.

"Fabulous! Absolutely exquisite! You must come. Jeffrey Donelson from Flatiron is just *dying* to meet you!"

Alex nods to the lady, then peeks up at me, giving me an apologetic look, though I've truly never seen a person so exuberant in my life.

"By all mean, go," I shoo her off with a smile. "Rock house, Al. I'll be here… sticking dots on stuff."

I show her my evil grin and she bites her lip, wiggling her brows at me as she stumbles away to greet her fans.

As soon as she's gone, I let out a swift breath. This is already the *best* night ever.

And it's just getting started.

Almost three hours later, I've spent a small fortune.

Within fifteen minutes of me being here, I had purchased five paintings. As it turns out, Alex's style is exactly my style, though I don't have many paintings in my apartment. My art is more photography and collectibles, and I've been in the market for some oil on canvas ever since I found out my new bestie was a painter. Now I have pieces for my library, my office, the guest room, living room… Just about every room in my house. They're all going to be decorated with Alex.

I'm practically giddy.

Seek Me

I knew people would be fighting over stuff tonight, so I wasted no time at all claiming mine. I even paid the desk right away to ensure no confusion as to what belonged to me.

I'm still staring at one I snatched up the second I saw it. It's highly intriguing to me; all oranges and yellows on the canvas with a swirling black mass in the middle, filled with two eyes.

The eyes are… strange. But in a good way. They almost look familiar. And they seem to be staring back at me. I'm not sure what they're trying to convey exactly… Maybe Alex can tell me how she interprets it later.

I've talked to Alex a few times since I arrived, but not for more than two minutes here and there before she was being pulled and yanked in all sorts of directions to schmooze with the art crowd of Manhattan. And I'm totally fine with it, only because I know I'm not letting her out of my sight tonight without some celebration. I fully intend to capture her when she's done here and bring her to dinner or out dancing. Whatever she wants to do.

It's her night, after all.

As for the other thing I planned on doing tonight, I haven't so much as peeped her husband anywhere. It would appear he's a no-show, which I don't understand in the slightest. How could he not be here?

I really wanted to "accidentally" trip him and send him flying into a table of canapés. That would be hilarious.

"Noah! Hey, pal!" My friend and fellow actor, Keith Fisher, sidles up to me with two girls hanging on his arms. One is a blonde singer who has been climbing the charts lately, and the other is a redhead I've never seen before, but whose boobs are so big, I swear they could be used as floatation devices should a tsunami overtake this art show.

"Hey, Keith. How's it goin, man?" I smile, giving him one of those half-hugs while the girls both flash oddly sultry looks.

"Good, good, bro. Can't complain. Cashing in on this new streaming shit everyone's talking about," he says casually. "Hey, do you know Layla and Amber?"

"Can't say that I do," I reply, feigning interest as I shake the girls' hands. "Nice to meet you both."

"*Very* nice to meet you," the redhead, Amber, croons, brushing her side against mine. "I'm a huge fan."

"Thanks. That's… cool," I grin. I hope I'm not coming off bored, because I hate to be rude, but I secretly can't stop glancing all over the place, checking for Alex or her fashionably late hubby.

"This artist is pretty bangin, huh?" Keith nods at the painting in front of us. "I saw a couple I wanted to grab, but they sold out faster than Cronuts in Williamsburg."

I chuckle and shake my head. "You snooze, you lose. I copped this one for myself."

"Her work is truly stunning," Layla adds. "So original. I haven't seen anything like this in... well, ever!"

My heart swells in my chest for Alex. She's so talented, I can barely wrap my head around it.

"Plus, she's a little hottie herself," Keith smirks, his eyes darkening a bit, which sets off a spark of jealousy in my veins. "I'd let her paint my canvas any day." His eyebrows waggle and I clench my fist to stop myself from punching him.

Why do I want to punch him for saying Alex is hot? She is *hot. He's not wrong.*

Layla beats me to the punch, laying a solid kidney shot on Keith that makes me laugh out loud.

"Well, *you're* clearly into her," Amber jumps in, running her finger along my side. "You've been watching her all night."

And it seems like someone's been watching me *all night...*

I turn to give her a look and she arches a brow, biting her lip in a display that would normally turn me on. But right now it's just making me uncomfortable.

And now why do I feel like I can't flirt with girls in front of Alex? This is getting a bit unnerving.

It would seem that I've lodged myself in some bizarre friend-zone with Alex, where we care about each other so much, and we occasionally make out, but then we're not together, and it all makes very little sense. I've never been so confused by a girl and my feelings for her, which is even more crazy because I've never actually *had* feelings for a girl like this before.

I brace myself to try and flirt with the redhead, just to see if I can, when my eyes catch sight of Alex from across the room. She's standing next to a very tall guy who has his hand on her back.

I blink a few times, registering this image. The guy is too good-looking to be talking to my Alex. Jealousy fizzles up my throat, scorching my chest like heartburn. And then I have a momentary thought...

Is that her husband??

Could be. They look awfully close to be strangers or even just normal

Seek Me

acquaintances. The way he's standing beside her, holding her... I'm convinced. That *has* to be her husband.

Suddenly I'm excusing myself from Keith and the girls, stomping over to Alex and the Doctor. What do I plan on saying to them when I get there? I have no idea. Hopefully I think of something soon, because I only have few more feet.

Nice to meet you, Dr. Glines. I'm Noah, Alex's best friend. Oh, and I'm going to chop your head off and hang it up in my office.

I reach them just in time to see his fingers slide along Alex's waist, sending my blood pressure through the roof.

"Hi, there," I grunt as I step in front of them, giving the guy a cunning smile. *I will destroy you.*

"Hi," Alex chirps, smiling at me and sounding much happier than I assumed she would with her abusive husband standing next to her. "Daniel, meet Noah Richards. Noah, this is Daniel Smart. He works for Anne Crawford's gallery in Bushwick."

I let out a hard breath and my body uncoils, the fury I was feeling two seconds ago being swept up in a wave of my own naivety.

"Pleased to meet you," the man, Daniel - who is *not* Alex's husband - rasps and shakes my hand.

"Likewise," I sigh, but when I go to release his hand, he holds onto mine for a second longer. My forehead creases.

"I'm a big fan," he growls and then I get it.

He's hitting on me, too. Damn, I must look good tonight.

I chuckle humbly. "Thanks, G." Then shoot him a wink.

"Alex, you have my card," he turns back to my friend. "Give me a call whenever you have your next collection started. I'd love to have you meet Anne."

"Okay!" Alex squeals, visibly ready to crawl out of her skin. *She's so cute, oh my God.*

"Enjoy your night," he says, giving me another once-over before wandering off.

I laugh to myself and grab Alex's hand, needing to touch her right away before I explode.

"He liked you," Alex giggles and I warn her with a look. "I can't believe you're still here. You don't have to stay, you know."

"Of course I do. I'm hanging with you all night. After this we're gonna go celebrate you selling out your first gallery!"

"Oh my God, Noah, I can't believe I sold out!" She grabs my shoulders and shakes me around while I laugh. "This is the best thing that's ever happened to me. Like, ever!"

"I know, baby. I'm so proud of you," I squeeze her hand, then glance at my watch one last time.

Show's ending in ten minutes... I guess he's not coming.

"Noah, what the hell are you waiting for?" She asks, perplexed. "You've been looking around all night. Am I missing something? Are they setting up a surprise chocolate fountain?"

I chuckle. "No... I just thought that maybe..." I pause and try to think of the right words to describe that I was waiting for her stupid husband to show up so I could look at him and maybe spit in his face. "I thought that... Roger might show up."

Alex gawks at me like I just told her I was waiting for Big Foot to arrive.

"Noah... he's not coming," she huffs a dismissive laugh and shakes her head. "Not that I even told him the date and time for him to come, but he'd probably rather light himself on fire than show up to this for me."

"Really?" I gasp, still surprised and I'm not sure why. I was just assuming that because she said he was outwardly supportive of her art career, he'd want to at least stop by. I guess that was foolish of me. Alex shrugs and nods. "Well, *I'll* set his dumb ass on fire for being such a piece of shit."

She laughs softly and wraps her arms around my waist, hugging me tight. "It's sweet of you to worry about me like that, Noah."

"I always worry about you," I kiss the top of her head. "You know that."

"What were you going to do to him if he *did* show up?" She asks, curling her neck to look at me.

"Nothing really," my eyes meet hers. "I just wanted to see his face. Maybe slip some Visine in his martini."

She giggles with her whole body vibrating into mine, giving me the warm and fuzzies.

"You rock so hard."

"Back at ya, showstopper."

A few minutes later, Alex is saying goodbye to people, still swept up in her zone, and I'm not admitting boredom or anything, but I'm just dying to get her out of here so we can go celebrate. Hopefully she's actually down to do something, because she hasn't said so yet.

I wander over to let her know I'll be waiting outside until she's done.

Seek Me

"You're serious about hanging out?" She asks with wide green eyes.

"I'm the most serious person on Earth, Alex. Don't ever forget it." Now she rolls them at me and I laugh. "No, but really. Whatever you want to do, we'll do it. I'll be out in the Navigator waiting for you. Take your time."

I kiss her temple then leave, and I can feel her, and the people she was talking to staring at me as I walk away. I hope I'm not coming off boyfriendy, especially because she *is* still married and if someone happens to tell her husband she was getting chummy with the likes of me, she could be in serious trouble.

I'm still second-guessing myself as I slide into the back of the Navigator, where Jimmy is waiting patiently in the front seat.

"She'll be out in a bit," I tell him, rubbing the back of my neck.

"You got it, boss," he responds, paying more attention to the magazine he's reading than my obvious and overwhelming insecurities.

It's just after eleven, so we probably won't be having dinner at any nice restaurants at this time of night, but we could still go to the club, or grab food somewhere else if she's hungry. We could go bowling or play pool, or maybe even find a last-minute show if she's into that.

Whatever she wants to do, I'll make it happen. Because she fucking crushed it tonight, and I want to celebrate with her.

As her best friend. That's it.

Not romantically. Just friendly.

Man, you're trying really hard to convince yourself of this, aren't you?

I'm telling my brain to shut up as Alex whips open the rear door and climbs into the back seat with me, closing it behind her. But she doesn't sit down.

Instead, she keeps crawling until she's on my lap, sitting nose-to-nose with me, her legs around my waist and a very sly smirk on her pink lips.

I let out a rough breath as my eyes lock on her mouth. "Jimmy, give us a minute, please."

I'm sure Jimmy shoots me a knowing look before he steps quickly out of the vehicle, but I'm not paying attention to him in the slightest. It isn't until I hear his door shut that I register that Alex and I are now alone inside this vehicle, and she's running her hands up my chest, then my neck, into my hair, grinning at me like she's in on a pertinent secret.

"Alex…" I whisper her name, and that's all I can get out before she cuts me off with a kiss.

A searing, scorching, face-melting kiss that has me groaning uncontrollably into her mouth.

Fuck. Yes.

Alex's lips attack mine, melding with my mouth, sucking all over while whimpering the hottest noises I've ever heard. She tugs my lower lip between her teeth, yanking until an *Ah* escapes me, and she giggles seductively, tracing the curve with her tongue.

Good fucking God, what is happening…

Any reservations I should feel flee when I grab her ass in both hands and hold on tight, squeezing and pulling her as close as possible while we devour one another. The surrounding air is steamy already, and my flesh is burning from the feeling of her tight little body grinding into me; the taste of champagne on her tongue as she takes over my mouth.

She wraps my tie around her fist then drags me closer with it, kissing and panting and kissing some more, her other hand slinking into my hair to rip it at the strands.

"Fuck, baby…" I grunt as I hold her, making her lips mine, kissing slow and deep, our tongues pressing together while we drink each other in. It's so hot I'm like a volcano waiting to erupt.

"You're fucking perfect, Noah," she whispers, fingers now caressing my jaw while our lips lock and we suck harder and needier than any kisses I've ever experienced. "I can't believe you stayed all night just so you could hang out with me after my show."

"I wouldn't miss this for the world," I tell her as my hand slips beneath the material of her dress to cup her smooth ass. "I mean, not *this*… But like, you. Your night." I pause my rambling to collect my thoughts while Alex kisses from the corner of my mouth, down to my jaw. "I meant what I said. We can do whatever you want tonight, Alex."

She holds my face in her hands, green eyes setting on mine. "Anything?" She kisses me softly and I let out a quiet moan as I nod. "Really?" Another soft kiss. I'm going out of my mind here. I nod again.

My dick is so hard it's going to break, since it's really smashed in an uncomfortable position between our bodies. But I barely care because Alex is giving me a tone with a look, and both seem downright filthy. And she keeps kissing me, slow and wet and warm and fucking delicious.

I don't know what she has in mind, but it better involve more of these kisses, because I'm not sure I could stop even if I tried.

She purrs, "Mmm… Noah," and moves back, but takes me with her by my tie, until she's lying on her back on the seat and I'm on top of her. "Your lips are like candy."

"You want this candy, baby?" I growl, giving her my tongue until she groans, my hips jutting forward to rub my aching dick on her through my pants.

Her dress is really riding up, but we're too hot and bothered to care about that, or the fact that we're still parked outside the gallery where she just finished her art show, in public. Or that my driver is standing outside.

All I'm thinking about right now is this perfect mouth and all the sexy things I want to do with it, starting with these yummy kisses.

Her fingers explore, sneaking under my shirt to trace my abs and chest, tugging my nipple ring, prompting a strangled groan as my dick flinches from the sensation.

Kiss kiss kiss.

She does it again, and I think my cock is weeping, he's so happy.

Lick suck lick suck.

Our tongues are wrestling, and it's so hot inside this vehicle the windows are fogged up. Alex is making sex noises and *God*, I'm really going to lose my mind if I don't get her naked soon.

"Noah, touch me…"

"Alex, if I touch you I'll come in my pants again, and I really can't have that. It's super embarrassing."

She lets out a soft laugh into my mouth, wrapping her legs around my hips to hold me with her.

"Okay, fine. Can we go to your place?" Her eyes are hooded with desire. That look has to be my new favorite thing in life.

"Are you sure…?" I ask, because wasn't it only a few days ago that she was telling me we couldn't? Which I totally understand, by the way. I just don't know what changed.

"Yes… please…" She breathes unsteady, imitating my own.

"Don't beg," I hum, dragging my lips over her throat. "Unless you're prepared to end this right here and now."

Erotic giggles leave her as she shakes her head. "No, I don't want it to end. That's why I want to go to your place." Her hands slowly sweep up my torso until they're on my face. "You said we could celebrate, any way I want. Well, this is how I want to celebrate… with you…" She tugs my face to hers, but presses her lips up to my ear. "Deep inside me." Then she licks the lobe and I almost explode all over both of us.

Seriously, I think I came just a little. That was like a mini orgasm, for sure.

Jesus, what the fucking fuck is this girl doing to me?! If this is best friends with a chick, I don't know why I wasn't doing it sooner...

Well, I *do* know. *I was waiting for Alex.*

I want to take her home more than I want to breathe, but I need some reassurance to ease my conscience. I need to make sure this is one-hundred percent what she really wants. And then I need to know why.

"Alex, baby... I think it's pretty obvious I've wanted that since the night we met," I start, my fingers running possessively up the length of her thigh. "But I just need to know... What changed?"

I lift my head to look down at her. She's all sparkling eyes, moist lips, and flushed cheeks. She looks breathtaking.

"I thought we agreed... we couldn't," I whisper in trepidation I need to squash before anything more happens between us. "I need to know you're thinking this through... I couldn't live with myself if I -"

"Noah, listen to me," she cuts me off with a touch of her fingers to my lips. "Since you came into my life, even though it wasn't long ago at all, I've felt things that I haven't felt in years. Some things I'm not sure I've ever felt." Her voice is low, but assured. "That's how you became my best friend so fast. Because you make me feel like my old self again... Like my *real* self."

I gaze down at her, mesmerized. And to my surprise, she's looking at me the exact same way.

"With you I'm happy, confident, strong... fun," her fingers trail my throat, onto my chest. "When you look at me, I feel *brilliant*. Sexy and badass and cool. All the things I know I am. All the things he took from me..." I witness her gulp and it forces me to do the same. "I trust you emphatically and let's be real here... I've been fighting this attraction the whole time."

She grins and I have to actively stop myself from kissing it.

"I know we're friends, and I know I'm married to the devil, and none of this makes any sense... But I'm already fighting the bad stuff all the time. I don't want to fight the good anymore. I want to savor it."

I sweep in a breath and hold on.

Sounds like she's thought this through...

I'm sold.

I lick the grin off my lips and kiss her slow, sucking her bottom lip until she purrs.

"As long as you're sure, baby," my voice slips into her mouth, "I'm here."

"I know you are," she yanks my face closer. "And I am."

Seek Me

This time she kisses me, and we don't stop. It grows deeper and hungrier, and it's not until I'm grating my erection between her thighs again that I realize we *do* need to leave.

We can't fuck in this car. *Although at this moment in time, I think I'd take the potential misdemeanor.*

I force myself to pull away from her before a light breeze blows and I erupt in my boxers.

"Alright, we're going home," I growl at her and she squeals, touching me everywhere, grabbing my hands and my hips and my ass. "But stop touching me! I know you like making me jizz on myself, but that's not happening tonight."

She laughs as I reach behind me and bang on the window to signal Jimmy. I sit back, minding my aching balls and pull Alex with me until she cuddles up, half sitting on my lap, half straddling my thigh.

"I'm serious, beautiful," I take her chin while Jimmy jumps back into the driver's seat, acting like nothing happened. *He's getting a raise.* He starts up the engine and peels off. *And a giant tip.* "Tonight's going to be different," I whisper to Alex who shivers, and I derail my train of thoughts away from how hard her nipples likely are. "I hope you're ready... You're my feast tonight, Alexandra. And I'm *starving*."

She whines and we spend the next eighteen minutes feeling each other up, touching softly, panting and teasing so good I can barely breathe by the time we reach my place.

I reach into my pocket, maneuvering around my hard-on to grab whatever bills are in there and toss them at Jimmy while he chuckles and we clamber out of the vehicle. I clutch Alex's hand tight in mine as we scamper like horny squirrels straight through my door, running down the hallway and into my house.

Once we're securely inside, door locked and alarm set, I'm pent-up, nervous and a little sweaty. This is such a huge deal for some reason, it doesn't even feel like it's really happening. I keep thinking I'm going to wake up, and it will have all been a dream.

Please let this be real...

Alex stands before me looking shy, but still so turned-on she's like a flame dancing in my foyer. Her skin is flushed, lips red and moist, eyes wide and twinkling green.

I swallow hard. "Do you want something to drink?"

She simply shakes her head and walks away, into the living room. And when

I think she might go for the couch, she turns and heads to the stairs. She kicks off her shoes and starts climbing.

Up the stairs. Up to my bedroom.

Fuck.

I follow her lead, stepping out of my Vans and removing my hat, tossing it as I make my way after her, slowly, so that by the time I'm in my room, she's already there waiting.

Standing at the edge of my bed, she slips her arm through the top of her dress and shimmies it down her body, over every slender curve, until it's around her feet, then nudges it away.

Alex Mackenzie is standing in front of me in just her panties.

Beautiful. Glowing. Exotic. Perfection.

My chest is already heaving. I can't help it. Anticipation is flying in and out of my lungs at a rapid pace, the same speed at which my heart is leaping into my ribs.

I undo my tie, leisurely, keeping my eyes on Alex, and hers on mine. When it's removed, I toss it at her and she catches it, draping it around her neck. Then she casually slips her panties down her legs and my dick throbs. *Wow...*

I take my time unbuttoning my shirt, building the anticipation. There's no rush tonight. Nothing else is going on. We're doing this and it's fantastic, and you better believe I'm going to drag it out as long as humanly possible.

Once my shirt is unbuttoned and shrugged off my shoulders, I go for my pants, nodding for Alex to lie down on the bed, which she does, without hesitation. Now she's gazing up at me from my bed, completely naked and gorgeous, the low light of my room's dimmers illuminating every curve and sinew of her small, toned body.

I pause unzipping my pants to turn on the music. I can't even be sure what the song is, but it's slow and sensual, adding another heady layer to this experience. Alex's eyes close briefly in a slow blink as she sinks deeper into my comforter, gripping it in her fists on both sides.

I gulp because I have to. My mouth is watering for this girl like she's a feast laid out before me. I can see all of her, and it's sheer magnificence. Round, perky tits with both nipples pierced; sultry slopes and peaks; her bare pussy with one small landing strip of light hair I want to touch so bad my fingers are actually twitching.

When I step out of my pants and boxers, Alex bites her lip. *Mhmm...* I'm so fucking hard my erection is painfully stretched and swollen. I crawl onto the bed, kneeling in front of her. We stare at each other for a while, accentuating the lust, thick in the air like smoke, surrounding us while we breathe and watch. I take a beat to study her tattoos because I love each and every one and I want to kiss them all a hundred times.

"Spread your legs," I growl, nudging her foot with my knee.

She does so, opening her legs for me so I can see my prize.

Fuck, I need that pussy like she's the cookie jar before dinner. *Delicious forbidden temptation…*

"So sweet…" I breathe, inching closer.

Alex's hands look impatient, her fingers curling around the comforter while her eyes dance between my dick, my abs, and my mouth. All things I want her to kiss, but we'll get there.

"Baby…" I whisper, moving closer still, until I'm hovering over her, without touching. "How bad do you want me?"

She moans out a soft noise. "So fucking bad, Noah… I've wanted you every day since we met."

A sharp hiss escapes my lips. "Show me."

Her head cocks a bit, and she looks like she wants to ask *how*, but I know she won't. This is Alex we're talking about. The girl who dry-humped me to orgasm on my living room floor and left me covered in hickeys. She knows what she likes, she's a bit of a fucking freak, and it's amazing.

If she wants something, she'll take it. Plain and simple. No shame in her game.

She lifts her hand and reaches out. For a second, I think she's going to grab my dick, which would be wonderful, but instead her hand creeps between her parted thighs and she drags her fingers along the slit of her pussy.

Fuck. "Fuck…" the grunt escapes me as I dig my fingertips into the bed.

"Oh my God, *Noah*…" She lifts her hips to give me a better view of her touching her body.

For *me*.

Her index finger circles her clit a few dozen times before it slinks lower and pushes gently inside herself.

"Alex… baby, that's so… good…" I croak, unable to say anything normal with my wide eyes stuck on what they're seeing.

She chomps her lower lip, breasts moving up and down with her panting; those barbells through her nipples begging to be sucked, hard. Her middle finger joins the other and they both press inside. I can see the glistening juices of her arousal dripping everywhere, making my cock jump as it twitches so hard it's moving on its own.

Alex gasps, brilliant green eyes gawking with hunger at my thick, heavy erection.

"Noah," she breathes my name like a lyric and I hum back to her. "Touch." She nods at my cock.

Oh fuck… If I touch it, I'll come…

No, you won't. Just focus. This is Alex. You're going to come with her. Just…

I curl my fist around my dick and pull, painfully slow, watching her watching me; fingers fucking herself as deep as she can… Nowhere near as deep as I'm going to be. *Yes…*

I hiss as I milk my cock, from the balls all the way up to my sensitive head and back, jerking myself for her; both of us touching ourselves for the other. It's such a turn-on, showing each other this side… It's naughty and dirty and so *fucking* hot my pulse is thumping in my neck, as are the veins in my cock, which I can feel in my hand.

"Alex…" Her name comes out like a harsh command. "Tell me how you want me to fuck you."

She cries out a breathy sound as her other hand cups her tit, and my balls are fucking *tight*.

"Deep," she mewls and I nod, edging her on. "So deep I can't breathe."

"God…" my eyelids droop. *Fuck me, this is amazing.* "My dick is going to claim you, Alexandra. So deep… so far inside your gorgeous body."

"Yes, Noah. I want it *all*," she moans. A pearl of precum pulses from my tip and I stroke with it. "You fucking me… So deep and so *hard…" Jesus, I can't wait to fill her…*

"Yea?" I bite my lip.

Her thumb grazes her clit and she groans, "Yea… I need you. I *need* to feel you inside me."

"How wet is your pussy right now?"

"So fucking wet for you."

For me…

My orgasm might sneak up on me if I'm not careful. So I stop with a growl and position myself over Alex, pushing her thighs open wider to wedge myself in between. I grab her hand to stop her teasing because I can't take it anymore. Keeping my eyes on hers, I extend my tongue slowly and lick her fingers, sucking them between my lips to clean off her juices.

She looks shocked and tastes like fucking heaven.

"Alex, you're sweeter than sugar, baby," I quickly drop my face between her thighs, before she can process what's happening, and give her a few strong licks.

She cries out loud, hips jumping off the bed, seeking my ravenous mouth. I slip my tongue inside her, swirling it a few times, then suck her clit with fervor.

As soon as her thighs tighten I stop, because that orgasm is mine to feel on my dick. *No coming on my mouth… Not until my cock has sufficiently explored every inch of her insides.* She whines out a noise, pouting down at me as I grin, wiping my mouth with my hand.

I begin my next journey to those luscious tits of hers, moving up her curves, kissing her pelvis, licking and nipping a path along her hip bone and up to her navel, where I stop to kiss the piercing in her belly button. It's so fucking sexy and cute, just like everything about Alex.

After that I kiss her chest, across her tits, flicking the steel with my tongue, lapping at it over and over before finally taking it between my teeth.

"Noah! Oh my *God…*" she cries, her hands flying to my hair. "I've always wanted your perfect mouth on my tits."

My heart pounds at that. "Really?"

On to the other breast, repeating the actions; lick, lick, lick, suck, suck suck, bite and tug until she squeals.

"Yes!" Alex is coming undone, and it's wildly encouraging. I can't help but rub my aching dick on her thigh for some sweet friction relief. "Your tongue is *so* good."

"You can have it for hours," I grin. "Here." I kiss her nipple once more. "And here…" My fingers tease the apex of her thighs and she shudders.

"God, yes…" she begs, her voice hoarse.

"But first, baby, I need to slide my cock in you before I come on your stomach." She makes a noise, as if she doesn't particularly care if I come on her stomach, which is adorable.

I roll away from her for a split second to grab a condom from my nightstand, and then I'm back, ripping it open with my teeth. I hand it to her, because I want to watch her do it. I *need* that image in my brain.

She sheaths my cock with the condom, all the way down and I'm momentarily bummed that I don't get to feel the inside of her body without the latex, which is a crazy thought to have because I *always* use condoms. I'm a responsible guy like that.

But with Alex, clearly all my reasoning and logic go out the window. I want everything with her. Everything I've never done with anyone else.

I gulp away the fear from where my mind is going and palm her breast, thumb grazing the nipple until I can feel her trembling. To be honest, I'm shaking too. This is so crazy.

Alex and I are going to have sex.

It's all I've wanted since the day I saw her at Maxwell's. She's quickly becoming one of my closest friends, despite only knowing her a few weeks.

And now I'm going to fuck her. I'm going to fuck my friend, hard, and it's going to feel so good, I already know.

Please, just don't let me come too fast.

I kiss her soft lips while she purrs into my mouth, meeting my tongue with hers. We kiss ourselves into a rhythm, and before I know it, I'm settled on top of her, with my cock resting over her warm, silky wet entrance.

"You have no idea how bad I've wanted this…" I tell her with a fuzzy brain, words pouring from my mouth against my will. "I want this with *you*, Alex…"

"Noah, I want it too," she whispers, holding my jaw while kissing my lips raw. "You're all I want… All I *need*."

I groan and grab her hip hard with my hand, looking dazed between our heated bodies to guide the tip of me inside, frantically needing to make us one. I give her a push, thrusting in just enough to engulf me in cloaked heat.

More than just my dick. My whole body is surrounded in an orb of fiery pleasure. *This is the most amazing feeling ever.*

"Fuck…" I whimper, falling apart while feeding her more, filling her slowly and stretching her skin to fit me. She's so tight it seems unbelievable.

"Oh, God!" She chokes out a cry, almost as if I'm hurting her, but I know I'm not because she's touching me all over, kissing and biting my neck, squeezing my ass.

"Baby… You feel like… *everything*…"

More of my cock, pumping into her until I'm almost up to the hilt.

"Noah… God, your dick is… deep. *Fuck*, it's so deep…"

Her juices overflow onto my balls while I move, pulling out and driving back in; working my length in her over and over while she screams and bites me. My face is buried in her neck and I'm panting, heaving, growling… Fucking her harder and deeper with each motion, determined to be everything she wants me to be. To make her come so good she'll never think about an orgasm from anyone else again.

Alex's hands slide over my torso and up my chest. She palms my pecs and brushes her thumb over my piercing until my dick tremors inside her.

"Does this feel good?" She's breathless and raspy as fuck as she tugs it and my cock swells. "Mmm... Fuck, that's *amazing*."

"Baby, keep touching," I plead, steadily thrusting, rocking my hips forward and back, swiveling to graze the sweet spot. She pulls my piercing a little harder and I gasp out loud. "Oh God, yes... *harder*."

She does me one better, and lifts her mouth to my nipple, sucking the barbell and yanking it between her teeth until I cry out a rough groan. *Jesus... this woman is... fucking... perfect.*

I force every inch as deep as I can, my cock so full and thick it's impaling her. "Fucking you is the best feeling on Earth, Alex."

A shaky squeak flies from her lips. "Noah, you fuck so good... Harder."

She gets what she wants. Pounding and aching and stroking and good fucking *God* this is intense. My bed is creaking, and even the nightstand is banging against the wall, all of its contents scattering onto the floor.

"Fuck!" I roar with my hips slamming into hers. My balls seize up and I think I may combust at any moment.

I lift Alex by her hips, legs wrapping around my waist as I hold her ass so hard I might bruise it. But she doesn't care, because she's too busy screaming my name and scratching my chest raw.

"Noah! Jesus I'm going to..." Her choppy voice gives out. I'm fucking her into a goddamned oblivion.

We're sweating and breathing ragged and holding each other for dear life.

Fuck me... Alex... Yes... Oh... God...

"Come for me, Alexandra," I demand, choked and panting. "Drown me, baby."

My hips are working overtime, pushing and pulling, deeper and deeper and deeper until I'm bottoming out and holy fucking *fuck... I'm coming.*

Alex lets out a loud yelp, her entire body tightening around me. "I'm coming... Noah... Fucking come with me, baby..."

Fuck... yesssss....

I chase her high as her body tremors and she comes, gracefully and so beautiful, setting me off like a rocket. I succumb to the sensation and release inside her, my orgasm ripping through my loins unlike anything I've ever felt.

My lips trail every inch of her dampened flesh while I sing her praises, my cock bursting at the seams, filling up the condom as I kiss her anywhere I can reach.

"Alex... Baby, I'm fucking coming so hard... *Yes*... You're the best ever... Fucking *ever*, baby."

She mewls, "You feel so good..."

"*You* feel so fucking good..."

My hips come to a gradual halt and I'm buzzing. I think my dick *actually* exploded. It's sore and throbbing. My whole pelvis is slippery and I fucking *love* it.

After minutes on end, the world stops spinning and I reacquaint myself with my surroundings. I've never felt anything like that before. It was *the* most intense climax...

I didn't know they could feel like that. Have I been coming wrong all these years?

I lift my face to look down at Alex and she's breathing so hard she's sputtering. Her skin is blushed pink all over, a sheen covering her marvelous complexion. She looks iridescent and so gorgeous.

"Al..." I croak, shaking my head. "Jesus... Wow..."

"I know, right?" She chirps and I giggle.

This girl's got me *giggling* now.

Oh boy... That orgasm turned you into a big mushy puddle of sap.

I don't even care. How could I care about anything right now? I'm in my bed with the best girl in the world and we just had mind-blowing sex! Nothing else ever needs to happen for the rest of eternity.

I kiss Alex's jaw and neck, nuzzling her sweet, slightly sticky skin and inhaling her scent. I hold her head in my hand and play with her hair.

"You're so affectionate after you come," she whispers a laugh.

I pull back to grin at her. "*You*... You're perfect, Alex Mackenzie."

"I think *you're* perfect, Noah Richards," she lays a sweet smile on me.

"Let's have sex like, a million more times," I murmur over her lips and she laughs hard.

I really love that sound.

But then she sighs. "I should probably get going soon. It's getting late."

I gape at her with wide, panicked eyes. *No! Don't leave!*

Internally, I falter. Why am I so opposed to her leaving? Typically, it would be me suggesting that exact course of action...

It's getting late, and I've got a long day tomorrow, so... Let me call you a car.

But the thought of Alex leaving right now makes me sad. I slept so well with her in my bed the other day. I cuddled the shit out of her and it felt like I was sleeping in a cloud that smells like strawberries and cream.

Seek Me

I want that again, preferably after a few dozen more orgasms for both of us.

"Don't leave," I huff, struggling to keep the vulnerability out of my tone. *Jeez, sex with Alex turns me into a major chick.*

She stares up at me, worrying her bottom lip as she's clearly deep in her thoughts. "Why?"

"Because I want you to stay," I kiss her lips softly. "I want to make you feel good more. And then fall asleep smothering you again." She giggles, and my mouth is swept up into an uncontrollable grin. "*Please*, baby..." I pout. "I've never begged a girl for anything in my whole life..."

"I believe you," she smirks, though her eyes are quite serious. "So... why me?"

It's an interesting question, one that I'm not entirely sure I have an answer for.

I decide to go with the candy-coated version of the truth. "Because... I want you. And I always get what I want." I move my lips back down her jaw and neck, leaving delicate little kisses all over her golden skin.

"I'm sure you do," she mumbles, her normally raspy voice even more gravelly from all the screaming she was just doing. "But Noah..." She stops my tortuous kisses by grabbing my face and pulling me back to look at her. "You and me... We're just casual, right?"

My eyes bore into hers and I say the only thing I know how to say. The first words that come out, like an instinct.

"Casual is my middle name, baby," I grin, winking at her, though for some reason it feels forced. "We're best friends with bennies. The ultimate relationship status."

She chews on her lip more. "Good... I think."

"It *is* good."

"Yea, because I couldn't stand to lose you, Noah. You're all I have right now," she whimpers and my heart clenches.

"I know, Al. I know," I nod slowly, stroking her hair.

"But I definitely don't want to stop having sex," she purrs, tracing some red marks on my chest with her fingertip. "Because that was... fucking *life-affirming*."

"Me neither, baby," I agree in a growl. "I've never come like that before... My dick turned into a firehose." We both laugh, and it occurs to me that I'm still inside her.

So I pull out, checking the condom. Sure enough, the whole thing is filled heavy... There's almost stuff spilling out of it.

"Jeez..." I remove it slowly, so as not to get it everywhere, tying it off and tossing it in the trash. "How is it possible to produce that much Noah juice??"

"Okay, so then we're in agreement," Alex ignores me, sitting up in bed and smoothing out her sex hair, which makes her look so pretty I just want to hug her forever. "We're best friends who happen to have sex with each other. No big deal."

"The *deal* is actually very big, beautiful," I smirk at her. "Don't forget it."

She snorts and covers her reddened face with her hands. "Noah, shut up! I'm trying to be serious here! We need to make sure this doesn't ruin our friendship."

"Okay, okay. I'm sorry," I sigh, scooting over to her and lying back against the pillows, tugging her onto my lap. "I'm being serious. We won't ruin our friendship, I promise, baby."

She shifts on top of me and I can feel her warm wetness settling on my slightly deflated cock; a feeling that makes it perk up in preparation for round two.

"Are you sure?" She squeaks, her wide eyes conveying some worry that I need to stomp out. But unfortunately, I'm not sure how to give her the reassurance she needs, because if I'm being honest, I'm already nervous about this arrangement.

"Well, I do have one concern..." I grunt, taking the material of my tie in both hands, which is still draped around her neck, and holding her close to me. "What about... seeing other people?"

She sucks in a noticeable breath and holds it for a beat. "Well, I'm still married... Until I can figure all my shit out..." Her voice trails off and she looks worried. But not about her complex marital issues.

She appears upset because she knows why I'm asking this - or at least she thinks she does. I'm a giant manwhore, an assessment I don't generally give to myself though it's entirely accurate. And I guess in her eyes, I'd want to make sure I can still bang other girls while banging her...

But that's not really what I want at all. I just want to make sure she doesn't get upset when she sees pictures online of girls hanging all over me, because it's bound to happen.

I don't plan on bringing anyone else home while I'm seeing Alex, even if we are just casual. I already haven't brought a girl home since the night before we had our cookie party in the car. And even then, I was thinking about her the whole time, to the point where I may or may not have shouted out *Alex* when I was coming... I really hope not, but I seriously think I did. That girl couldn't get out of my apartment fast enough after we were done.

The unhealthy truth is that I've got it bad for this tattooed little goddess, which is one giant reason why we *shouldn't* do the casual sex thing. But I'm finding it very hard to locate any fucks to give at the moment, especially when Alex is naked sitting on top of me, giving me that adorably timid look of worry.

"Do you think you and Roger would... have... sex?" I clear my throat about fifty times. *Why was that so hard to get out??*

"I doubt it," she scoffs. "We haven't done it in a few weeks, and right now he's on this kick of trying to win back my trust. I'm not sure why, but I'm just going to keep my distance until I have all my shit settled to get the hell out of there."

I nod slowly. I'm pacified enough by that answer. It makes me happy to know she hasn't fucked her husband since we've known each other, even though I'm not crazy about him trying to *woo* her.

"What about you?" She arches an accusatory brow at me, and I gulp, pointing a finger at myself. "You like to sleep around. Will you still be banging all kinds of skanky broads in between banging me? Because I don't know how I feel about that..."

I'm shaking a little, and my palms, which are resting on her thighs, begin to sweat.

As much as I want to tell her I won't see any other girls, that just makes things *more* complicated.

"Trust me, I don't want to see any other girls while I'm seeing you, Alex..." I start, my tone laced with uncertainty. "But if I don't, then we're exclusive. And that kind of muddies things up... No?"

She pauses to think for a moment while methodically trailing her fingers along my shoulders, which is wonderfully relaxing.

"I know!" She proclaims. "Here's how it'll work. No random sexing with other girls while we're doing it. I'm pretty sure we'll be able to scratch all our itches together, anyway." She slides her tongue over her lower lip and my cock is inflating quickly beneath her. *Ready for more...* I growl and she grins. "But if there's a girl you're interested in seeing for whatever reason, then me and you stop our thing so you can pursue it."

I stare blankly at her for a moment. "So you're saying that I don't see anyone else while me and you are fucking each other's brains out on the regs. And you don't sleep with your husband..." She nods. "But if something comes up and we want an out, it's as easy as just saying so?"

I watch her swallow hard. "Yea..."

"You don't sound very confident..." I whisper, eyeing her speculatively, even though I'm not sure how I feel about this plan either.

I'm not thrilled about the idea of her randomly breaking it off with me whenever she feels like it. I have a sneaking suspicion that I might easily become addicted to Alex. It's already sort of happening...

"Well, it's not something I've ever done before," she shrugs. "But the facts are that we need to stay friends, but neither of us wants to stop fooling around yet. So... What other alternative do we have?"

She has a point.

I breathe out hard. "Okay. So then the plan is settled. We keep fucking and remain friends until it doesn't work anymore. But even after that happens, we stay friends. No matter what. Right?"

"Right," she huffs and holds out her pinky.

I curl mine around hers and we pinky swear on it.

And just like that, the deal is done.

"So..." I rumble, gazing into her curious green eyes.

"So..." She touches her tongue to her teeth.

"Now the more pertinent question..." I tug her face down to mine. "Are you staying? Because I can think of a few hundred things I'd like to do with you right now... And every one of them requires you to still be here."

She giggles with those sparkly eyes stuck on mine. I'm probably fooling myself, but it seems like they twinkle a bit more when she's looking at me. *Don't get carried away.*

Finally she huffs out a soft noise. "What things did you have in mind?"

I grin and trace the curve of her lower lip with my thumb, ready to spend the rest of the best night ever buried inside my new fuck-buddy.

What's the worst that could happen?

Chapter Thirteen

Alex

EVER SINCE ROGER CHEATED ON ME FOR THE FIRST TIME, I've occasionally wondered what it would be like to sleep with someone else.

I don't know what kinds of girls Roger's slept with, and I really have no desire to. But in my imagination, they're always the opposite of me. Blonde and trashy, with big fake boobs and lip injections. Manhattan socialites and high-class escorts. They seem much more his type than I do.

But when I thought about getting some side-action myself, after my husband started beating me while he was also fucking other women, thus removing any guilt that I could possibly feel for wanting to sleep around, I always envisioned a specific kind of guy.

Someone hot and muscular, with kind eyes and a glowing smile. Someone with tattoos and piercings, like me. A man with nice hands and a gentle touch, and a killer sense of humor, who could make me laugh hard and come even harder.

Well, as it would seem, I've found exactly that in Noah Richards. My best friend, whom I am secretly banging.

I've tried to locate guilt inside myself for cheating on Roger. Believe me, I expected it to attack after the first time Noah and I fooled around on his living room floor. But much to my own surprise, it never did.

After we had sex, I was sure I'd feel shame and regret, mixed together like a bad cocktail. Despite everything Roger has done to me over the years, he's still my *husband*. We're still bonded by vows and holy matrimony, although our relationship is the biggest sham of all, and damn near every vow has been broken for years.

And yet when I left Noah's apartment last week, after our twelve-hour-long marathon fuckfest, there was no shame in my game. Zero regrets.

I felt no guilt, because I was buzzing on the high of having someone devote himself to me again. I haven't felt that since Roger and I were first married, and it's one of my favorite feelings in the world. Noah manages to do it in such a way that sets every nerve in my body ablaze.

Noah and I have the kind of chemistry you read about in love stories. We get along so well, sometimes I fear he's not even real. That maybe I've dreamt him up in some lonely, depression-fueled fabricated reality; an imaginary friend of sorts. Like my own, much happier version of Tyler Durden.

But by now I'm sure that Noah is completely real, and the best friend I've ever had. He's sweet, and caring, funny to the point of almost ridiculous sometimes, but he makes me laugh and smile every second that I'm with him, which is something to be truly admired.

And now I'm sleeping with him. Which could either be the best idea in the world, or ultimately the stupidest thing either of us have ever done.

That part is yet to be determined.

For now, everything seems hunky dory. I haven't seen Noah in a few days, because we're both busy. Him working on preparations for his upcoming project, and me basking in the aftermath of selling out my first gallery show.

I've been working nonstop since the exhibit last week. My phone's been ringing off the hook with collectors I met that night, other gallery owners and interested parties. Fortunately, I have a back-collection already essentially ready to go, so I can work on planning my next show. And in between all that action, I've been painting some new stuff that I really love.

I was able to sneak off and see Noah a few times, during which he's made me come so hard I can't believe I lived my entire life up to that point without experiencing such encompassing orgasms.

Roger and I always had a good sex life, or what I thought was good, anyway. He knew my body well enough to make me come, and I was always satisfied. But Noah is a completely different ballgame. You almost can't even compare the two. It's like comparing Major League Baseball to swatting at a wiffle ball in your backyard with a stick.

Just remembering the other day has my toes curling.

I met Noah at his place at lunchtime and he fucked me for forty-five minutes on his kitchen counter. I had four orgasms and then we ate cupcakes and talked about nonsense for a little while before he used his immensely skilled mouth to get me off three more times. And then sadly I had to leave.

Roger's been true to his promise about trying to prove to me he's *changed*, though I'm still not buying it. He must really think I was born yesterday. Just because he comes straight home from work every night, doesn't drink, and has been buying me more gifts than I can even count, it doesn't mean the last almost three years never happened. You can't erase history. You can only learn from it, which is exactly what I'm doing.

I have my guard up at home. I'm always on high-alert around Roger, because I know it's only a matter of time before he *relapses*, so to speak. He's been eerily kind to me lately, and it's putting me on edge more than anything. And I guess if he were to suspect anything about me sleeping with someone, he's refraining from confronting me about it.

I'm being careful with Noah, but still Roger's bound to pick up on the fact that I'm suddenly spending a lot more time out of the house, and even occasionally staying out all night. I have my excuses and alibis locked and loaded, but Roger hasn't asked, so I haven't said anything. The whole thing is incredibly bizarre, and I'm just itching to get the hell out now more than ever.

I recently started mentally devising a plan to leave Roger. I squirreled away all the money I made from my show in a separate account that I opened in my own name. I have enough for a top-notch divorce lawyer already, and now I just need to find somewhere to live; a place where Roger wouldn't be able to track me down. It'll be hard in the city, because he knows so many people. But Noah has repeatedly reminded me that I can also file a restraining order, if Roger does happen to go completely crazy, which I'm anticipating as a very likely possibility.

In the back of my mind I know Noah would help me with whatever I need to get the divorce rolling and safely extricate myself from Roger's world, but I need to do this on my own. I'm not a damsel in distress, and the one thing I hate the most is relying on other people. I've spent more than seven years as my husband's pet, and it took killing my first gallery show and meeting this slightly outlandish, fully adorable tattooed actor to finally realize that I'm my own person.

I can have my own life, and a great one, at that. I don't need anyone but me, myself and I.

I just got done showering after spending all day in the studio, and I emerge from the bathroom to find Roger pacing around our bedroom. I'm instantly tense.

"What's wrong?" I ask hesitantly, slinking past him into the closet to get dressed. He follows me.

"There are a series of away games coming up, and I'll have to go…" he murmurs, his voice sounding strange to my ear.

He has this tenderness in his tone lately that's so fake it makes my stomach turn. I just want to grab him and scream in his face that I know who he is, and he can try to act like he's changing all he wants, but guys like him don't change. You can dress up like a sheep, even pretend to be one. But at the end of the day, wolves will be wolves.

Regardless, I can't help the flutter of hope that tickles my chest at the thought of him being gone for long periods of time. I reluctantly drop my towel, knowing that he's standing there staring at me, and not really wanting to be naked in front of him. Especially because I think I have a hickey on my butt from a certain best friend, and I'm seriously hoping it's not noticeable.

"Oh?" I pull some panties on quickly, but not quick enough because he's wandered up behind me and is running his fingers over my naked back. I have nervous chills; not the thrilling goosebumps I get when Noah touches me. "How long would you be gone?"

"A few days to a few weeks, here and there," he answers, his breath warming my neck. "I'm going to miss you…"

Even a few months ago, words like that, in such a deep voice, would have spread fire through me, whether I wanted them to or not. But now all I can think of is how to get him to leave without wounding his ego and making him angry.

That spark from before, even the painful one I would use to get a quick high, has been fully stomped out by my new fling and reestablished confidence.

I dress fast, ignoring Roger's obvious desire to mess around, with my body and my brain, and leave him in the closet, praying he'll get tired of chasing and leave me alone. Unfortunately, no such luck.

"Can I take you to dinner tonight?" He asks, following me out of the closet. I can feel his eyes on me as I stand in front of my mirror, applying some light makeup.

I sigh internally out of frustration. I was hoping I could sneak out to see Noah tonight. He's already been texting me all day begging me to come over, but I had to keep telling him I wasn't sure, since my husband decided that being suddenly clingy is a way to make up for his years of abuse and infidelity.

"I'm not sure… I was planning to meet a gallery owner later for a drink to talk about a potential show," I lie, my hand trembling a little as I stroke mascara onto my lashes.

"Come on, darling," he hums, stepping over and leaning against my dresser. "I'll be leaving tomorrow. You'll have the rest of the weekend to meet with whoever you need to."

The tube damn-near slips out of my fingers. It takes everything in me to

Seek Me

act unfazed by what he just said, but my knees are shaking. The way he said that... It sounded faintly like he was calling me out. As if he knows I'm seeing someone, and he's throwing it in my face without actually doing so.

I'm startled and confused on so many levels. The real Roger would attack me for thinking I was screwing around on him. He certainly wouldn't tolerate his *perfect* wife out there spreading her legs for another man.

But it seems the mask he's wearing likes to play mind-games. In his effort to redeem himself as a *good husband,* he's going to allow me to get back at him and fuck someone else...?

It makes no sense. I don't get it. *What the hell are you playing at, you sicko?!*

"Please, babe," he whispers, inching closer and sifting his fingers through my damp hair. "Dinner, just the two of us? It'll be fun."

We haven't had fun since you started dipping your cock in other women, babe.

I peek at him and he smiles. It's such a cunning, manipulative smile I can't help but gulp over my dry throat and nod slowly.

I concede, only because I have to play my cards right. Turning him down could open a door to more violence, and I'm trying to keep him calm and pacified until my plans are in order.

"Alright, sure," I sigh with a forced grin, which he returns.

I'll go to dinner with my husband. After all, keep your friends close and your enemies closer.

Roger and I get to the restaurant at around nine. I didn't want to go to one of his fancy-shmancy places, so he decided to *surprise* me with something he thought I might like. But as soon as we were in the car on the way, I was hit with all kinds of anxiety.

He brought me to the Upper West Side, which is Noah's territory. I don't think we would run into him, but still I don't see why we couldn't have gone to literally any other neighborhood.

The restaurant is called Jacob's Pickles. I've heard of it before and it sounds amazing because it's a twist on southern food, and they make their own pickles and biscuits, two of my favorite things. So despite how antsy I am, I'm also excited to sit down and eat, regardless of who I'm with.

The hostess brings us to a table on the upper level, and we have a seat. The lighting is pretty dim in here, but it smells delicious and I'm already starving. We pick up our drink menus and I'm gazing over some yummy-sounding concoctions when I hear a familiar laugh.

The hairs all over my body stand up straight and my stomach twists into a huge knot.

I look up from my menu, across the room, and I spot Noah, sitting at a table in the far corner.

With a girl.

She looks like a model, which makes sense. If she's out on a date with Noah Richards, obviously she must be fucking perfect.

Blood rushes in my ears, and I feel the color drain from my face.

What the fuck is going on?? Why is he here, and who the hell is that bitch?!

Okay, he's obviously here to eat, just like everyone else in the restaurant. And he lives in this neighborhood, so it makes more sense for him to be here than it does for me. But still, I'm confused and hurt. Why would he be out on a date? We agreed we wouldn't sleep with other people while we're hooking up.

And no, I don't *know* that he's sleeping with her, or going to. But just the way she's playfully touching his arm and flipping her hair over her shoulder, I can tell she wants to go home with him. And Noah's all smiling and casual, like he always is, making it impossible to read whether he's actually into the girl.

Fuck that. He was supposed to tell me if he wanted to see someone else so we could end our fuck-buddy relationship. It's barely been a week since we made up those rules, and he's already breaking them.

This sucks.

I feel like I'm being punched in the heart. My chest is tight and I'm finding it hard to breathe normally.

I really shouldn't be staring at them. It's so obvious.

I lift my menu in front of my face so Noah won't spot me. Though he looks fully invested in his little *date* with the gorgeous bombshell.

My hands are shaking as I realize that Roger's trying to talk to me. I blink a dozen times, forcing my eyes away from my best friend who touches me like a boyfriend, and the girl he's flirting with, and aim them at my husband.

"What do you think?" Roger asks and my brows raise. "We could split the biscuits and gravy, since it's probably pretty heavy…"

I nod slowly, my eyes flitting back to Noah and his bimbo friend. Roger's back is to them, so he can't see what I'm looking at, but I have a full view of this tortuous scene, and it's really fucking me up. There's bile rising in my throat, and

Seek Me

I swallow repeatedly to keep it down.

And then the guy at the table next to us drops a glass, which smashes on the floor, causing everyone in the place to look in our direction.

Including Noah.

Fuck! You clumsy idiot!

My eyes dart away fast, but it's no use. I know he can see me now. I can physically *feel* his dark eyes on me, like flames scorching my skin from across the room.

I glance up again and this time our eyes meet. His forehead is lined in confusion, and what I'm perceiving as guilt. I can't be sure, because Noah Richards doesn't feel things like *guilt*, or *remorse*, but in that one split-second, I swear I see the unease flash over his face.

It's a look that screams *I just got caught*.

I chomp down hard on my lower lip and chew it vigorously while Roger talks about things on the menu and Noah stares at us. He's clearly registering that the man I'm here with is my husband. That part is now obvious. And even though I'm struggling not to look at him, I can't help but repeatedly peek in his direction while he watches us closely.

His date, seemingly dejected from having lost his attention, grabs his hand and locks their fingers. I feel physically ill. The first naïve thought that pops into my head is *those are my hands*.

But they're not. We'd agreed upon that. We were to remain casual. We're not *together*.

Then why does this hurt so much?

I can't do this. This is exactly what I'm not supposed to do… fall for him. Feel like he's mine.

He's my friend. That's it. Hooking up with him was a mistake for this reason. We need to remain casual, but every time I'm with him, he makes me like him a little more. And eventually, I'll be in way over my head.

I need to get out of here. I can't bear to see him looking at me like that. Like I'm pathetic. The girl who slept with him a few times and caught feelings.

"Roger, baby… I changed my mind. I'm not that hungry," I murmur, taking Roger's hand over the table, and using every bit of willpower in me not to look at Noah.

"You're not?" Roger asks with his brows pushed together.

"No, actually I'd like to go home. Maybe so we can… be alone," I trace his wedding band with my finger.

He gapes at me and I give him a forced look of intimacy, sliding my tongue over my bottom lip. His eyes fall to my mouth and I can see the dark hunger in them. On his face.

I have no idea what I'm doing. I don't know how flirting with my husband will in any way make me feel better about Noah boning that ditz, but I can't help how nauseated I am. My heart is being torn to shreds, and I need a high.

I need to feel something else. Something other than this gut-wrenching disappointment.

"Okay," Roger hums, his voice deep and hoarse with that wicked tone. It's scary, but familiar. "Let's go home."

He stands up and takes my hand, helping me stand beside him. As we're leaving, I can't help but glance at Noah one last time. His mouth opens like he wants to call out to me, but he doesn't. Because he can't.

It wouldn't change anything, anyway.

He stays seated with the model who's all over him, playing with his perfect hands while he gazes helplessly after me.

I knew our casual relationship would never work. It was doomed before it even started.

Roger and I leave the fun restaurant that I unfortunately didn't get to enjoy one bit, and get back into the car, heading straight home. I'm deep in my thoughts while we're riding in silence, and Roger takes my hand in his, tugging it onto his lap. It should give me comfort, but it just makes me feel worse.

All I can think about is that Noah will most definitely sleep with that girl tonight. That despite how amazing - and brief - it was between us, he's going to break the pact and fuck some hot slutty girl, because he's *Noah Richards*, and it's what he does. And if he's breaking the pact, then I suppose it would make sense for me to do the same...

I feel so low I should be living underground with the mole people.

Roger and I arrive at home, and we walk quietly, side-by-side, to our bedroom. He dims the lights, and I strip out of all my clothes, watching as he does the same. It feels like we're performing a scene; choreographed and sterile. Emotionless.

The opposite of the way it is with Noah.

When I'm with Noah, we're always giggling and smiling; touching each other constantly and kissing until we're breathless.

With Roger, I'm in a prison of my own heart. And he's the guard who holds the key.

Seek Me

My husband pushes himself against me until I fall back onto the bed and he crawls over me, moving slowly, forcing his large body between my legs. His eyes are so bright, illuminated in the dark room, watching my face, my eyes, with unwavering lust.

He slides his length over my slit and I tremble. It does feel good, in an obvious kind of way, but my heart's not in it at all. *Now I know how he feels.*

Roger kisses a slow trail along my jaw, then takes my earlobe between his teeth, teasing it the way he used to when I was a young, stupid teenager, who couldn't possibly believe she had won the lottery and caught this man. The nostalgia I'm feeling in my heart for my lost youth brings a tremor to my loins, my walls tensing in arousal.

I close my eyes while he works down my body, licking and sucking the steel in my nipples, and I imagine… I see Noah's shaggy head of hair there instead, using his perfect mouth to make me *his*.

I'm writhing beneath his big frame, lifting my hips to seek him out because I want him to fill me now. I want the high. I'm craving it.

Roger's face is back in front of mine, and he yanks my chin, forcing me to open my eyes.

Without saying a word, he guides his cock inside me slowly, sinking into me before retracting; building a rhythm.

"Mmm… I missed this…" he whispers, and my stupid heart flutters, believing him, like the fool it is. He kisses my lips softly. "I missed *us*."

I whimper, because I'm torn. His dick moving in me, stroking, feels good, but I don't want it to. He just keeps bringing me back to him, no matter how terrible he is. No matter how much of a goddamned monster he is… And I always go back like the lovesick puppy I so clearly am.

God, why am I so desperate for someone to love me? Why can't I just love myself?

I see Noah's face in my mind again. I see how gorgeous he looks when he's inside me, doing what my husband is doing right now.

And then I imagine him fucking the girl from the restaurant, and I want to retch.

Noah's hands touching her the way they touch me… Kissing her the way he kisses me… Holding her while he explodes into orgasm, panting her name into her neck…

I cry out loud in pain and sadness, though the pleasure rippling through my insides is the exact high I've been chasing.

"I know you love me, Alex," Roger holds my face while his hips thrust into me, over and over. "You'll always love me. You can be mad all you want, but we're made for each other."

I press my lips together and scratch his back hard, digging into his skin with my nails. He growls and picks up the pace, fucking me faster and harder.

"My beautiful wife," he rumbles, staring down at me, the center of a flame flickering in his eyes.

He's gorgeous, on the outside, there's no denying it. But his insides are rotten.

And yet here I am, giving myself back to him once more.

I hate you. "I love you," I breathe my lie, giving into the sensation. The high I need to survive.

"I know you do, baby."

Ring.

Check the screen. Swipe to ignore.

Leave me alone.

Ring.

Check the screen. Swipe to ignore.

I'm fucking serious.

Ring.

Grit my teeth. Check the screen. Forcefully swipe to ignore.

I'm about to go ape-shit.

At last. A moment of reprieve. No ringing.

Maybe he's finally done.

I suck in a deep breath and lift my brush to the canvas again, returning to my work after being interrupted for the last forty-five minutes with this nonsense.

I stroke the brush, leaving a trail of red behind it when…

Ring. Fucking. Ring.

My vision is suddenly as red as the paint in front of me.

I growl out loud and grab my phone again, swiping fast to accept the call.

"Oh my fucking God, what the fuck do you want?!" I bark, adrenaline coursing through me. I feel like I could murder someone; the someone on the other end of this call who won't leave me the fuck alone.

"Alex, just hear me out. I need to fucking talk to you!" Noah hisses, his typically easy-going voice now sharp with frustration and angst. I've never heard

Seek Me

him sound so tense before.

But I don't care. There's a reason I've been ignoring him for two days. I actually just turned my phone back on for the first time since the night I saw him out with that girl. And now he's harassing me.

Apparently he called and texted me about a hundred times that night, after I left with Roger. It was all the typical schpiel.

It's not what you think. We're not together. She's just a friend. You're being ridiculous. Please call me. I miss you. I need you. Whatever you think happened, I promise you it didn't. I CAN'T BELIEVE YOU'RE WITH HIM LIKE THAT! Followed by like a hundred crying face emojis.

Noah's just being dramatic. He'll get over it. Regardless of how internally upset I am about the whole thing, we're still friends. I just needed to distance myself from him a little, because my feelings were getting a bit too real for my liking.

"Noah, I don't have time to talk. I'm busy," I grunt, clenching my jaw so hard it's throbbing as I try to paint while he bothers me on the phone.

"Busy with your *husband*?" He seethes, and I hang up on him.

My phone is immediately ringing again.

This dude is an insufferable nuisance, and it makes me want to laugh.

"Are you done?" I answer the phone casually and I can hear his teeth grinding over the line.

"I'm sorry. I didn't mean that..." he mutters. "I just need you to understand what happened the other day. I wasn't doing anything -"

"Okay," I cut him off fast because I *don't* want to talk about this.

"Alex, let me finish!" He snaps. Now I can see him in my mind trying to calm himself down. It's sort of entertaining, and deep down in a place I'd never let anyone know about, I'm extremely satisfied that he's chasing me like this.

Noah Richards doesn't chase... anyone but Alex Mackenzie.

He takes an audible breath. "I don't want you to be mad at me over nothing, is all. The girl you saw me with is an old friend. A model I met like a million years ago. And yes, we did hook up at one time. And I suppose she wanted to hook up with me the other night, but I didn't know that when I agreed to have dinner with her!"

My eyes are rolling so hard.

"She showed up at my apartment unannounced and asked me if I wanted to go grab something to eat, and that she needed to pick my brain about an upcoming project of hers," he goes on rambling. "I didn't want to be rude, and I was starving so as soon as she mentioned JP's my stomach was grumbling like a fat kid in a Hostess factory. Anyway, when we got there, I realized she was more interested in flirting with me than talking about this alleged *project*. But it wasn't a big deal. After that we went our separate ways. She did *not* come home with me!"

I'm silent on the line, listening to him fumble about. I don't know what he's doing, but it sounds like he's banging things around in his kitchen.

"Alex? Are you there?" He shouts at me and I purse my lips.

"Yes. I'm here."

"Okay, so can you *say* something? Please?"

"I have nothing to say, Noah," I shrug, using every muscle in my body to remain cool and unaffected. My years of practice in faking things are coming in handy. "I'm fine. I get it. You didn't hook up with her."

"So why does it feel like you're still mad at me?" He huffs, and to be honest he sounds a little more broken than I would expect. It tugs on my heart significantly.

"I'm not mad, I just… Don't like the way I felt that night. I don't like those emotions… those feelings," I tell him in an uneasy tone. "I just needed a second to breathe."

The line is quiet again, this time from his end.

"You're over this…" he says stiffly, and I'm not sure why but it makes me want to burst into tears.

"No… I mean, maybe… I don't know," I sigh, rubbing my eyes hard with my fingers. "It's supposed to be casual, Noah. This doesn't *feel* casual."

"I didn't mean to make you hurt," he whispers, smashing through my chest so hard I can't breathe. "I *never* want you to hurt. Not for one second."

"It's not your fault, Noah," I utter, feeling lost. "You didn't do anything wrong."

"I did, though… I made you…" he pauses and clears his throat. "Come over."

"Can't. Working."

"After…"

"Not tonight, Noah."

"Then when?" He sounds desperate. I'm not secretly enjoying it anymore. I hate making him sound like that.

"Soon… I just need more time."

"Alex, you're my friend," he murmurs, his voice so deep and comforting, I just want to go to him, but I *can't*. "If you want to stop sleeping together, that's fine, but you're never getting rid of me as a friend, so you can just forget that idea right now."

I let a small giggle slip and bite my lip, so as not to encourage him. "I don't want to get rid of you, puppy. You're too precious."

Noah laughs out loud and I smile, wiggling around in place. It's just so hard to stay mad at him. He's a total sweetheart, and the best friend I've probably ever had in my whole life. Whether the sexual portion of our relationship ends up running dry, it's good to know we'll always have each other as friends.

"Al, I miss you like crazy," he whines. "You can't freeze me out like that. I need my Alex."

"It's been two days! Jesus, you called me like eight hundred times! You're basically a needy ex-girlfriend," I tease him.

"I'm going to chop off all my hair and mail it to you if you don't come over tonight."

This time I laugh out loud. *He's a freaking nutball. Honestly.*

"Noah..." I sigh, becoming nauseous from the internal game of tug-of-war that's always happening inside me when he's involved. This thing is already so hot and cold, I barely know which way is up. "I'm not sure if it's a good idea right now. I should really stay in and focus on this collection."

He grunts in frustration. I know he's not happy about what's going on because he's not the one calling the shots. For someone who claims to be so *casual*, Noah Richards certainly likes his control.

He's quiet again, and I can tell he wants to say something. I have a feeling I already know what it is...

"Are you... hanging out with *him* tonight?" His formerly agitated tone has gone dark and slightly hostile.

"No," I whisper, reticent. "He's out of town until next week."

Noah goes silent once more. As much as I'm fighting him, I really wish I could see his face. I just want to touch him; his stubbly jaw, his pouted lips, his defined chest and abs; velvety smooth skin draped over hard stones of muscle. I want to run my finger along the crease between his brows, which I already know is there because he's stressing out... over me.

"I just... don't think we should make any rash decisions," he hums, his deep, erotic voice slipping inside me through the phone. It makes me shudder, my nipples instantly peaking. "What happened the other night was just a stupid misunderstanding. And if you come over tonight, I guarantee I will more than make it up to you..."

God, he has the hottest voice I've ever heard. It's like creamy caramel dripping over a warm chocolate cake. *Sinful.*

I bite my lip hard. I should really try to resist... I shouldn't give in to him, especially after what happened with Roger the other night. I should be honest with Noah and tell him, just in case it changes his mind about us... About *me*.

"Noah, I need to tell you..." My voice gives out.

I don't want to have to do this. After all, Roger is my husband. If we were in a normal situation, he'd be the only one I should be sleeping with. But our situation is anything but normal. And yes, the other night complicated it a *lot*.

Fortunately for me, Roger left the next morning for his work travels, so we didn't even talk about how fucking ridiculous it was that we slept together. Not that he'll see it as ridiculous. He's getting exactly what he wanted. I'm digging myself further and further into a hole with him, and soon I won't ever be able to get out.

"Alex, hold that thought," Noah says, interrupting me before I can finish struggling to tell him I fucked my abusive husband. "You don't need to tell me anything right now, other than that you're putting your sexy ass in a car and coming across town. Do you want me to send Jimmy?"

I roll my eyes. "I'm more than capable of getting to your house on my own, thank you."

"Awesome! So then it's settled. You'll be here in what, like a half hour?" He chirps, all excitable and overzealous. He really is like a puppy sometimes.

Only puppies are most definitely not hot, muscley tattooed sex-Gods. Actually, they're not that great. I'm not a fan of dogs.

"Ugh, alright fine!" I grumble, giving in to his incessant pleading, although now that I've said yes I'm quivering in anticipation. I haven't seen Noah in almost a week, not including the other night at the restaurant, which I'm not because it wasn't fun in the slightest. I miss him more than I'll let myself think about. "But you owe me so freaking hardcore, Richards!"

"Yes! Yes, totally. Whatever you want. Name it, it's yours."

"I want a batch of weed brownies to take home," I tell him, and he laughs.

"Okay, you got it. Done."

"And your other can of Surge."

"It's yours."

"And I want you to do something embarrassing..." Now I'm grasping at straws. But I want to see how much he's willing to do for me. *This is a fun game.*

"Anything you want," he answers matter-of-factly.

"Anything?" My voice is more than just inquisitive. It's bordering on devious. But Noah doesn't flinch.

"*An-y-thing.*" He pronounces each syllable, and I can picture him crossing his arms over his naked chest. Because he never wears a shirt when he's home, I've come to realize.

And this gives me an idea.

Bingo.

"I want you to give me a lap dance," I say, daring him to object. He's actually quiet for a moment before he chuckles in my ear. The sound makes me wet.

"Alexandra Mackenzie… When are you going to learn that you have no idea who you're dealing with?" His smug voice rumbles into me and my vagina almost explodes. "Get that beautiful booty over to my place immediately so I can give you the best damn lap dance of your life."

I squeal. I can't even help it. The thought of Noah Richards touching me in any way is exciting. Him dancing? Sure, that's hot too. But him grinding on me while he strips?! *Yes, please.*

I can only imagine what his sexy brain is thinking up right now.

And just like that, I'm hanging up so I can clean my studio, then scampering downstairs to shower quick and get dressed. I'm going to Noah's and there's no deadline, or timer, or abusive husband waiting for me at home to worry about. I can't hide from my drastically improved mood.

Maybe friends with benefits will work out…

Cheers to optimism.

The second I set foot inside Noah's apartment, he attacks me.

He grabs my body and swings me around like a rag doll until I'm dizzy, from the spinning and the kisses he's planting all over my neck and face.

The swoon is real. My heart is frantic over the idea that I could have written him off in any way. He makes me feel light as air when everything else in life is weighing me down.

Well, accept my art career, which is just getting started, and is so thrilling I can finally breathe again.

So this is the first thing Noah asks me about. Because he's an awesome friend.

I tell him about my new collection, and the gallery director I've been talking to, and he listens attentively the whole time, smiling supportively like the caring little bean he is.

But I'm the one who's distracted.

I'm happy to talk about my work, because he's the only person I talk to about it. Or about *anything*, for that matter. But I'm also anxious because he promised me a lap dance. And I desperately want to cash out.

We wander into his living room, and I can't help but notice that he's grinning more than usual.

"Would you like something to drink?" He offers.

"You're stalling, Richards," I fold my arms across my chest and tap my foot. "You better not have lured me here under false pretenses."

He shows me a blithe smirk. "Not my style."

Noah steps up to me until we're so close I can feel the warmth radiating off him. He's actually fully dressed this time, in a Henley that fits the contours of his perfect body immaculately and his regular fitted jeans. The fact that he's wearing all his clothes actually gets me even more excited for him to take them off.

His hand extends slowly to play with the strands of my long hair as I struggle to keep my breathing in check. Then he takes my hand, brings it to his lips and kisses each one of my fingertips. How something so simple can set my ovaries on fire, I'll never know.

"Right this way, Ms. Mackenzie," he hums, tugging me over to his couch. "Your world is about to get rocked."

A massive grin takes over my face, though I try to smother it. Noah shoves me backward until I plop down onto the couch and a nervous giggle bubbles from inside my throat. Then he picks up a remote off his coffee table and I gasp.

"If you turn on *Pony* by Genuine, I'm leaving," I tell him, fully serious. He laughs out loud.

"Awww… give me a little more credit, baby," he sneers. My eyes are wide and stuck on his beautiful face which, as usual, gives nothing away. "That's song's for amateurs." Then he leans over me, caging me against the back of his couch and whispers, "By the time I'm done, you'll be wetter than a slip-n-slide."

He winks and licks my bottom lip, causing a tremor in my pussy so hard it registered on the Richter scale. My mouth is dry as I try to swallow, gripping the couch cushions with shaky fingers.

Noah's face is serious, his eyes lit up with playful arousal. It's my favorite look on him. He straightens and presses a button on the remote, the room coming alive with music. I know the song instantly.

The intro to *Grind With Me* by Pretty Ricky sets him up, and my jaw drops as he starts dancing for me.

Now, this isn't as you'd picture it. Noah can be very goofy sometimes, and he definitely knows how to make me giggle so hard I have to run to the bathroom before I pee on myself.

But that's not what's happening here. When Noah's being sexy, he has his game face on, and when it comes to building the anticipation, he's all business.

Warming up, his hips are curving in an easy gyrating motion as he moves to the music, sliding his strong hands down his torso to the hem of his shirt. He licks his lips, eyes stuck on mine the whole time, as tugs it up his body slowly, revealing muscles, tattoos and a fuck-hot nipple piercing like he's raising a curtain. *The show has begun.*

He tosses his shirt at me and I catch it with a wide grin, holding it to my chest and sniffing it without being obvious. And he's watching me, rocking his hips closer, swinging and rolling them in a way that makes me wonder if he's actually done this professionally before.

He looks *really* fucking good.

He pops the button on his jeans, standing above me and between my parted legs, eyeing me with curiosity and so much heat I'm burning in place. I bite my lip, shifting subtly because my insides are humming just from watching him. He closes his eyes in a slow blink, dropping his head back as he runs his own hands all over the muscles I desperately want to be touching, all the while grinding in the air to the music and that slow, seductive beat.

I stifle a moan, eyeing his crotch, the prominent bulge begging to be freed. Noah slides the zipper down, purposely taking an eternity, then spins around and bends at the waist while he shoves his jeans down his long legs, giving me a front-row seat to the best buns in town.

He shakes it slowly in front of me and I purr out a hungry noise, my patience running out as I reach forward to cup his firm, round ass. He kicks his pants away as he stands again, turning and shaking his head side-to-side as he *tsk tsk*'s me.

"Uh-uh," he admonishes with his eyes and darkly teasing tone. "No touching, bad girl. You gotta pay extra for that."

I gnaw on my lips to smother my massive smile, then pout as he climbs on top of me, kneeling over my hips.

"Hands down, young lady," he commands, and I oblige, placing my palms flat on the couch.

He's so close, rocking on me in slow motion, the heat surrounding us almost unbearable. He's practically naked, wearing only his fitted boxer briefs, and rubbing himself all over my body. His dick is solid; I can feel it smooshing against my pelvis and stomach as he moves to the music. Tingles zip through my limbs, my pulse jumping in my neck while he grips the back of his couch and does the slow-grind like the best damn stripper I've ever seen.

Noah leans his face in closer and nuzzles my neck, breathing hard, panting on my skin while my panties soak through.

"You want more?" He growls, sending a shiver between my thighs and across my chest.

"Yes," I gulp, resting my head back on the couch, watching his big, tattooed body with drooping eyes. "Please… let me touch you."

"Where?" He moans, the game clearly getting to him, too.

"Everywhere," I answer and ignore his earlier rule, grabbing his butt and squeezing.

He lets out a dirty chuckle, thrusting his erection into me. I'm all ready to move my hands around front and grab the big package, when he pulls back and quickly lifts my shirt over my head, whipping it across the room.

"Skin on skin," he demands, gliding his warm hands up my back and unhitching my bra, throwing that too.

Then he presses his bare chest up to mine and rubs us together, holding the back of my head while he breathes ragged into the crook of my neck. It must look hilarious, him sitting on top of me like this, since he's so big, and I'm much smaller. It's like he's trying to absorb me and make us one. And I'm fully on-board.

Unable to resist, my hands slink to his front and I yank his boxers down, freeing the beast. It springs out, ready for action, and Noah gasps.

I curl my fist around his length, between our writhing bodies, and stroke him, painfully slow. He whimpers in my ear and sucks my lobe while I work him from balls all the way up and back. Before I know it, he surrenders to my control and his hips move in-synch with my hand.

Noah letting me guide him, along with the little noises he's making, empowers me. He might be giving me a lap dance, but I'm calling the shots with this large hunk of man.

I've never felt more wanton and sexual. More *alive*.

Seek Me

"You want me to have this dick, don't you?" I bite his shoulder and he hums.

"Yes... Alex..." His deep, raspy voice saying my name is like the most beautiful music to my ears. "Use me."

I moan softly. "Lie down, sexy. Let me take what I want."

"Fuck..." he breathes and reclines quickly tugging me on top of him.

We're suddenly frantic, like we both want so much, but we're only two people.

I'm still gripping his dick while I say, "Undo my pants."

He does as I ask without question, sparking flames in my belly. *He's letting me control him. Mmm... This is going to be fun.*

My hand tugs eagerly on his length, warm and heavy in my palm. He gazes up at me, licking his lips as his eyelids droop with bliss.

"Take them off me."

Noah's hands push my jeans down my hips, sliding them as far as he can reach before I wiggle out the rest of the way. I pause what I'm doing to remove his boxers, then position myself between his long parted legs.

I'm aching to be filled by him, but right now there's something I want to do even more, which is something I haven't done in a while...

I hover over Noah's body, kissing his lips softly, causing him to rumble in my mouth. My tongue slides in to meet his, tangling while we kiss deep and hard until we're both without breath. Then I move my hungry kisses down his throat, licking the mound of his Adam's apple, down to his clavicle, stopping to bite it.

"Alex..."

"Noah..." My mouth continues to trail his delicious skin, licking and kissing all over his muscles, taking a moment to suck his nipple ring between my lips, toying with it until he shudders.

"Good fucking God..." his voice cracks, that big dick flinching against my stomach. I can't help but grin with pride.

Mmm he likes that. Jesus, he's so fucking sexy.

"I know exactly how good this feels..." I murmur, nipping at the barbell, licking circles around his raised flesh. "You like how I play with it, baby?"

"You're ruining me with that mouth, Alex," he growls, fisting his hands in my hair.

About that...

"Well, hold that thought, big guy," I smirk, continuing my trail of wet kisses down his abs, kissing his pelvis tats before eyeing his erection with the thirst of someone lost in a desert.

I haven't sucked a dick in a while. But I'm sure it's like riding a bicycle.

A long, pink, thick…

I lower my lips onto his cock and Noah groans out loud.

"Fuck! Jesus, Alex, a little warning before you -"

I suck the fat, smooth head of him and his words dissipate into a satisfied gasp.

I'm doing good.

"Shit fuck," he pants, tugging my hair with his fingers as I lick the crown, lapping at some silky, salty flavor that squeezes my walls like a vice.

I suck him between my lips, taking him in my mouth, cradling the underside with my tongue as I work up a slow rhythm. I'm getting the hang of it again, sliding him further into my mouth, deeper and deeper until he hits the back of my throat and I gag a little. I want to pout, but I think Noah liked it because he's groaning out all kinds of sounds and nonsense words. So I keep going.

My mouth fucks him, over and over, moving up and down, forward and back while his hips flex. I lift my gaze to watch him losing his edge, and it's the hottest motherfucking thing I've ever seen. His body is bowing to me. Head back, eyes closed, lips parted and quivering; his broad chest heaving through the pleasure he's so clearly feeling.

Lust overtakes me and I reach between his thighs, tugging at his balls with curious fingers. His fingers cup my jaw and I look up again to see his dark eyes set on mine, boring into me as he watches me blow him harder and deeper than I ever have before.

"You look like a fucking dream," he bites his lip, pushing his hips with my tempo. "Fuck, Alex… No one's ever… *Fuuuuck…*"

I can feel his muscles tightening all over, his cock throbbing between my lips as I vigorously suck with hollowed cheeks, chasing his orgasm. I want it. I fucking *need* it.

"Alex… baby, I'm… *really* fucking close," he hisses between gritted teeth.

I move faster, ignoring the strain in my jaw and the saliva that's getting everywhere. I don't even care. I just use it as lubrication while I slurp at him like he's a fucking milkshake I'm trying to get the last of.

Come for me, Noah. I know you want to.

"Seriously, if you don't wanna eat it, move now…" he rambles, his hoarse tone snapping as he moans and grunts, looking so gorgeous and sexy I physically *need* to taste him.

Seek Me

I've never wanted to drink someone as much as I do right now... For him.

"Alex... Alex... oh fucking *God*, Alex!"

And he erupts. While I'm sucking him, while his massive cock is sliding in and out of my throat, he fucking comes like an explosion, shooting hot, thick spurts on my tongue.

I swallow it because I want to, and because it's what I was working at. And it's a lot, but I savor it, because it's Noah and he's delicious, so nothing else matters. He's the best damn snack on Earth.

Also, the saltiness I'm gulping is accompanied by the view of him convulsing in front of me, gripping the back of my neck as every muscle in his body tightens and releases, his climax washing over him. I can feel his dick pulsing between my lips until finally he's done, and he melts into a puddle on the couch.

My mouth releases him with a flop of his tired cock against his abs, and I watch him in fascination. My big, sexy tatted movie star is flushed and panting, lying there like the sweetest thing I've ever laid my eyes on. And despite how raging my libido is right now, I just need to cuddle him. It's a necessity.

I crawl up his body and hug him, kissing his neck everywhere I can reach while his fingers trail lazily up and down my back. He's still struggling to catch his breath, and I use the opportunity to sniff his sweet spot. He smells like sweat and Noah, which is just the best scent a nose could ever ask for.

I move my face back to look at him and he's gazing up at me with twinkling eyes, lids wanting to close but resisting the urge. His soft lips morph into a killer smile, which I return, because damn... Sucking Noah Richards off is more reward than job, for sure.

"Why are you fucking *perfection*?" He drawls, taking my face in his hands and kissing my lips, gentle and warm.

"I'm glad I could return the favor for all of your spectacular oral skills," I squeak, grinning uncontrollably on his mouth.

I feel him swallow hard, and I open my eyes to watch as his brow creases briefly. I'm not sure what the emotion was that just slipped away, but it's gone before I can think about it too hard, and he's reaching onto the floor. I realize that he's rummaging through his pants with one hand, while the other grips my ass, his fingers slinking between my cheeks.

He finally locates what he's looking for, holding up a condom.

"Baby, I'm going to make you come so hard on my cock, you won't be able to move for hours," he growls, eyes shimmering dark, devious promises.

"Don't you need a minute?" I ask with a wild grin.

"It's been a minute," he huffs, tearing open the foil with his teeth.

I giggle with excitement as he hands me the condom, and I waste no time rolling onto his erection, which is either still hard, or hard again. I can't tell, but either way it's purely astonishing.

Noah reaches forward and, without saying a word, yanks at my panties and rips them clean off my body, the material crumbling at the seams.

"Jesus!" I shriek, mildly startled by how fast and effortlessly he did that.

"Panties are a casualty you sacrifice for me, baby," he says, lifting my hips and positioning me so I'm hovering over his. "Ready?"

He's breathing ragged again, and now so am I as I nod for yes, my eyes wide in anticipation. My body is trembling with need, so much that I can feel it coating my inner thighs.

In one motion, he brings me down onto his sheathed cock, slowly, so I can fully savor every hardened inch of him entering me. I cry out loud, my head whipping back as I absorb the sensation. He's so thick, stretching my skin to fit him; and long, reaching untouched depths of my body.

Noah sits up so we're nose-to-nose, chest-to-chest as he holds me tight, giving me a moment to get seated on him, before he squeezes my ass in his big hands and helps me move. He rocks his hips into me, steadily, while I thrust down, our bodies aligned in perfect harmony as we fuck, eyes locked on one another's. It's the most intimate thing I've ever done, but with Noah I don't feel embarrassed or self-conscious. I don't feel ashamed.

He makes me feel beautiful, and sexy. He makes me feel like a goddess.

"Kiss me, Alex," he pleads through a hoarse rumble, his breath warming my lips. "Please... I need you."

I moan as our lips touch, sucking gently, tongues pressing together while our hips move in tandem. His long dick strokes in me, easily with the natural lubrication, though still building that friction that's so magnificent it steals every ounce of breath from inside my lungs.

Every moan, every gasp, every whisper of mine is swallowed up by him, and he returns them, telling me how perfect I am, how amazing I feel around him, and that no one's ever made him feel the way I do.

It's so intense there are tears burning behind my eyes, but I push past it and allow the pleasure to shoot through my core. In this position, he's so deep, and his cock is grazing my G-spot in the absolute perfect way. Not to mention my clit is brushing his pelvis so good I'm ready to come in seconds.

My body is building and building, climbing higher, to the top of the precipice, and I'm about to plummet. Noah grabs my tits, cupping them and squeezing as breaths break from his lips on each forceful thrust.

"Baby, if you come right now… I'll totally be able to come again," he gasps a chuckle, as if he can't believe this fact. And neither can I. It's sort of extraordinary.

I grin, nipping his succulent bottom lip with my teeth. "Your dick works wonders, Noah."

"Mmm… you love this dick, don't you…" he growls, mashing my hips hard against his.

"So fucking much," I moan, combing my fingers deep in his hair and holding on for dear life. "Jesus, I'm gonna come."

"Come hard for me, baby," he grunts, teetering on the edge himself. The idea that he could actually come again after I just sucked his orgasm out with my mouth is a high all on its own.

And it pushes me right over.

My body free falls as my climax overtakes me, and I'm swept up in a cloud of sensation. Everything feels incredible, and I'm humming, riding the orgasm like a long wave.

I register that Noah is pressing his forehead to mine, whispering on my lips that he's coming inside me. But all I can do is gasp, and grip his shoulders for dear life while my walls quake and gush all over him.

Together we're coming down for a while. His hips gradually slow and we just breathe on each other's mouths and run our fingers all over the other's skin. I'm all sensation, and I think Noah is too, because he's shaking in a similar fashion.

He collapses onto his back and takes me with him, holding me there. And I cuddle up, treasuring his warmth, nuzzling his chest and singing quiet praises as I drift off to sleep.

Chapter Fourteen
Noah

I PEEL MY EYES OPEN AND LOOK AROUND, quickly processing that I'm in my living room. And I'm naked, lying on my couch, which is only momentarily puzzling before I remember what I was doing before I passed out.

A grin sweeps over my face. *Sexy little fucking woman.*

I will never forget tonight. It will live in infamy for the rest of all days as the first time Alex gave me head, and also the best blowjob I've ever received in my entire life. She made my fucking toes curl. *When does that ever happen??*

Followed by a sufficiently passionate, sweaty couch-bang, I think it's safe to say Alex and I have made up from our little hiccup, and are better than ever, which is more of a relief than I can even process.

My lunatic smile slips off my face as I look around. *Where is Alex?*

I get up slowly and step into my boxers but nothing else, stumbling off to go locate her. I notice that the door to my terrace is open slightly, and as soon as I get closer, a familiar scent tickles my nose.

I step outside onto the terrace and find Alex, wearing nothing but my shirt and swimming in it, sitting in one of the chairs smoking a joint. I can't help the smile that takes over my face at the sight. She looks beyond beautiful, in my clothes, hair all mussed up from the sex and cuddling on the couch, smoke billowing from between the curves of her lips.

I wander across the terrace and take a seat on the chaise lounge adjacent to her chair, leaning back and sighing a breath of cool air.

"Noah, you shouldn't be outside dressed like that," her raspy voice scolds me. "You could catch a cold."

I grin stupidly at her caring about my well-being as she gets up and walks over, holding out the joint for me to take.

"Then warm me up, baby," I open my arms instead and she smiles, this wide, beaming, firework thing, then plants herself right on my lap.

I wrap my arms around her waist, snuggling her up good on top of me as she drapes her arms around my shoulders, holding the joint up to my lips so I can take a drag.

We sit like this for a few, smoking and cuddling, being really fucking cute. It would worry me, how much I'm feeling like she's my girlfriend, but to be honest, after I saw her at the restaurant the other day, I decided not to let such things bother me anymore.

I just wanted to get her back into my life, as more than just a friend. And it would seem that in the days between then and now, I've stopped trying to freak myself out about my feelings for Alex.

I like her.

I like her more than I've ever liked a girl. And I will remain a friend to her, no matter what, because she needs it. But if I can help myself, I will always try for more, because I can't stand the idea of not doing all the things we did tonight with her, all the fucking time.

So there you have it.

Noah Richards has ventured off the bachelor trail and somehow wound up in a forest of feelings.

It doesn't mean I'll be professing my love to her, or ring shopping. It's not that serious, and I'm not sure it ever will be, or that I'm even capable of such things. But I care about her too much to give myself the yips over trying to define what we are. I just want to focus on happy, non-stressful stuff for now.

Alex deserves it.

All of that being said, there's still an apology I need to voice.

"Al, I just want to tell you again that I'm sorry for what happened the other day," I speak, the words rumbling out of me, knowing full-well she'll probably tell me they're unnecessary. But I'll see how many I can get out before she shuts it down. "None of it was supposed to happen like that, and I couldn't stand to upset you in any way, because you're so special to me."

She gazes down at me, her eyes slightly squinted, likely from the high. She blinks a few times, then reaches out to brush my hair away from my forehead.

"You're a good man, Noah," she whispers. "I trust you. I mean, *you* know you didn't really do anything, and it wasn't your fault that I got upset seeing you with another girl when we're not exclusive. But that you'd still apologize proves you're a true sweetheart, and a gentleman. So… thank you. And I'm sorry I ignored you for days. That was pretty immature."

"You're entitled to feel your feelings, Alex," I reply quietly, buzzing on her words. "You don't need to apologize to anyone for having them, especially not to me. I get you."

She grins a lazy, sweet smile at me, pressing an unbearably soft kiss on my lips that warms my whole body. My eyes stay closed even after she pulls back because the mixture of the buzz and her is enough to render me a floating mass of good vibes.

But when I do eventually open them, I see her smile has disappeared and my forehead instinctively lines with concern for whatever she's thinking. Based on the look on her face, it's probably not good.

"But I do need to tell you something..." she mumbles, flicking the roach onto the ground. "About that night... After I left the restaurant."

My stomach tightens, and a dizziness tries to overtake me. I think I know what she's going to say... And I don't really want to hear it.

She slept with her husband...

After she booked it out of the restaurant with Dr. Dickhead, and I left, dedicating the rest of the evening to texting and calling her with no response, I knew in my gut she was fucking him. It was just a wretched feeling I had in the pit of my stomach that I couldn't shake, no matter how much scotch I drank over the twenty-four hours that followed.

I won't say I'm happy about it... Because that would be a bold-faced lie. I won't even say it doesn't make me feel murderous, because that would also be a pants-on-fire move.

But I can understand it.

I may not have any experience with being in love, being married or, thankfully, with being in an abusive relationship. But the experience I *do* have is in using sex to make yourself feel better. It's something I'm actually quite familiar with.

So I know that Alex sleeping with her husband didn't mean she's forgiven him, or even that she likes him. It meant that she needed to feel something, to distract herself from the internal pain. The last thing she needs now is to feel like she owes me any kind of explanation.

"Alex," I take her small hand in mine, watching as our fingers thread together. "You really don't need to tell me anything. Trust me, it's all good."

My eyes come back up to hers and she's watching me closely. I so wish I could be inside her head right now. I have no idea what she's thinking. But I also don't want to subject myself to hearing her tell me she fucked someone else. If she doesn't say the words to me, I can pretend it never happened and we can just move forward.

Thankfully, she seems to get where I'm going with it, nodding in acceptance.

Seek Me

"Okay."

I take her jaw in my free hand. "Okay."

I kiss her for a few minutes; slow and sexy, solidifying that I made the right decision in going with the flow. There's no need to stress something that feels right like this. We should just concentrate on enjoying each other's company. After all, I've been doing it with multiple ladies my entire adult life. What difference does it make if I just stick to one for now?

"Are you hungry?" I ask once we finally peel off each other.

"You have the munchies?" She drawls and I laugh, nodding with zeal. "Me too."

"Let's order tacos," I murmur, watching as her face lights up.

We stroll back inside, order takeout, and spend the rest of the night blissfully together.

Maybe being exclusive isn't so bad... If it's with Alex.

I don't know how to say this without sounding cheesier than Velveeta, so let's just go for broke...

Life is so fucking good right now.

It's been three months since Alex and I started sleeping together, and suffice it to say, everything is going fan-freaking-tabulously.

We see each other often, despite the sneaking around, which I will say is becoming a bit daunting. But because she's still married to a wealthy, powerful, and also dangerous New Yorker, and I'm someone who gets bombarded by the paparazzi from time to time, most of our rendezvous are restricted to a small list of safe-zones. Basically, my apartment and the diner. And sometimes the park, depending on the time of day.

But it's not like Alex and I are a real couple anyway, so it's no big deal that we can't partake in PDA - public displays of anything. We have our own special little thing going on, and it works. No need to complicate stuff.

The Noah and Alex show has been going strong. So much so that time has simply flown by. Not that we haven't been busy.

I just got back yesterday from checking out houses in Georgia. I put an offer on one that I really love, and there isn't much of a question as to whether I'll get it. My costar and other new BFF - the one I haven't seen naked - Andrew

185

Nyla K

James, locked down a house that's only a fifteen-minute drive from mine. We wanted to be neighbors, but apparently shit in Savannah is pretty spread out. His place is on the water... I'm only the tiniest bit jealous.

We're all fully in prep-mode for filming in April. I've been meeting with a dialect coach weekly to work on my Southern accent, and it's coming along pretty well. Alex loves when I practice on her. She says it makes me sound like sexy hillbilly, which is *exactly* what I'm going for, since apparently my character on the show - who has been revealed to me as *Darren* - is just that; a tattooed bad boy from the wrong side of the tracks who trades car-jacking and petty larceny for scavenging and zombie exterminating in the apocalypse.

Every other awesome job in the world can suck it! Mine's the best.

Alex has been kicking butt herself these last few months. She sold out another show at a gallery downtown, which earned her rave reviews from some very fancy art publications. And she's been working on her next collection, deciding where and when to dole out more brilliance.

My girl is a damn rockstar, and not only when it comes to painting badass works of art that make me physically speechless when I see them.

We're in the car right now, driving back to my place. Jimmy and I just picked her up from a meeting with her divorce lawyer. No, I'm not kidding. Alex is making the moves she said she would, filing for divorce from her abusive husband.

I've seriously never been prouder of her, as my friend and as a strong, independent woman in general. She's so incredible, sometimes I just stare at her in awe. I try not to let her catch me doing it though, because she calls me creepy and smacks me on the ass.

Alex has been very clear that she needs to take care of everything related to her escape plan on her own, and I have to respect that. Still, she's my friend over anything else, and I *do* want to help her where I can. I know she can do this on her own. She's been doing it since she was eighteen-years-old. But I just like to continually remind her she's not alone in the world anymore. She has people who care about her now, like me, Brant, Jimmy, my cleaning ladies, Elsa and Phoebe, who are basically like family since they take care of Boots when I'm traveling. And the list is only growing. She's made all kinds of friends since her first art exhibit, and I think it's high-time the world realized just how wonderful a person Alexandra Mackenzie really is.

I got her a list of the best divorce lawyers money could buy here in the city, but that and coming to pick her up just now has been the extent of my

Seek Me

involvement in the matter. And I'm fine with it, as long as she knows I'm here. Which she does. Because she's sitting right next to me, gazing out the window, deep in thought.

According to Alex, the meeting went very well. Her lawyer told her he could have the paperwork together and ready to serve in less than two weeks' time. I almost can't believe it...

I haven't known Alex long. She's been married for almost eight years, and she's only known me for four months of that. But I'm so glad she could pull herself from the depths of hell she's been living in for years and win the fight. Although there's still work to be done...

Alex squeezes my hand and I glance over to find her staring at me.

"What's up, you beautiful thing you?" I ask, turning in my seat to face her.

She's gnawing on her lower lip, a sight that always fills my dick with excitement in the form of rushing blood. I decide to distract myself from the desire to maul her with an awesome song that just came on the radio.

"Jimmy, turn this shit up!"

And he does. *Light My Fire* by The Doors is now the soundtrack to Alex's adorable, worried face.

"Noah... I'm sort of... nervous," she murmurs.

I give her a sweet smile and continue to sing along with my boy Jim Morrison, all the while watching her closely.

"Like, trying to get all my stuff out of there is going to be really hard..." she keeps going. "Once he gets the papers, he's going to freak."

I'm still singing. Her brows knit together and it's so cute I just *have* to dance a little in my seat, too. I take her concerns very seriously, but she has to understand that I won't let anything bad happen to her, right?

I mean, how could she not know that?

"Noah, I need to talk to you about this," she grumbles in annoyance. "Can you please pay attention?"

"Hold on, this is the best part," I continue singing along to the music of the song, since there's more of that than actual lyrics.

"You mean the endless keyboard solo? Yes, it's great, Noah, but I need -"

"Alex, with this romantically obnoxious keyboard blaring in our ears, I would like to propose something," I grin then tug her closer to me. "And it's not that kind of proposal, so stuff your eyes back into their sockets please."

Her shoulders drop and she releases a breath, eyes returning to their normal size while I roll mine and scoff.

"We all know you can handle this on your own. No one's doubting that," I drape my arm around her shoulder. "But you're not alone, not anymore. Let me help you."

She tilts her face up to me. "How?"

"My realtor can show you some apartments. Once you settle on one, we start packing and moving your stuff in sections, so it's not obvious. And when the paperwork is served, when you decide you want to speak to him, Jimmy will go with you."

My eyes catch Jimmy's in the rearview mirror and he gives me a subtle nod. We've clearly already talked about this.

Alex glances between Jimmy and me. "Really?"

"Of course. I think you should file a restraining order as soon as you move, just to play it safe," I suggest in an easy tone. It's something that worries me all the damn time.

When Alex leaves me to go home to her psycho husband, I'm a nervous wreck. I rarely sleep, keeping myself up all night in fear that he'll hurt her again, or God forbid something worse...

I wouldn't be able to live with myself knowing I'd let her go back to him... And I don't want to live in this world without her, a fact that has me circling her block sometimes at four in the morning just in case.

And as much stress as it causes me, for Alex it's obviously a zillion times worse. She needs to get out of there. He's tortured her for long enough.

Alex hugs onto my waist hard, squeezing the air out of me, which makes me laugh. She kisses my neck over and over in the sweetest display of affection and gratitude. But she doesn't need to be grateful to *me*. I'm grateful to *her* for coming into my life.

"Thank you, Noah," she whispers, yanking my face to hers by my jaw and kissing me slow. "You light my fire." She grins on my lips and I chuckle.

"You *are* my fire," I hum.

She giggles into my mouth. "My one desire?"

"Uh-uh, Ms. Mackenzie. We are *not* going from the great Jim Morrison to the damn Backstreet Boys," I growl at her while she snickers away, slipping her hands inside my coat to feel me up a little.

"Noah, I'm agreeing with you!" She squeals. "I was just saying, believe when I say... that I want it that way!"

Now she's snorting from laughing so hard. It's the cutest fucking thing I've ever seen when Alex laughs hysterically. And I pride myself at being able to

Seek Me

make it happen often.

I squint at her for a moment, then sigh. "Ah, screw it. Tell me why!"

And Alex launches into singing the chorus of that damn Backstreet Boys song, while I give her a few background vocals because I know *some* of the lyrics, okay?

We're barely done goofing around by the time we reach my place, and even Jimmy is chuckling at us like we're ridiculous idiots, which is a fair assessment. Any time Alex and I are together, it's like what little filters we have disappear and all bets are off as to just how silly we can be.

But who cares, because screw being normal. Why be stuffy and boring when you can be a weirdo and be awesome? That's Alex and my collective motto.

As we're walking through my hallway, I recognize the distinct ringtone I use for texts and phone calls from people I actually want to answer my phone for, like Alex, Jimmy, my assistant...

"Baby?" I rumble while we walk inside the apartment, stripping out of our coats and shoes. Alex immediately turns the fireplace on.

"Yes, peaches?" She answers while making herself at home, sauntering into the kitchen.

I love how she walks around my apartment like she owns the place. It gives me a homey, comfortable gratification in my chest.

I feel myself hesitating, so I decide to jump in, head first.

"Would you come to lunch tomorrow with me... and my sister?"

Alex peeks at me over her shoulder. Her eyes are wide, but she doesn't look completely spooked, though I wouldn't blame her if she did. Family isn't something we've spoken about much since we've known one another. She's aware of my parents and sister living in Long Island, which is where I'm from. And she's aware that they're awesome.

Outside of that, Alex doesn't know my family at all. But believe you me, they know *all* about her.

I'm pretty close with my family. We don't talk or see each other anywhere near as often as we should, being that they're only a forty-five minute drive away. But when I do call them, or go to visit, it's like I'm back living there again, and it's great. We get along like four peas in a pod.

I went home for dinner one Sunday last month. Alex was hanging with some art friends, so I didn't invite her.

Alright, fine. That's not true.

Nyla K

I didn't invite her because I felt like she might freak out meeting my parents. It just feels very serious. But of course that didn't stop me from talking about her when I was there. Maybe too much. My parents are now convinced we're getting married someday, but that doesn't necessarily mean anything. They're just sick of me slutting it up.

My sister, on the other hand, was curious as all hell. She's thirteen, and pretty damn sharp. Actually, she's complete wise-ass. I have *no idea* where she gets in from.

Ever since then, Haley's been bothering me about meeting Alex. She wouldn't leave me alone, calling and texting incessantly, so I gave in and invited her to a spend a day with me in the city. I'm sending a car out to Rockville Centre to pick her up, and we'll do a bunch of fun stuff together here in Manhattan.

There was never a guarantee that Alex would want to tag along for our day of fun. I made Haley no promises, because I know Alex gets nervous about relationship stuff. Normally I do too, but for some reason I really like the idea of Alex meeting my family. And I think the reason is centered around her not having one of her own…

"Your sister?" Alex chirps, eyes unblinking, really showing off that bright green. It's a bit hypnotizing, but I force myself to move past it.

"Yea. Haley," I nod. "She's coming into the city tomorrow to hang out, and I think it'd be cool if you came along." I swallow hard, using my best acting abilities to project aloofness. "No pressure."

Alex is quiet for entirely too long and it's really making me question everything I've ever said or done in my life. I don't know how she manages to do that with a few seconds of silence, but I'm beginning to accept it as something inevitable that happens to me when Alex is around.

I've been accepting an awful lot of these personality changes lately…

"You said your sister is thirteen, right?" Alex's voice finally makes its comeback.

"Yes," I answer carefully. I'm not sure where she's going with this.

"She's not like… overly protective of you, is she?" She asks and I'm a bit stunned by this question.

Is Haley overly protective of me?

I don't think so. I mean, my family cares a lot about me. We're really close, because it's just the four of us. Both of my parents are only children, so I have no aunts, uncles, or cousins. Sure, they have friends they grew up with, and have remained close with over the years, but my immediate family is like an exclusive little club.

Welcoming Alex into that club is a bigger deal than I would ever admit to her.

"No, nothing like that," my head shakes from side to side as I step up to her, slowly. "She's a kid. She's sweet… maybe a little crazy. But I was the same at that age, so I can't really say anything."

Alex laughs and I reach for her waist, pulling her into me.

"I want you to meet them…" I whisper while burying my face in her hair, eyes rolling back in my head from the scent that's slinking into my brain through my nose, like a rush of endorphins pinging around my neurosystem.

"*Them?*" She squeaks, and my eyes shoot open.

Fuck.

I pull my face back to find her staring at me, hard.

"I… uh…" My brain scrambles for a way to save this, but it's really no use, so I sigh in defeat. "My parents… They want to meet you. At some point…"

"Your parents?" She gasps as her lips morph into this broad smile, sitting in the center of the joyous excitement radiating off her face. "That's so cute!"

I frown. "It's not cute. It's manly." She bursts into snorting laughter.

"Okay. Sure, babe," she breathes a grin, holding my face and brushing my hair back with her fingers.

"I know, it's a little serious," I gulp. "I just mentioned you when I saw them last month and they got all excited." *It's a half-truth.*

"How about I meet Haley for now, and we'll see how it goes," she whispers. Her brows raise expectantly so I nod along.

Whatever you want.

"Alex Mackenzie…" Smiling slow, my lips move to her throat.

"I love when you say my name," she purrs and I chuckle into the crook of her neck. My dick is already trying to force its way out of my pants.

"I love saying it when I'm inside you…"

She hums in a soft moan, "Don't tease me, Richards."

"Baby, you know I always deliver." Promises are made with nips to her sweet flesh as I slide up her shirt.

Which leads to more touching, more kissing, more gentle breaths of desire and unhurried lustful dedication. We spend the rest of the evening naked. My new favorite pastime.

And the next day we wake up and get ready for hurricane Haley's arrival.

While we wait, I make a call to my realtor and I give her the list of Alex's apartment requirements: Brooklyn, preferably Bed-Stuy, Williamsburg, or Greenpoint. Two bedroom, natural light, higher floor with an elevator, maybe a building with a doorman - that was my own request. I need her safety more than anything else.

She wants something with a studio if possible, and when my realtor asks what her price-range is, I turn away and whisper, "Don't worry about that. Money is no object."

Alex will kill you if you try to pay for her new apartment, my brain reminds me.

And I'm fully aware of that. But I want her to have everything her heart desires. She can't go from living in a huge co-op with her own studio, to struggling to paint in a spare bedroom. It just won't work.

The whole divorce thing is just such a process. I don't know how she's managing to remain so calm. I truly hope it has something to do with my assistance, but I'd just be guessing.

Not that Alex doesn't tell me how much she appreciates me. She does, all the damn time. It's just that I'm constantly toeing a fine line between giving her everything she wants and acting too much like a boyfriend. We're not *official*. We can't be official, because she's married and going through a divorce.

And I'm a bachelor who doesn't do relationships.

Right?

I shake my head. I'm still that guy. The past three months haven't changed who I am. The only difference is that I've gotten comfortable in a routine with my best friend. We spend almost every day together, we fuck nonstop and it's the best sex of my entire life, every time. We call and text each other about everything under the sun, and we have pet names for one another.

Is that a relationship?

Is Alex my girlfriend??

And now the walls are closing in on me. I'm losing my breath as the world around me goes blurry.

I can't have a *girlfriend*. I'm relationship stunted. I wouldn't know the first thing about being a boyfriend.

Fuck, what am I doing? I can't fuck Alex over. She's the most amazing person I know. And she's already been fucked over to the ultimate degree. I can't be like him... I won't.

My disparaging thoughts are silenced when Alex steps over to me and takes my hand in hers, tracing the lines of black in my skull tattoo.

"What did she say?" She asks, blinking up at me.

Huh?

Oh, right. The realtor.

"She has a few places she'd like to show you," I answer in a voice that's too gruff for someone who isn't having a secret panic attack. "We can look at some of them today if you want."

The face she's making is confusing, and it instantly has me wondering if I'm involving myself too much. I think this has been the problem lately, contributing to my numerous insecurities I never seemed to have before I met Alex.

I'm always afraid of pushing too much.

My problem with this *casual-yet-exclusive* thing we're doing here, which has remained unvoiced, is that I wouldn't actually *want* to screw any other girls while Alex Mackenzie is in the picture. Because she's the best I've ever had.

Hands down. No debate. *Don't @ me.*

Sex with Alex is like dipping my entire body in a vat of liquid euphoria, then lighting myself on fire and putting it out with rainbows and sunshine. Nothing has *ever* felt that good.

That being said, it's not the only thing I'm in it for, obviously, being that we're best friends. The sex may be a very satisfying cherry on top of the Alex Mackenzie sundae, but there's still a whole bunch of other stuff that makes it delicious.

It's because of all this that I'm constantly second-guessing myself. The last thing I want is to come off as too much... Which is hard for me because I'm so unfamiliar with everything I'm feeling. Even the way I act with Alex confuses the shit out of me. It's like I can barely recognize myself.

The thing is, though... I'm not sure if I mind.

"Won't that be boring for Haley?" Alex's raspy voice pulls me out of my head once again. "Looking at apartments?"

"No way," I scoff. "She's a teen living in Long Island. Anything she does in the city will trump whatever she would be doing back home."

Alex grins. "You have a point. Alright! Set it up. We can grab some lunch then go check out the places."

She smiles with satisfaction and my chest warms. I don't know why I'm doubting myself. I know Alex adores me, and I'm sure if I was being overwhelming, she would say something. She's not afraid to tell me how she's feeling at all, which is much appreciated.

Allegedly, I'm the one who got her talking; her first friend in years who got her out of her shell. And the pride I feel at that is enough to squash all the rest of the noise.

I'm kissing her face all over and she's giggling and hitting me when my door buzzes. We both look up in expectancy.

"You ready?" I ask Alex, smiling as I tap her on the chin, but not waiting for a response before I dash over to the door.

I glance behind me one more time to catch her fluffing out her hair and running her hands down her jeans over and over. That visible nervousness brings me joy. It's endearing as hell.

I open the door just in time for Haley to dart at me. I catch her and lift her up, swinging her all over the place while she squeals.

"Big brother boss man!" My sister shrieks in my ear, blowing out my eardrum. "I'm so happy!"

"I'm so happy you're here too, little slayer," I croon, placing her down on her feet then ruffling her hair, something she totally *hates*, which is of course why I do it.

Check this out. I always wanted a sibling, but for the longest time my parents told me I was so special they could have only one of me. It wasn't until after my mom got pregnant with Haley, when I was twenty-two, that I found out they'd been trying for years to have another baby with no success. Apparently, my parents stopped trying when I was ten, after years of disappointments, and doctor visits telling them there was nothing *wrong*; they just couldn't seem to get pregnant again.

And then one day, when I came home from a terrible audition, I found my mother openly weeping in the kitchen. I remember sighing out loud and pulling my hair so hard it hurt. I was in an awful mood from bombing my audition and I wasn't in the right state of mind to be dealing with anyone else's problems.

But I sucked it up, because this was my *mom*. She'd do it for me, and she had.

"Mom... Are you alright?" I huffed, stepping over to rub her back gently.

"Noah, sweetie..." she gasped, crying so hard she could barely breathe.

But then her face turned to meet mine, and she was smiling. Bigger than I'd ever seen anyone smile with tears flowing out of their eyes.

"Dude, what the hell is wrong with you...?" I grumbled, nervous and confused as hell.

Mom snorted out a laugh and took my hands. "It finally happened."

And she told me she was eight-weeks pregnant. It was insane.

Neither her, nor my father, me, or their doctors could believe that after years of writing it off as a *never gonna happen* situation, my mom somehow got pregnant again. I would finally get a sibling. As a fucking adult.

But I was pumped. Haley changed my life in many ways. Before her, I'd never been around babies. Her presence taught me how to change diapers, how to swaddle; how to feed, entertain and look after kids. It's a life skill I'm glad to have thanks to my awesome little sister.

Speaking of the sister, before I can say or do anything else, Haley is bum-rushing Alex. She launches herself at Alex, hugging so hard she almost topples over. I watch Alex's startled face from behind my sister's mane of wild brunette hair and smirk, shrugging a brief apology as she gawks at me with wide, round eyes.

"You must be Alex!" Haley jumps up and down. "Oh my God, you're so pretty! Noah said you were gorgeous, but he didn't tell us you were a *model*!"

Alex shoots me a look and all I can do is press my lips together.

"I'm not a model at all, but thank you," Alex giggles awkwardly, patting my sister on the head. "You're pretty damn beautiful yourself. Are you going to be an actress like your big brother here?"

Alex gives Haley an inquisitive smile and Haley flips her hair with teenage overconfidence.

"Nah, I'm not sure that would work for me," she answers. "I'm going to be a lawyer."

Alex's brows jump. "A lawyer?"

"Yea!" Haley nods enthusiastically. "I love to argue. I'm really good at it."

Alex laughs and peeks at me, to which I nod slowly, agreeing with my sister's self-assessment. *She's very good at arguing, yes.*

"So, Alex," Haley goes on, changing the subject in a way only a thirteen-year-old can. "Noah tells me you're a famous painter!"

Alex gives me a scolding look, though she appears more pleased than put off. "I'm hardly *famous*. I've done two exhibits here in the city that went well. Your brother likes to exaggerate." Green eyes, still on me.

"Her brother knows raw talent when he sees it," I growl at her and her cheeks flush.

God, I want to be in between those thighs right now. She needs a good tongue-torturing.

"Noah!" Haley shrills, and it snaps me out of my little trance. I clear my throat, seriously hoping I don't have a visible hard-on. It wouldn't be the first time I got wood from a simple look on Alex's face. "You must have some of Alex's paintings hanging up in here, right? Show me!"

I smile and nod. "Of course I have several of them."

Motioning for her to follow me, the three of us wander around my apartment, checking out Alex's special art exhibit displayed right here in my home. I feel exorbitant amounts of pride at being able to rep her artistic talent as a friend and a consumer.

Naturally, Haley is blown away. She keeps giving me these sneaky side-looks, every time Alex turns, and since she's my sister, I can essentially read what they say: *She's perfect. Don't let her go.*

She must think something slightly more serious is going on here, based on all the obsessive rambling I did to her and my parents when I was home. But that's okay... I don't blame her. It's all harmless.

Once we're done with the mini art show, Alex suggests, "Let's go get something to eat."

To which Haley returns, "We need to go to that place with the giant milkshakes! The ones they fill with candy and cookies and marshmallows!"

Alex peers at me.

"She's talking about Black Tap," I explain.

"Ahh..." Alex nods in immediate understanding.

My sister loves Black Tap, a restaurant in the West Village. Well, really *everyone* loves Black Tap. It's understandable, since their food is spectacular. But it's such a popular place that it gets crowded easily, and patrons have to wait outside on line until tables become available.

Of course *I* wouldn't have to do that, but me showing up and cutting the line could potentially cause a bit of a stir. It's not something I've ever cared about before, but with Alex and her situation, I can't have us being photographed.

"Um, Hale, I'm not sure if that's -"

"Noah, it's fine," Alex cuts me off with a knowing look. I return it, our telepathic conversation going back and forth while Haley watches us in bemused intrigue.

Finally, I concede. "Alright. You're the boss."

"Oh my God... He's never said that to *anyone* before," Haley squeals, gripping Alex's arm. "He's freaking smitten with you!"

Alex watches me struggle, grating my hands over my face, my chest caving like a two-hundred-pound body builder is standing on it.

"Noah Richards... *smitten?*" Alex sneers then bites her lip. "Are you sure?"

"Sooo sure," Haley giggles. "Noah and Alex sitting in a tree!"

She starts singing the stupid song and I grumble under my breath about getting their coats.

Why did I think this would be a good idea again?

Seek Me

Twenty minutes later, Jimmy's dropping us off in front of Black Tap. I had hoped that maybe lunch time here would be less of a circus than dinner, but I obviously miscalculated how much New Yorkers love cheeseburgers and over-indulgent milkshakes.

The line is wrapped around the corner.

We make our way to the front, and the hostess at the door's eyes light up.

"OhmiGod!" She squeaks, then quickly composes herself. "Mr. Richards! Hello! Welcome!"

"Hi," I grin, casually peeking around for any sign of people with cameras. I see none, but that doesn't mean anything. "Any chance you can fit three for lunch? We'll sit anywhere."

"Of course! Don't be silly," the young hostess, who is very blonde and very much giving off *I want to ride you like a merry-go-round* vibes in my direction, waves her hand. "We have a perfect spot for you."

She turns to a young man behind her who's fiddling with a bunch of menus and whispers something to him. His head springs in my direction and his face freezes momentarily before regaining his composure.

"Right this way, Mr. Richards," he chirps eagerly, and the three of us follow him inside.

On our way in, I wink at the hostess as she chews on her lower lip and pops out her chest. *And the answer to the question of why I've been single my entire adult life becomes much more apparent.*

"I'm a huge fan," the young man leading us to our table says to me over his shoulder. "Do you think there's any way I could get a selfie with you?"

The last thing I ever want to do is come off as rude, so I reply, "Sure thing, boss." Even though I'm not really feeling it.

We arrive at a table in the back of the upper level, which is a version of private, although it's not a large space and we're surrounded by people, all of whom are now looking right at *muah*.

Dude with the cell phone steps over to me and we do my signature pose: the middle finger. *Classy I know, but it's my thing and the fans love it.*

Alex and Haley are already sitting at the table watching me in amusement, and I experience a brief moment of panic when deciding where to sit in the booth; next to Alex or next to Haley. My hands sweat as I choose quickly, hopefully distracting from the fact that I'm struggling with something that theoretically isn't a big deal.

I plop down next to Haley and give Alex a look that's attempting apologetic, while also casual, just in case I'm overthinking things. I'm sure I am. I've been deep in my head all day and it's not what I'd call *fun*. All this worrying is going to give me crows feet.

Haley frowns up at me, but I change the subject before she can start criticizing me for whatever I'm sure she's about bring up.

"Which milkshake do you want, slayer?" I ask, flipping through the menu. "This one looks pretty cool. How the hell do they get all these candies onto the side of the glass like -"

"I'm so sorry to bother you, Mr. Richards," a voice cuts me off and my head slowly tilts in its direction. "But I'm, like, the hugest fan in the world! Is there any way I could get a selfie?"

I squint at the dude standing at the edge of our booth, and my momentary look of annoyance must be apparent because he adds, "I'm really sorry to interrupt you. Man, that was rude. My bad…"

"Don't worry about it, chief," I grin, using all my inner strength to remain cool. I'm good with this mask of stoner-esque casual indifference, so I pull it off well, since I've spent years crafting it to a tee.

The guy's face brightens as I stand up and we snap a quick selfie with our middle fingers up. He thanks me politely, and I sit back down with a huff.

"Sorry about that, guys," I mutter, flicking one of Haley's dangly earrings. "This is why I didn't want to come here."

"It's cool," she chirps. "I like seeing you with your fans. It reminds me that your famous. Honestly, sometimes I forget."

"Thanks, sis. You make me feel all warm and fuzzy inside," I grumble at her sarcastically, adding a teasing wink.

"You know what I mean!" She swats my arm. "You're very down-to-earth. You don't come off like an asshole celebrity."

"I would hope not… Shit," I shake my head. "If I ever start acting like an annoying egomaniac, I want both of you to slap me in the -"

"Noah Richards!"

"For the love of God…" I mutter under my breath. *This is not happening.*

"OhmiGosh, I'm so sorry to bug you! But it's my sister's birthday over there, and I was wondering if you could come take a picture with us…?"

The girl standing at the edge of our booth gapes down at me with wide, pleading eyes. Mine drift over to her table where there's a group of six other girls, all with brightly colored milkshakes sitting in front of them and eager looks on their faces as they attempt not to openly stare in my direction.

Seek Me

I suck in a deep breath and let the mask envelope my body, removing the snippy attitude I want to give this girl for interrupting lunch with my sister and my... Alex. I stand up with a grin as the girl squeals and cheers, grabbing me by the arm and dragging me to her friends.

The process takes more than five minutes. Getting all of their faces to the perfect *angles* takes that much time, not to mention a few extra minutes for each of them to touch me somewhere almost inappropriate and tell me how much they loved me in *whatever*. Eventually we take our picture, and I even record a quick video on the girl's Snapchat story telling her happy birthday while the other ones cheer and giggle, their voices hitting octaves so high local dogs are going nuts.

I make my way back to my own table with three phone numbers stuffed in my sweater pocket, shaking my head in irritation I won't let myself display. I'm the one who's never hassled or flustered by anything. It's just the way I am. Even if something does bother me like that, I'd never let myself show it to anyone, especially not these random fans.

After all, how douchey would I look complaining about the fact that people are interested in me? I should be so lucky as to have *fans*.

I slump back into the booth and I feel drained. My eyes instinctively find Alex, and she looks fine. Maybe slightly impatient, but she doesn't appear aggravated about those girls hanging all over me and disrupting our meal with my sister.

Not sure if that's good or bad...

"Sorry... again," I grunt, flipping open the menu once more even though I'm just going to order anything at this point.

"It's okay, bro," Haley smirks, though she's giving me a look I can't really interpret. "Man, those girls were all over you, huh?"

I blink a few times. "It's just part of the job," I shrug, peeking at Alex once more. She pulls a smile that seems forced, but I don't have time to comment on it because our waiter is now here, asking what we want.

The three of us order our own burgers and fancy milkshakes, each sampling a different one so we can all share and decide which is better. Thankfully, once our food arrives, no one comes over to ask for more selfies. Still, I'm hyper-aware of everyone around us, and I think I definitely spotted a few people snapping pictures with their phones, trying to be sneaky.

I can't and won't blame them at all. It comes with the territory. And I assume - even hope - that if *Hell Storm* becomes successful, it will get much more intense and complicated.

But I knew what I signed up for. I can't be mad at it.

The gushing over our food goes on for a while. It's just so appealing to look at, you almost don't even want to eat it. Accept that you do, because it's delicious. The burger and massive peanut butter cup milkshake improves my mood instantly, and maybe it's the sugar, but I find myself bouncing around in my seat. I wish I was sitting next to Alex so I could touch her thigh and play with her hair.

"Hale, we're going to check out a couple apartments for Alex after this, if that's cool," I tell my sister, chomping on an ice cream covered pretzel stick from my beverage.

"That's cool," Haley replies with her usual animation. "You're moving?" Her gaze slips to Alex.

"Mhm, I'm um... Getting divorced," Alex huffs, watching her burger as if she expects it to come to life and save her from the potential awkwardness of this conversation.

"Ohhh right. Noah did mention you were working on that," Haley nods empathetically, and I shoot her a fiery look.

Sister, read my mind and please do not *tell Alex that I told you, Mom and Dad all about her personal affairs.*

The word *affair*, even being uttered out of context in my mind, turns my stomach. I hate thinking of Alex and me being *adulterous*. It's almost the worst thing you can be, shy of a violent psycho, like her husband. Which reminds me of all his disgusting behaviors and dissipates the guilt significantly.

The guy's a worthless asshole who's been cheating on Alex for years. I don't think what we're doing is anywhere near as abhorrent as he is a human being.

To my surprise and relief, Alex doesn't look irritated that I told my sister she was going through a divorce. Which is all I told her, by the way. I would never disclose anything about her domestic situation to anyone. That's not mine to speak about.

"Yea, my husband is the worst..." Alex sighs, pausing to bite and chew an onion ring. "He's been cheating on me for years... I finally got up the courage to file for divorce, thanks to your wonderful brother."

She grins at me and I savor it. I love that I make her smile, and that she sees me as someone who gave her courage. To me, I've just been lucky enough to breathe the same air as her.

"No thanks necessary, darlin," I tell her with sincerity. "You've had this courage in you all along. You know that."

Her smile widens, lighting up the booth. "Well, I'm eternally grateful that you hit on me at Maxwell's."

"Excuse you. I did not *hit on* you," I grumble through a smirk. "I was simply striking up a conversation."

"Hmm, yes. You're very *striking*," she wiggles her brows and I laugh. "Should we tell your sister how the rest of that night went…?"

"Oh yea, that's fine. We talked for hours, getting our drink on, then went and ate waffles at the diner." I blink at Alex who's giggling under her breath, then peek at my sister. "And no parts of that story are being withheld. At all."

"*Really*?" Haley huffs. "You just ate waffles then went your separate ways? Noah, I love you, but let's be real here. There's no way that's all that happened."

"It really is though!" I defend myself. Alex is laughing hysterically and I gape at her like the evil, sexy woman she is.

"Okay fine. When was your first date then?" Haley asks, and now I'm gawking at her, wondering why she seems content to make me the world's most uncomfortable brother today.

"Hale, our burgers are already done. Stop grilling."

"You brought it up!" She squeals through a laugh.

"Did not!"

"Did too!"

"Okay, children. That's enough," Alex sighs. Haley and I scowl at each other for a few more seconds before returning to our food.

As much discomfort as I was originally feeling, it's been a great lunch so far. The food was wonderful, as promised, and the conversation between Alex and Haley flows effortlessly. I'm very pleased to have introduced yet another friend into Alex's world. I won't stop until everyone I know meets and loves her. That way she'll never have to worry about feeling alone again.

I mean, I'm thrilled to be her only friend, but I hardly think that's fair to Alex. I'm cool and all, but I'm not spectacular enough to fulfill all of her friend needs forever.

As soon as the waiter clears our plates, we're ready to go. The realtor texted me the address of the first apartment where we'll meet her, in Williamsburg, so I'm itching to check these places out and make sure they're good enough.

For Alex, not me. Obviously.

Unfortunately, getting out of the restaurant is slightly more challenging than getting into it was.

We're being stopped on the way out by just about every patron in the damn place. No one wants to let me leave without taking a selfie, and while I'm very good at playing the easy-going, chill dude part, my jaw is grinding excessively.

"Hale, please take Alex to the car, and try not to let anyone take any pictures of her," I whisper to my sister amongst more noise and commotion than I thought was possible in such a small space.

Haley nods and diligently grabs Alex by the arm, slinking through the crowd and out to Jimmy.

Once they're out of sight, I take a deep breath and smile.

Selfie time.

It goes on for a while. I'm trying to be patient, but I also know I need to leave. And I *want* to leave. Despite what some of these fans may think, I don't intend on moving into Black Tap permanently.

When I finally break free from the herd, my head is spinning and I've flipped more birds than KFC. Middle fingers everywhere. It was actually kind of cool seeing huge groups of people wearing enthusiastic smiles for me, throwing their *fuck yous* up in the air Noah Richards style. As stressful as it can be with the crowds, I'm buzzing on it just a tad.

I can't wait to see how these peeps react to Hell Storm. I can almost picture it already… Me, Andrew, Johnny Barthow, and the others… Rocking premieres and shit. I can't fuckin wait.

I hop into the car and close the door on more prying eyes and lifted cell phones, and Jimmy takes the hint, speeding us away to the address I texted him.

"Wow… that was crazy!" Haley chirps, and it's then that I realize she's sitting in the back row of the vehicle.

I turn over the seat and give her a quizzical look.

"Oh, I thought you might want to sit next to Alex," my sister's eyes widen for a moment, brows raised as she telepathically calls me out.

I cringe a little. "I'm sure Alex is sick of me by now."

My head tilts in Alex's direction to witness her lips curve.

"Not yet," she scrunches her nose at me. Unable to stop myself, I reach out and take her hand in mine, lacing our fingers.

I have an overwhelming urge to pull her as close to me as humanly possible; to sniff her hair and kiss her head, maybe do that thing where I slip my fingers underneath her shirt in the back just to feel her baby-soft skin.

But I don't.

I don't do any of that because my sister's watching, and I just know she wants me to be all boyfriendy with Alex to prove a point. And I won't give her that satisfaction. Mainly because I don't want to scare Alex by acting that way in front of my sister, but also partially because *I'm* afraid to.

Acting like a boyfriend to Alex is all peachy keen when we're alone, or just in front of Jimmy. But doing it in front of other humans means something else. It means we're veering off into some new territory that I'm still not sure either of us can handle.

I'll just hold her hand for now. That seems like the safe bet.

"So, what do we think?"

"Barbara, could we have a moment?"

Alex pulls me by the arm, dragging me into a giant empty bedroom and closing the door.

I breathe out hard and stare down at her face, waiting for her to give me the scoop.

What's going on in that big beautiful brain of yours, Alexandra?

"I really like the one by McCaren. I can totally see myself running there," she grins.

"You don't run," I chuckle, trailing my fingers along her shoulder.

"I could run. If I lived near McCarren Park." She lifts her brows assuredly.

"If you say so, muffin," I laugh as she punches me in the stomach. "But you're right. That place was amazing. I mean, this one's nice too…"

"They're all nice. But that one stands out," she sighs. "The studio was gorgeous. Incredible lighting, so much space. I could fit a couch up there, like I have now!"

She squeals and does a little hop, which is damn near the cutest thing I've ever witnessed.

"You have a couch in your studio?" She nods. "You're not taking that one with you?"

She swallows visibly as her smile fades. "Noah, I'm so nervous about moving my stuff… I just want to pack the essentials and dip the fuck out."

"I get that, baby, but you'll have help," I take her face in my hands, forcing her to look at me. "I don't want you to feel like you have to leave your things behind because you're afraid of him. Put that part out of your mind when you think about all of this."

She nods with her chin resting in my palms. *Let's add that to the list of adorable Alex moments, please.*

"And as far as the place goes, there's no need to rush," I continue, sifting my fingers through her hair. "It's your first day looking. You know Barbara will show you eight million more places. She's almost too excited."

Alex giggles. "She is. She's sweet, though. But I'm being honest, I really like that place. I've always loved McCarren Park. That area is awesome."

I nod slowly. *The building doesn't have a doorman... But there are cameras at the front so I guess that's something.*

"So... No to this place?" I rumble, glancing around the wide-open room. She shakes her head. "Mmm... that's too bad. I can totally picture us getting it on in here."

"Is that right?" She grins as I back her up into the wall.

"Yup." I trap her against it with my hips and kiss her neck, slowly.

"I think you can probably picture us getting it on just about anywhere," she breathes, fingers slinking underneath the fabric of my shirt.

"That might be true," I murmur with my tongue tasting her pulse.

"I know it is." Her nails graze from my lower back around front to my happy trail.

I let out a soft, eager breath as my cock twitches. It's been a long day, and the only thing I want right now is to be buried inside my girl. *If it has to be here in the empty bedroom of an apartment she's not even going to take, so be it.*

"How do you know that?" My voice comes out hoarse from the teasing way she's fingering the button on my jeans.

"Because I can picture it, too," she purrs, then pops it.

My patience runs dry and I tug her face to mine, kissing her fast. She gasps in my mouth and I suck her bottom lip, my tongue sneaking in to meet hers. I groan quietly while she writhes against me, begging for the friction between her thighs. But her hand is still at my crotch and now she's lowering my zipper and slinking said hand inside my pants and boxers.

"Fuck," I grunt as she takes hold of my solid flesh in her palm, stroking slow yet hard, just the way I like it.

She knows exactly what I like.

Fuck, she is exactly what I like.

"We probably shouldn't do this," she pants over my lips. "Your sister and the realtor are right outside." But she's not stopping.

"Baby, you can't just start jerking me off then say we need to stop," I grin, cupping her breast, circling the piercing in her nipple with my thumb.

"So what do you suggest?" She rubs my cock against her bare stomach, which feels insanely good. Her skin is so warm and smooth...

"I have some ideas," I rasp and she shudders. "But you'd have to promise to be really quiet."

"Being quiet is hard with you," she whimpers, before kissing me deep while pulling my cock so good I'm feeling lightheaded.

I reluctantly move back enough to catch her pout, which brings on a devious smirk from my lips. I undo her pants and tug them down to her thighs. Then I drop to my knees before her.

"Noah... They're totally going to -" I interrupt her with my tongue, tracing the length of her slit. "Hear... us..." It comes out like a moan mixed with a sigh of satisfaction; a sound I love all too much.

My lips kiss every spot they can reach, tenderly sucking her clit, apparently good enough for her hand to slap over her mouth. My grin is out of control, and my balls are aching because she tastes so fucking good.

I grab her ass hard and hold her as close as possible while I lick her in feathering flutters, slipping my tongue inside her a few times for good measure. Alex is trembling and quivering and yanking my hair, which just fuels me to eat her deeper and harder. Ragged breaths leave my mouth to tease her soaking wet flesh as I devour her like a starving man. I suppose I am...

I always feel starved for Alex. No matter how much I get, I'm always craving *more*.

I take that feeling and run with it, thrusting one, then two fingers inside her and curling them as I suck her clit between my lips until she explodes into a graceful orgasm, leaving even my chin drenched in her delicious juices.

I stand up on shaky legs and before I can process anything, she's spinning me until I'm up against the wall and dropping to her knees. *Wow... I guess Alex wants more, too.*

My dick is in her mouth even quicker as she wastes no time sucking the life out of me. And now it's my turn to cover my mouth with my hand.

Seriously, I'm biting my fingers to keep quiet. She's a fucking madwoman... *Jesus Christ holy fuck...*

Alex works my dick over and over between her plush lips, sucking hard with hollowed cheeks, keeping her eyes on mine the whole time. It feels mind-altering, and looks even better.

"Alex... fuck, I -" My moan cuts me off which is good because I'm not even sure what I was going to say, and I shouldn't be allowed to speak words when Alex is sucking my dick. My brain is too fuzzy to verify what it allows to exit my mouth.

I hold her face while she holds my balls, swallowing my cock until I burst. My dick pulses and shoots streams down her throat while I whisper all kinds of nonsense behind my hand. I don't know what I'm saying, but thank fuck she can't hear me because it's a lot of stuff I shouldn't be saying.

God, she's fucking perfect. There's never been anyone like her... I think I... I don't... know...

When she stands back up, she holds onto me and I kiss her for what feels like hours, both of us buzzing on the high of orgasms and each other.

Then we compose ourselves and leave the empty room to tell Barbara that Alex will take the place in Greenpoint.

I'm sure she and my sister knew what we were doing in there. But thankfully neither of them says a word.

Chapter Fifteen
Alex's Journal

I MAKE A SOLID EFFORT NOT TO CRY IN FRONT OF ROGER.

I don't want to show him my weakness, even though he knows I'm weak. Let's be real, Barnaby… If I haven't left him yet, and I'm still waking him up by grinding on his morning wood, that's pretty damn close to the actual definition of *weak*.

I really don't know what's wrong with me. It's been two years since my husband started abusing me, and even before that he wasn't a good man. God only knows how long he's actually been cheating on me, though I have my theories.

And yet still, I'm drawn to him. Part of me doesn't believe it's him I'm drawn to, but just the idea of a man who wants me. I can't help but feel pathetic even thinking these things. But it's the truth. Plus, this is my own safe space, and I can write whatever I want in here, to you, without worrying about the repercussions, or people thinking I'm a desperate loser who fucks a man who gives her bruises on the regular.

Anyway, last night I cried in front of him.

I tried so hard not to, but he was on a rampage. He burst through the bedroom door, completely shitfaced out of his mind, and I was immediately on edge, as I always am when he's around.

I had been reading in bed, so he crashed down next to me and plopped his head in my lap, breathing out a hard sigh. He smelled like a full-on brothel, prompting me to grit my teeth so hard they almost ground into dust.

Fuck you, disgusting pig!
I could find a man to fuck me too, you know? I don't need you or your charity dick.
You're the worst husband in the world, and soon I will leave your sorry ass.

"Do you want something to eat?" I forced myself to play the dutiful wife, in hopes that it could spare me any potential smacks he was looking to dole out. "I ordered chicken parm."

He turned his face upward and gazed at me, blue eyes glassed over in his drunken state.

"Why are you so good to me?" He rumbled, sounding like he was seriously asking.

"I don't know, Roger..." I sighed, because it was all I could do.

"I'm going to get better, you know..." his brows lifted slowly, his voice low and hoarse. "It's just a rough patch... Like, a disease or something."

My hands started shaking, and I felt the tears already threatening to burst from behind my eyes. I can deal with his asshole side. It's easy to hate him when he's hitting me and calling me a *worthless cunt*. I can pull a fake smile and know with absolute certainty that I will leave him someday soon, or die trying and be fine with it.

But when he shows his vulnerable side... When he gives me those big, sad eyes and speaks softly to me, like he had on the night he proposed... When he encompasses the Roger I fell in love with seven years ago, the one who most likely didn't exist, that's when I always break down. I can't handle it.

I'm not strong.

I'm broken...

"I will get help, Alexandra," he whispered, rolling over and climbing on top of me. He took my jaw in his hand, gently. Not like the monster in him does... "And I'll be the man you deserve. I swear, I can do it. For you..."

My eyes snapped shut as I shook my head over and over.

Why are you doing this? Just let me go...

"Stop..." I whimpered, tears rolling down my cheeks.

"Please don't leave me," he breathed, moving in as close as possible, until I could feel his warm, boozy breath over my trembling lips. "I need you."

He pushed his hips forward slowly, dragging his crotch against mine, and I had to actively stop thinking about all the other women he'd likely been with tonight... yesterday, the day before, or I'd become physically ill.

Roger took my forearms in his hands, holding them down hard on both sides of my hips. It hurt, but my body was numb.

Nothing could hurt the way my heart did as it pumped, despite all its open wounds.

"I know you could find someone better..." he grunted, writhing against me, the friction of him, long and hard between my thighs making me ache.

My stomach was churning, as it usually does when we fool around. I always feel a mixture of arousal and nausea when I sleep with my husband now. It doesn't feel *all* good... More like fifty-fifty.

Seek Me

"You could easily find a man who would treat you right, and not hurt you. But I... don't want you to..."

His hands curled around my arms, his thumbs digging hard into my flesh. It ached and throbbed, but I welcomed it. I needed the hurt to distract me from the sweetness in his words.

The empty promises and broken dreams.

His lips found mine, and I cried into his mouth while he held me down and made me come from simply rubbing himself against me.

A dream of *better* that would never come true.

This morning I woke up alone in bed, which was a relief.

Roger left early for some overnight business trip. He won't be back until tomorrow and I'm ecstatic. I'm going to a gallery today to check out a space for my first ever art show, happening in a few weeks. I think it could be really successful. The owner, Rafael, loves my work. It was only mildly humiliating that I couldn't take my sunglasses off during my first meeting with him...

Not that anyone would really care. I could be a dope fiend prostitute and it wouldn't make a difference to anyone in the art world, as long as my work sells.

So here I am. Freshly showered, dressed and ready to go. I hate to admit it, but I'm nervous. I want so badly for this to work out. My art is the only thing holding my life together right now.

I wish I had more than that, but it will have to do for now, Barn.

Say a little prayer for me. I'll try to write again later and let you know how it goes.

Chapter Sixteen

Alex

CHANGE IS ONE OF THE SCARIEST THINGS FOR SOME PEOPLE, and I never considered myself to be one of them.

But in the past two weeks, more things have changed in my life than in the last eight years. It's a lot to take on at once, and I can understand why certain people hate this so much...

None of these new changes are bad things, though. It's all stuff I need; moves I've been dreaming about making for years now. Ever since my knight in shining armor revealed himself to be a blue-eyed Satan.

And for years, following that revelation, I've been telling myself I'm going to get *out*. I'd spend hours lying awake at night thinking about it. Picturing myself leaving Roger and taking my life back. That feeling of weightless freedom was the ultimate high, and I promised myself someday I'd have it.

And now here I am. Standing in my new apartment, furnished with most of my belongings - some new stuff too, of course - divorce papers having been delivered to our place in the Upper East Side only moments ago.

And I'm hesitating.

I'm scared. Too much change.

Naturally my most rational fear at the moment would be my abusive husband murdering me. It's not an overreaction, given the events of that last two years. But outside of that, I'm also worried about this whole *divorce thing*.

What will my life be like without Roger? What if I miss him? What if he finds me? How will I paint without the fear?

That's probably the biggest one. I've been using the abuse for a lot of things, in order to survive. But what if it really is like a drug, and I need to detox?

So many stories of talented artists using actual drugs come to mind... *The music was better before he got clean. No junk, no soul.*

I'm praying the same won't be said about me. I couldn't bear to have Roger take this from me too. He's already taken damn near everything else.

Last week I saw a therapist for the first time. She's really sweet. Her name is

Dr. Rebecca. And as I expected, it felt truly serendipitous to speak to someone about everything I've been through. Other than Noah, I mean.

Don't get me wrong, talking to Noah is wonderful. He's the one who got me talking in the first place. He's my best friend, and the most supportive, caring person I've ever known. But every time I talk to him, I'm acutely aware that I want to screw his brains out.

I definitely don't feel that way about Dr. Rebecca. So it's a different dynamic.

Anyway, seeing the Doctor was exactly what I needed. I talked for the whole hour, straight through, and barely came up for air once. She listened and reinforced what I already knew: it's a life-or-death situation, and I need to get the hell out of there while I still can. But she also understood that it's not easy; not even a little. Leaving my husband after almost eight years of marriage isn't like tossing out a piece of furniture you've had for a couple months.

I know my heart still loves him because I can feel it, all the time. It's painful; as if I'm being stabbed, slowly and with precision. Like my heart is wrapped in barbed wire, and every single beat is laced with a singeing ache. That's how it feels to be in love with someone who does nothing but hurt me.

So Dr. Rebecca urged me to work quickly, but also at my own pace, which probably makes sense to no one but me. She also taught me everything there is to know about restraining orders, which is part of the plan now. I just know I'll need that peace of mind.

Everyone involved in my new apartment has been warned not to divulge any information about me to anyone asking. But even with that, and the restraining order, Roger could still find me. It happens all the time, and Roger's very powerful here in the city.

I'm trying not to worry about it too much, but it seems like worry has become a part of my daily routine.

Noah's already offered to stay with me the first couple nights here in the new place, with Jimmy and a few of his security buddies keeping watch. I want to tell them all they're overreacting, but the scary thing is that I don't think they are.

Roger had kept his word about showing me his *rehabilitated* side for a while. A bit longer than I predicted, but eventually he caved and let his anger out again. He hasn't hit me outright in a couple months, but he's definitely screamed at me, which is sufficiently terrifying, and grabbed me by the arm or hair.

I've refrained from telling Noah about this. I hate lying to my best friend - the guy I'm sleeping with, rather joyfully, I might add - but I think in this case it's necessary. I can tell it kills Noah inside when I go back to Roger. He's insistent on not *pushing* me or making me uncomfortable; on letting me find my way on my own. But I also know Noah. It hasn't been that long, but I know him pretty damn well at this point.

He keeps up his carefree persona with everyone else in the world. And yes, he uses it with me too. But there are moments here and there when it slips, and he lets me see his real feelings and emotions; his insecurities. And when this happens, I feel more special, more privileged than I ever have before. Noah showing me this side of himself, even if just for a split second by accident, is solidifying. It makes me feel like a different part of his world. Something more special, and dare I say, permanent?

Here's the other problem I've been dealing with lately... Dr. Rebecca has been asking me what life looks like for me in my mind after I leave Roger. Once the dust settles and I'm left living alone in my new place as an almost twenty-six-year-old divorcee.

I've been thinking a lot about this over the last couple weeks, while the paperwork was being prepared and the moving company Noah hired was helping me secretly sneak handfuls of my belongings out of Roger's home each day. At first it was like an impossible thing to visualize. What the hell would I do without Roger around, hitting me and keeping me as his little pet?

But then, slowly, I was able to picture it.

Obviously I would paint. I'll never stop painting, or drawing, or taking pictures. Whatever sparks me creatively, I know there's no way it'll just end because Roger's gone. After all, I'm sure he'll live on in my memories and nightmares, another reason seeing Dr. Rebecca on the regular will, I'm sure, be very important.

And then it started coming together. I could see me *living*. Throwing myself into my work, visiting with gallery owners, lunching with my new art friends, attending exhibits for other local artists. The life I was meant to have... It could be mine.

It will be mine.

And Noah. Our best-friends-with-benefits relationship works better than any other relationship I've ever had. We're so perfect together, I just know that as soon as Roger's out of the picture we'll easily slip into a real relationship.

It scares me almost as much as the idea of finally leaving.

Noah has been perfect, but I can tell sometimes he's in over his head. I don't know much about his past relationships, if you could even call them that, which I wouldn't. But from what I've picked up on, I think whatever it is we're doing might just be the longest relationship Noah Richards has ever had.

It's crazy, but then also not because I've never been with anyone other than Roger either. It's like we're two people completely ill-equipped to ever date anyone, let alone each other. But even thinking about not having Noah in my life makes me physically sick. I have no clue where I'd be without him. I might even be dead...

Still, falling into the boyfriend-girlfriend routine with Noah just because it's easy, and it feels right for now isn't a good idea. I know it's not, and I'm sure he does, too.

Noah has been acting a little weird lately, anyway. I know he's anxious for me to have the final showdown with Roger and get the fuck out of there hopefully unscathed - physically, anyway. But also his jumpy behavior leads me to believe that it's getting a little too serious for him. I wouldn't blame him if he felt that way.

The thought of escaping an abusive eight-year marriage and jumping immediately into a relationship with a celebrity manwhore makes me want to flee the country...

I shake my head and rub my temples. This is too much change... Too much *everything*.

I can do it, though. I'm not backing down just because it's scary. That's not me.

The thing that really sucks is that Noah and I are so damn good together. Sleeping with your best friend, when done right, seems to be the most blissful experience of all time. The problem is, though, that the blinding happiness never lasts. There's no way I can expect to turn Noah Richards into a boyfriend over the span of five months. He's hard-wired differently. It's not his fault, but the last thing I want to be is someone who tried to settle him down and failed, thus sufficiently ruining our perfect friendship.

I can't do that. And I won't. I just need to figure out what my new-life-picture looks like when it comes to Noah Richards.

Ringing chimes from inside my coat pocket and I practically jump out of my skin. My heart instantly races in my chest, so hard it hurts, as I tug the chirping device out slowly, expecting, and dreading, Roger's name on the screen.

I let out a heavy sigh of relief when instead I see my friend Evan's name. Evan works at one of the galleries interested in showing my next collection. He visited my last exhibit, and we instantly clicked.

I swipe to answer the call with a smile. "Well hello, darling."

"Miss Alexandra," his smooth, luxurious voice travels through the phone. "I have something very exciting for you."

"And what would that be?" I ask while traipsing slowly through my new hallway which adjoins my living room and home office. *This apartment is awesome. Hashtag blessed.*

"A friend of mine from SoHo District just called me," Evan goes on. "They have an opening for their eighteen-month art program in, get this... Budapest!" He makes an excited squealing noise and I freeze in place.

A what in where now?!

"An art program?" The words crawl from my throat.

"Yes! Remember when you told me you've always wanted to do one? Well, this one is incredible! They put you up in a luxury condo and you get to travel between Budapest and Prague, working with some of the most renowned artists in Eastern Europe! It's fantastic! Naturally once I mentioned your name, they were all jazzed up."

"Eighteen-months?" Is the only thing I can say while still processing all this new information.

My eyes are so wide I can feel them popping out of my head.

He's right. I've always dreamed of doing an art program or fellowship in another country. Traveling more is definitely part of my new-life-Alex picture. The only times I've traveled before were with Roger, and I'm dying to make new, exciting memories to erase those ones.

But eighteen-months is a really long time...

Could I really pick up and leave New York...?

The fact that Noah is the first thing popping into my head when I think about leaving makes me so uncomfortable, I'm worried I may collapse. We always agreed that we'd remain friends and keep whatever it is we're doing *casual*. Me leaving for eighteen-months would solidify the casualness for sure. Noah Richards isn't exactly the long-distance relationship type.

He's not the any relationship type, Al. Because he's a bachelor. And you two aren't dating.

I rake my fingers through my hair and tug at the roots, hard.

"Yes, the program is eighteen-months, but it's in *Hungary*, Alex," Evan uses his exaggerated tone to emphasize his point. "Your husband travels for work all the time, so you should too! Plus, he could come to stay with you, I'm sure -"

"Can I get back to you?" I cut him off, not wanting to get into all *that*.

Seek Me

"You'd need to let me know right away. They'll only hold this spot for me until the end of the month. It's a very coveted program. Lots of applicants. But they want *you*, my dear. So think about it, 'kay?"

I gulp over my dry throat as my phone slips in my sweaty palm. I nod, though he can't see me.

"Yes. Sure. I'll let you know soon."

"Please do. Kisses!" Then he hangs up, leaving me standing in my new apartment, facing even more changes than my fragile spirit can comprehend.

"Fuck…" I whisper to myself, and my phone buzzes.

I peek at it slowly, fearing Roger's name once more.

It's a text from Noah.

Fuck…

Noah: Hey sexy! Just checking in… Wanted to make sure you're doing good.

Noah: Let me know how everything goes. I'll be over tonight just text me when<3

I stare at his messages as tears push from behind my eyes. My bottom lip quivers and I chomp it, because this show of emotions is unnecessary.

We're *friends*. We've always been friends, over anything else. And I know that if I want to take this art program and leave for eighteen months, he'd be nothing but supportive.

Right…?

Of course he would. This is *Noah* we're talking about. He's the sweetest person I've ever known in my whole life.

So why would I want to leave that behind for over a year?

I shake my head, blinking back the tears.

It's not about that. I can't be Noah's girlfriend. I can't be anyone's girlfriend right now. I'm getting divorced and getting over the tragedy of the last eight years of my life. The only relationship that should concern me is the one I have with myself.

This is all too much stress for right now. I need a distraction.

I type out a quick message to Noah so I can settle in my new studio and maybe paint for a while. That will take my mind off all these changes…

Me: I'm good, thanks. I haven't heard from him yet but Jimmy is still waiting downstairs… I feel bad about him sitting out there all day tho. Just saying…

Noah: Don't feel bad baby. He's being paid handsomely and trust me when I tell you he cares about you a great deal. He just wants you safe and happy. As do I.

My heart lurches in my chest and I pout.

Me: You're very sweet. Both of you. I'll need to buy him a gift.

Noah: Lol. You're so cute.

Me: So are you ;) I'm going to paint for a bit. I'll text you soon :-*

My phone buzzes once more and I expect some sweet or dirty reply from Noah, my smile already growing.
Until I realize that the new message is not in his thread.
All the hairs on the back of my neck stand up.

Roger: Come home. Now.

Suddenly I'm so scared my hands are trembling and I feel like I might lose control of my bladder.
He got the papers. Oh God oh fuck.
This is it.
My stomach is twisting so aggressively I could gag, and I'm finding it hard to breathe. I try pulling air deep into my lungs and hold onto it, closing my eyes tight.
It's okay. This is happening. You have Jimmy with you. You'll be fine.

Me: He just texted me to come home. Noah I'm so scared.

My phone rings almost instantly.
"Babe?"
"First off, breathe for me, baby," Noah's deep, calming voice slinks inside me and it's uncanny how instantly calmer I feel just from hearing him. It's like I'm crumbling, but he's holding me together in his strong, tattooed hands. "You're fine. Everything is alright."
I breathe in deep and hold it, then exhale a shaky release, focusing on his words.

"You're so fucking strong, Alexandra Mackenzie. You're a goddamned badass."

I chuckle through my unsteady breaths because he's just the most amazing person on Earth. *How could I ever leave him?*

I cringe. *Don't think about that right now. One intense thing at a time.*

"You okay, baby? Talk to me," Noah pleads. I'm surprised by how sexy he sounds even when we're talking about very unsexy stuff.

"I'm okay, I'm just..." my voice gives out and I shake my head. "This is terrifying."

"He's not going to hurt you, Alex," Noah says with confidence. "Jimmy can handle him. And he knows to call the police right away if things get too intense. *His* police, not Roger's police."

I'm pacified by this because we've all talked about it at length. Roger is connected, but he's not above the law. Noah and Jimmy assured me that they know exactly who to go to so Roger can't have his cop buddies cover anything up for him.

"What are you going to do?" Noah asks and I stay quiet in thought for a moment.

"I'm going over there," I finally sigh, straightening my shoulders. "I'm going to get the rest of my things and end this, once and for all."

"That's my girl," Noah rumbles and I just wish he was here right now. I want to hug him and kiss him; have him wrap his big arms around me and take away all the bad stuff.

"I'll text you when I'm done," I whisper, fighting back tears from all the emotions bombarding my system.

"I can't wait to see you." I can picture his dark eyes shimmering at me as he says this. It fills me with warmth. And strength.

"Bring weed," I squeak, and he laughs.

Fifteen minutes of pacing around my apartment later, I'm downstairs and Jimmy is already out of the Navigator, greeting me and opening the door.

He gives me an expectant look before I hop into the backseat and I return it with a firm nod.

"It's time."

I settle in the vehicle, remembering to breathe as Jimmy climbs into the driver's seat and we pull away, heading to the Upper East Side of Manhattan. To my home which will no longer be my home after tonight.

The whole thing is so surreal. I think back to leaving Brooklyn, almost eight years ago. When I left my home to move in with my new husband, after having said goodbye to my parents for good.

I wonder what they would think about what my life has become. I'm sure they'd gloat. Tell me they knew I was making a horrible decision, and that I'm a silly, foolish, impulsive girl.

Which is why I don't care that they're no longer in my life. Despite the train wreck my marriage became, I don't regret leaving. It brought me to where I am now; realizing my worth, overcoming my obstacles and following my dreams. Sure, it took some horrible stuff to get me here, but I've also grown immensely.

I refuse to let anyone make me feel bad anymore. Not my parents. Not Roger.

No one will stop Alex Mackenzie from flourishing in this world.

And with that thought, I'm ready to face my husband. *Soon to be ex...*

"Jimmy?" I creak through the haze filling my mind.

"Yes, ma'am?"

"Thank you for doing this."

Our eyes meet in the rearview mirror. "No thanks necessary, Ms. Mackenzie. I hope you know I'm happy to help you with anything... And not just because I'm being paid to. Quite frankly, I'd do it for free."

"I know you would," I murmur, watching through the window as we zip over the bridge. "But I appreciate it, nonetheless. If I may, though... Ask you one more favor..."

"Anything."

"Whatever happens in there," I pause and swallow hard. "Whatever ends up happening... Please, I beg of you... Don't let me stay."

Jimmy's mouth opens, but I keep going. "No matter what I say to you... No matter how much I beg, or tell you things that sound sincere. I'm asking you... I'm *telling* you, right here and now. No matter what I say to you in there, *do not* leave without me. Please."

My eyes fill with tears as I stare up at the front of the car. Jimmy's are wide, and they bounce up to mine in between watching the road.

"Ms. Mackenzie, you have my word," he mutters, softly but with more assurance than I've ever heard before in a tone. He's very serious, and it's placating.

I blink and nod.

And we say nothing more for the rest of the drive.

Seek Me

When Jimmy and I enter the lobby to Roger's building, Javi is sitting behind the desk. He looks up and smiles when he sees me, but it fades a bit when his eyes dart to Jimmy. There's a realization in them, and he looks pleased, but sad, which makes me sad in return.

I step up to the desk and give him a weak smile. For obvious reasons, I'd refrained from telling anyone in the building about me leaving Roger. But I know they were picking up on it, since people have been covertly moving a couple items of mine out of the co-op each day for the past two weeks.

I didn't like keeping things from the building staff, because as sad as it sounds, they'd become my only friends over the last seven years. But of course I couldn't risk someone accidentally mentioning something to Roger.

Although being here now, and seeing the dismal look on Javi's face, who is by far my favorite doorman ever, I'm wishing I'd given him some advanced notice to my departure.

"Hey, Javi," I whisper. He puts down his iPad.

"Good evening, Ms. Mackenzie," his head cocks and he takes a breath. "So… This is it, huh?"

I nod slowly. "Thanks for all you've done for me."

"I should've done more…" he grunts, his tone oozing remorse.

"It wasn't your place," I tell him with confidence. "This is my life, and I'm taking it back. Finally."

Now it's his turn to nod. "Good luck to you, Alex. I wish you all the best in your new life."

I smile, unable to help the tears forming. I'm already such a mess and we're just getting started.

"I'll miss you, Javi. You were always my favorite." I wink at him and he chuckles.

I turn with Jimmy and we make our way in silence to the elevator.

The longest elevator ride of my life. Honestly, I never noticed just how long it takes to get up to our floor until now, with each second lasting an eternity. And yet I'm grasping at them, struggling to hold on because I'm dreading what happens next.

I'm so scared my knees are shaking, heart pounding against my ribs as we exit the elevator and I use my key to open the front door.

The co-op is quiet and dark. It's not unusual, but for some reason right now it's like I'm in a horror movie. The silence inside is deafening. And not that I expected utter bedlam when I walked in, but everything is just so *still*. I'm also now noticing how this entire place looks like a picture. Nothing ever moves.

It's not until I reach the kitchen that I spot the one difference.

The divorce papers. They're sitting on the marble island in a perfect, neat little stack. I don't need to look at them to know they haven't been signed.

I shoot Jimmy a look, which he returns, though his is much more stern and prepared. He's ready, whereas I resemble a scared little kid. At least that's how I imagine I must look.

We make our way quietly to the bedroom because that's where the rest of my things are that I need to get. I'm not even taking all my clothes with me, because that would require too much obvious packing, but I have a couple bags stashed in the back of my closet. Those bags have been ready and waiting to be packed for years, and it's crazy to think they're finally getting out of here. We all are.

This is it. Man up, Mackenzie. We're getting the fuck out.

Roger's not in the bedroom which prompts my sigh of relief as I rush to my things, grabbing them quick, along with a few other items I wanted to take; some jewelry, a few of my old concert t-shirts and my journal.

Jimmy carries my bags for me, and we turn to leave the room. We make it through the hall before I hear footsteps descending the stairs from my studio.

I squeeze my eyes shut tight and breathe.

"Your studio's empty," Roger's deep, ominous voice cuts through the silence of the wide open space. "When did that happen?"

I spin in place to face him, gulping over the saliva filling my mouth as if I'm preparing to vomit.

Once my eyes find his I freeze, like a deer in headlights. His bright blue irises twinkle in the low light, though the rest of him is cast in shadows. I'm not sure that I ever truly noticed how scary he is until right now.

His head flicks in Jimmy's direction, though his hardened gaze remains locked on me. "Who's this?"

I know I need to speak, but my voice won't cooperate. My entire body has shut down. It's gone on strike, and I'm just standing here, gaping at my violent sociopath husband like a frightened child, which is fitting since that's how he's always made me feel.

Seek Me

"Alexandra..." his tone is warning as he takes a small step closer. Jimmy instinctively puts the bags down on the floor, a movement which seems to have caught Roger's attention. He narrows his gaze at Jimmy for a moment, then comes right back to me. "We need to talk about this. About... those papers."

"Roger..." Finally my voice makes a comeback, but it's so small and timid I'm not sure he even heard me.

"Is this some kind of joke, Alex?" He begins to seethe, though he's still eerily quiet, like a rattlesnake, coiled and waiting to strike. "Seven years of marriage and this is how you treat your husband? Having some papers sent to me... As if what we have is *nothing*?"

He takes a few more steps, but before he can approach me, Jimmy moves in.

"That's close enough," Jimmy's voice, while remaining low and even, seems to boom through the room like thunder. I've never heard him so intimidating before.

And now I'm just standing here, watching the two of them, both several feet taller than me, feeling even smaller and more like a child.

"Who the hell are you, anyway?" Roger lifts a brow. "Are you fucking my wife?"

My blood boils at the obvious jab. Jimmy's old enough to be my father. Maybe even closer to my grandfather, because I'm not sure how old he is, but he might be in his mid or late fifties.

Jimmy scoffs, but my husband keeps going. "I'm not sure if you noticed, but she likes older men. Rich ones, too, so I wouldn't put it past her to slink into some unsuspecting old fool's bank account."

Okay. Fuck that. Now I'm pissed.

"Roger, stop," I summon all my inner courage and square my shoulders. "I've come to collect the rest of my things. Let's not kid ourselves anymore. This is over. So just do the respectable thing, sign the divorce papers and let's move on."

"Move on?" He barks and I flinch. "Alexandra, you're my *wife*. I'm not signing any ridiculous papers. Now, tell your friend here to leave us. We need to talk about this."

"We're well past talking, Roger," I huff. "It's over. Sign the divorce papers so we can avoid bringing this to trial. I know you don't want that..."

"What I want is *you*!" He roars, stepping forward again. Jimmy moves in front of me like a shield, but Roger continues to yell around him. "You're not leaving, Alex! You're going to stay here and we're going to work through this. Like adults."

"Adults?!" I shriek, side-stepping so I can glare in his eyes. "Roger, you've been beating the shit out of me for years! Fucking other women... Tons of them! Fucking thousands, for all I know. Jesus Christ, what kind of person would stay with you after that?"

He pales and for a moment he looks taken aback. He blinks a few times, as if what I'm saying is a complete shock. It's so ludicrous it makes me want to laugh.

"Alexandra... I love you," his soft voice makes an appearance and my stomach twists into a hard knot. This is the part I can't deal with... The fake compassion he uses to remind me of the man I fell in love with. "Don't do this, sweetheart. Please... You're my soulmate."

My head shakes over and over. "No... I'm not! I'm your fucking chew toy, Roger! I'm your punching bag. You've been using me since day one, and I just can't do it anymore. I deserve better. I don't deserve -" My voice cracks and I swallow repeatedly, begging my body not to cry in front of him. "*No one deserves to be treated the way you've treated me. No one.*"

"This is fucking bullshit. Alex, I made a mistake. I told you I was sorry... I thought we were going to work on it!" He keeps trying to get around Jimmy, but Jimmy's really blocking him, and I keep backing up.

"This isn't something that can be worked out, Roger," I sigh, defeated. "You're sick. You need help."

"Fine! Okay, fine. I'll get help," he grunts, grating his hands over his face. "We can go see a counselor. I'll find a doctor, or a psychiatrist... fucking whatever. Anything you want, Alex, please..."

I cover my eyes and tremble. *No. No no no no no... No, don't listen to him. Stay strong.*

"Alexandra, I love you. I know you love me. Please don't do this."

Stop.

Tears stream down my face, but I refuse to look at him. I can't see him right now. I'm so afraid my stupid heart will cave. I won't let it. I can't let myself give into him again. I'm not going back.

I'm. Not. Fucking. Going. Back.

"Alexandra! You are not fucking leaving me!" He bellows, his voice so loud it echoes off the walls. "I'm not letting you go!"

"It's not up to you!" I scream at the top of my lungs, releasing my eyes and

Seek Me

aiming my flaming gaze right at him. "*I choose to leave! This is my choice! I. Choose. It.*"

"Like fucking hell, you stupid cunt!"

Roger lunges at me. And without a single hesitation Jimmy reacts, and punches him right in the face.

Whoa.

My eyes widen.

It was loud. Something definitely broke...

It was like a crunching noise. That was wild.

Roger falls to the floor, gripping his nose, which is now bleeding all over the place. My adrenaline is jacked up so high I'm vibrating. But all I can do is stare down at my husband's large body, shaking on the floor as blood trickles from beneath his hand.

I wait a beat to see if he'll attempt to get up and fight back. Jimmy is clearly on high-alert. But Roger just stays at our feet, hunched over. He looks broken. I've never seen him like this before, and I wish I could say it's satisfying, but it's not. It's excruciatingly exhausting.

The last eight years just hit me, like Jimmy's fist to Roger's face. All the adrenaline has vanished in an instant and I'm so tired I can barely stand up anymore.

"Come on, Ms. Mackenzie," Jimmy says firmly. "Let's go."

"Alex, please..." Roger speaks again, though now his voice is ragged and pained. "Don't go. I need you. Please stay. I'll do anything... We can have a baby. We can do whatever you want. Just... don't... leave... me."

My heart snaps right now the middle. Inside my chest is bleeding, just as much as his likely broken nose. My heart is such a betraying bitch, I hate it with a fiery passion, because it actually wants me to stay with this asshole.

No. Stop. Don't even fucking think about it.

I peek up at Jimmy, mirroring the look I gave him in the car earlier. And he knows, without words, that I'm pleading with him to get me the fuck out of here before I ruin everything; all the hard work I've done getting myself ready for this.

All I've put into this fight.

Jimmy's eyes bore into me, saying so much without words. He picks up my bags.

"Alex," he mutters, in a tone that's firm while also pleading. His eyes are wide as he begs me not to give in with this one powerful look.

And I use every ounce of strength I have inside me to turn away from Roger and all his broken promises. And leave.

Roger's screaming and cursing at me is the last thing I hear as we exit the apartment.

Passing the threshold, I feel invisible chains and shackles falling from my body.

Inside the elevator, I feel them releasing my heart.

In the lobby, as I wave goodbye to Javi with tears and makeup staining my cheeks, I'm free.

And it doesn't feel glorious. It doesn't feel like a high; my heart doesn't soar with its newfound freedom. It feels painful and etched in sorrow.

But once I'm tucked securely in the car, heading back to my new home, I smile.

My insides are torn and broken; my heart more bruised and battered than my body ever was. But I'm smiling in repose because this is me. I'm finally Alex again, for the first time in my adult life. I'm victorious.

I won the fight.

I wake in the middle of the night from the sounds of screaming.

It turns out they were just in my head. Or in my dreams...

I'm panting, dragging air into my lungs with fervor as I blink in the dark.

A soft, warm hand runs across my naked stomach.

"You okay?" Noah's deep voice asks from behind me, raspy from just having woken out of a sleep more sound than my own, apparently.

"Mhm," I nod quickly, taking his hand in mine and wriggling myself up to him, nestling deeper beneath the covers in my bed.

"Not a convincing performance, baby," he murmurs, smooshing his hard, muscle-clad torso against my back. "I'm an actor, so I can say things like that."

I giggle out a soft sigh as my breathing regulates and I allow his calming heartbeat to rap on my shoulder blade. He's so warm, and his skin is so soft. Naked cuddling with Noah has to be my favorite thing ever, especially when I'm recovering from a particularly harrowing evening.

True to his word, Noah was waiting for me at my apartment when I got back from my final interaction with my soon-to-be ex-husband. Seeing his sweet face light up with pride when I got out of the car had me bursting into more tears I didn't even know were possible to produce. We stood there hugging for minutes on end until finally he took my bags from Jimmy and we adjourned to my new place.

Jimmy stayed outside in the car for a while until his friend, another security gentleman who's apparently an ex-Marine, came to relieve him of his watch duties. I tell you, if I was feeling even the slightest bit worried about Roger potentially coming to murder me, it's all completely gone now, what with Noah and his band of bodyguards here to protect me.

Let's get this straight. In no way am I saying I *need* or rely on these people for safety. I'm a strong woman, and I know I can damn-well take care of myself. But unfortunately the facts are the facts. Roger is very well-connected in this city, and he's a large man. So the idea of staying alone, especially after how terribly he took the divorce papers, was scarier than I'd care to admit.

If having this protection lets me get even a little rest, then I'll accept it, graciously.

So Noah and I spent the rest of the night relaxing. We smoked a joint, ordered Chinese takeout and watched reruns of all our favorite old shows. I passed out on his lap on the couch and woke up to him carrying me into my bedroom, which was adorable. He undressed me, then himself and we climbed into my new bed to spoon until we both fell into an easy sleep, which yes, was interrupted by my creepy nightmare.

But even more startling than that was Noah and me cuddling naked together without having sex. I know he just wants to keep me calm and help me feel safe while I deal with this extremely difficult process. But us not fucking makes it feel so much more serious than I know it's intended.

The even scarier part is how much I like it.

Being with Noah like this feels right, and it has ever since that first time we fell asleep cuddling in his bed a few months back. I mean sure, tonight he was rubbing his erection on me a little as we knocked out. But he always does that, and I absolutely never want him not to. It's almost my favorite part of cuddling with him. Well, that and how generally wonderful it feels to have his big, strong body with that smooth tattooed skin wrapping me up like a sexy blanket.

I hum out an easy noise as Noah nuzzles the nape of my neck with his soft lips and warm breath, perking my nipples up against the cozy comforter. His hand holds my waist, keeping me close and I register that his hard-on is feeling awfully rigid against the curve of my ass.

Nyla K

A breath slips out of me in the form of a gasp because as it would seem, the more his hips gently rock behind mine, the more his dick wedges itself in between my butt cheeks. It's purely divine, and while I know Noah isn't here to fool around - he's here to comfort me in my time of need, because he's a wonderful friend - it would certainly feel fantastic, and take my mind off the horribleness I had to endure earlier.

"You wanna tell me about your dream?" His voice purrs on my flesh, probably not intending to sound sexual, but I'm a bit wound up and craving him right now, so everything he says and does is going to turn me on. "You know you can... if you want..."

"I don't really remember it much," I whisper, scooting my butt back to him until he grunts. "I just remember feeling scared."

"I'll never let anything bad happen to you," he tells me with quiet certainty. And I believe him.

Why it's so easy for me to believe the things Noah says after all the hurt I've experienced from another man seems like something I should question, but I don't. Sure, Roger was pure evil dressed in an expensive suit, and he lured me into his web only to devour my soul later on. And I suppose Noah could be doing the exact same thing. How would I know, after all? He's an actor. They're probably pretty good at lying, I imagine.

But if we're being honest, there were immediate signs with Roger, all of which were ignored by my naive, love-struck teenage mind. Every warning that I can now see as plain as day was there from the moment I met him. And Noah Richards has exhibited none of those traits or behaviors. In fact, Noah seems to be the polar opposite of Roger in just about every way.

Still, that doesn't mean I should let my guard down. I'm not sure I'll ever be able to fully let it go after Roger. But with Noah, I need to guard myself from *my* feelings, rather than from *him*. Noah won't be the one to hurt me. I'll be hurting myself if I let the new and improved Alex fall for him hard and fast like she seems content to.

Maybe it's time to stop thinking for a bit...

I need a physical distraction from all the madness happening in my head. And I know the perfect place to get it.

I bend more at the waist, allowing that sturdy length to wedge itself between my ass. My arousal is dripping out of me, making a river of available lubrication for whatever his big, juicy dick wants to do.

"Mmmm... Noah," I hum his name because I love saying it, and he exhales a rough breath by my ear.

"You shouldn't let me do this…" he sounds like seductive mischief and it's hotter than my vagina can handle. "I want it *too* bad." His fingers trace a line up and down my thigh.

"I want it too," I pant, my lust-filled mind clouding me from thinking about anything other than the most filthy acts I'm craving. And it's so good.

No thinking. Just doing.

"Jesus, baby, you're gushing." There's some minute shock in his tone, but more awe than anything. "Do you want to be bad?"

I moan softly and grab his hand, bringing it between my thighs. "I love bad with you."

He growls and swirls his index and middle fingers around on my clit, rubbing tremors of pleasure through my belly. His dick is so full and thick it's wondrous, and judging by the wetness now on my lower back, I think he's *really* excited for whatever we're playing at, too.

"Fuck… Alex…" he rumbles into me from behind, using his arm to hold my body to his, toying with my nipple ring while his other fingers toy with my clit. "Tell me to stop now or I won't be able to."

The smooth crown of his cock slides over my forbidden area and it makes my spine tingle. If I said I've never done this before I'd be a liar, so I don't really have as many reservations as you'd think, although Noah's dick is the biggest that's ever been near that spot, which is only a little frightening. But clearly not enough to keep me from grinding into him even harder.

"Don't stop, baby," I say in what sounds like a plea.

Noah's breathing is harsh. I love the sound. It tells me he's so turned on he's about to burst, for me. *Mine.*

"I don't um…" he stops to groan out this gorgeous noise that spreads the burning below my waist into wildfire. "Do you have… lube? Or… something… fuck…"

I whimper and keep guiding his hand on my pussy, petting myself with his fingers until I'm quivering in anticipation.

"I don't know that we'd need it," I gasp when he tugs my nipple. "I'm so wet, it's everywhere…"

"I know," he moans and bites my shoulder. "It's awesome."

"Fuck me, Noah… Please get inside me before I die." *God… I want this so bad, it's unhealthy.*

"Don't die," he mumbles, pushing himself up to me until I instinctively clench. "I should get a condom though…"

"No don't stop," I whine in desperation, the three words coming out like one.

"I've never done that before," his voice cracks, which for some reason is even hotter, and now both of our bodies are stifling and sweaty. And we've barely gotten started.

"So then it's not a problem," I turn my face enough to catch his lips.

I kiss him and he practically melts into me, kissing me soft yet eager, trapping my lower lip between his to suck me greedy. I give him my tongue and he teases it with his, releasing hungry gasps in between kissing me with more raw desire than I've ever felt before.

"Alex," he breathes, running his slippery fingers back from my pussy to where his dick is waiting, anxiously ready to enter me. I can feel it coated in wetness, and I'm stunned that my body is able to produce the equivalent of a mini bottle of KY.

"Yes… Noah… please…"

"Stop begging or I'm gonna come in two seconds."

"*I'm* gonna come in two seconds."

"No way… This needs to last… *Fuck*, I want this forever."

My chest tightens at his words, my stomach fluttering in excitement and nerves and everlasting swoon for this big, gorgeous, hard-bodied man. In this moment, I think I want Noah Richards more than I want to breathe. *He* has become my oxygen.

Holding me tight, he glides the head of his cock over my entrance, kissing my back, my neck, my lips; everywhere. Then he gives a gentle push as I force myself to relax despite my insides clenching from how fucking good it all feels.

"Slow…" he whispers, tracing my lower lip with his tongue.

"Slow," I repeat, gripping the sheets in my fist.

He forces himself a little more, still so easy I find myself welcoming the intrusion much faster than I thought I would. That smooth, round ridge breaks through and it burns, but in the best possible way. I can't even control my voice box, and I yelp out some curse word mixed with his name.

"Sorry… does that… hurt…?" He sounds like he's falling apart already and it drives me to push back against him to take more. "Alex! God holy fuck, what are you doing to me…"

"Noah… mmmm so good…" I have no idea what I'm saying, but this is the most incredible feeling ever invented and I can't think.

Seek Me

He thrusts in deeper, moving his hand back around to play with my clit while his long dick feeds into me so slow from behind, I can barely comprehend what's happening.

All I know is that we're moving together, like one person; one body, one heartbeat.

Noah's more on top of me now, his weight pinning me to the mattress, his hands stroking my pussy, teasing my nipples, grazing my throat. He's touching me all over and it's ruining me. His cock finally makes it all the way inside and he just stays there for a beat. He doesn't even need to move. I can feel his balls where we're joined, and the orgasm is already about to sweep me up into a giant cloud of pleasure.

But then he pulls back. Only a little. Then thrusts. And moves out. Then thrusts again. I'm so fucking full I don't know what to do with myself, and Noah's grunting and panting, praising me with sounds.

He drills into me, slow and deep, unlike anything I've ever experienced; revering and passionate. He pulls himself up a bit and I feel his shaggy hair tickle my back while he grabs my ass and fucks it in the most dedicated strokes, it's like we were made for this.

"You look so fucking good, baby," he growls while moving in me. "This is euphoric."

"Noah… fuck me…"

He holds my body as I bow to him, his tongue tracing my spine until I scream his name. I'm about to explode. I'm dizzy and we're surrounded by hazy, sensual air made of breaths and erotic noise.

Then he slips two fingers inside my pussy, pressing on something that makes me whimper out loud.

"Feel it, baby," he moans, giving himself to me so deep I black out.

And then I come. Hard.

Harder than I've ever come in my life.

I cry out his name with tears seeping from my eyes while I quake down to my core. My body rocks itself like an earthquake, inner walls clamping on his fingers, drenching everything in the general vicinity. The feeling is so sublime I never want it to stop. And it almost doesn't. I'm climaxing for so long my limbs are numb.

Meanwhile, Noah is breaking down. I can feel him shaking with me, his hips bucking into me while he grips me for dear life.

"Alex! Fuck fuck Alex I'm gonna come," he groans, all ready to pull out which sends me into a panic.

"Come inside me," I demand, barely registering my words. All I know is that I'm still coming and treasuring this feeling and he better not make it stop yet.

"What...?" He gasps, but this is no time for talking, because he's coming too and I can feel his dick swell inside me, giving me aftershocks like a million little bonus orgasms. "Alex... fuck I'm... God... Yes!"

Yessss...

Noah growls out all kinds of jumbled words as his dick erupts inside me. He's barely even moving anymore; just trembling and gently rocking into me as he comes, still holding my pussy, his warm palm covering my clit and accentuating my bliss. I swear to God, I never knew an orgasm could be like this. It's an everlasting divinity coursing through my body; like fire and ice. I've been soaring for what feels like hours.

Eventually Noah collapses on top of me, basically smothering me into the mattress. But it feels good. His weight on me right now is comforting. And he's holding me so tight, it really is like we're one.

He pulls out of me gently, massaging my butt and thighs with his strong hands while we just lie there, him covering me, breaths flying in and out of his lungs like gusts of wind. His heart is leaping against my back and despite the fact that I think I'm crying, I smile so wide I think my lips might fall off.

That was... the best sex... of my life.

After several minutes of panting in the dark, he speaks. "How can it possibly feel like that?"

He kisses my neck and my jaw, rolling his weight off a bit, but hugging me into his chest.

"I never knew it could..." I rasp, my voice completely shot.

Then he shifts again, so he's looking down at me, his face visibly flushed even in the low light, eyes dark and shining at me, sex hair all mussed up and crazy. He looks so gorgeous I could openly weep, though I force myself not to.

"You're the most beautiful thing I've ever known," he whispers with nothing shy of pure astonishment in his voice as his fingers play with the strands of my long, tangled hair.

And we stare at each other for a moment, basking in the afterglow of the most fantastic sex either of us ever knew we could have. And the connection.

I don't doubt that I could do, or maybe even have done, what we just did with someone else, and it wouldn't even scratch the surface of what just happened with Noah and me. I don't know how it's possible, but together we make magic, and not just with the stupefying sex.

It's *us*. Noah plus Alex equals perfection.

And suddenly my heart aches in my chest because I know I can't keep this man. I can't hold on to this high until I smother it. I never want to ruin this one.

So rather than letting myself go where I know I will if we keep looking at each other in the dark like this, I grab his face and kiss him. We kiss for minutes on end so we don't have to worry about words trying to sneak out and destroy us.

When we finally pull apart, breathless and dizzy, I smile up at him and say, "Let's take a shower."

And he smiles back at me and nods. "Lead the way, baby."

Chapter Seventeen
Alex's Journal

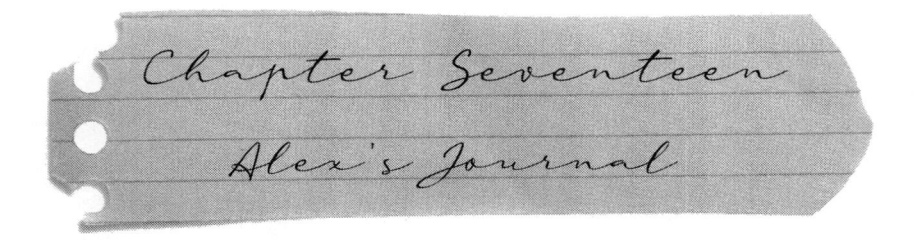

WELCOME HOME, BARN! I CAN'T BELIEVE WE MADE IT!

I would have written sooner, but my life has been a whirlwind lately, and for once it's all good stuff.

I know. Trust me, I'm just as shocked as you are.

Let me give you the scoop on the last three months.

I left Roger and moved into my new place in Greenpoint. And it's awesome. I truly love my new apartment, mostly because it's *mine*. I no longer feel like a guest in my own home because this home is all me. Alex's world.

After that night, the final showdown with Roger, he signed the divorce papers. But I know he only did it to avoid the scandal of going to trial and having me up there giving a testimony of his years of abuse and infidelity. Regardless, the story somehow broke and Roger lost his job.

He started calling me nonstop, leaving threatening voicemails, so I changed my number and took out a restraining order against him. I'm not sure if he knows where I live now, but I haven't seen him since that night. All the divorce stuff was done through our lawyers. Last I heard, he moved back home to Connecticut.

I don't know, and I don't care.

I'm done with that part of my life. I'm done with *him*. For good.

Of course I'll never forget about Roger. I'll never forget what he did to me, and everything he put me through. But my life now is more about moving on and healing. I have to say, it feels better than I ever imagined it could.

I've been seeing Dr. Rebecca once a week. She's helped me get out my emotions and piece back together my sanity. Well, her and my friends.

That's right, Barnaby. I actually have *friends*! Plural! Mostly people I've met in the art community, but they're awesome and cool, and we go out for brunches on Sunday mornings at Five Leaves, sipping mimosas and chatting about art and books and how much we either loved or hated so-and-so's latest exhibit. It's exactly the dream I had for myself since I was young. What I always knew my

Seek Me

life would look like.

As charming and hip as my new friends are, there's still one main person I prefer to spend most of my time with. And that's Noah Richards.

It's crazy that I actually haven't written to you about Noah yet, Barn. It seems bizarre to think about a time in my life when Noah wasn't around, though we've only known each other for about nine months. But still, he's become such a massive part of my world, it's hard to see any of it without him.

And recently, I've been feeling troubled by this.

Don't get me wrong, Noah is perfect. He's sweet, and funny, and sexy. And when I'm with him, everything is an adventure. I don't think I truly knew what fun was until I met Noah Richards.

The problem is that our friends-with-benefits relationship, while awesome, is seeming much less casual than when we first started it. I'm divorced now, and we don't need to sneak around anymore, which just makes it feel all the more like an actual relationship. And I love it... Deep down, I love it so much it scares the ever-loving shit out of me.

We spend just about every day together. Even on days when we're both really busy with work stuff, he always stays over my place, or I crash at his. We wake up together, cuddling like there's no tomorrow, then we have sex, either in bed or in the shower. Or sometimes in the kitchen before or after breakfast. We go out together, to little events or parties. We call and text each other constantly when we're apart. We laugh and kiss and hug, tease and play with each other endlessly. We're so adorably sweet it gives me a toothache.

For crying out loud, Barn, his stuff is all over my apartment! And I'm pretty sure I have at least a few outfits stashed at his.

I know he's my best friend on Earth, and that's probably why we're so close. But because we're sleeping together and not seeing anyone else, it feels like we're a couple.

And I can't be a couple right now, Barnaby. I just can't.

I want to, though... I *want* to be Noah's girlfriend. I want to stomp out that constant worrying fear that he'll eventually meet someone who catches his eye more than me and tell me he wants to pause our fuck-buddy thing so he can pursue her.

But I also know he's Noah, and it will definitely happen sooner or later. He doesn't do relationships. He never has... until whatever this thing is between us came up.

I'm newly divorced, and I'm finally learning how to be myself again. I can't just latch onto Noah because it feels like heaven when we're together. It's not right. I can't force him to be someone he's not. I care about him way too much to do that.

I've known this for a while. Which is why I enrolled in the art program in Budapest.

I accepted it a while ago, and I still haven't told Noah. I feel sick about it.

In three weeks I'll be moving to Europe for the next eighteen months to learn about art, to paint and explore. I'm so excited, but also so scared I don't know what to do with myself. What if Noah freaks out? What if he says he hates me for not telling him?

What if I never see him again?

Noah's leaving around the same time to film his new series. It was inevitable that we'd be seeing each other less. He'll be living on location in Georgia all summer, and after that he'll be crazy busy with all his premiere stuff and promo tours. Noah's schedule is about to be booked solid for a long time, so it makes sense that I would do this now. I need to go out and have this experience. I know it'll be good for me.

But I also need to tell Noah, and I'm just praying he won't be upset.

What will I do without Noah around all the time? How will I survive?

I guess that's part of the excitement. Noah brought me back to life when I was half-dead. He's my savior for that, but I can't keep relying on him for happiness. I need to get out there and stand on my own.

I'll miss him like crazy, though.

I live in constant dread that he'll meet a girl and fall in love while I'm gone. Naturally he'll meet tons of girls. He's Noah. It's his thing, and the fact that he's been exclusive to me for eight months, while fascinating, doesn't change the other fact that if I'm gone, he'll go back to fucking around. And if he could be exclusive to me, what's stopping him from doing it with someone else?

And what's stopping *me* from doing it with someone else?

It feels foreign and unnatural, thinking about being with someone other than Noah. That may be part of the excitement too, though it's a kind of uncomfortable, nauseating excitement.

Above all else, Noah is my friend, and I'm his. We need to do what's best for ourselves and be happy for each other in the process. And unfortunately right now, that doesn't include us being a real couple.

It stings to even think such thoughts in my mind. My heart is heavy and burdened with all this.

Seek Me

I need to talk to Noah. We haven't talked about him leaving for Georgia, and I think it's something we need to discuss. At which point I will tell him I'm leaving for eighteen months.

It'll suck being away from him, but I just know living in Europe will be the greatest adventure of my life. I can't wait to travel and see the world. To learn from some of the greatest artists alive. To eat different foods, explore different sceneries, learn new languages.

This is all part of *new* Alex's plan. She's moving on from the wreckage of her broken marriage and broken heart. It's time to start living again.

This seems even scarier than leaving Roger, Barn. All I can do now is live in the moment, like Dr. Rebecca says. Focus on rebuilding my present and my future. Wish me luck.

Chapter Eighteen
Noah

"Well, this all sounds great," I nod then take a sip of my mojito. This Mexican spot we're lunching in makes delicious ones with strawberries mashed up in there.

"How are you feeling? You doin okay with everything?" My assistant asks, giving me a wide-eyed look.

"Shut the fuck up," I scoff and he laughs, as does my publicist, Jeremy, and my agent, Lucas.

We're all having lunch together for one last meeting before we fly down to Georgia. There was a lot that went into getting my place set up, arranging my schedule and making sure I'm all packed and ready to move for the summer. But fortunately, I have people to do all that stuff for me, so I barely had to lift a finger. This way I can focus on the more stressful part in all this…

Leaving Alex and Boots behind.

I'm not sure I've ever been so excited about a job in my life. This show is going to kick so much ass. I'm itching to get down there; to check out the sets, do our first table read, meet the crew, see the wardrobe, my trailer! It's all so thrilling I keep feeling like I want to break out in dance moves for no reason.

Happy-dancing aside, of course there's the matter of being away on location for months at a time. My cleaning ladies always volunteer to take care of Boots while I travel, so that's not much of an issue. But I can't exactly ask them to take care of Alex while I'm gone. Our relationship is slightly different than what I have with Boots…

Okay, maybe it's a lot different, thank God.

As much as I've never really had a girlfriend, I've definitely never had a *long-distance* girlfriend. And I don't think anyone's ever had a *long-distance best-friend-exclusive-fuck-buddy*. Let's just say it's not one of Facebook's listed relationship statuses.

Things with Alex have been purely wondrous, especially since she won her fight and left her abusive husband. Their divorce went through, she loves her

Seek Me

new apartment... Everything worked out so well for her, and I'm so proud I can't even express it with words. My best friend is one badass chick; not to be fucked with.

Her art career is moving along swimmingly. She's made tons of friends. She laughs more and cries less. Alex is an all-around healthier person now, and it fills my heart with joy that I get to even be near her, experiencing her happiness by her side. As her *best friend exclusive fuck buddy...*

God, it sounds ridiculous.

I don't know what I'm doing with Alex. All I know is that I can't stand to be away from her, and I haven't even looked at another girl since we started hooking up. More importantly, I haven't *wanted* to. Alex is all I want, and it scares the bejesus out of me.

What will happen when I move to Georgia next week? How will we make this work?

I need to make it work. That's my newfound revelation. I can't stand the thought of not having what we have, all the time. It's possessed my mind so much recently that I had Brant look into leasing a jet so I can fly back to New York as often as aeronautically possible.

I devour my tacos as my lunch guests blather on about more Georgia and *Hell Storm* stuff, all the while deep in my thoughts. I want to plan out something fun for Alex and my last night together. It should be cool and romantic, and preferably private.

You bet your ass I'll be soaking up as much Alex time as I can before I leave, but that last night needs to be special. Because even if I can fly back to see her, the filming schedule is pretty intense, especially for the first couple weeks. Which means we'll be spending more time apart in the upcoming months than we have since we met.

It's frightening how depressed this makes me.

Maybe I'll cook dinner for her at my place... Alex isn't exactly a flashy girl. She hates all that fancy shit, so she'd probably enjoy a night in more than anything we could do outside my apartment.

Plus, if we stay in I can keep her naked. We'll need to bang out enough orgasms to last at least a month.

This really sucks. I don't want to leave her.

I don't want to lose her.

With my pulse suddenly thrumming in my neck, I suck down the rest of my drink and order another. I have no idea what I'm doing anymore. This thing with Alex is so fucking *not* casual, it's practically a black-tie gala.

She's under my skin, more than any woman I've ever known has been. It makes me physically sick to think about her finding someone else while I'm in Georgia, living out my dream of acting in a highly anticipated TV series. I don't want to spend my time down there worrying that Alex will be up here in New York meeting someone.

Do the rules of exclusive-friends-with-benefits extend to long-distance? Is it like a tri-state area only kind of deal?

My brain hurts. I feel a migraine coming on, and I think I'm breaking out into cold sweats. Or hives. Or both.

"Dude, you okay?" Brant asks, snapping his fingers in front of my face.

"What? Oh, yea, I'm great," I grumble then stand up fast. "Look, I gotta bounce. I'll talk to you later."

I leave the restaurant without looking back, because I need to be alone for a few. I need to take a walk and relax before I lose my cool.

I wave at Jimmy in the Navigator, signaling that I don't need him right now, and walk up the street. It's only three blocks to the park, so I stammer in that direction, hoping the cool breeze and fresh air will give me a little perspective.

And so I stroll through Central Park for a bit, just thinking. About Alex.

She's all I think about anymore. Every thought is laced with Alex, even the ones not directly related to her. She's on my mind day and night, even when we're together.

The other night I watched her sleep for hours. It was the creepiest thing I've ever done, and it felt fantastic.

She was all curled up in my bed, Boots at our feet, her arm draped around my waist; fully naked because we rarely sleep in anything, other than the occasional pair of underwear. The comforter was covering her just enough to make her look like a sleeping princess; dark hair all splayed out beneath her head like a wild mane. Long lashes fanned over her cheeks as her eyelids fluttered every couple seconds, as if maybe she was dreaming.

I wondered if she was dreaming about me. I still do…

Watching her lips part while she breathed soft breaths in and out, her chest rising and falling in an easy rhythm, was hypnotizing. I was put under her spell, and I have been since the first time I saw her.

I don't want her to fall asleep in some other guy's bed. I don't want anyone else in the world to have her the way I do.

Okay, so maybe I want Alex to be my girlfriend.

Seek Me

I stop walking. I stand there in the middle of the path in Central Park and blink, over and over and over until it makes more sense.

I want Alex to be my girlfriend.
I want to be her boyfriend.
I don't want anyone else. Only her.

I wait for the dread to attack me, like it usually does when I think of such insane things. But it doesn't. This time it all seems crystal clear.

That's what I need to do. I need to ask Alex to be my girlfriend. Ask her if she wants to be exclusive, *not* fuck-buddies. Just exclusive. Just us... together.

What if she says no?

Okay, there it is. The dread, filling me in seconds like rushing water. *Jesus... If I ask Alex to be my girlfriend and she says no... That would totally ruin our friendship. Like, obliterate it.*

"Fuck fuck fuck," I mutter into my hands, rubbing my eyes hard.

This is a truly shitty situation. I have feelings for my best friend.

That really cocks everything up.

A small smile tugs at my lips at the expression. That's Andrew's thing. He always says it. I guess it's British slang or something, who knows.

Maybe I could call Andrew. Ask him what he thinks I should do.

He's basically like my new best friend anyway, other than Alex. And I can't ask *Alex* what to do about Alex. No voicing any of this to her until I'm sure it's the road I'm going down.

Worse still, I can't talk to any of my other friends either, since they still think me and Alex are just casual naked pals. Which I suppose is the ruse we've been telling ourselves, too, although I now realize just how stupid I've been this whole time.

This thing is so fucked. I need help.

I tug my phone out of my pocket and place the call while walking in the direction of my apartment. It rings a few times, but eventually he answers.

"What's up, costar?" Andrew James chimes through the phone. "Ready to get your zombie on?"

I chuckle. "Oh, you bet your ass I am, *Rex.*" He laughs. "But actually, I... kind of need your advice on something." I swallow hard. This is already insanely difficult for me. I've never experienced all these *feelings.*

Who are you and what have you done with Noah Richards?!

"Shoot," he says casually, and I take a deep breath.

"So... Alex..." I grumble and my stomach flips just from mentioning her freaking name.

"You're in love with her," he sighs through a chuckle and I freeze in place.

"Whoa whoa whoa! Take it easy there, old chap!" I huff as my throat closes up. "No one said anything about *love*. Jesus Christ..."

Andrew laughs out loud. "Alright, alright. I'm sorry. You have *feelings* for her. Is that better?"

"Yes... I guess. God damn, dude..." I'm able to start walking again, but my legs feel all wobbly. I might come crashing down if he keeps this up.

"Okay, so what's the problem?"

"The problem is that I don't do *this*. I don't have feelings for girls. It's never happened before, so I don't know... And now we're going to Georgia for the whole summer... It's fucked."

"Hmm. Yes, it's a bit complicated. Have you talked to her about it?"

"No," I grunt, feeling suddenly very tired. "I don't want to ruin our friendship. I mean... what if she doesn't feel the same?"

"Noah, I'm sorry, but there's no way she doesn't feel the same," his tone is very matter-of-fact. "You two have been going on like this for what... eight months? And she hasn't so much as alluded to an interest in seeing anyone else?"

I swallow hard over my dry throat. "No."

"And you spend almost every waking minute together..." he points out. "She hasn't mentioned anything about taking some time apart?"

I shake my head slowly. "No..." He sighs in my ear, as if my obstinance is mildly testing him.

"I think it's apparent she's mad for you. That much is obvious. Granted, I've never met the bird, or seen you two together, but if it is the way you say it is, then she's likely feeling the same confusing things you are. The best thing to do would be to talk to her about it. Mention Georgia, being apart and all, and see where she stands. If it seems as though she's leaning toward wanting more, then that's what you'll do."

Rapid warmth spreads through my stomach and up to my chest, like I'm on a roller coaster and it's at the first drop; overwhelming but thrilling at the same time.

"And don't even think about this bloody *I don't do relationships* pish posh," he warns me and I huff. "You've been in a relationship with Alex for months now, whether the two of you call it one or not."

My eyes widen in a moment of sheer panic. *Oh God, he's right. Alex and I have* been in a relationship this whole time! Fuck, how stupid can we be?!*

"Okay…" I breathe, nodding to myself. "You make some valid points."

Andrew laughs at me and I curse under my breath. *Damn him and his smug, always right Britishness.*

"You'll be fine, Noah. And guess what? Even if it doesn't work out, you'll still be fine," he says in that blasé tone and accent that makes everything sound so simple. "I'll see you next week. We're making this show our bitch, aren't we?"

I chuckle as I cross the street from the park, heading to my building. "Definitely. Thanks, man. You're the best."

"I know." We both laugh then hang up. And I do feel much better.

I'm not sure what I was so scared about. I know Alex feels very strongly for me, and if she doesn't want to be exclusive, well then at least I can say I went for it.

No, but I really hope she doesn't shoot me down. That would be super embarrassing and painful.

I go inside and slip out of my coat, kicking my shoes off and making my way to the kitchen for a beer. But I come to a skidding halt when I see Alex, sitting at my breakfast bar with a glass of wine, reading a book. She hears me and looks up.

"Oh hi!" She squeals, hopping off her seat and scampering over. Her arms are thrown around my shoulders as she hugs tight. "I wanted to read this book, but I left it here. So I came by to get it, and then I started reading it and just got sucked right in." She laughs softly by my ear.

Instinctively I fold her into my arms harder, burying my face in her hair and inhaling that life-affirming smell. My eyes may be closing…

It's crazy that she's here after everything I was just thinking… About us. Seeing her right now is throwing me for a loop.

"I hope that's okay," she whispers and loosens her grip on me. But I only hold her tighter. *Not ready to let go yet.*

"Of course it's okay," I croak, squeezing her to death. "Hi."

She giggles. "Hi. You miss me a little?"

I nod into the crook of her neck and she laughs again. I pull back just enough to trail my fingers along her jaw, taking her face in my hand. She gazes up at me, wide eyes expressing curiosity and hope. Mine drop to her lips and I just need to feel them. To taste them.

I want more. I need more.

I kiss her gently, though surprising her enough to draw out a gasp on my lips; a gasp which evaporates into a satisfied moan while our mouths move, and I kiss her with slow dedication. She tastes like red wine and Twizzlers. It's delicious, and it feels heavenly, our tongues advancing on one another's before she does that thing I love where she playfully bites my bottom lip then sucks on it. My dick is already stiff and aching, more and more with every subtle pant and purr from her warm mouth into mine.

More. More. More.

More Alex. My Alex.

She tugs away, dragging air into her lungs as her hands fall to my chest. Her right one covers my heart, and she must feel it banging in there, because she gives me a look.

"I guess I should use my key more often," she chirps, tugging her lip between her teeth.

I swallow hard, choking on all the emotions swimming through me, and nod. "Yea."

Her brow furrows and her head tilts. "Are you alright? You seem a little... something."

My lips part, but I haven't the faintest idea what to say.

I know I just had this whole conversation with Andrew about it, but now that she's here, staring up at me with those wide, clover eyes, I'm transformed into a big, dumb sack of fear.

Something... Let me tell you about something, *Alex. I have feelings for you, and you're my friend. I have feelings I've never had for any other human person before, and I can't possibly express them to you, because I can barely wrap my head around them myself. I have feelings for you and we're supposed to be casual, because you've just been through a harrowing divorce, and I'm leaving for five months, and I don't want to be* just friends *anymore.*

I'm definitely something, *all right. Desperate and hopeless and inadequate. All those words seem to fit my current state of fucked.*

I clear my throat. I think I've officially lost it. *You see what feelings do??*

I need to speak words, because she's still just gawking at me and the longer I stay silent, the more awkward I am, so I just say the first thing that comes to mind.

"I'm going to miss you." It comes out rougher than I was going for.

Her eyes are even wider now, and I want to reach out, grab the words and stuff them back down my throat.

"Noah..." she gulps as her eyes dart to the floor. "You have *no idea* how much I'm going to miss you."

When her gaze lifts back to mine, it's glassy, like she might cry. I definitely don't want to make her *cry*...

But I can't ignore the warms and tingles everywhere from the concept of her missing me.

So be my girlfriend, Alex... That way when we miss each other it'll make a little more sense.

I keep my lips zipped tight to prevent more crazy from sneaking out.

I can't do this right now. I need more time.

I need to figure out how to even go about asking someone to be my girlfriend. It's a completely new venture for me and, if we're being honest, it's hardcore overwhelming.

Alex is still quiet, and her face is covered in some thick emotions that I can't decipher. It's making me uncomfortable. This whole *thing* is making me uncomfortable, and edgy, and I think I need to take a beat and chill before I have a nervous breakdown.

"You wanna go grab a drink?" I ask, taking her small hand in mine. "Happy hour at Easy's?"

Alex's expression remains unnerved for a moment, but then she breathes out hard and a small smile lines her lips.

"Sure. That sounds fun."

"'Kay," I huff and tap her chin with my knuckles.

We get our things and leave the apartment, walking four blocks to one of our local bars.

Easy's is full of the standard after-work crowd, but it's not overly packed. Alex and I have a seat in one of our usual tables by the bar and the waitress, who knows us, brings over our drinks.

I sit back in my seat and glance around the place. I don't really recognize anyone, and nobody's paying me much attention. That's why I like sticking to my regular spots. The patrons know this is my neighborhood, so I'm rarely bothered.

"So how was the meeting?" Alex's voice brings me back to her. She's watching me closely, sipping her drink.

"It was fine," I shrug. "Just a recap, sort of. This time next week, I'll be a southern gentleman." I wink at her and she laughs.

"Gentleman is a strong word," she teases with eyes twinkling at me in the dim light.

"Are you saying I'm not chivalrous?" My lips quirk into a wicked grin. "I open doors all over the city for you, Alex."

She giggles and nods. "Yes, that you do. Though I think Jimmy does it more often…"

"And I carry bags for you."

"Again, I think that's more Jimmy…"

"And there was that time I held your umbrella to cover you from the rain," my brows raise in expectance.

She shows me a wide smile that lights up the world around us, then leans forward.

"Yes, you did. But you didn't lay your coat over a puddle for me to walk on." Her eyes are bright and playful.

"No, no I didn't. But I lifted you up and carried you over it, did I not?" I smirk, catching sight of her tongue sliding along her lower lip.

"You did," she playfully cocks her head. "Wow. Noah Richards, a true gentleman. Who knew?"

I keep my eyes set on hers, though now my mind is running through all these memories. Andrew was right. I've been treating Alex like my girlfriend since day one, doing things for her I've never even thought to do for anyone else. And I'm not just doing it because I'm trying to get something from her. I do those things because I *want* to.

I'm shocked at how willing to change I am for this girl, though I know it's because she's so special that I want to treat her differently.

Like a girlfriend.

"So my flight is Tuesday afternoon," I start, forcing my voice to remain even. "I was thinking… I want to do something special on my last night. Just us…"

Alex's eyes widen briefly. "Oh… yea. That would be great." She pauses to chew on her lip for a second. "What did you have in mind?"

"Nothing crazy, just dinner at my place." It's a sudden struggle to keep my easy-going mask in place. "I thought I could cook for you."

She grins. "That's so sweet. But shouldn't I be cooking for you? Since you're the one who's… leaving…" Her voice trails, face growing still. Something flashes in her eyes, but I don't know what it is. It's almost like remorse, and I'm wondering why.

Maybe she is really sad to see me go… I don't want to leave her, but I don't have a choice. This is everything I've been working for my whole adult life.

"Do you cook?" I lift a questioning brow.

"Uh... no. Not at all," she shakes her head solemnly and I have to laugh. "I can't even boil water. It's awful."

"Aww, well that's okay, baby," I grin, taking her hand. "I'll do the cooking and you can just sit there looking pretty."

She tries to punch me from across the table, but I keep dodging her attempts, which is making us both giggle like fools.

"You don't cook anything other than weed brownies, Noah," she rolls her eyes. "You have a private chef who cooks for you."

"Not all the time! I know how to make stuff."

She folds her arms over her chest. "Like what?"

"What do you want to eat? You name it and I'll make it. *Myself.* I won't call Eloise, I promise." I draw an X over my heart with my finger.

Alex is deep in thought for a while and I'm beginning to regret this decision. Sure, I know my way around the kitchen enough not to burn the place down, but I'm no Gordon Ramsey. *Although, I do swear just as much.*

"Okay. I would like fried chicken and mac n cheese. Please," she smiles, clearly satisfied with her menu choice.

The waitress happens to be walking by at that exact moment and pauses by our table. "Oh, sorry. We don't have that here. But we do have twenty-five-cent buffalo wings for happy hour! You want me to put in an order?"

I laugh under my breath while Alex stutters, "Oh, um, no. Sorry, I was talking to... You know what? Yes, sure. We'll have ten wings. Thanks."

The waitress smiles and turns on her heel, scampering off to put in our order. I'm hysterical now, while Alex kicks me under the table.

"You're a douche," she huffs through an unrelenting grin.

"Fried chicken and mac n cheese, coming up for my little woman," I sigh, unable to crush the massive smile on my face.

She seems to falter for a moment, but recovers quickly enough that I don't think there's anything wrong. Still, she's being more fidgety than usual, and I'm not sure if it's just that she's bummed I'm leaving soon, or if there's something more going on.

"So what'd you do today?" I ask, hoping to draw out some information. "Other than break into my apartment."

She narrows her gaze at me and I wink. "Not a whole lot... Painted for a while. Almost done with that piece with the lips."

"I love that one."

"Mmm me too. But there's something missing and I just can't put my finger on it," she pouts, picking at some paint on her fingernail. "I've been thinking more and more lately that I need to get back with some instructors. There's still so much I have to learn, you know...?"

Her eyes shift to mine slowly and they're round; uneasy. I don't know what that look means, but if I can give her some peace of mind, maybe that would help.

"Alex, I think sticking with it and being consistent has given you great structure as an artist. But classes can never hurt. I'm sure you could find something, what with all your new connections."

Her forehead creases as she gapes at me, clenching my stomach in concern. *Why is she looking at me like that?*

"You're right," she whispers. "Maybe I'll find something... while you're away."

I blink because that's all I can do. "I think that would be good for you."

She nods slowly and kills her drink. I do the same to mine.

Something between us feels tense, and I don't know what it is or where it's stemming from. I think I'm doing a pretty good job of keeping my secret feelings to myself for now, but I can tell there's something else... Something she's not telling me.

I can only hope it's that she feels the same way I do.

I guess we'll find out Monday night.

The last five days have gone by in a flash.

It's depressing that I'm feeling so glum about leaving New York, because I really am excited as hell to get started on this project. But knowing I'll be saying goodbye to Alex tonight is making it hard for me to enjoy anything.

We've spent each of the last four nights wrapped up in each other; two lovesick patients in a quarantine of terminal lust. Whether we were at my place or hers was irrelevant. It's barely even mattered that we were in a *bed*, or an apartment. We snuck down a side-trail in the park the other night and I fucked her up against a tree.

I've never felt so at-one with nature.

Alex and I have been more inseparable in the last few days than in our entire time of knowing one another. And while it's been amazing, sexy as fuck and downright filthy at times, it's always looming over us that we're soaking up our time together because I'm leaving tomorrow. And after that, who knows what will happen?

Which is why I spent all afternoon *cooking*. That on its own is baffling.

I've never cooked a meal for a girl before. I don't think I've cooked for *anyone* before, other than myself and Haley, and yet here I am, wearing my cock apron, setting freshly fried pieces of chicken down on a draining rack, and removing a baked macaroni and cheese casserole from the oven.

It smells like a Martha Stewart Living version of heaven in here. I can't believe I made this stuff, *myself*, from scratch. I was tempted to call Eloise a few times and ask her why the fried chicken kept spitting at me. It was awfully rude. But eventually I got the hang of it, and the finished products look like what you'd find in Marcus Samuelsson's restaurant.

I set the large dish of mac n cheese down on the stove to cool, then make my way to the dining room to set the table. Phoebe, one of my cleaning ladies, told me I have placemats, which I honestly wasn't aware of, and where to find them. Eventually I locate them and set a place-setting for Alex and myself. I even find a couple candles to light when she gets here. *Make it nice and romantic.*

So I can ask her to be my girlfriend.

Each time I think about what I plan on asking her tonight, my chest sinks into itself and I have to pause what I'm doing to focus on breathing. But I know I want to be with Alex, and each second ticking us closer to me leaving is a reminder of how I can't possibly move to Georgia for the summer without establishing some kind of real relationship with her.

If we're exclusive, then I can fly back to see her on weekends, or even fly her down to my place in Georgia, if she wants. It wouldn't be that difficult. Anything will be an adjustment, going from seeing each other every day to only once a week or so. But if she's my girlfriend, I'm happy to do that. For her.

For us.

The *if* of it all is what's causing me to shake in my skinny jeans right now. Tonight I'll be asking Alex for something I've never asked of anyone before. And if she says no… Well, that's a big fat question mark, if I've ever seen one.

Gulping the fancy French white wine I bought three bottles of because I know Alex loves it, I continue on with my preparations. She's due here any minute, and I want everything to be perfect when she arrives.

One warning I must keep instilling in my brain tonight is to keep my hands to myself long enough for us to eat and talk. I don't want the food getting cold after I slaved all day over a hot oven like the pussy-whipped fool I so clearly am. Although taking her upstairs before I pop the GF question might make sense, considering that if she shoots me down I don't think either of us will be in the mood for sex. Rejection isn't my kink.

Oh God. I can't breathe. What if she says no? It'll be so awkward.

Maybe I can pretend I'm kidding? If she says no, I'll just be like, "Psyche! Haha! You should've seen your face! Big old jokester Noah's at it again!"

I'm not sure I can pull that off. Then again, I may not have a choice.

My door buzzes and my heart leaps up into my throat as if it's trying to escape before it's too late.

I wipe my hands repeatedly on my apron because they're too sweaty as I stalk to the door. I buzz her in and remove the stupid apron, throwing it somewhere before I open the door. And when I do, I freeze like someone said *freeze*.

I need a minute to compose myself after my first glimpse of Alex tonight. It's just too much sexy in such a teeny weeny package, she barely even looks real. Like a twisted version of a Disney princess, which coincidentally is exactly how I've always envisioned my dream girl.

She's wearing this black strapless corset dress that pushes her tits up, making them look like two ripe apples I *need* to sink my teeth into, like Adam. Some chunky boots that put her face in line with my chin, her hair long and flowing down her back. Olive skin with the shoulder and arm tats on display, that twinkly little ring in her nose, dark lashes and mauve lips…

She's a vixen. An exotic little beauty made, in my mind, just for me.

Alex smiles, like a meteor shower crashing down around me. "Hi."

"Hey." The jagged in my voice gives me away, but I can't even help it. I'm gawking. *Hard.* "Come here, beautiful."

I give in to the cravings and wrap her in my arms, hugging tight while breathing in that scent like a damn crackhead, eyes rolling back in my skull. I swear to God, she has some kind of pheromone coming out of her hair that works like a drug shooting directly to my brain's pleasure center.

She wiggles in my arms, fingering my hair at the back of my neck, which sends blood rushing below my waist. She knows I love that feeling; that's why she does it.

"It smells amazing in here," she whispers with her face smashed into my chest because I refuse to stop squeezing her.

"*You* smell amazing in here," I rumble and she laughs, her whole body

Seek Me

rocking in my arms as she does.

Be mine. Never take this feeling away.

I clear my throat and finally let go, though I can't resist playing with the strands of her hair while she gazes up at me, gnawing on that succulent lower lip like it's a Swedish Fish. It tastes like one, I would know.

"I hope you're hungry," I growl, eyeing her mouth.

"*I* hope you're talking about food, because I'm actually starving," she giggles and I smirk. "I saved my appetite all day for this."

"Did you?" *Aww. So sweet.*

She nods with diligence, so I take her hand.

"Right this way, baby," I murmur, guiding her to the dining room where my romantic display is all set up.

I let her go to light the candles and her face is priceless. She's stunned; green eyes wide and that pretty mouth agape.

"Oh my God, Noah!" She gasps through a laugh. "I can't believe you did this! This is so sweet... And romantic."

"Right?" I grin, internally second-guessing myself, which is par for the course with me and Alex.

"Babe..." she pouts and steps up to me, wrapping her arms around my waist. "This is amazing. Thank you so much."

She kisses my throat and my neck a few times, bringing some significant heat to the surrounding air. My fingers brush through her hair then across her naked back and she shivers.

"Anything for you," I tell her truthfully with a kiss to her head.

When she peers up at me, the smile is gone, having been replaced by a look of trepidation. She stares into my eyes while her hands come around to my front and she traces the muscles in my chest through my shirt. She's just gawking at me and I have no clue what's going on in her head, but she looks nervous, which is exactly how I *feel*, so I suppose we're on the same level.

"You want some wine, baby?" I change the subject fast before this bubble of tension swallows us whole. "I got that French white you like."

She nods slowly, though it takes her a moment to release me. "Yes, please. Thank you."

I swallow my nerves down and wriggle free to get the wine. We'll definitely need alcohol to get through this.

I refill my glass and pour Alex one, bringing it to her in the dining room. When I come back, she's standing by the table, staring at the placemats and tracing the silverware with her index finger. I even arranged the forks and knife in the right spots, which according to Phoebe is a big deal when you're putting on a fancy dinner. Though I stressed to her that I'm not going for *fancy* as much as *serious*, because I want Alex to know I am.

I feel like most of her reservations about us being together center on me being a relationship virgin. Sure, she's coming out of an eight-year marriage and is dealing with her own internal stuff, but I often think she sees me as someone too casual to ever be a boyfriend. I'm trying to change her perceptions on that tonight.

With silverware and placemats.

Jesus Christ, I'm going to crash and burn. Good thing I stocked the freezer with vodka and ice cream.

I extend a glass of wine to Alex and she accepts it graciously. Before I can say anything, she jumps in with her own toast.

"To amazing, life-changing opportunities," she rasps through a small smile that still seems abnormally unsure.

I return it anyway and we clink glasses, both taking long, drawn-out sips in awkward silence. *Okay, this isn't going great. I need to do something... quick.*

"Here. Have a seat," I mumble, pulling out her chair for her.

She sits down gracefully and I push her in, sneaking another sip of wine before I get the food.

I bring both of our plates out and set one on each of our placemats. I opt to sit next to her because I know she likes when we sit close, rather than across from one another. It's more comfortable, too. This way I won't be forced to look her in the eye while I struggle to formulate the words I need to tell her how I feel.

"My God, Noah. This looks fantastic!" She studies the food closely, examining the perfectly crispy, golden brown skin on the chicken, and the melted top layer of my three-cheese macaroni dish. "Are you sure you made this?"

I can't help but laugh. "Yes, dear. I made it. It took me all day, but I did it myself. No help from anyone."

"You worked on this all day?" She squeaks and I nod. "Baby, you're the freaking sweetest. It's your last night here. I should be doing stuff for you..."

"I'm sure you'll think of something you can do for me that doesn't involve setting fires in my kitchen," I grin, unfolding the cloth napkin that took me eight tries to figure out how to fold, draping it over my lap.

Alex grabs my hand unexpectedly and I look up. "I can definitely think of a few things to do for you on your last night... before you leave for months on location... because you're a big, sexy TV star." Her eyes twinkle as she brings my hand to her thigh.

I shift in my seat and clear my throat. *God, she's fucking sexy. How am I supposed to be serious when she's looking at me like that? And moving my hand awfully close to her...*

"I can't wait. But I want you to eat before it gets cold," I say in a hoarse whisper.

"Yes, sir," she breathes, then covers her lap with her own napkin, though my hand is still on her thigh and I'm not ready to move it.

My eyes travel up to her tits and I watch as they move up and down. Impatience piques my desire to be naked with her, and I think we should eat fast so I can say what I need to say, and hopefully still spend the night treasuring her beautiful body for the last time in who knows how long.

Alex digs into her food first and my ego is soaring because the noises she's making are oddly similar to the ones she makes when I'm inside her. I take a few bites myself just to confirm that she's not buttering me up. And yea, it's insanely motherfucking good. I'm not sure how I managed to pull this off, but I'm brimming with pride for my culinary skills right now.

"Noah... God, this chicken is perfectly cooked," she sings my praises in between scarfing down her food like a wild animal. But it's still somehow sexy. I don't know how she does it. "And the mac n cheese... I mean, damn. This shit is on point!"

I laugh humbly while smothering my out-of-control smile. "Thanks, babe. You know, I just did my thing."

She peeks at me and smiles while chewing. "You're so fucking cute."

I roll my eyes. "I'm a regular person, Alex. I just happen to be really good at certain things, but I don't deserve a parade. Maybe a small one, if you have time, but nothing crazy. I wouldn't hate a trophy either."

She giggles and swats my shoulder as we continue to eat side-by-side.

Once we're both sufficiently stuffed from my awesome meal, we've also killed a whole bottle of wine and started on the next, so we're a bit loosened up. I feel better now that she loved my romantic dinner, and we're enjoying one another's company as we always do. Although in the back of my mind I know we need to talk, and I'm stalling. I don't want to ruin the fun we're having together by bringing up serious shit.

But I have to. And soon.

"There's dessert, too," I tell her, placing my napkin on the table by my empty plate. "Nothing fancy, just brownies and ice cream. Regular brownies…"

She laughs. "I'm so full. I couldn't eat another bite."

"Well, I made enough to feed an army, so you'll have to take the leftovers home since they'll go bad here. At least you can have meals for the next few nights."

Her smile slips away, and she stares down at her fingers toiling in her lap. I can't get a good grasp on what's going on with her tonight, but she definitely seems anxious. I fool myself into thinking it's because she's bummed I'm leaving tomorrow, but I don't know… It seems like something more.

"Noah, I think we need to… talk," her barely audible voice wavers.

Oh boy, okay… Here goes. It's now or never. I need to ask her now if she wants to be my girlfriend.

"Yea, um, to be honest I was thinking the same thing," I rumble and turn in my seat to face her fully. She does the same. "Baby, look… uh, I know it'll be different with me gone…" My voice gives out and I stop, watching her face closely for a reaction while I work myself up to this.

I'm so nervous my palms are sweating profusely, and my heart is bouncing inside me like one of those Mexican jumping beans.

Alex nods, tucking her hair behind her ear, our knees touching as we face each other. "You're right. It will be… different…"

I swallow hard over the world's driest throat, summoning all my inner strength and courage to tell her I want to be *more*.

Just say it. You need to just tell her…

I open my mouth to speak, but she beats me to it…

"Actually, I um… I have some news," she says softly, then takes my hand in hers. My eyes are wide and locked on her beautiful, troubled face. "I got accepted into an art program. In Europe."

My whole body goes still. Even my heart stops leaping for a moment while I stare at Alex in shock.

I wasn't expecting that. I'm more than thrown off right now.

"Oh…" The word gusts from between my lips. "Really? That's great, baby. Congratulations."

She tries to smile, but it's not working, which leads me to believe there might be more to this. My stomach is already twisting and turning in unease.

"Thanks. It's in Budapest and Prague," she goes on, eyes blinking much more rapidly than mine. I don't think I've blinked at all since she started

Seek Me

speaking. "I leave on Friday."

Blood rushing in my ears is all I can hear. Everything around me feels dense and confusing, like I have no idea where I am or what's going on.

"Friday?" I gasp, trying not to sound as stunned as I obviously am. "As in, *this* Friday? The Friday coming up? Like, *four days from now*, Friday?"

Alex breaks our eye contact and nods quickly. "Yea. I um, wanted to tell you sooner, but it's been so crazy with your move and everything. I didn't want to stress you out. Plus, I figured... you'll be gone anyway."

I'm finding it very hard to breathe at the moment. My head bobs a few times in acceptance of what she's saying as my mind races to make sense of the newfound information flooding it.

Okay, it's fine. This doesn't change much. Still, when she gets back, we can be together. I mean, whether she's traveling too makes no difference. I still want to be with her, I don't care where she is.

"Wow, Alex... I mean, this is unexpected, but I'm still happy for you," I grunt, nodding. *Why am I still nodding?* "So, how long is this program for, anyway?"

Alex is quiet. The whole room is quiet. Actually, I think the whole world is quiet right now. Every noise on the planet Earth has stopped while I await her answer; while she figures out *how* to answer.

My heart is quaking aggressively because she's taking way too long to speak. Her eyes resemble giant, green saucers as she gapes at me, then looks away; then looks up, then looks away again. Up, down, up, down. Fucking torturous.

"It's for... eighteen months," she finally releases the words, like a hitman sent to kill the hopes and dreams I had in my head.

I'm suspended in time. I can't move any part of my body, and it feels like the walls are closing in on me. I refuse to gasp for air in front of her, but I seriously can't breathe right now... My lungs are tight; my chest is tight. Everything is fucking tight, and suffocating.

The empty, hollow thing in my chest, formerly known as my heart, has fallen out of my body, and is now lying on the floor of my dining room, pumping nothing.

My mouth drops open, but I can't even begin to formulate words. What would I say after a bomb like that?

She's leaving... for eighteen months?
Eighteen months?!
That's a year and a half! That's fucking forever!

I was going to ask her to be my girlfriend, and now she's going to Europe for eighteen goddamn fucking months? What in the honest to God fuck is happening right now?!

"Noah, I know I should've told you sooner," her small voice breaks the tense silence and the thickness of the air that's strangling me to death. "I feel awful. But this is such a huge opportunity for me."

My eyes are dry from not blinking for so long. I'm just gawking at her, watching the fretful look on her gorgeous face, those big eyes shining with guilt and sorrow. I don't want her to feel bad, but this is directly conflicting with everything I planned on telling her tonight.

Everything I planned on asking.

I have feelings for her and she's leaving.
I want her to be my girlfriend and she's leaving.
I'm leaving and she's leaving.
She's leaving. She's leaving. She's leaving.
There she goes.

My body finally forces itself to swallow and blink, but I can't get much else out of it.

"After everything I went through with Roger, I just need to do this," Alex sniffles. I now realize that she's crying, and my heart, still lying on the floor, breaks in half. "It's going to be new and scary, but I think I need that right now. I need to find myself... Figure out who I am."

If I know who you are, will you stay?

The sight of her breaking down snaps me out of my trance and I reach forward to hold her face. Her eyes bore into mine so deep I'm afraid she'll be able to read my thoughts, and she'll know what I was about to say...

What I was about to tell her right before she changed everything.

"Alex..." I croak with far too much vulnerability then clear my throat, stuffing all of it back down; shoving it deep inside and locking it up far away, where it can never get out again. "I'm so happy for you, baby. You'll have an amazing time. I know it."

Alex lets out a soft cry and launches forward, grabbing me and hugging on as tight as she can. It takes me a moment before I can wrap my arms around her, but I do, because I have to.

I hold the back of her head while she cries softly into my neck.

"I'm going to miss you so much..." she whimpers. I bite down hard on the inside of my cheek. "How am I going to survive without you?"

Squeezing my eyes shut as tight as possible, I will away the emotions. I count to ten in my mind; anything to stop them. I can't feel this. I can't let her know that I'm breaking inside.

I will wear this mask, forever. I'll be happy for her and support her. Because she's my friend.

That's it. She's just my friend. Nothing more.

No. More.

"You've been surviving all your life, baby," I grunt, tapping my foot on the floor over and over because this is killing me. It's *killing* me. "You don't need me for that. You're strong and brave, and badass. Don't ever forget it."

She trembles in my arms, but I feel her nod. I just keep holding her, breathing in and out slowly, letting it all fall away. Everything I thought I wanted... It's done.

And it's fine. Clearly it wasn't meant to be.

My heart lurches, fighting to keep beating, though it feels like I've been shot.

Her small breaths warm the flesh on my neck as she finally stops shaking and pulls back. I hadn't even realized until now that she's sitting on my lap, straddling my waist.

Her eyes are red and puffy, but she's so damn beautiful it hurts to look at her right now. She bites her lip and stares down at me, fingers gently teasing my jaw.

"I won't see you -"

I cut her off with my lips.

I kiss her hard and fast to stop the words because I just can't hear that. I can't think about it, *any* of it.

Nope. No no no. No more talking.

Talking is bad. Words ruin lives.

I whimper into her mouth because I'm broken, and it hurts. It fucking hurts; everything does. The pain in my chest is almost too much to bear, like slicing, gnawing exposed wounds.

But I'm going to keep kissing her, and we'll dull the pain. For as long as we can.

I hold Alex's face in my hands and devour her, drinking her in; all of her that I need so badly. I suck and bite her lips, giving her my tongue, kissing deep and furious; wrathful.

She grinds her body against mine, yanking my hair and pressing her breasts so hard into my chest we're one heartbeat. I groan into her mouth as she rocks the warmth between her thighs on my erection, so painfully stiff it might break.

My desperate hands reach for every part of her; her tits, her ass, her throat. I need to have her, now. I need to erase everything that just happened from existence. This is the only way to do it.

I grip her ass hard as I stand up, carrying her across the apartment to the stairs while she kisses, licks and bites my neck all over. I bring her upstairs to my bedroom and toss her onto my bed, immediately lifting my shirt over my head.

Crawling over her on my knees, I reach behind her to unzip her dress. Then I slide it down her frame, exposing her breasts first, her toned stomach, curved hips, her sweet pussy covered by a lacy little thong, swooping it down her legs and off her feet at last. Alex unbuttons and unzips my jeans, pushing them down fast over my butt, with my boxers, and I slither out of them the rest of the way.

As soon as I'm naked, her hands are all over me; touching my chest and my abs, curling her fingers around my dick and jerking it slowly. I kneel between her thighs, panting while I watch her stroking my cock. I run my hands up her ribcage to her tits and cup them, flicking the barbells in her nipples until she gasps out loud.

My head is cloudy, my movements driven by lust and the desire to make the agony inside me disappear. It's too much; all these feelings. I want them gone. I need this distraction.

I cover Alex's small body with my big one and I kiss her lips, softly, because I can't believe I might never get to do this again. Shaking those thoughts away before I can panic, I move down her body, grabbing her tits and sucking them hard. She's shaking beneath me, wrapping her legs around me as her hips lift off the bed, seeking my cock. I know she wants me inside her, and I want that, too. But for right now, I need to make her squirm a little.

I'm struggling to feel even the slightest bit of control. My whole world is spinning out, and the only thing I can do to feel better is tease the fuck out of her with my tongue, all over this gorgeous body that should be mine.

My lips cover her nipple and I suck it as hard as I can with a powerful, bruising force. She screams and her hands fly into my hair, fisting and pulling. But I don't stop. I lick the steel over and over, lapping at it, sucking once more, then taking it between my teeth.

"Oh fuck, Noah!" She cries, and I hum, soothing the pain with my breath and my voice.

The length of me drags over her slit, wetness soaking through her panties

Seek Me

as I roll my hips into hers until I can feel her coating every inch. My brain is going crazy. There are so many thoughts flying around in my head, and I need to keep them quiet. So I kiss and suck her breasts a few more times before I leave them trembling and slide down the rest of her body.

I rash my lips along her flesh everywhere, leaving a soft peck here, a little bite there; her stomach, her hip, her pelvis. I can't even stop myself. I'm possessed and burning alive. I need this so bad... all of it.

I slide her panties off slowly then kiss a trail up her inner thighs, hungrily sucking and lapping every drop of her juices that are overflowing from her body like the ripest piece of fruit on earth. My tongue extends and I trace her entrance, sipping and savoring her flavor because I might never have it again.

Fuck...

Forcing myself to block it out once again, I keep kissing; her clit, her lips, outside, inside; everywhere. I want it all. I want to eat her alive.

I circle her clit mercilessly, then suck so hard her thighs try to close on my head. I force them apart and go again, fucking her tight pussy with my tongue, grunting and groaning as I go, rumbling into her while I hold her thigh and ass in place. I slow down for kisses, then give her clit a little nip that makes her shudder. So I do it again. And again.

And when I can tell she's about to come, I stop.

"Noah..." She breathes my name like it means something, and my cock throbs against the softness of my blankets.

"Say my name... more..." I growl at her, riding her pussy with my mouth.

"Noah!" She squeals. "Noah, Noah, oh God, Noah..."

Her muscles tighten around me so I stop again, this time moving back up in line with her face. I kiss her and she whimpers between my lips.

"This is how you taste on my mouth, Alex," I grunt, sliding my dick through her silky wetness. "Promise me you won't forget it."

"I won't. I promise," she purrs, scratching my chest with her nails.

"Promise you won't forget how I feel..."

I don't understand why I'm talking. This is dangerous, and I don't want to think about it, but I can't stop the words from coming out.

"I could *never* forget how you feel," she whispers then sucks my bottom lip hard until I hum. "You're everything."

Don't say that... Don't say that when you're leaving.

I gulp as my chest draws up and down, sucking in air. I try to pull away from her and go for a condom, but she holds on tighter.

"Fuck me, Noah," she pleads through a raspy voice and unsteady breaths. "No condom. I want to feel you... all of you."

My cock leaks on her belly at that. I gaze down at her; rosy blushed cheeks, bright eyes threatening to close, plump lips parted and quivering. She's so perfect, and tonight wasn't supposed to happen like this, and now she wants me to fuck her bare, which I've literally never done before.

"Please, baby," she tugs me back to her and I go, willingly, under her spell.

She yanks my face down to hers and kisses me slow and soft; much more tender than just about everything I've done to her tonight. The feeling makes my heart swell. My stupid, idiotic heart.

"Alex..." I pant her name as our bodies move together, building up a rhythm. There's so much more I want to say, but I won't allow myself to speak a word of it.

Her fingers glides over my slightly damp skin, playing with the piercing in my nipple until my hips jolt forward and my full length throbs between her thighs. She leisurely continues touching me, down my abs, through my happy trail until she reaches my dick. She strokes it a few times with her soft hand, before pressing the head into her.

It's so warm and soft. And wet; soaking wet. I feel everything without the latex in the way and it's more marvelous than I could imagine.

"Are you sure about this...?" My mouth forces me to ask, because I still can't believe this is happening. It feels like I'm losing my virginity.

"Yes, trust me," she gasps, letting go of my shaft as I sink into her. *Alex... Baby...*

"Oh... *God...*"

This is the most incredible sensation ever invented. I mean, I know why I haven't been doing this all the other times, but now that I am doing it, I feel like I've been severely missing out on this euphoria all my life.

I feed myself all the way inside, her walls enveloping me like silk. She fits me like a glove and her walls squeeze tight like they're hugging me; welcoming me.

I pull back a bit then thrust in again, savoring the most amazing feeling I've ever felt while we move together, holding each other and whispering, panting out soft sounds.

"Alex..."

"Noah..."

"You feel so fucking good, baby." I stroke in her deeper and harder, though it stays slow; revering, cherishing.

Seek Me

"You feel incredible," she mewls, scratching my back, nails scoring my shoulders. "I've always wanted to feel you like this."

"God, me too," I hold myself up over her so I can watch her face, and watch me moving inside her. It looks life changing.

I hold her by her ass and pound into her so deep she screams, then locks her ankles at the top of my ass. Our bodies press together, heated and wet and trembling with passion. My lips skim her jaw, down to her neck where I kiss and suck and bite hard, marking her like she did to me when we first met. It wasn't that long ago, but it feels like forever has gone by since that night, and I'm not ready for it to end.

I never want this to end.

"Why are you going...?" I hum like a plea because I can't fucking help myself. For every ounce of pleasure I feel right now, there's a rippling pain coursing through my veins.

"I'm *sorry*, baby," she mewls, and she means it. I know she does.

But unfortunately it doesn't make it hurt any less.

"You promised you'd never forget how I feel... right?" My hips smash into hers over and over while I fuck her deep with every bit of myself.

That's what I've done for Alex. Given myself over to her, and it practically destroyed me.

"I promise, Noah," she says then moans out loud from the sensation we're both feeling. Her muscles are tightening all around me and I'm ready to let go. "You'll always be with me."

Her finger traces the word *Seek* on my chest.

"Remember how no one else can do this to you, okay?" I grunt, bottoming out. "Only me..."

"Only you, Noah..." she grips my neck as she cries out loud, her voice and the sounds of us fucking echoing off the walls. "*Only... You.*"

"Baby... fuck I'm coming..." I gasp, awestruck, then kiss her lips as soft as I can manage while my loins are being ripped apart by this killer orgasm. "I'm coming... inside you..."

"Yes... Oh God, Noah... Fill me, baby." I feel her coming on me in demanding pulses, like a vigorous wave.

The world becomes dark as I fall. I come hard in grueling throbs, pouring into Alex's plush walls, contractions aching in my balls from the intense release.

Coming inside her is the most spectacular thing I will ever feel in this lifetime. Like fireworks popping behind my eyes while my body is swallowed up by an endless impenetrable warmth. My hips are almost still, just barely stroking lazily inside her softness, balls deep as I empty every last drop into her body.

It's never been like this. I've never felt this before, and I probably won't again, a realization that makes me shake for a whole other reason.

Alex's pussy finally releases its grip on me, though her hands are still holding me close to her. Once the room stops spinning and our breathing evens out, I notice that she's comatose. I recognize the soft little breaths she makes when she's knocked out cold.

My body wants to smile, but it physically won't happen. I can't smile right now. I'm not happy.

I'm dead inside.

She's supposed to be *mine*. The first girl I've ever had feelings for, and instead of becoming my girlfriend, she's jet setting out of my life.

This fucking sucks.

I nuzzle her neck and kiss her creamy skin a few dozen times, committing her smell and feel to memory. She promised she'd never forget this, and I know a year and a half isn't long enough for her to forget me, but it is long enough for her to live many days of her life without me.

Long enough for her to meet someone else.

I feel like I could cry, and I can't do that because I haven't done it since I was nine years old... These emotions are too heavy. There's a reason why I avoid all this bullshit, and this right here is a prime example. Now I'm deep in Alex obsession and she's leaving. How the fuck am I supposed to function without her?

I try hard to push all these thoughts away and just keep cuddling her. It might be weird, but I want to stay inside her for as long as possible. My dick's never been inside a pussy without the latex pajamas, and it feels too good. I want to savor it for a little while longer.

I hold Alex's snoozing body against mine for minutes. Hours. Days, who fucking knows. It feels like a long time, of me just trailing my fingers on every inch of her skin I can reach, kissing and sniffing her hair. I'm tired, and I'd like to fall asleep, but I just can't. If I sleep, when I wake up she'll be leaving. And then who the fuck knows if I'll see her again.

There it is again, that overwhelming pressure behind my eyes.

I'm not doing this. I need to get up. I need to move.

I need to smoke.

I slide myself out of Alex slowly, which feels insane, then I roll away

Seek Me

carefully, so as not to wake my sleeping beauty. I cover her in a blanket, which one-hundred percent needs to be washed after this, and sneak into the bathroom.

Once I'm done in there, I tug on some sweatpants and go downstairs. I drink some water, blow out the candles, which fortunately didn't burn the house down, and grab a joint, making my way outside to the terrace.

I recline on my chaise lounge and light her up, taking a long drag and holding onto it. I stare up at the sky, which you can't really see from here, so it's mostly the sides of other buildings and all my millions of plants. But nonetheless, I stare, smoking until most of the joint is gone, and I'm sedated.

The little bit of sky I can see is turning light when movement catches my eye. I slowly pivot my head toward the door and find Alex, standing there in nothing but one of my t-shirts, looking all shy and adorable.

My heart skips in my chest. But then it remembers that it's dead and shrivels up again.

"Have you slept at all?" She asks, stepping timidly over to me.

I shake my head and say nothing, because I can't find my words and my mouth might be broken. She stands at the edge of the chaise lounge, but instead of crawling in next to me, she bites her lip.

"Do you... mind if I...?" She nods to where I'm sitting and my brow furrows.

She's asking if she can lay next to me?? Jesus, it really is over, isn't it?

"No, Alex, I don't mind," I grumble, gaping up at her with what I'm sure is hurt in my eyes.

I scoot over and she cuddles up by my side, resting her head on my chest. I snake my arm around her and pull her close; as close as I can possibly get her without smothering her to death. *This* is how I want her always, and I can't have it. It's devastating.

We're quiet for a while, just snuggling and avoiding the inevitable; that in a few short hours, she'll be gone. And then I'll leave, then she'll leave. And what will happen after that...?

"You'll always be my best friend, Noah," she whispers, tracing the lines of my tattoos. "I hope you know that."

I choke on the words my diseased heart tries to scream. *I want to be more than that.*

But it can't speak. It's all over, everything I felt. Everything I wanted...

So instead I take her small hand in mine and kiss her fingers. And I say, "I know."

Alex and I fell asleep outside on the chaise, which wasn't the best of ideas since it's still pretty chilly out. But we were snuggled together and warm, so I guess we didn't notice.

We woke up and had coffee in silence. And now she's getting ready to leave.

I have a flight to catch in a bit, so I need to get all my shit together. I need to get my head on straight before Brant gets here.

Alex comes downstairs fully dressed. Not in her dress from last night, but in some of her clothes she'd left here. She has a number of clothing items at my place... Also hair things, a toothbrush, and an assortment of cute little nose rings. The point is, she has stuff here. Because we've been *exclusive fuck-buddies* for eight months.

And now we're nothing.

Not nothing. Long-distance friends. She's not leaving forever, Professor Emo. She's going away for eighteen months. She'll be back before you know it.

I roll my eyes at myself. My brain is trying to make me feel better, but he's beating a dead horse. Who knows if Alex will even come back? There's no guarantee she won't fall in love with Budapest and decide she wants to live there full time.

Or that she won't meet a guy there and fall in love with *him*...

God... When is this sickening sorrow going to stop? I've been holding back emotional vomit since last night.

Alex saunters over to me looking particularly sullen, which reminds me of how gloomy I feel, and now we're both just standing here, staring at each other, looking pitiful.

I take her hand, because I need the contact up until the end.

"What are you doing with your apartment?" I ask, using humdrum chitchat to distract from my personal anguish.

"Keeping it," she answers quietly. "The rent is paid up, and the super said he'd pop in every once in a while to check on it. I could sublet I guess, but I don't really want some stranger living in my house." She huffs an awkward laugh then glances at her feet.

"I know what you mean," I rumble, working to shake off my grouchiness.

I need to not take my awful mood out on her. She's my friend and she's following her dreams. Just because I have feelings that are stronger than hers apparently, it's not like she's fucking with me on purpose. Realistically, she has no idea how I feel about her.

And now she'll never know.

"You want me to grab you a cab?" I ask, forcing my face to convey a normal, friendly attitude. I've gotta say, it's taking a lot of my best acting abilities to remain cool right now. I'm freaking out a lot on the inside.

For eight months, every time I've ever asked Alex if she wants me to call her a car or get her a cab, she always scoffs at me and says something like, *I'm not incompetent, Noah. I'm more than capable of getting a car myself.*

This instance, right now, is the first time that she's actually nodded and mumbled, "Sure."

It might not mean anything. But to my overtired, heartbroken state, it means that she thinks we might never see each other again. I'm practically crippled by hurt.

It's one thing if I'm mentally obsessing over us potentially never seeing each other again, but it's a much more serious issue if Alex is thinking it too.

God, what is going on? How is this even happening right now?

I sigh and take her hand, bringing her outside to the curb. Each step is more painful than the last. I don't want this. It all feels wrong.

It wasn't supposed to go down like this.

At the curb I flag a passing yellow cab and open the door. Alex gazes up at me with tears in her eyes, and it's the most heartbreaking thing I've ever seen.

I don't want to do this. I don't want this to be goodbye…

I brush her hair back with my fingers and fight to hold on to the mask. I use every bit of inner strength to keep it in place, because I need it right now. I can't let her see what's decaying underneath.

"Be good, Alexandra," I whisper, tone even.

Her lip quivers and she gasps, looking away for a moment as tears stream down her face. I suck in a silent breath, the dull ache inside building a permanent home in my chest.

She hugs me hard, crying softly into my neck while I hold her and rock gently.

"Hey… You're gonna be fine," I whisper through my fabricated voice of easy calmness. "You're Alexandra Mackenzie, remember? You'll make Europe your bitch."

She snorts a laugh on me and pulls back, nodding repeatedly.

"Thank you, Noah," she sniffles, wiping her eyes. "I'll see you when I get back."

She gives me a pointed look and I force the hardest smile I've ever had to produce.

"Can't wait," I wink at her. This whole performance has me wanting to retch.

She lifts herself up and kisses my lips quick, before turning and sliding into the backseat of the car, holding my hand until the last second. When her fingers slip from mine, my heart screams out loud, so hard I can feel it.

Don't go...

Alex shuts the door and the cab drives away, with her waving at me out the window as she disappears out of sight.

After standing outside for a slew of desolate minutes, I breathe deep and turn back toward my building. I go inside, wandering in a daze through my quiet apartment. It's my own home and yet it feels so foreign right now I can barely breathe.

I sway in the middle of the living room, staring at the floor; helpless and alone.

Alone when I never knew I didn't want that... Until it was too late.

The emotions are bubbling over... The mask is slipping.

There's a ringing in my ears as I rub my hands hard over my eyes.

Complete and utter fucking failure.

The only person I've ever wanted more from just walked out of my life, and she may never come back.

I'm fucking alone again.

Good! You're a bachelor, remember?? What the hell were you doing trying to make her your girlfriend, anyway? You're meant to be single. Relationships suck, clearly.

Fuck that. You're better off.

I tug my hair roughly with my fingers. I can't believe that happened.

I can't believe I let it happen.

What the fuck is wrong with me?!

I growl out loud and turn, grabbing the closest thing to me, a lamp, and hurling it across the room. It comes crashing down on the floor; the bulb shattering. But I don't stop.

I pick up a glass dish on my side table and smash it on the floor.

Struggling to catch my breath, my whole body is burning up. But I still don't stop.

I rip through my entire living room, throwing and bashing and breaking everything I can see. Everything that gets in my way.

I knock my flat screen over.

I smash my glass coffee table.

I heave a chair against the wall.

I destroy everything around me in a blind rage, because there's nothing else I can do.

It's all ruined, anyway. *All just a bunch of fucking rubble.*

Chapter Nineteen

Alex

Nine Months Later...

Lace up my boots with careful attention, making sure they're nice and tight before I tie them. I glance over my shoulder out the window. The sky is gray and overcast, and the noisy radiator in my place is currently clanging and rattling out the heat, making it toasty warm in here, while leading me to believe it's rather chilly outside.

So I grab my big fuzzy coat I bought last month from a small thrift shop my friend Chloe showed me, and bundle up, donning a scarf and my favorite black French Connection beanie that says *Don't FCUK With Me* on it.

I'm all ready to brave the cold when I see movement in my peripheral. I take a deep breath before I turn around.

"So... I'm heading out to meet Chloe for lunch," I utter to the being who just emerged from my bathroom in nothing but a towel.

Samson steps closer and my head tilts back because he's so tall he towers over me.

"Sure," he rumbles and leans down to kiss my forehead. "Can I call you? Last night was... fun."

He grins and I have to smile back because his accent is very unique, but I like it.

"Moka," I smirk and he laughs.

"Mhm, yes. *Moka*. Yet you sound so American when you say it." He teases me and I shove him away playfully.

"Can you lock up for me, please?" I ask, stepping away because I can feel my cheeks flushing out of awkwardness.

"Igen. Alex, you didn't answer me," he grunts, but I'm already at the door.

I peek at him one last time before I leave. He's just standing there, practically naked, with his arms crossed over his broad chest; eyebrows raised to where his dark, wet hair is on his forehead as he waits for me to say he can call me.

I'm not sure why I have to give him permission. He'll likely do it anyway if he wants to, not that it guarantees I'll answer.

"Bucsu," I wink and slip through the door casually, closing it behind me. Some weight lifts as I move through my hallway and out the front door.

As I anticipated, it's cold outside. Not freezing, but the chill is to be expected in winter. I'm sure it's the same in New York, probably even colder.

I walk the streets, passing the usual commotion of the city, heading to a local cafe my friend Chloe and I spend exorbitant amounts of time in. I'm famished after a long night, and I could use something warm and delicious to nourish what is likely a booze and sex hangover.

I went out last night with some friends from the program. We danced away the cold at a disco and as if that wasn't enough heat on its own, I brought home that giant, sexy thing for some fun between the sheets.

I enjoyed myself, and I think it was just the release I needed. Before last night I hadn't had sex in nine months, and I was starting to feel a little pent-up.

My time here in Budapest has been incredible thus far. To think it's only halfway through is crazy, because I've done so much already.

The art program has been life-changing. I've learned more in these past nine months than I have in my entire twenty-six years before that, and my instructors love me. I'm still sticking to my style, but it's very different now. It's matured a lot, and grown more picturesque. I never would have discovered this new side of my skill set if it weren't for the immensely talented instructors and my fellow classmates I get to work with every day.

There are people from all over in the program, and we've become quite the tight-knit little group. A few of them are from the area; Hungary and Prague. Some are from Germany, France, and London. There's a girl from Australia and a kid from Lebanon. The only other American is Chris from California, who I've definitely bonded with over our occasional mutual home-sickness. But we both agree it's amazing here and we're not ready to go back just yet.

I slink inside the cafe, relieved to feel heat once again as my eyes skim the tables for my friend. I spot Chloe sitting in the back and weave in between the tables to get to her.

"Why hello, mon amie!" Chloe croons in her elegant French accent, standing to kiss both my wind-burned cheeks before we take our seats. "You look refreshed." She smirks and I frown.

"It's cold outside," I grumble, shrugging out of my coat.

"Hmm... no, I think it's something else," she begins immediately berating me, though I can't say I'm surprised. Everyone saw me and Samson hanging all over each other last night, so I knew this would happen. She leans in on the table as her eyes go wide. "So how was it?"

"Chloe, Jesus... Can I at least get a cup of coffee first?" I rub my frigid hands together.

She looks up and makes a face at the waiter, who knows us well enough to understand we need lattes, and quick.

"I'm sorry, but I need to know how are his moves in bed," she wiggles her eyebrows and I giggle because her broken English is so cute, especially coming from such an adorable little blonde munchkin. "We've all checked him out since we got here and you, lucky little thing, you got to try him out. So I must know!"

I sigh and fight the urge to roll my eyes. Yes, Samson is very hot. And yes, we've spent the last few months getting to know each other out at parties and clubs. It started with some innocent flirting, and then one night a few weeks ago, he walked me home and kissed me at the door.

So naturally after that the flirting turned into some very heated makeout sessions at said parties and clubs. He kept asking me out, and I was hesitating.

I'm not looking to date. I just want to have fun. That's what I came here for.

Once I made that clear to him, and he accepted my terms, I agreed to go out with him. We went to the disco together last night, and we left together.

And we had sex.

Hooray.

Pardon me for not sounding more excited. I don't mean to feel unflattered or uninterested. Samson is a sweet guy, and he's certainly easy on the eyes. But deep down, a little voice inside me couldn't help but yawn.

Sam's not the only guy I've hooked up with since I've been here. There were a few others I made out with here and there, and one dude I let go to third base, which was pretty damn nice. But Samson's the first one I actually had sex with. I mainly did it because I got fed up with lulling myself to sleep at night with my vibrator.

The truth is that none of these guys, no matter how hot they are or how talented their tongues may be, can hold a candle to the one I left in New York.

My best friend. Who I miss so badly, I'm trying not to think about him because it only makes me regret being here, and I *don't* want that.

I love being here. I love this program and I love my friends. I love how much better I've gotten at painting. I don't want to have any regrets.

Missing Noah just comes with the territory. The homesick feeling that plagues me at night when I'm all alone. It can't just be about him... I miss New York, too. I miss how loud and crazy everyone is. I miss my apartment, and Noah's apartment, and Boots. But I knew I would feel like this. It was to be expected. It doesn't change the fact that I'm having a great time.

That's why I slept with Samson last night. And I was able to allow myself to enjoy it enough, so that's all that matters, I guess.

"It was fine, okay?" I murmur to Chloe, giving her a pointed look that she clearly doesn't understand, because she keeps going.

"Just fine? No spectacular? Was his sausage trop petit?" She holds up her thumb and index finger in a way that has me laughing out loud.

"No no no! No, his *sausage* was fine," I groan, rubbing my temples as the coffees arrive and I take a big sip, knowing full-well it's going to burn my mouth, which it does. "He was great. But it's just casual, okay Chloe? Nothing more will happen. Just one night."

She nods along, though I'm not sure she's following me. "Sam is the sexiest man in our group. Yet you say you don't want him?" She giggles and flips her hair. "I say you're a bit mad, no?"

I grin at her. "He is very sexy, you're right. And I do like him, but it's just... After everything I've been through, I didn't come here to meet someone. I came here to live and have experiences."

"Well, you're certainly doing that, l'amour," she gives me a warm smile.

We order some palatschinke, which is basically like a rolled up crepe filled with jelly or whatever you want. I get mine with Nutella, naturally. And we chat and eat, filling ourselves up and recovering from a late night out.

"Have you spoken with your friend?" Chloe asks just as we're finishing our food. "The one you miss very badly?"

I swallow hard, unable to stop the twisting in my stomach at where this conversation is going.

"No, I haven't spoken with him," I mumble, staring down at my plate. "I haven't heard a word from him since I left."

"I'm sure he's busy," she adds. "You said he's a famous movie star, oui?"

"Yes... Well, more of a TV star, but yes." I nod quickly. And now my mind is drifting to places I typically aim to corral it away from.

Not speaking to Noah at all while I'm out here wasn't part of the plan, but I didn't want to be the first one to reach out. My phone number doesn't exactly work here, but we could always message each other on Facebook or Instagram.

Stalking Noah's social media accounts has become a part of my daily routine. I just want to know what's going on with him, but I'm too afraid to put myself out there and message him first. It's been nine months. Surely if he wanted to talk to me, he would have made an effort by now. I'm worried he's mad at me, and that's what's keeping him from talking to me.

Or worse… That he met a girl and forgot about me completely.

I haven't seen any evidence that this has happened based on his social media, though he doesn't really use his much. The gossip articles haven't mentioned anything about him having a new relationship either, so I'm praying that's not the case. Still, I worry that us not having any communication for the entire time I'm out here could have a damaging effect on our friendship.

"This is why you can't enjoy your time with Sam," Chloe arches an accusing brow at me. "You love this other man."

"Well, of course I love him. He's my best friend…" I hum, finishing the last of my coffee.

"No no. You love him more than that," she signals the waiter for check, then begins pulling money out of her bag.

"No, I don't," I grumble, growing more tired by the second. "He's just a friend. Sure, he's also the best sex I've ever had in my entire life…"

I bite my lip and Chloe squeals. She loves talking about sex. It's basically her favorite thing. We've spent many a night in the last few months having sleepovers and dishing about guys. And because of my limited experiences on the subject, the only guy I talked about was Noah. So that must be why she thinks I'm in love with him…

Has to be it.

"So he's better than Sam?" She wiggles in her seat and I chuckle, tossing a balled up napkin at her.

"He's better than everyone. That's just Noah, though. He's the best person on Earth." She opens her mouth, but I cut her off before she can go there again. "And he's my friend! That's it. Just friends."

"You Americans and your casual sex," she giggles. "Like Sex and the City. You're like Carrie Bradshaw only you're a painter, not a writer."

I have to laugh at that. I'm literally *nothing* like Carrie Bradshaw, except that I'm from New York, which is enough to form the stereotype in her European mind.

"Yea, if Carrie Bradshaw was covered in tattoos and piercings and listened to Metallica to fall asleep," I smirk and she shakes her head. "I'm more like

Seek Me

Carrie White."

"Well, *Carrie*, I spoke to Simon and Trudy last night and it seems they are onboard to come to Edinburgh for New Year's Eve. Are you excited?"

I nod and clasp my hands together, mirroring her energy. But then I have a thought.

"Wait a minute... Simon is good friends with Sam..." I give Chloe a helpless look. "Do you think he'll invite him?"

She fiddles with her manicured fingernails. "I believe... he already did." She peeks up at me through a purely guilty expression.

"Dammit, Chloe!" I whine. "He's going to think I want to be there *with* him! It's a weekend trip! Make sure we get separate rooms, or I'll kill you."

Chloe giggles deviously while I resist the urge to swallow my tongue. I'm annoyed that Samson didn't tell me he was invited to come along with our group on this little trip to Scotland we've been planning for their giant New Year's Eve party. I can only hope he didn't mention it because I got through to him with my *keeping it casual* speech, but sometimes I wonder if he truly understands me when I speak to him. He's been fluent in English since he was a kid, but it's a very fluid language. Speaking *English* and speaking *American* are two very different things.

Chloe and I leave the cafe and brave the cold again, heading straight back to my place because it's closer. Thankfully, Sam is gone when we arrive.

I meander around the loft, making tea for us both while Chloe parks herself on my bed and glues her eyes to my laptop screen.

"Wow... I believe now I understand," she eventually sighs, and I plop down next to her. "He's gorgeous, Alexandra mon amie!"

My brow furrows as I peer at the computer to see what she's seeing. It's a picture of Noah, decked out in some Southern backwoods survivalist outfit on the set of his new show, *Hell Storm*.

Naturally I've already seen these pictures. Like I said, I've been actively subscribing to celebrity news articles lately.

According to many of them, the show's first season debuted to incredibly high ratings. Everyone in the States, and now many other countries, has been buzzing about this new gory, yet cinematically significant, zombie apocalypse drama.

They had a premiere in October that looked very exciting and fun. Thankfully Noah didn't bring a date, according to the pictures. That would've been a hard one to distract myself from, for sure. But just seeing him smiling on a red carpet next to his costars had me swooning and melting and beaming with pride. I wish

I could have been there with him… To celebrate his accomplishments like he did for me.

Okay, stop. We're not doing this. You're happy for him, and that's fine. But you can't wish you were back home when you're not. You're here and you love it, so just buck up.

"Does he always dress like this?" Chloe frowns at the screen and I laugh.

"No, he's in costume. For his TV show," I explain to her, admiring how damn good he looks in these pictures. Like a sexy redneck with muscles and tattoos and eyes so dark you can barely see his pupils.

Oh my God. Enough.

"He looks like a bad boy," Chloe grins, tugging her lip between her fingers. "No wonder you are so stuck on him."

"I'm not *stuck* on him," I huff, annoyed that I have to keep trying to prove this point to her. "He's my friend. I'm happy for him."

"Hmm yes. Well, will you still be happy to know about him seeing other women?" She peeks at me expectantly.

"It's kind of his thing," I shrug. "What I did last night with Sam, Noah's probably done just about every night since I've been gone. With different girls each time."

Surprisingly, this doesn't make me want to hurl everywhere like you'd think. I knew when I left that Noah would go back to whoring around. It was his default setting before we met, and there would be no reason to think he wouldn't return to it when we parted ways. Plus, I know that what Noah and I have differs from what he does with all the miscellaneous women. We have something deeper… Or *had*. Who knows.

But thinking about this now won't do me any good. I have nine months left here and until it gets closer to the end, I see no point in torturing myself over what will happen between me and my best friend when I inevitably return.

A few hours later, after a dinner of takeout paprika chicken from our favorite local spot, Chloe goes home, and I get ready for bed. I have an early class tomorrow, and I need to get some rest after the crazy weekend I had.

I strip the sheets off my bed because they still smell like Sam and it's bothering me for some reason. Once there are new sheets on, I climb in and turn off the lights. And I lie there.

I lie in my bed, in the dark, staring up at the bedroom ceiling of my little Hungarian loft, and finally give up the fight in my mind, letting it wander back to New York.

I wonder what Noah's doing right now. I think it's midday back home, so there's no way he's in bed. He's probably out, with his friends, or his assistant. Or with a girl.

Maybe they're walking through the park, like he and I used to. Maybe they're getting drinks at one of our usual spots. But no matter what they're doing, I know the girl would be having fun. Noah's a blast, after all.

He's probably making her laugh; teasing her about something, and finding little excuses to touch her, playfully. Flirting is an effortless art form for Noah Richards. Sometimes I don't even think he knows he's doing it. But it has girls powerless to resist him, and that's the part that makes my stomach twist in knots.

Noah will do him. He always does, whether it's with me in the picture, or with me thousands of miles away. All my wary heart can do is pray that whatever he's getting himself into out there, it's nothing serious.

And with that uncomfortable thought I drift uneasily off to sleep.

I'm giggling. Out loud. I can hear myself.

And I can feel it. Deep, full-bellied fits of laughter bubbling out of me while my stomach warms with excitement.

My fingers toil in his hair as he carries me in his strong arms, over the threshold of our penthouse suite. He slides gracefully through the foyer, but he's not stopping to put me down, and I know he won't until we're in the bedroom.

The anticipation is fluttering inside me like butterflies. I tuck my face into the crook of his neck and sniff him. His smell awakens something inside me, and yet it feels familiar. There's a nostalgia in his scent that confuses me.

But no time to elaborate on that because I've just been tossed down on the bed and he's crawling on top of me, eyes brighter than the sky and a smile so salacious it turns my limbs to jelly.

"My beautiful bride," he whispers, dropping his lips to mine and kissing me slow. Sensual and intimate, yet hungry. "I've waited a lifetime for you."

My heart skips in my chest and I reach up to hold his face and touch it everywhere with greedy fingers. I just can't believe he's mine.

What kind of saint was I in a past life to have won a man like him?

"I need you so bad, Alexandra…" he whispers over my mouth, sliding down the zipper of my white dress. "Do you need me?"

"Yes," I gasp with heat spreading below my waist.

He removes my dress, then my panties, all the while with my fumbling hands ripping at his tie, then dress shirt, then his belt and pants. He helps me as we kiss, ridding himself of his clothes until we're both naked, our bare flesh pressed together in the bed.

It's our honeymoon, and I can't wait to make love to my husband. I'm married and this is all so new. It's thrilling. I'm wet and shaking and ready.

He takes his time with me, cherishing my body, feasting on me as if he's been starved a thousand years. And when I look up at him in the dimmed light of the room, I see a man so gorgeous it feels unreal.

A nervous feeling settles in my gut. Something is wrong.

His blue eyes shine into mine as his hands travel up my body, massaging my breasts. I moan out a soft noise because it feels good, but somewhere in my mind, deep down in a place I can't fully understand, a voice is telling me to be afraid. It's telling me to run.

His hands find my throat and pressure builds. His fingers dig into my windpipe and it's hard to breathe.

I gasp for air, my face tight. I kick my legs under him, but he won't stop. His body weight is overpowering, and he's so much bigger than me.

All I can see are his eyes; deep glimmering blue, burning with rage.

With evil.

"Roger... please..."

I try to cry out, but I can't speak. I can't breathe.

My vision blurs and it all becomes dark.

"Now you're all mine," he growls and my body breaks out in a cold sweat.

I kick and punch and struggle to scream.

Get off me!

Help!

But it's no use.

I'm drifting. I'm falling... away.

I thought he loved me...

I gasp and shoot up in bed.

I'm panting, sucking air into my lungs fast and hard as my hands fly to my throat.

It's not sore, but that nightmare was so real, I can still feel his fingerprints there. Like they're etched on my body forever.

I blink my tired eyes in the dark and I can't see anything. I'm surrounded by complete blackness.

"Hello?" I whisper, though I'm not sure who I'm talking to.
Where am I?
Something about this feels familiar. It feels safe.
My pulse regulates as I register that I was having a bad dream.
It's fine. He's not here.
But then the bed shifts next to me and panic rises inside me once more.
I turn to my left and the wide, sleeping form next to me turns.
"You okay, baby?"
That voice. *That familiar voice.* It sets a longing in my chest and pacifies me at the same time. Just those three simple words sound like home and I let out a breath because everything is going to be fine.
Noah's here.
"I had a bad dream… about him," I whisper in the dark, cuddling up to his body.
I wrap my arms around him and he holds me back, stroking my hair gently with his long fingers.
"I'm here," Noah's tone is soft and raspy, and so comforting my mind and body are at ease. "I told you I'd never let anyone hurt you again. I meant that."
"I know you did," I murmur, lips moving on his warm, soft skin.
He kisses my head and rocks me gently.
"You're different from all of them, Alex," he tells me, and I believe him. "I wasn't looking for you, but I found you anyway."
I nod, because I understand. I know what he's saying. The words are in my mind before he even says them.
"My heart was seeking you…"
His voice becomes echoey. I feel him slipping away and I begin to tremble.
"Don't go," I whimper and kiss his neck over and over, committing his feeling to memory.
I can't lose this. I can't lose him.
He hums softly, that sweet little sound he gives when I make him feel good. So I keep going, sucking and licking his delicious skin. He brushes his hips against mine, and I can feel him; long and thick and solid. I grind myself into him, pleasure shooting through me.
"I want *you*…"
I think that was me, but it sounded like both of us.
"*Only you.*"
Noah pulls me on top of him and fills me. It feels glorious, as if every nerve

in my body has ignited in flames of bliss.

He thrusts into me deep and I cry out his name in the dark. I move with him, following his lead, building on his rhythm, holding him, kissing him; taking in everything he gives me.

"You're more than the rest of them, Alex," he groans, squeezing my butt hard with his big hands. "I never got to tell you…"

A quaking desire rocks through me and I gasp.

Then it all disappears.

My eyes spring open as my chest expands, breathing in and out hard. My walls are still pulsing through what was obviously an orgasm.

A sleep orgasm.

Good God…

I look around as my heart rocks in my body. I'm in my bed, in my loft, in Budapest.

Noah's not here. I was dreaming…

He dream banged me.

I scoff to myself and run a hand over my face. I just had a wet dream about by best friend. *A very wet dream from the feel of it…*

"Ugh," I pant, flopping back on my pillow. I feel empty inside.

Well, this sucks.

That was very strange. I had a nightmare inside a dream. That's never happened to me before. Not that I remember, anyway.

Tears push behind my eyes, because it felt so good to be with Noah… In his arms, hearing his voice.

I miss him terribly. That dream solidified what I've been hiding from these past nine months. That despite how much fun I'm having out here, I do still miss Noah. I don't think I'll ever not miss him when we're apart.

I roll onto my side and grab my phone off the nightstand. I pull up his Facebook Messenger contact and just stare at it for a while.

I want so badly to call him… I need to hear his voice right now. For real, not in dream form. I want to talk to him, to tell him about everything that's been happening and hear about what he's been up to. I just need to hear him.

I never got to tell you…

My chest tightens. I can hear his words so vividly. Something about them sounded pained.

I know it was a dream, fabricated by my subconscious, but it felt real.

I just want to talk to him.

Seek Me

I swipe at a tear rolling down my cheek. My fingers hover over the button on my phone, but I just can't bring myself to do it.

It's been so long. Why hasn't he tried to reach out to me? Why doesn't he want to hear from me as much as I want *anything* from him?

I slam my phone back down on the nightstand and turn over, pulling my covers up. I can't do this to myself. Not now.

I'm living out here. I'm doing this.

I knew it would be scary and maybe sometimes sad, but that was all part of the journey. It's for the best, and I need to see it through.

If I talk to Noah, he'll just make me want to come home. I'm finishing this program, and I'm going to enjoy it while I do. I'm doing the right thing.

Then why does it feel so wrong?

Chapter Twenty
Noah

Four Months Later...

The Network's newest hit series, Hell Storm, is filming a second season, and its rabid fandom is already abuzz!

Andrew James and Co are back! After airing to shockingly high ratings last fall, the cast takes to the Savannah woods to continue their zombie-fighting antics.

Georgia just got hotter! Andrew James, Noah Richards, and John Barthow put their boots back on for the filming of Hell Storm's second season. We have your exclusive, behind-the-scenes look right here...

I WIPE THE SWEAT FROM MY BROW with the back of my hand and look around. There's no way Nicola will need another take after that. She'd have to be impersonating Hellen Keller not to acknowledge how fantastically we nailed that last one.

I'm sort of tired, which is crazy because we just got here. In the grand scheme, I mean. We've been *here*, on set, since eight this morning, and the sun's just going down. So we've been doing this a while, and my body is craving a seat and a beer. *Or four...*

We actually just started filming season two of the show a couple weeks ago, which is why I shouldn't be allowing the work to wear me out just yet. Though I've really been bringing my A-game to this performance, more so than any project I've ever been in.

A second season is different. When you film the pilot season of a series, you're never really sure where it could end up going. The likely possibility, based on my years of experience, is that it'll go right into the garbage. But if you're like me, and you have a strong will to succeed in life, then you act your damn ass off anyway, all the while hoping and praying for the producer gods to throw you a contract bone.

Seek Me

That's exactly what happened with *Hell Storm*. Fans were instantly sucked in, like moths to the flame of a fire in backwoods Georgia. The critics were impressed. Seeing how quickly everyone began clambering about this Southern Sheriff and his band of badass zombie-wasting pals had their eyes gleaming with dollar signs.

So we all received contract offers, and the show was confirmed for at least three more seasons.

And here we are.

This job is much more physically demanding than I anticipated, which was foolish on my part because the scenes are almost exactly what I had pictured when I first began wondering what co-starring in such a show would look like. Andrew and I, along with our other awesome costars, spend our days covered in fake dirt and blood, running through the Georgia woods wielding fake weapons and perfecting the art of pretending to kill undead-human-makeup-covered extras. It's really bizarre.

And I *fucking* love it.

And I wouldn't trade it for any job in the entire world.

"Are you coming for a drink?" Andrew asks me, sauntering over from God knows where, raking his fingers through his slightly curly chestnut hair which is dripping wet after having a third bottle of water dumped on his head within the last two takes.

"Is the Pope a total pervert?" I smirk and he shakes his head slowly, though he obviously can't hide his amusement which has me bursting out in laughter.

"Where's Johnny?" My head bobs in search of our other costar and completing member of the trifecta that is our amazing friendship.

Johnny Barthow is the nicest, and loudest, person I've ever met. People have this assumption about him based on what they see in the media: that he's a heartless manwhore. More than myself, more than Andrew ever was, and more than just about every other narcissistic Hollywood actor on the scene right now.

And those assumptions couldn't be more wrong.

Yes, Johnny loves to enjoy the company of women. *Don't we all?* And he hasn't had a relationship in, *uh, well… let me check my watch…* Ever.

But that doesn't make him a bad guy. In fact, he's super supportive, kind, funny, and more of a sweetheart than the girls he sleeps with give him credit for. *But that's a whole other thing…*

"I think he's avoiding Erica," Andrew grumbles, attempting to squeeze more water out of the bottle onto his head, even though the thing is clearly bone-dry.

"Oh boy... That's why you don't sleep with makeup artists. They're always crazy," I hum, peeking over my shoulder.

"You just hooked up with Gigi last night," Andrew points out and I shush him aggressively.

"Yea, exactly. So I would know. Now, don't say her name too loud, or she'll appear out of nowhere like Beetle-"

"Hey, Noah!" Melody Davis, one of our costars, pops right in front of me and I practically fly out of my skin.

"Oh fuck..." I breathe out a hard sigh, slapping my hand over my heart before turning to Andrew. "You summoned the wrong monster." Andrew snickers.

"Ha ha, very funny," Melody rolls her eyes and flips her shiny blonde hair, which is caked with fake blood at its ends. "I heard Nicola say we're wrapping for the day. You have any plans for later?" She moves in closer and bites her lip, trailing her fingers underneath the hem of my sticky t-shirt.

"Yea, actually. We're doing a guys' night," I give her a look, hoping she'll understand what I'm saying, but she simply stares up at me with blank eyes. "No girls allowed." I wink and she giggles.

"That sounds sexy." She's still touching me and I'm internally itching for Johnny to get his big, crazy ass over here so we can bounce. "What I wouldn't give for an invite to that party."

She wiggles her eyebrows, and I peek at Andrew. He looks disturbed.

"And maybe throw in that new guy, too," she goes on. "He's a hottie. I'm surrounded by tens. What's a girl to do?"

"Pray more?" Andrew huffs and Melody shows him an evil grin that he brushes off effortlessly.

"Speaking of the newbie..."

I nod over to where the newest addition to our little family, Mike Beaumont, is following our director, Nicola Benson, around like an overly eager puppy. Nicola looks like she wants to hang herself.

Mike started with us at the beginning of this season, and he's a nice enough guy, I suppose. He's a new actor, so everything is all shiny and big in his eyes - his non-contract paychecks included. Andrew and I are trying to take him under our wing a bit; show him the ropes. He seems to be getting it, although he's ignored both of our advice about not bothering directors early on in the season.

"You guys should invite him along for your guys' night out," Melody suggests, repeatedly trying to grab my hand, though I'm not biting. "I think it would be sweet."

I shrug and aim my gaze at Andrew. "It's up to you, bossman."

"I hate when you call me that, and I don't give a tiny rat's ass who comes with us at this point, I just want to leave," Andrew grumbles, then looks up with wide eyes. "I mean, it's still guys only though," he throws in before Melody can start jumping up and down.

She pouts. "Too bad… I was looking forward to a repeat of last season."

She smooshes her boobs on me and Andrew shoots me an *I told you so* look over the top of her platinum blonde head.

Yea yea yea… I know, bro. You're always right. I get it.

Yes, I slept with my costar last year. And yes, it was stupid.

But what you have to understand is that I had just suffered a great tragedy and thus was not making the best decisions.

My best friend, the girl I thought I could make my first girlfriend of my adult life, took off for Europe for eighteen-months, leaving me alone to my own devices. I was goddamned inconsolable. I'm not sure I've used that much meaningless sex to ease my mind since I discovered that I could.

Sleeping with a coworker is never a good idea. Especially one you have to film with every day for five months, and then continue to see at press events, and act like you're the best of friends with. Melody and I are in close-quarters, filming some very physically demanding, often emotional scenes together. And based on how crazy the premiere stuff was for the pilot season, I'm willing to bet this fall they'll have an even more intense schedule lined up for us.

Sleeping with Melody was downright idiotic, but I did it anyway.

I really wasn't thinking at all…

It was late June last year, and we had just wrapped our mid-season episode ahead of schedule, so the whole cast and crew went over to Andrew's to celebrate with many beers. I got drunk fast, because I couldn't stop thinking about how badly I fucked up with Alex, and soon enough my mind was spinning out of control like a car on black ice.

I refused to let myself be that desperate loser who calls or messages her after only a month of her being away. So I set my sights on finding some new boobs with which to distract myself.

There were a lot of girls around, but I wasn't trying to be picky. In fact, I may have had awful beer goggles on at that point. Who knows. I was so wasted, I barely remember.

After watching me stumble about for a few, Andrew and Johnny put me to bed in the guest bedroom, and I was so sloshed for a moment I thought I might just pass out. Until I felt the bed shift…

It turned out to be Melody. She snuck into the room after Andrew rejected her and decided that rubbing up on me in my state of whiskey dick would make her feel better. Needless to say, my dick wasn't as fucked up as I was, and I banged the holy hell out of her. Thrice.

And she gave me head in the morning. It was ridiculous.

Feeling heartbroken isn't something I experience often, so when it happened I didn't really know how to act. I still sort of don't… I've definitely been drinking more than usual, and I'm not prepared to talk about it yet.

It's all just so ironic.

I was finally ready for something serious and the girl couldn't get away from me fast enough. It's been over a year and I'm still thinking about it. That might be the worst part.

"I'm going to find that wanker so we can get the bloody hell out of here," Andrew grunts and storms off. I can't help but smile. He gets so annoyed when he's hot and sticky and he can't continually dump bottles of water on himself. Almost as annoyed as I get when I have to do any physical work.

"Well, Noah, don't be afraid to stop by when you guys are done," Melody croons, which brings my attention back down to her. "I'll leave the backdoor unlocked."

She winks and my brow lifts in surprise. I don't know why she's still hitting on me. Last year we agreed hooking up was stupid and we would never do it again. Since we started filming she's been all over Andrew, and because he's married and not the slightest bit interested, she moved onto me. But I can't be mad about being her second choice, since she wasn't *my* choice at all. She just happened to be there.

A memory sweeps through my brain from that night… Of my costar bent over in front of me, her long blonde hair curled around my fist while I pounded into her from behind. She has a nice butt, I'll give her that. I liked how it jiggled when my pelvis slapped against it.

"*Fuck… Yes, Melanie.*"

"*It's Melody.*"

"*Yea, that's what I said.*"

I cringe and shake my head. *Stupid stupid stupid.*

"Mel, it's not gonna happen," I grumble and back away slowly.

"Right. No, I get it," she huffs, playing it off casually enough, though who can tell with an actress. "You're with Gigi now. I heard about you two…"

"No, I'm not *with* anyone." I look around for *anyone* who can save me from this annoying conversation.

Nicola stomps up to us with Mike on her heel and breathes out a frustrated sigh. *Thank God!*

"Sorry for the delay," she says and makes a face at me. I think she's telepathically asking me to get Mike away from her. "We're done for the day. Great work."

She nods subtly in Mike's direction and rolls her eyes so only I can see, which makes me smile. Nicola is my favorite director. She really gets what it's like to work with a diverse cast like us, and I don't want her losing her marbles before the show can truly hit its stride, so I'll gladly take one for the team and harvest the annoying newbie.

"Hey Mike, us boys are going for drinks," I tell him, patting his shoulder. "Why don't you come along?"

Mike's head snaps in my direction and his face lights up. I swallow hard, because I think I've made some terrible mistake.

"Okay!" Mike agrees animatedly. "I'd love to!"

Oh boy… What have I done?

I sigh out of whateverness and stammer off, nodding for Mike to follow me. Now I really need a drink. It's been a long week filled with physically exhausting work and I just want to lie down. But I can't do that alone, so I suppose I should figure out who's house I'll be lying down at later.

Not Melody's. One-hundred percent no.

Mike and I meet Andrew and Johnny at the set entrance, waving to the security guy, Bruce, as we hop into Andrew's SUV and he peels off. Everything in Savannah is far away, so the nearest shitty little dive bar that I absolutely *love* is a solid fifteen-minute drive from the set. As we cruise the streets, I'm quiet, staring out the window, watching trees pass while Mike blabs about one of the scenes he thought he nailed today.

"Nailed" probably isn't the right verb. "Pillow-fluffed" is more appropriate.

But I won't say that to him, mostly because I don't want to burst his newbie bubble. And also because judging from the awkward silence at the front of the car, Andrew and Johnny are two seconds from snapping and telling him themselves.

My lip curls slightly thinking about my friends up there. They're really the only reasons I've been able to enjoy the last year.

Then my wannabe smile fades and I close my eyes for a moment.

I can't let the depression sink me. My job here is too important to start wallowing in those nasty little thoughts that try to overtake my mind all day every day. It's a constant fight to keep myself upbeat these days; to keep the sadness at bay.

I don't know why I'm still obsessing over what happened with Alex. It was a year ago, for God's sake. It's time to forget about it and move the fuck on.

One would think from looking at me I've done just that. I'm burying the pain I feel inside by burying my cock in every girl I can find, so I guess to a layman, it would appear that I have no feelings left over for Alex.

But on the contrary, my feelings for her are still very much alive, and they make me miserable, hence the extracurricular activities. Honestly, screwing random women should be a part-time job for me at this point. I spend almost all my time outside of filming loading up my phone with endless options so that if thoughts of *Alex*, or *what I thought I wanted* ever try to sneak up, I always have a distraction on speed dial.

Andrew and Johnny are worried about me. They say I drink too much and sleep around with the ferocity of a man who has two weeks to live. But I've been assuring them this is just how I have to live my life.

It's what I was meant to do.

"*So*, baby blue, how's it going with the old ball-n-chain?" Johnny asks Andrew, cutting off Mike's incessant rambling.

Andrew sighs. He's been doing that more and more when preparing to talk about his wife, which worries me.

"She's good…" he mutters, and we all wait for him to keep going, but he doesn't.

"Is she gonna bring the kids out soon?" Johnny's voice is quiet, supportive yet curious, because we've all been wondering this.

Andrew's wife has yet to come to Georgia in the last year, since we started filming the first season. He had to live thousands of miles away from his own children for *five months* last year, which only worked because he was able to fly home every other weekend.

But still, it's my understanding that his wife doesn't work. I have no idea what's stopping her from getting off her selfish ass and coming out to support her husband, at the very least so he can see his kids without having to fly through several time-zones there and back.

Andrew was exhausted last year, and we all felt awful. Fortunately for everyone, he's a total badass, and he still crushed his performance enough to catch the Emmy's people's attention for a fucking *pilot season*. That shit is goddamn unheard of.

"I hope so…" he grunts before flopping back against his seat. "I'm flying home Friday night. Hopefully, this weekend I can convince her. The next three-plus years will get rather strenuous if she won't bend on this."

"I'll say," I chime in. "Does she even have a fucking reason for being insanely selfish?"

Andrew's eyes meet mine in the rearview mirror and they have this look of *watch it, that's my wife*. While also saying, *but thanks, bro*.

"I'm sure she has her reasons, but nothing she's offered to share with me," he answers and shakes his head subtly. "I'll try to make it work, though. I can fly home on the weekends if I have to. It's fine."

"Andrew, it's killing you and we're only just getting started," I huff in his direction. "You're exhausted."

"It forces me to work harder," he mutters petulantly.

"You're fucking fading!" I bark, and this time Johnny turns.

I don't know why I'm getting so worked up about this. It's possible I'm transferring some of my own issues into this conversation.

Andrew stares at me in the mirror for a second with his brows raised in concern.

"I can't just give up," he finally whispers and eventually I nod, my eyes slinking back out the window.

Relationships never work. My best friend is fucking doomed, just like the rest of them.

But what can I do? If he wants to try, then he's going to try. No use driving myself nuts over it.

Just let this serve as a reminder to your gullible heart next time it wants a girlfriend.

Fortunately, after that little dramatic scene, we arrive at the bar. The four of us hop out of the car and freeze for a moment in the parking lot, all staring at one another.

We completely forgot to change out of our wardrobe. We were so eager to get drunk we didn't even shower, or at the very least take off our fake-guts-covered ensembles.

We all burst out laughing at this. We laugh so hard for a second Johnny looks like he might fall over. I'm sorting. Mike may pee his pants.

I wish I could say it was the first time we've done something like this...

We're still cracking up as we stalk into the bar and everyone inside, all six of them, look up.

The locals are getting used to us. At first we weren't sure how they'd react to having a bunch of crazy, loud, rich and often overindulgent celebrities taking over their hometown for five months at a time. But when we started showing up around town this year, the people were very welcoming. I assume it'll get better as the next few years roll on.

We certainly bring their bars a lot of business, that's for sure.

"Larry! What's up, homes?!" Johnny shouts at a guy as we walk through the open space toward our favorite spot in the place: the pool table. "Frank! Haven't seen you since this morning! Going for round two, huh my man? Oh, shit! There's that crazy asshole... Bill! You sly sonofabitch!"

Andrew and I grin at each other in amusement as we watch Johnny make his rounds, high-fiving and slapping the backs of all the regulars. It's pretty hilarious to witness him bonding with middle-age alcoholics. But that's just Johnny for you. He can make friends with anybody, he remembers everyone's names and has to stop to talk to each one every time he sees them.

He takes forever to get through premieres. Press tours this fall will be brutal.

The three of us gather by the pool table and await our drinks while Johnny's booming laugh drowns out the jukebox. The waitress, Marla, brings over a bottle of scotch and four glasses as Andrew racks the balls.

"Did you hear Jason's coming out here this week?" Mike says, chalking a cue.

"Uh, you're in the presence of the Team Captain, noob," I grin, jutting my thumb in Andrew's direction. "He knows *everything*."

Andrew laughs and shakes his head, but Mike is staring at him with expectantly raised brows.

"He'll be here tomorrow at three," Andrew winks at Mike who can't help but appear very impressed.

"Well, maybe you can put a good word in for me?" Mike asks, jittering in place. "He's only ever said like two words to me. I want to make a good impression."

"I don't know him that well," Andrew starts, "But I do know that above all else, Jason DeWitt values talent, dedication and loyalty."

"I heard an actress tried to quit one of his shows a few years ago midseason, so he had her blacklisted," I tell Mike with wide eyes that are only sixty percent kidding.

"What? Really?" He chokes on his drink.

"I'm not sure how factual that story is," Andrew mutters, shooting me a look, unable to stop smirking. "But I definitely heard it, too."

"What are we talking about?" Johnny asks, rejoining our party.

"Jason," Andrew and I answer at the same time.

Johnny shivers intentionally, and I struggle to hold back my laughter. "Dude's stone-cold, man. Watch out for him."

I'm about to burst so hard I have to turn around. We're clearly fucking with Mike a little, which has become our new favorite activity since he joined the cast.

Jason DeWitt, creator of *Hell Storm*, is a super chill guy. I don't doubt that he has to get mean from time to time. That's just Hollywood. But overall, he's one of the more laid back dudes I've met in the business.

That being said, I definitely want to impress him too, though I won't be doing it in an ass-kissing way like Mike will be. I'll get the main man's attention with nothing more than my spectacular performances, my fanbase, which has already more than tripled since season one aired, and my ability to give his show my full attention. That's a big deal to showrunners.

Andrew and I have already talked about this. He wouldn't be able to take on any other projects while starring in this one, and I wouldn't want to. Johnny, on the other hand, is an incredibly active Hollywood actor. He usually films *at least* two movies a year, while also banging out a few little projects in between. I'm already predicting that his career on this show could be short-lived.

And that's fine for him. Johnny doesn't like to stay in one place for too long, project-wise. Andrew and I are different. If we find something that satisfies our hunger for performance, pays well, and allows us to build an image, we stay put. Personally, I plan to make *Hell Storm* my sole responsibility for as long as they'll have me.

We play pool for a bit, drinking more and laughing like the bunch of clowns we are. I'm having a great time, and I honestly couldn't be more grateful to this show and these guys for giving me peace of mind when I could be otherwise freaking out.

After our third game, Johnny suggests tequila shots and I already know someone will be putting me to bed tonight. *I should start planning which bed now. If the Boy Scouts taught me anything, it's to always be prepared. And never trust an old fat dude in cargo shorts who wants to pitch a tent with you.*

I'm still sucking on a lime wedge as I unlock my phone and try to focus my increasingly blurred vision on the screen. One of the new interns, Katie, gave me her number today. She's very hot, and small, like Tinkerbell with a rack so large she looks like she could topple over at any given moment.

I like it. So I pull up a new text to her number and make an attempt at typing, since I'm rather sloshed and there's no guarantee my fingers will hit the correct letters for what I'm trying to write. *Maybe I can get away with just sending emojis. Eggplant, erupting volcano, question mark.*

"Who you texting?" Andrew slurs, stumbling up to me and resting his chin on my shoulder as he tries to peek at my phone.

"Booty, baby!" I chuckle and shove him off me.

He frowns and looks at his watch. "Hmm... It's too early anyway, I suppose."

"Too early for what?" I ask, my face giving away how puzzled I am at his weird words. It's barely midnight. Just the right time to make sex plans in Georgia. *People here go to bed way earlier than in New York.*

"To message Alex. It's like six in the morning in Budapest," he hums casually. "Unless she has an early class..."

I swallow hard. "Why would I message Alex?" My voice is low and riddled with insecurity that I'm okay with him hearing, but no one else.

He sighs out hard and shakes his head like an admonishing older brother, even though we're basically the same age. "Noah, it's been a year. You're seriously telling me you have no desire to speak with her? At all?"

I pinch the bridge of my nose for a moment. "Of course I want to talk to her... But it's been a year. One *year*. And no contact whatsoever. I think... it's for the best." I shrug and he doesn't look amused.

"You're being immature."

"How am I being immature?!" I grunt defensively. "She hasn't tried to contact me either!"

"She left, Noah! I'm sure she figured you'd at least make an effort to find out how she's doing out there."

"Why am I the bad guy right now...?" I rake my fingers through my hair.

"You're not a *bad* guy... You're in over your head," he tells me, leaning up against the pool table. "I know this isn't easy on you, but you can't just write her off because she left. She's your friend."

"Exactly. She's my *friend*. That's it. And that's fine. Friends sometimes go years without talking." I pause to collect my jumbled thoughts. "If we really are as good of friends as I think we are, then it won't be a problem not to talk while

Seek Me

she's away."

Andrew is quiet for a moment, just staring at me. I can tell he wants to say something, or maybe hit me, but he's holding back, and I think it's because he pities me. Which feels much worse than a smack to the face.

I'd almost rather him just kick me in the nuts than keep looking at me the way he is...

"So that's it then?" He lifts a brow. "You're simply going to bang your way through every girl you can get your hands on for the rest of your life?"

That's a loaded question I can't answer right now. Honestly, I haven't been thinking about the future lately, and I need to keep it that way.

I thought about the future once. A year ago.

And it crushed me. So now I'm just going day to day, living my life the best way I can.

"I guess so," I tell him with a slightly pathetic smile. "And you're my best friend, so you'll just have to accept it."

"I'm your *best* friend?" He gasps, looking shockingly excited. He's fucking with me, but I don't care. He's a good dude, and basically my favorite person right now.

"Yes, Andrew," I roll my eyes and he laughs.

"Oi Johnny! Did you hear that? *I'm* Noah's best friend! Take that, bitch!" He shouts across the room at Johnny who's flirting with the waitress and paying exactly zero attention to us.

I chuckle and note the incoming text message on my phone. It's an address.

Time to bounce.

"Gotta go, bestie," I tell Andrew with a kidney shot and we spend the next few minutes punching one another and trying to get each other in headlocks.

"Dude, just let me take you home," Andrew grunts out of breath when we finally call a truce.

"Sorry, bro. You're a sexy mofo, but I don't feel that way about you," I grin and he scoffs.

"You know what I mean," he gives me one of his *I'm worried about you looks*, which I fully hate. "You don't need to go wherever you're about to go. Just call it a night."

"Andrew, it's fine. I have it under control," I tell him, though even saying the words out loud, I'm beginning to seriously question them. "I can stop any time I want."

I wink at him and he doesn't look pleased, but he gives me a reluctant smile anyway, and I leave the bar to get my Uber.

The ride to the girl's house is about fifteen minutes - go figure - the entire time of which I'm deep in my head. I can't stop thinking about what Andrew said, about how I don't need to do this…

Well, of course I don't need to. No one's holding a gun to my head. I want to fuck a bunch of random girls to make myself feel better.

Okay, that sounds really bad. Maybe never say that out loud.

I can feel myself spiraling, but it's too late. I'm drunk and this is happening, whether I like it or not…

God dammit, Alex… Why did you have to leave like that?

Why couldn't you have just let me tell you… Tell you I only want you and no one else will ever make me feel the way you do.

I slap my hand over my eyes fast and force myself to stop.

I can't go down this road. I barely even remember what it feels like to be with Alex anymore. It was so long ago, it's almost a distant memory at this point.

Of course screwing the life out of dozens of randoms doesn't help…

Should I just message her? Could I? Would it make a difference, or would it just make us both feel worse…?

It's too late. The damage is done.

The only thing I can do now is go inside the home of this sexy little intern, fuck her hard while trying like hell not to cry out Alex's name, which is typically what happens, and then go home.

And do it all again tomorrow.

Another beautiful day on set, and I'm only a little hungover, so stuffing myself into the fake trunk of a car with Melody isn't as misery-inducing as it potentially could be. That and the heat hasn't kicked off to its fullest degree yet, so it's still manageable. For me.

Andrew's having a little temper tantrum about the heat already, and I think it's funny.

Those London blokes can't hang in the south.

"Alright, great work, you two," Nicola nods at Melody and me. "Let's take five."

She stomps off while yelling something at someone, and before I can go to my trailer or find Andrew, Melody grabs my arm.

"You know, that scene reminded me of our sexy little night together," she pokes my nose with her fingertip.

I pull a confused as fuck face, because... *what??*

"How did that remind you of us fucking?" I grumble, and now I'm growing impatient because I need know, specifically, how being stuffed inside a small crate designed to look like the inside of the trunk of a car is in any way like having sex several times in the very large guest bedroom of a mansion.

She's about to answer when Andrew storms over, looking annoyed.

"Can we get some water over here?" He shouts into the air and several people scatter. "Bollocks. It's hotter than Satan's Bikram studio."

I laugh and disregard Melody so I can talk to my friend. "It's not that bad."

"So how was last night?" He asks, clearly trying to distract himself from his irritation.

"Good," I nod casually, like we're discussing a new restaurant I tried, not an intern I did very bad things to for several hours. "I found Katie to be quite flexible. At one point, she had her knees behind her -"

"God, please stop," he holds up his hand, making a face as if he's going to vomit, though he's still grinning. "I don't need to hear that. I'll never be able to look at her the same."

"Yea, me either," I smirk and wink at him as Johnny sidles up to us.

"What are we talking about?" Johnny grunts, bringing his bottle of water to his lips. "Boobs?"

I laugh, noting the salacious look on Andrew's face as he lusts over Johnny's beverage.

"Give me that," he grunts, snatching the bottle out of Johnny's hand and dumping it over his head.

"What the hell, bro?" Johnny grumbles, and I'm still laughing. He sighs and turns back to me. "Who'd you take home last night? The waitress from Chilis?"

"Katie, the intern," I keep up a prideful grin so fake I want to claw it off my face. "She has a huge mirror across from her bed, so the reverse-cowgirl was more dimensional..."

"Dude! Are you fucking serious?" Johnny whisper-shouts at me, eyes bugging out of his head. He looks very serious, which is an abnormal thing to see on his face. "You slept with... *Katie?* The *new* intern?"

I pause and swallow hard, my eyes darting between him and Andrew, who's also radiating concern. "Yea... What's the problem?"

"She's Jason's stepsister," he murmurs, then peeks around to make sure no one else is listening. Melody's still within an earshot, and I'm sure she's trying to eavesdrop. But I can't be bothered with her right now...

Because... *Fuck.*

"What?!" I gasp, my face falling in shock. Terror twists my stomach. "No... You're lying."

"I wish, bro," Johnny shakes his head. "Nicola told me. She was annoyed about having to deal with an inexperienced intern just because she's Jason's family."

Oh God... Oh Jesus. I'm so fucked.

I'm going to get fired. All because I can't keep my dick in my pants.

This is exactly what Andrew kept telling me would happen... My nonstop fucking would get me in trouble. *God dammit! How is he always right about everything?!*

"Fuck fuck *fuck*..." I rake my hands through my hair.

"You shagged Jason's little sister..." Andrew grumbles in disapproval, wiping his wet face. "How old is she, anyway?"

"*Step*sister," I grunt, keeping my voice down as I glance around in sheer panic and paranoia. "She's... twenty-one."

"Jesus, Noah," Andrew scolds me with his tone and angry blue eyes.

Johnny shakes his head as well, though it doesn't stop him from high-fiving me real quick, since... well, you know.

"Why the fuck wouldn't she tell me she was related to Jason?" I hiss as my entire career flashes before my eyes.

"Uh probably because she wanted you to bang her," Johnny chuckles and Andrew elbows him in the side.

"Mr. James, I got your water!" A high-pitched chirping voice comes from my right and I squeeze my eyes shut. "Sorry about that..."

It's Katie. Go fucking figure.

The three of us stare down at her with blank, expressionless faces. Andrew slowly takes the bottle of water from her.

"Thanks, Katie," he murmurs, remaining polite and gracious, though I can tell from the tightness in his lips that he's just waiting for this to blow up in all of our faces.

Please, God, no. I can't lose this job.

"Katie, um... Can we talk for a second?" I croak, stepping closer to her and eyeing my friends briefly, conveying that I need to try and smooth this over. And quick, before her stepbrother, my fucking *boss*, shows up.

Andrew and Johnny wander away from us as Katie peeks up at me with an

Seek Me

innocent smile. She looks much younger in the light of day, and it's sufficiently disturbing. Acid burns in my esophagus as I try to formulate a nice little speech to ensure she never breathes a word of last night to anyone.

"What's up?" She squeaks in her almost chipmunk-like voice.

"So... I just wanted to make sure everything is good with us," I gulp, smothering the look of dread that wants to take over my face. "You know... after last night...?"

She grins and bites her lip. "Yea, that was super fun."

"No, yea. Totally," I mutter through a seriously gravelly tone. "But it's not something you would like... share with anyone. Right?" I blink my panic-wide eyes at her. "Since it was just between us..."

"Oh. Yea, of course. Don't worry about that," she waves her hand in the air. "I've been with actors before, so I know it has to be sorta hush hush." She winks at me and I'm nauseatingly confused. "Your secret is safe with me."

Huh? What secret...?

My mind races over the events of last night. I was pretty drunk, as usual when I'm doing my booty call thing, but I don't think I did anything embarrassing... *Did I?*

"And uh, Katie," my brows zip together as I lean in. "What secret would that be?"

"You know..." her eyes twinkle before her tongue slides over her bottom lip. Her tone slips into a soft whisper, "How you like to... pretend." She raises her eyebrows at me expectantly, and I have no fucking clue what she's talking about, which is clear from my expression. She blinks a few times. "Like... *role-playing.*"

Jesus fucking Christ.

"You said you wanted me to pretend to be your best friend, Alex, when we did it," she goes on, smirking wickedly. "I thought it was a little weird at first, but it then it was crazy hot when I saw how excited you were..."

"Oh God," I cover my face with my hands as the noose of regretful guilt and mortifying shame tightens around my neck.

"Noah, it's fine," she reaches up to rub my back. "Like I told you, I've been with actors before. I get it."

My head starts shaking over and over. "No, I just -"

The surrounding commotion is suddenly amplified, distracting from this painfully awkward conversation. I look up and see people rushing around.

"Oh, look! Jason's here early!" Andrew's voice barks from a few feet away, and I catch him warning me with wide eyes.

Fuck!

I struggle to compose myself, because the showrunner is here and I'm standing next to his twenty-one-year-old stepsister with whom I engaged in some very dirty, and apparently humiliating, sex last night. My pulse is thrumming as I watch Jason DeWitt stomp closer to us, waving at people and checking out the set that's currently being transitioned.

Oh God, okay. Relax. You got this. Katie said she won't say anything. Just chill and be normal. You're an actor. You can do this.

I wipe my sweaty hands on my jeans over and over as Jason walks up with Andrew and Johnny stumbling behind him.

"Hey, guys!" He waves at all of us in excitement. "The place looks great, huh?"

"It does!" Andrew cuts in then dives in front of him, shaking his hand fast. "So good to see you, Jason. We're glad you could make it out today."

"Look at this frontman," Jason grins widely, slapping Andrew's back. "You're really killing it here, pal. Everyone's talking about how you're bringing this whole thing together."

Andrew's smile is gracious, if not slightly uncomfortable, and I feel like an asshole for making his cool moment with our boss uneasy because of my wayward dick. *What a scumbag you are.*

"I couldn't do it without my amazing costars." Andrew pulls off the breezy European thing so well. He's a great actor. And very British. "And this crew! They're fantastic. Each and every one of them."

"Yes! I see you've all met my lovely stepsister," Jason smiles and snakes his arm around Katie. "I hope Katherine's been taking care of you guys."

"She's very helpful here on set," Johnny jumps in, giving Katie a quick glance of approval for Jason's benefit.

He looks thoroughly pleased and I'm able to breathe a bit easier thanks to my friends.

The best damn wingmen on Earth.

"That's great," Jason hums, beaming at his sister. "I'm glad to hear it."

I step back slightly, hoping to extricate myself from this conversation for a minute to get some air.

"Noah!" Jason's voice booms at me and I cringe. "You, my friend, are making some serious headlines lately."

I swallow over the desert that is my throat. "I am?"

"Yes! The fans can't get enough of *Darren*!" He clasps his hands together. "I think we're gonna be playing on that some more in the upcoming seasons. The bad boy heartthrob of the group is making very exciting waves with the network."

I pull a forced smile, my eyes darting between Andrew and Johnny, who look nervous.

"Noah's such a phenomenal talent," Andrew says with confidence. "He makes us all look good."

My chest warms briefly at my new best friend's words. That he would put himself on the line for me is like a swift kick in the ass.

I need to get my shit together. I can't sacrifice this job and all the amazing stuff that comes with it because I'm suffering from a broken heart.

Maybe it's time to cool it with the girls...

I smile at Andrew and grab his shoulder. "Thanks, man. None of us could do it without you."

He smirks and winks at me, silently telling me he's got my back. *This dude is really something.*

"I hear that!" Jason says as Nicola walks over. "Well, let me see what you guys got! Nic, you ready?"

"Yeap," she huffs, glancing over the papers in her hands. "Places, everyone! Let's nail this next one."

And just like that, we're back to work, and my angst is swept away quickly because it's time to hustle. Making these next few scenes my bitch is more important than stressing over my pathetic love life, anyway.

So we work. For hours. Until the sun goes down, and then Jason takes us all to dinner. Katie's there, but it's not awkward. She's a sweet and rather mature girl, who I don't plan on speaking to again after today. It just needs to be like that. Add her to the ever-growing list of distractions that served their purpose at the time.

But today was a bit of a wake-up call. I can't keep going around screwing my coworkers. I can't go around screwing *everyone* like it doesn't mean anything, because that's a despicable way to act. I'm better than that.

Just because I *can* fuck around, it doesn't mean I *should*.

Don't get me wrong, I'm not settling down again. That ship sailed a year ago. If it didn't happen with Alex, it's not going to happen with anyone else. And I've accepted that. I just need to be a little more cautious and discreet with my comings and goings from now on.

After dinner, during which I only had one glass of wine, I arrive back home, alone. I enter my giant mansion by myself, and it's bigger and quieter than I remember it being since I moved in last year. And it occurs to me that I've been a version of tipsy ever since that day, hiding from the feelings I wouldn't let free.

But now I'm here... Home alone and sober. Left with nothing but my thoughts.

I meander through the wide-openness, glancing around, wondering what in the hell I'm supposed to do with myself. I end up deciding to change into my swim trunks and go to the pool.

My pool is massive and really nice, lit up from the inside, shining pale blue rippling water. I step in, wading through the coolness, which isn't cold since it's heated. I take a deep breath and submerge myself, staying under until my lungs burn, and my body forces itself to resurface.

I suck air in and float onto my back, gazing up at the night sky. The stars are bright and shimmering up there, in the vast everlasting space of black above. I let myself float in the water for a while, just staring, releasing the mask I carry around on me all day, every day.

I let myself just be *me*; the insecure, unsure, scared guy who struggles so hard not to let the world know he's not as happy as he seems. The hidden worries creep from all four corners of my mind, and as I float, I quietly obsess about it all; my job, all the girls, Andrew and his wife, Johnny and his reputation, Melody and Mike and Nicola, my mom and dad, my sister, Boots...

And Alex.

Will I succeed in this role? Will anyone ever love me? What will my life look like after tonight? What is my future?

The uneasy truth is that I don't know. I can't see myself doing anything other than what I have been. When Alex left last year, it changed *everything*, just like I knew it would. Before that night, I could see a future, rife with a scope of colorful possibilities.

But now, I see nothing more than a deep, black sky. An endless darkness, sprinkled with a few shining stars.

And me, alone.

Chapter Twenty One
Alex's Journal

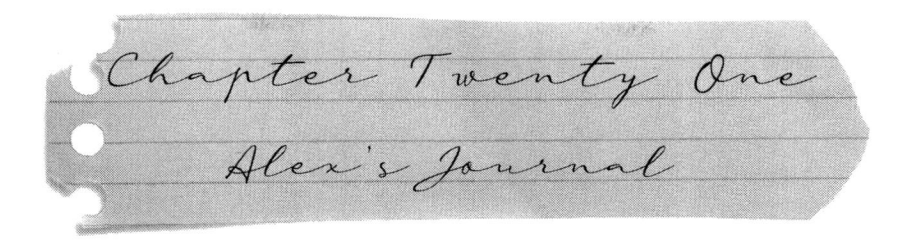

I'M TIRED, AND YET WIDE AWAKE. Anxious. Jittering with nerves... Fear. Anticipation. Unease. Excitement. Worry. Thrill.

I just walked into my apartment, in Brooklyn. I'm home. For the first time in eighteen months.

No need to throw a welcome-home party, Barnaby. I'm just glad to be back.

My time in Budapest was life-changing. I'm a different person than I was when I left, which is all I could have asked for.

Don't worry, I'm still me. I'm the same Alex I always was before, but I've managed to reclaim myself. I've grown into the person I knew I could be. The person my ex-husband tried to strangle to death.

Walking through my foyer into my living room felt weird. I haven't been here in so long. I suppose that's why I set my bags down and immediately started writing to you, Barn. It was a long flight home and I'm exhausted and jet-lagged. But I'm also wired.

Because I'm *back*, in New York. After being away for a year-and-a-half, I'm finally where I belong again.

And go figure, the only thing I can think about is...

I'm not going to say it. You already know who I'm thinking about, Barn. The name that never once left my mind in eighteen long months. The name that haunted my dreams every single night; the one I cried out in my sleep, when I would wake up clutching my pillow, and more often than not, humping it.

So here's the deal, Barnaby. I'm going to be honest.

Part of my new life is not hiding from what I want and not shying away from the truths in my life. I came to a blinding clarity one night six months ago when I was painting in Prague.

Life is full of so much pain. For a gift, more often than not it can feel like a curse.

I've experienced a lot of said pain, so I understand now that I need to scrape as much joy out of this life as I possibly can. That night when I was painting, overlooking a gorgeous city of jagged buildings beneath a dark night sky, I realized that it's up to me to *live*.

I came back from the dead, Barn. Despite what happens on Noah's TV show, people don't just come back to life after they die. But *I* did.

Roger tried to kill me, and it almost worked. For so long, I was stuck. I'd planted roots in a world of pain and suffering; sadness and cruelty. And loneliness.

Yet, despite what I almost let myself believe, my life was not over. It wasn't then, and it still isn't. It's my time to breathe and laugh and dance. To paint and love and sing. To experience every beautiful thing this world has to offer me; all the good I missed out on when I was decaying in what I thought was my truth.

But that wasn't it. My truth is here and now.

My truth is what I'm living today, divorced and moving on. I'm home, and I'm fucking *happy* to be back. I loved living in Europe. I learned so much; I laughed a ton, and I grew exponentially. It was a time I'll never forget because it helped me heal. And now I'm back in New York, and I don't know that I've ever been gladder to be here.

It doesn't startle me as much as you'd think that the first thing I want to do is see Noah. Over the course of my ten-hour flight, I came to terms with the need to be back with him, even if it's just as a friend.

I don't know where Noah and I stand in our romantic relationship. I mean, I left for over a year… I hardly expected Noah to wait for me, not that we were official before I left or anything. I understand that my leaving may have ruined whatever feelings were growing between us. Thinking about it makes me so nauseous I could be sick… But I have to accept it.

He might be totally over me.

Still, despite all of that confusing shit, I need to see him, as my best friend. I've missed him so bad, it's been cutting a hole in my heart for eighteen months. And now that I'm back, I'm desperate to see him smile, and hear his laugh; to tell him all my stories and hear all of his, spoken in that raspy voice and tone laced with wicked humor, like he's holding back a dirty secret.

I need my best friend.

I'm wondering what I should do. I need your help, Barn. I'm so nervous about reaching out to Noah, I just want to curl into a ball. We haven't talked at all since I left. Any number of things could have happened while I was away…

I made it an irritating habit to obsessively check gossip articles and social media to stay updated on all things Noah. Twitter proved helpful in verifying that, at the very least, he's still alive. But as much as people love to pry into the lives of celebrities, I know to take it all with a grain of salt.

For all I know, Noah could be married with a child at this point, an image that makes me want to puke all over my living room floor. I'm praying with every bit of faith inside myself that he's not involved seriously with anyone. Noah being an unattached bachelor was the only thing holding me together the whole time I was gone. Coming home to him in a relationship would surely crush me.

Though it shouldn't. We're *friends*. As long as he's happy, I should be happy. His happiness is all that matters.

And yes, Barnaby, you know me, and you know I'm full of crap.

I want to see Noah, and I don't just want to casually hug him like a long-lost friend. I want to kiss him. So freaking bad. I don't think I've wanted to kiss someone this bad since I was a teenager and I had an unhealthy crush on Johnny Depp.

I'm craving the feeling of his soft lips on mine like a fiend; the powerful, almost bruising way he kisses me with hunger and lust, holding my face in his firm grip and devouring me. Making me *his*. It was all I could think about on the plane.

For ten hours, I squirmed around in my seat imagining my best friend claiming me with his warm, wet mouth. Tonguing me slow, biting my lip and panting those sexy fucking noises he makes, like the mere act of kissing me is so satisfying he can't possibly stop, not even for one second. Not even to breathe.

Breathing is overrated where kissing Noah Richards is concerned.

I miss his taste, like brandy and caramel and rich, decadent deliciousness. I miss gripping his shaggy hair in my fist, feeling his hard body pressed up against mine; holding me tight with strength and devotion.

I haven't stopped craving him in all this time. Like an addict, dreaming of a next fix that may never come.

I didn't want to spend my entire time out there wishing I was with Noah, so I tried to recreate some of these lascivious desires with other guys, but it was really no use. It didn't matter how hot they were, or how many tattoos they had. How defined their muscles were, or the fact that one of them had his tongue pierced. In my mind, they might as well have been fatties farting in their moms' basements.

None of them compared to Noah, and now that I'm home, I can feel his presence again. I can physically sense him all around me like an aura. New York City is Noah's domain, and it's impossible not to associate everything about this place with him. Especially because his stuff is still all over my apartment.

And yes, I may have immediately grabbed one of his t-shirts he left here and sniffed it like some kind of weird psycho. But it still had his smell lingering on it. And now I'm really wound up.

I'm being foolish. Noah might not even be in New York right now.

His show has really taken off, from what I've been reading in all the hundreds of online articles and Twitter threads. They wrapped filming the second season last month, so he could be in LA, or London, or Tokyo doing promotional stuff. He could still be in Georgia for some reason, finishing up show-related things. He could be celebrating with his costars in Fiji or Belize.

The point is, Noah could be literally anywhere right now, and I would have no idea. Because we haven't spoken a word to each other since I left him, unexpectedly like some flighty, selfish little tease.

Ugh, sorry, Barn. I'm getting carried away. I swore I wouldn't feel bad about leaving. Traveling was always a part of my plan, and in no way am I saying just because I'm happy to be home that I won't be leaving again. Actually, Chloe and some of my art program friends want me to come to Tel Aviv with them next year, and I'd be a fool not to go.

So it would seem that Noah and I are living separate lives, and it's just the way it has to be. We're both young, though I'm a bit younger than he is. But still, we're both following our dreams, and it's fantastic.

So then why do I want nothing more than to go to Noah's apartment and stay there with him forever?

I don't know what's wrong with me. But something inside is just telling me Noah's not traveling. He's here.

It's like I have The Shining for my best friend. He's in the city. I can feel it.

I know I sound like a lunatic, Barnaby. You don't have to point it out, okay? Jeez.

Instead of being a judgy judgerson, why don't you just help me??

Should I call him? What would I even say?

Hi, Noah! It's been a while, huh? Yea, right. Long time! So… you wanna make out?

God, that's pathetic. And then he tells me he has a girlfriend. Or a fiancée. Or a fucking wife. And the ground swallows me up and I die of embarrassment.

I couldn't stand it if any of that happened, but even more so, I can't stand the idea of being home and not seeing him.

Seek Me

I *need* to see him.
Alright, that's it. I'm calling him.
No. I'll text him, because I'm a total chicken-shit.
Okay. Here we go. Say a prayer for me, Barnaby.
I might be doomed.

CHAPTER TWENTY TWO
Noah

Alex: I'm back

I GAPE AT MY PHONE SCREEN FOR A SOLID FIVE MINUTES. Just staring. Vacuously. My body is stone. I actually might have died for a second there, until my brain reminds my lungs to take a breath. They suck one in and hold it. Eyes, blink.

Again. Blink blink.

I'm back.

Fuck me, is this real?

I go out of the message and re-click on it, just to make sure it *is* from Alex, and not some weird phone malfunction.

Nope, it's real. Alex texted me. She's back.

I'm back.

HOLY FUCK.

After eighteen months of no contact, Alex just texted me that she's *back*, which I can only assume means she is *back* from her trip to Budapest. And is here in New York again. I may not be much of a detective, but my brain is rifling through any other possible meanings for that text, and it's coming up blank.

There's only one meaning. She's *back*.

She's home. *Alex is home. Alex is home.*

Alex.

Is.

Home.

I'm two seconds away from jumping up and down, squealing and peeing my pants. I'm barely kidding, that's the scary part.

Okay. Calm down, loser.

Right right. My brain is right. I need to relax. It's just Alex. My friend. We're friends.

She's home from her eighteen-month art program in Budapest, and she probably wants to tell me all about it. And fuck, I want to *hear* all about it. I can't wait, actually.

So I should probably respond to her message and make plans to get together. That would be the normal thing to do. I should reply to her message and say, *That's awesome! Can't wait to see you, Al. How about dinner tomorrow?*

I'm sure you see where I'm going with this...

That's not what I'm going to do. At all.

I press *call* on her contact in an instant, and bring my phone to my ear with my heart slamming against my ribs as I chew on the inside of my cheek. It's pretty loud here, so I walk away from the noise to hear better.

I'm making my way to the exit of the club when Alex's sweet, soft voice serenades me through the line, and my chest warms in a split second before gravity gives up. I'm fucking flying.

"Hi..."

I choke on everything that wants to tumble out of my mouth, coughing as I push open the back door of Sensay and stumble out into the alley.

"Hi," I whisper, then clear my throat. "Oh my God, is it really you?"

She giggles softly and my eyes flutter shut as I lean up against the brick wall, my body overcome with revelation. *Fuck, that sounds good.*

"Yea, it's me," she hums, and I can hear her smile. I can fucking *hear* it... And I haven't heard it in so long, I could burst into tears. But I won't. "Fuck... Noah. Holy shit, I missed you."

My heart swells up so big it's pushing through my chest. "I missed you so fucking much."

She sniffles and I hate hearing it, but at the same time I'm so glad to hear *anything* from her at this point. Eighteen months is too long. It's a fucking *eternity* without Alex Mackenzie.

"I don't even know what to say," she murmurs. "I just needed to let you know I was back."

I nod, though she can't see me. "I want to know everything."

"Are you free tomorrow?" She asks hesitantly, and it occurs to me that while hearing her voice seems to transport me right back to eighteen months ago, before everything changed, we haven't in fact time-traveled.

We're very much here, now; a year and six months having passed since we last saw or spoke to one another. For all she knows, everything could be different in my life. And for all I know, everything could be different in hers.

The time apart happened, and we can't pretend it didn't. So it would be wise to go into this with a shield up. It's a sucky way to think about my reunion with my best friend, but I'm worried I'll get carried away. I'm already so excited that she's home, I can see us easily slipping right back to where we were. And that absolutely cannot happen.

The last year-and-a-half almost killed me. I can't go through that again. I need to stay strong and guarded. I can see Alex, of course. I can talk to her and hug her, and maybe kiss her... Maybe even fuck her, because good *God*, I need to do that. I've missed more than just her words and her voice, her laugh and her smile.

I've missed the feeling of pushing myself inside her; feeling her skin tremble while I fill her with every inch of myself...

Okay, I might be getting carried away. *See?* It's already happening. This is not good.

Get your head on straight, Richards.

"Fuck tomorrow," I grunt, stammering toward the street. "What are you doing now?"

"Now?" She squeaks, and her voice sounds awfully breathy.

If I were a betting man, I'd say she's equally excited to potentially see me. Which makes my dick even more antsy. He's practically dancing in my pants at the thought of reuniting with Alex tonight.

"Yes, now," I growl as my hunger gets the best of me. "Can you come over?"

"To your place?"

Why is she hesitating so much?

"I still have the same place, Alex," I chuckle. "That hasn't changed."

She's quiet for a moment. "What has changed?"

I gulp and my head shakes subtly. "Nothing. I missed you a fuckload... You're my best friend and you've been gone for eighteen months. That's all that matters right now."

"Okay. Can you come over here? I'm super jet-lagged, and the idea of getting into another vehicle makes me want to cry." She giggles softly and I can't help it. I'm smiling so big it's distracting passing airplanes.

"Of course. I'm getting in the car now," I tell her as I stomp up to the Navigator. I slide inside and tell Jimmy, "Take me to Alex's, please."

Jimmy's eyes dart to mine in the mirror and they're much wider than I've ever seen them before. I'm sure he can tell by my unwavering grin that this is good news, and he looks ecstatic. He shifts into drive and pulls off, speeding us

Seek Me

toward Brooklyn, barely trying to hide his excitement at not having to deal with whatever dumb bimbo I was planning on picking up at Sensay tonight.

I can't be mad at him. He has a point, after all.

Seeing Alex trumps any and all skanky potential one-night stands.

Sure, I've toned it down with my sleeping around over the last five months. But I'm not *dead*. I still have needs, ergo the reason I was out at Sensay tonight with Brant and some friends. *Oh, shit. I should tell Brant that I left.*

Alex's voice distracts me from my thoughts. "You're in the car right now? Coming over?"

"Yes. Why is that weird?"

"Uh... It's not. I just... I don't know, I guess I expected you to be busy or something..." Her voice trails off and my stomach fills with rampant warmth. *She's so fucking cute, I can't even deal with it.*

"Alex, I'd never be too busy for you," I rumble, leaning back. "You just got back from your trip. I need to see you. Don't you... need to see me?"

"Yes!" She blurts out before I have a chance to feel insecure. A slow grin sweeps over my mouth. "I mean, yes, I really want to see you."

I chuckle. "Good. Then I'll see you in a few."

"Okay!" She squeals, and her excitement has me ready to crawl out of my skin. "I'll see you soon."

"Bye," I hum, shifting in my seat.

"Bye..." Maybe my eagerness is playing tricks on me, but I swear her voice sounds like a moan.

She hangs up before I come in my pants, and I groan out loud, falling over onto the backseat, curling up into a ball while covering my face with my hands.

Jimmy laughs. "So... She's back?"

I nod, face still covered. "She's back."

"That's great, Noah. I'm really glad."

I pull my hands away. "What am I doing? This isn't exactly going shields up... Racing to her apartment the second she gets back."

"It is what it is," Jimmy shrugs. "You two are the most fucked up couple I've ever met. I just assumed it was your thing."

I narrow my gaze at the front of the car as I sit up slowly. "We're not a couple."

He rolls his eyes. "Okay, then. What are you?"

"I don't know," I huff and flop back hard, wearing a petulant pout. "We're friends. Over anything else, we're friends."

"Alright. Just remember that, then. You can't get mad at her for disregarding feelings she doesn't know about." He shoots me a pointed look in the mirror and I scoff.

"Just drive, smart ass."

We arrive at Alex's and I hop out of the car like it's on fire. I rush inside her building, using the key I still have and still keep on the ring with my own house keys, and take the elevator to her floor. And when I get there, I stop outside her door to take a breath to compose myself.

Friends. We're friends.

Just…

I knock on the door, and Alex opens it shockingly fast, launching herself at me.

Friends?

Lips are assaulting mine before I can even process what's happening. She kisses me so hard and fast that I almost fall backward, but I steady myself and hold onto her, reacquainting with how incredible it feels to kiss her. *Man*, does it feel divine. I grip her waist tight then squeeze her butt as she sucks my lips over and over, mewling and whining out these needy noises that make my dick jump and throb.

She threads her fingers through my hair, tugging my face as close as humanly possible while we kiss into a stupor. Hard and deep, wet and hot. It's a makeout session to make up for all the makeout sessions we've missed over the last eighteen months.

It's fantastic and my whole body is buzzing with shivers of magnetic warmth.

Alex slams me up against the wall of her doorway and grinds her body against mine, yanking fistfuls of my hair as she nips my bottom lip gently, sucking then slipping her tongue over it to meet mine. It's a treasure how soft her kisses are, even when she's devouring me like I'm anything fattening the day after a cleanse.

"Noah," she pants in my mouth. "Tell me now if this should stop."

"Whaa… huh…?" I'm incapable of forming normal thoughts or words right now. My hands are too busy roaming this perfect body I've missed for *fucking* ever.

Her luscious ass, her hips, her waist, her sweet fucking handful tits. *God*, this is perfect. I don't care about anything I was thinking before. *This* is all I need.

"If we can't do this, you need to tell me right now," she whimpers, hitching a leg around my waist which I catch and use to hold her up on me. "I won't be able to stop once we go inside, so please, just…" She breaks to gulp and take a breath. "Speak now or forever hold your peace."

Her dazzling green eyes lock on mine and I gaze into them like an oracle. I can still barely believe she's here right now. I'm actually *physically* touching her, feeling her, tasting her and smelling her. She's awakened my senses after far too long of coasting by on just average.

This is what I've wanted since she left; what I've been struggling to convince myself I could do without the whole time, and not fooling me one bit.

Fuck everything else. I just need *her*.

I won't get lost in thinking I want to make her mine again. That was a mistake I made last time, and I can't do it again. We're friends who fuck. It's fine if that's all we can be, but I need her in my life like this.

So no. We don't need to stop. We need to go. *Go go go.*

"Alex, please don't ever stop," I grunt breathlessly, and that's all the go she needs.

After that, we're a whirlwind of kissing and touching, squeezing and pulling, licking, sucking, breathing, moaning. It's happening fast, and I sort of want to slow down to savor it, but we can't. It's impossible to simmer right now.

We kiss our way inside and I kick off my shoes while Alex undoes my jeans. Shirts, off. Pants, down. Bra, gone. Boxers, see ya.

By the time we're at her living room, we're completely naked and too starved to make it any further, so I wind up seated on the couch with her straddling my hips. My naked hips. With hers also naked. She grinds that wet warmth I missed so much all over me and before I even know what's happening, I'm inside her.

Bare. No condom.

I probably should say something… Ask if it's okay that we're doing this, and make sure she's up-to-date on her birth control. But she initiated it, so I have to assume she's good to go. *I'll check in before I come, just to confirm.*

Holy Jesus on a sailboat, this feels magical.

Alex builds to riding me slowly, sucking my neck hard, biting me and twisting my nipple piercing until my balls seize.

"Baby, I fucking missed you," she groans, kissing my lips rough while she bounces up and down on my cock like she's riding a hippity hop. "It sounds cliché, but I never stopped thinking about you, the whole time I was gone."

My chest tightens at her words and I gasp out loud. I bow my head to her tits and suck her nipples like I've dreamed of doing every night since she left me. Plus, my mouth needs the distraction before it says something crazy.

I've become partial to saying insane things during sex since Alex left. All the girls I've been with in the last eighteen months probably think I'm a nutbag, but at least it serves as a reminder for them of why I'm incapable of a relationship.

Alex... My Alex... You're perfect. I only want you, baby. Only you... forever...

"Did you miss this?" She purrs, pulling my face back up to hers so we can look at each other while she rolls her hips, working me over like the goddamned sex goddess she is.

Her green eyes twinkle at me and my cock pulses. I only do this with her... Looking deep into someone's eyes while we fuck. It's so intimate, and she's the only person in the world I've ever experienced it with.

Fuck... She wants me to say words to her? That's dangerous. I say a lot of cuckoo for Cocoa Puffs stuff when my dick is buried inside this kind of silky wet tightness. Especially with no condom. Another thing I've only done with Alex...

"Every. Fucking. Day." I tell her, because it's true, and it earns me a raspy moan followed by more piercing love.

"You fuck so good, Noah," she hums, then takes my hand in hers and sucks my index finger between her lips.

"Fucking holy fuck..." I groan, watching how deliciously dirty she's being with wide eyes that I should probably close because the sight of it will make me come in approximately three more pumps. "Alex... I'm gonna come soon, baby... I can't... Don't let me come yet."

I use my free hand to hold her steady, maybe slow her down a little before I blow. Her voice vibrates on my finger while she sucks it like she's sucking my cock, then pops her mouth off bringing my hand around back... To her ass.

"Don't hold back, Noah," she demands through heavy panting, sliding my now wet finger between her cheeks. *Holy mother of God.* "I've dreamed about this every night since I left."

She lifts her brows at me, signaling that she wants my digit in her from the back, and obviously I'm totally willing to oblige. This girl is my exact fantasy. She's gorgeous, sexy as sin, and sweet but with the filthiest side of freak I could ever desire. It seems like being apart gave her an itch. I know the feeling... I've certainly been conjuring up a million salacious scenes in my mind for a while, in case she ever came back to me.

And would you look at that... She did.

My finger presses inside her tight ring and she moans, resisting for a moment.

Seek Me

But I kiss her pouty, swollen lips softly and whisper, "You're so damn sexy, Alex. You *are* my dream, baby." And she relaxes enough for me to penetrate her naughty place with my hand.

Her body tremors on top of me as she rocks slower on my dick, writhing against my finger that's up to the knuckle. I can feel it on my cock. I'm so fucking ready to erupt.

"Baby... I'm not kidding," I rumble, holding her close, both of us glistening with sweat and breathing so hard the room is filled with sex-sounds. "I'm gonna come deep inside you. Is that okay, or should I pull out?"

She squeals out loud, her pussy clenching on my dick, squeezing it so hard I know she's about to explode.

"I'm good, I promise," she breathes and grabs my face. "Come with me."

Fuck...

"Anything for you," I growl and we both let go.

Our bodies quake together as she gushes all over me and my orgasm bursts, throbbing every drop of the world's hottest fucking climax deep into the girl of my dreams. We're both crying out garbled curses mixed with each other's names, and her neighbors are probably scarred for life. But it feels so good I can't find it in myself to lower the volume. And clearly neither can Alex.

I wait until she's done before I take out the finger, keeping her wrapped tightly in my arms as our breathing normalizes and we eventually stop moving.

My brain is hazy and my mind is jumbled. I can't believe we just did that. I can't believe she's here. She's really *here*, naked, on top of me, sweaty and huffing soft breaths on my neck, stroking her fingers lazily in my hair.

Alex is back. And that was the best reunion I could have ever hoped for.

After a few minutes of reveling in the post-orgasm bliss, I recline on the couch and bring her with me, cuddling her up on my chest, leaving my dick where it is, lest we release the probable gallon of *happy stuff* I made inside her. I kiss her hair, nuzzling my nose in it, the softness and the smell bringing on a wave of memories.

I missed her hair. Is that weird?

Don't answer that.

"I wasn't lying..." she whispers, and I curl my neck to look down at her. She lifts her head. "When I said I dreamed about this... I did. I thought about you constantly, Noah."

I blink and swallow hard. "Me too."

She rewards me with a pleased smile - yet another thing I missed more than

I can even express - and rests her head back down over my heart, kissing my tattoo. We lie like this for a while longer until I think she might be dozing off.

My heart is so full. It feels like I've been put back together again.

I have to acknowledge how dangerous this feeling is. I know I can't get myself swept up in wanting her again. I can already tell it'll be a problem if I don't control it. There was a time when such a mind-numbingly perfect moment would have prompted me to tell her I want her as my girlfriend. It wasn't that long ago, but it still feels like a small lifetime has passed since then.

And that's why I know I can't, and won't, go down that road again. I'm not the same person she left eighteen months ago. Of course I *am*, in the larger sense. But when it comes to wanting an actual relationship with Alex, I've changed.

I'm living in the moment and seizing joy where I can. And because of that, I won't allow myself to dream about what we could be. I have to keep going with the flow. Because I'll never forget how bad it hurt to watch her walk away without knowing how I felt.

So until Alex tells me she wants more from me, I'm content to keep it casual. It's in my best interest to refrain from putting myself out there. Plus, she's been through enough stress. I refuse to let myself be like her scumbag ex-husband. I'll never make her do something she doesn't want.

She's my best friend, with benefits. And that's fine. As long as she's happy, I'm happy.

"I was worried that maybe you'd have a girlfriend," Alex's quiet, sleepy voice chirps from where she's breathing on my warmed skin.

I pause for a moment, because *what did she just say?*

She raises her head again. "That's why I asked if we should stop kissing before. I thought you might... not be single anymore."

It takes me a minute to figure out how to respond to that. "Me? You thought *I*, Noah Richards, might have started dating someone...?"

Someone who isn't you?

Her head bounces in a shy nod that's so adorable I can't stand it.

"Don't get me wrong, I was... seeing some girls..." I gulp, feeling guilty for no reason. "I mean, you were gone a while, so..."

"I know," she whispers, stopping my unnecessary excuses. "I wouldn't expect you not to date because of me."

"It wasn't exactly *dating*..." I mumble as my eyes fall away from hers because I hate telling her about me sleeping with other women. We're friends, but we're also *us*. We have a sort of *don't ask, don't tell* policy to our fuck-buddy relationship.

"Yea, that sounds about right," she giggles then takes my hand in hers.

I smile, because she's seriously the best. I never have to feel guilty with her. She gets me, and she's not judgmental about my fucking around, even though she easily could be. It's just the weird nature of our situation.

But a sudden curiosity ripples through me, and I have to ask...

"Did you see anyone? While you were there...?"

She stares at our joined hands while methodically pressing her fingers up to mine.

"Yea," she sighs. The burning that runs up from my stomach to my chest makes me very uneasy. "Not many. Nothing crazy. I was just... having fun. Living the life I missed out on for all those years, I guess..."

I nod slowly, though it hurts to hear this, and I don't know why. It's hypocritical for me to expect her to be fine with me banging my way through a small village-worth of ladies, while also being all pissy about her getting her swerve on with a couple Euro-dudes. And I won't let myself be that guy.

So I push past the whiny jealousy and macho-guy rage that wants me to Hulk-out, and kiss her head again.

"I'm glad you had fun," I tell her with sincerity. "I missed you every fucking day, Alex. But I'm glad you did that for yourself. You deserve all the adventures in the world."

She gazes up at me and I allow myself to get lost in her vibrant green irises for a few minutes. So many times I saw bright green vegetation in Georgia, and it always reminded me of Alex's eyes. I'll admit that I spent many days and nights wishing she would come back so I could look at them again.

And now that she's here once more, I'm pacified. Even if she leaves tomorrow, at least I'll have this memory. This night with her to soothe the ache she caused when disappeared that first time.

And yet I know my heart is a liar. Because I don't want her to leave. I don't want to lose this feeling again. But I have to brace myself because it could happen.

I'll just have to soak up as much of her as I can now, until she decides to go again.

"We should get up," she hums, lifting herself slowly on shaky arms. "My couch is covered in sex leftovers."

I laugh and she bites her lip. "Okay. Let's take a shower, and then I want to hear all about your trip. Beginning to end."

Nyla K

"That'll be a long story," she pushes my hair away from my forehead.

"I guess we'll have to make some coffee then," I give her an eager look and she smiles, like a lightning rod shooting straight through my soul.

"Sounds like a plan," she kisses me quick, but I grab her face and hold her there, to keep it going.

To make it last.

CHAPTER TWENTY THREE

Alex

Six Months Later...

"NOAH, IF YOU KEEP PESTERING ME, I'll never make it to the airport on time."

"First of all, it's a private jet, *Alexandra*. They will wait for you to arrive before they fly away. And second of all, I need a favor."

"This better be an actual favor, and not just a request for naked pictures," I sneer. He laughs and my insides hum. *Love that sound.*

"No, you already lost my subscription on that. You were supposed to send them last night, and I fell asleep waiting."

"You're a pervert." And yet my grin is wild.

"You love it. I'm serious, though. I need you to swing by my place before you go to the airport. I want you to check on Boots."

I pause with a bikini in my hand. "Is he okay? I thought Phoebe was taking care of him?"

"She is, but she said he's been a bit... I don't know, lethargic?" Noah doesn't sound worried, so I try to uncoil my stomach. "I think maybe he's just a little depressed. He probably misses me, and I feel sorta guilty. I haven't spent this much time traveling in a while, and he's older now, so maybe he's not used to me being away." He pauses to breathe out hard. "I don't know, I'd just feel a lot better if you would pop in and make sure he's alright before you come down."

I nod as if he's looking at me with his gorgeous coal eyes. "Of course I will. I'm happy to check on him and report back."

"Thanks, baby. You're the best," he huffs. "Now get that sexy ass ready, and I'll see you in a few hours."

I try to stifle my out-of-control smile, but it's no use. I'm vibrating with anticipation. I can't wait to see him.

"Mhmm... And then you won't need the naked pictures because you'll have the real thing," I purr into the phone, knowing it drives him crazy in the best possible way.

"Don't get me started, beautiful. It's been a month... I'm going to ravage you." His tone is deep and dangerously sexy. I have to press my thighs together to stop the river that wants to flow from between them.

"That better be a promise, Richards," I whine and he growls. "I'm so hard-up for you, I'm calling floor sex, then second I get to your place."

He chuckles in that wickedly seductive *Noah Richards* way that always prompts me to let him do whatever he wants to my body. It's given us some fun memories over the last couple years.

"I love you missing me, baby..." he murmurs and my heart thumps in my chest.

Because for a second I thought he was saying *I love you*, and *oh my God*, what is wrong with me?? That's where my mind goes?! *Get it together, Mackenzie. Quick! Say something dirty to cover up your weirdness!*

"I'll tell you what I miss. That big, long, delicious -"

"Alex, please..." he whimpers and I giggle.

"Toblerone! Is what I was going to say... I love buying those huge Toblerone's at the airport. You want me to grab you one?"

"Fuckin wise ass," he rumbles, but I can hear the smile in his voice. I can't wait to finally see it again in person.

I'm over FaceTime. Noah left almost five weeks ago for Georgia, to film season three of *Hell Storm*, and while phone sex and video calls can be fun, I miss touching him. It's crazy to think last year we were apart for so long, because now I hate not seeing him for more than a week.

And clearly I'm getting a bit carried away, what with thinking he was telling me he *loves* me a minute ago. *Jesus, imagine?? That would be insane... Wouldn't it?*

"Alright! I have to go! I want to get there sometime tonight, and now I have to go out of my way into Manhattan." I change the subject before my mind can spiral out any further.

"Okay, okay. Tell Boots that Daddy loves him and misses him, and I'll be home before he knows it," he says, and I swoon so hard I almost collapse.

"Will do, *Daddy*," I smirk, licking my lips.

"Alex, don't make it weird," he grumbles and I laugh out loud.

"See you soon, superstar!" I squeal, and we make a dozen or so kissy noises before hanging up.

It's gross how much of an adorable couple we are without actually *being* a

Seek Me

couple.

I used to worry that Noah and I would fall back into the relationship-zone that we were at one time dancing around, being that we were inseparable from the moment I came home. But now, we have an effortlessly chill thing going on. We're still casual best friends with benefits, who don't see anyone else. We both go out and do our own separate things, and I suppose we could date other people if we wanted to, but it never really comes up. I guess it's because we don't need to. We satisfy our needs together.

We date, we attend things together as friends; we support each other and fuck like there's no tomorrow. It's unnecessary to pursue outside parties when it's this damn good between us.

I finish packing quick and drag my travel bag downstairs where Jimmy is just pulling up along the curb in front of my building. He jumps out of the vehicle and dashes over to me, snatching my large bag in his hand.

"Alex, why on Earth wouldn't you text me to come upstairs and carry your bag down for you?" He asks, sounding annoyed, which I think is too cute.

"I can do things on my own, Jimmy," I roll my eyes as he tosses my bag in the way back. "Might I remind you, it's not the nineteen-thirties."

He laughs and opens the door for me. "No, it's certainly not. Now come on. Let's get you to the airport, unless you'd like to do that on your own, also?" He lifts his brow teasingly.

I purse my lips as I hop into the backseat. "You're *so* funny. By the way, we have to make a stop real quick at Noah's. He wants me to check on Boots."

Jimmy freezes with his hand on the door before he can close it. "Is he okay?"

So I'm not the only one who immediately panics about Noah asking me to check on Boots. But we're all overreacting. We have to be. I'm sure he's fine.

"Yea, yea," I wave Jimmy off. "Just misses Daddy that's all." I smile, but my insides are suddenly balmy. *Why is that so hot??*

Jimmy gives me a relieved grin, not picking up on my perverted thoughts about his boss, and closes the door, reclaiming his place in the driver's seat and carting us off to Manhattan.

When we get there, he waits out front while I go inside. As I walk through the foyer, it's very quiet. There's no one in sight, and no noise happening whatsoever, except maybe the washing machine at the back of the apartment.

"Hello?" I call out, walking slowly. "Phoebe?"

"Alex?" Phoebe's voice calls from the back.

"Yea! Um, Noah wanted me to come by and check on Boots…"

Phoebe emerges from the laundry room and darts over to me. Her face is more serious than I'm used to, but surely it's nothing to be alarmed about.

"Oh. Right…" she pauses when she's standing in front of me and clears her throat. "I didn't want him to worry. He's so busy with work and everything. The last thing he needs is… This."

I try to swallow, but it's not really working. I feel like my throat is closing up.

"What's wrong…?" My voice squeaks out of me.

"Well, nothing. Not really," she waves for me to follow her, which I do.

We ascend the stairs up to Noah's bedroom, I assume because Boots is sleeping on his bed. That's always where he is these days.

Boots has been a cuddle-bug since I met him almost three years ago. He's not the most energetic cat in the world. He likes to sleep and snuggle, which I've always thought was just how he is.

But now that I'm digging deeper with the paranoid mind of someone who thinks there might be a problem, it dawns on me that I haven't seen him play since I got back from Budapest six months ago. Usually we could count on him to get up at night and scamper around, or bring us his fuzzy catnip toys while we're trying to watch a movie. Or wake Noah up to feed him at odd hours.

But I can't for the life of me remember the last time he did any of that. He's just been… tired. He cuddles us at night, and purrs a lot. But I now understand the whole *lethargic* thing. He definitely seems… off.

"I had a vet friend come over and check him out, just to see if he thinks we need x-rays or anything," Phoebe breaks the silence as we stand in Noah's bedroom, gazing down at Boots, who's exactly where I guessed he would be. Cuddled up on Noah's bed, right by his pillow.

Poor thing… Maybe he does miss Noah.

Wait, did she just say x-rays??

I glance at Phoebe, unable to hide the distress on my face.

"He said everything looks normal…" she continues, rubbing her eyes hard with her fingers. "Vitals are fine, no abnormalities. He took a blood sample, so he'll give me a call tomorrow and let me know if there's any cause for concern."

I hold back my worry and lean over Boots, petting his soft little head. "Does Noah know?"

Phoebe's quiet, and I peer up to see her shifting in place.

"No, I didn't tell him," she mutters, looking and sounding extremely guilty. "Like I said, I didn't want him to worry. You know how important his performance is down there... He can't be distracted. I'll tell him when the results come in, though. I promise."

I nod slowly and return to Boots. I know I have to leave, but this is more important.

I crawl into the bed next to him and cuddle his small, fuzzy body next to mine. He seems to notice, though he doesn't do much in the way of regarding me. But he's purring. *That's gotta be a good sign, right? Purring means happy...?*

A nervous and twitchy Phoebe leaves the room and I stay there, snuggling Boots and telling him everything Noah told me to say to him. And maybe some extra stuff about what a good boy he is, and how special he is, and how we really want him to feel better.

I finally drag myself out of the bed and leave, heading back downstairs. I feel pretty confident that Boots is just going through something. Maybe he needs a change in diet, or Noah needs to help him get some exercise. I know the less *I* work out, the less I want to move at all. The same could be happening to poor Boots.

Phoebe's right not to alarm Noah. Boots seems perfectly healthy to me, and until we get the blood work back from the vet, there's no reason to freak out.

Noah's baby will be just fine. I'm sure of it.

In the meantime, I need to get my ass down to Georgia to see my man. It's been way too long, and I'm missing him something fierce.

I hate missing Noah... Although I suppose I should get used to it...

I have a bit of a bombshell to drop on him while I'm visiting, and I seriously hope he doesn't get upset. He's entitled to his feelings, but unfortunately in this case, they won't change anything. It's a done deal.

Jimmy drives me to LaGuardia, where I board a private jet Noah rented, so I don't have to deal with the hassle of an airport, or flying on a packed-ass plane. My excitement is kicked up to high. I've never been on a private plane before, and I feel like such a classy bitch. I can't wait to crack the Dom.

I'm on my way, baby!

When I exit the super fancy G6 at Savannah/Hilton Head International Airport, I expect to see another car waiting to drive me to Noah's house.

What I don't expect is Noah himself, standing in front of a silver Maserati, and holding up a sign that says *Alexandra Mackenzie aka Noah's Baby Boo Thang.*

I can't help but die laughing. And then attack him and dry-hump his hard body against his sexy sports car.

Almost three years and we still haven't gotten over the dry-humping.

I know. It's hard not to be jealous.

Rather than fucking me on the hood of his car in the middle of an airport tarmac, Noah refrains from sexual activity until we're securely tucked inside his vehicle. At which point I take the opportunity to tease him and torture him until he eventually caves and pulls down a side-street so we can engage in some hot, sweaty car sex.

The limited space of the Maserati just serves to turn us both in even bigger raging sex fiends, since we have no choice but to wear each other like a second skin. It's so spine-tinglingly perfect, I manage to get off three times, and get Noah off twice.

It was exactly what I needed. And let's be real, I wouldn't have been able to make it an entire forty-minute drive from the airport to his house.

When we arrive at his place, I'm blown away more than Noah was in his car just now.

He lives in a fucking *mansion*. And I'm not just saying that because he's my best friend, and I'm trying to be supportive of his life down here.

His house is so big, my face is tilted at a right angle and I still can't see all the way up. I've never felt smaller than when I'm standing next to this house. Somehow, it looks larger than the skyscrapers in Manhattan, which I know makes no sense. Maybe it's because it's surrounded by wilderness. It just makes the whole thing look a zillion times more huge.

"Home sweet home!" Noah cheers and grabs my bag, motioning for me to follow him inside.

There are a ton of wise-ass remarks I'd like to make about this place, but nothing will come out of my mouth at the moment. I'm just dumb-staring at the monstrosity before me.

Going inside isn't much of a difference. I feel like I'm in a mall. There are so many rooms, and they're all so *big*. Noah offers to give me a tour, and it takes us a solid half-hour to get through the whole place.

"So we have a few minutes to relax now, but we should probably leave for Johnny's by seven. He's having us over for a little barbecue," Noah tells me when we come full-circle back to the kitchen, the size of which resembles those they compete in on *Top Chef.*

Seek Me

"Oh cool," I nod, more eager than I have been in a long time about finally meeting Noah's costar besties. "Who will be there?"

"We're keeping it casual. Just Andrew, Mike, and Sarah. And Johnny, obviously," he tells me. "Johnny might have a date over. I can never be sure."

I giggle and Noah steps up to me, pinning my butt to his marble island as he grips it on either side of my waist. I peek up at his beautiful face and allow myself to get lost in every perfect thing about Noah Richards.

From his deep, dark eyes, like the night's sky out here in the country, to his soft, candy lips, which are surprisingly full for a guy's; sharp jaw lined with sexy stubble that he never grows out too much. His silky, ear-length hair that's always a mess in the hottest possible way; a color that, if it were a bottled dye, would be named *brown sugar honeycomb*.

And all of this is only above the shoulders. Once we trail down his delicious body, it would take another several hours to describe each magnificent part of Noah in detail.

He's a phenomenon. A treasure. The eighth wonder of the world.

And he's mine. In a sense...

Noah's hand slinks up my side, twirling in my hair before caressing the flesh of my neck, and up to my face, his fingers tracing the line of my jaw while he stares so deep into my eyes I feel like I'm drowning in him.

"Do you have any idea how much it means to me that you're here?" His voice is soft yet insistent and laced with fascination. His brow lifts, and I think he wants me to answer him.

But I can't. Not only do I not really know how much it truly means to him, I wouldn't even begin to know how to answer such a question. Not to mention, the whole notion of producing words right now... While he's looking at me like that. It's a tricky one.

So I settle for a slow and subtle head shake.

He presses his forehead to mine, minty breath warming my lips. "I'm going to tell you something that will make me sound like a complete and total sack. But you know every part of me, so chances are you already know just how much of a wuss I am deep down." I huff a quiet giggle, and his lips curl.

"So here goes... When you left for Budapest last year it fucked me up a little. More than you know..." He pauses to gulp and my knees begin to shake. "I was always so happy for you, don't get me wrong, but I really wanted you in Georgia with me. At least a couple weekends, here and there. I couldn't stop thinking about how much you'd love this house, and how much I wished you could enjoy it with me. I started fantasizing about you being here... In the backyard, fucking with the pot plan I've been trying to grow without much success. Lying by the pool, reading. Curled up in the theater, watching *Goodfellas*. In my bed with me... Or in that giant Jacuzzi tub.

"Andrew's wife hasn't come out here once since we started filming three years ago. And he has kids, so it's totally fucked. He's trying to hold it together, but I know he's really upset about it. And I always thought about how if you were still around, I knew you'd drop everything to come be with me out here, and share this awesome time in my life."

He folds his arms around my back and pulls me flush against him. He's so warm, with hard muscles pressing into me through his thin t-shirt. It feels magnificent, and yet I'm so tangled up in my own guilt, I can barely enjoy it.

"And now here you are," he whispers, his lips moving on my neck, sheeting my flesh with goosebumps. "Last year, I wasn't sure if I'd ever seen you again. I was afraid you might fall in love with Europe and decide you had no reason to come back. I only want happiness for you Alex, but I'm still selfish because I couldn't stop myself from wishing, every chance I got, that you'd come back, and that someday I'd be able to see you in this place with me, for real. And it happened."

He presses a soft kiss on my pulse, which is rapping in my throat. "You're here." His voice is dripping in fascination; like a child whose birthday wish came true.

Unable to stop myself, I run my hands up his back, holding his shoulders and pulling him even closer. I burrow my face in the crook of his neck and kiss the same spot on him as the pressure builds behind my eyes.

"I'm here," I tell him in a timid voice that wants to quiver because I'm holding something back. And I know it's going to hurt him.

I can't bring myself to ruin this moment, or the wonderful night I know we're going to have. So I keep my confession to myself for now, and kiss Noah's skin, everywhere I can reach. I just care for him so much sometimes it hurts, which is a feeling I remember well.

It scares me down to my core.

I hold Noah harder and tighter, hugging onto him and praying that regardless of what I do in the future, I won't lose this.

I *can't* lose him. But I also can't have him.

"I'm sorry if that's a sort of heavy thing to say..." his voice rumbles into me. "I never want you to feel bad about following your dreams, because I wouldn't be here if I didn't follow mine. But I just... I can't take this feeling for granted. I'm so grateful I got you back, Alex... Even as a friend."

"You know how grateful I am to you, Noah," I hum and he nods, his hair tickling my face. "I wouldn't miss being here with you for anything in the world."

He abruptly takes my jaw in his hands and kisses my lips so sensually and tender, I'm melting all over the place. We stand in his kitchen for minutes on end, kissing and touching, absorbing each other for as long as we have.

Because even though he might not know it now, this high will have to end. But not yet.

Finally he peels off me and sucks in a breath. "We should get going."

I give him an easy smile, sliding my thumb over his bottom lip. "I can't wait to meet your friends."

He smiles back, and it's such a spectacular thing to see. Like fireworks over calm waters.

"They've been dying to meet you," he locks our fingers.

"Well, in that case. Let's do this."

We hop back into the car, driving for fifteen minutes to his friend Johnny's house, which is yet another massive mansion in the woods. Johnny's has a five-car garage, which is stocked with lavish, brightly colored sports cars. There are a few other vehicles in the driveway which I'm guessing belong to his guests, and Noah parks right beside them.

He jumps out of the car and sprints to my door to open it for me, prompting a giant smile I try to conceal. Then he immediately takes my hand again, and we walk around back, following the music.

The back patio of Johnny's place is quite spacious, and he has an Olympic-sized swimming pool that's bigger than Noah's. But I like Noah's better, because it has those cool lights at the bottom, it's surrounded by rocks and even has a waterfall in the corner. I can't wait to swim in it. We have all day to relax and chill by the pool tomorrow.

As it turns out, I'm grateful to Noah for this little getaway, too.

Nothing like a weekend vacation in Georgia with my hot friend before reality sets in again.

As we walk through the back gate, I hear some chatter over the music, followed by a loud laugh that echoes off the surrounding trees. It occurs to me that this is the first time I'm meeting Noah's close friends and costars at an actual private gathering. I've met plenty of people in his life before, but these are the people he's been spending a majority of his time with lately; enough for him to classify them as his *best friends*.

And I'm his... well, whatever I am to him. It all feels rather serious, and I swallow repeatedly while my nerves buzz, mentally pep-talking myself to make a good impression.

"Yo! The party's officially here!" A deep, booming voice shouts at us, and before I know it, a giant man is bounding toward Noah and me.

I squeeze his hand harder, which makes him chuckle.

"Johnny boy!" Noah croons at the huge person who hugs him so hard, he almost tackles him to the ground. *So that's Johnny.*

"And you must be his little vixen," Johnny's face is plastered in a beaming smile that's sweet and kind, yet slightly devious.

I take a brief once-over of this big hunk of man, trying not to be obvious. Of course I've seen John Barthow before, on TV and in movies. Everyone knows this guy's face. He's a hugely popular action star, and a fully drool-worthy human. Every inch of him is made of muscle and sin. He's got an angled jaw that could cut glass, and deep molasses eyes that match his trimmed up brown hair and beard.

He reaches forward and grabs me in a bear-hug that could probably be used to kill actual bears, though it somehow manages to be warm and enveloping, not scary. He's just such a behemoth, it's almost overwhelming. But I can already tell he's a total muffin.

I pat his back a few times before he releases me, and I realize once I'm out of his grip that I've been planted back onto my feet. He actually lifted me up without me even noticing. *Wow...*

It's also once I'm on solid ground again that I feel Noah's fingers still strangling mine. He was holding my hand possessively the entire time Johnny was hugging me, which has to be the cutest damn thing this side of the Mississippi.

"Um, hi," I blurt out, struggling to sound normal. "I'm Alex."

"Hello, Alex. I'm Johnny. Best friend number two. Or I guess three, after you." He winks at me. "Come on, love birds. Let's get you some drinks."

"Don't say *love birds* ever again," Noah grumbles and Johnny sneers over his shoulder before guiding us to the rest of the party.

As we enter the patio, I can already smell grilling meat and my stomach gurgles because I've barely eaten anything today.

"Are there hot dogs?!" I squeal, picking up my pace and dragging Noah with me.

"I've got a sausage with your name on it, sweetheart," Johnny drawls and

Seek Me

Noah shoots him a look laced with daggers. "Relax, bro. I'm just saying I saved her a weiner."

"Johnny, leave the poor girl alone," a smooth voice with a British accent croons from beside the grill. As we approach, the deck lights illuminate another familiar face. "And you're making Alex uncomfortable, too."

Andrew James lets out a laugh at his own joke that sounds like smooth jazz on vinyl.

"Hardy har har," Noah rolls his eyes, going for a hug. "You two are a regular comedy duo tonight, huh?"

Andrew smacks him hard on the back, then turns some very intense blue eyes on me. "Hello, dear. Can I just say, I am bloody *ecstatic* to finally meet you."

He gives me a warm, friendly hug, that dazzling smile never once leaving his lips.

"Hi! It's very nice to meet you, too," I beam, fidgeting in place. *Oh my God. It's Andrew freaking James! Be cool, bitch.* "I'm Alex Mackenzie."

"You're all hugging her for way too long," Noah huffs. "Three seconds each. That's unacceptable."

Andrew throws his head back in a laugh that makes most other laughs sound like nails on a chalkboard. "Hi, Alex. Ignore him. I'm Andrew James, best friend number one. Or two...?"

He lifts his brow at me and I giggle like a dumb ditz.

"You can be best friend number one. I'm cool with it." I peek at Noah and bite my lip. "I think I win anyway, since I'm the best friend that goes home with him."

Noah winks at me and uses his free hand to give me a little smack on the butt.

"You've got us beat there, darlin'," Johnny adds, handing Noah and I each a glass of brown liquor. "Noah keeps trying, but I'm just not into him like that."

Noah yanks his hand out of mine just long enough to punch Johnny hard in the kidney, causing him to groan out loud. Then his fingers thread gracefully back through mine.

"Wow, I still can't believe we're finally in the presence of the famous *Alex*," Andrew rasps, ignoring them. "I've heard so much about you, I feel like I know you already."

Noah's eyes widen at his friend, whose eyes narrow in return, and they share some telepathic conversation which fascinates me to witness.

"Tell me about it!" I jump in. "Noah talks about you guys all the time. It's actually very sweet. I even know your kids' names and what they do for fun." I grin then take a sip of my drink.

"Aww!" Andrew reaches out to pinch Noah's cheek, who then slaps him away.

"Hands off!" Noah growls, gulping his drink all the while shaking his head. I can't help but laugh.

"Oh thank God, another female!" A melodious voice calls out as a tall, slender woman with short silver hair floats over to us. "It's a damn sausagefest in this place! Hi, I'm Sarah."

The woman gives me a generous hug, and I must say, I'm really digging how friendly all these people are. For famous actors, they're insanely nice and down to earth.

"Hi! Alex," I introduce myself, admiring how well-put-together she is.

"Hi, Alex! I'm Mike." A guy jaunts over and hugs me before I can process what's happening, though Noah pulls me away from him before we can even really make contact.

"Simmer down, newbie," my best friend seethes, though I think he's kidding.

"When are you going to stop calling me that?" Mike frowns and I catch Andrew chuckling behind him. "I'm on my second season!"

"You're still a newbie," Noah, Andrew and Johnny all say in unison and I can't fight the laugh that bubbles from inside my throat.

Mike seems like a sweet kid too, and he's also dressed very well, in skinny jeans, a fitted button-down, and high-top sneakers the brightest shade of yellow I've ever seen.

It's like I'm standing around in a magazine cover, all of them rocking expensive designer labels, as if they're a collective ad for all the designers on Fifth Avenue.

I would feel insecure, in my combat boots, ripped jean shorts and crop-tank covered by one of Noah's flannels, except that Noah is dressed pretty casually himself. Though he never really *looks* casual because he wears the most unique things and still looks sexy as fuck.

He's toned it down tonight in a Gucci t-shirt, torn-up skinny jeans and the red Supreme hat with the black paint smudges I made. But this *is* Noah we're talking about, so naturally he's wearing his Ray Bans. At night.

It's kind of his thing.

"I propose a toast!" Andrew raises his glass, and we all follow his lead. "To finally meeting the remaining member of our little group. Welcome, Alexandra.

Seek Me

Thank you for making the journey to Savannah."

We all murmur *cheers*, *Salud*, or in Noah and my case, *nostrovia*, then clink glasses. I sip my scotch slowly, already buzzing on the excitement, and glance at Noah, who's watching me. He pulls me closer to him, snaking an arm around my waist and pressing his lips to my temple.

I have to admit, even though we're not a real couple, I love that he's acting this way in front of his friends. I know he's happy I'm here, especially after what he said before. And I've never been happier to be some place in my life.

The conversation flows smoothly from there. The group of them regale me with stories from the set, which I really enjoy hearing. According to Andrew, Noah is lazy, and according to Noah, Andrew is a baby with the heat. The two of them bicker like brothers, but then feed off of one another, and it's just the sweetest friendship I've ever encountered. They seem like they've known each other their whole lives, even though they only met shortly after Noah and I did.

But I suppose it makes sense. Noah and I have the same kind of thing going on, although we've been sleeping together for years, so that would account for our intimate relationship and how well we know one another. Still, there's a reason why I can call Noah my best friend, and it has nothing to do with the fact that we spend almost every night screwing each other silly.

It's because we've spent years growing and learning together. We've shared our deepest, darkest secrets, and have been there for one another through some very intense stuff. Just thinking about it now makes me regret the time we spent apart, which is something I hate feeling.

I don't like regretting the decisions I've made for my new life. I know I have to be independent. It's the only way I can build myself back up after spending the beginning of my adult life trapped in a cage. And yet when I'm with Noah, I only want to be with him… And be *his*.

But I can't think like that. I still have more life experiences to make.

I'm distracted from my worrisome train of thought when Johnny shoves a plate of hot dogs in my face.

"You're small, but Noah says you can put away the meat," he smirks, and this time he anticipates Noah's kidney shot, dodging it. "Come on! No, I just mean, let's see how many hot dogs you can eat in ten minutes. It'll be fun."

I'm actually considering it for a moment, because I'm starving. But Noah snatches the plate away.

"Dude, she's not a carnival attraction. Baby, how many hot dogs do *you* think you can eat in ten minutes?" He smiles wide and I bite my lip.

"Ten minutes? Oh jeez, I don't know. Ten?" I lift my brow at him, waiting for him to react either with a face of disgust or approval. And because it's Noah, he looks elated.

"One hot dog a minute?" Andrew gasps, leaning up against the table. "I have to see this."

"Yes! Eating contest! Let's do this!" Johnny shouts, waving his arms in the air as Andrew shushes him.

"Only if you think you can do it without puking," Noah sings as his head cocks to the side. I can't see his eyes beneath those glasses, but I just know they're wide and challenging. And I know why he's so confident in my abilities…

It's because he's seen me eat ten hot dogs in ten minutes before. From our favorite hot dog cart, the one at the Central Park entrance on 81st. *Best hot dogs in the city.*

It's one of my favorite memories with Noah. He challenged me to a hot dog eating contest and failed miserably. I beat his ass, and then we both puked. *What a great night.*

"Game on, bitches!" I cheer and the rest of them whoop and wail.

Everyone is so excited, the pressure is definitely on. I don't want to fail, and I'm certainly hungry enough to eat at least five without a second thought.

Let's do this, Mackenzie. Show these punks what you're made of.

They sit me down at the table with a plate of ten hot dogs in front of me, like a mountain of potential. They smell so good, my mouth is watering, but I have to remember to pace myself. If I go too fast, I'll end up choking down the last few and that will make me ralph for sure.

"Got the timer ready," Mike says.

"Get her some water," Sarah adds, and Andrew appears with a glass.

"You got this, baby," Noah says, kissing my head. "I believe in you."

I give him a sweet smile as they all count down.

"Three… two… One!"

And I'm off. Chomping them back like a champ and wondering why I never entered the Coney Island contest because this shit is fun *and* delicious.

The first four go down as easy as I expected, and I'm not full yet, which is a good sign. They all cheer me on as I get through five, then six, then seven, before we reach the halfway mark.

"This is the best thing I've ever seen!" Andrew grips the edge of the table.

"Bro, your girlfriend's a beast," Johnny says to Noah with amaze in his voice.

Seek Me

"She's not my girlfriend," Noah whispers and I choke through a hot-dog-filled laugh.

Chewing the last bite of number eight, I feel suddenly woozy. I think I'm hitting the wall, but I'm so close. I can't give up yet.

"Come on, baby," Noah rubs my back. "Only two more. Three minutes left. You're golden."

"Fuck…" I groan and finally swallow the last of eight. "I don't know… if I can…"

"You totally can!" Johnny bellows then starts the chant. "Alex! Alex! Alex!"

The rest of them join in and I summon all my strength and inner hunger. I pick up the ninth dog, taking a generous bite and chewing, slow yet with dedication. I eventually swallow and eat the rest.

Only one more to go.

"She's gonna do it!" Sarah shrieks.

"One minute left!" Mike calls out.

"Go for it, babe! You're home free!" Noah's encouragement pushes me to chomp down the final hot dog, the act of chewing becoming more strenuous than jogging. I force myself to swallow as they scream out *thirty seconds*.

I can do this! I can… do… it.

Oh God, I'm gonna hurl so bad.

No! Don't admit defeat!

"One more bite!" Andrew and Johnny blare from behind me.

I stuff it into my mouth, ignoring the strong urge to vomit, and chew hard, my palms sweating as my stomach screams for me to stop. But stop I will not.

They count me down from ten.

And with three seconds to spare, I swallow the final bite. And I shoot up out of my chair in victory.

I did it!

"She did it!" They all scream together, huddling around me, jumping up and down.

"Baby, you did it! You're the motherfucking champion!" Noah hugs me, but not too hard, because he knows I could erupt at any minute.

Johnny turns on *We Are the Champions* by Queen and we all sing together. It's a fucking masterpiece of a night. I've never been gladder in my whole life to have met these people.

And let them watch me eat ten hot dogs in ten minutes.

After that bizarre, amusing feat, the night goes on, and I don't vomit, which is good. Although I eat nothing else because I'm still so stuffed I could pop.

Noah breaks out a joint and we all smoke a little, continuing on with our drinking as we move the party inside when it cools off outside. Johnny has a massive fireplace in his sitting room, and he gets a nice one going so we can roast marshmallows. I roast a few for Noah, because I can't even think about eating one. And we all talk, getting our buzz on and enjoying each other's company.

It's been hours since we arrived, and we're all relaxed and cozy. Noah's talking to Mike and Sarah, arguing about something in their last script they all seem to disagree on. Johnny's across the room, parked on a big chair, texting.

And I'm with Andrew, on the couch, listening to his Noah stories. I have to say, I freaking love this guy. Not in a romantic way, obviously, though it's kind of scary how dreamy he is. But more than that, he's a total sweetheart, and he loves Noah to death, which is so cute it leaves a permanent warmth in my belly. *Maybe it's all the scotch and weed.*

"It was a true shame they couldn't use that footage, because he really nailed it… right before he fell into the creek," Andrew tells me through a laugh, wiping his eyes as I do the same.

We've been giggling for a while at all the embarrassing things that have happened to Noah on set. Not that we're making fun of him or anything. It's just so satisfying to be involved in this part of his life. It's the one part of Noah I haven't seen yet, and I love feeling included in his world.

"It sounds like you guys have a blast down here," I sigh, resting my head against the back of the couch. "I wish I could spend more time…" I stop myself before I blurt out any details on why I can't.

"Well, at least you're here now," Andrew mutters, and his smile disappears as he stares at the fire.

I pause for a moment. I really want to talk to him about all the problems he's been having with his wife, but I'm not sure it's my place. Then again, I'm practically an extension of Noah, and maybe Andrew needs a woman's point of view on what's happening.

"So… she hasn't been out here at all?" I ask hesitantly, my eyes gliding slowly over to him. I half expect him to look angry or offended. But he doesn't.

He looks vulnerable, and it sucks to witness. Sure, I don't know him well, but Noah talks about him all the time, so I kind of feel like I do.

"No…" he grunts then turns abruptly so that his whole body is facing mine, and I do the same. "What do you think it means? That she doesn't want to be here with me…" He stops and swallows visibly. "Do you think it means…

we're over?"

"Andrew, I couldn't tell you that," I whisper, unable to stop the sympathy in my tone. "I don't know your wife, but I do know that it doesn't take much effort to fly down to Georgia every once in a while."

"Right. You did it," he scoffs. "And you and Noah aren't even officially together, although no one's buying that." He freezes and his eyes widen. "Uh... I'm sorry. I shouldn't have said that. I take it back."

He's gaping at me now, as if he just let some horrible secret slip. I don't know what to think about what he just said.

My chest tightens suddenly as I stare back at Andrew, considering what it must look like to everyone else. Noah and I claiming we're not a couple when we do literally everything that couples do together... Of course his friends think there's more going on.

"Do you think... Noah thinks we're more than just friends?" I ask, unsure of what answer would make me happy.

I'm torn in half right now... Between wanting Noah as mine so badly and knowing I can't possibly have him as more than a friendly fuck-buddy.

"I don't... I think..." Andrew stutters then shakes his head. "It doesn't matter what I think. What would I know about relationships, anyway? I'm just some bloke whose wife doesn't even want to be near him anymore."

I pout and rub his arm. "Do you want to be near her?" He's silent for a generous amount of time, so I have to add, "If it takes you that long to think about it, you probably have your answer."

"I know, but it's not that simple," he rakes his fingers through his hair. "I have my children to consider. Am I really going to put them through a divorce? What sort of damage could that cause?"

"The only damage to them will be from seeing Mom and Dad fighting all the time," I tell him. "Children are smart. They catch on. Maybe not right now, but when they get a little older, they'll be able to tell you're not happy. That could cause more harm than doing what might be best for both of you."

He huffs out a hard breath and flops back. "I was thinking if we could just wait until Lucy was a bit older, then maybe..." He peeks at me and I give him a look. "No, you're right. It's a Band-Aid. Alex, I miss feeling for someone the way you and Noah feel for one another. I love that feeling... Being inseparable. Never wanting to spend a moment apart. Why couldn't it just be like that with Viv and I?"

"Because life isn't perfect," I answer. "It's messy and complicated and..."

I stop talking and chomp my bottom lip. It might be the lack of filter from the buzz, but I really need to talk to someone about what's going on in my head. I'm not sure if Noah's best friend is the right person to share this with, but I need some advice, and he could be the perfect person to ask for it.

"If I told you something, would you promise not to tell Noah?" I lift my brow and he blinks several times.

"It depends what it is…" he murmurs. "I don't want to see him hurt again."

"It's something I'm going to talk to him about it before I leave Georgia, so you won't be keeping a secret. I just need to get this off my chest before I explode."

Andrew looks wary of my potential confession, but he nods reluctantly.

"I'm leaving," I whisper, my eyes darting across the room to where Noah is still deep in conversation with his friends. "To travel some more. I'm going to Tel Aviv for six months."

Andrew gawks at me for a solid minute of silence before he finally says, "Fuck."

"Yea," I nod.

"When are you leaving?"

"In two weeks." We're both quiet again. "Do you think Noah will be upset?"

"If he is, he'd never let you know about it," he replies in a knowing tone that has me nodding again. "Look, I don't know about what you've been through, but Noah told me you're divorced and that it was a difficult time. And I understand that you need to live your life and do what makes you happy. But I need to ask you something, and it should only be a one-word answer." My pulse picks up as I stare back at him, barely breathing. "Does Noah make you happy?"

My crazy heart answers before I have a second to think. "Yes. Without a doubt."

"Then… what more do you need?" His face is caring and attentive; his tone not prying or accusing. He's genuinely making a point, and it's one I've thought about myself for years now.

But the truth, *my* truth, is one I haven't voiced to anyone aloud. One that I barely ever let myself think. And yet for some reason, I'm going to say it to this person I just met.

"I'm… scared."

Andrew simply nods and drapes his arm around my shoulder, nestling me up to his side.

He gets it. And there's not much else that can be said.

Seek Me

Fear is a powerful emotion. More often than not, it's stronger than even the most blinding happiness.

So we just sit in quiet thought, our truths existing between us. Both equally upsetting.

"Before, you said you don't want to see Noah hurt *again*..." I speak softly, and I feel Andrew tense. I swallow hard. "Was it really that bad?"

"I think you already know..." he whispers, and I nod. Because I do. "Noah has a lot of pride, Alex. Getting him to admit certain things is like pulling teeth..."

"Did he admit it to you?"

He's silent for a moment before he answers. "It's not my place."

But that's all the answer I need.

"Dude, if you're gonna mack it on my date, the least you could do is wait until I leave the room," Noah's voice bursts through our little pity-party, and we both look up.

"Get in here, bestie," Andrew grins and scoots over, allowing Noah to plop down between us.

He takes my hand in his and tugs it onto his lap. "You wanna get going soon?"

For a moment I just admire his face, the contours of which are shadowed by the dull glow of the fire.

I know with absolute certainty that he's the perfect man for me. And I know if we gave it a shot, we could be truly happy.

But life *isn't* perfect. And it's definitely not easy. It's downright terrifying at times.

If I were to stay with Noah, now, I would be giving him a version of myself that's too unsure. And I could never do that to Noah. He deserves everything.

It's all or nothing, Alex.

I give him a soft smile and nod.

We say goodbye to his friends, who I now consider my friends, and we head back to his house, where we spend the rest of the night devoted to each other. I have to give him everything while I'm still here. Because two days from now, I'll be gone again. And it's always a coin-toss when I leave.

That's the thing about me getting these life experiences... They're a gamble. I'm playing Russian roulette with my heart. Leaving again, but at what cost?

There's no guarantee that what Noah and I have will endure this tug-of-war. And yet I'm unable to stop myself from pulling.

"You really don't have to drive me to the airport," I tell Noah as he hops down the stairs with my bag.

"Oh, I'm not doing it for free," he says pointedly. "I'm an Uber driver on weekends. You didn't see the illuminated *U* on the dash of my sweet ride?"

I laugh and try to punch him while he teasingly fights me off.

"Well then, I expect a discount," I wrap my arms around his waist. "Because I let you do some very filthy things to me last night."

"Do I get a five-star rating?" He smirks, dropping my bag so he can feel up my butt with both hands.

"You get a million-star rating," I breathe and he hums, kissing my lips, soft and warm and so *Noah*. It still amazes me that he can be so sweet after doing the things we did this weekend.

My muscles are aching and sore all over, reminiscent of that last Pilates workshop I did. Noah Richards is a workout in his own right.

Plus, if we're being honest, I was soaking up as much of him as I could, knowing I won't be seeing him for a while after this.

Speaking of such things…

"Babe… There's something I need to… tell you." My stomach twists into multiple knots, and I'm already sweating.

"Oh no… You're fourteen?" He pulls a faux-horrified face, and this time I land a punch right to his gut, which makes him *oof* before bursting into a laugh.

"No, dumbass. I'm being serious."

"Okay. Let's be serious." He gives me his undivided attention, and I suddenly want to go back to joking around. More than anything.

Ugh… Here goes…

"I'm um… Going to Tel Aviv. With some friends from the art program," I gulp, running my hands down his chest as my eyes seek out anything in the world other than his.

Noah becomes stiff and quiet. It feels like he stopped breathing.

I know I need to look him in the eye, but I'm so scared he'll be mad, or worse… That he'll be hurt. But I finally give up the fight and connect my eyes with his. They're wider than usual, but he doesn't look angry, or devastated. Just a bit surprised.

Seek Me

He purses his lips. "And let me guess, you're leaving tomorrow?" He huffs out a small laugh that was probably meant to be teasing or playful, but it comes out sarcastic.

"No…" I squeak, then clear my throat. "In ten days."

He nods a few times. "Oh. Okay. Well, that sounds fun." His shoulders do a little shrug thing. "Eighteen months again?"

This time he's not sarcastic or snarky. He's seriously asking, forehead lined as he braces for impact, like he's waiting for me to slit his throat. I absolutely despise that look.

"No, no… Nothing like that," I rush the words out and his muscles relax a bit. "Six months."

"That's not too bad," he mutters low, almost like he's consoling himself. "I've heard Tel Aviv is beautiful. I always wanted to go… Maybe I could come see you one weekend…?"

I open my mouth, but before I can say anything, he starts rambling some more.

"No, ew. What am I thinking? That's ridiculous. You're going to do… your own thing. That was stupid. Pretend I didn't say that."

My gut is heavy, like it's being filled with concrete. I'm just gaping at him with round eyes and my mouth hanging open, because I *loathe* what I'm doing to him right now. I hate making him feel like this. I'm never more guilty than I am when I tell Noah I'm leaving him.

"You'll have a great time, Al. I'm sure of it," he smiles, though it seems forced, and it doesn't reach his eyes. "So… ten days, huh?" It's all I can do to nod slowly. "Well, then I guess I should plan to fly home next weekend so I can say goodbye."

My lip trembles a bit and I bite it before it's noticeable. "Noah, you don't have to do that. You're so busy right now with filming. Please, don't let me keep you from work."

"Alex, you're not keeping me from work," he rumbles. "I want to be able to say goodbye…" His voice trails. "Or… this was the goodbye, wasn't it? This weekend? Is that why you came?"

"Stop," I grab his face in my hands. "I came because I wanted to. Because I missed you and I wanted to be with you."

"Before you leave," he adds. "Don't worry, Alex. It's fine. I'm good, trust me. I'm happy for you. You're living your dream, remember? We both are… So it's fine."

Each time he says *it's fine* feels like a knife plunging between my ribs. He looks anxious and uncomfortable, as if he doesn't know how to deal with what he's feeling. I can't say I blame him.

"Tell me what you're thinking," I plead, desperate for him to stop bullshitting me and give it to me straight.

If he's mad, or hurt, I want him to tell me. I'd rather that than him acting like he's fine now, then going on benders for six months while I'm away.

And in some small, secret part of my brain, a teeny tiny little voice is begging him to ask me to stay.

It's ridiculous. I *want* to travel. No one's forcing me to go. I can't wait to see Tel Aviv and experience another new part of the world with my art friends.

But I can't ignore the strange desire lurking in my chest for him to ask me not to go.

Noah takes a deep breath and smiles, his mask sliding back into place. "What I'm thinking is that I'm proud of you, and I'm glad you're doing this. Of course I'll miss you, but it's like you said, I'm super busy, anyway. It's a good thing."

His hand roams into my hair, and he holds the back of my head as he presses his lips softly to my forehead. He keeps them there for a moment, grasping me hard and tight, which has me suddenly fighting tears.

Tell me to stay. Just say it, Noah. If you ask me not to go, maybe I won't need to...

"We should get you to the airport," he whispers then lets me go.

The moment is gone.

And so am I.

CHAPTER TWENTY FOUR

Alex

Six Months Later...

I GOT HOME FROM TEL AVIV LAST NIGHT.
It was late, and I was so exhausted from sixteen hours of travel, plus the time-change, that the second I hit my bed, I was out like a light.

I slept myself from Israel time back to New York time, and when I finally reopened my eyes ten hours later, I barely even knew where I was.

I got up and moseyed around the apartment, throwing out my plants that had died while I was away, because I totally forgot to ask someone to water them. I unpacked my bags in my mind, but didn't have the gusto to do it for real, so they're still sitting there.

Made myself some lunch, watched a little TV, and now I'm staring at my phone in my hand. Trying to muster up the strength to call Noah.

We didn't speak at all the entire time I was gone. Again.

It seems like that's our thing. Maybe we're emotionally unequipped to talk when we're not able to see each other. Or maybe we're just so scared that one another will have moved on while we're apart that we make it a point to pretend the other doesn't exist, hoping it will somehow soften the blow if that does in fact become the case.

Who really knows, but either way, I'm back now, and I'm itching to talk to him. I need to know if he's still my best friend with benefits, or if he's now my friend Noah who's dating a tall, blonde Swedish supermodel with perfect skin.

I don't know why, but I always picture him moving on with someone breathtakingly gorgeous and foreign. The kind of girl who always wears Louboutins and has contoured makeup and stylishly blown-out hair.

I shake my head to myself and pull up Noah's contact in my phone. It's already almost dinner time. I need to determine now whether I'll end up wallowing in a pit of despair surrounded by empty ice cream containers tonight, or if I'll be seeing my best friend. I'm desperate to hug him and smell him; to tell him all about my trip and hear what he's been up to for the past six months.

I'm sure it's been a lot. He wrapped season three of the show and they did a whole press tour thing, according to my inside source known as Entertainment Weekly. The tour did not include Tel Aviv, much to my disappointment.

Just like last time, I won't say I didn't enjoy my travels. I very much enjoyed it. Exploring Israel was a once-in-a-lifetime opportunity. The culture was unforgettable; the food was some of the best I've ever had, and the art... Well, that made my incessant missing of Noah just the slightest bit worth it.

I did miss him, though. A ton. I couldn't even look at another guy the whole time I was there, so to say that I'm also feeling the burn of built-up sexual frustration would be an understatement bigger than Noah's perfect...

I press call and bring my phone to my ear, listening to the ringing while I chew actual layers off my lip. My heart is racing faster and faster every second that passes without an answer. And then the unthinkable happens...

It goes to voicemail.

Well, shit. That just shattered my entire universe.

I'm beyond wound up now, envisioning all the worst possible scenarios.

Noah out at Sensay, talking up a hot girl. No, four hot girls. And they're all Swedish supermodels. And they're touching his arm.

No, they're touching his body. He's screwing them. Noah is banging all four of the supermodels at once, even though it's physically impossible, but he's found a way to do it, because he's Noah and he's perfect and he's over me, and *oh God*, why did I have to leave when I so clearly wanted to stay with him??

Hey, you've reached Noah's phone! I can't answer you right now because, well, quite frankly I'm doing something more important. The truth hurts. Leave it awesome at the tone and hope I get back to you!

Beep.

Fuck! Say something!

"Uh, hi! Noah, it's Alex. Um... so... I'm home. And um, I just wanted to say hi and see... how you're doing, I guess. But you're probably busy. It's cool. I'll just... talk to you later. Have a great... um... night! Okay. Bye..."

I hang up fast and toss my phone down onto the couch before I can see the look of pity it's giving me.

God, that was the most awkward message anyone's ever left anyone! Why didn't you just hang up?? Why the hell would you leave that ridiculousness on his voicemail? That's great. Just fucking great. Recorded evidence of how much of a loser you are.

I cover my face with my hands, mind swirling with images of Noah banging hundreds of blonde models while my embarrassing message plays on speaker and they all laugh at me.

But then my phone rings.

I gasp out loud and grab it fast.

It's Noah. *Oh my God! Okay. Calm down.*

I suck in a deep breath and answer the call.

"Hello?" I'm going for casual, but it comes out like the last chirp of a dying bird.

"Hey! Oh my God, Alex! Are you back?!" Noah's sweet, deep and sexy voice rumbles through my phone directly into my brain. He sounds so excited.

And I melt into my couch.

"Yea... Hi. I'm back," I whisper, surrendering to the smile that's swept over my mouth.

"Thank fucking God," he breathes and I giggle. "Sorry I missed your call. I just got out of the shower and heard my phone ringing, and I thought, *there's no way*. But then it's been six months and I've been hoping to hear from you, so I ran to grab my phone completely naked and dripping wet, you're welcome for that image, by the way. And it was you! I'm so psyched you're home!"

Now my beaming smile is actually hurting my face. He's just the most adorable thing in existence. And I've just been informed that he's naked and wet, so pressing my thighs together is necessary.

"Can I see you?" I blurt out, then regret it. "I'm sorry. You're probably busy. We can get together sometime this week if you -"

"Alex, come on," he cuts me off. "Do you honestly think I wouldn't drop anything and everything in the world to see you when you come home from your travels? I could be in the middle of a winning round on *Wheel of Fortune* and I'd dip out in a heartbeat for you. Although that's a bad analogy because you know I'm a *Jeopardy* man."

"Aww. Yes, I know. It's Trebek or nothing."

"Right?? God, I fucking missed you."

I swoon and giggle, because he's fully ridiculous and just the sweetest treat in the whole gosh darn world.

"Noah, I missed you so bad."

"Stop. I don't want to hear another word until I'm with you," he huffs, and I can't stop picturing him naked, standing around in his bedroom, all tattooed and muscley and beautiful. *I need to see him right this fucking minute.* "Now, are you coming here, or am I going there?"

"I'll come over to your place," I tell him, jumping up and dashing to my bedroom to pick out an outfit that's sexy and revealing, but won't make me look like I'm trying too hard. And maybe disguises the fact that I haven't gotten stuck in six months, twelve days, and fourteen hours and I'm ready to slut it up on him the second I set foot inside his apartment.

"Should I... stay naked...?" His tone is deep and dark, curious, questioning and a bit hesitant.

It's the hottest thing I've heard since I left.

"It doesn't make a difference," I tell him, shimmying out of my leggings. "You'll end up that way, regardless."

"That's what I like to hear," he chuckles. "See you soon, beautiful."

"Bye." I hang up fast, out of breath from the anticipation coursing through my body, quaking me from my chest into my panties.

I'm so motherfucking ready to see my man again, I can hardly contain myself.

Yes, I said my man. Just let me have this one, okay?

Approximately thirty-seven minutes later, I'm walking through Noah's hallway. My limbs feel like they're made of jelly, and I'm just trying to concentrate on not tumbling over.

I decided to wear my skin-tight faux-leather pants I know Noah loves, and a slinky backless top with no bra. The fewer items of clothing separating us the better, although I am wearing my leather jacket because it's a bit brisk out on this autumn evening.

Like clockwork, Noah's door opens before me, and he's standing there in his ripped jeans and a zip-up hoodie, which is hanging open, showing off the definition in his chest and abs.

I'm immediately drooling and panting like a dog in heat. *Has he been working out?? Sweet mother Mary, look at all those curvy muscles. Rawr.*

As I step up to his front, before I can throw my arms around him and attack him with hugs and kisses, I notice another difference in his torso.

"Oh my God, you got a new tattoo?!" I squeal, reaching out to graze his abs with my fingers.

Seek Me

He has some sexy-as-fuck new ink in the form of the word *Hellion* curved above his navel. The letters look woven together and almost decayed, like that of something decomposing into the ground with vines crawling over it. It's amazingly detailed. And I really want to kiss it.

But that'll come later.

"Yea! You like it?" He grins, but before I can answer he grabs me and lifts my body effortlessly against his. He hugs me as tight as humanly possible, sniffing my hair and kissing my jaw and neck repeatedly. "I fucking missed you so bad. Jesus…"

"I missed you too," I whimper, combing my fingers through his hair, which I can tell from the feel is shorter. "You got a haircut?"

"Yea, it got a little long over the summer," he carries me inside his apartment before setting me on my feet. Then he looks me up and down slowly, eyes significantly darkened. "You look fucking edible."

A tremor pulses below my waist. "So do you. You got bigger."

I chomp my lower lip as my eyes covet his broad shoulders and chest; those long arms that I just *know* have veins bulging out everywhere, despite them being covered by his sleeves.

Yum.

"Physically demanding job," he shrugs. "Gotta keep up. So, I want to hear everything about your trip."

"Well, first of all, I got a new tattoo myself! Wanna see?"

"Um, fuck yea!"

I remove my leather jacket and lift the left side of my shirt to reveal my new side-tat. It's an elaborate hand with all five fingers as paint brushes, leaving behind lines of paint, like it's brushing my ribs.

"I drew it myself," I tell him with pride as he gapes at my ink, trailing the fingers with his own.

"Wow, that's incredible, baby!" He gasps, laying a path of tingles on my flesh in their wake. "You really drew that?"

I nod, unable to stop my cheeks from flushing at his obvious appreciation for my work and from his gentle touch, which has somehow lit my whole body on fire. He's still examining the tattoo, while so close to me that all I can smell is him. *Everywhere.* My vagina is practically crying out for him already and I just freaking got here.

Slow your roll, little lady. Don't be a thirsty bitch.

Noah's hand runs down my hip, away from the tattoo. So now he's just touching me for fun, which has me giddy. I missed his touch so bad, having been starved for months. My stomach is ensconced with a kaleidoscope of butterflies, and there's a heat sinking deep below my waist that causes me to suck in a breath and hold it.

His index finger traces the top of my pants along my belly and then circles my navel.

"I missed this thing..." he whispers, so low I can barely hear him, but I think he's talking about my belly button ring.

He flicks it playfully, but then his fingers dance lower, slipping beneath the hem of my pants.

His eyes lift to mine and he blinks slowly. "Fuck..."

"Yea," I pant, because it's really all I can say. The heat surrounding us is stifling and I'm getting sweaty.

"Just... tell me you had fun," his deep voice commands. "Tell me it was worth it... You being away. Because if I'm being honest, I hated every second."

So did I.

No. Wait... No you didn't! You had a great time.

What the hell are you talking about, you loon??

"I... I did have... fun," I gulp the last word, because for some reason it feels like a lie, even though it's not.

I really *did* have fun. I enjoyed the entire six months with my friends, eating and laughing and painting. It was amazing.

So then why does it feel like I just got out of prison or something?

"Good," he nods, eyes wide and voice rough. "I'm glad you enjoyed yourself... But I'm also glad you're back."

"Me too."

He plays with my hair in that *Noah* way he always does, and once again it's like no time has passed at all. We're right back where we were, standing in his kitchen, touching and looking and preparing ourselves for a night of sex hotter than all the layers of hell.

"I'm sorry I never called you," his forehead creases in a look of guilt. "I always wanted to, but I was just afraid it would make me miss you so much more."

"It's okay," I reply in an equally remorseful tone. "I'm sorry I didn't reach out either... I should have, what with your premiere and all." I glance at the floor between us, feeling like such a crap friend.

"Hey, it's alright," he murmurs, lifting my chin with his fingers so he can capture me with those dark irises. "You were doing your thing. I get it."

I sigh. "I love seeing the world... Painting and learning and having experiences. But I do wish I could have been there for your premiere. I mean, three seasons already?" I huff a soft laugh and he smiles. "Where has the time gone?"

"I know, right?" He hesitantly nods, but then his smile slips slowly from his lips. "Well... The time didn't go as fast for me as it did for you, apparently."

I witness him swallow visibly and my brows push together.

"I mean... you were gone for a while," he adds, and if I didn't know any better, I'd say he's calling me out. "You could have made it back for my premiere if you really *wanted* to."

"What's that supposed to mean?" I ask, my pulse picking up the pace.

He remains quiet for a moment, then takes a deep breath. There's a noticeable tick in his jaw.

"It means six months, Alex," he grunts and runs a frustrated hand through his hair. "You didn't have to go for *six months*."

"But my friends -"

"Plenty of people travel," he interrupts, his tone shifting to one more accusing. "I travel myself all the time, but for like, a couple weeks. Shit, even two months. Or three. But no. You have to leave for these long, drawn-out amounts of time. It's almost like you're... running away."

I'm so shocked by his words, I can't speak. Or move. I'm frozen, staring up at him while he glares back, and now he looks *angry*. He's pissed, and I'm so confused, because if anyone should be pissed it's me.

He knows why I'm doing this... *Right?*

"Noah, I'm not running," I finally find my voice again, though it's small and unsure. "I'm -"

"I know, you're having life experiences," he digs his palms into his eyes. "I get that. But you're my best friend, Alex. Why does it feel like you can't get away from me fast enough?"

"Are you fucking serious?" I squeak, eyes bugging out at how insane he's being. "How could you even say that to me?! Noah, you know why I'm doing this. It's not to get away from you... It's not about you at all!"

"Oh trust me, I know you'd never think about me for a *second* when you make your escape plans," he mutters, aiming those dark orbs of vexation he calls eyes right at me. "God forbid you even *consider* it."

"Consider what?!" I bark and he looks taken aback, like he doesn't know how to answer the question himself, or what would have even made me ask it. "Noah, I'm sorry about leaving. And I'm sorry about missing your premieres... I know I should have been here."

He scoffs out loud, and it makes me shiver with regret and the frantic desire to somehow fix this.

"I'm not some kid whose mommy missed his little league games, Alex. It's not about the fucking premieres. I had my other friends there with me anyway, so don't sweat it."

"I know you have other friends. I have other friends, too. And they wanted me to travel with them, so I did. You said it was fine!"

"Well, I fucking lied, okay?!" Now his chest is heaving, and he appears more distraught than I even knew was possible.

I don't know what to do. I can't believe we're fighting right now. We never fight.

What the fuck is happening??

My whole body feels heavy, yet I'm singeing with fear. Fear at the idea that he's been truly hurt, and I might have actually ruined us when I left... Twice.

"Why would you tell me it was fine if it wasn't...?" I ask, afraid to death of the answer.

"Because, Alex. You mean more to me than any of my other friends! Don't you get that?" He starts pacing around in front of me. I'm so angry and sad and wrecked with guilt I don't know what to do with myself. "But obviously your *new* friends are more important than me."

"That's so not true!" I gasp, and my fingers are twitching. Tears try to force their way out from behind my eyes, but I refuse to let them. "Noah, I've been doing this for me. I told you, I need to live my life and experience everything I missed out on."

"I know. I know that," he nods over and over, though his tone is anything but pacified. "And I'm expected to just be here when you get back. Always waiting around for Alex. Well, guess what? That sucks! How would you feel if I kept disappearing on you? Every six months, just taking off for extended periods of time, never knowing if you'll see or hear from me again??"

My bottom lip quivers and I bite down on it hard. "Noah, I -"

"And yes, I know, I could have called you. But... Fuck, Alex. What about me? You couldn't send me *one* goddamned text? A fuckin DM on Instagram? Do I mean that little to you??"

I can't hold back anymore. My face is tight and hot, and I have to keep swallowing over and over to fend off tears. The dam is about to burst, and I won't give him the satisfaction of breaking down in front of him.

"Fuck this," I sniffle, then grab my coat and storm off, toward the door.

"Oh, perfect! There she goes again, folks!" He roars from behind me. "Couldn't even stay the night this time! No, you're not running *at all...*"

Whipping open the door, the tears are falling. I slam it behind me so hard it rattles the wall, and I scurry down the hallway as quickly as possible, puffing heavy breaths as my vision blurs from the sadness streaming out of my eyes.

I think I can still hear Noah shouting, and then there's a crash, like he may have thrown something. But I don't care. I need to get away from him right now. I need to leave...

And the frustrating, rage-inducing fact that I know he's right is tearing my heart to shreds inside my body.

"Fuck you..." I mutter at nothing as I leave his building, stomping down the stairs, onto the sidewalk.

How dare he say those things?? Like he has no idea what I've been through, or why I needed to get away.

And no, of course I'm not trying to get away from him. It's not always about him!

Okay, I guess it's never really been about him. He's sort of the most selfless person I've ever known in my whole life.

And how do I repay him for his endless support...? By taking off, every chance I get.

"Ugh!" I grunt and tug my hair at the roots.

I stammer up to the street, looking around for a cab. My stomach is rolling with guilt that feels like potential throw-up. I'm just so angry... With Noah, myself. Everyone.

These feelings are wretched and I want them gone. I can't unsee the look on his face in there. I've never seen him so upset... So hurt.

And it was all my fault.

I mean, *Jesus*. He started the night by telling me he'd literally drop anyone and anything to be with me the second I get home. Who knows if he had plans tonight? He very well could have, and tossed it all aside to be with me, just like last time.

I feel like scum. *The next car I see, I'm throwing myself in front of it.*

"Alex!" Noah shouts at me from his front door.

I refuse to turn around and look at him, but I can hear him storming closer. And some idiotic part of me wants to jog away and make him chase me. *What in the name of all that is holy is wrong with you??*

"Alex... wait. Please," he huffs as he inches over to me. "Don't go. I'm sorry... Can we please talk about this?"

The second I hear the apology, my head springs in his direction.

"Baby, I'm really sorry I got upset with you," he breathes, his broad chest lifting and falling with forceful breaths. He stops right in front of me, so I have to tilt my chin to look up at him. "I shouldn't have said those things... I was an asshole. Please don't leave again. I just got you back."

Tears are fully streaming down my cheeks and all I can do is blink at his gorgeous, worried face.

He apologized to me. He... the guy who didn't do anything other than stop his whole world for me and then speak his mind for a very brief moment when he was feeling hurt. Apologized to me... The girl who makes it her life's mission to put oceans between us and tell him we can only be friends. The liar girl.

I cry even harder.

"Fuck my life..." he mumbles and grabs me hard, pulling me into his solid chest. "I made you cry. I'm such a piece of shit. Oh Alex, please forgive me. I feel like such an asshole."

I'm crying so hard I'm practically convulsing. This is all *my* fault. And he's still apologizing. *And* he feels like an asshole.

"No... Noah, stop. I'm the... asshole," I hug him even tighter, squeezing until I hear him grunt. It makes me want to smile. *If I wasn't such a big, fat lying asshole.* "Everything you said is... right."

He rocks me gently, stroking my hair with his fingers. "Shh. No, it's not. I was just... I don't know, excited to see you or something and I got my wires crossed. This wasn't how tonight was supposed to go."

I shake my head a bunch of times. "No. It wasn't. We were supposed to be humping right now."

He laughs softly, and it's like music to my ears. It stops my crying instantly, and I tug my face back to look up at him.

"I miss humping you," he pouts, though it's laced with humor. It's the cutest damn thing in the world.

"Noah, I'm *so* sorry I made you feel that way," my words come out jumbled, because I want them out faster than I can speak them. "I know I'm a shitty friend. I guess I just assumed you were okay with me leaving because you knew why I needed to do it, but it's still not fair to just take off like that, especially when we're..."

My voice gives out quick, evaporating inside my throat. I'm not sure what I

Seek Me

was about to say, but I'm fairly certain no good can come of it.

Noah swallows visibly. "When we're... what?" His tone is quiet and curious, with a dash of fear.

I blink some tears off my lashes, my lips parted and shivering. His dark eyes drift to my mouth.

"I... I don't..." My head shakes back and forth.

"What are we, Alex...?" He's nudging me, emotionally and physically, our bodies practically melded together as we stare at one another.

We're more.

The look on Noah's face mirrors how I feel inside. He appears starved for whatever it is he wants me to say, but also so terrified of its potential he could pass out right here in my arms.

My mouth is bone-dry and my heart is leaping in my chest, as if it's trying to jump out of me and into him.

"Noah..." I whimper his name while the battle royale wages inside me.

My heart is screaming for me to tell him what I want... What I've always wanted. What I've been running from for three years while convincing myself I'm not.

But my mind has pulled the rip-cord. I'm too overflowing with doubt to utter the words out loud. I'm worried it could change everything... Especially if he doesn't feel the same.

Honestly, based on the way he's looking at me, it could go either way.

"You and me..." Sneaky words push their way out, but before I can say any more, his mouth comes crashing down on mine.

A startled gasp flies out of me, but quickly dissolves into a moan as he kisses me wild and hungry. My bottom lip is being sucked and nibbled so vigorously, and I'm fairly confident I'm not standing on my own anymore. He's holding me up, with one hand squeezing my ass and the other gripping my neck.

I find myself writhing against him, parting my legs to get his full, thick erection in between and rub my clit on it. I can feel the entire shape through his pants, and I'm coming undone. Every nerve in my body is sizzling like bacon in a skillet.

Noah growls into my mouth while he kisses me deep and hot, wrestling my tongue into submission with his. I use the opportunity to touch every inch of him I've missed so badly, combing my fingers through his hair, grazing his jaw, his throat, then down to his chest. *God*, I love his chest. It's so wide and defined and his nipples harden when we're kissing which makes me feel like the sexiest girl in all the land.

"Baby," he hums, but doesn't stop licking and sucking, not even for one second. "I... mmmm... fuck, *Alex*..."

Jesus, he sounds so hot. He doesn't even need to say anything relevant, and it scorches my panties to ash.

We're kissing so hard and aggressive, the inside of my pants feel like a rainforest and my lips are tingling, about to melt right off my face. Noah's hands roam up my back, then around to my front, over my silky top to cup my breasts. He groans into my mouth when he realizes that I'm braless underneath it and his cock swells up to an almost unhealthy thickness. I can feel it throbbing through our clothes and it makes me want to rip them off and ride him in the street.

Oh fuck, the street. We're outside... In public right now. And we're basically fornicating.

"No... no no no..." Noah shakes his head steadily, forcing his lips from mine while he holds me by my ribcage. "We need to go inside. I refuse to come in my pants again. Seriously Alex, how do you do this to me?"

I giggle out a breathless laugh, unable to stop my hand from sliding down to his generous package.

"Mmm... no. Please..." he whines, dropping his head onto my shoulder. "Don't touch it. I have no control over it where you're concerned."

I'm not sure in what world a guy blowing a load in his pants over you is a good thing, but for some reason to me, it's the ultimate compliment from Noah. He's had more sexual partners than most people probably have in a lifetime, and we've had a *lot* of sex, so I know exactly how long he can last. On Valentine's Day he screwed seven orgasms out of me before he broke once.

But when we're all hopped up on each other, teasing and touching and kissing like fiends - especially after we've been apart for a while - I have the uncanny ability to make him nut himself without much more than a few subtle grazes in the right spots. And I fucking *love* it.

I hum out a needy breath, not ready to stop just yet, using the motivation of how much I get to him to fuel my actions. Then I glide my fingers along his shape, down between his thighs and back up, making his whole body shudder. He kisses my neck slowly, moaning as he licks the hallow and caresses it so softly, my insides squeeze and pulse.

"I'm sorry..." I whisper, glacially moving my hand up and down. "I don't want you to lose control..."

"Mhmm... that's why you're still doing it," he calls me out, his voice gruff

Seek Me

and stuffed to the brim with arousal.

"No, you're right," I slink my hand to the waist of his jeans and shove it inside. "Let's go in."

"Uh-huh," he nods, kissing my neck and shoulder, then biting me until I gasp. "But you have to let go of my dick so we can walk."

I giggle deviously right by his ear, then suck the lobe between my lips. "Not necessarily true."

He finally pulls his face back to look at me and his eyes are blazing with raw, carnal need. His cheeks are flushed, lips moist and puffier than normal. I think I could come just from looking at him.

He arches his brow and I'm pretty sure I have a mini orgasm.

"You're so done for, Mackenzie," he growls with the most wickedly salacious look on his face.

Then he abruptly hoists me up by my ass, forcing my legs around his waist so he can carry me inside. Which he does, all the while with me stroking his cock from within his pants.

"I've been waiting six months for this," he says as he walks through his hallway. I can't see his face, but I can tell he looks determined. "If you knew how pent-up I am right now, you'd understand why I'm two seconds away from coating your hand."

I waver for a moment at his words.

What does he mean by that? Is he saying... he didn't hook up with anyone while I was away?

I'm too afraid to ask, so I bury my face in his neck and sniff him, allowing his mouthwatering scent to open me up as if I'm a lock and he's my key.

I'm desperate to know if it's true... If he really hasn't been with anyone else the whole six months. I know I wasn't... But I'm scared to know the answer. If I'm wrong, then I'll feel silly and stupid for assuming someone like him would ever not sleep around for any reason. But if I'm right...

Well, what in the world would that mean?

So I push away all the nagging thoughts and tell him something true.

"I love making you come," I say with a possessive suck of the sweet flesh on his throat.

This little hickey means you're mine...

He kicks his door shut with his foot then makes a beeline to the stairs.

"You... are... *destroying*... me..." His words are pained and elated; both amazed and troubled, one in the same.

When we're in his bedroom, I expect him to lie me down on his bed and impatiently climb on top of me. But instead he stands me up at the edge and takes a moment to compose himself. I'm hypnotized watching his chest rise and fall. I love his heavy breaths of excitement. I guess I love anything that lets me know how much he wants me.

Noah shrugs out of his sweatshirt, then steps out of his pants and boxer briefs, until he's fully naked and oh-so beautiful. I'm trying to play it cool, but I can't stop my eyes from falling below his waist to check out his length.

Every time we're apart and I see his dick again for the first time, it briefly startles me. It's just so impressive. And it still amazes me that all of it fits inside my body. You'd think after a certain point something would stop it...

"Strip please, Alexandra," his voice is as soft as cashmere, but the erotic gleam in his eyes gives him away. *He's thinking some very bad things right now...*

I gulp and lift my shirt over my head, tossing it away. I hear a sharp inhale of breath from him, and I realize he's gazing at my tits like he wants to eat them.

But he doesn't. He stays stock-still, burning in place as he watches me eagerly, hands clenching into fists by his sides.

I shimmy out of my leather pants, feeling like if it were colder in his room there'd be steam coming from my lady parts. The panties came down with them since they're soaked through, so I'm standing before him, just as naked as he is; ready and waiting for him to devour me.

But he doesn't do that either.

He stares at me for a beat, his Adam's apple bobbing in his throat, marked by my love bite, which turns me on more than it probably should.

Then he nods behind me and says, "Lie down at the edge of the bed and spread your legs. Please."

Mmm... so polite.

I do as he commands, because he said *please*, sitting down at the edge of the bed then plopping onto my back, spreading my legs as wide as they'll go. I'm trembling with excitement as I stare up at his ceiling, wondering what he's going to do next. My nipples are pebbled and pert in the air, just begging to be attended to. As is my throbbing clit.

I feel the warmth coming from Noah's body as he kneels on the floor between my parted legs. He lifts them and drapes them over his shoulders.

Good God...

"Do you know... How many times I've thought of this? Over the last six months..." His breath warms the apex of my thighs when he speaks and I gasp out loud. "How many nights I woke up in the dark... burning through my sheets... moaning your name like a fucking prayer?"

His voice is hoarse and dangerously seductive. And I'm panting so hard I'm practically seizing.

He grabs my hips hard in his hands and scoots my pussy closer to his mouth, causing me to squeak out of surprise.

"Alex, you do things to me that *no one* has ever done..." he whispers into me, his breath and the vibrations of his speaking sending a jolt through my loins. "That's not something you just forget."

"Noah..." I mewl his name, reaching for his face. But he takes my hands in his and laces our fingers, pushing them down on the bed.

"Shhhh..." He blows on my clit and I tremor. "Is this how you feel when you're away from me?"

I whine softly and nod, lifting my hips to his mouth, but I can't get him. He's purposely refraining from touching my pussy, and the teasing is like torture. But it feels divine.

He blows on my clit again and a soft, reluctant wave of pleasure brushes me, like a paintbrush on a canvas.

"Did you miss me, baby?" His lips hover over my trembling wet flesh. I bob my head repeatedly. "Mmmm... You missed this so bad, didn't you?"

I can feel them moving as he speaks and I just want him to talk forever. I want him to recite Shakespearean sonnets into my pussy right now. I'm already building and he hasn't even touched me yet.

"I can taste you from here, Alex," he growls and his tongue flicks my clit when he says my name. I cry out and squeeze his hands. "You taste like warm cherry pie and vanilla ice cream. So... sweet..."

He kisses me once. A very brief yet immensely soft peck. And I'm ready to fall.

"Noah... oh God, *please*..." I can barely process what I'm saying while seeing spots behind my eyes.

"Do you... *like* this?" On the word *like* his tongue brushes my clit, and I moan, loud. "Or do you... *love* it?" Another featherlike stroke on *love*.

Jesus Mary and Joseph... I'm so fucking close.

"*Like*... Or *love*..."

"Love..." I pant, grinding my hips into the air, chasing my orgasm. I'm right on the edge. I need more...

"You *love* it...?"

"Yes!" I squeal, rocking forward and back. "I love it. I love… it."

Whoa, that was close.

"It's okay, baby," he murmurs, and his voice becomes echoed. "I *love* it, too."

His tongue swirls in slow, punishing circles around my clit, over and over until my thighs tighten.

"My Alex… All mine…" He grunts, kissing and licking and nipping. "My… love…"

My body explodes. I'm crushed by the slowest, most intense orgasm I've ever felt. My thighs close on Noah's head, but he doesn't seem to care, because he's lost in his own little rhythm of lapping and lashing in between praising me with words spoken straight into my body. The climax completely shatters me, shooting through my loins like white-hot fire.

Noah hums and stops long enough for me to recover, only about thirty seconds, before he plants a series of delicate kisses on me until I come again.

And again. And again… And a-fucking-gain.

By the time he's done with me, I don't know who I am, where I am, or what time, day, year it is. All I know is that I'm a fucking slave to this man. He just claimed my body with barely any movement at all. And it rocked my goddamn world.

He subdued me like a lion-tamer, or a dog-trainer, or fucking Paul Abdul on American Idol.

I have no fucking idea about anything other than Noah fucking Richards being a fucking *god*.

When I get sensation back in my extremities, I feel Noah's warm body of rippled muscles sliding up me, kissing my stomach then my tits. He nuzzles the piercings in my nipples, humming as he goes. It sounds almost like he's humming a song, but I'd have no clue what it is. All I know is that it sounds sexy, especially when he's dropping slow, wet kisses all around my neck.

He rocks his hips into me a few times, stroking his solid cock in the wetness that has gushed out of me all over the place. He still has my hands in his, and he lifts them over my head, fingers still laced together, pinning them into the comforter.

He stares into my eyes, so close the ends of our noses are touching, then cocks his head to the side, regarding me with a faithful and mischievous yearning. It's the kind of covetous look you would give a particularly alluring article of clothing. Wondering how good it might look on you, and how good you would look in it.

Seek Me

"Baby..." he whispers, slowly pressing his hips into mine, shooting little lightning rods of pleasure through me every time that smooth, fat head brushes my sensitive clit. "I was wondering... And feel free to say no..."

"Noah, I don't think I could say no to anything right now," I rasp and he chuckles, the sweetest and sexiest little noise ever given.

"You know how, *occasionally*, I've found my way inside you... bare?" His voice is hesitant though he's still unable to lose the small grin on his full lips.

I nod slowly, gazing up at him. "Uh-huh."

"Well, I know it's not exactly *responsible*... But I really want to feel you on me like that. Right now..." He tugs his lip between his teeth.

"I want that too..." I lift my hips and he gasps.

"Really?"

"Yea..."

"Can I...? If I pull out..." He's practically begging. "I won't make it a habit, I promise."

I can't help but grin at how adorable he is, while also being the hottest human being ever made.

I've been on birth control since I was sixteen, and I've never missed a month, even when I was asking Roger about babies all those years ago. Still, I know it's not responsible to go bareback, so we rarely do it. It's only ever happened a handful of times, with no one other than Noah and my ex, who I'm not trying to think about right now.

But Noah asking me like a kid asking to go to the ice cream parlor after dinner has to be the most charming and mystifying thing I've ever experienced. After all, Noah doesn't do bare sex... with anyone but me.

And it makes me feel like the most special girl in the entire damn world.

"Baby, I'm good on all fronts," I say, needing to touch him, though he's still holding my hands. So I lift my foot and run it up and down his calf. "You don't have to pull out..."

He bites his lip again and his eyes sparkle.

"Or... do you *want* to pull out?" I lift my brow. He nods, somehow appearing shy and ravenous at the same time. My lips quirk. "Where do you want to come, baby?" He lets out a breath and slow-blinks. "On my stomach... Or my tits..." He groans, smashing his erection into me. "Or in my mouth...?"

"Fuck me..." he shivers. "Alex..."

"Where?" I whisper, rubbing my nipples on him.

"That's for me to know..." he kisses me softly. "And you to find out."

351

He bites my bottom lip and yanks it until I moan.

"Noah... I need you inside me," I plead and he kisses me once more, before rearing his hips back.

"I need to watch me pushing inside," he looks between our heated bodies as he guides his head into my entrance, no hands. *That's skill, right there.*

It's so round and smooth, and engorged, it's an instant pleasure shot, which causes me to groan out his name. He slides in further, sinking into me, slow; so slow I'm able to fully cherish every curve and ridge of his solid, warm skin owning me.

"God, *yes...*" his voice cracks as he pulls back then thrusts in again, holding himself at arm's length above me so he can watch. "You're fucking *perfect,* Alexandra."

"Mmmm... baby, so are you," I tell him, moving my hips with his methodical strokes. "Your dick was made to be inside me."

"It so was..." he drawls, pumping in deeper, stretching me around him. "Look how well we fit together."

"A perfect fit," I gasp and he leans in to kiss me, doing so while he flicks his hips over and over, feeding me every inch.

I wrap my legs around his waist, locking my ankles atop his delicious ass, which I really wish I could see right now, because I'm sure it looks wholly fantastic when he's thrusting. Breaths escape him with every movement as he goes harder, loving my body into a puddle on the bed.

I can feel my whole world winding up again while Noah squeezes my hands, groaning into my mouth while he sucks my lips and it all starts to fade again.

"I'm... almost... gonna... fuck, *Alex...*" he whimpers and I give into him once more.

I whisper to him that I'm coming again, my walls holding his cock with all their might. My body is buzzing as I spiral through outer space.

Nothing has *ever* felt this good.

"Baby, I'm going to..." he stops to moan. "Come..."

And when he's sure I'm sufficiently done with my masterpiece of an orgasm, he pulls himself out of me and releases one of my hands to keep up the strokes.

It probably seems insanely slutty, but I really can't wait to find out where he wants to come. Seriously, I'm so enamored with this man, I'll let him do it wherever at this point.

He drags the head of his cock between my breasts while he jerks hard, but

Seek Me

slow. He bites his lip and our eyes meet and he looks positively devious. *God, he's such a freak, I can't get enough.*

I part my lips and touch my tongue to my teeth, catching his attention. He lets out a soft, growly noise of approval and his eyes flutter shut, in that way that lets me know he's about to blow.

So I lean in, fully ready to let him mark me his way. And he meets me in the middle, kneeling over my chest as I wrap my lips around the head of his dick, sucking nice and hard. I can taste me on his skin, and it serves as more naughty motivation.

"Fuck, Alex," his voice shakes as his hand milks up to where my lips are and he pulses into my mouth. "Alex... *Alex*... Baby... fucking swallow me..."

I do, but he takes it away before he's done, shooting the rest on my chest and all over my tits.

"Jesus, you fucking *own* me, Alexandra," he croaks as his hand finally comes to a gradual halt. "You own every *single* part of me."

He collapses on top of me and holds me tight, not even caring that we're both sweaty and covered in slick. He kisses my face while we both pant in the dark, walking on rainbows and sunshine.

His words replay over and over in my brain, like my favorite song on repeat. *You own me.*

I've never wanted something to be true so bad in my life.

Chapter Twenty Five
Noah

I wipe the sweat from my forehead with the back of my hand and finish off the water in my bottle. Getting up slowly, I feel the burn in all my muscles as I make my way out of my home gym, done for the day.

I've been working out a bit more lately. Not because I feel the need to bulk up or anything. I think leaner muscles look better on me, and my body's always been built good like that. I'm no Johnny.

Dude's a beast. I honestly don't even think he notices that he lifts people up when he hugs them.

Andrew and I are the more toned and cut ones. But I've been taking to my home gym on the regs lately so I'm not huffing and puffing when we have to run around or lift things on set. I never would have known how theoretically out of shape I was if I hadn't almost died filming season one. To others that would seem like an overreaction, but it sure as fuck felt like a form of death to me, when I was keeled over, wheezing after seven takes of Andrew and I *fighting*.

The stunt doubles did most of the work. But I was sweating just *watching* them.

So I started strength training more on hiatus, doing some cardio here and there. I feel better, and I'd be lying if I said I don't enjoy the lingering looks I've been getting from the ladies. I mean, I always get looks. But now they appear downright *hungry*. And Alex has a fondness for touching my chest and licking my abs when we're fooling around. So that on its own is worth the extra time spent straining and sweating. *Much like we do in the bedroom.*

Speaking of Alex, I need to call her and see when she's coming over. Tomorrow's Thanksgiving and we have plans to eat here at my place, just the two of us. I could've gone home to Long Island, but I wanted to spend the day with Alex since she doesn't have family to gather with. And no, I'm not bringing her home to meet my parents for Thanksgiving. That's a suicide mission I'm in no place to attempt at the present moment.

I stumble through my apartment, heading for the kitchen so I can inhale

Seek Me

some protein and muscle recovery yadda yadda. I don't do the whole *clean eating* thing, so Eloise made me some prepared meals and post-workout snacks, shakes and all that crap, to make sure I'm on the right track. When I get to the kitchen, I'm reminded that it's time to feed Boots.

He's been on a new diet himself. After the vet did some blood work on him a few months back, we found out he's at high-risk for kidney issues, so he advised we start giving him more fresh salmon and avocado. Stuff that I guess is good for his kidneys, which Eloise also prepared. *She's a damn saint, that one.*

I'll admit, I was worried about my baby boy for a bit there. When I got home from Georgia, he was very mopey, and I hated seeing him like that. He's always been a chill little dude, but there was something... off. He didn't want to play, or even really get up at all. He'd just sort of lie there.

But I've been spending more time with him, and that, with the new diet, has noticeably improved his mood over the last few weeks. He seems to be in better spirits and though I don't say it out loud, or show it to anyone, I'm beyond relieved. I know it's a little silly for a grown man to be so attached to a cat, but he's my buddy. Boots has been the only constant in my life for a solid decade. In a weird way, he's like my kid. Only way easier to look after.

I scarf down one of the bars Eloise made, then scoop Boots's dinner into his little green dish with the fishies on it. He likes that one. *I know, I know. My inner mom is showing. Lay off.*

"Bootsey boy!" I call out to him, even though he's probably upstairs snoozing on my bed. "Dinner time, you handsome devil."

I take his dish and meander around the first floor, calling him over and over. Phoebe stammers inside from the terrace as I'm heading to the stairs.

"I was just taking off for the weekend," she huffs, wiping her dirty hands on her overalls. I assume she was tending to the plants.

"Alright, cool," I nod. "Have you seen Boots?"

"Umm no. Actually, I haven't seen him all day," her brow furrows, but I ignore it.

"It's cool, I'll find him," I shoot her a quick smile over my shoulder. "Happy Thanksgiving!"

"Same to you!" She shouts at me, but I'm already climbing the stairs, making an effort not to spill the pungent salmon-avocado mixture all over myself.

"Boots?" I call out again, glancing around the hallway. "Come on, homie. Time to eat."

I step inside my bedroom and I'm surprised to see he's not on my bed.

That's his go-to cuddle spot. *Hmm... Weird.*

I try not to let myself panic as I search for my cat, checking the bathroom, then the office and the open closets. I go back downstairs and check the library, the guest room, the laundry room, where his litter box is kept. I can't seem to locate him anywhere, and now my heart is sneaking into my throat.

"Boots?" I continue wandering around, now much faster, checking under the couch, the chairs, under the guest bed. I call him over and over with no sign of his furry little ass anywhere until I'm practically running with my heart thumping in my chest.

I go back upstairs, dropping to my knees quick to look under my bed. I almost have a fucking heart attack when I see him lying under there.

And for a brief moment of sheer devastation, I think he's dead.

I hesitantly reach out to touch him, and release the hardest sigh ever when I feel that he's still warm, and very much breathing. He lifts his head slowly, his eyes a bit glazed, and gives me a quiet *meow*.

I squeeze my eyes shut for a second and regulate my own breathing. "Boots... What the heck are you doing under here, man? You scared the shit out of me."

I grab his dish I'd left on the floor and place it in front of him.

"You want some dinner, buddy?" He sniffs it a few times, but is slow to react. I push it closer to his face. "You want to eat under the bed...?"

He finally lifts his head and gets up a bit, though he doesn't seem very excited. I can't say that I blame him. I wouldn't really want to eat that either. But he goes to it, casually lapping at some fish. I tug the bowl a little at a time, luring him out from under the bed. He follows the food, eating one small nibble at a time.

"Okay, I guess we'll leave your dish here then," I hum and pet his head a few times. "You're a good boy, Bootsey. I just want you to feel better, man. You're my special little guy. I know you don't want to eat healthy and exercise. Trust me, I don't either. But we have to take care of our bodies so we can last longer. You feel me?"

He doesn't respond, as usual, but I hope he knows I love him. I sit next to him until he's eaten his fill, then I grab him before he can try to slink back under the bed. I kiss his soft head a bunch of times, and he purrs while I lay him down on my bed in his usual spot.

"There we go, pal," I scratch under his chin and he looks happy, so I'm pacified. "You rest up. Maybe later we can play with that catnip mouse guy you love so much."

I get up and release a long breath I wasn't aware I was holding, then head to the bathroom to shower. But I call Alex first.

"Hey, killa," she answers right away, her soft, raspy voice creeping into my chest to fill me with much-needed tranquility. "What are you up to?"

"Just about to shower," I say as I step out of my sweats. "You wanna come join me?"

"Mmm... I'd love to," she sounds wicked, and I can't ignore the swelling that's happening below my waist. "But I'm just putting the finishing touches on that piece for Dan's show. Can we meet up when I'm done?"

"But of course, my dear," I turn on the shower. "I was thinking maybe we could hit Sensay tonight. Some friends invited me."

She's quiet for a moment. "Are you sure you want me tagging along?"

She always does that.

"I wouldn't have asked you if I didn't want you there," I tell her honestly.

"Okay, cool," she chirps and I can hear the smile in her voice. I can picture it, too. It's hardening my dick even more. "Meet at your place?"

"Yes, please."

"Alright then. It's a date." She sounds so sexy it has me itching to see her and touch her. I just want to grab a handful of her ass and pull her as close to me as humanly possible.

"You're so lame," I tease, though my tone is doing a terrible job of remaining aloof.

She giggles and I know she wants to punch me. "See you soon."

"Can't wait."

We hang up and I take a second to lean up against my bathroom counter and soak in the bliss that comes from talking to her. It's so bizarre that even after all this time, I still feel this way. A two-minute conversation gives me butterflies and aligns the pulse in my erection to the steady beat of house music.

Truth be told, Alex and I are in an odd place. We spend a ton of time together, as usual, and when we're not together, we call and text each other like a codependent high school couple. And yet, we're not *any* kind of couple, and we both know that. So in between all the cuddling and laughing, date nights that aren't really *date nights* and more sex than our bodies know how to handle, we have these weird moments when we both freeze up and feel the need to pull away.

It's confusing as hell, and probably the furthest thing from healthy. I can tell Alex likes me... maybe more than she's liked anyone in a long time. I would know, because I feel the same way about her. But it's been so long... We've been doing this *casual best friends who fuck* thing for so damn long I'm beginning to think we're stuck like this.

I won't claim that I haven't thought about Alex and me being exclusive again. It slips into my head often, usually after we both come and I'm holding her in my arms, her heart beating steadily into my chest, fingers trailing along my bare skin as if all she wants in the whole world is to touch me. I allow my mind to wade back into dangerous waters, and consider telling her that what we're doing is stupid, and immature, and we should just be together because *we* make more sense than anything else ever has.

But then I remember all the times she's told me we need to remain casual. How she needs to be out living her life and learning how to be on her own again. *Really* on her own, not just lonely and tied to a crazy, abusive asshole. How she finally feels like the real Alex again, and it makes her so happy and scared she wants to burst into tears and jump for joy at the same time.

I won't be the guy who pushes her. I can't, even if I know we could have the real thing, and I'm fairly confident we could make each other happy for a long time.

But that's rain on the Macy's parade, right there... That there's no guarantee if we entered a real relationship it would even last. I think of my friends and all their failed marriages; all the fighting, the depression, the insecurity, the divorces and custody battles, lawyers and alimony. I've seen it all. It's happened to damn-near every one of my friends.

Shit, poor Andrew is getting the brunt of it right now. He's fucking miserable in his marriage. I talk to him almost every day, either on the phone or via text. He says he and his wife are like strangers. He sleeps in his study most nights, and when they do talk to one another, it always results in screaming matches. He said they barely even have sex anymore, which according to him was the one thing he was holding onto; the one last shred of hope for the flame of their marriage that's all but fizzled out.

I couldn't live with myself if that happened to Alex and me. Not that I think we would ever get married, but even if we started dating officially... I can't turn us into her second failed relationship. I won't be another man who lets her down.

Our friendship means the world to me. I can't risk it for a bunch of *what-ifs*.

I force all these annoying thoughts out of my head and get into the shower, washing away the sweat from my workout, and the stress of not knowing what the fuck I'm doing with my love life.

Alex and I are better off as friends. That's how it has to be. And I can live with that.

I just pray that in our struggles to keep from ruining us, we don't ruin us.

The club is packed. It makes sense, because it's the night before Thanksgiving, which is a huge party night. Everyone's home for the holiday, looking to get drunk and hook up, as if a booze and sex hangover somehow makes the food taste better.

Alex and I are in a booth in the back with some of my friends. Brant is here with his cousin and a couple girls they're talking to, along with a few other random people I've known in the city for years. I would barely classify them as *friends*, but they love inviting me out, so every now and then I throw them a bone.

Plus, I don't really care who else is around at the moment, because I'm sitting next to a tipsy Alex, who's been playing footsie with me under the table for the last twenty minutes. She thought it would be fun to do tequila shots, and with each round she's gotten friskier. I can't stop laughing because her face is so damn cute when she's drunk. She gets all flushed, really showing off her complexion and those light, scattered freckles on her cheeks I just want to kiss.

The girls Brant and his cousin brought are yammering on about something no one who's not trying to bang them cares about, and every few minutes words will come up so exciting to them they apparently warrant a loud *wooo!* Which in turn makes the rest of us cringe. I keep checking my watch because as soon as the clock strikes two, me and Alex are fuckin outta here.

"Hey..." Alex distracts me from my countdown with her hand, trailing up and down my thigh. "The night we met... You dry-humped me right over... there." She points across the dance floor to the spot where we danced our first dance as best friends-turned fuck buddies.

"Um, pretty sure you were the one humping me," I lean in closer to her, locking us in a staring contest that blesses me with a front-row seat to the most glimmering green ever housed by two eyeballs.

"False. You were all over me," she slurs a bit, slinking her hand between my thighs.

"Oh please," I growl. "You wanted it so bad you were ready to strip down right there on the dance floor."

She laughs softly then tugs her lower lip with her teeth. It causes a significant stir in my jeans, which she obviously feels, and her face lights up. *Dammit. My dick is always salting my game with Alex. He's too hopelessly obsessed with her to play it cool.*

"Maybe we should go dance. Recreate the moment you turned into the Alex-crazed stalker you so clearly are." With a slow display of licking her lips, she has me on the ropes. She knows full-well I can't resist that perfect mouth of hers.

Every time she bites or licks her lips - shit, sometimes even when I watch them moving while she speaks - I can't help but picture all the things that mouth has done to me over the years. It's done *a lot* of very sexy, very filthy stuff. I won't bore you with the details now, but let's just say I have my own personal porn folder in my mind dedicated to Alex's mouth; each and every memory serving as eternal jerk-off material.

"I would love to dance with you right now, beautiful," I hum, taking her small hand in mine to stop her from rubbing my rapidly hardening erection before I'm unable to leave the table for a while. "Recreate the moment when you were introduced to the dick that would live inside you for the next couple years."

"I want you to live inside me right now…" she breathes as she moves in even closer until she's practically sitting on my lap.

"You think anyone would notice if I sat you on my cock right here at the table?" I whisper by her ear. She moans quietly, music for only my ears to hear, and it sends a chill across my body. "If I slid inside you, filling you all the way up until you're stuffed to the brim with my swollen cock…"

"Fuck, Noah…" she gasps, grabbing at my face. "My panties are drenched. You always do this to me." She whines, her tone a mixture of innocent irritation and pent-up lust. I can't help but laugh.

"I'm sorry I make you so wet, baby," I faux-pout at her. "Should I try to be less irresistible?"

"Not possible," she smirks, then presses a quick kiss on my lips. "Come on, let's go dance. I'll have to take my panties off soon, anyway."

I chuckle and oblige, scooting out of the booth and taking her with me. We don't bother saying anything to our friends, because we didn't really care what they were doing in the first place. I drag Alex over to our spot, in the far corner

Seek Me

of the dance floor, where it's slightly less packed, and dark enough for some secret humping.

I'm not sure exactly what song is playing, but it's a good beat and I tug her close to me as she sways on her feet, steadying herself with palms on my chest.

"This is *so* your move," she grins as my hands slide to the top of her plump ass and I move my hips gradually with hers. "You lure unsuspecting women here, feed them a bunch of booze and then grind with them until they're powerless to resist."

"You sound like you're speaking from experience there, Cuervo," I grumble and she giggles. "And yea, you're right. It's totally my move. I grind with every girl I meet in the club before they storm off then I chase them and we eat waffles in a diner then spend weeks forming a lifelong friendship followed by years of fun, adventures, fantastic sex and cuddling. It's standard behavior at this point." I roll my eyes and she laughs out loud, her fingers toying with my hair at the back of my neck.

"Mmm… you're right about the fun. And the adventures. And the fantastic sex," she purrs with those brilliant irises set on mine.

"Fucking mind-blowing, right?"

She nods emphatically. And we continue to dance, holding each other close, our bodies becoming one as we move to the music together, like the easy waves of a calm ocean.

"I'm so glad I stopped at Maxwell's that day," she whispers. "When I think back to it… I can't even imagine where I'd be right now if I hadn't gone in there for a drink to celebrate booking my first gallery show."

I swallow hard as I watch her face, the dim light illuminating her in shadows and deep colors. She looks fascinated; thoughtful, mesmerized. And grateful.

I've always known that Alex sees me as someone who saved her, in a sense. She sees that night as one which monumentally changed her life for the better, because apparently meeting me, and us becoming friends, gave her the courage to take her life back.

But me? I see that night as one when I was fortunate enough to meet a girl who changed *me*. I found something that day I hadn't even been looking for. Something my heart was seeking, without me even knowing it. And on a deeper level, I think maybe it was meant to happen like that. It wasn't just dumb-luck; two people meeting in a bar, hoping to get laid. It was all part of a bigger plan.

Seek and ye shall find.

Staggering need suddenly overcomes me. I'm not even sure what I need exactly, but I'm restless and buzzing with intense longing. I press myself into Alex, firm and possessive, holding her hips on mine to move deeper, as if we really are fucking through our clothes. But it's that slow, desperate kind of fucking, when you want so much more than your body can take, and you drive at it, chasing the high with every covetous stroke.

Alex grips me in return, her fingers greedily exploring my neck, jaw and throat while she breathes harsh gasps on my clavicle. I bury my nose and mouth in her hair, and her neck, inhaling her scent that drives me absolutely fucking wild. My lips press featherlike kisses on her warmed flesh, concentrating on the spot where her pulse taps. I love licking that spot. I can taste her need for me in her heart's gentle cadence.

"I've never been more grateful for anything in my life," I speak so softly that I'm unsure of whether she even heard me.

I know we're getting swept up in the memories, and drifting further from our *casual fuck-buddy* label with every second we spend dancing like this; holding each other and reminiscing about a night that changed both of our lives forever. But the truth is that it's been three years since that night, and every single day after it has built us to where we are now. Like bricks stacking up, one by one, to create something strong and sturdy. Cementing us in this relationship that's not quite love, but far from *just friends*.

Who knows what the future holds… What each new brick will raise us toward.

The idea scares me. It frightens me to my core, and I know it's because my heart craves the one thing it's been seeking, behind my back, for the past three years.

More.

"We should leave," Alex mewls while grinding herself into me with fervor.

"The panties have to go, huh?" I ask in a devious chuckle. She nods vehemently, which makes me laugh again. "Alright, let's leave." I pull back enough to gaze down at her beautifully blushed face. "So I can get you out of your panties."

She bites her lip as she stares up at me with a look that is so far from casual, it's not even on the map anymore. My heart races at the thoughts bounding through my brain; so many things I've tried so hard to keep at bay. It's a constant struggle to stop my mind from going where it is right now, and it feels like a rubber band that's being pulled and stretched so far, eventually it has no choice but to snap.

Emotions rush inside me, coursing through my veins, and my body aches to catch them and turn them into words. Words that could destroy us if spoken out loud.

So I force myself to stop and shove them all back where they came from. Instead, I focus on bringing my best friend home and sliding my dick into her admittedly wet pussy.

Because that's what we do, after all. We ignore the feelings bottled up inside us, and we fuck each other as if our friendship depends on it.

And I think in many ways it does.

"Happy Thanksgiving!" Alex's cheery voice rings into my ears that haven't fully awakened enough yet to accept such sounds.

I grunt at her, because I'm a bit hungover and won't be thoroughly alive until I inject some caffeine directly into my bloodstream.

"Ooh, someone's grumpy this morning," she sings, fluttering around my kitchen like a dark-haired, tattooed fairy. "How can you be Oscar the Grouch after the night we had? I found it to be quite refreshing."

She looks up at me as I amble over to the counter and pour the world's largest cup of coffee.

"Oh trust me, I'm very refreshed," I mumble. "I just went against my better judgements last night and mixed tequila and scotch, which has to be the worst combination of all time. Worse than that place that puts Nutella on a cheeseburger. I mean, I'm all for experimentation, but that's just yucky."

She giggles then slides a bottle of Excedrin and a Gatorade over to me. I smile graciously, popping two pills in an attempt to combat this dehydration headache attacking my brain like a crazed group of bargain shoppers at Walmart on Black Friday.

"I'm sorry... I know the shots were my idea," she pouts.

"Well, considering how hungry you were for my cock last night, I'd say it was worth it," I wink at her and she laughs.

"Yea, it was. I have hickeys on my inner thighs, by the way," her darkened eyes glide to me and she raises a brow. "And my tits."

"I guess you weren't the only one who was hungry," I growl and grab her by the waist. She's wearing my cock apron. Something doesn't add up here...

"Mmm... Well, I hope you're still hungry," she squeals, yanking away from me and going back to her task.

It takes my sleep-deprived and groggy mind a moment to piece together what I'm seeing. Alex is mixing something in a bowl. And my kitchen looks like it's been run through by a tornado.

"Where's Eloise?" I mutter, looking around with my forehead lined in concern.

Alex's face is beaming unbridled excitement. It causes me to gulp down the unease filling my throat.

"I gave her the day off!" She squeaks and does a little hop. It's adorable, but now I'm terrified. "Surprise! I'm cooking Thanksgiving dinner for you!"

My eyes widen as distressed realization floods me. "Um... Really?"

"Yea!" She gasps, obviously not picking up on how potentially disastrous this could be. "I think it'll be fun. I've never done it before."

"Baby..." I murmur, using my supportive and loving tone reserved for calling her out. "That's because you can't cook."

"Noah, don't be such a butthead," she grumbles, which makes me laugh. "I know, I'm not a *chef* or anything, like you. But I can do this! I wanted to... cook you a special dinner."

My heart melts inside me and I can't fight the beholden smile. "Aww... babe. That's so sweet. Okay, sure. Whatever makes you happy."

She lets out another elated noise and kisses me quick. "Yay! This is going to be so great. Thank you, baby."

She returns to her mixing, but I wrap my arms around her waist from behind and press myself into her while she does whatever the hell she's doing. I'm not sure what she's mixing, but it doesn't look like any Thanksgiving food I've ever eaten.

But that doesn't matter, because she wants to cook for me. And Alex gets what Alex wants.

I kiss her neck slowly, nuzzling my nose in her hair that smells like strawberry shortcake, which is making me hard for some reason. She wiggles in my arms.

"Noah, you have to stop distracting me. I need to make sure this comes out right," she admonishes, though her breathiness alludes to a desire for me to bend her over. "Go sit down and watch football or something."

"I want to help you," I rumble, and it's clear that I'm referring to helping her out of her clothes, not helping her cook the meal. She pushes me away and I sigh. "Fine. Are you sure you don't need me for anything, though? Thanksgiving dinner is a big meal."

"I know it's a big deal, but are you saying you don't think I can do it?" She narrows her gaze at me.

"No, I said it's a big *meal*. As in lots of food."

"Oh. Right." She blows a strand of hair out of her face. "Well, I think I can handle it. I mean, how hard can it be?"

She's not instilling a lot of confidence right now.

I must be giving her a worrisome look because she turns away fast. "Noah, get out of the kitchen and let me work. I've got this under control."

"Okay, baby..." I murmur, stepping back slowly. "If you say so."

"And if you call Eloise, I swear to God -"

"I won't call Eloise! I have faith in you, beautiful. You can do this." I show her a sweet smile which she returns, before sauntering out of the kitchen with my coffee.

I release a swift breath as I wander through the apartment trying to think of ways to occupy my time while Alex cooks. I decide to call my parents, which I naturally end up regretting five minutes into the conversation.

"So Alex is cooking you Thanksgiving dinner?" My mom asks, sounding as surprised as I was, only for a different reason. "Things are getting serious with you two then, hm?"

"No, nothing is serious," I grumble, sitting on the floor of my walk-in closet next to Boots. He keeps getting in here to hide under my stuff, and it's unnerving me more than I want to think about. "We're just friends."

"Oh my God, you've been saying that for years, Noah!" Haley shrieks over the line. They have me on speaker so I can talk to all three of them at once. "You guys are obviously meant to be together, so man up!"

"Hale, let your brother work out his weird relationship on his own terms," my dad sticks up for me, though now I'm frowning at my phone.

"It's not weird," I mutter defensively. "We're perfectly normal."

"Sure you are, sweetie," Mom patronizes, and believe it or not, it doesn't make me feel better.

"It's not normal to be friends with benefits for three years, dumbass," Haley interjects.

"Language!" Mom and Dad scold her in unison, which makes me laugh.

"Noah, I think what your sister is saying in a less than supportive way, is that you and Alex should be clear about what you mean to each other," my mother croons, and my chest is growing increasingly tight from the direction of this convo. "Do you really see the both of you just being friends forever? Because if so, you should let her move on to pursue a real relationship."

Ouch. Jeez, Mom.

I run a hand down my face. "Our relationship *is* real. Alex was married for a while, you guys. She doesn't want to jump back into anything after the divorce and all the crap her ex put her through."

"So you're saying if she *did*, you would want to be with her?" Haley prods, making me want to reach through the phone and noogie her to death.

"I'm not saying anything," I dismiss them. "In fact, I'm done talking about this. Let's talk about you, Hale. How's that guy with the eyebrow piercing you've been seeing?"

I grin with wicked pride after that bomb explodes all over my meddling little sister.

"Haley Lynn! What is he talking about?" My mom shrieks and I can practically see the evil glare my sister would give me in my mind, which is very satisfying.

"Noah!" She whines and I laugh out loud. It's only minutely maniacal.

Suddenly there's an alarm going off downstairs.

"Oh boy. I've gotta go. Love you guys! Miss you!" I shout at my family then hang up fast, thankful for the escape from all their prying questions about my confusing-ass love life, even though my apartment could very well be on fire.

I dash downstairs fast, swinging into the kitchen. There's smoke billowing from the stove, but Alex doesn't look as flustered as you would think.

"Oh, hey. How do you shut this thing off?" She asks, waving a towel toward the smoke detector.

"By not starting fires," I reply like the wise-ass I am. "What is that smell?" I cough. *It smells like burnt ass in here.*

"I spilled something," Alex mutters nonchalantly. "It's no big deal. Can you just shut this stupid thing up please?"

I leave the kitchen and open the door to the terrace, hoping to get some smoke, and God willing, the smell out of my place. It's going to need a deep conditioning after today. Especially the kitchen.

Then I make my way back to Alex, taking over the towel waving for a bit while she rectifies the situation with the stovetop. The alarm finally stops, though the burners have seen better days. I don't even know what she spilled, but whatever it was, it's still bubbling inside a pan, looking equally inedible.

My face is giving away my worry, not about the kitchen, since I pay people to clean here and they'll certainly have their work cut out for them tomorrow. But because Alex will expect me to eat that stuff, and I really didn't plan on vomiting today.

As soon as she glances at me, I plaster an eager and encouraging fake smile on my face, purely for her benefit. I don't want her to feel bad. This is important to her, so if I have to ingest whatever she's burning right now to make her happy, then I'll do just that.

I'm an actor, so I'm sure I can swing some yummy noises and stomach rubs, regardless of how gross it tastes.

"You sure you don't need any help?" I ask flippantly, so as not to offend her.

"Um... no," she bites her lip while scouring the pages of a cookbook.

Jesus, this is going to be brutal.

Yet despite knowing I'll be forcing down her nasty version of a turkey and trimmings in a bit, I can't help but smile. She's just so cute and she's trying so hard. For me. What did I do to deserve this kind of devotion?

I'm sure I'll be asking myself that same question when I'm bent over a toilet later...

I chuckle and bite my lip to smother my delirious smile. This girl is really something else.

"What's so funny?" Her brows knit together. "Are you laughing at me?"

"No, baby," I murmur, stepping over to hug her because I just *need* to. It's like an impossible itch that must be satisfied immediately. "You're so fucking adorable and sweet. I can't believe you're cooking me dinner."

"I'm trying to..." she pouts, and it's clear she's doubting herself.

Let's give her some reassurance.

"You are. You're doing a great job. Everything smells delicious," I kiss the words across her jaw and behind her ear.

It's not even a lie. *She smells fucking scrumptious. I can just eat her tonight and be fully satisfied.*

"You're distracting me again," she purrs as her fingers slink underneath my shirt.

"Mmm... but I'm hungry now," my voice is hoarse as I go for her lips.

And then something starts sizzling on the stove and Alex jumps.

"Oh shit! It's overflowing again," she darts away from me and lifts the lid of a pot that has white stuff bubbling out of it.

Dear Lord...

"I'm just gonna get out of your hair, baby," I tell her as I back away and she waves a distracted hand in my direction.

I laugh to myself and watch her for a minute, stirring things and adding spices to stuff, undoubtedly with no clue what she's doing at all. But it's so enchanting to witness that I'm melting inside, more than the plastic handle to the mixing spoon she just left too close to the burner.

I'm in awe of this girl. She has not the slightest idea how to cook a bag of popcorn, let alone an entire Thanksgiving dinner. But she's doing it for *me*. She's trying something wholly out of her element because she wants to make me happy.

Like people do when they're in a relationship...

I'm guessing. I mean, I've never really been in one, so I'm just going on things I've heard.

And then I remember a conversation we had when we first become friends... From the first time she told me about the abuse.

Alex said that when you're in love, you barely recognize yourself. You act differently, and do different things, because the other person makes you crazy.

My eyes are glued on Alex's back as she scurries to and fro, dumping things here and chopping stuff there. She looks like a nut. She looks *crazy*.

For me. *She's crazy... for me?*

I blink a few times as an odd sensation floods me, starting in the pit of my stomach and rising all the way up to my throat. It's an unnerving and morbid exhilaration, thrilling and uncomfortable, overtaking my body. Saliva fills my mouth and I swallow over and over, squeezing my sweaty hands into fists.

I need to move. In an instant, I'm so jittery I can't be in one place.

I turn away and stalk out of the room, heading for the terrace. Maybe I just need some fresh air. It's too hot in here. I'm suffocating.

I go outside and sit down on the chaise, sucking in a deep breath and holding onto it. Against my will, my mind is flashing over all the crazy things I've done for Alex...

Buying thousands of dollars worth of art because she made it.

Driving up and down her block all night when she lived with her ex because I feared for her safety.

Renting a damn G6 so she could get to Georgia easily and comfortably.

Jesus, I fucking did *exactly* what she's doing right now when I cooked her dinner for the first time. Sure, mine definitely came out better than hers is, but I had very little experience in preparing a gourmet meal, and yet I read up on it and spent an entire day in the kitchen.

I must have thrown away six or seven pieces of chicken that didn't come out right until I finally got the hang of it. I folded napkins and bought candles and a twenty-dollar piece of cheese just on the off-chance that it would make her smile for even one fucking second.

And all of this combined makes me crazier than any one single thing I did. I completely changed who I am... For Alex.

I started calling and texting her like an obsessive teenager. I dropped everything and everyone just to be with her when she needed a friend. I let her sleep in my bed, *and* cuddled with her, no sex involved. And I fucking *loved* it.

I've been blocking the girls who text me for booty calls, and at this point, I haven't had sex with anyone who isn't her in longer than I can even remember.

I'm an entirely different person now. And I'm not even mad about it. I actually like this version of me *better* than the old me.

I think I know what all of this means...

In the blink of an eye, my breathing is so aggressive it's hurting my lungs. I'm convinced I'm having a heart attack. I flop onto my back and cover my eyes with my hand.

I knew this would happen. It was inevitable.

It's been brewing since the first time I saw Alex; since our first conversation. We talked for hours at Maxwell's, and then we danced, sensually, and I sniffed her hair and kissed her neck. That was the first night we met, for fuck's sake. And after that, I began craving her smell and her touch, the sound of her laugh and the way it feels to stare into her evergreen eyes.

I was a goner. I never stood a chance.

Reaching underneath the chaise lounge, I pull out the cigar tin I have stashed under there for emergencies. Then I remove a joint and light it fast, taking a long drag, letting the drugs settle inside me, and calm me a bit.

The truth is, even though after the first time Alex left me without knowing how I really felt I told myself I would shelve my feelings for her and let her do her own thing, it hasn't stopped them from growing inside me. Like a sapling that spent the last couple years being cared for under the sun and the rain, sprouting and budding into a tall tree filled with life.

Alex took up roots in my heart, and now I'm surrounded by an overgrown forest of her.

I smoke my joint in silence until I'm relaxed and docile. And when I'm sure more than an hour has passed, and I'm getting a little cold, I know it's time to go back inside and face the music.

But before I can, Alex walks outside. She looks uneasy as she joins me on the chaise, sitting down by my feet. She lets out a long sigh, and I sit up.

"Okay. I'm admitting defeat," her shoulders slump. "I can't do it."

I clear my throat. "No, don't say that. I'm sure we can -"

"Noah... I messed up," her eyes meet mine and they're wide, shining with guilt. "I messed up bad."

I can do nothing more than blink at her a few times. "What happened?"

She doesn't respond. She simply stands up and walks toward the door, so I get up and follow her back inside. She leads me to the kitchen, which smells like a myriad of burnt things.

We both stop in front of the stove and Alex crosses her arms over her chest.

There's a turkey... Or what I'm guessing *was* a turkey at one time, though it now resembles a large, eighteen-pound lump of coal. It appears to have burned itself into the pan, the two of them melding together in a hardened black mass of pure nastiness.

I peek at Alex, and she's just staring at the destroyed bird, sitting amongst a whole slew of mess. She appears defeated, and kind of sad; like she wants to recite a eulogy to the poor thing she slaughtered in vain.

I press my lips together. I really don't want to laugh, with her feeling insecure, but this entire scene is one of the most endearing and heart-warming things I've ever witnessed.

I can't help it. I let a small giggle slip.

"Noah," she whines, her lower lip jutting in the cutest little pout that's fully destroying me. "It's not funny."

I laugh harder and wrap my arms around her waist. And now she's chuckling too, reluctantly, because she's still downhearted from being unable to make it work. But I can't stop myself from chortling into her neck and it's causing her to giggle in return.

She gives up the fight and hugs me back, burrowing her face in my shoulder while we both crack the hell up, laughing harder and deeper until we're breathlessly dying over how damn hilarious this situation is.

Minutes later, we finally sigh and wipe our eyes as I inch away so I can look at her beautiful face. She appears a bit crushed, but she's an optimistic girl, and she's confident enough in herself now that she wouldn't let one small failure get her down.

Just one of the many things I...

I swallow hard, not ready to say the word in my mind yet. It's still too fresh.

Seek Me

"What do you think, beautiful?" I ask softly, combing my fingers through her hair. "Indian, Mexican... Thai? Or maybe burgers?"

Her lips sweep into an appeased smile before she bites her lip. "I love the Tom Yum soup from that place on 79th."

"Mmm me too," I nod with enthusiasm. "You go turn on the fireplace and pick a movie. I'll Grubhub it."

"Noah, I..." her voice trails off as she gazes up at me, something so severely appreciative in her eyes that my stomach bottoms out and I'm free falling into what I now know with absolute certainty is what I feel for her. "Just... Thank you."

I take her face in my hands and lean in, watching her eyes until the last second when I kiss her, tender and slow, as my brain releases every endorphin it has to offer. I can't help the involuntary groan that passes through my lips into hers, professing things I never knew a sound could.

Alex kisses me back, harder and hungrier, swallowing up my confessing moans and returning them with her own. She slides her hands up my chest and neck, into my hair, fisting them and pulling me as close as possible, sucking my lips and seeking my tongue.

I'm in agony, dragging her to me as I tremble with all the nerves and lust and confused emotions. I'm feeling so much and I know Alex is feeling it too. Her desperation mirrors mine.

I force myself to stop, breaking our intense kiss and hauling air into my lungs fast. I'm afraid my filter has dissipated and I'm one more kiss away from declaring things to her that I'm still way too unsure to let out.

"Um..." I croak, shaking my head a bit to remind myself to hold it together. "I should uh... order the food."

"Right," she breathes and nods, stepping back, but not without first swiping her thumb over my lips. Even that has me coming undone. "I'm gonna go change real quick."

My head bobs in return. "Okay."

And before I know it, she's scurrying away from me and going upstairs, likely to commandeer some of my sweatpants and a hoodie. I'm obsessed with Alex in my clothes. It makes her look like mine.

It seems like it should be the easiest thing in the world for us to be together... But then why does it feel so impossible to grasp?

I rake my hands through my hair and ignore these thoughts for now, ordering our Thanksgiving dinner of takeout Thai food.

We end up sitting on my living room floor, eating and laughing, watching movies and just being us. I couldn't have asked for a better holiday with my best friend…

Who I am hopelessly, desperately, painfully in love with.

I stomp inside my apartment and shake the snow from my boots in the foyer.

I didn't exactly want to go out today. It's really coming down out there, and staying in front of the fireplace all day watching TV was part of the original plan. I don't get much time for rest and relaxation now, since the show has taken off the way it has. Our schedules are always jam-packed these days, many events, appearances and photoshoots often eating into hiatus.

But Christmas is in two weeks, and we all agreed not to partake in any work stuff until after New Year's. So I have some free time right now, and there's something I've been obsessing over, which drove me out into the winter wonderland today.

I need to buy Alex a Christmas present.

I know, I know. I'm probably doomed. I mean, what the hell do you get for the girl you're secretly in love with?

Many ridiculous things come to mind, and they all get shoved right back out faster than they can plead their case.

Jewelry? No. That's too cliché.

Clothes? Pass. Alex can pick her own clothes, and she does a damn good job of it, if we're tossing out opinions.

A puppy? Absolutely not. Alex hates dogs.

I need to find something unique and special. Something that will allude to the fact that I'm infatuated with her, without actually having to say the words out loud.

So far, I'm coming up blank.

I shrug out of my coat, then remove my boots, leaving everything wet by the door before making my way into the apartment. I move straight to the fireplace and warm my frigid hands over it, smoothing fingers through the snowflakes in my hair.

I hear sudden footsteps clunking down the stairs and I already know it's

Seek Me

Phoebe. She's been here all day cleaning and looking after Boots. Which reminds me that my trip wasn't a total loss. I got him a cool little string toy with a feathery guy on the end.

Hopefully, it'll cheer him up. My boy's been a bit sullen lately, though I still can't determine why.

"Hey," I say to Phoebe while rubbing my hands together. "How's it going?"

She remains silent, which I think nothing of, until I realize she's walking straight toward me. So I look up.

Her eyes are red-rimmed and puffy, with mascara smudged underneath.

The dizziness that fills me is instant and so overwhelming I'm caught off guard.

"Noah, um..." her voice gives out as she stares up at me with wide eyes. I can practically feel her shaking from where I'm standing. "I... I don't know..."

She fumbles, sniffling over and over. My body goes rigid and I swallow thickly as terror chills rush across my body.

"What is it...?" The words scrape from inside my throat. "What... happened...?"

Her bottom lip quivers visibly and she shakes her head. Then she turns without further explanation and walks toward the stairs, so I follow her mindlessly, blood rushing in my ears as I prepare myself for devastation.

My mind is a jumbled blur as we ascend the stairs and make our way into my bedroom. I'm trying so hard not to freak out, but I don't know if I can handle this... Whatever is about to happen when I set foot in my room.

I'm not ready.

My body quakes in fear and potential anguish, limbs stiff and heavy as I follow Phoebe to my bed. She stands before it, and I can't help but almost collapse from the stress of not seeing Boots in his spot. Something in my gut feels so wrong I could heave.

Phoebe looks up at me again and her eyes convey many things, not even one of them good. Her lips part, but nothing comes out. And I can't say anything either. I just stare at her because I'm afraid.

I'm fucking scared shitless right now.

Eventually she whimpers and looks down at the floor. So I drop to my knees and peer under my bed. And realization crashes, weighted like the entire world, down on top of me, damn near smothering me to death.

I see Boots, lying under my bed, which he's taken to doing the last couple days. He's been crawling under there almost every chance he gets lately. And now I know why…

I don't need to touch him to know he's stiff. But I do… Just to make sure.

And when I feel his normally soft, warm body, now cold and unmoving, I think I black out.

For a moment, I can't breathe. Everything around me goes dark and I'm spiraling and retching in pain, though I haven't moved at all.

I'm still just staring at my boy… My pal… *My Boots.*

Dead under my bed.

He's gone, and I'm fucking hollow.

I run my hand over him once more and press my forehead onto the floor.

Fuck… No. No no no… Why??

I struggle to take deep breaths and compose myself, but it's not working. I'm sputtering for air as my heart snaps, crumbling to jagged bits inside me.

I reopen my eyes and peek at him again. His eyes are open.

Jesus fucking Christ.

The sight scares me. Startles me enough to jolt me backward and I crawl away quick, horrified at having to see him like that. It's wrenching my gut and now I can't get the image out of my brain. I stand slowly beneath the crushing turmoil on my shoulders, rubbing my eyes hard with my hands as I let out a ragged breath that's completely unsatisfying.

Nothing feels right. Everything feels so fucking *wrong.*

He's dead. He's gone.

Dead. Gone.

Dead and gone.

And I wasn't even fucking here.

"Noah, I'm so… *so* sorry," Phoebe whimpers with tears streaming down her face.

"It's -" I croak and then clear my throat, grasping at every bit of strength I have not to break down. "It's okay. It was…" I hum out a pathetic noise because I can't fucking help it.

I'm being torn limb from limb.

Phoebe reaches up and hugs onto my shoulders, pulling me into her. I gradually, lifelessly, wrap my arms around her small body and hold her close. She shakes against my chest, sobbing into my shirt while I rock her gently, resting my cheek on her head.

"I'm sure he's in… a better place…" I expel the words as some bullshit consolation and squeeze my eyes shut, willing myself not to cry.

Seek Me

"Noah..." she squeaks, shuddering as I tighten my grip. I physically need this contact right now. My heart has been chopped into severed chunks. "He's at peace now. He was such a good boy..."

I wasn't fucking here.
I should've been here.
I let him die... alone.

I gasp out loud and chomp on my lip so hard I taste blood. I'm going to burst and I can't have her seeing me like this. I need to be alone. Alone with my guilt and grief, mixed together and stinging my stomach like acid.

I release Phoebe quick and step away.

"I just... need a minute," I grunt through a cracking voice and stumble into my bathroom, closing the door fast and locking it behind me.

My breathing has become erratic as I fall backward against the door and slide down it until I'm crouched on the floor.

"Fuck..." I huff, tears welling in my eyes. I don't want them to... I don't want to let them.

But I don't really have a choice. They're coming, whether or not I want them to.

I press my forehead onto my knees and cover my head with my arms as the dam bursts and I break the fuck down. My tears fall and I struggle to breathe through the pain lancing in my chest. Maybe it's immature or foolish to be so torn apart over the death of a pet, but anyone who says so clearly hasn't experienced it.

I just lost my goddamn *son*. I loved that animal like I'd love my own kid.

And now he's gone. He's fucking *gone* and I have nothing left.

So I cry, on my bathroom floor, like I'm nine-years-old again. That was the last time I lost a pet... My rabbit, Mitsy. And coincidentally, that was also the last time I cried.

I'm not sure I've hurt this bad since then, and it feels exactly the same.

Like I'm spinning out of control. Like I'm fucking *lost*.

Boots is dead.

And I'm fucking broken.

CHAPTER TWENTY SIX
Alex

I BREAK OFF A SMALL CHUNK OF MY CANDY CANE, sucking the minty sweet flavor, swirling it with my tongue as I surf the internet.

My eyes are glued to my laptop screen while I scroll through hundreds of items on Amazon. I've been searching for over an hour with no avail. It's frustrating, as is the notion that I'm still no closer to finding what I'm looking for.

I'm Christmas gift shopping for Noah. And it's fucking impossible.

I have not the slightest clue what to get him, and it's making me angry. He's my best friend in the whole world. And my casual fuck-friend who I secretly wish was my boyfriend. But we're obviously keeping that part quiet, hence the whole *secretly* bit.

I know everything there is to know about him, and yet I can't for the life of me figure out what to get him for Christmas. It needs to be something cool and special, something different, because that's what Noah is. He's a snowflake; unique and rare and elaborate.

Whatever gift I choose for him should be indicative of that. I suppose I'm putting a wee bit too much pressure on myself, though. I should probably think simple, being that even though he's my sexy snowflake man, he's still a guy. And guys value simplicity over the complexities often conjured up by the female mind.

Noah and I have never spent a Christmas together, so we haven't ever exchanged gifts before. The first year, I was still with Roger, so we didn't see each other. And last year I was in Hungary for the holidays.

But this year I'll be very much around, and even if we don't see one another on the day - I assume he'll want to spend it with his family in Long Island - we'll definitely cross paths at some point before or after, and I want to give him something. Even though I'm not sure what it is yet, I still know exactly how I'd like his face to light up when I give him whatever I end up choosing.

I briefly thought about giving him sex, because that always makes him light right up, in many delicious ways. But we've already done so many dirty things together that I think giving him sex as a gift is a cop-out. I will drop my panties for him regardless of what day it is, so that idea doesn't allow for much surprise.

I frown and shake my head. Christmas is in two weeks, and I'm still drawing a blank. What do you get for a rich and famous celebrity, anyway? Surely just picking something expensive is banal. He can afford to buy himself houses and boats and cars, so spending money on him doesn't mean *special* in the slightest.

Plus, Noah deserves better than that. He deserves something straight from the heart, because that's where he lives. Right inside mine.

Ever since Thanksgiving, my feelings for Noah have been magnified. I've known for quite some time that I have feelings for him, stronger than those you should have for your *casual* best friend with benefits. But after that night, after how purely, irrevocably selfless he was to me, I just couldn't stop thinking about how perfect we'd be together.

The main reason I've been stopping myself from actively trying to pursue something more with Noah has always been fear. Fear of my past tainting my present and future. But on Thanksgiving, when I fucked up his kitchen and ruined our dinner and Noah barely batted an eye, I realized once more just how truly different he is than my ex-husband.

Noah is wholly the sweetest, kindest, most caring person I've ever met. And I can't even pretend he's not the best sex I've had in fucking *ever*. He's gorgeous and strong, talented and charming, and the funniest damn tattooed hottie a girl could dream up.

But most importantly, he's *good*.

He's so mother-loving good, and not damaged or psychotic, and that alone is worth grabbing ahold of and cherishing for as long as humanly possible.

Does it sound like we'd be perfect together? *Of course.*

Does that mean I'm going to run over to his place right now and declare my love to him? *Are you fucking high?*

I'm terrified of my feelings for Noah, still, even after all this time. Because while I haven't physically witnessed him dating other girls in years, or even showing interest in them, I can't help but worry that he's incapable of committing to anything more than fuck-buddies. And as per usual, our friendship takes precedent over everything else going on in my overstimulated heart.

If I were to tell Noah how I feel, I'd need to be one-hundred-million percent sure that he feels the same, and that he would be in it as much as me. I can't get my heart ripped out by another man, and I really can't lose my best friend.

And unfortunately Noah rejecting me would make both those things happen.

Ugh! Why does this have to be so hard?!

I sullenly crunch the small sliver of candy cane in my mouth and go for another bite when my phone rings.

I pick it up and see *Phoebe*, Noah's cleaning lady, come up on the screen. I squint at it in confusion, but answer quick, despite being puzzled as to why she'd be calling me. Phoebe's a sweet woman and I adore her, but she's only ever called me once, and that was to ask if I wanted her to dry-clean my dress I left at Noah's.

"Hello?" I rasp with curiosity in my tone.

"Alex? Hi. It's Phoebe..." She sounds strained in duress, and I'm immediately standing up.

"Hi, Phoebe. Nice to hear from you," I gulp politely. "Is everything okay?"

She takes a long breath, and before I even know what's happening, I'm pulling on my shoes.

"No... Everything is really *not* okay."

I get to Noah's apartment in record time and use my key and knowledge of his security code to let myself inside. I dash through the hallway faster than my legs want to carry me, almost slipping on the snow caked to my Uggs twice on my way in.

I shed my coat and everything else in the foyer, head darting around frantically. I hear a noise and follow it to the kitchen where I find Phoebe stirring something in a mug. I stomp over to her and before she can react, I throw my arms around her in a massive hug that's more for me than it is for her.

She seems startled for only a moment and then we're gripping each other tight and crying softly into one another's hair.

This totally fucking sucks.

I still can't believe it.

Boots is dead.

My tears fall on Phoebe's neck, but I force myself to get it together. I can't do this right now. I need to stay strong.

"Where is he?" I ask, pulling out of our embrace and wiping my eyes as she

Seek Me

does the same.

"He locked himself in his bathroom," she sniffles, her brows laced together in so much worry it hurts my heart even more than it's already ripped up. "That was almost two hours ago. I've tried knocking a few times, but he won't even answer me. I'm worried, Alex. I know he won't be upset that I called you. He probably really needs you right now and -"

I shush her gently to interrupt her rambling. She takes a breath.

"And... Boots?" I can't help the whimper that comes out when I say his name. I'm a fucking wreck right now. I can only imagine what Noah must be feeling...

Oh, God... my poor, beautiful, strong man is breaking apart upstairs. How am I going to help him?? I'm the least emotionally capable person to deal with death.

"He's still under the bed," Phoebe whisper-cries and I pout, patting her hair. "I didn't want to move him without Noah..."

I nod in agreement with what she's saying and then I turn away, because I need to get to Noah right now. I need to be with him; to comfort him in his time of need, like he's done for me countless times since the moment we met.

I practically run to the stairs, climbing them fast. But when I get to the doorway of Noah's bedroom, I come to a screeching halt. A chill washes over me and I'm rooted to the ground.

I can't believe Boots, my sweet, soft little orange baby, is actually dead... Under Noah's bed right now. It makes my knees want to give out.

I swipe at more tears falling down my cheeks and straighten my shoulders. Summoning all my inner strength, I move my feet, slowly stepping into Noah's bedroom. My eyes creep to the floor by his bed, but I can't see anything. It's a minute relief. I can't see Boots like that, not right now. Not yet.

I need to get Noah first. I need to make sure he's alright. He locked himself inside the bathroom for hours, which leads me to believe he's very much *not* alright, and it pains me inside. He's always so strong; sturdy and secure, like a rock. Nothing breaks him.

But this is another story. This is his baby boy...

Fuck... I can't even...

I shake my head. No time for that. Time to focus.

I suck in a long stream of oxygen and knock gently on the bathroom door. Of course there's no answer.

So I knock again and lean in, "Noah? Baby... It's me. I'm here."

I hold my breath and wait for him to acknowledge my presence and hopefully let me know he's okay. I want him to let me in so I can cuddle him and hold him and try with all my might to take away his pain. I need to do that for him... God knows he's done it for me.

I hear something rustle behind the door, but still no words.

"Phoebe called me..." I say, keeping my tone steady. "Take as much time as you need, baby. I just wanted to let you know... that I'm here."

I stand there fidgeting in place, praying for any response. Even just one word to let me know he's not completely lost in there.

Noah does me one better. I hear the lock click and the door creeps open.

The first things I see are deep, dark eyes, peering through the crack in the door at me. They're red and glassy and it tears my heart wide open. The poor thing looks exhausted.

"Alex..." Noah breathes and then before I know what's happening, he's lunged at me, and is hugging me so hard to his chest I'm being crushed.

But I welcome it, because I'm here to comfort him, in any way he needs me.

His face burrows in my neck and I can feel him trembling as my arms circle his waist, my fingers running up and down his back. Tears spring from my eyes again and I can't help it. I cry softly and quietly, not wanting to upset him anymore, but also not really being able to stop myself. Noah's whole body shivers and I think he's crying too, which is to be expected.

This loss is a big one. My man is feeling it, in every crevice of his broken heart.

He sniffs before pulling back, taking both my hands in his. His eyes are wide, his forehead lined in such agony I want to do anything in my power to make him feel better. I would slice my wrists open and bleed for him if it would take away this pain he's feeling.

We stare at each other for a moment, speaking an abundance without having to utter one word. Then Noah's eyes dart over my head, into his room, and I see his Adam's apple bob in his throat. He abruptly yanks me into the bathroom fast and shuts the door behind me, breathing so hard it's as if he's run a marathon inside.

"I'm sorry..." his deep, raspy voice sputters. "I can't..." He shakes his head over and over and I grab him again.

"Shh... I know. It's okay, baby. We can stay in here as long as you need."

His eyes slam shut, lips twisted into an unintentional pout that it kills me to see.

"Alex, I wasn't here," he hums, shoving his hand into his hair and tugging it hard at the roots. "I wasn't even *fucking* here."

"Noah, you cannot blame yourself for this," I tell him with surety. "It was just his time."

"I could've done something," he whimpers, stumbling backward until he's sitting on the edge of his tub, then drops his head into his hands. "I *should* have done something."

"Baby, there's nothing more you could have done," I hum and crouch down in front of him.

I take his hands and move them away from his face, forcing him to look at me. His coal eyes cut me deep, and my mind races through anything and everything I might say to pacify him. I'm coming up blank. So instead I stroke his face softly, pushing his hair away from where it wants to flop over his forehead. I don't know how, but he's even more gorgeous when he's in despair.

"He was… my friend," he mumbles, his eyes darting to the floor between us. "I know it sounds stupid… But I've had him for a decade. He's been with me through *everything*…"

"It's *not* stupid, baby," I whisper, tracing the line of his jaw with my fingers. "He was the fucking best. And trust me, he knew just how much you loved him."

He chews on his lip for a moment, as if considering my words. But then he scoffs and shakes his head.

"I wasn't here. I left him alone for so long…"

"Noah, you can't beat yourself up over this," I remain firm, yet caring still. "You gave him a wonderful life. I've only known you for three years, and I have tons of memories of him, playing and cuddling with us. Running around like a damn knucklehead at three in the morning and scratching the side of the bed while we were having sex."

That earns me a little chuckle, and I'm over the moon at being able to make him laugh and crack a smile right now.

Noah's eyes slide back up to mine and he watches me closely, emotions shining in his inky irises. I can't help but notice how soft his lips look, curved in a slight frown which has wiped away the hesitant grin from a second ago. Maybe his lips get softer when he's upset… Maybe they taste like his tears.

I need to know, and I lean forward, pressing mine up to them, which prompts a strangled sigh from deep in his throat.

They are soft… And sweet, and sad. My Noah… Let me kiss your pain away, baby.

Our lips part just a bit, and I suck ever-so-slightly on his bottom while he does the same to my top. But I stop it and pull back, so as not to get carried away. I just want to make him feel better, but kissing those perfect lips for even a second gets me muggy, and I need to focus.

I swallow hard and breathe out slowly while Noah clears his throat, our eyes melding together, green meeting brown so swarthy it's basically black. He's looking at me like he's immensely grateful I'm here, and yet he's tortured in this moment, twisted up and needing someone to guide him.

And it reminds me of the exact thing to say, to give him just that.

I take a seat next to him on the tub and turn so I'm fully facing him. He does the same.

"Did you know I had a cat when I was younger?" I speak, a rhetorical question of course, but I still pause to admire the symmetrical lines of his face, chiseled and contoured in all the right places, like a work of art.

Noah shakes his head slowly.

"When I was about ten, my parents finally gave into my incessant begging and got me a kitten," I go on, unable to help the small smile that shows up from the memory. "He was the sweetest, softest little calico in the world. I named him Barnaby."

Noah's lips twist into a hesitant smile, as if he likes what he's hearing, so I go on, needing to see more of that look.

"He was my best friend in the whole world," I sigh, remembering. "I wasn't the most confident kid at school. I was shy and artsy, so I didn't have that many friends. But I had Barnaby. I would come home from school every day and tell him all about what happened; what I'd painted in art class, or drew in math when I was supposed to be learning."

I chuckle and Noah's smile grows. But then mine quickly slips away.

"My parents didn't really give a fuck. They were always tired from work, constantly fighting. If I tried to show them one of my drawings, they'd just mutter *that's great, sweetie, but focus on your homework, please*. So I'd lock myself away in my room and talk to Barnaby. For hours, I'd tell him about my dreams of becoming a famous painter. Of traveling the world and seeing as many things as possible. And Barnaby always listened. I mean, maybe he didn't respond…" I grin at Noah and he huffs a small laugh.

"But he truly was my best friend. He was so special to me, it didn't matter if he was *just a pet*. Because he wasn't *just* that. He was a part of my life, and he was there for me when no one else was."

I stop and swallow hard. "But then a few years later, he got hit by a car. And

Seek Me

I was crushed."

My forehead lines and I bite my lip. Noah reaches over and takes my small hand in his big one. He squeezes it, giving me a look of empathy. He knows that pain, maybe not even just from today. And he's here for me, just like I'm here for him.

We can share each other's pain.

"After Barnaby died, I felt alone for a while. I had no one to talk to. My confidante was gone. Until one day my teacher gave me a journal. She told me that writing down what's going on in my mind could help me feel better. So I did it… But I didn't just write my thoughts. I wrote *to* Barnaby. I began writing in my journal any time I needed to tell him something. And it felt like he was still there with me. In fact, it still does… Because I still do it."

I give him a sheepish look and his eyes widen.

"Really?" He asks, looking and sounding a bit fascinated. I nod slowly. "You still do it now?"

"Yea," I sigh, my thumb grazing over his. "It's sort of an old habit at this point. But any time I've felt sad or alone over the years, I could always count on writing to Barnaby to make me feel better. The point is that a friend is a friend. It doesn't matter if they're a pet, or a real person. Sometimes we just need someone to listen. Whether they're here… or gone away."

Noah swallows visibly, giving me a wide-eyed look of determination and understanding, which seems to have overcome a bit of his sadness. Just a bit.

"You'll never be alone again, Alexandra Mackenzie," he whispers, slinking his free arm around my waist and pulling me into him. "Because you have me. And I'm not going anywhere, I can promise you that. Even when we're apart, I'll always be with you."

My heart leaps in my chest as the pressure builds behind my eyes once more. This man is just so compassionate. I don't understand how in the world I found him, but I know I'd be a complete fool to ever let him go.

"I know," my head rests on his shoulder. "And I'll be with you. Always."

Noah kisses my hair then leans his cheek on it. And we sit in silence for a while, just listening to one another breathe, comforting each other with presence. Sometimes that's all it takes.

I'm not even sure how much time has passed, but eventually we're both stiff from sitting still for so long. I stand up first and stretch my arms before holding my hand out for Noah. He takes it and rises slowly, like the weight of it all is burdening his broad shoulders.

"How am I supposed to say goodbye to him?" He asks quietly, looking down at me for answers I don't know how to give. "What do I even -"

"I'm here, baby," I grip his hand. "Whatever you need. I'm right here."

He lets out a long breath and tugs me with him over to the door. He stops in front of it for a moment, as if he's still afraid to go back out there and face reality. I reach up to rub his shoulder with my free hand, and I feel them relax a bit.

He finally opens the door slowly and we walk into his bedroom. We stand before the bed, frozen in time, both of us wishing so hard it didn't have to be like this.

"Hold on," I murmur and he glances at me. "I have an idea."

I leave him and go down the hall to his office where I know he keeps most of Boots's stuff. I find his favorite fuzzy blue blanket and a small chest with a latch. I dump its contents on the floor and bring the items back to Noah's room.

When I return, I think he realizes what I'm getting at and he squeezes the back of his neck, forehead lined in grief. I place the chest on the floor by the bed then take a deep breath and drop to my knees. I didn't even notice my eyes were closed until I know I need to open them, though my body struggles to do it.

I feel Noah kneel next to me, and I can hear him breathing heavy. He takes the blanket from me and my eyes peel open as I watch him wrap Boots's lifeless body in his blanket and place him carefully into the chest.

Tears are streaming uncontrollably down my face and Noah's practically whimpering out loud, which makes it all the more devastating. He shuts the chest fast and I hug onto his waist. He pulls me closer, holding my head over his heart while we both break down.

It's wholly one of the saddest, most awful moments, almost more than I can stomach. It feels exactly like when Barnaby died, and I'm heavy with sorrow.

We eventually bring Boots downstairs in his makeshift casket. We agree that he needs to be cremated, since we don't have anywhere to bury him, and Phoebe calls in a favor to her friend the vet, who has someone who will come to pick him up tonight.

In the middle of a snowstorm. As far as I'm concerned, Phoebe is a saint, as is her friend.

We decide to bring the casket outside to say a few words. When we're out on the terrace, Noah disappears for a moment, only to return with a bottle of scotch and a toy that he apparently bought today for Boots as a Christmas present.

Seek Me

I'm a fucking blubbering mess and I can't even help it. I know I need to stay strong for Noah, but this is so heartbreaking.

He places the toy inside the chest with his baby boy then closes it again, immediately opening the bottle of liquor. He's quiet for a while, and I just stand beside him in silence, feeling the pain ripple off him like vibrations.

"Boots... I can't say I'm happy to lose you, buddy..." Noah starts, clearing his throat more than normal in his attempts to keep from crumbling. "Actually, I'm pretty fucking miserable. But I know you lived a long, comfortable life. You were such a cool dude... My fuzzy little guy. I still remember the day I found you... All battered and scared. You looked at me like I was crazy for even getting near you."

Noah pauses and lets out a strained chuckle. "I've always been a little crazy, I guess. But seeing you alone, I knew all you needed was a friend. I was determined to be that for you. And then it turned out that you were my friend right back. You were always there for me, pal. You were such a good friend... The best. And I just hope you know..." More throat clearing. "How much I love you."

His voice finally gives out, and he rubs his face. I wrap my arms around him and squeeze with all my might.

"I love you so much..." he whispers at the chest on the ground. Then he tilts the bottle slightly. "Rest in peace, little homie." He takes a generous swig, then dumps some out on the ground before handing it to me.

"Boots, I'll miss you a lot," I squeak, my nose stuffy from all the crying. "I'll miss playing with you and cuddling up with you in bed or on the couch... I'll miss your cute little meows when you're hungry or excited that we're home. I'll miss you jumping up on the edge of the chair when we're watching movies, effectively scaring the crap out of me, every single time."

Noah snorts a tiny laugh, and I release a tired one in return.

"But mostly, I'll miss how happy you made your daddy. Because he just loves you so much, and I know he always will, no matter what. It doesn't matter if you're gone from this world. Because you'll always live on in our hearts and our memories."

I raise the bottle to our furry friend. "Rock on, Boots. And say hi to Barnaby for me. I know you two will be the best of friends."

I take a sip of scotch then pour some out like Noah did. And when I look up at him, he's smiling at me with the most grateful eyes, lined with staggering sadness. I reach up and hold his shoulders, hugging onto him with every bit of strength I have. And he returns it.

We gave Boots his send-off, and sure, it sucks we had to do it. I know that Noah is distraught, and he probably will be for a while.

But I also know that my man is strong. I can't count how many times he's carried me, emotionally, and shared my pain to ease me of the burden. He can handle this, even if it seems to him like the worst has happened. He'll bounce back.

He has to.

I awake in the dark, my mind sifting through the images in my head; parts of an uneasy dream where Noah was writhing in pain and I wanted nothing more than to help him, but I was bolted to the floor.

I blink a few times as my eyes adjust to the lack of light in the room. I'm in Noah's bed, but I quickly realize he's not here with me. So I sit up and look around.

I don't see him anywhere. And I hear nothing but quiet.

After the animal hospital guy came to take Boots, Phoebe finally went home, and I urged Noah to get some rest. I'd honestly never seen him look so tired, and he wasn't talking much, which is so unlike him. Hearing him answer me with one-word grunts had me determined to get him to bed so he could sleep off this waking nightmare.

We put the TV on in his bedroom and zoned out for a while until he passed out clutching me for dear life. I fell asleep stroking his hair, and from what I can tell by the time on the clock, that was about three hours ago.

I get out of the bed and stumble down the hall, checking the office quick to see if Noah's there. He's not, but I can't help noticing that all of Boots's stuff is gone, which prompts me to swallow hard over my scratchy throat.

I go downstairs, padding my bare feet across the hardwood floors, noting that the fireplace is still going. The dull glow illuminates the room in shadows, the only sounds to be heard those of the cracklings flames.

Then something rustles in the kitchen.

I drift, following the noises until I find Noah crouched on the floor, rummaging through a cabinet and tossing items into a cardboard box.

"Hey," I whisper, so as not to startle him with my presence. But he doesn't flinch, nor does he turn around, so I'm guessing he already knew I was here. "What are you doing up? Come back to bed."

"Sorry… I just need to clear out all this stuff," he mutters, and then I realize what he's doing.

He's getting rid of everything cat-related.

Oh, Noah…

I step over to him and reach out to touch his hair. "Baby, you don't have to do that right now. It's three in the morning. You should be sleeping."

"Can't sleep," he grunts, shoveling cans of cat food into the box.

"Okay… Well, let me make you some tea then," I hesitate before turning to grab the kettle.

He doesn't respond to my tea offer, but I need to do *something*. I need to help him in some way, because right now I feel more than useless.

I fill the electric kettle with water and turn it on, then take out two mugs and some chamomile tea bags.

"So… What are you going to do with that stuff?" I ask, to get him talking.

I know Noah. If he bottles up his feelings, he'll retreat into himself and grow more despondent with every aching emotion that floods his system. He'll throw up a mask, and act like he's fine. And to everyone else in the world, he'll seem like his usual, cool self. But I see through his masks, as if they're made of cellophane.

I'm his best friend, and it's my job to help him grieve in a healthy way.

Noah makes a noise that sounds like it means *I don't know*, then stands up with a shrug.

"Probably just… donate it or something," he mumbles, then comes closer to me.

I tilt my face up to see him; this tall, godlike being in sweatpants and nothing else, the intricate lines of his muscles covered in soft skin and marked with ink. If I didn't know him, he might look dangerous, what with the brooding scowl he's wearing on his pillowed lips, dark brows pushed together and eyes deeper than infinite space.

Instinctively, my body leans into him, craving his touch, even now, when he's feeling lost. *Especially* now. I need him to show me he'll be okay.

His eyes meet mine for a moment, and I can see in that one look that he's twisted up, and that the pain he's holding onto is so much worse than physical hurt.

It's in his heart, and that's a feeling I know all too well.

I take in a small breath as he inches closer, his hand moving out slowly. I shiver in anticipation.

But then he reaches above my head and opens a cupboard, taking out a small green dish decorated with fish. I blink slowly. *Boots's favorite food dish.*

Noah stares at it for a few generous seconds, his face moving from a fond reminiscence to a strangled disappointment before he dumps it into the cardboard box with a huff.

He shakes his head and grumbles something under his breath, lifting the box like he's about to continue tearing through his house in the middle of the night to get rid of everything that reminds him of Boots.

Well, I'm not letting him do that.

"Noah, put that down for a minute, please," I ask of him, grabbing his biceps.

"Alex, I just need to do this..." he argues, though he looks and sounds almost too exhausted to protest.

"Why? Why must you do that right now?"

"Because, I just..." he stops to chew on his lip for a moment. "I can't stand the thought of waking up and remembering he's gone. I can't deal with seeing his stuff and knowing he's fucking ash. It... sucks."

"I know it does," I commiserate, yanking him closer to me until he gives up the fight and sets the box down, his eyes sliding up to mine, shining with insecurity and doubt. "It sucks so hard, baby. It really does. But running through your apartment at three a.m. dumping his things into a box won't make you feel better about him being gone."

His wide gaze remains locked on me. "Then what will...?"

"You have to let yourself feel it," I say, sympathizing with him deep in my gut, because I know this shit is *way* easier said than done.

He dips his chin and squeezes his eyes shut tight, releasing a shaky breath before nodding and dropping to his knees. He wraps his long arms around my waist, holding me by my hips and resting his head against my stomach.

"You have no idea how much it means to me that you're here right now," his lips move on my skin, exposed by the crop-tank I'm wearing. "You're a fucking saint, Alexandra."

"Noah, I would never dream of letting you deal with something painful on your own," I run my fingers through his impossibly soft, mussed up hair. "Your pain is mine, just like my pain is yours."

His face pivots as he gazes up at me.

Seek Me

"You're perfect…" His voice cuts off a bit at the end, as if there was more to that statement, but he caught himself before he could let it slip.

Perfect what? Please finish that thought… I really need to hear it.

But he doesn't continue. Instead, his eyes fall back down, landing on my belly button. He nuzzles the piercing there with his lips, pressing a small kiss on the barbell.

"Come on, baby," I sigh, taking him by the hands. "Let's go lay by the fire."

He nods slowly in agreement and stands up, allowing me to lead him back into the living room. He has a seat on the couch, but I push on his hard chest until he reclines, and I snuggle up on top of him. My body rests between his parted legs, my head on his chest, rising and falling in easy tandem as I hold his hand up in front of my face and play with his fingers.

We're quiet for a while, just cuddling in relaxed silence, him no doubt thinking about his sadness, while I think about his pain, and how easy it is for me to share it. It comes naturally to me.

Everything does with Noah. Being with him is the easiest thing in the entire world, and yet somehow we still can't manage to make *us* real.

Though I want to. *I want to be his so badly.*

"Come home with me for Christmas," his deep voice rumbles from within his chest so I can feel it on my cheek. "Please?"

I lift my head in line with his. "Really?" He nods. "You want me to come to your… parents' house? For Christmas?"

A nervous elation simmers in my belly. I haven't been with an actual family on Christmas since I was seventeen.

Noah nods again. "Yea. My parents are dying to meet you. And honestly…"

He pauses to swallow visibly while I'm suspended in mid-air, all my internal doubts sprouting to the surface of my mind.

He's taking pity on me. He doesn't want me to be alone for Christmas. He just feels bad for me, that's why he's asking.

"I don't want to be without you," his words slice through my self-deprecating thought bubble, causing me to gasp. "I don't want us to spend this one… apart."

"Noah," I whisper his name because it's all I can say now. Well, other than, "Yes. Of course I will come with you. I'd be honored."

"Yea?" He lets a small grin slip, and it's the sexiest, most comforting thing I've seen all day.

"Yea," I nod, finally allowing myself to smile, for the first time in hours. I trace his jaw tenderly with my fingertips.

"Alex, thank you so much," he breathes in relief then yanks my face to his, kissing me slow and sweet. "This means so much to me."

It means so much to him? *Wow...*

A warmth spreads rapidly through my chest, and words are threatening to erupt from inside my throat. Words that I most certainly cannot say.

So I kiss him fast before they sneak out, and he groans into my mouth, a tasty vibration that sheets my skin with goosebumps. Our kisses grow deeper and hungrier while we writhe around, touching everywhere our needy hands can reach.

And before I know it, I'm licking the divots in his abs and tugging his sweatpants down below his butt so I can take him in my mouth.

Noah's entire body bows to me while I worship him with my lips, easing his mind in the best way I can, while also thanking him for being the best person I know.

The man of my dreams... The one I can't live without. The one whose smile breathes life into my lungs.

Only while my mouth is occupied like this do I allow myself to think the words that have been itching to escape my lips... The words that grow stronger and bolder with every second we're together. The ones I have no business saying to my best friend, that will undoubtedly change the course of our friendship if uttered out loud...

Three little words for three years of our lives spent holding back.

I love you.

I'm all packed up and waiting in my living room. And I'd be lying if I said I wasn't nervous. A lie that no one on Earth would believe from looking at me right now; hands shaking, bottom lip being gnashed between my teeth, knee bouncing rapidly up and down.

When I agreed to go to Noah's family's home in Long Island for Christmas, I wasn't aware it would be an overnight trip. But according to Noah, it's a tradition for them to have dinner on Christmas Eve and then wake up for breakfast Christmas morning, opening presents and enjoying some loving family time.

This whole concept is new to me. Not only did my ex-husband have no real family, so we never went to any gatherings like this while we were married, but my own family didn't really care much about the holidays. Sometimes we'd go to my aunt's house for Christmas, but that stopped when I was around thirteen years old. After that it was just the three of us, celebrating a quiet, unenthused holiday that my parents never seemed to care much about.

And now here's sweet, perfect Noah, my best friend who was raised by parents who actually gave a shit about him, and still do, enough to want him around for the holidays, even after he's grown into an adult. Despite all that's been going on with him in the past two weeks, he's seemed more excited than ever to go home and see his family for Christmas.

And he'll be showing up with a stray.

I pick anxiously at some paint around my fingernail. I'm not even his *girlfriend*. What if his parents think I'm weird? What if they hate me because I'm preventing their son from finding a *real* relationship? What if I don't fit in with their happy, most likely caroling-while-wearing-Christmas-sweaters family?

I have little time to fret internally over it, because my door is buzzing, which means Noah and Jimmy are downstairs. My Christmas chariot awaits, ready to cart us like a sleek-black sleigh to the wonderland of Long Island.

God, this could be so disastrous. I really hope Noah brought a forty or at least a few edibles for the ride.

Wait, what am I saying? This is Noah Richards we're talking about. He's always packin.

I grab my bag, complete with a change of clothes, my Christmas jammies, and Noah's present, locking up and heading downstairs.

That's the one silver-lining of this whole ordeal. I'm very confident in the gift I bought for Noah, and I just know he'll love it.

Eee! I can't wait to see his sexy face light up! Who knows… He might be so grateful he immediately drops to his knees and kisses me into orgasm. But not in front of his family… I'm trying to make a good *impression.*

In the lobby of my building, Noah rushes over and grabs my bag, smiling and pressing his lips to my temple in a way that makes me feel like a princess. He takes my hand in his and we walk out to the car, the cold wind whipping our smiling faces.

"Hi, Jimmy!" I squeal as he opens the door for me. "Merry Christmas! Why are you working?" I scold him with my eyes and he laughs. Then I narrow my gaze at Noah, who's tossing my bag in the back.

"As soon as I drop you two off I'm heading to my daughter's house in Connecticut," Jimmy tells me.

I nod, pacified by this information. The last thing I want is him to miss Christmas with his family because we need to be carted around and theoretically *protected* from nothing.

"That means some weirdo will be driving us home tomorrow," Noah frowns, hopping in next to me as Jimmy closes the door. "I don't know how to feel about that…"

I shove him playfully and he grins, grabbing me by the waist and tugging me into his side so he can tickle me until I'm breathless and my stomach is sore from laughing.

The drive to Noah's hometown isn't very long. There's much less traffic than we all anticipated, which is good and bad. Good, because we're making great time, but bad because I'm really enjoying riding in the car with my best friend. As we cruise down the parkway, Noah points out places that spark memories from his childhood.

"You lived here your whole life?" I ask, brimming with curiosity, hungry for more glimpses into what made him who he is.

"I was born in Huntington," he says with his fingers examining my thigh through the rip in my jeans. "We moved to Rockville Center when I was three and lived there ever since."

I'm not sure why thinking of a baby Noah being moved into a new house makes me all warm and fuzzy inside, but it does, and I find myself nestling up to him even closer as we gaze out the windows.

"Here's something I've always wondered but never asked you," I murmur, tilting my face to grin at him. He peers down at me with his brows lifted patiently. "If you were born and raised in Long Island, why do you sound like a California surfer when you talk?"

Noah laughs out loud and my cheeks blush from how much I love the sound and sight.

"I like to keep people on their toes, fairy girl," he winks at me and my face reddens deeper.

I'm baffled by wherever that nickname came from, but now that he's said it, it's all I can hear in my mind as we gaze out the window at his old stomping grounds.

This area of Long Island is so confusing to me. One second we're driving through what looks like the projects in a Spike Lee movie, covered in graffiti and scattered with burned-out abandoned buildings, and the next we're surrounded by cute little suburban houses decorated with Christmas lights and blow-up

Seek Me

Rudolphs.

New York is a fun-house mirror of diversity. It's as if the entire state couldn't seem to decide what it wanted to be, so it said *Fuck it. Let's be a little of everything.*

"There's my high school," Noah points out animatedly and my head springs to catch a peek.

It looks like any regular high school, but to me it's fascinating because it's where Noah Richards, my best friend and secret love of my life, went to school. That's where he probably slacked off in class and flipped off his teachers. Where he made out with cheerleaders under the bleachers at the football games, most likely while their quarterback boyfriends played.

I snicker to myself. I can picture it all in my mind. Noah was exactly that bad boy your parents warned you about back then. But underneath his rebellious exterior is the kindest heart; the most fiercely loyal soul.

I glance up at him with playful eyes. "What were you like in high school?"

He looks down at me and his little smirk gives me chills. "Exactly like you think I was."

My smile is uncontainable.

Eventually we arrive and Jimmy helps us with the bags. The fun I was having on the drive is gone in a flash, and I'm trembling down to my core, so nervous I can barely stop myself from peeing.

I'm desperate to make a good impression on his parents. I so badly want them to accept me.

Noah locks his dark eyes on me and gives me a quick wink before knocking on the door. But then he opens it and walks inside like he owns the place, because I guess in a way he does.

"No need to worry, family. Awesome has arrived," he calls out into the foyer and his mom, dad and sister instantly scamper over to attack him with hugs and kisses and squeals of excitement.

I stand there next to Jimmy, fidgeting in place while they all say their hellos. Jimmy sets down the bags and I give him a grateful hug.

"Merry Christmas, Alex," he whispers to me, patting my back. "Don't worry. They'll love you."

He smiles at me and I feel much calmer already.

"Thanks, Jim. Go be with your family," Noah tells him, and slips what I'm assuming is some cash into his hand when they shake. "Tell the girls I say Merry Christmas."

"Will do, boss," Jimmy winks at him and turns to leave, but he doesn't get far before Noah's mom grabs his arm.

"Not so fast!" She demands and his eyes widen. "I have a lasagna for you to take home. And some cookies."

Jimmy's smile goes wider than I've ever seen as he chuckles humbly then nods. My heart warms at the sight, and because Noah's mom cooked for Jimmy and his daughters. It's the sweetest damn thing ever.

Mrs. Richards disappears into the kitchen, but Noah isn't waiting for her.

"Dad, this is Alex," he murmurs through an apparently pleased smile, his hand resting on my lower back. "Alex, my dad, Tom. He's alright."

Tom swats his son's shoulder and rolls his eyes, though his smile is delightedly friendly.

"So nice to finally meet you, Alex," he shakes my hand. "We've heard so much about you."

"Likewise, Mr. Richards," I chirp in the most proper voice I can manage.

"Oh God, please call me Tom," he huffs. "*Mr. Richards* sounds like a high school principal."

I giggle and he smiles. It reminds me so much of Noah I'm almost taken aback.

I can see where Noah gets his good looks from... Damn.

"Dad, you're a dean. That's basically a principal," Haley pushes him out of the way and engulfs me in an overzealous hug that gets hair in my mouth. "Hi, sis! I'm so happy to see you again!"

Did she just call me sis?? Oh my God... I'm going to pass out.

"Hi, Haley!" I try not to sound like I'm shaking, though I most certainly am. "I'm so glad to see you, too."

"When Noah told us he was bringing you for Christmas I was so excited you have no idea!" She squeals, jumping up and down while clutching my hands in hers. "I knew he'd smarten up, eventually."

She shoots Noah a look and his eyes widen at her as they share a telepathic sibling conversation.

"Haley, leave your brother and his *girlfriend* alone," Noah's mom sneers as she returns, holding a tray for Jimmy.

He takes it graciously and we all wave goodbye as he leaves with his food to go enjoy Christmas with his family.

And then I'm left alone with the Richards family. All staring at me, like they're waiting for me to do a backflip or start juggling.

Seek Me

"You have a lovely home," I whisper, and they all laugh.

"It's *okay*," Noah's mom teases then hugs onto me in such a lovingly matriarchal way, I almost burst into tears. *I guess I missed being hugged by a mom...* "I'm so happy to meet you, dear." She whispers the words by my ear and I'm practically falling apart.

She finally pulls back and strokes my hair, "My name is Gemma, by the way. Or you can call me Mom." She lights up and I hear Noah's throat clear, loud.

"Mom," he grunts, running a frustrated hand through his hair.

"See? He gets it," she winks and I can't help but laugh.

"Alright, can we all be normal, please?" Noah mutters, pulling me away from his mother. "Don't overwhelm Alex. Jeez, two minutes with you psychos and she'll be running directly into oncoming traffic."

"Aw come on, son," Tom says, slinking an arm around his wife as they study me with curious and captivated eyes. "We're not that bad. We'd never do anything to scare away your girlfriend."

"Okay, that's twice now," Noah warns. "I let the first one slide because you're all obviously excited, but three strikes and you're out. Don't test me, Father."

I can't help but grin at how defensive he's getting over them calling me his girlfriend. It's clearly struck a nerve, and I'm willing to bet my favorite leather jacket it's because he's never actually brought a girl home before. I could not possibly feel more special if I started laying golden eggs.

Tom and Gemma giggle in obvious entertainment as their son squirms. Yet I'm busy observing them closely, like animals out in the wild.

Happy parents. Who are truly in love... You can tell by how they're holding onto each other, watching their only son, all grown up, bringing a girl home on Christmas. They're beaming with pride, and it's so foreign to me, it's like I'm watching aliens do their taxes.

They're also a very attractive couple for their age. The fact that Noah is the most gorgeous thing I've ever seen, and Haley is a supermodel in training, doesn't surprise me now that I'm looking at their beautiful parents.

Their family portraits must look like the pictures that come inside the frames when you buy them.

"Sorry, kiddo," Tom replies first to Noah's whining. "We'll be good, I promise."

His mom draws an *X* over her heart, and it's as if I'm seeing Noah do it. Because he does that, all the damn time. My eyes are alight with intrigue, and I'm beguiled. I can barely move or speak. Just watching.

"Alex, would you like some cocoa?" Gemma asks, and before I can answer she scurries off while Tom adds, "I'll bring your bags up to your old room."

Then we're left with Haley, who's bouncing around in place, grinning at us like we're life-sized hipster versions Barbie and Ken, with our tattoos, piercings, ripped jeans and Ray Bans.

"Come on," Noah sighs, taking my hand. "I'll show you around the home where I grew into the most awesome badass of all time."

I laugh and nod joyfully.

Noah drags me all around his house, which is pretty big, though it's exactly what you'd expect in a suburban Long Island home. Everything is so comfy and welcoming, the interior decorated informally and sprinkled with Christmas cheer.

I have to admit, I expected the place to be set up similarly to Noah's. But apparently their son being a rich and famous actor didn't convince Tom and Gemma to trade their cheerful, homey decor for some more luxurious and chic. I like it a lot. I love that they're still so down-to-Earth, because Noah is too. And now I see where he gets it from.

The last stop on the tour is Noah's bedroom, which is where we'll be sleeping tonight. I guess his parents don't have any misconceptions about us not sleeping together, because they didn't even bat an eye at letting us stay in the same bed.

Then again, why would they? Look at who their son is…

"So… this is my room," Noah hums, glancing around while I do the same. "A lot of memories in here…"

"Like what?" I grin up at him, tugging the waist of his jeans. "You discovering your sexuality by humping all sorts of inanimate objects?"

His head drops back as he laughs out loud, and my insides shudder. "What's going on in *your* head, you sexy little pervert?"

I giggle as he presses me up against his dresser. "Did you bring girls in here? Pretend to be studying while you make out and try to grab boob, with your parents right downstairs?"

"Mmm… no, not exactly," he whispers, his lips trailing my jaw. "I mean, maybe a little…"

I laugh and grip his strong shoulders. "Were you always this bad?"

"I was bad enough," he rumbles and his hips surge forward to rub his hardening erection between my thighs.

Seek Me

I can't help the eager gasp that flees my lips. I want him so bad right now. I haven't gotten stuck by that perfectly majestic piece in two days and I'm yearning for it. My body is craving him, like it craves nourishment. My need for Noah is just as strong as my need to eat and drink.

"Oh my God! Get a room!" Haley's voice shrieks from the doorway, and I freeze, but Noah barely moves away.

"Uh, this *is* my room, turd face," he grumbles, glaring at her, though he's still holding me flush against him, maybe to block his sister from seeing his very visible hard-on. "Get the hell out."

"Mom and Dad wanted me to tell you guys to come downstairs," she says, leaning against the doorframe, making herself comfortable. "They want to grill Alex. I mean, *get to know* her." She shows us a purely wicked smile.

"Okay," Noah says, his tone unaffected and never once breaking his cool as he lifts a lazy eyebrow. "We'll be right there."

God, even the slightly bored way he talks to his sister is making me wet. Good thing I brought extra panties.

Haley finally leaves, not without first sticking her tongue out at Noah. I breathe hard and gaze up at him, eyeing his lips with the starved hunger of a person who hasn't eaten in days.

"I guess we should get this over with," Noah huffs, finally placing a soft kiss on my lips, which is enough to light my blood on fire like it's cut with kerosene. "Tonight is going to be excruciating… I'm dying to get inside you, baby."

I moan at his words, and the feeling of his pouted lips teasing mine.

"Wait… Are you saying we can't have sex here?" The look on my face must be one of sheer panic, because Noah smiles with satisfaction.

"Oh no… Trust me, that would never work," he growls, and I release a sigh of relief. "I just mean we'll have to be really quiet. That headboard rocks like a mofo."

"Sounds like you have some experience with that," I smirk, and he kisses me again.

"Mmm sounds like you're itching to find out, huh bad girl?"

My needy hands drift uncontrollably down to the curve of his butt and I pull him into me so we can rub our stuff together for another minute before we finally have to peel apart.

Noah steps back and breathes hard, getting himself under control so we can go back downstairs to his family. I go to move away, but he grabs me by the hand and squeezes it tight. My gaze slides up to his, and he's regarding me with wonder and perplexity in his coal eyes.

"You being here..." his voice is gruff and hesitant. "It's almost astonishing. I guess I don't need to tell you this has never happened before..."

I shake my head slowly, fully immersed in the look he's giving me. It's as if we're on our own planet, where nothing and no one else matters.

Just us, in this moment. It's just *us*.

He bites his lip, looking like he wants to say so many things he won't allow himself to say. And I want to hear every last one of them.

We finally stop staring at each other and leave the room, going back downstairs to rejoin his family for Christmas Eve dinner.

The words will have to remain unspoken for now, though I'm not sure how much longer we can keep them in.

Sooner or later, they're bound to break free.

"My God, Gemma, that pie was so good, I could cry," I hold my stomach as if it's carrying a food baby.

"Don't cry," Noah's mom giggles, apparently quite pleased with herself.

As she should be. She fed us all until we're ready to pop, with the most scrumptious home-cooked food that's ever touched my lips.

And she made Noah Richards. For that alone, she deserves a parade and her own holiday.

We've spent the last few hours eating and conversing, like normal families do on Christmas Eve, I assume. I still feel very much out of my element, but Noah's parents are so cool and sweet and kind that any insecurities I had before today about meeting them have been sufficiently squashed.

They did grill me a bit earlier, but not in an interrogating way. More in a *we want to get to know the girl who's spent the last three years getting to know our son* kind of way. They were very excited to hear about my art and how my career is going, although I got the sense that Noah has already told them about a lot of it, which makes me swell with pride for my best friend, and how proud he is of *me*.

They didn't ask me about my ex, or why I'm not with my own family for the holidays, again, as if Noah had instructed them to stray from such topics, which is also appreciated. I try not to think about those things, *especially* around the holidays. I often wonder if my parents will eventually try to reach out to me.

Seek Me

It sure as hell won't be me reaching out to them...

I suppose they won't try. As far as they know, I'm still with Roger, and still a failure daughter, so why would they want to check in? They're too busy living their lives as if I never existed.

The second I feel myself spiral into these painful thoughts, Noah's hand reaches for mine under the table. I glance at him and he's watching me closely with that calming smile which lets me know everything will be fine, and as long as he's here I'll never be alone.

I can do nothing more than smile at him, and he winks in return.

"You two are so cute together," Gemma swoons, batting her eyelashes at her son, who frowns.

"I think Noah's finally met his match," Tom adds, sipping his coffee.

"Enough from the parentals," Noah sings.

"That fact that you brought her home for Christmas just proves my point, kiddo," his dad continues. "You haven't brought a girl home since your senior prom. And even that was barely a real date."

"Hm yea. Donna Larson. She was a cool chick," Noah reminisces, a casual smirk playing on his lips. "Turns out her boyfriend wasn't very excited about me taking her to prom. Dude attacked me the second we got there." He laughs softly at the memory and his parents shake their heads in disapproval.

"He had blood on his tux in their picture," Gemma mutters, then gets up, I assume to go find this picture to show me.

"It wasn't my blood," Noah shrugs.

"Damn, man. You stole the dude's girlfriend at prom then kicked his ass?" I chirp and Noah chuckles, wearing an unapologetic grin.

"I didn't know they were still together, and *she* asked *me* to prom," he explains. "Clearly he wasn't handling business."

"Noah," his dad scolds him with a look. "Be serious. What if Alex went to prom with someone else? Would you beat him up over it?"

Noah leans in on the table. "I would tear that whole goddamned school apart."

I can't help the tremor that runs through my belly at the idea of Noah beating guys up for me.

"Wow... So you were a hell raiser, huh?" I ask, disguising my arousal for simple curiosity.

"God, it was stressful," his mom breathes an uneasy laugh as she rejoins us, handing me a framed photo of Noah and his prom date. "He had quite the mean-streak for a while there. Always fighting over something or another."

I'm surprised at what I'm hearing. My sweet, lovable, lighthearted Noah was a fighter?

Though, I'd be lying if I said I couldn't picture it. I've seen him angry before, and I've definitely seen him act it out on his show. I always just assumed he could give someone a piece of his mind if need be, but as it turns out, Noah likes to scrap. Or at least, he used to.

"Mom, you don't know what it was like growing up around here," Noah jumps in. "All the kids are trying to prove how *hard* they are. If you show them weakness, then it's four years of being tormented. Like a prison sentence."

Haley scoffs and flips her hair. "Maybe for you. I'm effortlessly popular."

I laugh softly and Noah rolls his eyes. "I grew up in a different time, slayer. This city wasn't always as civilized as it is now. And let's be real, there's definitely the same kind of hierarchy now, only kids rely on their social media accounts. We didn't have that when I was growing up. You had to prove yourself."

"So you proved yourself by getting into fights?" I ask, cocking my head to the side, fully invested in hearing more about what this badass high school version of Noah was like.

"If I had to," he shrugs. "And I stood up for the smaller kids who couldn't protect themselves."

"So you were like Robin Hood?" Haley giggles.

"Or a mob boss… What kind of hell did we raise you in?" Tom looks horrified and Noah laughs out loud.

"Look, I obviously turned out fine, so don't worry about it," he sighs.

I glance at the picture in my hand of a much younger Noah, smiling that devilish smirk he's wearing right now, in a white tux with blood smeared on the lapels, a girl who isn't his hanging on his arm.

I would expect nothing less from Noah Richards' prom photo.

I realize that Tom's whispering something to Gemma about how Noah is *relationship stunted*, and they both snicker. Noah glares at them until they stop, pressing their lips together. It's comical to witness the four of them together, and I must say, I'm really vibing on this family.

"Alright, well let's go have some eggnog by the fire," Gemma says, and everyone stands up, moving sluggishly from the heaviness of our full bellies. "Alex, the tradition is we each get to open one present tonight. And I already know which one I want you to open." She claps her hands together, face illuminated with zeal.

But I'm stunned in place, because did she just say she has a present for me? Really??

She bought a present... for me? My God, this really is a family. And they're welcoming me into it with open arms.

Oh, no... here come the tears again. Hold them in!

"Okay, thank you, Gemma," I squeak, swallowing down my irrational emotions. "That sounds great. I brought some gifts for you guys too."

"Oh, sweetie, you shouldn't have," she waves me off, but Haley shushes her.

"Mom, shut up. Thanks, Alex! I can't wait to open my present from you!" Haley cheers, then peers at Noah. "It better be a painting."

I have to laugh. *I love these people so much already.*

As we walk toward the living room, Noah whispers in my ear, "I hope you don't mind, but I got you something." I stop and aim my wide eyes up at his face. "I think you're gonna love it."

My smile threatens to break my face in half.

Not that I hadn't expected him to get me something. Noah loves buying me things, but usually they're just little trinkets, art supplies or books he thinks I'd like; occasionally a sex toy we can use together or a piece of lingerie he wants me to wear for him - the memory of last Valentine's Day springs to mind and my toes instinctively curl in my fuzzy socks.

The truth is, I would have been perfectly happy giving him the gift I bought for him and getting nothing in return. But since he did get me something, and it's something he thinks I'll *love*... Well, that just adds to the endless list of factors that are making me feel special right now.

"Baby, you didn't have to get me anything," my hands slink up his chest, feeling indurated curves of muscles beneath the downy fabric of his shirt.

"You know that's just not true," he rasps while playing with my hair.

"I got you something too," I tell him quietly, feeling suddenly shy, which makes no sense. "And I hope you like it... I mean, I think you will."

"You got me a gift?" His brows peak in surprise, so I nod. "Beautiful girl... You're making this the best Christmas ever."

If I wasn't already melting from those words, and the honey-like tone in which he said them, I'd definitely be muddying up over the way he kisses me; soft and chased by one of his hums I love so much. The ones that assure me he's feeling what I am.

Just as my fingers slink up into his hair, though, he breaks it and pulls away, his eyes darting above my head.

"Sorry. I can't kiss you like that in front of my family," he huffs. "They'll never let me hear the end of it."

I whine and pout, to which he chuckles that smug little thing, tracing the under curve of my bottom lip with his thumb.

"Fine, but you owe me more of those later when we're alone," I step back, giving him a demanding look which has him biting his lip.

"Oh, that's a guarantee, you sweet, delicious thing," he growls, and my panties soak through.

We rejoin his family in their living room by a crackling fire, and Gemma hands us each a cup of eggnog spiked with brandy. I smile when I notice my drink is in a *Hell Storm* mug with Noah's face on it.

So damn cute.

Noah and I cuddle up on a love seat while Haley plucks two gifts from under their large, intricately decorated Christmas tree, handing them to her parents. They open them and gush over the thoughtfulness; a very nice Prada tie for Tom from Haley, and a white gold necklace with a flower pendant for Gemma from Noah. This earns both of them loving hugs from their parents and it's such an adorable thing to witness, I sniffle when no one's looking.

I see Noah suddenly rummaging around the presents, his fingers grazing over my gift to him, which I stashed under the tree before dinner. My insecurities had urged me to keep it upstairs, so we could exchange our gifts alone later, but I convinced myself to grow a pair.

If I want his family to accept me as I've accepted them, then I can't hide. I can't stow away and be timid, or act like someone I'm not. I need to be myself. And if they love Noah, then they'll love me by association. Because that's how family should work.

"Mom, if you don't mind, I'd like Alex to open my present now," Noah says to his mother then glances at me. "Sorry, I'm too excited to wait. Plus, I want you to use your gift tomorrow."

I chew on my lower lip, because now my curiosity is winning out and I *need* to know what he bought for me. I'm vibrating in anticipation.

"Of course I don't mind, sweetie," Gemma rubs Noah's back. "I think that's very thoughtful."

"Calm down, Mom," Noah mumbles, though he has pride and eagerness all over his face.

He picks up a large box from the back of the pile and my mouth drops open. I don't know where that thing was in the car, because I'm sure I would

Seek Me

have seen something so big and covered in candy cane wrapping paper.

He jaunts over to me and we sit on the love seat, side by side, as he places the heavy box on my lap. My eyes dart between his and the box, my stomach fluttering with exhilaration.

"Open it," he whispers, all but shimmying next to me. "Hurry. I'm so excited."

I force my shaky fingers to tear open the paper and as soon as I glimpse the brand name on the box, I gasp out loud.

"Oh my God... Noah!" My voice creaks as I frantically rip all the paper away and have a mild heart attack.

Noah laughs beside me, bouncing around in place.

It's a camera. But not just any camera... It's the *best* fucking camera.

The exact model I told him I wanted, so I could start taking more professional photos.

"It comes with the detachable lenses, a tripod, *and* all the software you need to upload so you can develop them on your laptop." He leans in closer. "But we could get you a printer or whatever goes with it if you want. If you decide that's how you want to do it. We could set it up in your office."

I peek at him and tears spring to my eyes. *So many we's just now.*

My heart is bursting. I don't even know what to do with myself.

I have no choice but to grab him with my hand that's not holding my amazing new camera and hug him so hard I hear him hiss. Then I quickly take his jaw in that same hand and kiss him, hard and passionate and right in front of his family. And I don't give the tiniest fuck if they make assumptions about us, because how could anyone not after something like this? I'm making those same assumptions in my mind, right now.

Oh my God, Noah... I fucking love you.

I whimper into his mouth to stop myself from saying it. It's the hardest thing I've ever done not to let those words out. After this... I'm feeling it more than I ever have.

I struggle to pry myself away from a dazed-looking Noah and squeal like a kid who just got the exact toy she'd been begging Santa for.

"I can't believe you did this," I go back to examining the box of my brand new Nikon. "How did you even remember this was the one I wanted? It must have been, like, *years* since I mentioned this to you!"

"I never forget what's important to you," he replies with confidence in his words, because he knows as I do how true they are.

"Noah, I..." Words fail me as I gape at him, wanting to say so much and struggling not to. "I just..."

"Tell me you love it," he murmurs with eyes illuminated in gratification for seeing me happy.

And I am, so damn happy, from something he did. *He makes me so fucking happy.*

"I love it." It takes every bit of restraint I have to say that word... *It.*

"Noah, that's incredible!" Haley shrieks, jumping up to join us in opening my camera up and taking it out. "Wow, that looks expensive."

"It is, so of course I got you a lifetime warranty," Noah tells me with a knowing smile.

"We raised such a good boyfriend," Tom says to Gemma as they smile at us from across the room.

Noah attempts to scowl at them, but he can't stop smiling. I know the feeling.

While Noah and I are still distracted by my shiny new toy which is, in fact, the coolest thing I've ever held in my hands, Gemma gives Haley a gift to open; a makeup palette she'd apparently been pleading for since it came out three weeks ago. She's in seventh heaven. *Again, familiar feeling.*

And I know I have to give Noah my gift now. There's no possible way I can wait until tomorrow. Not after this.

I hand him my camera to hold while I stand up and pluck his present from under the tree, my reluctant timidity making a comeback. I'm not doubting myself, or my gift, because I put a ton of thought into this, and I know he'll love it. It's nowhere near as expensive as his was, but it has more meaning than any gift I've ever given in my life.

"Okay, so... um..." I stutter, handing him the box wrapped in reindeer paper with a big green bow on top. "This is for you. Merry Christmas, babe."

His face is etched in delight and enchantment as he places my camera back in its box and takes my gift. I have a seat next to him as he opens it slowly, with dedication, to find a matte black box.

He glances at me, eyes having grown serious over the course of the ten seconds it took him to do that, and now he almost looks nervous. I want to take a picture of him this way, to savor it because he's just the sweetest thing to look at. But I don't want to ruin the moment, so I take a mental picture instead.

Noah sucks in an audible breath and lifts the top of the box, pushing aside some tissue paper before his jaw drops. I have to sit on my hands to stop them

Seek Me

from trembling.

He removes the gorgeous, leather-bound journal from inside the box and his eyes sparkle as he gapes at it like he's never seen anything so special in his life. Then he notices the silver and black Mont Blanc pen tied to the front with a ribbon.

He unties it and studies it, reading his name engraved on the side. His thumb brushes it and I see him swallow.

"This…" he croaks, eyes darting to me. "This is for…?"

I nod slowly. "Open."

My eyes drop to the journal and he runs his fingers over the cover, which is so soft and smooth, made of real leather, some of the best I've ever seen or felt. Then he unhooks the clasp and turns the cover.

And now it's his turn to gasp.

Inside the cover, I've attached a picture I took of him and Boots. It was from a lazy Sunday afternoon two years ago, when it was raining hard outside, so we stayed in all day, watching movies and cuddling by the fire. I'd honestly never seen Noah so happy, and he passed out on the couch with Boots on his chest, the two of them snoozing so soundly, I couldn't have resisted if I wanted to. I snapped the picture, and I used to look at it all the time when I was away, remembering that perfect day with my boys.

"I had the picture developed at a special shop," I tell him, because he's still too stunned to move or speak. "They glued it on for me. So now you can write to him."

I swear I see his lip tremble as his brows knit together in so much emotion for a moment I fear I've done something terrible.

But then he sets the journal down it its box and he lets out a little noise before grabbing me and hugging me so hard it almost crushes my ribs.

"Alex… Oh my God…" he breathes in my neck, a large hand holding the back of my head. "This is so incredible… Thank you. I can't even… I just… Thank you so much."

"You like it?" I sniffle and he nods against my cheek.

"It's everything…" he whispers. "Now I can write to him, like you do to Barnaby. It's like… he's still here. You brought him back, baby. This is the best gift anyone's ever given me."

Then he pulls back slightly and adds, "No offense, Mom and Dad."

I snort a laugh and grip his back tight, holding him close and soaring inside at my wonderful, thoughtful gift, which he loves and is exactly what he needs.

I knew it in my heart, the minute I had the idea.

The night Boots passed, when I was lying awake, stroking a broken Noah's hair while he shivered and slept, I knew this would be the perfect way to help him heal. Because really that's the best gift I could ever give him. Helping to ease his pain.

Noah's family gets up to check out the gift, and they're all so moved by it that Gemma actually bursts into tears. Noah can't seem to stop touching me, and smiling, so I'd say this has been one of the more fantastic nights of my life.

I've never been so full of joy, watching these people talk, and laugh, and include me in their special family moment. It's truly astonishing to think that having Noah in my life has given me this gift.

Eventually we all go back to sipping our drinks, playing with our new toys, hearts overflowing with love. We nestle up in front of the fire, and listen to Christmas carols, growing quieter and more mollified by the minute.

And just as I'm beginning to doze, my heart replete and my mind at ease, Noah pulls me tighter into his side.

He kisses behind my ear and says, "You know I love you, right?"

My heart stops beating.

And I tell him, "I know. I love you, too."

Chapter Twenty Seven

Alex

Three Months Later...

I SIP MY GLASS OF CHAMPAGNE, smoothing a hand down my cocktail dress. It's tight, black and backless, and I know it makes my ass look great, so I'm not surprised by some of the looks I've been getting from miscellaneous guys tonight. Not that I had gaining male attention in mind when I picked my outfit. I just wanted to look sophisticated and sexy, maybe a little mysterious.

But most importantly, I wanted to look like New York City's newest up-and-coming artist, because that's what I am. At least that's what everyone keeps telling me…

This is officially my third solo exhibit. My fifth show altogether, in three years, which is impressive. The press are here tonight, and I already gave a quick little interview with some photos to be published in a magazine next month.

I feel high. Honestly, I wasn't sure if the gratification I feel from being in the galleries would fade after the first time, or the second. But much to my delight, it hasn't. Each time is better than the last, and I just can't wait to see where my career will take me next.

And yet despite how glowingly pleased I am with how much has changed for me in the last few years, how much I've grown and how far I've come, I can't help but watch the door.

"Darling, you've outdone yourself here," my friend and philanderer of the art community, Evan, saunters over and takes me by the elbow. "This show is truly exquisite."

"Everything looks so chic," my other artist friend, Audra, joins us, flipping her red hair over her shoulder. "And the food is actually good! That on its own is a feat."

"Right? What are those? Pigs in blankets?" Evan gasps, his eyes lighting up. "Genius. Though, half of Manhattan isn't eating meat right now."

"Thanks, guys," I murmur, smiling as my eyes dance over the sea of captivated faces. "It really turned out amazing, didn't it?"

"Totally," Evan squeals. "And that hottie over there in the Tom Ford suit has been eyeing you all night." He wiggles his brows at me and I flush.

But when my gaze lifts to the tall, handsome guy with the slicked back hair, my stomach rolls in protest. And I glance at the door once more.

"And yet you're eyeing... the door," Evan huffs in disappointment and squeezes the bridge of his nose. "Alex, he's not coming."

"I know. I don't care," I mutter petulantly, practically stomping my foot like a child.

"Really?" Audra snarks. "Is that why you've turned down every hot guy who's approached you tonight? Because you *don't care*?"

"Alright fine, I care," I roll my eyes and kill what's left of my glass. "I just thought... maybe he'd come."

"Al, it's been three months," Evan sighs, petting my head like I'm an elderly animal he's trying to pacify. "I think maybe it's time to move on."

"I'm sure he has..." Audra mutters under her breath and I shoot her a wounded look. "I'm just saying, sweetie. You two have barely spoken since New Year's. I know it sucks that it didn't work out, but you can't sit around wallowing. You need to be out living your life."

Evan nods in agreement and I feel like I'm being ganged up on by my own friends, which isn't fun.

"You guys don't get it," I mumble, staring at the floor. "He's my best friend."

"I know he is, Alex," Evan croons. "And I'm sure you guys are still friends, but it's not healthy to be pining over someone like this for so long. You should get the hot guy's number. What's the worst that could happen?"

"Really?" I scoff. "Well, a lot of things could happen. To start, he could be a murderer. Or he could have bad breath. Or he could think Pollock changed the face of American expressionism. Take your pick."

They both laugh and I flag the waiter for more champagne. I'll need a stronger buzz to get through this level of inter-friend-tion.

The unfortunate fact of the matter is that they're right.

What happens when your best friend, the one who you've been quietly falling in love with for three years, finally tells you he loves you?

The assumption, one I made myself at the time, is that you both kiss romantically, and fall into each other's arms with hearts in your eyes, holding onto that feeling for the rest of your life. You move in together, get married, have some babies, and live happily ever after.

That's how it should work, right?

Well, maybe in a Hallmark movie. But this is real life, and real life is a cold, heartless son of a bitch.

When Noah said that he loved me, it was as if every broken shard of my heart, which was smashed to bits by my abusive ex-husband years earlier, had finally been glued back into place. I was complete, and whole.

Noah's love had healed me.

We spent that night making blissful, quiet love in his childhood bed, and nothing had ever felt more perfect, or more real, before.

And then we came back to the city, and we went our separate ways. It was to be expected, really. Just because we said we loved one another, it didn't mean that anything had *actually* changed between us. We were still best friends who fuck. I suppose we still are.

We stepped back into our normal routine without missing a beat, and that was the harshest reality we could never have overcome.

Love *didn't* conquer all. Not in our case.

The words being said out loud didn't magically make us different, or change our circumstances like the wave of a Harry Potter wand. In fact, the opposite was true. We were in the exact same boat as before, because the problem was never that we didn't love one another. The problem was and always will be that we're friends. *Just* friends.

I knew I wanted to be more. I've known in my heart that I want Noah as more than a friend since the moment we met. And back then, there was a concrete obstacle in the way, in the form of my abusive husband. But once I made the leap, and tore down that wall for good, it left an even more complicated obstacle in its place; fear.

My fear mixed with Noah's fear is like a giant, angry monster that lives under your bed; always waiting to scare you the moment you finally begin to feel safe.

And so me *knowing* I want to be more than Noah's friend and physically voicing it to him are two totally different things. The worst part of it all being that I truly have no idea where he stands.

Noah is the most frustratingly difficult person to get a read on. He keeps his emotions so intricately hidden behind his mask of friendly, casual indifference, there's no way to tell what he really wants. And because he's such a caring and selfless human, I know he would never push me into something he thinks *I* don't want. So even if he did want a relationship with me, which again is purely speculation on my part, his fear of hurting me would force me to be the one to admit it first. And my fear won't let me do that.

We're fighting fear with fear, a war that will always end before it even starts.

Add to that Noah's bachelor status, and his repellence of all things relationship, and we were doomed to fail from the beginning.

I felt Noah pulling away after the *L*-bomb was dropped. Classic move for a guy who doesn't do feelings. And of course, because I'm no more privy to relationships than he is, I did absolutely nothing about it. Though I could have. I *should* have. Us admitting love would have been the perfect time to tell him I want more. And yet I stayed quiet.

It was as if I'd been stranded on a desert island for years, and I finally saw help; a passing ship, coming to save me. Only when it came time for me to call out for rescue, I couldn't do it.

I've failed *myself* more than anything.

So that's that. We've seen each other here and there, we text and call from time to time, but the whole thing seems to have ended before it began, and it's killing me inside because all I can think is *he loves you as a friend. He's not in love with you.*

Apparently there's a difference. I must have been absent when they taught that in relationship class.

Where's the class on how to tell your best friend that you love him more than just a friend? Because I'll gladly sign up at the novice level.

I shake my head free of all these thoughts and zone back in on Evan and Audra's discussion about whether the hot guy who's been looking at me is a serial killer.

"He's too clean cut," Evan argues. "There's no way he's chopping people up."

"Um, hello! Have you *seen Dexter*?!" Audra flails. "That's exactly how a dude who's dismembering bodies in his spare time would look!"

I chuckle and then jump when my phone vibrates in my clutch. My heart lodges in my jugular as I whip it open and pull the device out fast, praying for Noah's picture on my screen.

I sigh in disappointment when I see an unknown number, then swipe to decline.

Rats.

"Alex, you need to forget about him and enjoy your night," Evan insists, handing me a new glass of champagne from the waiter's tray.

"Yea, aren't you excited for Barcelona?" Audra's eyes shine with her question.

"Of course I am," I sigh, letting a small grin slip. "It's going to be a blast. A whole summer in Spain… It sounds like a dream come true right now."

Except I haven't told Noah yet… Not that he'll probably even care.

"It will be," Evan smiles and pinches my cheek. "Alright. Come on, mopey ass. Let's go mingle. You can't waste that Dolce lying around feeling sorry for yourself."

I breathe out hard and nod. He has a point.

A couple hours later, the show is over, and it's time to go. Evan, Audra and I leave together, and they're begging me to come out dancing with them.

"It'll be so fun!" Evan shrieks, spinning his way out onto the sidewalk while Audra and I die laughing. "We're gonna dance our troubles away!" He sings this, which has us in stitches.

I'm considering going with them, for the simple fact that going home alone right now sounds like the most depressing thing on earth, when I hear a familiar voice.

"Hey, can I get an autograph?"

I look up and my stomach flips when I see Noah, leaning against the next stoop over. I can feel wind in my mouth because it's hanging open, but I can't seem to close it.

I walk over slowly, glancing back at my friends, who give me looks that I think say either *good luck,* or maybe *you should slap him.* Could go both ways.

"Noah…" I whisper as I approach him with caution, struggling not to get lost in how dangerously good he looks. "Hi. It's good to see you."

"It's *really* good to see you," his deep voice croons at me like my favorite melody. "You look stunning."

I give him a once-over, admiring his tousled hair that I just know feels like silk beneath my fingers. His eyes almost as dark as night, those cushioned lips, twisted into the slightest smirk that makes him look like he's withholding a secret. His body; tall and lean, covered in hardened slopes of muscles that show themselves through his fitted designer clothes.

I now realize I never stood a chance. With a best friend that looks like him; who flirts like it's breathing, makes me laugh with his wit and dazzling personality, and who kisses like he was put on Earth to do just that.

There was no hope of me not falling in love with him.

I realize I've been staring at him in silence for way too long when he clears his throat and looks at the ground between us.

"I'm sorry I'm late…" he mutters, rubbing the back of his neck. "I didn't know if I should come…"

"I'm glad you did," my pitchy voice cuts in and his eyes raise to mine. "I mean, I wish you'd gotten here for the actual show. It went really well."

He smiles, melting me with those straight white teeth and that curious little dimple peeking out on the left side.

"Of course it did," he hums, and when his hand reaches out to play with my hair, I stop breathing. "I miss you, Al."

"I miss you too," I whisper like a reflex, throwing my shields away and stepping to him, sliding my hands up his frame and around his broad shoulders.

He embraces me with hands on my lower back, basically the top of my butt and pulls me flush against him. I rest my head over his heart and take him in; his warmth and scent the closest things to home I've felt since I was young and stupid.

Maybe I still am…

I want to ask him so many things. *Where have you been? What have you been doing? Why haven't we spoken? Who was that blonde skank on your Instagram story the other day?*

But I can't say any of it. Not while he's here. Not while he's holding me and touching me and telling me he missed me.

He bends to me and tucks his face into the crook of my neck, inhaling a long breath that tells me he's sniffing me back, and it makes me swoon. His body shudders as he hums, gripping me tighter, his muscles melding into me and hardening my nipples with sensation.

Then his lips caress my throat, my jaw, my cheek… Until they're hovering over my mouth and I can feel him trembling ever-so-slightly.

My clit is suddenly aching with the desire to be touched by him. It's been weeks since we've seen each other, also the last time we hooked up, and I'm so desperate to feel him inside me I'm dizzy.

As much as I know it's flawed logic, and it's not getting us anywhere, I need this connection. I need to keep this part of us. I'm clinging to it; hanging on for dear life, so afraid to let myself fall, even though I should.

"Come home with me," his voice is hoarse and I know he's breaking too because I can feel his erection on my waist. "You're like a drug to me, Alex. I need my fix."

Seek Me

I whimper and make the move to kiss his soft, pillowed lips, causing him to groan. The sound and the vibrations zap me like an electric shock, igniting deep in my belly.

I can't resist him. I never could. And more importantly, I don't want to.

"I'm yours," I tell him in a purr and he gasps. "Have me any way you want. I'm made for you, Noah Richards."

I walk up to Noah's front door and a brief wave of panic washes over me when deciding whether I should let myself in or ring the bell.

If this was four months ago, I wouldn't have even hesitated. I'd use his code to get in the front, and his key to get inside his apartment, and he'd see me when I walk through the foyer like I own the place, and smile and hug me against his shirtless body.

Apparently a lot can change in four months, because now I'm ringing his doorbell and waiting to be buzzed in.

I smooth out my hair in preparation for Noah opening his door, but when I see a certain blue-eyed British stud in his place, I grin less like a girl trying to hide her secret love, and more like a girl who's amped to see a friend.

I scamper over to Andrew James and hug him hard, almost toppling him over into Noah's foyer. He chuckles and hugs me back, then pulls away and gives me a studious look.

"You're blushing," he squints at me, pursing his lips. "Does Noah know you're secretly in love with me too?"

I growl and shove him. "Shut up. And ew, that's like incest. You're basically the big brother I always wanted."

"Glad to hear it, sis," he pokes my side and I swat him away. "You're just in time to hear Noah complain about the script like the spoiled nancy he so clearly is."

"I'm not complaining, I just don't understand why we would be talking and running at the same time," Noah grumbles, emerging from the kitchen with three beer bottles. "Can't we wait until we're done running to have the conversation?"

"Sweetie, let's be honest," I murmur, stepping over to him. "Are you more upset about the talking, or the running?" I grin up at him and he narrows his gaze at me, a look that never fails to moisten my panties.

"The running," Andrew cuts in then grabs one of the beers from Noah's hand. "Definitely the running."

"Don't you start with me, beautiful little tattooed fairy girl," Noah rumbles then leans in slowly before attacking my face with a flurry of kisses.

I squeal and pretend to fight him off, though there's no chance I want this to stop. But it does, after a long hug wherein I believe Noah is rubbing his junk on me.

He hands me a beer and the three of us clink before taking our respective sips.

"So Andrew, you excited to get back to Georgia?" I ask joining them in the living room where they've been *running lines*, though really I think they were playing video games. "Season four, bitch! It's going to be madness, right?"

He grins and nods, though there's some pain behind his expression and I know it's about his failing marriage. Dude tries to hide it the best he can, but we all know it's killing him inside, not being able to fix his relationship with his wife.

"Okay, no, this is good. We need a female perspective on this," Noah starts, then turns to face me as I sit in between the two of them on the couch. "I think Andrew should get laid. Thoughts?"

"Noah!" Andrew barks, though it appears his cheeks are reddening a bit. It's subtle, but it's there and I think it's adorable. If only we weren't talking about adultery while it's happening.

"I don't know… I might be a little biased in this case," I answer. "I want you to be happy, Andrew. And I also cheated on my husband a little so I don't think I'm the best person to ask."

"How to you cheat *a little*?" Andrew raises his brow at me, then Noah, who shrugs.

"My ex was cheating on me for years. And he was an abusive psycho. So I don't really feel bad for giving up on us," I glance at Noah for a moment, who gives me a sympathetic smile, and squeezes my hand.

When I turn back to Andrew, he's gaping at me like I've just revealed my true identity as Super Girl.

"Your ex-husband abused you…?" He whispers, blinking about a hundred times. "Like, physically?"

"Yea…" I mutter, swiveling my head between him and Noah. "You didn't know that?"

"No!" He gasps. "How would I have known that?"

I look to Noah. "You never told him?"

"Is that a real question?" My best friend scoffs. "What kind of friend would I be if I was out there spreading your business around like some loose-lipped floozy?"

I giggle as my heart is engulfed in warm vibrations. "Noah... that's so sweet. I just assumed since you two are such close friends..."

"We are, but still," he tucks me into his side. "You're my *best* friend. And your story is yours to tell."

I pout and yank his face down so I can kiss his sweet, loving best friend lips.

"Aww. You two are so cute," Andrew sings from the other side of the couch and we both look up to scowl at him. "Well, if it worked out for you guys, then maybe finding someone new could work for me. Since, you know, you're both completely secure in your relationship... right?"

He blinks accusingly at us, more so at Noah than me, which has my stomach twisting up into an unforgiving knot.

Noah clears his throat and sits back. "Anyway, I think if Andrew and his wife are ready to move forward with the divorce, then it shouldn't be a problem to do, at the very least, a tiny bit of flirting."

"Are you and Viv talking about divorce?" I ask Andrew, my insides heavy with sympathy for my friend.

"That would require actual *talking*," he rakes his hands through his hair. "All we do is fight, or she ignores me completely. I think she may have cheated, but I can never be sure. I tried confronting her about it and said maybe we should separate..."

"What did she say?"

"She locked herself in the bedroom for eight hours," he closes his eyes and flops back against the couch. "My marriage is over. Ten years of my life, down the bloody drain."

"Hey," I grab his hand and his eyes peel open, aiming that effervescent blue in my direction. "You can't think like that. Your marriage was not a waste of time. You made two beautiful children, and you learned about yourself. You learned how to be strong, and how to fight. How to love selflessly. That's something you should never take for granted."

I feel Noah stiffen beside me, but I choose to ignore it.

Andrew sits up, and when I go to release his hand, he squeezes mine tighter. "Has anyone ever told you you're a badass?"

I grin and peek at Noah briefly. "I may have heard that once or twice."

Noah wraps his arms around me from behind and kisses my neck. And if I could suspend this moment, hold on to this feeling for as long as possible, I would in a heartbeat.

But just like every moment of bliss for Noah and me lately, it eventually comes to an end, and we're left awkwardly maneuvering around each other, like two moons in an axis around the same uninhabited planet of our dysfunctional relationship.

The three of us chat for a little while longer. Andrew asks me about my experiences with my ex, and I tell him the story, hoping maybe it'll give him some solace toward his own troublesome situation, which is not quite the same, but equally disappointing.

Then the boys finish going through their script, while I putter around the apartment, smoking a joint and baking cookies.

A little while later, Andrew goes out shopping for his kids, and Noah and I are alone, which is dangerous. I'm half tempted to screw his brains out to squash the stiff tension between us. But that's the solution we've been using ever since Christmas, and clearly it's not doing us any good.

Plus, there's something I need to tell him, and once it's out, he probably won't even want to have sex with me. Maybe ever again.

Oh God, don't even think like that!

"So what are your plans for the summer?" Noah asks, as if he's reading my mind, which is the scariest damn thought I've had since two seconds ago. "Any shows or exhibits in the works? Let me know now, because Brant's figuring out my schedule and when the jet will be free. I was thinking you could come down for Fourth of July."

I stare at him blankly for a moment, because I'm being torn to shreds, and it's prohibiting me from moving or forming words with my mouth.

I honestly can't even comprehend the level of friendship I have with Noah. Despite us fucking for years and dancing around our feelings; regardless of us saying *I love you* and it confusing our relationship status even more than before, it still doesn't make him want to be around me any less.

He's planning out his summer on location and including me in it, in spite of how little we know what we're doing together. It's bewildering, and now I need to sit before I fall to my knees and cry until I'm nothing more than a puddle at his beautiful feet.

"Actually, Noah, I need to tell you something…" I squeak out the words, planting my butt on the edge of his big leather chair while he looks down at me

Seek Me

with his forehead lined.

Much to my surprise, and dismay, he scoffs a little laugh and shakes his head to himself.

"How long this time?" He lifts a brow with his question, and for minutes on end I can't speak. I simply stare up at him, pressure winding up so tight behind my eyes I fear my head will pop.

But finally I swallow hard, choking on the acid stinging my throat, and say, "Four months. Just for the summer."

He nods and his jaw ticks, though his unaffected mask remains tightly in place. "Where to? *Hm*? Tokyo? Peru... Kenya...? Wait, no don't tell me... You're going to Mother Russia!"

His tone has some serious bite to it, but he's playing it off like he's joking, and I'm sick to my stomach.

I hate this... I fucking hate this so much I can barely breathe.

"Barcelona," I whisper, my gaze dropping to the floor as I study our feet. Even his shoes look like they hate me right now.

"*Barcelona*... ooh. That's gonna be sweet." His words are friendly, but I know from one look into his eyes he hasn't been this angry, or hurt, in a long time. *All because of me...* "Lotta hot dudes out there. Better stock up on your condom supply, Mackenzie."

I shoot up fast, glaring at him. "Why are you being such an asshole?"

"I'm not," he laughs, and it hasn't even the slightest bit of amusement to it. "I'm just fucking with you, Alex. That's what we do, right? We're *friends*."

Why does that word sound like a threat when he says it now?

He slaps my shoulder and I shove his chest.

"Fuck you," I spit. "You'll be in Georgia all summer, but I'm not allowed to travel with my friends? What do you expect? For me to just sit around and wait for you to get back?!"

"No, Alex! That's my fucking job," he barks and then recoils a bit, like he wasn't supposed to let that vulnerability slip. He blinks hard and take a breath. "*You're* the one who leaves, remember?"

"But you're leaving too," I say in defense, grasping at straws. It's a weak argument, because I already know how he'll respond. The drawbacks of knowing someone like you know yourself.

"Oh okay. So it's cool if I come visit you in Barcelona, right?" He seethes, dark eyes shooting flames of impuissant rage. "Fourth of July, what do you think? I've never been there... I think it would be a blast."

His accusatory brows arc as he waits for me to say something.

And I should. I know I should say *anything* right now, but I can't make the words come up. Because I don't have any to give him.

He leans in closer to my face. "Your silence speaks *volumes*, Alexandra."

I press my lips together as I tremble. I can't cry, not now. Not in front of him when he's so angry with me and I'm pushing him away yet again.

And for what? Another trip alone?

I mean, sure, I'll be with my friends the whole time, but why wouldn't I want Noah to come out and spend at least a few days with me? It could be so wonderful. What's stopping me from making that happen?

It's like I'm paralyzed in self-doubt. I don't understand what I'm doing with him anymore, but I see now that no matter how much we *love* each other, it won't stop hurting.

I duck around him fast and focus on breathing through my meltdown as I scurry toward the door.

"Alex, don't leave," he shouts at me, though when I get to the foyer I see him still planted in the same spot, prohibiting himself from chasing me this time. I don't even blame him.

"Why would I stay?" I whimper, shaking my head. "You're leaving anyway, Noah. It's fine. I'll be back in August. Maybe I'll see you then."

"Alex, *please*..." he begs, his tone wrought with the suffering I've caused. "Come back."

I don't know if he means right now, or in August, but I'm too confused to tell and too emotionally beat-up to stay and find out.

I just need to go. *Like always*, I hear Noah's voice in my mind, and I shudder.

"Bye, Noah," I murmur with all the empathy in the world, though it makes no difference.

Because two seconds later, I'm gone.

My mind is on the text message from yesterday. The one I never responded to.

Add it to the collection of calls and texts from Noah, to me, that have gone unanswered in the last week.

I'm pacing around my bedroom, all dressed up and ready for a party. A party I probably shouldn't attend, but one I wouldn't be able to keep myself from if I had all the strength of a thousand Fezzik's from *The Princess Bride*.

Noah has indeed been calling and texting me all week, apologizing for snapping at me, and saying it makes no sense for us to spend our last week before we both leave apart. And that we're *friends*, and this argument is *stupid*.

All these points are valid, and yet I haven't been able to answer him once because I know he's right. He has every reason to be mad at me for flitting off constantly, never once considering coming back to see him, inviting him out, or even promising to call when I'm away.

The traveling, or the *escaping* as it should be called, since that's exactly what I'm doing, has become like an addiction for me. A sadistic pain I can't seem to stop inflicting on myself, like cutting.

Each time I'm away from Noah, I miss him even more. And how we leave things always ruins my trips a bit, paired with the fact that I won't let him visit me, and I insist on severing all contact.

My stupid, immature mind yells at me that he could easily contact me first. He could track me down if he really wanted to, thus completing his endless Alex Mackenzie chase.

But my heart, the one I should listen to, reminds me it's not right to do that to him. Noah has promised me since day one that he would never push me into anything. He needs me to initiate the contact, or to just stay with him, and prove that I want what he wants - or at least, what I think he wants... What he *might have* wanted.

And yet each time I tell myself I need this. I'm still getting over my ex, and what he took from me. I'm piecing myself back together, despite how whole I've felt since Noah told me he loved me.

You have no idea what you're doing, crazy pants. You've gone off the deep end and you're flailing in a bottomless ocean.

The final text from Noah came yesterday afternoon. He informed me that he's having a celebratory going away party at his place tonight, since he leaves for Georgia tomorrow to film season four of the show, and apparently he's very excited about it. As he should be. It's a huge accomplishment, and the best friend side of me is blindingly happy for him. But the insecure wannabe-girlfriend side is worried he's mad at me for blowing him off, and for leaving once again with no intention of communicating with him through another four months.

Hence why I'm wearing a scandalously short dress and hesitating in my apartment. My hair is styled, makeup on. I've applied that body shimmer dust all over myself that makes me smell like a cupcake and sparkle like a unicorn, hoping that maybe I can make him forgive me enough to earn a naked going away party of our own.

I just want him not to hate me. That's the bottom line. He's my best friend, and I can't keep hurting him. If I'm not careful, it'll drive him straight into someone else's arms, and that final thought has me grabbing my bag and leaving the house.

When I get to Noah's there's a bouncer by the door. As if his apartment is now a club.

My stomach and bladder are simultaneously shivering with nerves.

I give the large man my name and he lets me in. I walk through the hallway, following the loud music, which gets a hundred times louder once I enter the apartment.

Noah's place is packed. I've never seen this many people in here. Sure, he's had parties before, but he usually likes to keep them mellow.

This is not mellow. *This* is a fucking Manhattan rager.

I wander through the sea of unfamiliar bodies and faces, feeling incredibly out of my element. I wasn't prepared for this. Not even slightly.

I grab a scotch from a passing waiter and take a large gulp, ignoring the burn that springs tears to my eyes. I catch people watching me; noticing me, as if I'm the most recent celebrity addition to this party, and I know for a fact it has nothing to do with my recent success as a painter, and everything to do with me being Noah's well-known fuck-buddy.

I ignore the whispers from a group of nearby girls, who are wearing even fewer clothes than me, and seek out my best friend.

"Alex!" I hear Noah's assistant, Brant, before I see him, and I turn to find him sucking tequila out of the belly button of a topless girl who's splayed out on Noah's breakfast bar.

I raise my brow. *What the actual fuck?*

"We didn't think you'd show!" Brant slurs, biting a lime out of the girl's hand then spitting it across the room.

"Where's Noah?" I ask impatiently because even this is longer than I want to be talking to him at the moment.

"Oh God, who knows," he huffs and goes back to his girl, but not without first shouting, "Hey! Have fun in *Barcelona*."

I roll my eyes, stifling the rage that's burning a hole through my chest as I

Seek Me

turn and stalk toward the living room. I look around for Noah, or even Andrew or Johnny. Someone I know, other than fucking *Brant*, but there are so many people everywhere and I'm too short to see over anyone, even in my wedge boots.

I recognize a few of Noah's friends we've been out with before, and they wave me over. I'm about to join them and ask if they've seen Noah when I hear a familiar voice howling like a wolf which echoes through the whole damn apartment.

Everyone cheers. And I look up to see Noah at the top of his spiral staircase. With a fucking blonde girl hanging on his shoulder.

The sharp stab of pain that hits my gut is instant and crucifying.

It doesn't look like they're doing anything, not really, but they are coming from upstairs, which is where his bedroom is, and my knees wobble at all the horrific images flooding my brain.

Noah descends the stairs to rejoin his party, and he looks… Well, I'm not really sure how to describe it. I can only tell you what he's wearing and you can make your own assessment.

He has on his black skinny jeans, the ones that are all torn up and sit shockingly low on his hips. No shirt, as per usual, so his rippled and tatted torso is on display and covered by a large, extremely immodest fur coat that makes him look like a nineteen-seventies pimp.

I know it's faux-fur, because Noah's an animal lover, like me. But still, it's excessive, though I can't deny that he looks like a much younger, far hotter Mick Jagger.

And of course he's wearing his Ray Bans inside. That's probably the most normal thing about how he's dressed.

It's paining me to see him with that girl, but he's just so fucking sexy to look at, between my thighs clenches a little. The coat is hanging open to expose his muscles, and tattoos, and that god-forsaken nipple ring. He's so confident in himself and his body. His somehow charming cockiness and eccentric style just add to the layers of his drastically unorthodox persona.

It makes him damn-near irresistible, and clearly I'm not the only one who feels this way, because all the girls in the vicinity are swooning for him like an *actual* god just stepped into the room.

Especially the one hanging on him as they step off the stairs and move through the crowd.

Who the fuck is that bitch, anyway?? A leopard-print dress? Is this Halloween, and she's going as Fran Drescher circa 1995??

Noah shoves the girl off him and she scuttles over to another group of girls who all proceed to surround her and grasp at her arms, likely demanding to know what happened.

If anything... Is what my mind tries to tell me, but I'm almost tempted to eavesdrop on their conversation to find out for sure.

Rather than doing that, I push my way through all the people, drunk and high, bouncing around and dancing to the music of a DJ.

Yes, there's DJ here... *Wow, Noah. Really going all out for this one, huh?*

I'm salty. I can't help it. I fully *hated* seeing him with that girl, and now as I grow closer to where he's standing in the midst of his loyal subjects, I see a new girl, redhead this time, pressing her boobs into his side while he drapes his arm casually around her shoulder.

If I had eaten anything today, it would all be threatening to come up.

But no. I'm drinking on an empty stomach, which reminds me. I gulp back the rest of my glass and shove it at a guy whose frown I ignore as I stomp over to the star of the show.

Taking a page from my best friend's playbook, I warp my face into one of friendly, casual indifference as I stand right in front of him. He stops talking to whichever random dude he was speaking to mid-sentence when he sees me, and I swear I see him falter just the tiniest bit.

I wish I could say it's satisfying, but he's still touching some slutbag and all I want to do is rip her off my man and kiss him in front of everybody; to make it clear to each and every one of them that *I'm* the one he chases.

Not them. Me.

Noah cocks his head to the side, then slides his sunglasses down the bridge of his nose enough to peek at me over their top.

"Am I trippin balls, or is Alex Mackenzie here staring at me?" He rasps through a smirk that only I would know is a bit hesitant, as some guys laugh.

"You invited me, right?" I force myself to project a confident tone of voice. "Well, here I am."

Noah's arm slides off the redhead like she's nothing more than a beam he was supporting himself on, and he steps over to me slowly.

"Hey, fairy girl," he whispers. "Nice of you to show."

"I wanted to see you before you left," I mumble, because it's the truth.

"And before *you* leave," he adds, and it's now crystal clear that he's still very much upset with me. I assume the unanswered calls and texts didn't help.

Seek Me

I nod because it's all I can do. I'm hypnotized by him, which is bizarre because he's been my best friend for over three years. We've seen each other at our highest and lowest. We've made each other come, probably hundreds of thousands of times, and done things together that neither of us have ever done with anyone else.

You said you love me...

And now I'm just staring up at his gorgeous face, hidden behind those dark glasses for a reason. He's hurt. And if he feels like being vindictive, then this will be a very painful night for me.

"Looks like you're having fun," I nod behind him at the girl and he chuckles.

"I always have fun, baby. You know that." He twirls a strand of my hair around his finger.

"Yea, I do. Listen, could we maybe go somewhere and talk for a minute?"

He tugs on the strand, harder than I'm prepared for, and I gulp.

"Maybe in a bit," he brushes me off then turns back to his group of friends. And the girl. "Come find me later, pussy cat."

He winks at me then leans up against the wall next to the redheaded skank and gives her his undivided attention. Her eyes flick to mine and that bitch fucking *grins* at me, before squeezing herself in close to my best friend, trailing her fingers over the tattoos on his pelvis.

I'm sick. Sick to my motherfucking stomach.

I want to retch. But more than that, I want to attack her; rip out her goddamn red hair and shove it down her throat.

But I don't. Of course I don't. What would that get me anyway, besides some momentary gratification? My beef isn't with the girl, it's with my *friend* who just snuffed me in front of a crowd of assholes.

So instead I do the only other thing I can at a time like this. I do the thing I'm best at.

I leave.

I turn away from the snickers of Noah's fuckboy crew and shove myself far away from him and whatever the hell he's doing with that girl, and probably countless others tonight. I rush off, keeping my cool, pleading with my body not to show any emotion until I'm securely stuffed into a taxi on my way home.

Man, I feel bad for whatever poor, unsuspecting cab driver picks me up tonight.

I feel my phone buzzing in my clutch as I scurry, huffing and pulling it out to note an incoming call from an unknown number.

Who in the hell...?

I'm so distracted by whoever the crap is calling me during my non-dramatic exit that I bump right into the front of someone.

"Oh, shit! I'm so sorry!" I grumble and look up to see Sarah, Noah's costar and the only person I'm actually glad to see tonight.

Where was she ten minutes ago?!

"Alex! Hey!" She cheers, steadying me with her hands on my arms.

"Hi, Sarah," I breathe, tucking my phone away as I attempt a smile that doesn't quite work since I'm currently battling an emotional breakdown.

"I didn't know you were here!" She smiles, but it slips. "Are you leaving?"

"Yea…" I breathe.

And my eyes, my stupid betraying bitch eyes, slide back over to where Noah is standing, with the redhead, plus some new girl, both whispering things in his ear which I'm sure make them even sluttier than they look, while he graces them with a dreamy, if not remotely uninterested smile that they eat up like benzos.

Sarah follows my line of sight and her brow furrows in empathy for me and annoyance at her dumbass friend and costar, who's being the world's biggest dickhead right now.

"Are you okay?" She asks, and I know she means well, but it just makes me feel worse.

"Yea, I'm fine. I just need to leave." I force a small smile and give her a hug.

And then I peace the fuck out, not making the mistake of looking back again.

CHAPTER TWENTY EIGHT
Noah

Four Months Later...

I TAKE A SIP OF MY SCOTCH and let the burn slide down my throat. It's welcomed, the feeling. I almost wish it hurt *more*.

I glance at the knife the bartender has next to the limes he was just cutting, and I find myself wondering if I could sneakily pick it up; maybe press the blade into my thigh a little. Just as a distraction from what I'm feeling inside... Nothing major.

No scars, no slicing, no *suicide*. No, nothing so dramatic or permanent. Just a quick poke to my leg to release the noise that's built up inside my head.

I close my eyes and squeeze.

Am I really thinking about cutting myself right now? Is this really happening?

You need to get a grip, dude.

I take a deep breath in, hold it, then breathe out, surveying the crowd at Maxwell's once more. The rooftop deck is bustling, naturally, since it's a Saturday night in August. The city's burning from the inside out and rooftops are the only place in Manhattan where the breeze starts to resemble air conditioning.

I'm here with Andrew. We wrapped filming season four of the show a few weeks ago, and we get a bit of a break before the premiere and all the press tours begin. They're anticipating the highest attendance in years for our panels at SD Comic Con.

I can't wait. It's going to be so rad.

Needless to say, we deserve to blow off some steam before all that chaos ensues, which is why Andrew is staying with me until Tuesday. We have a small interview/photoshoot thing lined up for Monday, but it's nothing too serious. He's mainly here to avoid the situation with his wife, which apparently has gotten pretty dicey.

He told me that before he left for the airport yesterday, she told him she didn't care if he never came back. Imagine your wife, the mother of your children, saying that to you.

Hence why I'm not, and probably never will be, married.

Andrew's in a bad headspace right now. And I'm no better off, personally, but I'm used to wearing my upbeat, life-of-the-party mask to cheer up my friends. There's no reason I can't also use it to cheer myself up at the same time.

Two birds, meet stone.

Though I'm not exactly sure *how* to cheer myself up when all I can think about is inflicting small, secret pain on my body to distract myself because we're currently sitting in the exact spot where I met Alex four years ago.

Alex, my best friend and the best sex of my life.

Alex, the girl I'm in love with.

Alex, who flees the country every six months to get away from me.

Alex, who I hurt by acting like a selfish, immature asshat.

My eyes drift to the bartender's knife again and I swallow hard over the growing lump in my throat.

"How old do you think Slash is, anyway?" I ramble mindlessly to Andrew because *Jesus fuck,* I need an actual distraction.

I turn my gaze across the rooftop to Slash from Guns n Roses, who's here with a bunch of young hot girls, looking like the biggest mack daddy pimp on Earth. I can't help but grin to myself.

I could probably be like that someday. If I wasn't so desperately in love with my best friend.

"He's gotta be at least fifty-five, right?" I keep going, though Andrew has yet to answer me. "Sixty? I mean, Axl's at least fifty and I think he's younger. Or maybe he just did fewer drugs... What do you think?"

My friend is still silent to my right, so I swivel on my barstool to see why he's ignoring me and maybe kick him in the shin. And when I face him, I see exactly what's got his tongue.

Pussy.

Andrew is fucking *drooling,* almost visibly, over two girls who just walked onto the rooftop. One is blonde, wearing a yellow dress that accentuates what appears to be a nice plump handful of booty. And the other is this short, stacked little dark-haired thing in a strapless blue dress. Together they look like two pieces of the rainbow that got separated from the rest of the gang.

I glance at Andrew again and an evil grin tugs at my lips. He's clearly trying not to be obvious while checking out shorty in the blue dress so thoroughly that, with his hat on as he goes for inconspicuous, he really looks like a serial killer.

I chuckle to myself and shake my head. But my eyes dart back to the girl in blue, then return to Andrew. Then over, then back. I do this a few times, watching him watch her closely. And that's when I notice that I've *literally* never seen him so enthralled by anything before.

As much as he doesn't know this girl one bit - for all we know she could be married... *Okay, well maybe that's not the best example.* But still, he's seems like he's seeing something in her. Something he either hasn't seen in so long that he forgot what it's like to see it, or quite possibly something he's never seen before in his whole life, until this girl in the blue dress walked into the bar.

And if that's the case, I owe it to my best friend, who's been sinking deeper and deeper into his misery every day since we met, to help him meet this girl. Even if it's just for some casual flirting to ease his mind and get his confidence back, or some casual sex to cleanse his palette and remind him of what he's been missing.

Not that I condone people cheating. Adultery is a harsh word, but it's also hard to not to feel biased when you're watching your best friend bleed to death on a daily basis.

Nothing in this world is black and white. There are gray areas all around us, and as his best friend, I think I need to give Andrew a little nudge in any direction. Who knows if it'll be the right one, but if it gets him unstuck, I'd call it a victory.

"Wow," I lean closer, hoping he'll start paying some attention to my words. "Did you see those two girls who just came in?"

"No," he stutters fast, and I have to bite my tongue to hold back the laughter. "Where?"

He fakes looking around, acting like he has no idea who I'm talking about, making it clear he didn't catch me catching him.

"The two over there, in the blue and yellow," I nod to where the girls are having a seat on one of the benches.

He allows his eyes to land on the two lovely ladies, though it's apparent he's only seeing one of them.

"Right," he rasps, feigning disinterest. *I see right through your game, brother.* I'm about to ask him if he wants to go talk to them when he blurts out, "Which one do you like?"

I almost laugh out loud because he's *so* obvious, but I hold it in and force myself not to say I like Shorty Blue-Dress just to fuck with him.

I fight to smother my amused grin as I say, "The chick in the yellow is my type for sure. You know how I feel about blondes."

"Yes, I do," Andrew sighs in relief that widens my smirk.

He physically can't stop looking at her. This is going to be entertaining.

"Let's go talk to them," the sound of my voice startles him out his thoughts and his eyes widen.

"I don't know…" he brings his drink to his lips and takes a large gulp.

I can see the hesitation and insecurity all over his face, and it tugs on my already significantly fucked-up heart. I hate seeing him like this. I despise watching my best friend, a man who's so strong and poised, and also a total fucking badass, reduced to a nervous and melancholy shell of a human being.

Once more I look to the table where the girls are sitting, and I know I can take one for the team. I told Andrew that coming out tonight he'd be my wingman, but really I had very little intention of hooking up with anyone. I haven't been with anyone other than Alex in two years, and I've gotten comfortable in my state of crestfallen self-pity. Of course I would never let anyone know about that…

Gotta keep wearing the mask.

But now it seems the tables have turned, and I have a chance to be the wingman for Andrew. Who knows what will happen tonight, but if there's even the slightest chance something I do can bring him some joy - bring a little color to his world of gray - then I'm all in.

Who knows? It might end up being a good night.

Just as I'm devising a plan for us to approach the two girls, the one in the yellow dress stands up and begins walking right over to us, though it doesn't appear she's noticed us in the slightest. She just spotted an opening at the bar right next to yours truly and is coming up to get a drink.

I look away fast, so as not to reveal that I was just staring at her and her friend, and I see that Andrew is doing the same thing. I sip my drink and give her a moment to get settled in her spot, before I turn and plaster on my most inviting smile.

I'm doing this for Andrew.

"Hi," I say to the girl, who peeks some very sparkly hazel eyes at me. "What are you drinking?"

She faces me and smiles, polite yet slightly resistant. "Actually, I'm getting drinks for me and my friend." She nods over to the table where her friend is sitting alone.

Okay, making me work for it a little. I can appreciate that. "So, what are you *and* your friend drinking?"

Her eyes soften a bit while the smile remains intact. "I'm having a Grey Goose and cranberry, and my friend is having a whiskey ginger."

I nod to my bartender, who gets the hint right away and begins pouring their drinks.

Yellow-Dress Girl lifts her brow, and I can tell she's intrigued, though she's already playing me more aloof than any girl ever does. *Except Alex...*

I swallow hard and hold my mask in place. I will not lose my composure and blow this for Andrew because my mind is stuck on my absentee best friend.

"I'm Fiona," the girl tells me her name and holds out her hand to shake, which I do.

"Noah. And this is my friend, Andrew." I nod behind me at Andrew, assuming he's still there and hasn't left me to bum-rush the girl in the blue dress.

Yellow-dress, now revealed to me as *Fiona*, slips her hand out of mine and shakes Andrew's, confirming that he's still with me. *That's good. I'm doing this meaningless flirting for him, so the least he can do is stick around.*

"Thanks for the drinks," she grins. "Do you guys want to come join me and my friend, Tessa?" *Ah, and the object of Andrew's obsessing has a name. Andrew and Tessa. Has a nice ring to it.* "We found a seat over there. There's definitely enough—"

Fiona's invitation stops short when her gaze finds her friend. "Oh, you've *got* to be fucking kidding me."

I watch as her eyes narrow, more focused on her accent than what's suddenly bothering her. *Is she from Long Island? Too weird.*

"Something wrong?" I ask Fiona, wondering why she's going all Strong Island out of nowhere.

"Yea, I'll tell you what's wrong," she huffs, and I half expect her to pull out her earrings. *I don't recognize her, so there's no way she's from Rockville.* "We've been here all of five fucking seconds, and already this hipster douchebag thinks he can harass my friend."

She turns back to the bar to grab their drinks, as if she's about to high-tail it back to her table. Glancing over to check what has her so angry, I see a guy with an awful mustache sitting across from Andrew's new girlfriend.

Uh oh.

When I peek at Andrew and he looks enraged. Part hurt, part jealous, and maybe a little psycho-possessive over someone he *hasn't even met yet!* I really want to laugh, except that I'm a tad worried. I really can't be bailing him out of jail tonight.

For the sake of being the only rational person out of the three of us, I ask, "Are you sure she's being *harassed*? I mean, what if they're just talking?"

To which Andrew almost shouts in my face, "He looks like he's bothering her."

I press my lips together as my eyes widen directly at him in a *dude, really?* look. He simply shrugs and grabs the whiskey ginger ale meant for Tessa, squaring his shoulders in a newfound aura of determination. I know that look…

My best friend has a plan. Dear God, this could be dangerous.

Fiona looks puzzled for a moment as she stares up at Andrew with curious eyes. He winks at her and a slow smile spreads over her lips.

"What are you going to do?" She asks, sounding downright devious.

The girl is a nut, too! Am I the only one who's normal in this damn place?? Don't answer that.

"Watch and learn, kids," Andrew rasps, having fully regained his bravado. I must say, it's a welcomed improvement.

He stalks away without another word, and I turn to the bartender. "You got any popcorn?"

Fiona giggles, though now she seems a bit unnerved. "He's not going to kick that guy's ass, is he?"

"Honestly, your guess is as good as mine," I chuckle, then take her arm. "Come on. Let's go watch the show."

We scamper over just in time to see Andrew standing awfully close to Tessa with his hand on her waist. She's gazing up at him like the clouds have just parted and there are rays of sun shining down on his head. Like he's an *actual* white knight, saving her from a dragon.

I'm stunned fucking speechless right now. As hard as Andrew was drooling over this girl a moment ago, I'm about to hand her a napkin to wipe her mouth.

She's so fucking into him, too! Wow. Fascinating.

Andrew's gaze is on the mustached goon, seated at the table like an unsuspecting dumbass, and he looks pissed. More than pissed, he looks murderous. Now I'm a wee bit nervous again. I'm too drained to pull my best friend off this scrawny genius-bar-reject right now.

"Is there a problem here?" Andrew scowls at the guy, who's practically shitting himself under Andrew's death glare, which looks shockingly like his *Rex-stare* from the show.

Seek Me

"Oh my God... Andrew James!" Fiona whispers to herself, then turns her wide eyes up at me. "And you're Noah Richards."

"Guilty," I smirk, but I'm distracted from Fiona when my ears catch what Andrew is saying to the guy. "Wait, did he just say, *my wife*??"

We watch in fascination as Andrew takes Tessa's left hand in his and says something about how she's off-limits to everyone but her husband. *He's pretending to be her husband... Dear God. This dude is too much.*

"Isn't that right, baby?" Andrew says to Tessa in such a warm, affectionate tone it seems like they've been together for years.

I bite my lip, because it's so obvious from how they're looking at each other... How his hand is resting on the small of her back. How she's gazing up at him with hearts in her eyes.

He's a goner. Instant, immediate connection. I know the feeling...

I shake my head at where my thoughts are going and focus on the mustache guy, who's stuttering an apology to Andrew's dagger-eyes. He stands his lanky ass up and scurries off in defeat, with Andrew's protective watch locked on him until he's fully out of sight.

Fiona gasps at my side, which reminds me of her presence. She's practically giddy that my friend just put on such a performance to save hers. Really though, it was quite the scene.

A meet-cute if I've ever seen one.

Andrew and Tessa are gazing at each other like love-sick bunnies; he's hungrily trying not to stare at her rack, while she's biting her lip and popping out her chest. It's abundantly clear if you're paying attention to them, which it seems no one else is.

Andrew talks to Tessa, though they're speaking soft enough that I can barely hear what they're saying. Before I can try to distract the friend, wingman-style, so my boy can have his little introduction with his new crush, Fiona skips closer to them.

"That was amazing!" She cheers, clapping her hands together. "Did you see the look on that guy's face? Talk about getting shot down!"

I weigh in with my own encouragement. "Yea, holy shit, man! You fucking owned that guy."

Andrew grins with pride, but I'm not sure Tessa even heard us. She's still too busy ogling my best friend like he's wearing a suit made of her favorite treats and she wants to eat his clothes until he's naked.

Andrew *finally* introduces himself to Tessa and they shake hands. I hear

Tessa mention that she works for the network that produces *Hell Storm*, which is a pretty interesting coincidence since neither of these girls even recognized us until just a moment ago.

The new pair are flirting pretty hard already, so it seems like I'll have my work cut out for me tonight. I might not even have to hook up with the friend, although I'm beginning to wonder if that would be such a bad thing...

I might need a palette-cleanser myself. It's been a really long time since I've had casual sex. Plus, I'm still single and I haven't gotten laid in four months. My balls are constantly screaming at me to give them some relief that doesn't involve my hand and my imagination. Or equally pathetic, pictures of Alex on my cell phone...

I'm distracted out of my strange thoughts when I hear Fiona's voice telling Andrew she recognized his dangerous scowl from the show, which is amusing because I was having the same thought myself while watching him telepathically rip that dude a new one. So I laugh to make her feel funny, which she seems to appreciate. Then Andrew laughs because I'm laughing. And the next thing I know, we're all giggling up a storm and I'm thinking this dynamic little foursome will be my entertainment for the night. A nice distraction from the fucked-up-ness happening in my love life.

Truthfully, I don't mind. I'm doing this for Andrew, and he deserves it. Just seeing him smile and laugh now, his eyes brightening every time he looks at Tessa... He's like a completely different person from the downtrodden guy I was pep-talking not an hour ago.

If he has a good night, this will all be worth it.

"Do you guys want to sit down with us?" Tessa offers, and we obviously accept.

We all sit together at the bench table, and I set out to be the best damn wingman my British friend has ever had.

Hopefully, it works out for him.

I'm man enough to admit when I'm nervous.

I don't particularly subscribe to the idea that guys need to be *macho*, or *alpha*. I don't believe in the whole *asserting your dominance* thing. Okay, sure. Maybe occasionally I have moments when my testosterone gets the best of me. It

Seek Me

happens. But in the grand scheme of things, I roll with the punches.

I'm very comfortable in my own skin, and with who I am as a person; as a man.

So it doesn't make me feel like any less of a dude to admit that I'm shivering the slightest bit because I just kissed a girl who isn't Alex for the first time in two years.

It was a nice kiss. I didn't hate it.

What I do hate is the instant gnawing feeling of guilt that grips my stomach from my lips having touched lips that don't belong to the girl I'm in love with. Guilt is one of my least favorite emotions. Next to jealousy...

We brought the girls back to my place after spending hours at Maxwell's, chatting and drinking enough to put an elephant to bed. I could tell Andrew was dying to be alone with Tessa, and it's hard to get any privacy out in public when you're us.

So in my quest to be a damn good wingman, I invited Fiona and Tessa to my apartment for more drinks in a more intimate setting. When we got here, Fiona suggested doing tequila shots, and the warm and fuzzies from all the booze, mixed with seeing my best friend flirting mercilessly with a girl he clearly wants more than he wants to breathe, drove me to take a leap and go for a kiss.

I'm not really sure why. I guess I just wanted to see if I would like it; to see if kissing someone other than Alex gave me even ten percent of the feelings I get when I kiss her.

It wasn't ten. Maybe three or four.

But now Fiona's pressing me up against my breakfast bar, running her hands all over me and I'm so light-headed I'm seeing spots.

"Um... sorry..." I blink slowly and attempt to compose myself. "I'm not sure if I can..."

"Are you alright?" Fiona asks, sounding genuinely concerned, which is sweet.

I don't want to lead her on, because she seems like a great girl. But I should tell her the truth. Anything I were to do with her tonight, my heart definitely wouldn't be in it.

"Yea, I just need you to know that... I'm hung up on someone," I murmur, chewing on my lip. "She's not my girlfriend or anything, but it's... complicated."

She nods, her fingers still trailing along my shoulders. "I get it. I'm kind of in the same boat." I raise my brow at her, signaling that I want to hear more. "There's this guy back home in Boston... I've been waiting for him to ask me out forever, but I'm starting to think maybe he doesn't like me like that."

Her lips twist into a sad little frown, which is really cute for some reason. So I take her chin in my fingers, lifting her gaze back to mine.

"No offense, but he sounds like an idiot," I tell her, and she beams.

"Look, how about this," she starts, the confidence in her tone commanding and sort of sexy. "We have fun tonight. Do whatever feels right... But with no strings attached. I'm not looking for serious, and I know you aren't either. We play wingman and wingwoman to our friends and enjoy ourselves in the process. And then after tonight, we can go our separate ways and hopefully figure out our messy love lives."

An appreciative grin forms on my mouth. "You mean like, a *palette-cleanser*?"

"Exactly," she nods.

I consider what she's suggesting for a moment.

Maybe this is just what I need. It could even help me better understand my feelings for Alex. After all, she's likely hooking up with many a hot Spanish dude right now, a thought that makes me feel murderous, so I block it out fast before I can lose my mind any further.

Fiona is hot. And she's nice, and a little crazy, which is to be expected since she's from Hempstead. We basically grew up right near each other, even though I'm a solid thirteen-years older than her, a fact which neither she, nor Tessa, seem to mind very much about their present company.

Who's to say I shouldn't be living my single life to the fullest while Alex is doing the same thing in Barcelona? Especially since I toned it down exponentially in the last couple years. I practically turned it off completely, for everyone but my best friend.

But I've been sullen and brooding for four months now. It's time to get back out there. To be *me* again.

I'm done wallowing. I'm making the best of this.

"Okay," I've decided. "I'm in."

Fiona and I shake on it and she kisses me this time. It's up to five percent now.

I glance behind Fiona's head at Andrew, who's grinding himself in between Tessa's parted legs, and I bite my lip.

"Let's give them some privacy," I whisper and take her hand, dragging her quietly into the living room.

"You should put on some music," she suggests. "Ooh! Can I hook up my phone? I have a great playlist."

Seek Me

My inner whiny bitch wants to protest, because what's wrong with my music?

Alex likes my music.

I shake my head and force a smile. "Sure. I think I have a cable somewhere…"

I could probably just hook it up with Bluetooth, but I'm too preoccupied with thoughts of missing Alex to think rationally right now. I'm distracted, and I don't want to be.

Fiona hands me her phone with the playlist up, and before I can comment on at least three songs I see right away that make me nervous, a frazzled looking Andrew stalks through the room with his phone in his hand, making a beeline for the guest room.

Oh boy… I wonder what that's all about.

Tessa meanders slowly into the room to join us, her face flushed and dismal.

"What's wrong?" Fiona asks, comforting her friend with an arm around her waist.

"Can we talk?" Tessa whispers, eyes darting to me quickly, as if she can't say whatever she needs to in front of me.

"You guys can go out on the terrace if you want," I offer, then nod to the door.

Fiona gives me a gracious smile and takes a woeful Tessa outside, leaving me alone with a useless auxiliary cord in my hand and a myriad of confusing thoughts swimming through my brain.

When Andrew finally reemerges from the guest room, he informs me that his wife called right as he and Tessa were about to kiss, and he seems torn up over it. So I give him some reassurance and set out to get the music going so I can step up my wingman game.

Andrew goes to get Tessa, and Fiona comes back in to let them hash it out. I feel bad for my friend, because I already know what he's up against. His situation is anything but easy, and I can only imagine the guilt he must be feeling at lusting over someone who isn't his wife. He's been with the same person for ten years, and now it's over between them and he wants to be happy again. I don't blame him in the slightest.

And yet there's a ton standing in his way. He's got an uphill battle ahead of him, and tonight could be just the motivation he needs to finally move on. I just hope Tessa will give him a chance to prove himself.

"Are they gonna be alright?" I ask Fiona, scrolling through her music in search of anything that isn't Ariana Grande.

"Yea, I think so," she huffs. "Tessa's been through a lot. She deserves to have a little fun. But I know Andrew's still married, and it's a tough situation…"

"Yea. He's been so unhappy," I mumble. "I don't think I've seen him smile as much in years as he has in the last two hours."

Fiona grins then bites her lip. "That's sweet. You obviously care a lot about him."

"He's my best friend," I shrug. "Well, him and…" My voice trails off and I clear my throat.

Fiona gives me a sympathetic look. "We should drink more. Like, *a lot* more."

"Agreed," I chuckle.

Tessa and Andrew return from the terrace hand-in-hand and I'm relieved. I was hoping this whole thing wouldn't end for him before it even got started.

Tessa, the former bartender, makes us all some drinks, and we bring them into the living room.

I'm staring off into space, absentmindedly grazing my fingers up and down Fiona's arm as she leans against my side. I have to appreciate how low-maintenance this girl is because I don't think I could handle someone in need of constant attention right now. I'm way too in my head.

I'm not even sure what it is I'm thinking about. It's almost as if I'm in a trance. I'm pretty drunk, but still coherent, and my mind is flashing through memories of the last time I saw Alex.

And how much of an asshole I was to her.

I don't deserve her. I'm glad she's in Barcelona, living her life. Probably kissing tall, dark and handsome guys while sipping Sangria and forgetting all about her douchebag, bachelor best friend, who loves her but can't find it in himself to ask her to stay…

I'm awoken from my hurtful inner monologue when Fiona jumps off the couch and scrambles to her purse. Her newest idea is that we play strip poker. And I'm hesitating… *Again.*

But when I see how excited Andrew looks at playing strip poker with Tessa, I force myself to get on board, for my friend.

We play. We laugh. We flirt. Well, I flirt with Fiona and Andrew flirts with Tessa.

It's fun. I'm having *fun.*

Really trying to convince yourself, huh bro?

I'm teetering on the edge of my emotional sanity, so when Fiona loses her hand, and then her panties, I make a snap decision, and I take her upstairs to

Seek Me

my room.

I tell myself I'm doing it to leave Andrew alone with Tessa. I'm giving my best friend an excuse to get closer to the girl he can't stop watching and touching, and that's more pertinent than whatever Fiona and I are going to do…

Alone. In my bedroom.

I gulp as I bring her inside and shut the door. My breathing is heavy already and nothing's happened yet. It doesn't even feel like I'm here right now. I'm outside myself; watching the whole scene unfold like a movie.

Fiona bites her lip as she stares at me with wide, glassy eyes. The lighting in my bedroom is dim, shadowing her curves as she slips the yellow dress over her head.

Now she's standing in front of me, completely naked, and I could pass out from the anxiety rocking me down to the core. I lock my eyes on hers, because I'm afraid to look anywhere else as I squeeze my hand into a fist repeatedly.

"Noah, I know you're unsure about this, and you're probably just doing it so Andrew can be alone with Tessa, which I think is the sweetest thing ever." She steps closer to me and I'm so stiff, I'm a Noah sculpture. "If you tell me you don't want to do anything, that's fine. We can just hang out in here and let them do their thing. But honestly, I kind of need this. And I think you do too."

I suck in a deep breath and hold on to it for dear life. She's standing right in front of me now, and my weak, curious eyes slide down to her tits; round and perky, nipples pert from the chill of the air, and probably the thrill of this heady, confusing moment.

She reaches up and brushes her fingers through my hair, her breasts pressing into my chest. I close my eyes and whimper.

Fuck, I don't know if I can do this…

What the hell happened to me?? Alex ruined me for casual sex.

"Use me, Noah," she hums, tugging my face slowly down to hers until I can feel her warm breath on my lips. "Let's make each other feel better."

And then I black out.

Not really. It *feels* like I've blacked out, though I'm fully aware of what I'm doing.

But I go on auto-pilot. A robot version of the old Noah takes over, and I kiss the blonde girl, hard and fast, wiping away all my thoughts and emotions, and just focusing on the physical.

I've done it so many times before, it becomes like a reflex. Like riding a bicycle, I get used to the motions again, and after only a few frantic, hazy moments, Fiona's in my bed, and we're panting and touching and tasting, and doing all the things I remember doing with dozens of women before the one who made me want to stop.

But I don't stop, because this feels necessary.

I'm not in love with this girl. She's not the one I want to be with, exclusively, for as long as she'll have me. But that girl isn't here, and this one is. So I don't stop, not for any reason, until I'm fucking Fiona hard from behind, and she's screaming my name, loud.

And when I come, I don't cry out Alex's name, because this is an awakening of sorts.

I'm not in love with this girl. But for right now, she's exactly what I need.

I let Fiona sleep in my bed last night, but we didn't cuddle. She didn't try to spoon me, and I didn't instinctively gravitate toward her the way I do with Alex. I suspect that Fiona understands what this is about, and I'm beyond grateful to her for giving me my space.

I wake up before her and shower alone, washing away the guilt and shame that always accompanies a night of drinking and fucking someone I have no feelings for, other than what seems to be a mutual appreciation for one another's bodies and if I'm being honest, a budding friendship.

Fiona's a cool girl. She's not like other casual hookups, in that she has no presumptions about getting me to fall in love with her. It's just sex, and it's fine. We're playing wing-people for our best friends and getting our rocks off in the process. It could easily be depressing, but I'm trying not to go there.

When I come back to my bedroom in just a towel, Fiona's snooping around my dresser and I watch her for a moment, grinning with her blissfully unaware that I've caught her red-handed.

She picks up a framed picture of Alex and me at Great Adventure and studies it for a moment. Her face doesn't appear jealous, or put-off. She actually smiles, and I think now's a good time to clear my throat.

She startles and almost drops the frame. "Jesus. You scared me." She breathes out hard and sets the picture back down.

"Whatcha doin?" I sneer, narrowing my gaze at her.

"I know you told me last night, but I have to ask again because I've been lied to enough times to know answers are always different the next morning..." she says with conviction as she stares at me. Her eyes are a swirling mix of green and brown, and it's a surprisingly nice combination. "Do you have a girlfriend?"

I step closer to her and sigh. "No. I don't have a girlfriend. That's my best friend. Alex."

She nods and lifts her brows. "Hm. Interesting."

She seems like she wants to say something, so I change the subject before she can. "Shower's all yours. Clean towels in the closet."

She pulls a hesitant smile and scampers into the bathroom without another word.

I get dressed and sneak downstairs to get us some coffee. I hear the shower running in the guest bath as I pour two cups. And then I hear muffled moans that echo, as if they're coming from said shower.

I grin stupidly, because my boy's getting it in, and as complicated and taboo as their mingling is, I'm happy for Andrew. I saw the way he was looking at Tessa last night. I'd be willing to bet my entire collection of Ray Bans he's already in it for more than just the one night. And morning.

I scurry back upstairs with the coffees just as Fiona is turning off my shower. I sit on the edge of my bed and wait for her until she eventually emerges wearing her dress from last night, because she has nothing else to wear, which makes me feel bad that she's probably uncomfortable.

"I got you some coffee," I offer her the cup, and she takes a seat next to me, accepting it with a lustful expression on her pretty face.

"Thank you," she sips, and we sit in silence for a few more minutes.

It's not as awkward as it should be. In fact, her presence is calming me down a lot. At least it's stopping me from obsessing and moping like I otherwise would be.

"Last night was fun," I tell her with an easy smile.

She smirks in return. "Oh, it definitely was."

"I was thinking, Andrew will probably want to spend the rest of his time here in New York with Tessa..."

"You think?"

"I *know*. Dude's smitten with your bestie. I can already tell he won't be letting her out of his sight as long as he can help it."

"Awww!" She squeals, giving me a pout complete with puppy dog eyes that make me scoff.

"Alright, simmer down," I laugh. "I'm just saying, if she wants to spend the night here again with him... It'd be cool for you to stay."

"Really?" She scrunches her nose, and it wrinkles up like a bunny rabbit. She's very cute, this girl. She looks like a Barbie, the polar opposite of my dark-haired fairy girl. "So you'd let me stay here again just so your friend can get with my friend some more?"

I shrug and nod. "Yea. Extending wingman duties over the entire weekend isn't something I've explored before. But I know Andrew needs this."

"You're basically the best friend on Earth," she says matter-of-factly. "Not a lot of guys would volunteer their whole weekend like that just so a buddy can get laid as much as humanly possible in two days."

"I do what I can," I bow and Fiona giggles. "When are you going home?"

"I was going to leave tomorrow sometime," she answers, sipping her coffee again. "I haven't checked the train schedule yet."

A train? No, that doesn't work for me. We can think of a better way to get young Fiona here home, I'm sure. It's the least I can do.

"Okay, then it's settled. You guys will stay here, and we'll make this a weekend affair." I pause and cringe. "Oh, God... please don't tell them I said *affair*."

Fiona chuckles. "My lips are sealed. And I think you're right. I know Tessa needs this just as bad. She's been fucked up for a while now herself."

"What's the deal with her husband?" I ask without thinking and she freezes, her eyes widening in unease. "Okay, sorry. Forget I asked." I hold my hand up and she lets out a steady breath.

"It's not my place to talk about it," she mumbles with her gaze stuck on the floor.

"Message received."

"All I'll say is that you better make sure he doesn't hurt her," she warns, turning a protective glare on me. "Or I'll chop both of your balls off. Meaning you *and* Andrew. All four balls. One. At. A. Time."

I laugh, but she doesn't, which makes me gulp. "Okay. Hurting Tessa equals ball removal. Got it."

This time she laughs, and I allow myself to smile, though I have a strong suspicion she's not joking. Not one bit.

Gotta watch out for those Hempstead girls, man. Their hotness is always served with a heaping side of crazy.

We wait a little while longer in my room, to give the love birds their private time. I turn the TV on and we watch some boring reality show that Fiona seems

Seek Me

rather invested in.

As much as I'm unsure about having her here all weekend, I can't deny that she's an easy person to spend time with. She's cool and interesting, and we've bonded over Long Island stuff, so I already have a bit of a kinship with her, though it's not romantic, despite how we spent last night.

When we eventually make our way back downstairs, I notice that Andrew and Tessa are sitting on my couch, breathing heavy with flushed, guilty faces.

They were totally just banging on my couch.

I can't help but laugh to myself as Fiona and I split up, and I take Andrew into the kitchen to interrogate him. He caves after two seconds, and tells me about him and Tessa's naked adventures, culminating in an unfinished poke session on my leather couch.

And even though he gives me a flimsy apology, it's obvious that he's not sorry, not even slightly. Because he's really feeling this girl a lot. It was obvious from the moment they met last night that he wouldn't be able to keep himself from her, regardless of society strictly forbidding them from being together right now.

But fuck society. When it comes to my friend's happiness, I'd rather do everything in my power to help him be with the girl that makes him smile so much he looks borderline insane.

After that, we agree to spend the day gallivanting around the city. Andrew comes here to visit me a lot. More now that his home life is sufficiently strained, but there's still so much he hasn't seen. So I decide part of my wingman duties will include a day-long double date to all the fun places I haven't yet taken him, and that he obviously hasn't explored with Tessa.

Our first stop is Charlie's diner, because we're all famished and hungover.

The moment we sit down, Andrew and Tessa are whispering things to each other, and sneaking little touches under the table, thinking no one's noticing when they're actually the most undeniably love-struck people I've ever seen together.

And not five minutes later, Tessa is stalking off to the restroom, looking flustered.

Andrew taps his fingers on the table for about thirty seconds, fidgeting in place before he scoots out of the booth, muttering a weak, "Excuse me."

And he goes after her.

I take a deep breath and settle into my seat. "Well, they'll probably be gone for a while."

"They're fucking inseparable already," Fiona giggles, flipping through her menu. "It's really cute. I don't think I've ever seen Tessa like this before. Not even with Devin…"

I consider this for a moment.

I've only met Andrew's wife, Vivian, once before. We were doing a convention in London, so I had dinner at their house, and met the famous Michael and Lucy, Andrew's adorable, picture-perfect children. I've also talked to Vivian on video chat a few times, when she'd call Andrew in Georgia, early on in filming seasons one and two.

While she seems like a nice enough person - she certainly has that posh, prim and proper yet slightly detached British lady vibe going on - not once did I ever witness her and Andrew interacting the way he has been with Tessa, and after only knowing her for barely a full day, no less.

That has to mean something. What, I have no idea, but I'm thinking he won't be letting this end when he goes home on Tuesday.

"Tessa wants Andrew to stay at her place tonight," Fiona continues talking to me, oblivious to my never-ending train of complex thoughts. "She wants to be alone with him. I was thinking I could get a hotel -"

"What?" I cut her off fast, and she looks taken aback. "No fucking way. You came here to hang with your friend. If Tessa's out, then I'm in. You're staying at my place. Don't be ridiculous."

A slow smile stretches over her lips and she nods. "Okay. Thanks."

"Not necessary," I mutter, and as casual as I'm making this whole thing seem, my stomach is tightening up in angst as I wonder what we'll do all night, alone in my apartment.

Sure, the sex last night was refreshing. It was different, and it took my mind off the Alex of it all for a little while. But I'm not sure if I should do it again. I'm not even sure if I *could*…

Well, of course I could. My dick is still fully functional, after all.

But it feels like giving up on casual sex with strangers for two years changed things a lot. I'm not the same Noah I was before Alex came back from Budapest. My whole life feels different now, and I can't tell if I resent Alex, or love her even more for it.

Either way, I need to get the hell out of my head, and back down on planet Earth.

"What are you getting?" I ask Fiona, fighting against my distractedness tooth and nail.

Seek Me

"Hmm... I don't know," she murmurs. "How are the waffles here?"

My head springs in her direction as my heart lurches inside me.

"That bad?" Her forehead lines with worry, the look on my face likely giving her the impression that ordering waffles here could mean food poisoning.

I open my mouth to speak, but I'm finding it difficult to produce words at the moment. It's more than odd that something as simple as *waffles* can send my heart crashing into my gut. But now my mind is flooded with memories of the night I met Alex...

In this very diner, eating waffles and trying to get a read on her. The mysterious, raven-haired, tattooed beauty with bruises on her arms and her soul.

Something about her called to me on such a deep level that I instantly changed. And I see that now.

It wasn't some slow development that happened over months and months of continued friendship. It smashed through my world like a brutal and dazzling hurricane, tearing apart the person I was before and forcing me to see everything with new eyes.

My life. Myself. *Everything* changed that night, all thanks to Alexandra Mackenzie, and her beautiful, broken heart.

The desire to hear her voice comes at me like a wrenching need, one that demands satisfaction; a longing in my bones. I've never felt something so powerful, and yet hopelessly out of reach. It settles uncomfortably in my chest, and I clear my throat before I start openly weeping for no reason.

"No..." I grunt, swallowing hard as I go for my glass of water. "Actually, they're really fucking great."

Fiona shrugs off my pensiveness and closes her menu. "I think I'll just have a salad. Same as Tess."

I breathe out in secret relief. *Thank God.*

Hours and a whole slew of New York City-themed activities later, Fiona and I return to my apartment. We parted ways with Andrew and Tessa, saying our goodbyes for the night so they could enjoy a private sleepover at Tessa's place in Brooklyn.

Andrew and I agreed to meet up tomorrow morning for the magazine interview, after which we'll all have dinner together, and I'll see to it that Fiona gets back home to Boston safely and comfortably.

If someone had asked me years ago if I would ever play host to a miscellaneous girl for an entire weekend just so my friend could pursue her friend, I would ask who kidnapped me and if the ransom note was made of letters cut out from magazines, because I've always found that interesting.

Fiona putters through my living room hesitantly, and I fidget around with no idea what to say or do next.

"I'm gonna go smoke," I tell her while wandering toward my terrace. "You can join me if you want."

When I get outside, I'm more thankful than I'll admit that she chooses not to.

I sit on the chaise and light up a joint, smoking to calm my nerves while I pull my phone out of my pocket. I bring up Alex's contact on WhatsApp and stare at it for a long time, with my thumb hovering over the call button.

I've still never actually called Alex when she's away, nor has she ever called me. It's like an unspoken agreement between us, that when she's traveling we just let each other be, and save all the words and feelings for when she's back, and we can express them in person.

But the more I think about it, the stupider I feel. How differently would things have turned out if I had just called her when she was away that first time? If I had told her I missed her; that when she comes back, I want things to be *real*.

I shake my head and tuck my phone back in my pocket, putting to rest with it the idea that Alex and I could overcome this distance with one measly phone call.

It won't change anything. I'm beginning to fear that we're too far gone.

I go back inside and see Fiona on the couch, watching TV. I take a seat on the other end and we watch the dumb reality show in silence, every once in a while laughing at something that happens, or making hum-drum conversation about *who* did *what,* resulting in *no one cares.*

This goes on for a while until my eyelids are heavy and I'm fighting back sleepiness. I stretch my arms behind my back and stand up slowly.

"I'm gonna crash," I shift my weight back and forth. "The guest room's all yours. Or if you want, you could sleep in my bed again. Um… I don't know if that's weird, but whatever makes you comfortable."

Fiona stares up at me, waging some kind of internal war that's apparent from the way her brows are stitched together.

Seek Me

"It's okay. I'll take the guest room," she finally utters, and I can't tell if I'm relieved or disappointed.

I'm so out of my element right now.

"Okay," I nod. "Goodnight."

She mutters the word back to me, and I'm a few steps in before I turn around and go back to her. I lean down to where she's sitting and kiss her lips. Just one small, quick kiss, because I feel like it's necessary for reasons I truly don't understand.

"Sleep tight, Fi," I whisper, and her slow exhale is the last thing I let myself hear before I'm darting to the stairs and heading up to bed.

Once I'm there, I strip down to my boxers, a restlessness churning in my belly. I pace around for a few minutes, debating what I'm doing.

There's a hot girl downstairs. A girl whom I've already fucked once, during which we both enjoyed ourselves. I could potentially do it again. Why not?

I'm single, she's single. It makes sense. If tonight is her last night here, then why wouldn't we make the best of the *reset weekend*, then go back to our regular lives and figure our shit out? I'll probably never see her again. Wouldn't it ease my mind and bring me some reprieve, like it did last night?

I huff out hard and shake my head, climbing into bed and burrowing myself beneath the covers that shield my exposed skin from the chill of the central air. Turning off my thoughts is a challenge, but they're so cluttered and congesting my head, that it eventually sets me adrift.

My eyes are closed, sleep settling over me when I hear a noise. It sounds like a knock at my door.

I blink groggily in the dark and whisper, "Come in."

I'm doubting whether she heard me, but then the door opens and Fiona steps inside, padding over to my bed. It's dark in the room, so all I can see is the halo of golden hair flowing from her head, and her gleaming hazel eyes.

She climbs into my bed and cuddles under the blankets. She turns on her side to face me, and we stare at each other for a moment, saying nothing. Just breathing and staring, staring and breathing. This has to be one of the most bizarre encounters I've had with a random sex partner. Really, this whole weekend has been strange in many ways, but it's still a promising distraction.

Neither of us says a word, but after a few more quiet breaths I realize that we're inching towards each other. Soon enough, she's slipping her leg in between my thighs and running her hands up my chest.

Fiona feels me up for a bit, so I return the favor, cupping her butt and bringing her flush against me so I can grind my hardening erection on her. She rolls on top of me and kisses my neck, trailing her tongue down to my nipple and sucking the piercing between her lips.

"Fuck..." I hum, reaching inside her boy-short panties she bought earlier while we were out shopping, and slide my fingers through her wet slit.

She moans, but takes it away from me when she continues down my torso, yanking off my Calvins and covering the head of my cock with her mouth. I groan and thrust, feeding it between her lips while she sucks, harder and deeper, blowing me as I close my eyes and clear my mind.

It's working. I'm no longer stressed, that's for damn sure.

Fiona fucks me with her mouth until I'm grabbing her hair by the roots, then she stops and removes her panties quick, scrambling over me before going for the drawer of my nightstand.

"In here?" She asks breathlessly, and I assume she means *is this where the condoms are?* So I nod, swallowing hard as she pulls one out and tears it open with her teeth.

Everything quickly becomes blurry. We're both in somewhat of a daze as she rolls the condom on me and wastes no time getting seated with every inch of me buried inside her plush walls.

And then she holds herself steady with palms flat on my pecs and rides me into a naked, sweaty stupor.

It doesn't take us long to get off, and after we do, we roll onto our backs and pass out, side-by-side in easy, comfortable silence.

Crazy weekend, man, is all I can think as I say goodbye to Andrew and Tessa after dinner.

He's staying at Tessa's again tonight before his flight back to London tomorrow morning. They also made plans to see each other in three weeks, when Andrew comes back to New York to hang out with me and Johnny, thus confirming my suspicions that in the span of forty-eight hours, he's been swept away by this little teal-eyed beauty, more than he has been by anyone or anything before.

I'm happy for Andrew. Ecstatic, really, and not jealous *at all*.

Why would I be jealous, anyway? Because it took him two days to meet and admit his feelings for the girl of his dreams, while I've been tip-toeing around my secret love for my best friend for four years and can barely even admit to myself, let alone her, that I want to be her boyfriend?

Not the slightest bit jealous. Stop looking at me like that.

I hug the both of them goodbye, as does Fiona, and then they hop into the Navigator with Jimmy, who drives them back to Brooklyn.

And I'm left alone with my new *friend*. The sorbet.

I'm trying not to let things be awkward with me and Fiona, but part of me is antsy to get her back to my place so I can put her in the car and send her on her way. Not that I didn't have fun this weekend. I definitely did, especially because if I'm being honest, I really needed to get laid.

But despite the sex-factor, I also happen to think Fiona's a super cool chick. Whoever she ends up with will be a lucky guy. But it sure as shit won't be me.

Sorry to anyone who's been shipping us. Fioah ain't happening.

We take a cab back to my apartment, where the car service I hired to bring Fiona back to Boston is waiting. I take her hand and walk her to the vehicle, the most confusing anxiety thrumming in my blood. For someone who spent the last two nights having sex, I'm certainly wound up.

"Thank you so much for a kick-ass weekend, Noah," she smiles, hooking her arms around my shoulders in a friendly hug. "You're a really awesome friend. I hope it works out with the girl."

"Same to you, though I think you should hold out for someone who knows exactly what he has when he's with you," I say by her ear, squeezing her tight. "You'll meet someone like that someday. And when you do, the chemistry will be so undeniable you won't need to worry about waiting for him to make a move. Because he won't be able to *not* move for you."

Fiona pulls back and gazes up at me, a look of gratefulness shining in her eyes. "Noah... enough dicking around. Go get the girl."

I huff a small laugh and kiss her lips softly. It's a sweet goodbye kiss, though it feels more platonic than anything.

And that's good. My mind is finally clear thanks to this monumental weekend.

I know what I want now, and I don't think anything will change that. But getting it will be a different story.

"Get home safe, girl," I pat her on the butt then open the door for her.

She smirks at me. "I will. Thanks for the ride."

She winks and I laugh as she closes the door and the car drives off.

I watch it go, breathing in the summer air. As soon as the car is out of sight, I turn and run into my apartment.

I walk straight to my terrace and sit down outside on my favorite chaise lounge, lighting up a joint and shimmying my phone out of my pocket. I take a drag, my fingers shaking as I tap on Alex's contact.

But this time, I don't hesitate.

I press call.

The phone is ringing, and I'm fucking *trembling*. It's so unnecessary, I take another long drag hoping the weed will tone down my blood pressure just a tad.

The phone continues to ring, and it occurs to me that I have no clue what time it is in Barcelona.

Fuck... This was a stupid idea. She's probably sleeping... She's not even going to answer. You idiot.

Oh God, what if she's out with a guy?? What if she's fucking him right now?!

Man, you're a dumbass. Why don't you ever think before you -

"Hello?" Alex's quiet, raspy voice comes through the line and my heart thumps so hard I have to lie back to stop it from knocking me over.

I take a moment to find my words, but eventually I rumble, "Hey. Hi... Sorry, am I waking you up?"

"Yea, a little..." she whispers, and I feel bad, and stupid, until she says, "But I don't care. I'm so happy to hear your voice. I'm only fifty percent sure this isn't a dream."

I chuckle through an unwavering smile. "It's not a dream. Alex, I miss you so much... I know we don't do this. We don't talk when you're gone... But I just couldn't fucking stand it anymore."

She whimpers. "Me either. I miss you more than words can describe."

My chest warms as my heart opens right up for her. "Baby, I'm so sorry... For the way I acted, the night you came over. To my party..." I gulp over my shame. "I was such a fucking asshole."

"It's okay, Noah. I accept your apology. I know that's not you." She sounds so sure of this, it has me levitating off the chaise, weightless from how much she cares about me. And how much she knows me.

"I was just hurting... But I shouldn't have taken that out on you. It was immature. God, I felt like such a dick for treating you that way."

"Hey. Stop it." I can tell by her voice she's waking up more now. And I love how I can tell things like that just from her tone. "I know I haven't made things easy on you..."

Seek Me

"None of this is your fault," I hum, staring up at the sky peeking through the trees that surround me. "Look, I've had a lot of time to think... And what it all comes down to is how much you mean to me."

She's quiet for a moment before she responds. "How much?"

"More than all the soccer balls in Spain," I grin and she giggles.

"That's a lot."

"I know."

"I can't stop thinking about you, Noah..." Her tone makes my toes curl and my dick throb. "No matter what happens, it always comes down to you and me."

I nod as if she can see me. "It does."

So then why the fuck can't we just be together?

"I'm coming home in two weeks," she tells me and I startle at how quickly I'm overcome with staggering excitement.

"Is that right?" I try to play it cool, though I'm wiggling around more than I can stand.

"Yea. I can't wait to see you," she purrs in my ear, stiffening my cock. "Will you drop everything for me again?"

I grin stupidly. "Mmm... I don't know. I think I'll have some pretty important plans in two weeks..."

"Please?" Her voice is downright erotic, and she's begging for *me*.

I might need to jerk off when this conversation is over.

"Don't beg... You're driving me crazy," I growl, adjusting my hard-on in my jeans while forcing my hand not to linger.

"Sorry... I just..." she gives up and sighs. "I just want to be in your arms again."

My full heart aches behind my ribs. "Alex, I told you I'll drop anything and everything to be with you, you know that. It won't change, not ever."

"You're right... I do know that." She breathes out a soft noise. "I'll call you when I'm back. I'll come to your place right away."

"I'll be counting the fucking minutes, baby." She makes a satisfied huff, then yawns into the phone. "There's so much I want to know about your trip, but you're clearly tired, so I'll let you get back to sleep."

"No, Noah, wait," she rushes the words out. "Can you please just leave me on the phone? Until I fall asleep?"

I press my palm down hard over my heart, to make sure it's still intact. "Of course, baby."

"Keep talking to me..." she drifts.

Savor this moment. "Anything for you, beautiful fairy girl."

CHAPTER TWENTY NINE

Alex

Two Weeks Later...

Me: Be there in 10

Noah: I'm going to pee my pants

Me: Is that supposed to turn me on?

Noah: You're literally the only person I'd be willing to pee on. Or let pee on me.

Insert Ron Burgundy meme *Well, that escalated quickly.*

Me: I was just telling you I'll be at your house in 10 mins!

Noah: LOL sorry! I'm very excited to see you

Me: Clearly.

I bite down on my lower lip, attempting to smother my ridiculous smile.

Me: I'm excited to see you too...

Noah: I have a boner already

I laugh and roll my eyes, though the unrelenting grin on my lips beams like a neon sign.

Me: Keep it on ice, loverboy. I'll see you soon

Noah: ... Do you really want me to ice my dick?

Seek Me

Noah: Because I will. For you. *Insert several heart-eyed emojis*

I giggle like a cheerleader, then glance up to see the cab driver's eyes on me in the rearview mirror and press my lips together. *This guy thinks I'm weird. I guess I sort of am...*

I'm more than weird. I'm in love with my best friend, and I'm on my way to his apartment to see him after being away for four months.

I'm downright stupefied.

Me: No, I like him warm ;)

Noah: Jesus I'm so fucking turned on right now

Me: We're sex-crazed maniacs. That much is clear.

Noah: True story bro

Me: Turning onto your block

Noah: Alright use your key cuz I'm naked and covered in whipped cream. K byeeee!

I cackle out loud, with zero fucks given to the cab driver who thinks I'm nuts.

Because I am. Lookin so crazy in love, Beyonce-style.

Uh oh Uh oh Uh oh, oh no no.

I jump out of the cab like it's about to blow. I almost tuck and roll while it's still moving. Then I jaunt up the stairs to Noah's building, keying in the code and twitching like an antsy fiend all the way down the long hall. My shaky hands will barely allow me to insert the key into the damn keyhole.

Calm down, Alex. Breathe. It's just Noah. He's your best friend.

Above all else, remember?

The second I step inside, my body is immediately thrust into the door, effectively shutting it with a slam as my *best friend* pins me to it with his hips.

I barely have time to gasp before his lips are on mine in a searing kiss that makes me forget my name. *Alex? Who's Alex?* All I know is that I'm melting against his strapping hard body, fingers lacing in his hair to hold his face to me.

Noah's lips absorb mine, his tongue tracing the curve of my bottom lip before slipping into my mouth to seek my tongue. He shudders as he grinds against me, bruising my mouth with his forceful need, hands gripping my waist so hard it's as if he doesn't trust them not to go straight for my tits. Not that I would object to that...

"*My* lips..." Noah breathes, warm and minty, into my mouth, and I can't help but bite him just a little. "*My* Alex. Mine mine *mine*."

The word is like a prayer; a devotion that he chants with every soft breath in between sucking my lips with fervor. It synchronizes with my pulse, until I can feel it in every rhythmic beat.

Mine mine mine mine mine.

"Living without you..." he pants, a hand finally leaving my hip to slide up to the base of my throat, "Is like living without oxygen." I whimper as his lips trail to my jaw. "I can finally *breathe* again."

"I missed you," I hum because it's my truth. "Every day without you felt like an eternity."

"I'm here," he rumbles, placing his hand over my thumping heart. I do the same, feeling his rap against my palm, beneath the soft material of his t-shirt, and the hard muscle of his pectoral. "And now you're here."

"We're here," I speak breathlessly as he rests his forehead on mine.

"Finally."

Noah unexpectedly lifts me up by my butt, wrapping my thighs around his waist as he carries me to the living room, all the while with me kissing his neck and jaw, sucking his earlobe. His smell is overtaking me. I feel like I just huffed paint, and I'm soaring into an abyss of colored lights and blinding euphoria.

He lays me down on the couch and crawls over me, nudging my legs apart with his knee so he can wedge his big body in between them.

"Hi," he whispers through an elated smile, then kisses me softly. "Mmm... God, you taste like heaven."

"I had a dream about you on the plane," I ramble mindlessly, succumbing to the sensation of him rubbing his erection on my clit through our pants.

"What was I doing?" He bites my lip almost possessively. *Mine.*

"What you're doing now," I slink my hands up under his shirt and scratch his abs. "Only on my kitten."

He pulls back enough for me to see the salacious gleam in his coal eyes, so dark I can barely tell where his irises end and his pupils begin.

"That sounds like fun," he cocks a brow, then wastes no time licking down my throat.

He nips the peaks of my nipples through my top, under which I'm braless,

Seek Me

because why the fuck not? I dressed for Noah's easy access tonight anyway, in some of his gray sweatpants that I stole last year and a tight white crop-tank. No bra, no panties.

No illusions about playing hard-to-get.

I landed at JFK only eight hours ago. I went straight home, took a quick nap, showered and came here. Because fuck literally *everything* else in the world that isn't Noah Richards.

"Can I fuck your tits?" He mumbles, practically motor-boating me through my shirt. "Ooh, and your mouth? And your sweet, tight pussy… *Yes…* and your even tighter -"

My groan cuts off his erotic demands. He's killing me right now, with his words and his clearly pent-up lustful fantasies, and the way his dick feels like steel inside his pants, rutting into me slow and hard. I'm so and flushed everywhere as he kisses down to my stomach, licking the line right above my pants. Or rather *his* pants.

"I knew you stole these," he grins, tugging them at the waist while kissing the ring in my navel. "Are you getting them all wet?"

I whimper as he yanks the fabric away from my skin to peek inside.

As I'm wrapping my legs around his back, Noah's phone rings on the table next to us. And it's not the regular ringtone. It's the special one he sets for calls he actually wants to answer.

He ignores it for a moment, kissing down my pelvis. But then his eyes dart to the screen and I can see him waging an internal war. To stop this right now means physical torture for both of us.

But even I can see Andrew's name on the screen, and he's one of the few people I know Noah doesn't like to ignore. He takes a deep breath and peeks up at me with an apologetic look on his adorable sexy face that I just want to maim with kisses.

Then he grabs the phone and answers it.

"Hello?" His hand slides up my waist, desperate to touch even while we're on pause.

I can't help rocking my hips leisurely up to him, not willing or able to stop myself.

But now Noah's face appears worried, and it forces me to halt my grinding motions.

"Slow down, bro. What's going on? Is everything okay?"

He sits back on his knees, forehead lined in concern, and I swallow hard, straightening up a bit. I watch him closely as he listens to whatever Andrew is saying, and I can already tell it's not good. My stomach twists into an uneasy knot.

Suddenly Noah jumps off the couch and adjusts his clothes. "Andrew, breathe. Where is she exactly?"

She? Who's she?

He grabs his sneakers from beside the table and steps into them, running a distressed yet somehow calming hand through his hair. I can tell from his face he's devising a quick plan in his mind.

"Don't worry, bro," he grunts in a confident tone. "I'm going now."

Going?? Going where? What the hell is happening!?

"I'm going now," he says again, then walks away. I get up off the couch fast and follow him, confusion and panic lancing through me. "Seriously. I'm out the door. I'm running, not even waiting for a fucking car or anything."

My face is bound in hopelessness as I watch Noah, and he stares at me, though he's still listening to whatever scary shit Andrew is saying. I'm shaking with fear of the unknown. Any number of things could be wrong right now. I have so many questions and not enough time to ask because Noah opens the door.

"Don't stress. I'm on my way," he comforts his friend over the line. "Call Fletch. Now."

He hangs up the phone, tucking it away, and I finally have his attention, though it appears he's about to bolt.

"What's -"

"Baby, I gotta run real quick," he cuts me off, pressing a chaste kiss on my cheek. "I'll be right back, and I'll explain everything. I promise, okay?"

He raises his brows in an attempt to console me, though he's still inching away.

"Okay..." I mutter, anything but pacified.

"Stay right here," he speaks in an easy command that has me doing exactly what he says. "I promise I'm coming right back. I just need to handle this."

Handle what?? I want to yell. *Are you in trouble? Is Andrew okay? Who were you talking about and where are you going??*

But there's no time to ask any of that, because Noah darts down his hallway, leaping through the front door and out of sight.

I huff out of frustration from all the unanswered questions swarming my brain. My body is keyed up from the sexual tension and daunting notion that I

Seek Me

have no idea where Noah just went, or if he'll be safe.

I decide to distract myself with wine and go to the kitchen. I smile when I see two bottles of the French white I like in the wine cooler. I take one out and pour myself a glass, all floaty with giddy relief at being back here. In Noah's apartment.

Where I belong.

I had a wonderful time in Barcelona. It was one of the most beautiful places I've seen, and it was a treat to spend four months with my friends.

We partied a lot. Leaving Noah on not-so-great terms gave me a renewed desire to go wild at first. I couldn't stop thinking about the way he acted on that last night, when he brushed me off and flirted with girls in front of me. Of course I knew why he was doing it, and I would never hold something like that against him. But it still hurt like hell and lit a fire inside me.

So I spent my first month in Barcelona going out almost every night, drinking and dancing, and hooking up with insanely hot guys. I didn't sleep with them, because I knew that would just make me feel worse. But I also knew it was necessary for me to clear my mind.

I needed to hit the reset button and *cleanse my palette*, if you will. Which I did, with some very tall, very muscular dudes.

But when all was said and done, after waking up in a mysterious bed with a pounding in my skull like a fucking jackhammer, I realized that the point in all this partying wasn't to sate my desires for the one I can't have. It was to guide me back to him.

I had been led directly to my truth. The one truth I haven't been able to ignore in four years. The one that's consumed my heart this entire time.

I'm in love with Noah. And I want to stay.

After that, everything came together.

I felt like Bella in *Breaking Dawn*, when she finally becomes a vampire. My vision was clear. Colors were more vivid, sounds crisp and melodious. Every song on the radio reminded me of him, and every other guy who looked at me had me craving Noah Richards like my very own bloodlust.

The only problem was that I assumed he was still mad at me. So I prepared myself to grovel a little when I came home. Not much… I'm still a lady, after all. But I accepted that I would need to apologize to my best friend and pray, once more, that he was still single and interested in seeing me.

And then he called.

It blew me away so hard, and my heart was restored to full capacity when he broke our unspoken pact.

He still chases me, even after all this time. And now I need to stop running.

I can't do this to him anymore. I need to stay and tell him how I feel so we can finally figure out what in the holy fuck we're doing.

Sheesh... Maybe it's a good thing he had to leave. These thoughts are intense.

Liquid courage, activate.

I kill my glass of wine in one big sip then pour more, pacing around the kitchen. I can't tell if I'm more nervous about Noah being out somewhere, doing God knows what, or about him coming back. Because once he does, I'll need to talk to him. And that right there is a scary fucking thought.

How do you tell your best friend of four years that you're finally ready to be exclusive? Is there an app for it? Maybe a Wiki-how page?

I grumble to myself and down more wine. *That's if he even wants to be with me like that...*

For all I know, Noah could have been spending the last four months dipping his cock in every hoebag imaginable, like he's trying to beat a world record. I would certainly hope not, but then he is a bachelor, and it's kind of his thing.

So I guess I also need a Wiki-how page on turning womanizers into boyfriend material.

Maybe it's like a male version of Pretty Woman. Not that I'm a millionaire, or that Noah takes money for sex. Although at this point, nothing would surprise me.

In any other situation, that thought would be horrifying. But with Noah, it makes me smile.

He's just so cute and sexy, with his shaggy hair and crooked smile and tattooed body that I just want to lick everywhere.

I can't even find it in myself to be mad about his whorings around. I love him too much. He's my best friend and also my perfect match.

I just hope he sees it, too.

The sound of the door opening sends my stomach into my throat. I hear more than one set of footsteps and I turn the corner from the kitchen to see Noah... And a short girl with dark, wavy hair in a gorgeous black and gold dress.

"Hi!" I chirp, awaiting an introduction.

The girl's big teal eyes land on me and she looks stunned. Shocked and frozen in place.

She looks like I'm the last person she expected to see here in Noah's home, which has my inner crazy girl - the one who's overly jealous and oddly ratchet - urging me to accuse him of something. Like for example, bringing another

Seek Me

girl home while I'm here waiting for him, as if he *actually* expects us to have a threesome, when he knows damn well I told him the only threesome we're ever having is with another dude, a stipulation that made him vow never to bring up the threesome thing again.

But I shut it down fast because Noah may be a womanizer, but he's not evil, or stupid.

He saunters over to me and plants a kiss in my hair, grazing his fingers on my lower back, allowing me to relax a bit and smile at the girl, cocking my head.

"Hello…" she speaks warily, still studying me as if I'm a mermaid who just hopped out of the Hudson and crawled onto Noah's lap.

"Tessa, this is Alexandra," Noah introduces us, wearing his signature smirk. "She's a… friend."

I peek up at him and his eyes twinkle. So naturally I elbow him in the stomach, and he laughs.

"Nice to meet you, Alexandra," the girl - *Tessa* - says with a friendly smile as she clunks to me in her insanely high heels and shakes my hand.

I can't get over how pretty she is, even more so up close. The heels make her an inch or so taller than me, since my feet are bare, but you can just tell she's a little peanut person without them. Still, she's all curves and long, flowing hair that's like a dark waterfall coming from her head, complete with the most gem-like eyes which sparkle in the low light.

"Please, call me Alex," I tell her politely and her smile widens.

"How long have you two known each other?" She asks, and I'm still not sure *who* the heck she is or why she's here, but Noah seems comfortable with her presence, and I'm getting nothing but sweetheart vibes from her.

She arrived here with Noah after Andrew called so… Maybe she's his cousin, or… Does Andrew have a sister? But she's not British…

"Oh, God… Feels like forever!" I kid in response to her question, tilting my chin up at Noah who grins like the world's most adorable Big Bad Wolf.

"Yea, she just can't seem to stay away," he sighs and slings his arm around my shoulder, pulling me in close. My favorite place in the world is smooshed up against him.

"Mhm," I narrow my gaze at his sexy, smug face. "If I was smart, I would've stayed in Barcelona with that six-foot-four soccer player with the tribal tattoos."

I giggle because I like prodding him just a little, especially after what he did before I left. And this joke is based on real events. *What was that guy's name again? Javi? Jorge?*

Noah rolls his eyes, and his obvious jealousy is making me giddy. *Doesn't matter what his name was, because it's not Noah.*

"Shit! I have to call Andy!" Noah frantically pulls his phone out of his pocket and taps on the screen faster than any of us can blink. He brings the phone to his ear then stalks into the living room. I can hear him talking for a second, and I watch Tessa closely, the mystery and intrigue getting the best of me.

Who the hell is this girl? How does she know Andrew?

She chews on her lower lip incessantly as she watches Noah on the phone, her brows zipping together in worry and what appears to be guilt. Noah waves her over and she goes like a puppy being called to its master. But not for Noah.

I think her master is on the other end of that phone call.

She takes the phone from Noah and brings it hesitantly to her ear, sinking down into the big chair while she talks. I don't think I've ever been more curious about anything in my life, and I fully intend on prying answers from my best friend as soon as humanly possible.

Noah returns to me and takes my face in his hands, kissing my lips, then my cheeks, then my chin. And I've completely forgotten what I was just thinking about.

"I'm sorry about that, baby," he huffs, taking my hand in his and threading our fingers. "Long story I can't wait to tell you."

I bite my lip, desperately wanting to hear his story, and tell him all of mine from Spain. But then I also want to get him naked and hold him down while I ride him like a mechanical bull.

Maybe we can talk and hump at the same time??

"Let's go upstairs," I whisper while walking my fingers up his torso.

He glances at Tessa again, and I follow his gaze. I frown because it looks like she's crying.

"Yea, we should give her some privacy," he murmurs, tugging me along.

"But she has your phone…"

He shrugs like it makes no difference. I like that about Noah. He's not one of those guys who's always on his phone. When we're together, I always have his full attention.

I really do love him. And I think he loves me, too.

My head is swirling with thoughts as Noah and I sneak quietly through the living room, past a sobbing Tessa, and up the stairs to his bedroom. I feel really bad for the girl. I wonder what happened to her tonight… Why Noah

Seek Me

had to run off and bring her here, and why she's now crying on the phone with Andrew.

Noah closes his bedroom door behind us and locks it, then flops backward into his bed, pulling me on top of him by my butt. I giggle and straddle his hips, my hair draping around us like a dark curtain. He reaches up and tucks it behind my ear.

"So... Who's the hot girl?" I ask with a grin and he chuckles.

"Get this... She's Andrew's new girlfriend," he tells me and my jaw drops.

"You're fucking with me..." I gasp.

He shakes his head. "Nope. They met two weeks ago when he was here visiting me. Spent an entire weekend shacked up together. Alex, I think he's in love with her."

My mind is running a mile a minute.

Our friend Andrew, the one who's married with children, is *dating* that girl?

There are so many questions that want to flow from my mouth, and I can't settle on which one to start with. Unfortunately, the stupidest one comes out first.

"How old is she?"

Noah grins. "Twenty-seven."

"Wow, good for Andrew," I blink. "So what happened tonight? Why did you have to run out and get her?"

"I'm still not exactly sure. All I know is that she's in a bad marriage too, and her husband has some crazy job where he's always gone. Andrew's coming back next week to see her again. And Johnny's coming out too, so be ready to party."

He pauses while I squeal. I love hanging out with the three of them together. Now four, with the addition of Andrew's new love interest.

"Anyway, Andrew called me spazzing that some guy stopped Tessa on her way out of Sensay. He was a total creeper, so I had to get up in his face a little. Tessa said he's a friend of her husband, or more like an enemy, I guess..." Noah frowns. "It's a very complicated situation. I'm worried about what Andrew's getting himself mixed up in. I just hope this doesn't fuck with him."

I nod slowly. "Jeez... I go away for four months and all hell breaks loose." Noah hums through a grin.

I have a zillion more questions about this whole thing, but I figure now's not the time. We can talk about it more later, or next week when Andrew's here.

I move my face in closer to Noah's. "So you rescued her from some stalker dude?"

"Yea, I had to," he shrugs casually, as if his secret identity is a superhero who saves girls from weirdos. *A tatted Superman. I like it.*

"You're kinda badass, huh?" I whisper and flick my tongue on his lower lip, which earns me a breath that catches in his throat.

He squeezes my butt in his wide palms, pulling my crotch down to his. "I would rescue you from all sorts of danger, baby."

"Mmm I know," I hum then press my breasts hard on his chest, bringing my lips to his ear. "You already have."

"Alex, I fucking *need* you," he grunts, abruptly flipping me so I'm beneath him. "I can't wait one more second."

"Don't wait, baby," I whimper and he groans, kissing me fast and hard.

We kiss ourselves into a rhythm, panting and touching, building friction and heat until the air around us is hazy and stifling.

Noah lifts my shirt off, then I do the same to his, salivating over his sculpted body. I can't help but run my fingers over all his tattoos I've missed looking at and kissing.

"Oh yea... I wanted to ask you something," he's out of breath, sucking all over my neck and throat while I unbutton his pants.

"What's that, sexy ass?"

He chuckles and I swoon. "I was thinking of getting some new ink. You wanna come with?"

"Um only fuck yea!" I cheer. He beams at me, then wiggles out of his jeans. "Where are you gonna get it?"

"Hmm... Not sure," he shows me a wicked grin. "Where do you think?"

I use this as a cheap ploy to touch him more, my fingers exploring all the unmarked spots I can reach.

I graze the right side of his ribcage. "How about here?"

He trembles and I feel his dick swell between us.

I tickle down to his hip. "Or here?"

"Mmm..." He hums and appreciative sound and slow-blinks.

I tug his boxer briefs down below his ass then reach around him feel it up, drawing circles on his lower back with my fingertip.

"Or maybe here..."

"You want me to get a tramp stamp?" He smirks lazily and I giggle.

"You should get *Alex's Bitch* right here," I say with my hands on those sexy muscle dips above his butt.

His smile is lethal and almost taunting. "Don't even test me because you know I'll do it."

An erotic laugh bubbles from my throat as he shimmies out of his boxers the rest of the way, then yanks his sweats clean off my legs. He settles between my thighs, his long, solid length resting on my slit as arousal coats him, making me wish he would just push it inside me and stuff me to the brim with every perfect inch.

Noah hypnotizes me with soft kisses, turning my brain into mush before he trails those magic lips down my throat and onto my tits.

"I've missed these," he laps my nipple in a hungry stroke of his warm tongue, as if he's licking an ice cream cone. Then he takes the steel between his lips and sucks hard, drawing out a groan. "I think about this when I jerk off, you know."

"Oh yea?"

He sucks again, this time giving it a gentle bite, which shoots lightning into my groin.

"Yea…" He moves onto the other one and does the same thing, while cupping my breasts with his hands, squeezing tenderly and circling the nipple with his thumb. "You're the only porn I can come to, baby."

I don't know why him saying this is so hot, but the words, and the way he says them, in that deep, raspy voice that sounds like sex for your ears, plus images of him fucking his hand to thoughts of me, tighten my insides like a vice.

"What else do you think about…?" I ask curiously, reaching between our writhing bodies to make a fist around his thick shaft. "When you touch yourself like this…"

I jerk him, painfully slow yet firm, the way he likes it, and he growls with his mouth covering my nipple.

"Last night I came so fucking hard… Thinking about fucking you with my tongue," he tells me while he pumps his hips with my hand. "The way your tight pussy clamps around it… And your sweet juices coat my lips. You taste like strawberry ice cream."

"Fuck, Noah…" I moan, pressing my head back into the comforter. "More…"

"I want to fuck your mouth… while I eat every drop of that sweetness, baby." His tone is demanding, rightfully so because he doesn't need to beg me for a thing.

I'm fucking ready, for all of it. Every dirty, filthy, depraved thought he has,

I'm down. He can use me any way he wants.

I push on his chest, signaling for him to turn, which he does, his long, toned body moving gracefully on his bed, like a panther; cunning and dangerous. He lies on his side, and I do the same. Except that now I'm face-to-dick with the stunningly long, impossibly hard piece of him that makes me a hundred times wetter with just my *eyes* on it.

Noah holds my thigh hard in one hand, while the other touches me, cherishingly tender. His finger teases my hole, swirling in the wetness as his mouth inches closer. I know I'm supposed to be doing similar things to his cock right now, but I can't stop watching him through the narrow space between our heated bodies.

He presses his index finger inside me a little, then licks my clit, twirling his tongue around it, over and over. Then he withdraws the finger and slips it between his lips, sucking my juices clean off before planting more warm kisses all over my pussy.

It feels mind altering, and looks like the dirtiest, hottest act I've ever witnessed. He's alternating between fingering me while licking my clit, then sucking his finger, and I feel like I could come already. I have no choice but to seal my lips over the smooth head of his dick and suck hard.

"*Fuck*, Alex," his voice vibrates into me as he stuffs two fingers inside.

I moan on his cock, sucking deep and unyielding, giving him back what he's giving me in strides. His length throbs in my mouth, a feeling that makes me gush because it means I'm pleasing him, and that's what I desire most of all. When Noah feels good, I feel good. Our pleasure is linked together by an unbreakable chain.

With his face wedged in the apex of my thighs, those plush lips eating me alive, he curls his fingers and sends a jolt through my loins. I cup his balls and squeeze gently, letting him push further down my throat as he sings my praises directly into my body.

I open my legs as wide as I can in this position, resting one on his shoulder while I suck faster, determined to make him come first. It's like a race, and I really want to win. I want his orgasm almost more than I want my own.

Noah removes his fingers, replacing them with his tongue, fucking me with it like he said he would. And then it sneaks back… To my other spot. The bad one.

He spreads me open and licks like he's starving, sinking a wet digit inside, fighting the resistance. It burns like usual at first, but I welcome it because I

Seek Me

fucking love when he does stuff like this, and I really don't have a single care or reservation in the world when we're naked in his bed.

The finger penetrates, slow and steady, while his mouth works on my clit, rolling it between his lips and sucking so vigorously I go cross-eyed. I whimper with his dick sliding in and out of my face, hoovering him like he's doing to me, until I feel him shaking.

"God… fucking… *Jesus*…" he groans on me, his abs tightening. "Baby, don't make me come…"

It comes out like a plea, which is so damn sexy I want to deliberately disobey. I slurp off and stroke him with the lubrication. "I want you to come."

"No… I wanna come in you…"

"You will come in me…"

"In your pussy, smart ass."

"I love your dirty talk."

He growls out loud and stops everything, pulling away and making me pout.

"Get the fuck over here," he straightens back out, so he's kneeling between my legs, then curls one around his waist.

He looks so good I'm in pain just from seeing him. His hair is all mussed up and sexy as fuck, eyes dark and hungry, lips moist, sweat glistening on the muscles in his chest. *Holy motherfucking sex-god.*

"Is this okay?" He pants and lifts a brow. "Should I get a condom?"

And because it's Noah, my only answer is, "Please put your bare cock inside me."

He lets out a ragged breath and his eyes droop shut for a moment, looking like he could come just from me saying that. And for him, I'd be totally fine with it.

He yanks me closer and guides himself in, slowly, savoring each inch as it moves inside my body. He groans and watches with hooded eyes as his aching flesh disappears between my walls, which clench from the welcome feeling of him filling me; the feeling I've missed for so many months it felt like years waiting for this moment.

"Alex… Your pussy is so tight," he drawls, reaching for my breast, holding it while he draws back then thrusts in all the way, so deep I'm stuffed to the hilt. "It's swallowing my cock."

"Fuck me, Noah…" I mewl and scratch his abs with my nails.

He rocks his hips into me, building up the motions, forward and back, until he's balls deep and pounding. I can't help but scream his name through a voice choppy with his ravaging thrusts. He leans over me so his pelvis brushes my clit because he's so fucking deep it's as if we're one person.

He brings his mouth to my tits and sucks my nipples while grunting breaths for every smack of his hips into mine. I pull his hair hard until he moans, then he bites me and I cry out. It's so hot and dirty, and amazing; we're both sweaty and hoarse, fucking each other raw.

"You're the only one I want, beautiful," he squeezes my ass hard, his fingertips bruising me in the best possible way. "Only you… forever. Do you want me?"

"Yes!" I gasp without even needing to think. The word is a reflex.

Of course there's only him. There will never be anyone who can make me feel the way he does, with his body, his heart and his soul.

"Only me?" He demands, crushing me with his weight while he bucks into me over and over and again until the world around me grows dark and hazy.

"Only you, Noah," I take his jaw in my hands and watch his face. His gorgeous, perfect face that belongs to me.

Mine.

"Tell me you're mine," he swells to a thickness I didn't know was possible, and the walls are about to come crashing around us.

"I'm fucking yours," I squeal, then gasp as the orgasm looms. "I'm yours forever, Noah."

"*Fuck*… fuck fuck fuck I love you fuck I'm *coming*." All his words come out as one long stream, and it sets my body ablaze.

"I… God, I love you…" Tears spring to my eyes as my climax tears me apart. "Come with me."

"I'm coming with you, baby," he tremors over me, kissing my lips fast, roaring into my mouth.

Quaking, my walls grab hold of him like they never want to let go. Which they probably don't… *I* don't.

"Mine…" He hums, his thrusts slowing as I feel all his love pouring deep inside me. "All. Fucking. Mine."

I see sparks behind my eyelids, even though they're open. They want to close instinctively, but I refuse to stop watching him for even one second. He looks so beautiful when he's giving himself to me. Every single fantastic part is…

"Mine," I rasp, sucking air into my lungs. I'm tingly everywhere and my toes are numb.

Seek Me

For several minutes he's still stroking, barely a movement, but I think his orgasm went on longer than normal, and I'm cherishing it because it feels wondrous. My body is humming, coming down from a mind-altering high, and everything around me is pure magic.

Noah eventually curls up on me, hugging me to his chest, both of us sweaty and so hot our skin is burning. I can't even comprehend how intense that climax was.

And I'm pretty sure we just said we loved each other while coming...

I'm dazed, and only partially sure that actually happened, but I would believe it if it did. *That was the best sex that's ever been had by anyone. Ever.*

Noah nuzzles his face in my neck, kissing my flesh, and maybe licking me a little too. I can't be sure because I can barely feel anything other than fuzziness. But he might be licking. And I'm cool with it.

More than cool. I want this.

I want *him*. I want everything he has to give for as long as I can get it.

"Nothing has ever felt as good as *everything* feels with you," he murmurs through a sleepy voice, then pulls out of me slowly, cuddling my body into him.

I don't want him to see, but I'm crying a little. It's super embarrassing, but I can't help it. My wires are crossed, emotions going haywire.

Does he really love me? Or was that just the orgasm talking?

Does he really want me... forever?

"Noah..." I whisper, lips moving on his chest while he plays with my hair.

"Mmm...?" His movements are sedated, and I think he's falling asleep.

I should go get cleaned up, because I'm all gushy and I'm sure it's getting everywhere. But the last thing I want to do right now is move.

I'm mollified. Almost tranquilized.

"Noah," I say his name again, because I can't stop saying it.

"My name on your lips is like a lullaby..." he croons.

My eyelids grow heavy as his steadying heartbeat rocks me to sleep.

Mine. All mine.

I wake with sun streaming in through the partially drawn curtains, right in my eyes. I groan and try to smash my face into the pillows, but I can't move because Noah's giant, long-limbed body is wrapped around me like a weed.

I'm used to his monopolizing cuddles at this point - I even welcome them - so I lean into it and kiss his chest, right where the word *Seek* is tattooed over his heart. I love that spot. Not to mention his skin smells like heaven; part manly, part sweet, with a hint of something like a baby's smell. Maybe it's baby powder or fabric softener that reminds me of baby clothes, who knows. But it opens my ovaries up like a blossom. It's actually alarming, but I'm trying not to get lost in overthinking it.

Noah makes a sudden humming noise and I think he's waking up. When I pull back to look up at him, I see that his eyes are still closed, though he's doing what I wanted to do and burrowing his face into the pillow. I trail my fingers up and down his back, mischievously rubbing his butt a little because it's just so nice.

"I missed this so bad..." his sleepy voice rumbles into me, and I can't tell if he's talking in his sleep or just teetering on the edge of consciousness.

"Me too," I whisper, then brush his ridiculously soft hair away from his forehead with my fingers.

"I never want it to end," he murmurs, causing my heart to swell behind my ribs.

"Me neither, baby," my lips kiss the words onto his skin.

"You always leave me..." he says with an audible pout and I freeze.

I swallow hard, sudden unnecessary tears filling my eyes. I blink them away and nestle harder into his chest. He squeezes me, protecting me with his big arms. Keeping me safe from the outside world.

Why do I always leave him?

Ah, the unavoidable question I have no more answers for.

There's a voice in my heart, one louder than any other internal voice I've ever heard. And it's telling me, insisting that maybe it's time to stay put.

Maybe this time there's nowhere else to go.

I'm done running. I've spent enough time escaping the past. My past will always be a part of me, but I need to start thinking about my present and my future, and I can't see either of those things without Noah.

He means the world to me. Why would I want to leave that again?

I have to tell him all these things, but I don't think doing it while he's half asleep is a good idea. I should get my head on straight and figure out how to finally voice to him all the stuff I've been hiding from for so many years.

I trail my foot up and down his calf, deep in my head, and he finally shifts enough that I know he's awake.

Seek Me

"Why is it so bright in here?" He grumbles, shoving his face into the crook of my neck.

I giggle as my fingers toil in his hair. "Summertime sunshine."

"Is that the title of a song you're writing about my morning wood?" His body wiggles around as he laughs at his own stupid joke and I really can't help but fall even harder for him.

The dude is just irresistible in every way. *So perfect.*

"No, that would be called *A Rod Through My Heart*," I snicker and he laughs even harder.

"I like that!" He cheers, rolling me on top of him.

"I thought you might," I grin down at him with hearts in my eyes.

He holds my butt in his strong hands, gazing up at me like my face holds the answers to every mystery that's ever needed solving. It's a great look, and I never want to lose it.

I want to see it every morning.

"Shower?" He grumbles as his eyes turn dark before slipping down to my mouth.

"Are you saying I smell?" I tease and squint at him, to which he chuckles.

"You smell heavenly," he leans up to sniff my neck, which quickly turns into heated kisses accompanied by sexy growling noises. "Shower with me. I missed you and I need my fill."

My body clenches in response to his request, but before I can speak he sits up, rather effortlessly with me on top of him, straps me to his torso with those muscular arms and rolls off the bed. A squeal escapes me, because he's really just tossing me around, and I fucking love it.

He carries me into the master bathroom and turns on the shower, stepping inside while still holding me. He checks the water temperature for a moment, my sweet, thoughtful man, before submerging us both in the cascading waterfall of the massive shower head.

And the next thing I know, my back is pressed up against the wall, and my best friend is showing me just how much he missed me with glorious, steamy shower sex.

It's a good time to be Alex Mackenzie, folks.

I make Noah waffles for breakfast.

And by *make* I mean heat up the already-cooked waffles his chef made. It's the one thing I can do in the kitchen without starting a fire. Although Noah had to save me from putting tin foil in the microwave, just in the nick of time.

When we came downstairs, Tessa wasn't here. Noah assumed she had spent the night, since Andrew apparently asked him to let her sleep in the guest room, to which Noah happily obliged. But she must have left super early or something, because the only evidence of her having been here was Noah's phone resting on the living room table.

We eat our waffles together at the breakfast bar, all the while chatting, laughing, and teasing one another, touching, kissing and being the most playful, adorable people in the whole universe.

I said it. Have you met anyone cuter than Noah and Alex? I don't think so.

Noah calls his tattoo artist and schedules him to come over later and ink us. I'm so excited I'm vibrating like a tattoo gun. Noah and I both love tattoos and collectively we have a lot of them, but in our four years of friendship, this is the first time we're getting something together.

And apparently, something matching.

"Are you sure you want us to get matching tattoos?" I ask hesitantly. "What if someday you hate me and you always have to look at your ribcage and remember the girl you despise."

Noah gives me a face that's so wrought with horror, some confusion, and maybe a bit of hurt, that I can't even really look at him. It's as if he just swallowed something gross it made him want to die.

"First of all, are you fucking kidding me?" He gasps. "How in the world do you ever think I would hate you?? I mean, Jesus, what do you plan on doing to me, Mackenzie?"

"Nothing," I murmur, hopping off my stool to stand between his legs and hug his waist as tight as possible. "You're just… I mean… You're so…"

"I'm what?" His voice is low and uncertain.

"You're *you*. You're Noah Richards…"

"We've been over this. And you're Alex Mackenzie. What's your point?"

I kiss his bare chest over and over because him repeating his words from the night we met makes me want to burst into tears.

"I'm always afraid you'll realize you're too good for me," I whimper and he sighs, closing his arms around me so tight I'm being suffocated in the best possible way.

"That's the dumbest shit you've ever said," he whispers, and I snort a laugh onto his skin. "You're a part of me forever, Alex. Just like Boots was, God rest his soul. Which is why I'm getting a tattoo for him, and I want you to get one, too."

I nod repeatedly. "Okay. Understood. Loud and clear."

"Good."

"What's the second of all?"

"Hm?"

"You said *first of all*, are you fucking kidding me..." I squeak and he laughs.

"Oh right. Second of all, I could always just cover it up with some stripper's name to forget you." He giggles wickedly and I punch him in the kidneys. "Okay, okay! I'm kidding, obviously. Even if I were *mad* at you, we're unbreakable, Alex. Plus, it's a Boots tattoo. It'll be epic."

I peek up at him and he gives me the *you know I'm right* Noah Richards look that makes me weak in the knees.

"You're right."

Hours later, the day is coming to an end, and I'm blissfully sated. From all the orgasms, yes, but also from being back with Noah again and having a purely wonderful day, as we always do.

We went out shopping for art supplies for me, and some books we've been wanting for the library. Then we came home and got each other off a few more times before the artist came by.

And now I'm staring at Noah's latest ink, a detailed paw print with *Boots* written inside it in a fancy script, on his left side. Knowing that I have the exact same thing on my thigh, only with the addition of *Barnaby* scrawled in there as well, makes me feel anchored. It's a feeling I only get when I'm with Noah, and before recently it scared the crap out of me.

I used to think being anchored meant I would get stuck in something I wasn't ready for, especially so soon after divorcing an abusive, cheating monster. But now I welcome the stability. I crave it, like every second I'm away from Noah I could potentially float away.

I don't want that. I want to stay here with him and put down roots in this world of undying happiness.

We're lying on the couch watching *The Hangover*, a blanket of calm delight warming us when Noah's phone rings. It's Andrew, so he answers it.

"Hey, bud," Noah says and puts the phone on speaker. "You're on speaker and Alex is here."

"Alex! You're back!" Andrew cheers in his deep voice and swoony accent. "That means you'll be there next week when Johnny and I come to visit, yes?"

I smile in excitement. "Yes! I can't wait to hang out with you guys! We're going to have a blast. Especially with your new *girlfriend*..."

I snicker and Noah smacks my butt.

"Oh my God... You guys, I'm rather fucked up here..." Andrew grunts, and he sounds stressed. "Noah, thank you so much for going last night. You're honestly the best friend anyone could ask for."

"No thanks needed, and yes, I am," Noah sighs, prompting me to peek up at him. "Have you heard from Fletcher at all?"

"No... I have no idea what happened, though I'm quite afraid of what he may have done," Andrew mutters. *What are they talking about?* "But um... there's another problem." He sounds hesitant, so Noah and I share a look. "I screwed up. I screwed up horribly."

"What do you mean?" I respond, while Noah asks, "What happened?"

Andrew is quiet for a moment. He takes a long audible breath, then grumbles something to himself. I'm a little terrified of what he's about to say.

"I'm fucked Vivian last night..." he whispers and Noah's eyes widen in a shell-shocked expression, which I think is mirroring my own.

"Oh..." Noah gasps.

"Shit," I breathe.

"I don't know why I did it... It just happened and I feel sick about it," Andrew begins rambling, and it's clear he's wrought with guilt. It's a strange notion, considering that sleeping with your wife shouldn't be a problem. *Theoretically.* "It meant nothing. I think it was just some closure or something, and I was so upset and stressed about everything with Tessa that when Viv initiated it, I... couldn't stop."

He huffs out a pained noise and my heart breaks.

"Oh, Andrew..." I murmur, wishing I could console my friend in some way.

"I'm such a bloody moron," he whimpers, sounding like he could break down. "I ruined things with Tessa. It's over before it even started, all because I'm a piece of garbage."

"Wow..." I hum, gaping at the phone in Noah's hand. "You're in love with her."

He lets out a strangled sigh. "I am."

"Bro, I think you should give yourself a break," Noah says with compassion.

Seek Me

"I mean, I'm not saying Tessa won't be angry, or hurt, but you owe it to both of you to tell her what happened and explain yourself. If she loves you too, I'm sure she'll understand."

"You'll have to do some serious groveling," I add. "But this isn't a simple situation, not even slightly. You guys are both going through the ringer right now. But you can't give up over one stupid mistake." I pause. "It was a mistake... right?"

"Yes! God, I wish I'd never done it," Andrew gulps. "It wasn't even satisfying. It left me with nothing but guilt and shame."

"Yea, that's not how you should feel when you fuck your wife," Noah scoffs and I shoot him a look. "I just mean I think this is evidence that you need to sort out the divorce. It's time to move forward, bro. No more dwelling on the past when you have a future right in front of you."

Tightening seizes my chest when I hear these words. The same could be said to me.

Stop dwelling on the past. Move forward to your future.

I stare at Noah with curiosity swimming through me. *I wonder if he wants to be with me... I wonder if he's ready to move forward, too.*

"You're right," Andrew sighs over the line. "I know you are. Thanks for being awesome, you two. You're the best non-couple I know."

Noah and I chuckle together, though it feels forced in every sense of the word. We look at each other and it seems to linger, our eyes holding one another's gaze in something tense, maybe a little awkward, and riddled with nervous fear.

Noah's Adam's apple dips in his throat. I blink slowly.

"Anyway, I'll see you Friday," Andrew goes on, unaware of the black-hole of uncertainty that's swallowed us up. "I'm picking Johnny up from the airport and then we'll come right over."

"Alright," Noah murmurs, his eyes still stuck on mine. "We'll see you then, pal."

"Bye, Andrew," I chirp.

"Bye, guys!"

He hangs up, leaving Noah and me gaping at one another, wondering what the hell we're supposed to do now.

Noah clears his throat. "That's crazy, huh? About Andrew and his wife..."

"Yea... Quite the pickle." I chew my lower lip.

"Hey, um... Last night you mentioned something about a guy from

Barcelona..." he mutters, suddenly going to great lengths to avoid eye contact. "Were there... a lot of guys? I mean, not like it's any of my business. You have every right to do you..."

"Do I?" I ask, my forehead lined and my tone genuinely wondering, because I'm not even sure anymore.

"Yes...?" His response comes out like a question, which only serves to confuse me further.

"I guess I've been doing me like you've been doing you," I shrug, dizzying with vagueness.

Noah nods reluctantly. "So... we're just doing us."

"Right."

"And doing each other," he lifts his brow.

Normally I'd laugh at his little reference, but I can't seem to find it in me at the moment.

"Yea..."

"So this is good," he mutters, sounding more unsure than I feel.

"It's great." I rest my head back down on his chest, and I can't ignore how hard his heart is jumping against my cheek.

How shaky his fingers are as he plays with my hair.

We go back to watching the movie, drifting into an uneasy sleep on his couch. And the only question now plaguing my mind is, *What are we doing?*

"Hey, sweetie!" My friend, Keira, hops over to me in her giant black Louboutins, wrapping her arms around me for a generous hug.

"Hi! I'm so glad you could come out tonight!" My face nestles in her abundance of illustrious blonde hair, and I pat her back a few times before we separate.

"Are you kidding? I miss the crap out of you, gorgeous little thing," she smiles wide, pinching my cheeks.

I giggle as we lock arms, walking up the block so we can catch a cab to Hell's Kitchen from Keira's loft in Midtown. We're only a few avenues away from the rooftop where we're meeting the crew, and I'd love to walk since it's nice out tonight. But I already know Keira won't want to in those overly-indulgent high-heels. So a cab it is.

Seek Me

"So how have your travels been?" She asks me with enthusiasm. "I heard you just came back from Barcelona! And where before that?"

"Tel Aviv," I answer, smoothing a hand over my dress. "It's been incredible. Tel Aviv was life changing, and Barcelona... My God. You *have* to go there. It's beautiful and the food? Please." I shake my head in a serious fashion which makes her laugh.

"And the guys?" Her eyes sparkle. "I'm sure you met some Spanish hotties over there."

I swallow hard, my cheeks warming a bit, though inside I feel nothing but discomfort.

"Yea, there were a few," I sigh and she squeals. "But truly, I'm glad to be home. I always miss New York when I'm away."

"I'm sure it's just New York you miss," she gives me the side-eye and I smack her in the boob.

We're still giggling as I hail a cab and we hop in, giving the driver the location of Hudson Terrace, the rooftop bar where we're meeting Noah, Andrew, Tessa and Johnny.

I'm so excited to see my friends, I'm bordering on hysterical.

Of course Noah I was with earlier today when he insisted I join him for brunch with Brant. But I haven't seen Andrew since before I left for Barcelona, and I really miss his sweet British self.

Johnny I haven't seen since the first time I met him at his house in Georgia while he was still working on *Hell Storm*. He's since left the show to move on to other things, but Noah and him remain close friends, which is why I feel like I know him well enough to set him up with my friend Keira here.

And let's not forget the newest member of our little group; the lovely Tessa Woodrow. Also known as *Andrew's soulmate*.

I'm extremely excited to get to know her more. Noah seems to think she's awesome, and perfect for Andrew, so I have to trust both of their judgements. She came off sweet enough when I met her at Noah's last week, though it's my understanding she wasn't having the best night. I look forward to spending more time with the girl who's captivated our British heartthrob bestie, and find out what's underneath those designer clothes and all that hair.

"So, tell me about this guy I'm meeting tonight," Keira turns to face me, her eyes lit up with excitement. "Is he an actor, too?"

I chuckle and nod. "Yup, he's an actor. You definitely know of him..."

"Oh my God! Has he worked with Noah on the show?" She wiggles.

"Yes…"

"Holy shit! I'm going out with a TV star!" Now she's fanning her face over and over, pulling a compact out of her purse to reapply her lipstick.

"You'll need to relax," I tell her. "They're just regular people."

"You're just saying that because you've basically been dating a celebrity for four years," she waves me off.

"We are *not* dating…" I mutter. *Cue the eye-roll.*

"Whatever, Alex," Keira rolls her eyes. *Called it.* "Okay. Tell me his name. I promise I'll be cool."

I sigh. "John Barthow."

Keira's eyes widen so fast she looks like one of those rubber stress relief guys you squeeze and his eyes pop out.

She takes a deep breath and closes her bugged-out eyes, whispering something that resembles a prayer to herself. I can't hear what she's saying, but it sounds like she's reciting a penance to the patron saint of casual dick.

She finally reopens her eyes, and I can't help but note the devious look in them.

"I'm sure we'll have a lovely evening together."

When we get upstairs to the rooftop of Hudson Terrace, I immediately spot Noah before anyone else.

I feel creepy, as if I have some kind of radar detector that seeks him out at all times, but I just can't help it. I'm drawn to him.

It's hard not to be, since he's sex on legs. I watch heads turning in his direction every time we're in public together, including right now. And it's not just because he's famous.

How could anyone ignore something that looks that good?

Sure, there's also the teeny tiny little matter of me being hopelessly in love with him, bordering on obsessive infatuation. But we'll just forget about that for right now.

Noah is over by the bar at the far-end of the rooftop, talking animatedly to Andrew and Tessa. I don't see Johnny just yet, but I can hear his voice, which must mean he's around here somewhere. Keira and I make our way over to them, and I can't take my eyes off Noah.

He just looks so inconceivably sexy, in dark skinny jeans, a pink sleeveless Gucci top that has holes in it on purpose and fits him much more snugly now that he works out regularly for the show. Not to mention all the tattoos on display, his messy head of silky hair covered up by a black Louis Vuitton hat, and always the last piece of the puzzle that is Noah's idiosyncratic wardrobe: the Ray Bans.

I'm startled out of my ogling when my phone rings in my purse. I tug it out and see *unknown number* flashing on the screen, huffing in annoyance because I've been getting these calls for months now, and I have no idea who it could possibly be. All I know is that I'm not answering because whoever it is refuses to leave a message, or text me like a normal person.

Whatever you're selling, I ain't buying, homie.

We step up to my friends and Noah displays a wide, pleased smile directly at me.

"Hi, fairy love," he murmurs, taking my face in his hands. But his smile fades fast as his forehead lines in concern. "What's wrong, beautiful?"

"Um nothing," I breathe, melting under the heated gaze that comes with his full attention. "I just keep getting these calls from an unknown number and it's skeeving me out."

Noah frowns, but before he can comment, I'm being enveloped in a giant hug.

"Hey there, sis," Andrew rasps to me, pulling back and giving me the mother of all charming smiles. "Missed you."

"Missed you too, mate," I grin and he chuckles.

"I hear you already had the pleasure of meeting my gorgeous little woman here," he gazes down at Tessa, and she up at him, and *holy fuck*, I don't think I've ever seen two people look at each other the way they are right now.

"Hi again!" Tessa squeals then hugs me hard. I can't fight my smile, because I thought I was short, but she's *so* tiny, and just about the sweetest damn thing around. Like a little elf with big boobs and impeccable makeup.

"It's so good to see you, Tessa," I murmur, then tug away to introduce them to my friend. "Guys, this is Keira. Keira, this is Andrew and Tessa, and you know Noah."

They all shake hands, wearing polite smiles.

"Where's Johnny?" I ask, looking around while following the sound of his loud voice.

"He's saying hello to everyone here," Andrew huffs through a laugh, which

Noah joins him in. "He should be done by the time we're ready to leave."

"We're getting a table," Noah tells me, slinking a possessive arm around my waist. "It'll be ready soon."

"'Kay..." I hum, making googly eyes at his face because I want to kiss the crap out of him right now, even though that's not something we normally do.

Don't get me wrong, Noah and I definitely partake in displays of touching and flirting in public, since they're behaviors we can't just *turn off*. But as far as openly making out goes, we're not a couple. So it doesn't usually happen, unless we're at a specific party or maybe out at Sensay.

Though at this moment in time I'm ready to throw all caution to the wind for those positively delicious lips.

I bite mine to stop the drool.

"Hey! There she is!" Johnny booms from behind me somewhere, and I brace myself for the completely innocent and friendly manhandling I'm about to receive.

Sure enough, I'm scooped up in his huge arms and lifted into the air as if I'm on some carnival ride, and he spins me all around in a way that I don't even think is intentional. I have no choice but to bury my face in his shoulder and try not to get motion sickness.

"Hi Johnny!" I croak as he sets me down, fumbling against Noah to regain my balance. "It's so awesome to see you! This is my friend, Keira."

I wave my hand at Keira and Johnny turns, looking her up and down with just the right amount of subtlety.

"Hi," Keira flushes, and I get it. It's hard not to be overwhelmed by Johnny's hotness.

Fortunately, he doesn't really do it for me. I like my guys a little more tatted, a little less bearded, and a whole lot more *Noah*.

"Hello there, beautiful," Johnny winks at her, then takes her hand, holding it for a moment.

I've never seen Keira redder. *Tonight's gonna be a good night, I can already tell.*

"Mr. Richards, your table," a man addresses Noah and nods to a private table for us in the VIP section.

"We'll meet you over there," Johnny says, distracted by Keira and the artful way she's popping out her chest.

Andrew and Noah chuckle to themselves then proceed to follow the guy toward the table. But before I can join them, Tessa takes me by the arm.

"Actually, I'm waiting for a round," she says to Andrew, who tilts his head.

Seek Me

Then she turns to me. "Buy you a drink?"

Her eyes are so captivating, I'm finding it hard to say no to anything she suggests. She could be asking me to perform the dance of the seven veils with her, and I'm pretty sure I'd just nod along in hypnotized agreement.

"Sounds good to me," I smile, then peek at Noah and Andrew who appear pleased that we're getting along.

"We'll be at the table," Andrew says in his standard casual tone, though his eyes are slitted in a protective gaze that lingers on Tessa until he absolutely has to turn and walk away.

She takes a deep breath by my side and ruffles her hair. "I can hardly contain myself when he looks at me like that..."

I grin widely. "You're not kidding."

Tessa giggles and we stand at the bar beside Johnny and Keira, who are deeply invested in whatever conversation they're having that requires them to stand mere inches apart.

It would seem that love is in the air here in Hell's Kitchen tonight. I wonder what that means for Noah and me...

My stomach flutters as Tessa orders us two of the bar's specialty *fuzzy navel* shots. She hands me one and lifts hers.

"To finding love when you least expect it," she smiles and I almost choke, but compose myself enough to clink my glass on hers and take the shot.

It's pretty strong, and it goes down with a burn, but I welcome the immediate calm the booze is giving me. Maybe that's how I'll get through another night out with my best friend, pretending I'm not head-over-heels... By getting sloshed.

Tessa flags the bartender for another. "I'm really glad you're here, Alex. To be honest, I was nervous thinking about getting through tonight with only Andrew and his guy friends."

I give her an easy smile. "Well, I think you'd be fine, regardless. Noah adores you. He only has the nicest things to say..."

She flushes and bites her lip. "It's crazy to think I've only known them for three weeks. Noah is just the sweetest person on Earth. He's the kind of friend we'd all be so lucky to have." I nod. *Ain't that the truth.* "You know he actually called me a couple days after Andrew left, to make sure I was okay?" She huffs and shakes her head.

"That sounds like Noah," I reply quietly, struggling to keep the dreaminess out of my voice.

"You're blessed to have someone like him in your life," she goes on, picking up our next shots and handing me one. "Not that Noah isn't lucky to have you, obviously. I just think the two of you make the cutest pair."

My blinking becomes rapid as we clink our shots and whip them back. I release a ragged breath, a little from the alcohol, but more so from where this conversation is going.

"I mean, I don't know you guys well or anything, but I can feel the chemistry between you. It's like what I have with Andrew. A strong force of nature that pulls you together like magnets."

I nod slowly, really *feeling* what she's saying. "I suppose that's what makes Noah and I such good friends. We've basically been inseparable since the day we met. Aside from when we were both traveling, of course."

Tessa aims her teal eyes at me. "Are you planning any more trips soon?"

My head moves in a distinct shake. "No… I don't think so. I want to stay put for a while. I've got an art exhibit coming up, and I just… I missed the city a lot over the summer. It's good to be home."

"And to be back with Noah?" She asks, innocently enough, though I still feel like I'm under a microscope.

It's not her fault at all. She doesn't know what's going on with Noah and me. What's *been* going on for four years now… Hell, *I* don't even know what's going on with us, which is probably why I'm becoming sweaty and fidgety all of a sudden.

"Yea," I answer honestly.

I don't know what it is about her, but I feel like I can open up to this girl. Maybe it's her eyes, all big and round and inquisitive. Or the way she stares at you while you're speaking, her face still with the desire to hear what you're saying thoroughly.

"I always miss him when we're apart, but it's sort of become a part of our relationship. Noah and I…" I pause to sigh. "We've been casual for so long, sometimes I wonder if we're stuck like this…"

"Has he said anything to you about wanting more?" She asks, her voice low and curious.

"No. But lately it's felt different. I don't know how to explain it…" I glance across the room at Noah, who's laughing at something Andrew is saying. "Something shifted, and it feels like he's nervous about it. Like he's realizing he might want…" I stop and shake my head. "You probably have no clue what I'm talking about."

"No, trust me, I do," she says assuredly. "Like I said, I haven't known you guys long, but I could tell just from seeing you two interact the night when I met you that Noah sees you differently than everyone else. There may be a million women in New York, but there's only one Alex Mackenzie. He knows that."

I press my lips together before I can get emotional. I've already got a nice buzz going, and if we keep talking about Noah and my crazy relationship status, I just know I'll start blubbering. So instead I give Tessa a friendly hug and thank her for the drinks by getting our next round to bring to the table.

We walk over to our guys, mojitos in hand, and join them in the middle of some debate they're having about one of their costars. I scoot in next to Noah, and Tessa does the same with Andrew, and when I see the look he's giving her, like he's finally found something he's been searching for his whole life, I can't help but nestle up even closer to Noah.

We chat and drink more, laughing and teasing one another, which is practically a second language for us. Noah and Andrew talk about their upcoming premiere, and all the crazy conventions their people have been lining up for them. Then I tell them about my next exhibit, which is happening before the holidays at a gallery in TriBeca, and is set to be one of my biggest showings ever.

Noah is over-the-moon. He's been beaming with pride for me about this show since the other day when we found out it was happening. I know I could be misconstruing his friendly enthusiasm for boyfriend-like support, but it makes me feel too good to care.

I'm talking about the gallery owner, Jean-Paul, a very ostentatious art critic-turned gallery mogul who just so happens to love me, when Noah slides his hand onto my leg. Normally, this wouldn't be a big deal at all, but for some reason tonight it makes me shiver inside.

He's smiling at me, fully engrossed in what I'm saying, while Andrew and Tessa are in their own little world across the table, so it truly feels like it's *just* Noah and me. Just us, on our own private island. Just me and my best friend who makes my heart race, and my nerves rattle. Who looks at me like I'm doing him some great service just by being here, talking about whatever.

When I'm done with my little story, he chuckles and leans in closer, whispering, "You look so beautiful tonight."

That's it. My heart is done-for.

He delivered the knock-out punch. And now I know with absolute certainty I'll never be able to be *just friends* with this man.

It has to be all or nothing.

My eyes dart across the table once more, where Andrew and Tessa are whispering to one another, looking flushed and ravenously afflicted. Noah follows my gaze, and I feel a vibration from his small laugh.

"They're hooked, aren't they?" He murmurs, making circles on my thigh with his thumb. I nod slowly, because I'm not sure I can speak right now. "It really makes you think…"

I turn my face upward to gape at him with my pulse thrumming in my neck. Then his eyes slide off the love birds across from us and land on mine. And I hear him take in a sharp breath.

Holy fuck… What's happening…? I might pass out.

We're snapped out of our trance when Tessa scoots off her seat, but before she can make it more than a couple inches, Johnny flops himself in next to her, effectively shoving her onto Andrew's lap.

"What in God's name are you two whispering about over here?" Johnny chuckles and lifts a brow.

For a moment I freeze in sheer panic and awkwardness, thinking he's calling me and Noah out. But then I relax when I realize he's talking to Andrew and Tessa. Though I don't think I was the only one preparing to make excuses, since I can feel Noah's shoulders drop in relief next to me.

Andrew and Tessa gape at each other, sharing the look of two people who were just busted.

Sorry guys, but better you than me.

Noah leans in on the table. "I'll tell you what they're saying. It goes something like this: I love you more. No, *I love you* more!" He mocks his friends, doing a high-pitched Tessa voice and a rumbling British Andrew. We all laugh because it's adorable as hell, and factual.

"Sounds pretty accurate," Andrew smirks, then winks at Tessa.

My chest warms at the sight. It's amazing how seeing two people so in love can make you question every thought you've ever had about your own relationships.

After that, Johnny demands that we focus on him, asking us if he should go home with Keira. I tell him about how she's recently been through a divorce and not looking for anything serious, to which he mentions that she's already invited him home with her. *That was fast. And not surprising at all.*

Then Johnny asks Andrew if him and Tessa are getting ready to leave soon, because he's *that* friend who says what we're all thinking. The couple exchanges some eager looks, eyes gleaming with anticipation for spending time alone together, and it's crazy, but I really get it. Because right now, more than anything, I just want to be alone with Noah.

"You two are so adorable," I have to say, and they smile.

"We can stay..." Andrew hums, though it's clear this is the last thing he wants to do.

"No way, don't be silly," Noah insists. "It's your first night back together. Go enjoy it. We'll all still be here tomorrow."

"New love," I sigh and flutter my lashes, which makes Andrew laugh.

"I know, right? You're making us all jealous anyway," Noah chuckles, and then he winks at Tessa. It fills my belly with eager and curious butterflies.

Is he really jealous of their relationship? Does Noah want what they have? Maybe he and Tessa have talked about it...

Please tell me! I need to know!

I'm jittering like a whacko as we all say our goodbyes to Andrew and Tessa. We agree to get dinner tomorrow, and Johnny engulfs Tessa into one of his bear hugs, whispering something in her ear that makes her smile so wide she's beaming. And I've never been more ecstatic, because it seems like our little group has added one new, very important member.

Once the two of them leave, Johnny takes Keira home, and it's just Noah and me. I'm relieved to be alone with him, but I'm also more nervous than I have been in a while. The air around our table is thick with tension, and I'm not sure why. I could potentially throw up.

Noah sips his drink, appearing cool, calm and collected. And I'm sure everyone else in the world is buying it.

But not me. I know him better than that.

"What's on your mind?" I ask, having summoned all my internal courage, and that which I've borrowed from the multiple drinks.

Noah's eyes lock on mine, boring into me so hard I'm lost in the depth of his irises. He tugs me closer to him, until I'm sitting on his lap a bit, then leans in by my ear, releasing a shaky breath.

"I'm just... thinking," he mumbles, sounding more unsure, more scared than I've heard him in a long time. "Seeing Andrew fall in love so hard, and so fast... It's making me consider things..." His voice trails off as he plays with my hair.

"Noah... I know you're not a relationship guy," I whisper, trying so hard not to let my voice quiver. "And it scares you to think about being in a real one. But it's totally normal to see your best friend getting serious with someone and wonder what it would be like to have that for yourself."

He makes a little noise that slithers inside my heart. "Alex, I'm not that guy anymore…"

And then I go still, because I'm not sure what he's saying, and if it's good or bad.

Fortunately for me, he continues before I can really panic. "That bachelor, womanizer you befriended four years ago… That guy is long gone. I mean, sure… I went a little crazy when you left for Budapest. I was dying inside from losing the best girl I've ever known, so I covered up my emotions the only way I know how. But when you came back… I realized that no amount of meaningless sex will ever satisfy the Alex-shaped hole in my heart."

I'm afraid to look at him again. I might crumble to pieces.

"Do you know how many people I've slept with in the last two years?" He asks, and now I have no choice but to gape up at him, because any variation of terrifying number could come out of his mouth. His lips quirk and I hold my breath. "Two."

"Two…?" My brows are so high they're almost at my hairline.

He nods sheepishly. "Two. And one of them is you. The one I *want*… Is you."

My body breaks out in a tremble as I blink up at him over wide, wet eyes with tears straining behind them. I can't believe what I'm hearing right now. I want to shake my head like a cartoon character who just got hit with a mallet.

"Who's the other one?" My small, stupid voice asks, like a little green jealousy monster, sneaking out when all I really want is to revel in what he just revealed.

Noah laughs softly, charmed by my possessive concern. "Just… someone I met a few weeks ago when I wasn't sure if you were coming back."

His smile slips away, and he looks down, swallowing visibly in guilt.

I take his jaw in my hand and force his eyes to connect with mine. "You know that's never mattered to me, right?"

"I know, Alex," he breathes. "And that's why you're so amazing. You see me. The *real* me. You always have. And that's why I need you to understand that you didn't force me to change who I was. You helped me become who I *am*."

I'm shaking everywhere. My hands, my legs, my lips. I bite the bottom one hard to stop it and Noah pulls it gently with his fingers, before leaning in and kissing me so slow, so full I think I may pass out.

"So all this time…" I whisper on his mouth, my mind racing through

Seek Me

everything that's happened in the last two years, since I came home from Budapest. I'm seeing it all so much clearer now. "All this time, I thought you were..." He nods, breathing heavy. "But you weren't...?" He shakes his head. "Why didn't you tell me?"

"I'm sorry, baby," he takes my hand and places it over his heart so I can feel it leaping in his chest. "I didn't know what you wanted... I didn't know if it would change anything."

Noah... You silly, wonderful, perfect man.

It changes *everything.*

My heart is soaring. I can't believe Noah Richards, Bachelor King of New York City, has stopped whoring around. For *me*.

It's almost unfathomable.

And then, because I'm an unsure girl with low self-esteem, I gulp over my own guilt. "It's not exactly like I'm innocent either, Noah."

He pulls back to look me in the eye. "Have you hooked up with anyone other than me while you've been in New York? Since your ex, I mean..." My head shakes hard and fast, which has him wearing that dazzling, overjoyed, cutest-thing-ever smile. "You only wanted me...?"

"Only you," I hold his jaw and kiss him, sensually, drawing out a sweet, satisfied hum. "Can you promise me one thing, though...?" I ask and he blinks. "Have you ever hooked up with any of my friends?"

"Never," he tells me with sincerity. "I promise." I sigh out hard in relief and he chuckles.

And then we kiss it out. Long, drawn, passionate kisses, filled with more hunger, more love than any kisses I've ever been a part of.

We're in public. In front of dozens of people. And yet it's still just *us*.

I'm more thrilled than I can even comprehend. I don't know what any of this means, but it has to mean something. Noah has grown up for me. He's ready for more... And I *know* for the first time since Roger, I'm ready, too.

When we finally peel off each other, we're breathless and burning up. I can feel Noah's erection throbbing on me through his jeans, and I want nothing more than to go home with him and do what we do best. But a part of me thinks we need to finish hashing this out before we distract ourselves with sex.

"So um..." I swallow, tracing his muscles through his shirt, because I can't not. "What does this mean?"

His eyes are hooded with lust, but he still looks nervous. "Baby, I swore to myself I would never push you into something you don't want... Something you're not ready for. I'll never do that to you, as long as I'm breathing. So if you want this, I'm gonna need you to tell me so."

Anxiety ripples through my stomach. *He wants me to admit my feelings first?? That's a scary thought.*

But I nod. If that's what I need to do to let him know how I feel, I have no choice but to do it. I'm not hiding from my truth anymore.

"I think we should talk about this," I chew on my lip. "There's a lot going on. I mean… this is crazy."

He chuckles and I laugh with him. It almost feels like we're being naughty; like we're doing something forbidden. We've been friends who fuck for so long. Admitting we have feelings for each other and talking about being exclusive? That's taboo for us.

"Trust me, baby. If you could see inside my head, you'd know it's really not as insane as one might think." He caresses my butt with a large palm, sending tingly sparks across my skin.

"What do you mean by that?" I ask, my tone eager, giving away how desperate I am for him to tell me his feelings first.

"There's something I never told you…" he hums with reticence. "Something I almost… did…"

He's hesitating and I'm growing impatient and antsy.

"Please tell me," I beg. "I need to know."

He kisses my jaw then shakes his head. "No way. I'm not telling you yet. Not until you tell me what I want to hear."

I growl and kiss his neck, slow and soft, running my lips over his throat. "*Please* tell me."

"That's not fair," he shifts under me. "You can't use your perfect lips as a weapon."

"You'd have to get used to it…" I purr on his warm skin that smells like every scrumptious treat I've ever craved. "If we were…"

My voice trails off and I gulp. How am I still so nervous about admitting that I want to be with him? I might have some serious emotional problems here. It's the only explanation.

"If we were what?" He asks, cocking a sexy eyebrow. He looks so smug I just want to smack him on the ass.

"Noah…" I whine and he laughs out an erotic, growly thing.

"It's getting late," he murmurs, kissing my temple. "We should get you home."

I gape at him in hurt and rejection. "Home... To *my* home?"

He smiles wide, combing his fingers through my hair. "We shouldn't sleep together again until we know where we stand."

"Oh my God, you're milking this so hard!" I squeal and he laughs again. "You're really going to make me declare my love for you before you'll have sex with me again?!"

His smile falls and his eyes widen. "Is that what you want to do...? Declare your... love?" He whispers the word *love* like it's a line from a communist manifesto.

"Noah, stop," I pout. Now I'm grouchy.

It was one thing wrapping my head around confessing my feelings for him first, but now he's withholding sex when he looks like that. It's completely unfair.

"Tell you what, fairy girl," he takes my hand and laces our fingers. I'm awestruck by how amazingly sexy he is. And the things he says... I've become more than a little obsessed the nickname. "I'm throwing a party at Maxwell's tomorrow. I started planning it the other day. Something fun to celebrate with all our friends since Andrew and Johnny are here. Tomorrow at the party, you tell me what you want, and when you do, I'll give you whatever that is."

I stare at him, flabbergasted at how this night has gone.

"You hear what I'm saying, Alexandra?" His dark eyes reach into my soul and instinctively I nod. "What you want... You're going to get."

My stomach does a somersault as my heart pounds in my ears.

He's telling me he wants to be with me... But I have to go first.

Damn him. He's the sweetest, most incredible, frustrating man in the entire world.

And come tomorrow, he might be my boyfriend. If I can muster up the courage to give in.

"What if I tell you now?" I rasp. "Can I stay over?"

He laughs and even though I'm grumpy and sexually frustrated, I can't get over how fantastic he looks and sounds when he's laughing like that.

"No. You have to tell me tomorrow. I think it'll be more special that way." He smiles victoriously, and I want to punch him. Then kiss him. Then bite those tasty lips right off.

"You're being an idiot."

He leans in close to my ear and whispers, "Love you too."

Chapter Thirty
Noah's Journal

Hey, Boots. How's it going, buddy?

I hope kitty heaven is fun. I'm so curious about it... Are there fish everywhere for you to catch? Mice? Endless bags of Temptations treats for you to snack on whenever you want?

What about string? Has catnip been legalized? I have so many questions, Bootsey boy. I wish I could see it for myself.

At this point, I'm not sure I'd necessarily mind going to heaven myself... Even a cat-themed one.

Anything would be better than staying here on Earth, with all the death and destruction... And the love of my life who keeps leaving me.

I know what you're going to say, Boots, and I already don't want to hear it. You think I need to tell Alex how I feel about her. You think that if I let her know I'm crazy about her, she'll stay and we can be together.

Well, as much as I appreciate the advice, you're a little out of your league here, pal. Sure, I don't know exactly what you got up to before I took you in, but I can't imagine you let me rip you away from some super fulfilling relationship. So you don't exactly know what it's like to be in love with someone who has dealt with so much pain in their past.

I made a promise to myself a long time ago that I would never hurt Alex in any way. I'll never be like her scumbag ex. I won't rope her into staying here, or make her give up on her dreams of traveling just to make *me* happy. Her happiness is a zillion times more important than mine will ever be.

If Alex wants to be with me, she'll have to figure it out on her own terms. I know I sound like a broken record, but I won't push her, Boots. Not ever.

That's why I didn't tell her about my feelings before she left for Budapest, that's why I've never called her while she's been away, and that's why I refuse to ask her not to leave when all I want in the world is for her to stay.

Because *she* needs this.

I still remember the first time I saw her with bruises on her face. It felt

Seek Me

like the sky was an infinitely large sheet of rubber that had come falling down on top of me, making it impossible to breathe. I was being strangled to death. Suffocated.

Seeing someone I care about being hurt was like the most frustrating helplessness of all time, and I experienced that for months on end while Alex was with Roger. But I would go back and do it a thousand more times if I had to, because she means that fucking much to me.

After helping her through that trauma, after all the blinding inadequacy that comes with wondering if there's more I could be doing... More I *should* be doing... After seeing her finally emerge victorious, like the beautiful tattooed ass-kicking princess she is, there is no fucking way I could ever stop her from following her dreams.

So I stayed quiet. I shut my fucking mouth and let her do her thing. And yes, it's killed me a little bit, slowly, over the last three years. But again, I'd do it a million more times.

I will endure this pain forever if I have to. If it means she gets to be happy. Even if that happiness comes from being away from me. Because that's what love is, Bootsey. Being completely and utterly selfless. Putting the needs of someone else above your own without a second thought.

And so that's what I'll keep doing. Though I have to try and keep my cool a little more with it... It's hard to stop the jealousy and the hurt from bubbling over sometimes.

I did something really abhorrent last night, Boots, and I'm kind of sick over it.

I was mad that Alex was leaving again, so when she came to my house where I was having my going away party, I sorta brushed her off... And flirted with girls right in front of her.

I know, dude. You don't have to rub it in. I'm Captain Douchenozzle.

Of course I didn't sleep with any of those girls, who were all a little put-off that I made them leave after that performance. I don't know what came over me, and I don't blame Alex for being mad. Although she'd probably forgive me in a heartbeat. She's so sweet and understanding, that girl.

She'd tell me it's *okay*, and that she knows I *didn't mean any harm*; she knows that's not *me*. And maybe we'd try to convince ourselves that it's because we're *just friends*, so what does it matter if I flirt with girls?

But I feel like we both know that's bullshit. We're more than friends. We always have been.

When I think about me and Alex... *Really* think about us... I don't see two best friends who have been casually fucking for three plus years. I see a *couple*. A boyfriend and a girlfriend who have put themselves and each other through the ringer for years and still manage to smile and kiss and fuck like we were made to do just that.

Alex and I have always been *more*.

Now I just need her to admit that, so we can end this production we've been putting on and finally be together.

Man oh man, buddy. I tell you. If Alex only knew the things I've been dreaming about since pretty much the first moment I saw her...

If she only knew how she brightens my day just from being alive. Just from existing.

If she knew that not a day has gone by since I met her at Maxwell's where I didn't crave just being near her. That the sound of her laugh is my favorite song, and her big, sexy brain is my favorite part of her, despite how every inch of her body makes me harder than a goddamn calculus exam.

If she knew that I watch her sleep a lot more than a normal person would cop to, and that when I sleep alone, I wake up hugging my pillow wishing it was her, which is another insanely embarrassing thing to confess.

If she knew that her smell awakens my soul... Enlivens me. Like a psychedelic drug, it twists at the nerves in my brain and makes the world feel like a painting. That her eyes are my favorite color on the planet, and that every green object I see I compare it to them. And her eyes always win, by a landslide.

If she knew that I think she's the funniest, cutest, strongest and most phenomenal person I've ever had the good fortune of meeting, and that she changed me down to my core, in the best possible way. That I'm not just a bachelor anymore... I'm not just the life of the party. The guy who lives wearing a wicked smirk to cheer his friends up, taking them out and showing them a good time, because I'm forever single, and it's my thing.

Ever since I met her, I stopped wanting to be that. She showed me my worth, and who I really am just by being *herself*. She made me see that I'm not just a bachelor, or a chronic partier, or someone who laughs in the face of all that is serious. That I haven't even slept with anyone who isn't her in longer than I can remember, and it feels... *good*. Better than good.

It feels right.

If Alex only knew that I found in her something my heart has been seeking my entire life, I know she would stay.

Seek Me

And I can't let her do that. Not until she's absolutely sure it's what she wants.

Because Alex is the only person who makes decisions for Alex now.

So until the time comes, when she tells me what she wants, I'll sit quietly. Bide my time and store up every ounce of love I have to give. I'll save it all for her.

So that when she seeks me, Boots, I'll be right here for her to find.

Chapter Thirty One

Alex

I DIDN'T SLEEP A WINK LAST NIGHT.

I think it was safe to assume that after the way I left things with Noah, when he had Jimmy drive me home, alone, giving me no more than a very brief, very frustrating kiss by the car before I was pushed inside and carted back to Brooklyn by myself, I wouldn't be getting any rest whatsoever.

I lied awake in my bed all damn night staring at my ceiling, alternating between thrilling happiness and blinding pessimism. My mind was running a mile a minute, replaying our conversation on the rooftop over and over and over again until my emotional sanity was jagged and my vagina was so hungry it was ready to chew off my hand.

Noah basically admitted to wanting to be with me last night. And I say *basically* because he's being a giant tool and forcing me to admit my feelings first. I swear, if he wasn't the most gorgeous, adorable and sexy human being who's ever walked the earth, I would punch him right in his stupid, beautiful, perfect face.

Over the course of my obsessing last night, I came to a few conclusions I'll share with you right now.

First, I'm obviously going to tell Noah how I feel tonight, at the party at Maxwell's. I'd have to be the biggest dope on the planet not to, especially after I made up my mind before I even returned from Barcelona that I'm done traveling for a while. The next time I travel somewhere, I want it to be *with* Noah. I've had enough solo adventures to cleanse myself of every wicked memory from my failed marriage. I've let them go, and I've forgiven the universe for sending me a wolf in sheep's clothing as my first great love.

Which brings me to my second conclusion; my next great love. *Noah Richards.*

It's obvious to me now that Noah and I have been dancing around our feelings for one another for years. I would even go so far as to say we fell in love at first sight. Unfortunately, there was always too much standing in the way of

Seek Me

us realizing it before.

But now that I've let go of all my bullshit, it's time to claim my prize for enduring the world's worst first marriage. And honestly, is there any better prize on earth than Noah Richards?

I think not.

My final conclusion from last night has to do with Noah's insane request that I get down on metaphorical bended knee and confess my feelings for him tonight. I know exactly why he's doing it.

He's always been afraid of forcing me into a relationship before I'm ready. While I assumed his fear was of being exclusive to *anyone*, because he's a known bachelor, his revelation last night that he hasn't slept with anyone but me - and one other skank-tron I don't wish to think about right now - since I returned from Budapest two years ago, proves that people can, in fact, change.

I've felt in my heart since we met that Noah is capable of real change. I just never thought he wanted it. But apparently he does… He's already changed his ways for me, or rather, *because of* me. And if that's not the ultimate declaration of love, then I don't know what is.

So tonight I'll go to his party at Maxwell's. I'll accompany him as his date, per his request. We'll hang out, and have fun with our friends, like we always do, because us loving each other will never erase the fact that he's my best friend.

We'll drink, we'll laugh, we'll dance. And I will tell him I'm done running. That I'm ready for us to be the real deal, just like we've always wanted.

And according to his words last night, he'll give it to me.

It would be a big fat fib to say I'm not nervous, so I won't even bother saying it. I just know that while Noah and I being *official* probably won't change our lives at all, it's still a big deal.

What will it be like to say that Noah Richards is my *boyfriend*? Just thinking about it is making me all tingly.

I jump out of bed, where I've been laying wide awake for hours, and take a shower. I change into some of Noah's clothes he left here, because I'm already getting myself used to the idea of us being a couple, and I love it so much more than I could have anticipated, then I go to my studio to paint.

I'm working on pieces for my show in a couple months, and they need to be perfect. This show will be a monumental step for me, just like the thing I'll be engaging in tonight at Maxwell's.

The word *engage* sticks in my mind for a moment, and I have to shake it out of my head.

That this will all be going down at Maxwell's - the place where Noah and I met four years ago - makes me so antsy I could scream. I check my watch, and I'm disappointed to find it's still eight-thirty in the morning. *Only twelve more hours until I can go see my man... And make him my man. Officially.*

I squeal and wiggle on my stool. This whole thing is *so* me and Noah. Rather than just voicing our feelings last night and celebrating with some hot and mildly kinky sex, we're going to wait until a party full of people to lay it all on the table. We're the most unconventional couple who's ever existed.

And that gets me thinking. And then I'm painting what I'm thinking.

And before I know it, three hours have gone by, my back is stiff, and my arms are shaking. But this painting is fucking killer. One of the most fantastic things I've ever done. I don't know if I'll sell this one.

I stand up to stretch and get some circulation back into my limbs, and my giddy excitement wants me to text a picture of the painting to Noah. But I refrain.

I think I'd rather show it to him when it's done. In person.

He might even cry. Oh my God, that would be so great!

I snicker to myself as I clean up, then I check my phone for texts from Noah, which there are, as usual. Potential love-professions aside, we're still *us*, and it's perfect.

Noah: Jimmy will be w A&T tonight so I'll send a car to your place around 8.

Noah: I hope you got some sleep last night beautiful

Noah: I missed you... *Insert sad, pouty face emoji*

Me: Well you should. You're the one who sent me home *Insert eyebrow-raised emoji*

Noah: Lol sorry not sorry. Tonight is a big night for us... I didn't want to mess it up by screwing you into a coma

I snort out a laugh.

Me: Oh I'm sure that's the reason. I'm sure it has NOTHING AT ALL to do with the fact that you're nervous. And you wanted to pee the bed alone.

Noah: Is this what it'll be like when we're a couple? You dogging me constantly?

Seek Me

I suck in a hard breath while my heart rate increases to that of a hummingbird's.

Noah: Because I really fuckin like it

I bite my lip until it's swollen.

Me: You seem awfully confident there Richards. You have no clue what I'm going to say tonight...

Noah: A guy can dream Alexandra.

I'm swooning so hard I have to lean up against the wall before I collapse into a buzzing ball of ditz.

Me: Hmm... Okay well you go prepare yourself. I'll see you tonight.

Noah: Can't wait

Noah: Oh and Alex?

Me: Yes...

Noah: Remember the panty rule

My face splits in half and my toes wiggle.

Noah's *panty rule* means he's allowed to destroy any pair of my panties he wants in order to get my vagina naked, if I'm *inconsiderate enough not to go commando,* his exact words.

And seeing as how he's already *dreaming* about us becoming a couple by the end of the night, I'd say there's a good chance we'll end up in a corner somewhere banging it out like besties-turned-significant-others.

Now for the most *significant* decision of the night: to go bare-booty or not?

I choose to wear panties.

The panty rule will be honored regardless, so I made sure not to wear any of my favorites.

And since I was informed this will be a *semi-casual* event, I've also decided to wear leather pants and my fave Jim Morrison t-shirt that I ripped up and cut into a crop top.

It's my thing.

I'm just finishing up applying some shimmery gloss over the lipstick color I chose for the night, when my door buzzes. I already know it's the car Noah sent for me, so I grab my bag and head downstairs, getting used to the fluttering sensation in my stomach.

Let loose, boys. You've earned it.

When I get down to the lobby of my building, I see my car waiting at the curb. Just as I'm walking to it, a hand grabs my arm to stop me.

I look up and all the blood drains from my face.

Ice-cold chills wash over me even in the August heat. I blink hard, willing away this nightmare I'm trapped in. But unfortunately it won't end.

This is *fucking* real.

"Hey, little one."

I should run.

In the past, my instincts were sharp. I could always anticipate strikes and brace myself to soften the blows. Or maneuver and steer conversations to achieve the least painful outcome.

But now, as my ex-husband stands before me, staring down at my face with the same fluorescent blue eyes that captivated me twelve years ago, I fully believe I've gone soft.

Roger regards me with caution, as if he's prepared for me to flee, and will use necessary tactics to keep that from happening. It's terrifying me so hard I can barely breathe.

"W-what are you doing here?" I ask, my mind frantically racing through every available escape.

I know the car is only a few feet away. I can't chance looking at it, but I remember where it sits. And the driver would have been instructed not to leave without me, and to call Noah if there's a problem.

Noah...

God, I wish he was here right now. He'd go all Tarantino movie on this asshole before he could breathe his next word.

"I just came to see how you're doing," Roger speaks slow and calculated. He seems casual enough, but then that was always his MO. He's calm and cool... until he's not.

He's a goddamned psycho. I need to get away from him. Quick.

"You're a hard girl to get ahold of these days," he goes on, lifting his brows at my face.

And the new realization dawns on me. *It was him. All those unknown number calls.*

Jesus Christ...

"I've been busy," I reply, fumbling to keep my cool.

"Clearly," he hums, and there's a tiny shimmer of something very scary in his eyes, imperceptible to anyone but me.

"Well, Alexandra, I just came to tell you there are no hard feelings. About you leaving me and ruining my life." I swallow hard, inching away as slowly as possible.

His gaze skims me generously. "You look wonderful. Hot date?"

I sprint.

I don't even run. I just turn as fast as possible and *sprint* like my damn life depends on it, which it probably does.

I get to the car and whip open the door fast, diving into the back seat.

"Drive! Drive! Hurry!" I shout at the confused driver, who immediately shifts the car and pulls away with a skid.

I peek out the rear window as we speed off, but Roger's already gone. I'm panting, aggressively sucking air into my lungs as I flop back in the seat and close my eyes.

"Is everything alright, Ms. Mackenzie?" The nervous driver asks, and suddenly I miss Jimmy. More than I ever have before.

"No... Not really," I whimper and rub my forehead. "Do you work for the same security company as Jimmy Lopez by any chance?"

"Yea, ma'am," he nods. "Mr. Richards hired us. You may not remember me, but I was at your house a few years ago for a security detail, organized by Mr. Lopez."

Oh, thank God.

I breathe a sigh of relief. "Thank you for that, by the way." He nods at me in the rearview mirror. "That man I was talking to... I'm not sure if you saw... Anyway, that's my ex-husband. The one you guys were protecting me from back then..."

"Oh shit," he whispers, then peeks at me. "Pardon my language."

I chuckle. "It's fine. The guy's a fucking asshole. My restraining order ran out last year, and I never bothered to renew it because I hadn't heard from him in years, and I thought he was in Connecticut… Sorry, I'm rambling. I guess now he's back and who knows what he wants."

"Probably nothing good, I imagine," my new driver friend mutters.

"Until I can get a new restraining order, I might need you guys to keep watch again."

"Ms. Mackenzie, part of our job is to always watch out for you," he says with sincerity. "Any time any of us chauffeurs you, Mr. Richards pays us to make sure you're safe."

Wow… I may have gone soft, but Noah hasn't.

"Thanks a lot, um… What's your name?" I ask, feeling bad that this guy's been protecting me from my crazed ex-husband for years and I don't even know his name.

"It's Phil," he says with a kind smile.

"Nice to officially meet you, Phil. I'm Alex. Is Jimmy your boss?"

"Yes, ma'am."

"I'll be sure to put in a good word." I grin.

"Thank you, ma'am. Or you could… you know… put in a good word with the jefe grande."

My Spanish isn't fantastic, but I know he said *big boss*.

I pause for a moment before my eyes widen. "Oh, you mean Noah!" He chuckles and nods, to which I laugh softly. "I can do that, too. I'm on my way to his party to tell him I think we should be a real couple."

I have no idea why I'm telling him all this.

"You're *not* a real couple?" Phil asks, apparently bemused and skeptical.

"Alright, Phil. Just shut up, okay?" I grumble through a stupid smirk while Phil laughs at me.

Almost thirty-minutes and some annoying traffic later, Phil parks in front of Maxwell's and gets out to open my door for me. As if the nerves I was feeling tonight weren't already too much, what with the looming task of finally telling Noah how I feel and my abusive ex showing up out of nowhere to scare the crap out of me, now there are paparazzi swarming the vehicle and the entrance to the club.

Great.

I hop out of the backseat and the cameras flash, blinding me while random people shout personal questions. I will never understand where some of these weirdos get the audacity to ask such bold questions at complete strangers. One time a hack actually asked where me and Noah like to do it best.

Thank God Noah wasn't with me, because I'm sure he would've ended up settling out of some stupid lawsuit for that fucker. Instead, I just smiled at him and replied, *"Your mom's house."*

I'm already too far in my head to pay attention to what any of these fools are shouting. I simply allow Phil to guide me inside, where he hands me off to more of Noah's security, and Maxwell's security. I should have guessed this would be like Fort Knox to get into, since a majority of Noah's friends are famous and super rich.

Once I'm upstairs, I meander through the crowd of people on the rooftop, searching for Noah first and booze second. But before I can look too hard, a warm, muscular body is wrapping me up from behind, and the delicious scent that's invading my nose tells me it's my man.

If all goes accordingly.

"Embarrassing confession time," he whispers in my ear, giving me goosebumps. "I've been watching the door for you since I got here."

I spin in his arms because I just *need* to see his face before I die. I run my hands up his frame, locking my eyes on his and allowing him to swallow up all my doubts and fears with just that one look.

He's dressed as he always is, in something flashy and bizarre; something only *he* could pull off. And of course it's working for him. He's the hottest man in this whole damn place, no debate.

"Alex, um..." he stutters and his brows pull together. "I know we're supposed to figure *us* out tonight, and I'm super excited about it. But... do you think..." He pauses and bites his lip. "Can I kiss you?"

My knees quake and I hold on to his strong shoulders to keep from falling. "You're so fucking cute, it's *killing* me..."

He laughs a rumbly one and leans in, pressing his soft, full lips to mine. My hands fly to his jaw like a reflex and I hold on, feeling it move, tighten and adjust as he kisses me deeper, claiming my mouth like only he can.

Because it belongs to him. *I do.*

He whimpers as he forces himself back, breathing ragged over my mouth. "Baby, I *really* want to be alone with you right now..."

"I know. Me too," I tell him, sifting my fingers through his hair.

He opens his eyes and gazes at me, the tenebrosity of them possessively ravenous. And yet I can see his angst, his uncertainty. It makes me want to tell him what I want right this second so we can move forward.

"What's wrong, my dark fairy?" He cocks his head to the side, then runs his thumb between my brows. "You only get this little *v* here when you're nervous. Am I putting too much pressure on you? Alex, I swear I'm not trying to make anything difficult, I just need to hear you say the words so we can -"

"Noah, it's not that," I interrupt his rambling, and I can't help but smile because believe it or not, I'm really excited.

All I've wanted for so long is to hear Noah tell me he wants to be officially mine. I can make that happen tonight, and I've never felt so giddy.

"Oh..." he breathes. "Then what is it?"

I clam up a bit, my eyes darting around in every which way, looking for a waiter. Noah catches on and waves a hand at some guy who scampers off in search of drinks for us.

"Roger showed up at my place," I let the words out, and I'm still in some minute shock.

Seeing my ex-husband's face after years have passed... After I've done so much to move on from him. It's fucking with my mind a little.

The last time I saw him was the night I moved out, when Jimmy kicked his ass. Throughout the entire divorce process, I didn't have to see him once, though he *did* call me for a while afterward, leaving all those lovely voicemails, which is why I changed my number.

I haven't the slightest clue how he found out my new number, or where I live. But I suppose anything is possible when you're rich and well-connected. Apparently everyone finding out he's an abusive cheating monster didn't rob him of his ability to buy information.

Noah's entire body is so still, you would think I was standing beside his wax figure at Madame Tussaud's. He's staring at me with many emotions cluttering his face, I don't know what I could possibly say next. So I just keep quiet.

"Did he..." He pauses to swallow. "Was he... inside?"

"No," I huff, shaking my head repeatedly. He breathes out of relief. "Nothing like that. He was outside my building. He stopped me before I could get into the car."

"Jesus..." Noah cringes. "Are you alright?"

He pulls me closer to him, touching me everywhere and inspecting for some evidence of harm we both know isn't there. It's so sweet I could cry.

"Yes, I'm fine. He just said there are *no hard feelings* for me ruining his life. And then I ran away to the car as fast as possible before he could say anymore."

"What a fucking pile of shit," he seethes, his already shadowed eyes growing darker with rage.

"I know, right?" I mutter, because I'm still not sure what else to say.

"Well, you'll stay with me until we inform the police. Get that restraining order sorted out again," he rakes his fingers through his hair. Then he blinks at me. "Right?"

"Yes! Of course," I nod vehemently, so he doesn't think I secretly *want* to see Roger again.

Noah hums and grabs me hard, hugging onto me with all his might. "Baby, I'm so sorry this happened to you. I shouldn't have made you go home last night. It's all my fault..."

"Noah, that's ridiculous," I murmur, burying my face in his chest and inhaling a nice big whiff of his mouthwatering smell. "It's my apartment. Obviously I would have to go back there, eventually."

He grunts, and I turn my head up to look at him. But he won't stop hugging me, so I settle in and let him.

He finally removes his strangling hold on me and says, "Johnny's around here somewhere. Andrew and Tessa should arrive shortly."

I nod and chomp down on my lip. He keeps staring at me and I'm not sure if he wants me to just shout out my feelings for him now and get it over with, or if he wants to go somewhere so we can do it alone.

The waiter brings us drinks and I take a massive gulp, needing the lowered inhibitions for what I'm about to do.

"So... Maybe we should go talk," I whisper at him and raise my brows, lifting on my tippy toes to kiss his chin.

Noah's lips curve into an elated little smile. But then out of nowhere he's tackled so fast he becomes a blur of shaggy hair and a flying Supreme hat.

Johnny laughs hysterically, helping Noah up and dusting him off. Noah coughs like he had the wind knocked out of him, but chuckles anyway. This must be their thing they do... Attacking each other for fun.

"Hey, look! It's Noah's other half," Johnny grins. "And I'm not talking about Andrew."

He pulls me into one of the circus-trapeze-flying hugs, forcing giggles out of me like I'm a damn toddler or something.

"So where is my baby blue and his woman?" Johnny asks Noah, looking around as if expecting to spot Andrew and Tessa.

"On their way," Noah says, and I pout internally. *So much for our talk. If*

Andrew and Tessa are coming, that means Noah will be distracted with them for a while. He takes my hand and pulls me with him. "Come on. Let's go say hi to our friends."

My pout quickly morphs into a grin, because we're already a couple.

He just doesn't know it yet.

Roughly an hour later, Andrew and Tessa grace us with their presence. They both look stunning, as usual, and radiant with that new-love glow, though I can't help but notice they appear a bit tired, and slightly stressed. *I know the feeling.*

Once they arrive, we all hang out and drink for a bit. Andrew brings Tessa all around the party, introducing her to people, and I know this because I'm paying more attention to them than I want to be.

I think Noah is avoiding me. I haven't really seen him much in the last hour, and every time I try to snag him away from what he's doing so we can *finally* talk, he makes up an excuse about some party crisis in order to dip out.

I know he's not fleeing on me. He's just nervous, which I think is so adorable. But I've decided I'm not chasing him anymore tonight. He can come to me when he's ready. After all, this whole stupid love-declaration thing was his idea.

Outside of that, I'm still very uneasy about Roger showing up earlier. I can't stop looking over my shoulder every two seconds to make sure he hasn't followed me here. This place is as crowded as balls in a Speedo. I've never seen the rooftop at Maxwell's so packed before. I have to assume it'd be pretty easy to sneak around unseen, although Noah has a list at the door and Roger's name is most certainly *not* on it.

I spot Andrew and Tessa again, talking to a guy, so I decide to join them. I wander up to Tessa and place my hand on her shoulder.

"What are you guys up to?" I ask, noting that Tessa looks hella uncomfortable.

"Oh, Alex!" She chirps, then introduces me to the man they're standing with as her Supervisor from work.

Me and the dude shake hands and I give Andrew a look, telepathically asking if his girl needs saving. He widens his eyes and sips his drink, which definitely means *yes.*

"Tess, I wanted to introduce you to someone," I lift my brow at her. "Can I steal you for a minute?"

Seek Me

"Um, yea! Sure." She glances at Andrew. "Be right back?"

Andrew nods, showing her a sweet little smile that makes my heart swell. They're just so cute together, it's impossible not to look at them like two characters in a Disney fairy tale.

I lock my arm with Tessa's and lead her away, through the crowd and over to a table. We both have a seat across from one another and I take a gulp of my drink.

"Sorry. You looked like you needed to get out of there," I say to her with a small smile.

"Yea, thank you," she sighs. "That was so awkward. I never expected to see anyone I work with here. Thank God Andrew's good on his feet."

I really want to make a dirty joke, but I hold my tongue. *Noah's clearly rubbed off on me.*

"He'll distract him for a bit," I laugh. "So how's it going with you two?"

Tessa's eyes drift down to the drink in her hands and she appears distraught.

"It's complicated..." she murmurs and I pout at her words. "We love each other so much, and we have the most incredible chemistry I've ever experienced in my life, but there are just so many things..."

It's uncanny that Andrew and Tessa are dealing with relationship drama similar to Noah and me. Of course, our situation is less complicated now...

And I feel momentarily ridiculous that I'm sitting around, whining about not being able to be with the guy I love when really the only thing standing in our way is fear. Which is such a stupid reason not to be with someone.

Andrew and Tessa have real problems holding them back. They're in the midst of a superstorm, while me and Noah are complaining about a light drizzle.

"I hear you," I say to Tessa. "Do you feel like you're gonna stick it out?"

"I honestly don't think I'd survive if I tried to walk away. I've never felt like this before. Frankly, it's kind of overwhelming. But in a good way. Like, I feel miserable when we're not together, but then when we are, it's..." A massive smile creeps over her lips. "I don't know, but it's something else."

I grin at her. *I know the feeling, girlfriend.*

"I've definitely seen it!" I chuckle, which makes her smile bigger. "Honestly, I've never seen two people so connected before."

Tessa's eyes widen and she gapes at me, as if I've just said something ground-breaking to her. It's perplexing, but the more I think about it, the more it makes sense. She and Andrew seem like two people who have found exactly what they were looking for. But you can never see yourself as others see you.

Maybe she needs someone else to cosign with what she already knows in her heart.

"He's going to see a divorce lawyer on Monday…" Tessa whispers.

I'm shocked, but only for a second before I realize there was never any doubt this would happen.

"That's a good thing, right?" My brows lift.

"I think so…" She looks unsure, and now I *know* it's my job to give her the reassurance she needs. *I can help this girl.*

"Hell yea it is!" I cheer, optimistically. "Listen, if there's one thing I've learned it's that sometimes marriages don't work out. It's no one's fault. People change. They grow apart. What was good for someone eight years ago isn't always going to stay good for them for the next eight years."

Oh, crap. I totally didn't mean to bring my own shit to this conversation.

"Or, you know… some other amount of time." I take another big sip of my drink, knowing full-well she won't let that go.

"Were you ever married?" Tessa asks.

I peek up at her, mouth agape, and I very briefly consider lying. But then I straighten my shoulders and buck the fuck up. She needs to know about this, and more importantly, I need to tell her about it.

After all, it could help.

"I've been divorced for… about four years."

And the next thing I know, the floodgates have opened, and I'm telling Tessa my entire story. From falling for the sports doctor when I was seventeen, to my parents disowning me. The cheating, the abuse, and ultimately meeting the man who saved me, right here in this very bar.

We bond over that fact, because apparently she and Andrew met here too. I'm beginning to think they put something in the drinks here at Maxwell's.

I go through my long-winded tale, of how even though I won the fight and freed myself, I couldn't be Noah's. Not then… It was still too fresh. And in my mind, as I'm recanting the epic battle that has been my adulthood, I realize it all worked out exactly how it needed to.

It was painful for me, and Noah, this whole time. But if I hadn't left, over and over again, we might never have discovered just how much we mean to each other.

By the time I'm done speaking, a massive weight has been lifted. Tessa is fascinated, and there's a renewed sense of determination flowing through me.

So I decide to leave her with a piece of advice which is actually for me, too.

Seek Me

"Don't be afraid to move on. I know it's hard, but if you've met someone who makes you feel the way I know Andrew does, then you need to go for it. Don't waste any more time. Life is too short."

Tessa stares at her hands for a moment, and it looks like she might cry, which makes me want to off myself. But then her gaze lifts to mine, and she has a knowing look in her eyes. There's something that she wants me to understand...

"You need to give it a shot with Noah."

My lips part and I'm momentarily dumbfounded.

"As much as we know there are some guys who are chronic bachelors, I personally think all it takes is the right girl to make them finally settle down. Noah was unsure for a while that he would ever want a serious relationship, but I know he does now. And not just with anyone... He wants it with you."

Fuck...

I'm blown away. It's as if I've been hit upside the head with a blunt object, and finally it's all coming together.

They've obviously talked about this. Noah must have told Tessa something about us... About him wanting more.

My heart is ready to burst out of my chest and start flying around the room like a damn bird.

How could I have been so blind as not to see it? It's been there, plain as day, this whole time. Noah's wanted more from me, but he's been too afraid of pushing me when I needed space to recover. Because he's the best friend... *No.* The best *human* I've ever known.

Fully selfless. Patient, dedicated, and in love. With *me.*

Now I think *I* could cry. But I won't. Not yet, anyway. *We'll see how the night goes.*

At that moment, in true Noah fashion, because he's perfect and he can always sense when I need him, he walks over to us and plops down next to me.

"Man, I am getting *drunk*," he sighs then rests his head on my shoulder, slinking an arm around my waist.

Tessa shoots me a clever look, smirking and arching a brow.

Okay, I get it, honey. You were right. You totally called it.

"What are you guys doing over here?" Noah asks, lacing his fingers through mine on the table.

I stare at our joined hands, swallowing over a very dry throat, with eagerness and apprehension bubbling inside me.

I know it's time for us to talk. I can't believe this is finally about to happen...

"Just girl talk," Tessa stands up, smiling. "I'm going to go find Andrew."

She winks at me and I mouth *thank you* to the awesome little matchmaker as she walks away. *I think I just found a new best friend. Good thing I have a spot opening up...*

"Hmm... Girl talk," Noah hums, moving his lips to my ear. "Hot."

I elbow him and he laughs wickedly. Then he takes a breath and turns his whole body to face mine. I mirror his body language.

"So, beautiful," his coal irises set on mine as I use this opportunity to study how magnificent they are. "You have something you wanna tell me?"

I giggle a nervous, breathy thing. "Yea... But for the record, I was ready to tell you this last night."

His smile turns a bit chagrined. "Well, maybe *I* wasn't ready last night..."

"Baby..." I whisper and he bites his lip as I run my hand up his chest. "Are you nervous...? *You?* Noah Richards?"

"I know my name, *Alexandra*," he narrows his gaze playfully and I laugh. "Yes, okay? I was... nervous. You were right... This is crazy. It's a big deal."

"For someone who's so nervous, you still seem awfully confident about what I'm going to say..." I smirk.

He blinks over his wide eyes and I watch his throat adjust as he swallows hard.

"Okay, baby," his head bobs subtly. "Tell me what you want then."

The world slows around us until time is standing completely still. All I have right now are my words for this gorgeous man, who has given me so much in so long that the only way I could possibly repay him is by giving him all of me.

"I want *you*, Noah," I speak softly, my voice shaky as it carries the weight of what I'm saying. "I want only you. I want us... I want *more*."

Noah lets out a strong breath and looks down. He closes his eyes tight for a beat, squeezing them before reopening to look at me. And I feel as though I can see myself through his eyes. Every perfect thing I love about him, he mirrors for me. It's awakening.

He pulls me by the waist until I'm on his lap, holding the back of his neck.

"You're sure?" His forehead creases. "You're ready for this? Because Alex, I wasn't lying when I said I'll give you what you want. I'm *dying* to give that to you..."

A jittery chuckle escapes me as I press my forehead to his. "Noah, you already have. You've been giving me what I want since the day I met you on this rooftop. But yes, baby, I'm ready." I kiss his lips gently and he whimpers. It has my body tightening from my chest all the way down. "I'm finally ready to be yours."

"Mine?" He whispers, kissing me slowly. I nod and purr. "Only mine?"

"Only yours, Noah Richards," my fingers sift through his hair. "I've been yours for four years."

"Baby, I love you," he gasps on my lips, then kisses me, harder and with more reverence than I've ever felt. But then he stops, leaving me desperate for more. More kisses, more words. *More Noah.* "I have loved you for *so* long. And last time I said it, we were still so fucked up. But that doesn't mean I didn't love you, because I did. I do."

"I know, baby," I place my hand over his heart. "I love you too. So fucking bad."

He hums a laugh, quiet and deep, the vibrations rumbling into me. "We're so corny right now, but I'm not even mad at it."

I giggle in his mouth then kiss him again, tasting his smile. It's delicious, and it fills my whole heart with joy.

"Don't ruin this for me, Richards." I bite his lip and he chuckles through it, which is the cutest thing ever. "I have a boyfriend for the first time since I was eighteen."

"Oh my God, me too!" His eyes light up.

"You had a boyfriend when you were eighteen?" I tease him and he growls. "No, wait, I'm serious though. I think you need to *officially* ask me to *officially* be your *official* girlfriend."

"That word sounds weirder and weirder the more you say it," he grins and I tug his chin to make him focus.

"I'm serious!"

"You mean *official?*"

"Anything I want, I get, remember?" I sing and he hums, still wearing that elated smile.

"Alexandra Mackenzie," he sighs my name *perfectly*. "Will you *please* be my official girlfriend?"

I press my lips together, willing myself not to cry. *I will remember this moment for the rest of my life.*

I open my mouth to shout an emphatic *yes* in his face, when suddenly there's a commotion.

People are rushing past us, and there's a large crowd gathering around across the rooftop, at the far end by the second bar. Noah and I share an uneasy look, before I slide off his lap and we race over to see what all the fuss is about.

As we grow closer, I realize everyone is standing around a dazed Andrew and Tessa. I see Johnny darting over to them and Noah takes off, shoving people out of the way to get to his friends.

"Andrew!" Johnny shouts as he and Noah approach, two large security guards having appeared out of nowhere at their sides. "What the fuck happened?!"

I maneuver through the crowd, my stomach twisting in fear when I realize there's a random dude on the ground in front of Andrew, clutching his bloody face.

"Who's this?" Noah asks, observing the kid who's keeled over, grumbling behind his hand.

Andrew and Tessa peek at one another, their eyes wide in distress. Tessa is holding Andrew's right hand in hers, and I'm piecing together the puzzle.

"He called me a cunt," Tessa tells Noah, who gasps in disgust.

"Jesus..." Noah's gaze narrows at the dude on the floor, and I see his eyes darken.

I finally get through all the onlookers and stomp up to my friends.

"Tessa! Andrew... are you guys okay?" I grab Tessa's shoulder in a comforting caress.

"None of us know this fucking loser," Johnny grunts at the bouncers. "How the fuck did he get in here?"

The security guards gape at one another, mouths hanging open as they shrug. I have to roll my eyes, because all the security they have here and still any psycho can stroll in off the street. It has my knees wobbling at the thought of Roger being in here, too.

Useless fucking idiots!

"Well, get him the fuck out!" Noah barks at the guards, waving an authoritative hand through the air that has them springing to action immediately.

"Yes, sir," they both mutter quickly, then pick up the rando off the ground and carry him away.

This is not at all the time, but I can't ignore the rush inside from seeing my man boss people around. He's so commanding and sexy when he's mad.

That dude's my boyfriend? Go me!

"Wow, that was crazy," Johnny grips Andrew's shoulder. "Are you okay, bro?"

Andrew nods, though he really appears out of it. "Yea..."

Seek Me

He turns his attention back to Tessa, as if he's programmed to attend to her at all times, and they mumble back and forth while she checks out his hand.

I grab Noah by the arm and squeeze, prompting him to give me a confused look. We still don't really know what just happened with our friends, but I'm guessing there's more to this story than some guy calling Tessa a *cunt*.

"Noah," Andrew's voice calls and my boyfriend looks up. "I can't have these people watching me like this."

Noah needs no further instruction. He stammers over to the crowd of people who are itching to get in on the drama and gossip, diverting their attention to him.

"Alright, guys. Let's move it along," he says in a powerfully captivating voice. "Nothing to see here. I've got pizza coming from Mama Leoni's. I hope y'all are hungry!"

And now everyone is focusing on Noah, who leads the group away from his friends like the gorgeous altruist he is.

I sigh out hard and watch as Andrew and Tessa grumble things at each other.

"Fletcher?" Johnny says in confusion, and now it appears we've been joined by an older man, tall and stocky, with gray hair and a gray mustache. He looks like Magnum in twenty years.

The guy - Fletcher - rushes to Andrew and Tessa to see what's going on.

"Fletcher, what are you doing here?" Johnny asks the man while giving him a friendly hug.

Now it all makes sense. This must be the famous Fletcher Serpone I've heard so much about. A private investigator friend of Noah, Andrew and Johnny. I've never met him before, but I've certainly heard enough about him from Noah.

Wait, the other night, Noah asked Andrew if he'd heard from Fletcher… Regarding what happened that night when he had to rescue Tessa…

This is all so weird.

I zone back in when I hear Fletcher say that someone followed Andrew and Tessa from her apartment.

"Wait a minute. *Followed?*" Johnny asks, sounding just as confused as he looks.

"Fuck…" Tessa mutters, her face etched in guilt and insecurity.

"Guys, what's going on?" I ask, brows high as my eyes dart back and forth between the couple.

I need to know what's happening. I want them to be okay, but it seems like there's a lot they haven't been telling us... About Tessa's marriage problems, most likely. I'm thinking my earlier advice isn't quite enough to cover what they're going through.

"We have to go," Andrew blurts out, his voice firm and not to be argued with. "I'm sorry, guys. I'm not feeling well. I'll explain everything later. Come on, Tessa."

He drags Tessa away, though he stops to hug Johnny and kiss me on the cheek.

"Dude, are you sure you're okay?" I've never seen Johnny look so worried before. "At least stay for a little bit longer."

"I can't," Andrew grumbles with finality. "I'm sorry, I have to go. I'll see you tomorrow for sure." His eyes dart to mine briefly. "Tell Noah I said goodbye and thank you. I'll talk to him tomorrow."

I nod because it's all I can do, watching as he pulls Tessa toward the exit with his left hand.

"Um... okay," Tessa mutters in uncertainty, like a kid who's preparing to be scolded by a parent as soon as they're alone. "Bye, guys. Thank you for everything..."

She waves at us, and we wave back, but they've already disappeared through the crowd, Andrew rushing to get them the fuck out of here.

Johnny and I share a look.

"That was really..." I whisper, and then Johnny finishes my thought, "Weird."

I peek up at the older gentleman and decide to introduce myself.

"Hi there! We haven't officially met," I extend my hand to him politely. "I'm Alex Mackenzie. Noah's girlfriend."

"Fletcher Serpone," he smiles at me as we shake.

But I feel a burning glare just above my head, and pivot to see Johnny staring at me, wearing a sly smirk.

His brow quirks. "*Girlfriend?*"

I nod slowly and swallow. "Yes..."

"Well, it's very nice to meet you finally," Fletcher croons. He has this sweet grandpa vibe about him, although based on what Noah's told me, he's actually a very scary man. "I've heard a lot about you."

"Likewise," I grin, my eyes darting back to Johnny, who looks like he wants to implode. I sigh out hard and roll my eyes. "Yes, it just happened. Jeez, why

Seek Me

are you so excited?"

"Because!" He shouts, and five or six nearby people turn around. "You guys are finally official?! That's fuckin awesome! Fletch, how long has Noah been pining over this girl?"

"The whole time I've known him, that's for sure," Fletcher smiles warmly.

My heart thumps. *The whole time...*

Noah saunters over to us, running a stressed hand through his hair. "Alright, so about a hundred pizzas just arrived. It seems like a lot... But my munchies are wilding out right now so I took down three slices in like two minutes."

He pauses his rambling and looks around. "Where are Andrew and Tessa? And why is Johnny looking at me like he's about to -"

Tackle.

I laugh hysterically watching Johnny straddle Noah on the ground and shake him repeatedly. I should probably help my man out, but I don't think I could move Johnny with a forklift, so I just stay put and smile like a goon.

"You have a girlfriend!" Johnny sings while Noah tries to fight him off. "Dude, you know what that means right?"

"Yea, that you're trying to get me to cheat on her with you already, and it's not gonna happen," Noah grunts, giving Johnny a final shove that sets him free.

He stands up and brushes himself off. "Hey, Fletch! Good to see you, man!" He hugs his friend. "What are you doing here?"

"Long story..." Fletcher sighs, appearing concerned. "But you might want to check in on Andrew soon. This stuff going on with Tessa's husband is... a bit much."

"Maybe they just needed to go home and fuck away the drama," Johnny shrugs. "I'm sure they'll be good in the morning."

"Stay for a drink," Noah insists to Fletcher, who concedes, him and Johnny ambling off to get one.

I breathe out to release some of this adrenaline coursing through me as Noah's arms circle my waist, pulling me flush against him.

"Crazy fuckin night, man," he kisses my forehead.

"Yea..."

"So... we were interrupted before I could get your answer," he blinks at me. "I'm gonna need that."

I sigh out a giggle and scratch his jaw with my nails. "Yes. Yes, Noah, I am already your girlfriend, and I'm so damn happy to be that."

His smile is as bright as a meteor shower raining through the cosmos. "Four

509

years later… Here we are."

He leans in to kiss me, and it's soft, and passionate; loving and tender, yet packed with sizzling lust, just like all our kisses have been over the last four years. Our chemistry is something that will never cease to astound and astonish me.

"I'm so glad we finally made it," I whisper and he hums.

When we pull apart, I realize that we've separated ourselves from the rest of the party, and are standing at the entrance of a corridor that leads to the restroom.

I look up at Noah and treasure the way he's gazing at me right now. My mind is still circling through everything that's happened in the last twenty-four hours. And as hot as I am for him at the moment, I want to hear all about everything he's kept himself from telling me.

This *whole time*, when I thought he saw me as just a best friend and a fuck-buddy, he was actually waiting.

"Last night, you said there was something you almost did…" I stare up at him.

I know he knows what I'm talking about, because he's chewing on his lower lip, eyes darting between us, though it seems more like he's staring at my rack.

"The night before I left to film season one," he begins, speaking slowly, "When you told me you were leaving for eighteen months, I had planned to…" His voice trails off and he swallows.

"Planned to what?" *I need to know this right now or I might die.*

"I was going to ask you to be my girlfriend that night," he mumbles, fidgeting in place. "I planned to ask if you wanted to be exclusive. But then you told me you got accepted into that program… So I just…" He shakes his head a little, brows zipping together.

Once again, I'm stunned. My eyes are so wide I think they might fall out of my skull.

I feel like such a fucking idiot.

How could I not have known?! It's so obvious now! The dinner… The way he was acting… How devastated he was when I told him I was leaving…

Holy fuck.

"Noah… Oh my God…" I squeak, barely even aware that I'm clenching his shirt in my fist.

"Alex, I don't want you to feel bad," he rushes out. "It all worked the way it needed to. You had to travel and find yourself. It was part of the plan. I get that now. So just… Don't think you stopped me from having what I want. I have you now. That's all that matters."

"You wanted me as your girlfriend three years ago..." I hum and drop my head to his chest, pressing my forehead right over his beating heart. "Jesus... If you had asked me..."

"You would have said yes," he stops me. "You would have given up your plans and stayed for me. I know you would have. But I couldn't let you do that. Alex, you're the most important person in the whole world to me. Your happiness is all I care about."

Tears flood my eyes, choking back in my throat. I'd say I can't believe he did that for me, but of course I can believe it. Add this to the list of self-sacrificing things Noah Richards has done for me since I've known him.

His arms envelope me and he holds me tight, kissing my hair. "Baby, don't cry. I love you. I've always loved you, and I had absolutely no qualms about waiting for you."

I lift my gaze and give him a look.

"Okay... maybe I freaked out on occasion..." he grins and I laugh, squeezing the air out of him with my arms around his waist. "But you were worth the wait, fairy girl. You always have been."

"I love you so much, Noah," I whimper, then tug him until my back hits the wall, holding his tall, strong body on mine while my hands slink up underneath his shirt.

"I love you, Alex," he kisses the words on my lips. They taste like *home*. "You're the only girl I've ever said that to, who isn't my mom or my sister."

"I'm honored to be your first," I smile, and he rumbles a low noise, pinning me to the wall with his hips.

"My first... My only..." he pants, sucking my bottom lip until I moan. "My *forever*."

Chapter Thirty Two
Noah

I'VE ALWAYS CONSIDERED MYSELF TO BE A HAPPY PERSON.

I was raised by parents who love me, in an environment that was safe and supportive. They instilled me with proper morals and values; encouraged me to follow my dreams, and I took all that compassion and loyalty with me into adulthood.

I have friends and family who care for me a great deal, a career that kicks more ass than Jason Statham, a sick apartment in the best city in the world.

What's not to be happy about? My life rules.

And yet despite all that greatness, I never knew I could experience the kind of mind-blowing, soul-vindicating joy I'm feeling right now.

Because Alex Mackenzie is my *girlfriend*. And she's in love with me.

It may sound silly to some, but this is a yearning that has dwelled in my heart and mind for four years. I've tried to fight it; resisted these feelings at all costs to spare myself the broken heart I never wanted or knew I was even capable of.

But that's the thing about masks. You can wear them to fool everyone in the whole damn world, but you can't lie to yourself.

Alex finally telling me she wants to be mine - for *real* this time, no more games or *casual fuck buddy* whatever the hell - ripped the mask clean off my body. I'm exposed for the first time in my adult life, and as scary as it may seem, I'm excited about it.

I actually like being real, as long as it's with her.

We're still standing against the wall by the bathrooms on the Maxwell's rooftop. Well, *standing* is an exaggeration. We're more like, lying vertically, gyrating into each other as if we're trying to rub enough friction out of our clothed bodies to start a fire. Which seems fully plausible, since my skin is scorching and all I want to do is rid myself of all my clothes. And hers. Preferably somewhere hidden, but if people have to see us, that's a risk I'm willing to ignore while I get my girlfriend off. And maybe me in the process. But mostly her.

She's the only one who matters.

Alex gets what she wants. Forever.

"Fuck, baby…" she rasps in that deliriously hot voice that has my dick scheming to escape my pants and seek refuge inside her perfect body. "I've never wanted a cock in me so bad in my life."

I groan into the crook of her neck while kissing, licking and sucking her creamy skin like it's made of gourmet candy. "Don't tempt me, beautiful. This cock wants nothing more than to fuck you so hard you can't walk right for a week."

She mewls for me like the sexy kitten she is, those naughty little fingers gripping my length through my jeans until I throb in her hand.

"I wanna ride my boyfriend's dick," she purrs, stroking me harder while I rumble and bite her collarbone. *Fuck yes, baby…*

"Your boyfriend wants to make his girlfriend come on his dick," I growl, out of breath and so fucking ready to find a closet or something so we can consummate our relationship that's been four years in the making.

"You're such an asshole," she hums and grabs me by my jaw, pulling my face up to hers. "You knew I wouldn't be able to resist you and now we're in public and we can't fuck like I want to."

I laugh softly on her lips and she kisses me hard, sucking and biting and tasting. She's starved right now and I love every second of it. I love how desperate she is for my dick, although this time feels different, and new. It's more than just wanting to bang each other into an early grave. We're in fucking *love*. As dirty and sweaty and rough as it'll undoubtedly be, we'll be making love. As a couple.

That thought has my cock weeping. I *need* to be inside her before I explode everywhere.

"Alex," I can't help but whimper her name into her mouth. "I need you, baby. I need to feel how much you love me."

She pauses with our lips hovering over one another's, ragged breaths flying in and out of both of us. I can tell she's thinking about where we could go, and how we can do what we need to do to each other without having to leave the party.

Just then, some people walk by us toward the bathrooms, and one dude shouts, "Yea, Noah! Get it in, homie!"

He and another guy laugh as they stumble away, and Alex peers up at me with reticence in her pastoral eyes.

"We shouldn't do this here..." she whispers, though it sounds like she wants to argue with herself about that comment.

"You're probably right," I nod, sucking in air and attempting to compose myself.

I pull back enough to run my hand through my hair as Alex does the same to herself. She's so undisputedly gorgeous, especially when her face is all flushed and her lips are swollen from eating me alive.

My smile overtakes me and I hold her cheek, kissing her once more softly, on the lips, then the chin, then cheek; each freckle gets a kiss. Then that cute little gold hoop in her nose, her temple, her forehead.

Fuck it. I'm just kissing every kissable surface on her face, and I can't help myself.

She giggles and pushes me away playfully, but keeps a grip on my shirt as she gazes up at me with more love and devotion in her eyes than I've ever seen on a person. She sucks her bottom lip and I take her hand in mine, placing her palm over my heart.

"This is for you, Alexandra," I whisper and she blinks over tears she's trying to keep at bay.

"I'll keep it forever," she gleams.

Once we've acknowledged that we won't be banging yet, I have to wait a few minutes before I can rejoin the party because of my raging hard-on, which Alex thinks is cute. I don't, though, because my balls are aching like they're snared in barbed wire.

"Baby, how do you think that guy got in here?" She asks as I experiment with which way to stuff my dick so it's least visible. "The guy Andrew hit."

I think for a moment. "I'm not sure. He probably just said he was with someone coming in, I guess."

"Do you think other people could do that...?"

Her uneasy voice causes me to glance at her. She appears worried, so I give her my full attention.

"What's wrong, love? Talk to me," I insist and she breathes out hard.

"I'm scared that Roger could have snuck in here too," she huffs, and the fearful look on her face makes me want to find that asshole ex of hers and toss him into a wood chipper.

"Well, my security knows about him," I hold on to her for comfort. "But you're right. Clearly these morons aren't paying enough attention. I'll go talk to the bouncers and make sure they sweep the place."

Seek Me

She nods reticently. "I wish we could just go home."

The pout on her lips is my undoing. *I think I'm over this party.*

"Okay," I twirl her silky hair around my fingers. "Whatever you want, baby."

"No, Noah, I don't want to make you leave your party..." she mutters.

"Babe, honestly. Do you really think I'd rather be hanging out with these people than going home with you?" I lift my brow at her and she smiles. Then I take her chin in my fingers and lock my eyes on hers. "Whatever *you* want."

Alex hugs me, and we end up kissing for several more minutes before we pry ourselves apart and I set out to find Johnny. I don't imagine everyone will leave just because I am, so I'm passing the torch to him, until he decides to leave for round two with Erica the makeup girl, and then it's anybody's ballgame.

I spot him over by the bar, whispering something into Erica's ear that makes her laugh. I don't exactly want to interrupt him laying the mack down on this girl, but I need to say goodbye at the very least.

Just as I'm about to sneak up behind him and smack his ass, my phone rings, and I'm able to make out my special ringtone over the melodious sound of The Killers floating through the speakers. I yank my phone out of my pocket and squint at the screen when I see Jimmy's name.

That's odd... He was bringing Andrew and Tessa back to Brooklyn. I shrug because that was a while ago, and he's probably just wondering if he should come back here and wait for us.

"Hey, Jim," I answer the call, strolling toward the bar where Johnny is doing some kind of ballerina twirl that has me questioning his sobriety. "What's going on, chief? You back from Tessa's?"

"Uh no... Actually, I never made it there," Jimmy mumbles in my ear and I freeze. He sounds much more serious than usual. "I'm at your place. With Andrew."

"My place?" I grunt, making a distinctly confused face, like he can see me. "Why would Andrew be at my place?"

"I think something bad happened..." Jimmy sighs, the sound of which, mixed with every terrible conclusion I'm jumping to in my mind, twists my stomach into a knot. "It's a weird story, and I'm not sure it's my place to tell you what's going on. I think you just need to get over here. And fast."

My mouth is suddenly parched, and I'm having a hard time staying still. I can't help but focus on, and obsess over, the fact that Jimmy didn't mention Tessa once in this conversation.

Fuck fuck fuck... This is not good.

"Okay... I'll be right there," I tell him, rushing over to Johnny.

"Do you want me to come get you?" Jimmy asks.

I shake my head. "No. Stay there and keep an eye on him. We'll hijack one of the drivers outside. Thanks, Jimmy. I'll see you soon."

I hang up fast and grab Johnny by the back of the shirt, yanking him away from Erica, though he barely moves.

"Dude! Simmer," he wriggles out of my grip, aiming a bemused glare at me. "No distractions. She's making me work for it for some reason."

I scoff. "Maybe it's because you slept with her two years ago and never called her again." I rake my fingers through my hair and cut Johnny off before he can argue. "Look, you're gonna need to say goodnight to your rerun. Jimmy just called. Andrew's at my place. And he's alone. I think something happened..."

"Oh, fuck..." Johnny mutters. He blinks twice, then turns back to Erica, placing a chaste kiss on her cheek. "Gotta go, doll. Something came up."

Johnny and I run around looking for Alex, and we finally locate her talking to Sarah. I grab Alex by the waist and my movements are clearly frantic because she gapes up at me with wide eyes.

"We gotta go, babe," I tell her, glancing at Sarah who looks lost. "Something might have happened... We need to leave. Now."

Without a single hesitation, Alex nods and waves goodbye to Sarah. Not that it's the time for swooning, but I love how much my girl trusts me. I could be bringing her outside to say Papaya King is about to close and we need to move fast before they throw out all the corn dogs, and she wouldn't even bat an eye. Where I go, she goes, and vice versa.

I only wish this excursion was about day-old corn dogs, rather than our friend experiencing some kind of traumatic event.

The three of us leave the rooftop in a hurry, barely saying goodbye to anyone on our way out. Once we get through the security, and the lingering paparazzi outside, one of the chauffeurs offers to drive us uptown, and we pile into an Escalade.

The ride to my place is tense. We're all just wondering what's going on, hoping it's nothing too serious, and praying that Andrew is all right. He's been through enough grief in the last few years. He doesn't need anymore heartache.

Unfortunately, when we arrive at my brownstone, and see him sitting on the front steps with his head in his hands, we come to terms with the likely possibility that something very bad did happen, and brace ourselves for turmoil.

We all creep slowly over to our friend, so as not to startle him, though he barely moves or acknowledges our presence.

"Hey, buddy," I place my hand gently on his shoulder. "You okay?"

No response.

"Baby blue?" Johnny leans in. "What are you doing here, bro?"

Still nothing. The only thing letting us know he's alive is the way his broad shoulders are moving up and down with his rapid breaths.

I snap my fingers in front of his face, but he still doesn't react.

"We should get him inside," Alex whispers to us and we agree.

Johnny and I get on each side of him.

"Alright, killa," I murmur as we each grab an arm. "Let's go in and get a drink, whadya say?"

He grunts out a noise of despaired disinterest, and now I'm really fucking worried. *Jesus... What the hell happened to my friend?*

We carry him up the stairs to my front door as Alex opens it for us. Andrew is technically walking on his own, but he's stumbling a lot, leaning on us for support. It seems like he's shitfaced or something, but he doesn't smell like booze at all.

"Andrew, did you take anything?" I ask to cover all bases. "Did you have too much to drink?"

He shakes his head subtly, which is a relief, and not. Because if he's not fucked up, then there's something much more serious going on here.

Shitballs.

Alex opens the door to my place and we guide our friend inside. As soon as he's in, he lifts his head slowly, looks around as if he's contemplating something painful, and then drops his face into his palm again.

"Alex, grab a bottle of scotch and some glasses, please," I ask of her and she darts away to get it. "Johnny, you got any cigarettes?" Johnny slaps his pants pocket then nods. "Okay, let's go sit on the terrace."

We bring Andrew outside and get him seated on the chaise. He's staring at the ground, eyes exhausted and unblinking. They're bloodshot, and his hair is all over the place. He looks like a wreck.

Johnny lights him a cigarette, handing it over in hopes it'll get him at the very least moving, which it does. He takes a drag of the cigarette and puffs out smoke, though he's still staring at nothing.

Alex rushes outside with the scotch and pours a big glass for Andrew, handing it to him slowly. He regards the glass for a moment like it's a foreign food he's never tried before. But then he finally accepts it and kills half the thing in one gulp.

We're all just gawking at him, waiting for him to do anything other than what he's doing; Johnny on his right, Alex on his left with her hand rubbing his back. And me, plopped anxiously on the table across from him struggling to recognize my best friend.

I've never seen him like this before. He looks like a ghost.

"Andrew…" Alex whimpers next to his head. "Talk to us. What's wrong?"

"Yea, dude, what happened?" Johnny asks.

"You can tell us anything," I plead.

His head finally lifts, sky-blue eyes locking right on mine.

"It's over."

He said the words calmly enough. Actually, he sounds almost lifeless, which is immensely troubling. But not as much as the words themselves.

"What is…?" I blink, my stomach rolling like I might be sick.

His jaw clenches visibly, and his brows pull together. He looks like he could cry, and it's wholly awful. But then he growls out loud, like the roar from some feral beast, and tosses his glass at the wall across my terrace, smashing it to pieces.

His voice bellows again, and he stands up, pacing around in circles in front of us, ripping his hair at the roots while muttering to himself.

"It's over… It's *fucking* over. We're done. Jesus Christ… what the fuck happened?! He's… he's… *No*… She can't…"

I stand up slowly. "Andrew, bro, talk to me. Just tell me what happened -"

"Don't you get it?!" He gets into my face and for a moment, one very brief, very ugly moment, I think he might hit me. And I would probably let him.

Fortunately, he doesn't. Instead, he whimpers and drops his head onto my shoulder. And I have no choice but to pat his back slowly.

"Tessa and I… We're over." He sniffs.

I gape at Alex and Johnny who are standing behind him, on high alert. I mouth *what the fuck?!* To which they both shrug.

"Hey, Andrew…" I whisper, squeezing his shoulder. "We're here for you, alright? We're not going anywhere. Just… talk to us."

He straightens up and grabs the bottle of scotch, taking a large swig. Then he rips on the cigarette he's been pinching to death between his fingers.

"There's something you guys need to know…" he grunts, pausing to swallow more scotch. "About that bloke I punched tonight."

The three of us listen attentively as our best friend tells us a long, very

Seek Me

complex and devastating story. About how people have been coming after Tessa, since the night I rescued her on the street by Sensay.

About how her husband is actually a military sergeant who's been in a coma for six months, as the result of some rogue officer's vengeful plan, coincidentally the same guy I almost had to toss around a little.

About how the people responsible for this are now harassing Tessa to pull the plug on her dying husband's life support and using threats of harm against Andrew and his family as collateral to get her to cave.

About how he and Tessa ended their relationship tonight because they couldn't find a way out of this together.

By the time he's done, my heart is shattered for him.

All the gaps have been filled in. That guy I threatened for Tessa two weeks ago... The dude Andrew punched tonight... Fletcher's part in all this.

It all makes sense now. But it doesn't make it any less awful.

"She fucking ended it... to keep me safe," he shudders, slugging away at the bottle, putting down more scotch than I would want, though I don't have the heart to stop him. "She ended it for my family. She's so strong and brave... And now we're done. And I'll never see her again."

He coughs and waves a tired hand at Johnny, we assume for more cigarettes. Johnny gives him the whole pack.

"I'm a fuckin idiot," he scoffs, swaying on his feet as he tries to remove a cigarette from the pack, four of them falling out onto the ground as he does. "I actually thought we could be something... I actually thought she was my... my..."

He covers his face again and stumbles backward like he's about to sit on something, but there's no furniture behind him. I grab him by the waist to keep him from keeling over.

"Dude, easy," I hum. "Maybe you should get some rest."

"Fuck rest. Noah, I'm in love with her! I'm in love with her and it's over. We're over before we even started..." He lets out a strangled sigh.

Wretched sympathy swarms my gut. *He doesn't deserve this.*

"How can we help?" Alex asks, looking as helpless as we all do right now.

Andrew lifts his head and squints at something none of us can identify.

"I need to get out of here," he grumbles, stammering toward the door. "Noah, I can't be here. I'm sorry, but this whole place reminds me of her. There's no way I can stay here. I see her everywhere here, Noah, bloody everywhere!"

He's breathing heavily and I shush him, nodding with determination. "Okay, buddy. It's fine. I got you. Johnny, we can go to your suite, right?"

Johnny nods enthusiastically in response. "Yea, yea, of course! I'm at the Four Seasons."

"Let's go," Alex agrees, and we help Andrew back inside, just to usher him out to the car.

We get him settled in the back, gripping his bottle of scotch like it's a baby, and tell Jimmy to drive us to the Four Seasons, which he does, as quickly as possible.

When we get there, we all go up to the penthouse suite, where Johnny's staying, and Andrew's first words since we left my place are, "John John, you have any more booze?"

Reluctantly, not because of cost, obviously, but because we don't want him getting alcohol poisoning, Johnny relinquishes the mini bar to our heartbroken friend, and even calls down to the hotel bar so we can buy a big bottle of scotch to replace the one Andrew killed on the way over. We drink with him, because honestly, we're all sort of shaken up over this news. And plus, the last thing we want is for him to get drunk alone.

But the three of us are still in babysitter mode. Andrew's not doing well at all. And we need to stay conscious enough to make sure he doesn't hurt himself.

Alex and I are parked on Johnny's bed, watching Andrew as he tries to kick his shoes off his own feet from where he's lying, sprawled out on the couch. Johnny sighs out of inevitable frustration and rips the shoe off for him, but when he goes for the other, Andrew accidentally kicks him in the nuts.

"Ow! Jesus fuck!" Johnny groans, thumping to the floor and keeling over on his side.

"Shit! I'm sorry, bro," Andrew mutters weakly, but then a small drunken giggle slips through and it's the most refreshing thing I've seen since we found him on my stoop.

I start hysterically laughing, unable to help it, and Alex follows suit, both of us leaning into each other as we snort at our friend's expense. Andrew lifts his head slowly and peers over at us. His brows raise and he sips from the bottle of scotch while watching us closely.

"What?" I ask, my chuckles evaporating in fear he's about to throw up everywhere.

Andrew nods between Alex and me. "You two. You're bloody perfect together."

I swallow hard and glance down at Alex and my joined hands, feeling like maybe we should separate out of guilt. I don't want to be flaunting my new relationship that makes me so giddy I could sing *Shiny Happy People* at the top of my lungs in front of my best friend who's going through a gut-wrenching break-up.

I peek at Alex and she up at me. She smiles and I can't help but smile back. I'm not sure there will ever come a time when her smile won't have me mirroring it.

"Alex... Are you done running?" Andrew grunts, ripping from the bottle again. His blunt, no-nonsense inebriation is somehow both endearing and worrying right now.

I give Alex a nervous look, mainly because I don't want her to feel uncomfortable or interrogated. But also, in the back of my mind, I'm desperate to hear the answer to this myself.

We're a couple now. Tonight, after four years of build-up, Alex finally told me what she wants - *me* - and I gave her that, gladly. There's no way she would ever turn around and tell me she wants to travel more without me...

Right?

My pulse thrums in my neck as I stare at her, and she stares back. If Alex wanted to leave to travel more, I wouldn't stop her. Of course I wouldn't. I've always cared about her happiness more than my own. And we could make long-distance work, I'm sure...

Fuck... Just thinking about it makes me want to beg at her feet for her to stay.

But before I can, Alex whispers, "Yes. I'm done running."

I swallow hard, finding my lips twisting against my will. "Really?"

She nods, eyes the color of green pastures locked on me. "Really. Noah, I can't leave you again. I won't. I've seen everything I needed to see on my own. The next time I travel somewhere, I want it to be with you. Every time, from now on... I never want to go anywhere without you."

I'm having a mini heart attack. Or I'm hallucinating. Surely this can't be right. How did everything change so drastically in one night?

But as I'm gazing deep into her greener than green eyes, I discover that maybe it didn't happen overnight. Maybe this is something Alex has been feeling for a while...

"I can't wait to see the world with you," I whisper, triggering an even bigger smile to take over her face. I hold her jaw in my hands and kiss her softly while she giggles.

"Dude, having a girlfriend in your late thirties is barely acceptable," Johnny, who has recovered from groaning in pain on the floor, and is now leaning against the couch, cupping his balls and staring at us, teases. "You're gonna have to propose soon, you realize that, right?"

Alex's smile dissipates so fast, it's as if someone physically ripped it off her mouth. We both turn to Johnny who is evil-laughing from the floor at the horrified looks on our faces.

"At least I *have* a girlfriend," I grumble at him and he pouts.

"Wait, so you two really are official?" Andrew slurs, rolling off the couch and stumbling over to us.

Me and Alex nod together, seriously hoping this doesn't upset him. I know it shouldn't. We're best friends, and our relationship beginning the night his ended is an unfortunate coincidence, but he must know it wasn't intentional.

"Yea," I sigh, standing up to grab him because he looks like he could fall over. "It just happened tonight. Okay… come sit here. You're fucking stressing me out."

I push him down onto the bed next to Alex, where he slumps over, but not without first pulling her into his side.

"I'm so happy for you guys," he raises the bottle, sloshing it all over the place.

"Are you really?" Alex whimpers and reaches out to smooth back his out-of-control hair. "I'm sorry about the timing… But you know how long we've been dancing around this."

She peeks up at me and I bite my lip to stop the corniest smile of all time from overtaking me again.

"No no no… Alex, please," Andrew hums, shaking his head a bunch of times then blinking hard out of what appears to be dizziness. "You deserve one another. I love you both, and I only want you to be happy. I mean, someone should be, after all…" He scoffs and goes still, staring at the floor in silence.

I feel so fucking bad for my friend, it's killing me inside. I really wish there was some way to make him feel better. But there's nothing I can do. I'm more than helpless and I hate it.

"Bro, you're going to be fine," I tell him, crouching down in front of him so he's forced to look me in the eye. "I promise. I know it sucks now, but it'll get better."

"How? How will it get better?" He asks in an almost pleading tone, blinking over glassy blue eyes. "Remember how you felt when Alex left for Budapest?

Seek Me

Well, this is like that. Only worse, because there's nothing anyone can say or do that will bring her back to me."

I can't help my eyes from darting to Alex for a moment. She looks taken aback. I really didn't want her to know the extent of how fucked up I was the first time she left. I would've gladly downplayed it for the rest of our lives, now that she's mine and it doesn't matter what happened in the past.

But our drunk and bitter friend seems to have completely lost his filter, and I know he'll just keep revealing things until he passes out. I suppose I should brace myself for him to tell Alex about more embarrassing shit I didn't want her to know, like the time I ran gut first into a giant oil drum on set and it hurt so bad I threw up everywhere.

"I get it, man," I sigh, because there's nothing else I can say. "Let's just keep drinking."

And so we do.

Johnny passes out first, in his bed although we're all still lying on it together. After that, me and Alex take Andrew into the living room where we try literally anything that might distract him from the meltdown that keeps running through him in cycles.

TV doesn't work. Every commercial seems to remind him of Tessa. The same goes for music. Alex suggests playing *I Never*, which strikes some kind of nerve for him and he ends up hobbling into the bathroom with his pants undone, where he eventually passes out in the bathtub.

"Well, at least he's asleep," she murmurs as we stand over him, watching him clutch the bottle of Macallan to his chest, eyelids fluttering while he mumbles incoherently.

I swipe a hand over my face. "Yea… Jesus. What a fuckin night, huh?"

I turn to leave the bathroom and walk face-first into the wall. Alex laughs at me, but I shush her incessantly because I don't want to wake up Andrew.

"How sloshed are you right now?" She whispers, guiding me back toward the living room.

"God, I don't even know…" I grumble, tripping over Andrew's one shoe. "I've been drinking for hours. What time is it?"

"I don't know," she chuckles. "Like four…?"

"Fuck," I huff and crash onto the couch, tugging her on top of me.

We both laugh, as quietly as we can, until I register that she's straddling my hips, palms flat on my chest, while mine hold her waist. Our laughter fades and we stare at each other for a moment in silence.

"You're my girlfriend…" I rumble, pulling her until she's flush against me.

"I know… It's crazy." She tucks her hair behind her ear and bites her lip. And now I can stop watching her mouth.

I'm pretty damn drunk right now. And Andrew is suffering from the worst night of his existence. And Johnny's passed out only a few feet away…

But still… It's Alex and my night. We're supposed to be celebrating our officialness with nakedness. I still want that. I need it.

"Take your pants off," I growl, burrowing myself further into the couch.

She giggles timidly, but stops when she realizes I'm dead serious. "Johnny's right there."

Her eyes lift for a moment, I assume so she can check to see if he's still knocked out. He obviously is. I can hear him snoring.

"Mhm," I grunt and cock my head. "Pants off, Mackenzie. Or are you really going to deny your boyfriend on our first official night together?"

Her eyes sparkle at me in the low light as she shakes her head. "No."

"Good girl."

She slowly trails her hands down my torso before unbuttoning her pants. Then she sits up so she can shimmy her way out of them, all the while glancing up to Johnny's bed every two seconds.

"What if he wakes up?" Her tone is innocent and devious at the same time, and it's driving me absolutely crazy.

"Then I guess he might see something…" I shrug casually. "Depending on what we're doing."

Alex lets out a soft purr as she comes back to me, pressing her breasts down hard on my chest. I grab her jaw and bring her mouth to mine, tenderly kissing her soft lips until she moans.

"Quiet, baby," I whisper then nip the bottom. "Or my friend will wake up."

I palm her ass in my hand and yank down harder, to which she immediately catches on and rubs her crotch on mine. My dick is so stiff already, since I've been waiting to get her alone all night. And no, we're not technically *alone*. But Johnny's drunk. I'm sure he'll stay passed out. And if not, well then he'll be in for a surprise. Because I'm not waiting one more second to slide inside my girlfriend.

Alex lifts my shirt up, tossing it on the floor, then I do the same to hers. She unbuttons my pants, all the while kissing me mercilessly, panting in my mouth while she strokes my aching cock through my jeans.

I unclasp her bra, but before I can rip it off her, she hesitates.

Seek Me

"What's wrong?" I breathe, chest moving up and down as my fingers trail the silky soft skin of her stomach.

She gives me a look like she's not sure, but I can tell she's still concerned because of how technically not alone we are. I huff out a small laugh and lift my hips so she can really feel my arousal for her.

"Do you know how fucking turned on Johnny would be if he saw you like this...?" I hum, combing my fingers through her long, beautiful hair. She mewls and releases her bra, dropping it off to the side. "You're so damn sexy, Alexandra. Any of my friends would be itching to catch a glimpse."

She gasps then pushes my jeans down enough to pull my dick out. "Does it make you jealous? To think about them seeing me?"

Her mouth finds my jaw, then my throat, sucking and biting, I'm sure leaving small, possessive marks in its wake. I groan softly, gliding my hand up to cup her breast.

"Mmm... Not if I'm inside you." My voice is rough as she fists my erection, stroking firm. "Not if they see me owning you with my cock."

A quiet moan leaves her lips with breaths warming my flesh. "I love how your cock owns me, baby."

I'm practically vibrating with need as I lean forward and kiss her tits everywhere, sucking her nipples between my lips, tugging the steel with my teeth.

"Fuck... God, I love your tits," I flatten my tongue over her nipple and she bites her lip to keep quiet, which prompts a wicked chuckle. "You want him to hear you, huh bad girl?"

She doesn't answer me, but it could go either way at this point. She's trying to stay quiet, but her inhibitions have completely dissolved, so much so that she moves her warm, wet kisses down my chest, sucking my own piercing for a moment, before working her way below my waist.

Unlike Alex, I'm not checking for anyone. I don't give a flying fuck who sees this right now. My parents could walk in with a priest and my third-grade teacher and I'm not sure I'd even bat an eye.

The head of my dick is sucked between Alex's lips, soft and yet forceful enough for me to let a groan slip. Her wide eyes twinkle up at me with amusement.

"You want him to hear, too?" She cocks a brow at me and I growl, grabbing her jaw and guiding that smart mouth back onto my dick.

She resumes her sucking and my head drops back in euphoria. It just feels so fucking good. I can't even help gripping her hair in my fist and thrusting myself down her throat a bit. But I know Alex loves it because her hand is between her legs.

She likes when I use her mouth. Mmm... Fuck. Yes.

"Suck me, baby... Fuck, swallow it whole," my voice cracks as she pushes me all the way down her throat, and *holy fucking shit*, how is it even possible for her to suck that deep?

I'm being blown away. Literally. She's fucking me with her mouth, stealing my edge, and it's awesome. So awesome, in fact, that I might just blow my load down her sexy, tight throat any second.

"You wanna make me come, baby?" I keep talking to her in a hushed tone and she nods with my dick sliding in and out, eyes watering but remaining locked on mine. "Is my girlfriend desperate to drink me?"

She moans *yes* with me in her mouth and it's so fucking hot I groan uncontrollably, louder than I should have. So I slap my hand over my mouth and bite it to stop myself from crying out her name.

"Alex... fuck fuck fuck Alex, baby, I'm gonna come," I ramble behind my hand and Alex's eager vibrations ripple into my shaft.

I can't fucking take it anymore. It feels *too* good.

My balls seize up as Alex slurps me again and again until I burst. My orgasm erupts and I pulse it all between my girlfriend's lips. And of course she swallows it, because she loves me and she's fucking amazing.

I can't help but whimper as my cock throbs, shooting a staggering climax on her tongue and down her throat. I barely even noticed that we're holding hands, our fingers laced and gripping one another to death while the pleasure rocks through me.

By the time I'm done, I'm panting for air. Alex comes up to cuddle me, but I'm not finished with her yet. Not even close. I hold her face and kiss her deep, tasting myself in her mouth, which is so fucking hot I can't stand it.

"You taste good, right?" She grins on my mouth and I shudder.

"Don't test me," I grunt and effortlessly rip her panties off with one solid tug. *The panty rule, baby.* I thrust a finger inside her and she gasps then bites my shoulder to keep quiet. "Are you mine, Alex?"

Another finger and she quivers. "Yes, Noah. All yours."

"That's good, baby," I bite the words on her lips, my fingers priming her, although she's so damn wet, it's not necessary. But it feels wondrous.

I finger fuck her for a few more minutes, until my cock is aching again, then

I pull her hips toward me, wrapping her legs around my waist and sinking inside her, slowly, but hard enough for her to squeal out loud.

"Shh..." I cup her tits with my needy hands, feeding inches into those slippery, plush walls. "Johnny could wake up any minute."

"Fuck... Noah... Oh my God..." she whispers by my ear, holding me close to her while I fuck her into the couch and she marks up my back with her nails.

"Jesus, baby, you feel so good," I tell her, rocking my hips, each time moving deeper and deeper until my balls are pressing against her soaking wet flesh on my thrusts. "You're so warm and wet. I missed you last night... This is all I could think about."

"Me too," she hums, then kisses my lips, surprisingly soft, considering how hard I'm pumping into her right now. "This is our first fuck as a couple."

"I know. It's perfect."

"So perfect."

I hold her legs open as wide as they go, drilling into her deep as we talk filthy to one another.

"Noah! Baby, your cock is so big. You're tearing me apart," she pants in my ear and this whole experience is bringing me to the brink again.

"Mmm... *yes*... Take this dick, baby."

"I love this dick. I want it forever."

"You do, don't you? *Fuck*... Bite my shoulder... Yes, right there... *Harder*. Jesus, I'm gonna come again."

"I'm gonna come... I'm so close."

I slink my hand between our writhing, sweat-slicked bodies to rub her clit with my thumb. She's breathing heavy. I'm breathing heavy. Together we sound like we're running out of oxygen completely.

And then I freeze. Because Johnny's up. And he's walking right past us.

Me and Alex stop moving for a minute, silently watching over the top of the couch as Johnny stomps past us toward the bathroom.

"Did he see us?" Alex asks in a breathy whisper.

"I don't think so..."

Then we hear the sound of Johnny peeing, and Alex laughs, which clenches her vagina muscles enough to have me groaning into the crook of her neck.

"*Please*, baby... I'm so close to coming," I say to her as she fists her hands in my hair, holding me against her body.

I can't stay stopped for much longer or I'll lose my orgasm and get swept up into blue balls, which no one's trying to deal with right now. So I thrust again, slow and gentle, and she whimpers.

"God, *Noah*... I'm gonna explode," she tremors as my thumb circles her clit slowly.

The toilet flushes and Johnny stammers back into the room, walking right past us, either half-conscious, or just oblivious to what we're doing, or both. Then I hear him collapse on his bed again and I sigh out of relief.

"Thank God..." I kiss Alex's lips and resume my stroking. It only takes a couple before I'm moaning into her mouth, "I'm gonna come... Baby, I'm gonna come inside you."

"Fucking come inside me," she gasps and her insides clench on me so hard I can barely even move anymore.

That is, until she comes. And everything gets a million times more slippery. And then I come. And we're just gushing all over the place.

"Fuck yes... *fuck yes fuck yes*," I pant over and over, while Alex rips my hair so hard it hurts. But the pain turns me on even more, and doubles up on the electric shocks pulsing through my loins.

"Noah... I love you so hard, baby!" Alex squeals, trying to be quiet, though she could be screaming for all I know and it would still sound super echoey.

"I *flove* you..." my words jumble together. I kiss my girlfriend's neck and throat while she giggles, our bodies slick with sweat and sex.

And love.

The next morning, Alex and I wake up before the other two, and decide to go grab some stuff that might cheer Andrew up. We run around all over Manhattan, getting him bagels and newspapers and magazines, Snapples and cookies. Everything he could only get in New York - for the most part.

I just don't want his visit tainted by the crumbling of his first new relationship in eleven years. I mean, I know it will be. But he's my best friend, and I just really want to help.

When we get back to the Four Seasons, Johnny is force-feeding a disheveled-looking Andrew pancakes. He's still cuddling with the bottle of scotch, but at least he's getting some food down, too. I'd call that progress.

"Do any ring shopping while you were out?" Johnny sneers at us, and I scowl.

Seek Me

He needs to stop fucking with my relationship. Just because Alex and I have basically been falling in love with each other for four years, it doesn't mean we're indestructible. If Johnny's marriage comments scare Alex away, I'm going to punch him in the dick.

"Johnny, I told your mom we were just casual," I rumble at him through a wicked smirk. "She can beg all she wants... which is what she's good at, by the way." I wink and his brown eyes narrow, shooting daggers at me. "You started it," I shrug.

"Guys, shut up for a second," Alex murmurs, staring down at her phone screen with a creased forehead.

God, she better not be upset about his teasing. If he makes her even the slightest bit uncomfortable, he's dead.

And then it occurs to me that Johnny's joking isn't making *me* uncomfortable. Like, at all.

I squint at the floor and swallow hard. Why am I not more nervous about all this proposal talk? Is it because I know Johnny's just fucking with me?

Or is it because the idea of marrying Alex isn't actually scary...?

My mind races through concocted images of me getting down on one knee and giving Alex a ring. What would I say? What would the ring look like? Would Alex cry? Would she giggle and jump on me and kiss me everywhere while screaming *yes yes yes*?

Would she say *no*?

Oooh... That's no good. I don't like that thought one bit.

But the rest of them... I do like. My stomach is flipping over and over like I'm on a carnival ride. I set eyes set on my girlfriend and the warmth that surrounds my heart is stronger than any sense of love I've ever had in my life. It's startling, because does this mean I love Alex more than my own family?

It's probably just different.

This whole thing goes to show how relationship stunted I am. I know nothing about what I'm feeling. It's all brand new, as if I've just opened up a present I've been anticipating for years, and now I actually get to play with it. The possibilities are endless.

Alex stands up, and the worried look on her face distracts me from fumbling over how overwhelmingly in love with her I am.

"What's up, baby?" I ask softly and she takes my arm.

"Come here," she mutters and pulls me into the next room.

I go willingly, my head spinning and dazed as I watch her closely.

"Roger texted me," she mumbles and all the joy I was just feeling dissolves in an instant, being replaced with unkempt rage.

My jaw clenches so hard it hurts. "What did he say?"

She holds up her phone to show me the text.

Unknown number: Alexandra, we need to talk. There's something important to discuss.

"What the fuck could he possibly need?" She barks, throwing her phone on the floor in a huff. "Nothing he has to say is *important*. He just wants to mindfuck me some more, and I'm not fucking having it!"

I force myself to settle the anger coursing through my veins and focus on my beautiful girlfriend. This isn't about me wanting to murder her ex, it's about me needing to take care of her. To make sure she's alright.

I hold her face in my hands and her eyes lock on mine. "Alex, we'll get through this together. I don't want you worrying about him. You're right, he's just trying to get into your head again, and it won't work."

"But what if he keeps showing up at my place?" She hums, then pauses to chew on her lip. "It will take at least a few days to get the restraining order back…"

"I'll send Jimmy's guys over to check the place out," I assure her, using my thumb to tug her plump bottom lip from between her teeth. "And you can stay at my place for as long as you want. Or I'll come to your place with you. It doesn't even matter. Whatever happens, we're in this together, right?"

She nods, blinking over wide, green eyes. "I'm so happy you're mine."

Then she launches herself at me, hugging onto me as hard as possible. I fold her small body into my arms and hold the back of her head in my palm, sniffing her hair and letting my mind drift again.

What if we got married? What would that be like? Would it be any different than us dating?

We eventually peel off each other and head back into the living room, where Andrew is pacing around the room with his cell phone plastered to his ear.

"Alright… Cheers, mate." He hangs up and releases a steady stream of air before turning to face me. "Jimmy's going to Tessa's in a bit to get my things…"

I witness him swallow and all the bliss I was just feeling with Alex is once again smothered, this time by a commiserative gloom. My best friend looks tortured, more so than I ever saw him look before, even when his crumbling marriage was his only worry.

He's still dealing with that, and now on top of those stresses, he's going through a break-up from the girl he considers his soulmate.

How can I help him through this? What can I do?

The hard realization is that there are no magic words I can utter to take his pain away. This isn't like what I've done for my friends in the past. I can't take him out to a strip club, or call some random girl in my phone to get him laid.

This is different. Andrew's in love with Tessa, and the only way I could help is to get her back.

But I'm not sure that's even possible.

Andrew stays at Johnny's again that night, while Alex and I go back to my place. There's a dark cloud settled over our mood, but we don't let it impede celebrating our newfound relationship. And for the first time ever, witnessing someone I love's failed relationship doesn't seem to scare me. Because I know in my heart this is the real thing.

Even though nothing has really changed between Alex and me with the new label, it all feels monumentally different. We're no longer hiding from our feelings, and it's like the best kind of high I could ever imagine.

That night, we make love more times than I can even count, and the words *I love you* are on our lips like a song that's perpetually stuck in our heads. And in bed in the dark, after Alex falls asleep in my arms, beautifully naked and soundly sated, I delete every single girl's number from my phone, minus of course the ones I need, like my family and work people.

But it feels like a milestone. Noah Richards, chronic bachelor, is now Noah Richards, Alex's boyfriend.

And nothing has ever been more *right*.

Chapter Thirty Three
Alex

I GRIP THE ARM OF MY COUCH with white knuckles as my hips rock forward and back; the movements being guided by wide palms on both my butt cheeks.

Noah's fingers are digging into my flesh, bruising me in a way that only serves to turn me on more and ignite flames deep below my waist. His bruises are the sexy kind, not the awful kind I used to get, which would make me cringe.

A mark left on my body by Noah Richards is done so with love and lust, and is always fully consensual, because we're partners, and he worships every single thing about me.

A groan escapes him, and I glance down to see deep, coal eyes glowing up at me from where his face is tucked between my thighs as I ride his mouth, those perfect lips teasing and sucking, his skilled tongue plunging inside me and making me tremble from head to toe.

I move a hand down to comb my fingers through his soft hair, prompting a slow-blink that makes him look even more painstakingly gorgeous than I can stand, and my insides shudder as I press myself down harder on his warm, wet mouth.

He lets out an *umpf* noise, buried in my pussy, eating like he's starved, while sending chills across my already-pebbled nipples. One of his hands releases my ass and glides up to cup my breast, fondling gently, those shapely, masculine fingers brushing the steel barbell until I quake.

"God Noah… Jesus, your mouth is too good for real life…" I whimper and my head drops back, skin glistening as my body steadily climbs to its near orgasm.

Noah uses the strength in his muscular arms to move me how he wants, grinding me on his face. I reach behind me to where his long, pink cock is lying on his abs, stretched so hard the veins are almost visibly throbbing. I make a fist around it, jerking him slow and firm, just how he likes it.

"Alex…" he gasps my name, though it's muffled by my pussy he's devouring, which triggers a moan to shoot from inside my throat. "Mmmm…"

"You wanna come while I ride your face, sexy?" I grin down at him, our eyes locked as he nods quick, kissing the lips between my legs the way he kisses the ones on my face; deep and reverent, hungry and devoted. "You're *so* fucking hot."

He whimpers as his eyelids droop shut briefly, I think because he's close to coming himself, which is insane. I've barely even been touching his dick since we started fooling around less than fifteen minutes ago. Him being so turned on he could come just from me riding his mouth and jerking him off a little has me ready to erupt on his pretty, pouted lips.

Noah extends his tongue long, thrusting it inside me while his upper lip brushes my clit in a way which brings me right up to the brink of climax. I tug harder on his dick, stroking him from balls all the way up to that smooth, fat crown, teasing the underside until he squirms. His broad chest and shoulders are moving with forceful breaths and it's watching him that gets me off in the end.

He just looks so damn good it's unbelievable. I'm still shocked that he's my boyfriend. I'm in awe that *I* actually get to have him.

Mine.

I cry out loud as my orgasm crests and I buzz from the inside out, coating his lips and chin with my arousal and screaming out his name over and over again. The only name I ever want to shout out in bliss as long as I have a voice.

"Mmm… Mmm… *Mmmmmmm…*" He rumbles beneath me as his cock swells in my hand.

I force myself to look away from his sexed up, love drunk face so I can watch him coming, which he does, shooting his orgasm in my hand and all over the divots in his abdominals. He squeezes me as hard as possible, moaning into my pussy while he comes, which keeps my climax going longer and harder, until my body is vibrating so intense I come crashing down on him.

Noah laughs out of breath, lifting me by my thighs and scooting me down before I smother him to death with my vagina.

"I'm sorry!" I squeal through my rapid panting, curling up on his chest, ignoring all the sticky stuff between us. "I almost suffocated you."

"If there's a best way to go out, I think that would be it," he chuckles, then releases a breath, kissing my neck.

I pull his face back and kiss his lips, making him sigh. I love the way he tastes with me on his mouth, and I know he loves when I kiss him with my flavor on his lips. It's this kind of dirty, sexy stuff that makes us perfect together.

Our lust and chemistry will forever captivate me.

I'll never get enough Noah Richards.

"I love you, dark fairy," he murmurs, holding me close.

"I love you forever, dark prince."

His smile is unrelenting, and it's melting me more than the stupefying orgasm.

Suddenly my door is buzzing and we both grumble.

"Who the hell would that be, interrupting our sexy times?" I frown.

"I don't know, but you should tell them to fuck off," he grins with sparkling eyes that make me shiver, because it's clear he's not done with me yet. Not even close.

I lick my lips as my fingers trace the silky orgasm he made on his own hard, tattooed stomach. I slip one between my lips to taste him and he growls, leaning forward to bite my bottom lip.

"Girlfriend is insatiable…" he rasps and I'm so hot for him again, I can't help but slide my finger over his lips, to which he responds with another growly animal noise.

Fuck me, this man is so damn hot I can't stand it. I'm fucking addicted.

"Boyfriend wants to play more…" I purr, and he nods slowly.

The door buzzes again, even longer this time.

"Ugh! Annoying!" I grunt, then kiss him quick before hopping off to see who the hell is cockblocking me right now.

I grab Noah's t-shirt and tug it over my head, stumbling around the living room on shaky legs to locate my panties. I pull them on and stammer to the door, pressing the intercom button.

"Hello? Who dares interrupt me right now?" I grin, assuming it's an Amazon delivery or something that is way less important than doing dirty things with the sexiest guy in the whole damn universe.

There's no answer for a moment, and I see Noah approaching in my peripheral vision, wearing only his fitted gray sweatpants that sit low on his hips and make him look like a mussed up, tattooed sex god. I bite my lip because I can't seem to stop ogling him. And now that he's my boyfriend, it's totally acceptable for me to check him out constantly, a thought which is completely enthralling.

"Alexandra," a familiar voice comes over the intercom and my heart sinks.

My smile falls away just as fast, eyes widening in shock and fear and confusion, and every other negative emotion that has appeared to ruin my sex-

Seek Me

filled afternoon with my man.

Noah and I stare at each other for a moment in silence as I hold the button, listening to the sound of my ex-husband down in my building lobby. Before I can process the fact that he's here to fuck up my life more, and formulate the best way to tell him to jump into oncoming traffic, I hear two other distinct voices.

"Alex... It's Dad," my father's voice is first, followed by, "And Mom. Let us up, honey. We need to talk."

"What... in the name... of all that is..." My own voice comes out in between jagged breaths as I stare at my boyfriend, who looks more stunned and appalled than I've ever seen him before.

Noah opens his mouth, but nothing comes out.

"What do you want?" I mutter into the speaker, struggling to keep the anger and restless fury out of my words, though it doesn't quite work.

"They're here to speak with you," Roger answers calmly, and even that is pissing me the fuck off. "You never answered my text... So we decided to come by. We need to talk, Alex. Please."

What the fuck would they ever need to talk to me about?? Why the hell are my parents here? And why are they with Roger? Is this real fucking life?!

I shake my head repeatedly, staring hard at the intercom as if it will give me some clue as to what I should do next.

The intercom won't do that. But Noah will.

I turn to him and blink, silently asking what he thinks. His mouth is still agape, but he gives me a little shrug which I know means *it's up to you, baby. Whatever you want to do.*

I take a deep breath and press the buzzer to let them in.

It's a potentially stupid decision, and I know I'll probably regret it. But the fact that Noah's here makes the thought of facing the three people I hate most in this world tolerable.

He takes my hand and squeezes. "We've got this, baby. We're together, in everything."

My bottom lip trembles a bit as I stare at his beautiful face, flushed from the activities, which reminds me we just came all over each other, and my ex-husband and parents are on their way upstairs.

"Shit," I mumble, and drag him to the bathroom where we wash up quickly, and not very thoroughly.

Just enough to not have visible traces of what we were doing on our bodies, although I don't really care that we smell like sex right now. Maybe that will give them the hint that I'm not interested in whatever they think they need to talk to me about. I'd much rather be fooling around with my hot-as-fuck shirtless boyfriend.

I'm cleaning Noah's muscley torso with a washcloth when there's a knock at the door. I groan and roll my eyes, to which he gives me a small smile.

"Babe, I don't want you to worry, okay?" He cocks his head. "You can hear them out, but it doesn't have to mean anything. You're in charge of your life, and you always have been. They can't tear you down anymore. You're so far above them, beautiful."

I smile back at him graciously and nod, tugging his face to mine for a soft kiss which has him humming. And just like that, the stress and uncertainty evaporates.

As long as I have him, I don't need anyone else. He's my family.

They're knocking again as I approach the door, and despite my newfound confidence, my hands are shaking while I open it.

And as soon as I do, I'm eighteen again.

It's bizarre and surreal, seeing my parents now after not seeing them for so many years. My mind still pictures them exactly as they looked that day in the front yard, when I sat in Roger's car, watching him talk to them, before they let me go. The day they sacrificed their only daughter for their pride.

In reality, they look much older. The last twelve years have clearly aged them a bit. My mother has circles under her eyes, and a streak of gray in her jet-black hair. And my father's hair is almost completely white, as is the stubble that lines his jaw; the wrinkles on his forehead and around his mouth giving away his state of perpetual disapproval.

And then there's Roger, who looks exactly the same as he did when I saw him last week, but still much different than when we were married. He too looks exhausted. His five o'clock shadow is overgrown and those bright blue eyes are murkier than they used to be.

Three people who used to mean the world to me stand in the doorway of my new home, my new life, where they aren't wanted.

So we don't hug. We don't exchange pleasantries, or voice fake banter about how *it's been so long*. We actually don't speak at all. I simply give them a bemused expression and step aside, motioning for them to come in.

I lead them into the living room, waiting for them to have a seat. And I almost smirk when Roger sits on the couch right where Noah and I just fooled

Seek Me

around. It's minutely satisfying in this very unappealing situation.

Mom and Dad sit on the love seat adjacent to him, and I stand. Because I don't plan on being a polite host, inviting them to stay awhile or offering them a beverage. I'll hear what they have to say, and then they can leave. I don't want them here for one second longer than they need to be.

When I catch Roger's eyes roaming over my bare legs, I remember that I'm dressed in nothing but Noah's t-shirt, which I instinctively tug down. My parents look uncomfortable with what I'm wearing, but I really don't give a fuck. They're the ones barging in on my afternoon. I didn't ask them here.

We're all just staring at each other for moments in silence, and as if sensing my discomfort like he always does, Noah saunters around the corner from the bathroom, still wearing only those sweatpants that make him look oh-so delicious. I can't help but gaze at him for a moment, because he's a picture of pure perfection; muscles inked, nipple pierced, and honey-golden hair ruffled from my fingers while he was kissing my special place that belongs to him.

He steps up to my side and winks down at me. I can feel Roger seething from the couch, something that, in the past, would have completely terrified me. But now, I'm nothing more than a little smug mixed with some mild disgust and pity. Because he's here, trying to mess with me, and I'm over him.

I have my prince here with me. My protector. The holder of my heart. Roger can't do anything to me anymore, and that thought gives me the resolve to look down at the three of them and raise my brows in impatient disinterest.

"Well? What do you want?"

My mom and dad appear a bit shocked by Noah's presence, and our collective lack of dress. Also, I think they're all recognizing him, which is odd to me, being that I've been photographed with Noah hundreds of times in the last few years, so if they kept up with any kind of celebrity news, they would be well-aware of my presence in Noah's life, and vice versa.

Roger lets out an audible sigh that I think is supposed to be condescending, but it comes out more jealous than anything. "Alexandra, this is a private conversation that needs to be had between myself, you and your parents. While I'm sure they appreciate the show, why don't you have your friend wait outside or -"

"Are you fucking kidding me?" I bark at my ex-husband and his fucking audacity. "You're in *my* home. I didn't ask you here, and quite frankly, you're interrupting our afternoon." My lips quirk ever-so-slightly and Roger's eyes blaze, which lights a fire of victorious satisfaction inside me. "By the way, this is Noah." I peek up at my boyfriend. "Noah, this is my ex-husband, Roger, and my ex-parents, Dan and Cara."

Noah's face is etched in protective dissent, though he also wears that casual little smirk, his Noah-mask very much in place for our unwanted guests. He doesn't respond, doesn't say *hello*, or *nice to meet you*, or shake their hands. He simply glares, mainly at Roger. I have to say, that look is giving me life, and making me wet.

"Alex, there's no need to be rude," my dad grumbles, though he doesn't come off anywhere near as confident as I believe he's trying to. "We just came to speak with you. It's been... too long, and well, Roger told us about the divorce, and we wanted to make sure you were doing okay. Clearly, that's debatable..."

I laugh out loud. It's not even really bitter, although it probably should be. It's just a laugh of amusement, because these assholes came here to *my* home uninvited, and now they're insulting me. And I'm not even surprised.

"Okay, Roger. So you went to my parents?" I look directly at him, and he takes a moment to pry his eyes off of Noah. "And you told them we're divorced? Why?"

He straightens a bit. "I thought they'd like to know."

"Did you tell them why we divorced?" I ask, my tone even and eyes locked on my ex-husband's. He narrows his testing gaze at me. I scoff and shake my head, then look to my parents. "I left him because he was cheating on me and physically abusing me for years."

To their credit, my parents don't appear shocked by this information, though it's clear Roger didn't tell them that part.

"So... Now that you're aware, is there anything you'd like to say?" I go on. "Any opinions you'd like to voice about my failed marriage? Get it all out now, because this will be your one and only chance."

"Alex, we were always worried about you," my mother speaks quietly, her voice coming out strained. Her words slink inside me just enough to make me momentarily dizzy, but I push past it. "We've only ever wanted the best for you."

I laugh again, this time more aggressive. "Okay. Duly noted. So why are you three here now, together? How can we be of assistance? I mean, surely if you'd wanted to see me or speak to me you could have called... It's been over a goddamned *decade*. If you wanted to gloat over being right about Roger, why would you come here *with* him?"

My parents share an awkward look, then glance at Roger, and my brow furrows in confusion. I can't get a read on them at all. I have no idea what

Seek Me

the hell they want. And Roger is still just staring at Noah with flames of hate burning in his blue eyes.

"We're not here to make you feel bad," my dad says, and it's then that I notice the vulnerability on their faces. The guilt and shame.

It brings my blood to a rolling boil.

"The day that you moved out... Well, we didn't want to let you out of our lives," my mom says, her fingers knotting in her lap. "We thought you were making a mistake, but we could have lived with it. You were always an impulsive girl... Wild with imagination and defiance. We didn't want to watch you make mistakes that could negatively affect your future, but we had no intention of cutting you out *completely*..."

And then my mother glances at Roger again. My dad does the same. They look at each other, and there's something suffocating in the air; something unsaid, that they're hiding. A secret that will hurt me. And go figure, it seems to revolve around my ex-husband.

I grit my teeth as I watch him, sitting quietly, cocking his head in that sociopathic way he does, which reminds me of how he used to look at me after he'd hit me. No remorse; no guilt or regret for his actions, his eyes radiating bemused curiosity for the aberrance he's witnessing.

I take a step closer to him and whisper, "What did you do?"

He blinks. "The day I took you home with me was not the last time I've spoken to your parents. Actually, Dan, Cara and myself have been in communication for years."

The wind is knocked out of me, like someone whacked me in the stomach with a sack of potatoes. I almost stumble backward.

"For what...?" I breathe out of consternation. "Why?"

My glare flits between Roger and my parents, who now refuse to look me in the eye.

"What did you say to them?" I speak louder, more insistent. "That day... The day I moved out. What the *fuck* did you say to my parents?!"

"I offered them money," he answers calmly, sitting back and folding his hands in his lap. "To stay away from you."

All the air leaves my lungs and my head swims. My knees buckle and I become unsteady on my feet, wobbling until Noah catches me.

"You..." I gasp, my wide eyes finding my parents. "You accepted this...?"

"They did," Roger answers for them, because my cowardly parents can't even look at me, let alone respond. "I've been paying them for years. To cut you out of their lives. So you would be fully mine."

Fuck. I can't breathe. I can't even find any oxygen to take in. Everything around me is blurry and uncomfortable. The only thing giving me any semblance of ease are Noah's hands on my arms, holding me up against his tall frame.

And it's then that I feel him squeeze. He's gripping me so tight it might hurt, if I could feel anything, which I can't. My entire body is numb, and my mind is simultaneously blank and riddled with anxious thoughts.

I peek up at Noah and the look on his face is unnerving. He looks like if he weren't holding onto me, he'd be lunging at Roger and strangling him to death. I can feel his heart beating into my back, and it brings me into the present once more.

It reminds me that I'm fucking enraged.

"How fucking could you?" I grate the words out, like metal scraping together to cause sparks. "You fucking *sold* me?! You sold your only child to someone you didn't trust!?"

My body surges forward, but Noah holds me in place. "You're fucking evil! You're just as bad as he is! I mean, he's the goddamned devil, and you fucking sold your souls to him! Jesus Fucking Christ… Holy fuck…"

"Alex, please," my mother begs, and her look of disgraced regret makes me even angrier. "It wasn't that we… It was just…"

"You wanted to be with him! You were in love with him, remember?" My dad jumps in. "We couldn't have stopped you if we tried!"

"So you just took his money and said good fucking riddance?" I hiss, fisting my hands at my sides. "I'm your *daughter*! All these years I thought you didn't love me enough to come back into my life, but really it was so much worse! You care so little about me you accepted money to stay away from me!"

My mother is crying now, and it makes me want to smack her in the face. *No, fuck that. I'm going to hit her. Fuck you and your fucking tears!*

I lunge forward again, and Noah wraps his arms around me from behind. I fight against him, flailing about, yelping and wailing nonsense at them. I don't even know what I'm saying, but it's a lot of *fuck yous*, and *you're disgusting*, and *I fucking hate you.*

For the first time in what feels like hours, Noah speaks.

"Why would you come here with this?" He growls, his tone resembling the careful snarl a jaguar who's two seconds away from clawing someone's face off. "What's the fucking reason?"

Roger stands up and steps closer to us. I'm trembling, but for the first time

Seek Me

since I met him, it's not with fear, or lust. It's with pure, unbridled rage.

"I thought you deserved to know the truth," he says, blue eyes set directly on me. "I told you I would do anything for you, Alexandra, and I meant that. I only ever wanted you all to myself."

I swallow down the bile rising in my throat. "Get out."

"Alex, you and I are meant for one another," Roger keeps going and now I'm gripping Noah's arms, digging my nails into his flesh, though he doesn't flinch. "You can leave me, humiliate me, divorce me… Whatever you wish. But you can't deny that no one else would ever do for you the things I've done." His eyes flick behind me. "He wouldn't. You know that."

A small huff escapes me. I blink a dozen times to reacquaint myself with reality, because I can't even comprehend how insane this man is. Now more than ever, I realize that he's not well.

He's mentally unstable.

"Oh my God," I breathe, unable to say anything more.

I'm suddenly so exhausted I can barely keep myself upright anymore. I whimper and turn in Noah's arms, holding onto him for dear life. I bury my face in his chest and tremble through hushed cries. He rests his chin on my head and hugs me hard, rocking me slowly and whispering, "It's okay, baby. They can't get to you, remember? You're so strong, beautiful. So fucking strong and I *love* you so much."

"Make them leave," my pleading voice shakes. "Please. Get them the fuck out of here."

"It's time for you to go," Noah says with no hesitation, his voice deep and firm. It's actually pretty scary, but not to me. To anyone who doesn't do what the fuck he says. "All of you. *Leave* and never come back."

My parents say nothing else. They know there's nothing left; no more words they could speak that would erase their actions. I hear them get up and walk to the door, leaving in quiet shame.

And I'm now fully aware that I will never see either of them again. When my parents walk out the door, they walk out of my life for good. And it's almost freeing.

Everything I was holding onto, all the wondering, about whether they still loved me, or if they would someday set aside their pride and come back into my life, it all evaporates.

The door has closed.

Roger lingers. He's still standing in my apartment while Noah holds me and comforts me. I don't want to look at him, but I have no choice, because I know this will be the last time I see him, too. And I have some very serious thoughts about what needs to happen to Roger Glines, none of which include him being anywhere near me, or anyone I know, for that matter.

He's still just staring at Noah and me, looking confused, and hurt, and angry. The old Alex would keep quiet, to protect herself from him and his unpredictable outbursts. But after what just happened, I can't find it in myself to care.

Plus, I fully intend to call the police and get that restraining order reinstated immediately.

"You said you'd do anything for me, Roger," I whisper, gripping Noah as hard as possible. "Well, you need to leave me for good. Leave me to be in love with someone who actually deserves me. Someone I deserve."

He glares at me, and I see his jaw tick. Then he huffs out a breath and stalks to the door, leaving fast without looking back.

And I collapse in my prince's arms and cry.

Despite my earlier reservations, this party is sort of fun.

The drinks are good, and strong. The company is friendly and casual, regardless of how much press is here, and how *official* an event it really is.

And best of all, I get to see my man in action.

Noah is the star of the show so far tonight. Since the moment we set foot at the Hard Rock Cafe here in Manhattan for *Hell Storm's* Season Four Pre-Premiere party, he's been pulled every which way, doing interviews, taking photos, talking to people. It's overwhelming for *me* and I'm not even the one who has to deal with all the fuss.

But my boyfriend is a consummate professional. He goes where he's asked, answers questions with all the right charming words, and wears his casual smile the whole time, whether he's actually enjoying himself remaining a secret that only he will know.

Fortunately for me, I'm not alone while my Noah does his thing. We came with Tessa, who over the last couple weeks has become one of my closest friends.

Even though I have many friends nowadays from the art community, people

Seek Me

I hang out with on a regular basis and whose company I very much enjoy, I can't deny that it's still hard for me to form tight bonds with new people. I recognize that I keep a wall up to protect myself, though it's not done intentionally. It just happens, and outside of Noah, Andrew, and Johnny, I never let my *friends* get too close.

But all those hidden insecurities and unnecessary shields dissipate with Tessa Woodrow. She's just such a cool chick. She's sweet, loyal and fun, and she listens way more than she talks, which is something I don't get from any of my artist friends.

And most importantly, in the last few weeks, she's needed a girlfriend just as much as I apparently have.

After everything that went down with Roger and my parents, I felt a little out of it for a bit. It wasn't the heartbreak you would expect, because I've been over Roger for years, and I had written my parents off the day they let me go. But it still felt weird, knowing that they'd accepted money from him to stay away from me. To be honest, I lost some faith in humanity after that revelation.

But rather than letting it sweep me into a depression, I focused on all the good in my life and let it drive me. I threw myself into my painting, getting ready for my next solo exhibit, which I'm beyond excited for. I continued seeing my therapist once a week, and it's been enlightening. I renewed the restraining order against Roger and even petitioned to have the courts perform a psychological evaluation on him, because at the end of the day, I think he needs a lot of help. They can't force him to take one, but if he volunteers I think it could be good in getting him away from other people whom he might harm.

I know that Roger will always be a part of my life, which is something that stings like bitter salt in a wound deep in my soul. But I've moved on from that pain, and being with Noah has allowed me to savor the happy moments, and harness the joy. That and my relationship with my new potential bestie, Tessa.

We've been hanging out a lot lately. We go to yoga once a week, we go shopping and out for meals. Last night Noah and I went to her place for takeout and movies, and I *finally* got to meet her friend Brandon Cruz, a sexy beast of a man Tessa has dubbed her *gay soulmate*. We had a great time, although every great time we've had in the last three weeks has been tainted by the heartbreak she's still suffering.

Hence the other reason tonight is such a big deal.

Noah, being the scheming best friend he is, insisted that Tessa come to the party tonight to have some fun and get out of the house. But what she doesn't know, what Noah has covertly distracted from, is that Andrew is attending this party as well. Actually, he should be here right now, though none of us have seen him yet…

My boyfriend is just the sweetest friend in the world. We all know this by now. He couldn't stand seeing both of his friends so upset about their break-up, so he stepped into action and concocted this little plan to tell both Andrew and Tessa that the other wouldn't be attending the party, thus forcing them into the same room together.

It's the classic ruse, used countless times before, and almost never ending successfully. But maybe this time will be different.

Now if we could just locate Andrew…

I'm standing in a small circle made up of Tessa, Noah, Mike Beaumont, who is checking Tessa out a little more than I'm comfortable with. *She's spoken for, homie!* And a few more of Noah's cast and crew members from the show, all of whom are gabbing about *Hell Storm* stuff.

Thankfully, our current group is minus one blonde hoe-bag named Melody Davis, Noah's costar and apparently a fling from the first season, right after I left for Budapest, during a time which Noah refers to as his *shameful slut months.*

One of the first nights after we became an official couple, me and Noah decided that we didn't need to talk about the people we've hooked up with while we were avoiding our love for one another. He was an open book to me about everything, and it was doing nothing more than making me jealous and stabby, so I told him we should leave all that stuff in the past, and focus on *us*. *Our* present, and *our* future.

That being said, he mentioned to me that he was a bit of a *shameful slut* after I left for Budapest, and that he regrets many of his hookups, but none more than Melody Davis. Hooking up with a coworker is never a good idea, especially when said coworker was just using you to get a rise out of your married best friend.

So I went into tonight planning to avoid Melody Davis like the plague, and fortunately for all of us she left before midnight.

Still now, the place is crowded as heck, and Noah keeps subtly looking around for Andrew, though it's really not subtle at all because Tessa has been watching him like a hawk. She might be onto something…

I really hope this plan doesn't blow up in our faces.

It's not that we don't understand why Andrew and Tessa had to break up. That part was abundantly clear. It's just that we don't want to see them torture themselves anymore when the issues have slightly resolved themselves...

That sounds terrible, but it's true.

The fact is that none of us are sure if it will be safe for Andrew and Tessa to get back together, what with all the drama surrounding their marriages. But their separation seems like unnecessary pain now that Tessa's a widow and Andrew's divorced - well, almost.

I get where Noah is coming from. They've been staying apart because they think it's what needs to happen, when in reality nothing makes more sense than Andrew and Tessa. They're like Ross and Rachel. Destined to be together despite all the bullshit.

I notice that everyone is staring over at a group of people huddled across the club by the other bar, so I grab Noah's shoulders and hoist myself up on my tippy toes to see what they're seeing.

It's Andrew. He's up at the bar, talking to a few people.

That's when I catch the look of horror on Noah's face. And Tessa's.

The woman standing next to Andrew is tall, blonde, and gorgeous, and while I've never seen his soon-to-be ex-wife before, I gather by the way Noah is now trying to distract Tessa that it must be her... *Vivian James.*

Holy fuck. Code red.

And Tessa takes off. Ignoring Noah who's fumbling behind her, she makes a beeline right over to her ex and his wife. I gulp down the unease that's trying to rise in my esophagus like bile as Noah shoots me his panicked eyes before immediately rushing after our friend. Mike Beaumont starts to follow them, but I grab his arm and hold him in place.

"I wouldn't," I whisper to him and he gives me a confused look that I can't be concerned about, because I'm too busy watching Noah stalk after Tessa, who is practically running directly at Andrew and his wife.

"Jesus... this is so bad," I pace, wondering if there's anything I can do to help.

But I stay put. I have to assume Noah will smooth things over. It's one of his secret talents, after all.

I decide to just wait for the inevitable Andrew and Tessa bomb to explode all over the party, at which point I'll be there to help clean up the mess.

Once Mike is distracted, I leave him and slink closer to the action, hoping to pick up on what's going down. I see Noah slink his arm around Tessa's waist, and I have to bite my lip to keep from laughing.

I can already tell just from watching them that they're probably pretending to be a couple in front of Vivian, since she can't know about Andrew and Tessa. And it's just so funny to witness. I love them both, but Noah and Tessa look absolutely nothing like a couple. They look more like cousins, standing there acting as if they're dating, while Noah's face is radiating tension and Tessa can't stop glaring at Andrew.

I'm dying to snap a picture of this moment, but I think it might blow their cover. So I just stand by and wait.

And sure enough, not five minutes later, Tessa is high-tailing it to the ladies' room. I consider following her, to make sure she's okay. But then, of fucking course, Andrew takes off after her. I watch him follow her into the restroom and giggle to myself.

Noah will be so excited. His plan worked.

I make my way over to where he's standing, with Andrew's wife and one of his directors, and I'm two seconds away from wrapping my arms around him. But I freeze before I can, because if he was pretending to be Tessa's boyfriend, I won't be the one to ruin the act. So instead I tap him on the shoulder.

He turns fast and smiles awkwardly. "Hi." He's making a weird face at me and I laugh because I already know. And he's just so adorable I can't stand it.

"Um, Viv, this is my... friend, Alex," Noah gulps and I can do nothing more than smile like a lunatic as I shake her hand.

We spent four years calling each other just *friends*, but now that we've been officially dating for three weeks it's excruciating to go back to it.

"And this is Nicola," he introduces me to his director, whom I've heard so much about. "She's my favorite."

I shake her hand, wearing a polite smile. "So nice to finally meet you! According to Noah, you're a genius."

Nicola laughs buoyantly. "Well, according to me, Noah's a genius. I'm seriously the luckiest director of all time. Between him and Andrew it's like, when does the work start? Ya know?"

She giggles and I laugh along, peeking at Noah who's chuckling humbly and waving off her compliments. I can't help but notice that Vivian looks bored, and I'm wondering why on Earth she came to this party if she and Andrew are over.

It's my understanding that she's taken no interest in being a part of his career before, which is baffling to me. I mean, sure... I haven't been to any of Noah's premieres yet. But that's only because I wasn't around for them. They always conveniently happened while I was traveling, the exception of course being the one that's happening in three weeks.

Seek Me

It will be my first time attending a TV premiere, and also the first time I'm going as the date of one of the stars. I'm so excited, and also so nervous. *What will I wear?!*

We continue to chitchat for a bit, and I'm itching with the desire to touch Noah. I just want to hug him and kiss him and hold his hand. It's ridiculous, because we're not the couple who's all over each other in public, but not being able to do it makes me want to so much more.

I'm secretly grazing my fingernails along his lower back under shirt while he talks, and he keeps scolding me with his eyes, a look that makes me wet, prompting my hands drift lower so I can rub his butt a little. And then someone tugs on my hair and I turn over my shoulder to see a flushed Tessa, aiming her wide, sparkling teal eyes right at me.

I grin wickedly and grab her arm, yanking her away from the group so I can grill her about what just happened. We scurry over to the other bar and I order us a round of shots. We both rip them quick and Tessa coughs, pinching her lower lip between her fingers as she tries to smother the smile of a completely insane person growing on her face.

"So…" I smirk and cross my arms over my chest. "Have fun in the bathroom?"

"Alex!" She squeals then wraps her arms around me in a giddy wiggling hug that fills me with joy. I'm so happy she's not pouting or sulking, it's almost like I just got laid myself. "He said he still loves me! He loves me and he wants to be with me and *oh my God*, I've never been this happy before!"

She jumps up and down while holding my hands, and I can't help but jump with her. I'm mirroring her excitement because this girl is basically my best friend now, and it hurt a lot to see her so sad. Even worse was knowing that Andrew was equally depressed on the other side of the Atlantic.

But now he's back where he belongs; in New York with his woman. And all is right with the world again.

"Why did his wife come?" I ask Tessa once she finally settles down and orders us another round.

"He said she just wanted to tag along," she shrugs, handing me a shot glass filled with pink liquor. "I guess his kids are here, too. This is so much, Al. It's like feelings overload. I don't know if I can just jump right back into it with him, but then I don't think I'd be able to stop myself if I tried."

We clink and take our shots, and while the alcohol is burning me inside, I consider what she's saying.

"Well, you have to see him tomorrow for that interview anyway," I tell her, and she focuses those big eyes on my face. "Wouldn't it make more sense to straighten everything out tonight?"

She nods while chewing on her lip. "You're right. Lay it all on the table."

"Exactly."

Once we're done girl-talking, and drinking more shots to get loosey goosey, we set out to go find the guys. Tessa is visibly nervous about being next to Andrew again, which I think is too cute, seeing as how they just had sex in a bathroom stall.

We approach Andrew and Noah, and it takes everything in me not to smack my boyfriend on the ass. Andrew's wife isn't really paying attention to any of us, so I'm sure it wouldn't matter, but I don't want to ruin all the mediocre work they've put into this barely-believable lie.

So instead I brush Andrew's back and he turns to give me a sweet smile. I'm so glad to see him, and looking much better than when we were together last. You know... when he was drunkenly stumbling around Johnny's hotel suite in the throes of an emotional colostomy.

Andrew and Tessa are back to looking at each other with those eyes, and I'm so relieved to see it, my heart is soaring. *The world needs these two together. It's better for us all.*

"Sweetie, I think we should be going," Tessa places her hand on Noah's shoulder in amusement, speaking loud enough that Vivian would hear her, if she were paying attention, which she isn't. "We need to bring Alex here home also."

Tessa grins at me and I giggle, watching while Andrew pouts and scowls at his best friend. It's so funny, I want to die laughing, but I refrain and keep up the charade.

"Well, aren't you just the luckiest man in all the land..." Andrew grumbles at Noah, who shrugs unapologetically, to which Tessa and I laugh under our breath.

Noah and I say our goodbyes to everyone in the general vicinity, including Mike, who's hand definitely lingers on Tessa's lower back for a few too many Mississippi's. Actually, I think he's checking out her ass too, which makes me want to gut-punch him.

But before I can, Andrew and Tessa are back within a few inches of each other, shaking hands like two people who just met tonight, not two people who are going to get married and have a bunch of babies, probably sometime in the

Seek Me

near future.

After that, the three of us leave Andrew at the party, all the while wishing we could bring him along. The four of us haven't had anywhere near enough time to double-date as couples, and I'm hoping after tonight, all that will change.

We climb into the Navigator and Jimmy drives us to Brooklyn, to drop Tessa at home. Within five minutes of the ride, Tessa's phone is out, and she's texting with a beaming smile on her face.

I cuddle up to Noah and he kisses my temple. "Well, everyone officially thinks we're having a threesome tonight. Thanks, Tess." He grins and I giggle.

"Uh, that was your doing," Tessa replies, tucking her phone back into her purse. "I didn't fake ask *you* out."

"Yea, and thank God I'm an amazing actor and even better at improv," Noah huffs. "You stomped up to Andrew like you were about to throw a drink in his face. I had to do something!"

Tessa laughs and shakes her head. "I never would've thrown a drink in his face…" Her voice trails off and she bites her lip. "But I did slap him."

Noah and I gasp in unison.

"You *slapped* him?" I shriek through a surprised laugh.

Tessa covers her face with her hands while nodding. "Yea… I was hurt, okay?! I thought he brought his wife as his date!"

Noah bursts out laughing. "Oh my God, that's amazing! Was it hard?"

Tessa's forehead lines in appall. "Ew, Noah! That's personal."

"I meant the slap, you damn pervert," he laughs at her and I can't help the giggles pouring out of me. *I might be a little drunk.*

"No offense, but you two are the worst fake couple in the world," I sigh and they both pout at me, still looking like cousins, or siblings, or some other completely nonsexual pairing.

"I can't help it. I'm in love with someone else," Noah croons, then takes my jaw in his hand and kisses me, soft and sweet and so fucking perfect.

I love him so hard.

"Awww!" Tessa squeals, watching us with heart-eyes. "I hope me and Andrew can get that back…"

"I know you will," Noah smiles at her, and I smile too, resting my head on his shoulder.

There is absolutely no doubt in my mind that they'll be back together by morning.

The future is looking bright for our little group.

I can't wait to see what surprises it holds.

CHAPTER THIRTY FOUR

Alex

Seven Months Later...

Jimmy helps me carry the large frame covered in paper and protective bubble wrap into Noah's apartment. He sets it down in the foyer and leaves fast, before Noah gets home and sees him.

This is a surprise I've been waiting to give my man for months, and I finally seized an opportunity. I can't wait to see the look on his face when he opens it...

I breathe out a sigh of relief that we weren't caught sneaking this huge thing into the apartment, and I meander to the kitchen for some wine. It's barely lunchtime, but I think after wrapping the giant painting and getting it over here, I deserve a glass or two.

Noah is out to lunch with his publicist, so I knew this would be the ideal time to bring over my gift. And being that we're heading down to Georgia in a couple days, this is the exact right moment for me to give my boyfriend a beautiful gift that signifies everything awesome about our relationship.

Things with Noah and me are as perfect as perfect gets. Honestly, sometimes I can barely even comprehend how happy I am.

When we decided to get our asses in gear and be together for real eight months ago, it was the best thing either of us had ever done. And since that wonderful, dramatic night at Maxwell's, we've grown our relationship into something strong and vibrant.

We're still best friends. But now we're best friends who basically live together, mostly here at his place because, let's face it, his is much bigger and nicer than mine. We're best friends who support each other in everything, like at his premieres and my art shows, and when it comes time for him to film on location in Georgia, I will fly back to New York a bunch over the next five months, but me moving into Noah's place down south was never a debate. I can't stand to be away from him for even one day, so I had no intention of doing

Seek Me

long-distance with my sexy actor boyfriend.

We're best friends who spend exorbitant amounts of time with our couple friends, also known as Andrew and Tessa, and Brandon and William, Andrew's assistant and Brandon's adorable love interest. The six of us are practically inseparable, especially now that we all live in New York. A lot changed in the last seven months, all for the better, and I wake up every morning thanking God that I chose to stay here with Noah.

We're best friends who have massive amounts of sex, day and night, all over the damn place. Anywhere that it's acceptable for us to bang, we do. And maybe some places where it's not... Like behind a rare ficus at an exhibit in the Brooklyn Botanical Gardens two weeks ago.

I wish I could be sorry, but it's really hard to give fucks when your man looks like mine does.

In short, Noah and I are the best kind of best friends there are. Because we're in love, and we're unbreakable. Even our fights are adorable, and they end rather quickly when we give up whatever stupid thing we were arguing about to play Mario Kart and hump each other on the floor.

Yes, we still do that. Maybe we're the weirdest couple in the world, but for us it works, and I wouldn't trade ours for any *normal* relationship on Earth.

I go to the kitchen and pour myself a glass of wine, deciding to do a triple-check of our list for Tessa's surprise birthday party we're having here tomorrow. Because of who her husband is, I know everything has to be perfect. Andrew wouldn't have it any other way. And while he did most of the planning and arranging himself, he left Noah and me with two responsibilities: food and booze.

The booze is for us, since homegirl is three months preggers, which also means that the food is insanely important. Tessa is at a ravenously hungry stage in her pregnancy, which is adorable because of how small she is, but also scary at times, because if you get near her food she might bite you just a little.

Noah already hired a catering company with one of the most renowned chefs in Manhattan and made sure to order cases of only top-shelf liquor. But I want to check the receipt for the Hamptons vineyard he ordered the wine from and make sure he got enough. Just because most of us love scotch, it doesn't mean everyone else will.

I notice a couple notebooks open on the breakfast bar, with invoices scattered around them, so I assume this is what I'm looking for.

I pick up the first notebook which is opened to a page with some catering companies' info. I gaze over it for a moment before setting it aside to check out what's underneath.

It takes a moment for my brain to process what I'm looking at, but once I do, there's no unseeing it.

It's Noah's journal. The one I got him for Christmas two years ago.

And it's open to a page he's written in.

And on that page, which I'm totally not reading by the way, the only word that jumps out at me is *marry*.

I close my eyes quick and shake my head. This is wrong.

I shouldn't be looking at this. I can't read someone else's journal. It's like the most fucked-up thing you can do.

But now that my brain knows what word is there, I can't even help myself...

My eyes creep open slightly, enough for me to see a few more words around it.

I want to marry Alex.

My stomach is in my throat. I feel as though my whole body is being swept away in a cloud, drifting me up into the air. I'm light and floaty, and suddenly there's a world of endless possibilities laid out in front of me. A future I hadn't even been thinking about, in all honesty, until just now.

Noah and I don't talk about marriage. I'm divorced, so to me it's not something I'm trying to rush into a second time. And I always figured Noah would freak out at the idea of marriage, so I never bring it up.

And it's totally fine. We don't need any validation from the government, or a piece of paper. We're blissful in our eight-month relationship, living each day as happy as two people can be together.

But now that I've read those words... those tiny words, written in Noah's jumbled, manly handwriting, I'm seeing it all so very different.

Sure, we've been *official* for only eight months, but we've been in love with each other for almost five years. We've been sleeping together for that long, and we're still so undeniably attracted to one another, we can't keep our hands, or private parts, to ourselves, even in public. If that's not a reason to get married, then I don't know what is.

Plus, if you want to get cultural, Noah's forty, so it's understandable if he's starting to consider things that people often do as they get older. Not me, necessarily, because I got married super young. But I have to admit, Noah considering such things makes me want to consider them, because he's my everything, and I can't imagine my life without him.

Fuck, what am I doing?? I'm going all Bridget Jones after reading a couple words on a page. A page of my boyfriend's private journal! What is the matter with me?? I need to put this away and never look at it again.

I'm sure you can see where this is going…

I don't put it away.

I let my eyes drift to the top of the page, and I start from the beginning, because despite how wrong it is, my curiosities have piqued, and there's no turning back.

And so I read…

Dear Boots,

Let me tell you about something that happened to me in February…

Chapter Thirty Five
Noah's Journal

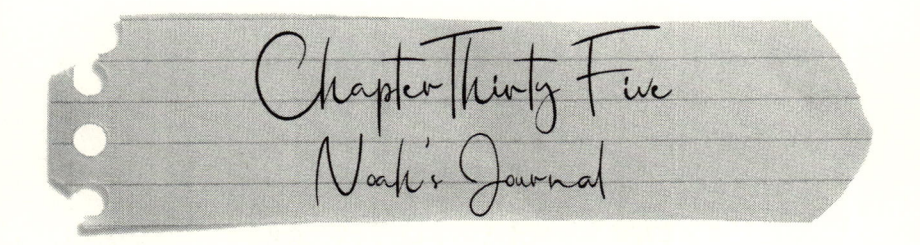

Dear Boots,

Let me tell you about something that happened to me in February.

My best friend got married.

Well, married for a second time. But this is the one that will stick, and I don't even need a crystal ball or some tarot cards to be certain.

I know in my heart that Andrew and Tessa are going the distance. And if you're wondering how I know, all you need to do is see them together.

I'm telling you, Bootsey, I've never witnessed two people so entranced with one another. It's actually alarming sometimes. We joke with them often about how codependent they are, but really, it's fascinating to be around. They're just so painfully in love, in a way that's selfless and fully magical. Like the stars aligned just for them, and fate plucked them out of their shitty lives to deposit them together in greatness.

When I saw them looking at each other on their wedding day, which was completely gorgeous by the way, in Fiji on Valentine's Day, they had this mirroring mesmerized wonder on their faces. As if they themselves couldn't believe they had found each other and were blessed with the mystical presence of divine intervention.

The wedding ceremony, as beautiful as it was, is not the instance I'm telling you about right now. Not the reception either, which was such a blast. It's hard to comprehend a wedding with only eight guests being such a fantastic event, but it was. Everything about that night was perfect, but again... Not what I'm writing to you about.

I'm writing to tell you about the night before the wedding, and the day after.

The night before, we had Andrew's *bachelor party*, if you can call it that with no strippers, in a little island bar in Fiji.

That night, when we were sufficiently shit-cocked beyond all recognition, we had to flee the bar after a bunch of crazed fans started chasing us. It was weird, but still not the most bizarre part of the night. What happened next, now

Seek Me

that's the kicker.

We stumbled upon a huge waterfall at the top of an embankment. It was one of the most incredible, most picturesque things I've ever seen. And Andrew got it into his head that he wanted to jump.

I know, I know. Cliff-diving is already dangerous. Add alcohol to the mix, and you've clearly got a death wish, or a startling suicide pact going on.

Well, I assure you, Andrew, Johnny and me didn't have any of those. And yet still, for reasons I didn't understand until after, my two psycho best friends were itching to jump.

So after I examined down below for a moment to make sure there were no sharp rocks we could impale ourselves on, I agreed. And the three of us jumped.

I'm not even kidding you, Boots. We fucking *jumped* down what we thought was a fifty-foot waterfall!

The day after the wedding I went back to it sober, and it turns out it was just barely pushing thirty-feet. But still! In our drunken minds, it was the highest thing we'd ever seen. And we jumped it!

When I crashed into that clear blue, tropical water, with my stomach in my throat from the gravity, it was the most magnificent thing I'd ever felt. Unfortunately, also in the harsh reality of the next day, it ended up feeling much worse, because I didn't close my legs enough and the impact of the water definitely bruised my taint.

But still! It was amazing, Boots. I had never felt so free, despite the ass-pounding pain in the morning. It was a high I never could have expected, and it changed my life.

After that, we trudged our sopping-wet asses back to our luxury huts, put Andrew to bed at Brandon's, and I made my way home.

To Alex.

She was passed out drunk when I got there, in nothing but a sheer *Bridesmaid* t-shirt. And I stood in the doorway for a half an hour, just watching her, and thinking, *This is my home. Wherever this girl is.*

After a while, I couldn't stand not touching her, so I stripped out of my soaking wet clothes and climbed into bed with my woman. She woke up the second I started spooning her against my freezing cold skin, which I felt sort of bad about. But then, not really, because she warmed me up by rubbing her perfect tits all over me.

We had mind-blowing sex that night, as we always do, and when she was lying in my arms, her quiet breathing relaxing me while our joined heartbeats synchronized, I took her left hand in my right, and I gazed at her ring finger, wondering what it would look like with a ring on it.

My ring.

See, I suppose the other thing I should mention about that night is that while we were out at the bar, I told Andrew and Johnny I wanted to ask Alex to marry me.

I had been thinking about it for a while. Actually, ever since we became an official couple, months earlier. But I always figured waiting was the way to go, since we'd just finally declared our love for one another, and I didn't want to appear eager, or crazy.

And yet the more I thought about it, the more sense it made in my mind. I've been in love with Alex Mackenzie since the night we met, and nothing would make me happier than spending my life with her.

So when Andrew and Tessa invited us to be a part of their special, intimate destination wedding in Fiji, I decided that the next wedding we all attended together would be ours. And Boots, when I jumped that waterfall alongside my best friends, all I could see while the wind was rushing around my body, and into that cool splash of water, was Alex saying *yes*.

I want to marry Alex.

I want to spend the rest of my life with her, laughing and kissing and growing old together, and who knows, maybe starting a family.

I want to cuddle her when she's upset and kiss away her tears when she's sad. I want to take the brunt of her anger when we're fighting, and I want to hold her hand when we make up.

I want to spend hours, days, weeks, months making love to her in every way imaginable, and I want to make her feel gorgeous and sexy every second of every day, because she has to know how fucking perfect she is. She just *has* to.

There are a million things I want from Alexandra Mackenzie, but most importantly, I want to dedicate my life to her. I want to give her, and only her, my body, my heart, and my soul... Forever.

That's why the day after Andrew and Tessa's wedding in Fiji, I bought a ring. I found a jeweler on the island, in an unexpected place at an unexpected time. But the second I saw it, I knew it would look perfect on that little finger.

So I bought it and I held it with me on the plane back to New York, with my woman sitting right next to me, snuggled up while we watched *Ace Ventura* with Johnny, Fiona, Brandon and William. I kept it in my pocket the whole time, and

Seek Me

she had no clue, and that makes me feel all the more privileged.

That I have this beautiful, special dark-haired, tattooed fairy girl in my life, who lights up my world. And she has no idea I'm going to propose to her, or that when I do it'll blow her freaking mind.

I just hope she says yes, Boots.

I just hope she says *yes*.

Chapter Thirty Six
Noah

I stroll through the hallway to my apartment. My heart is racing pretty quick, considering that nothing has even occurred yet to make it do so.

I pause outside my door, wiping my sweaty palms on my jeans. I laugh breathlessly to myself and shake my head, because this is so crazy. And I really hope my plan works.

My shaky fingers turn the doorknob, as slow as possible, because I'm trying to be super quiet. I need to channel all my sloth-like agility to get inside the apartment without Alex hearing me.

Here goes…

I'm in. I look around the foyer, but I don't see her. This is good. This could work.

I tiptoe inside, stepping out of my shoes to stifle the additional sounds, then slink past the living room, toward the kitchen.

I see Alex at my breakfast bar and I almost lose bladder control. This is so exciting, I really might pee my pants. I truly hope it doesn't come to that, since it would most definitely be a deal-breaker.

No one says yes to marrying somebody who just peed themselves.

I stand at the entrance to my kitchen for a moment, controlling the breaths that want to shoot in and out of my body like a cannon, and watch Alex.

She's fallen right into my trap, and I've never been happier that she disregarded my privacy and read my journal that I left open for her to read. I'm ecstatic right now. I'm trembling from head to toe.

How the fuck am I going to pull this off?? I'm so nervous already!

I wait, watching in silence to make sure she's done reading the pages I wrote, specifically for her. I can tell when she's done because she lets out an audible breath and covers her face with her hands, whimpering some curses behind them.

Alright, Richards. Your entire acting career has led you to this moment.

"Alex…" I rumble her name and she startles so hard she gets air when she jumps, turning around to face me, wearing the guiltiest expression I've ever seen in my life.

Showtime.

She lets out a squeak which isn't words, so I step forward, witnessing how the color has drained from her cheeks. For show, I gawk at my journal, opened to the last page I wrote, in front of where she's standing, and I purposely crease my forehead.

"What are you doing?" I ask, cocking my head to the side as I blink at her beautiful, worried face.

"Um... I..." she stutters, turning over her shoulder to glance at the journal, as if she expects it to admit to opening itself up and reading its words aloud to her.

I take another step. "Is that my journal?"

Alex gulps visibly, and it takes some serious skill not to smile at how damn cute she is.

"Noah... I'm so sorry..." she whispers, her voice quivering. "It was opened, and I didn't mean to read it, but I..."

"You read it?" I gasp, keeping my tone more insecure than angry. I don't want her to think I'm *mad* about her reading it. Just worried that I may have scared her away.

She does a little nod and I cringe on cue.

"Oh, no... fuck fuck fuck... You weren't supposed to see that," I rake my hands over my face in mock humiliation.

"Holy fucking shit, Noah, I'm *so* sorry. I really didn't mean to," she breathes, closing the gap between us and grasping my shoulders. "I thought it was something for the party, and then before I knew it I was... reading it..."

She flinches in remorse and I bite my lip. *I know exactly what you thought, baby, because that's exactly why I left it like that.*

I blink at her. "So... You saw... all of it?"

She shakes her head, but still answers, "Yea..."

"Oh... So you read everything... about Fiji?" I lift my brows.

"Yes," she hums, those brilliant green eyes locked right on me. It's so bewitching, I have to remind myself to play it cool.

"And about... me wanting to marry you?" My voice rumbles low and I hear her breath catch in her throat as she nods. "You read about how I want to spend every single day for the rest of my life with you...?"

Alex gives me a confused look, but nods again. So I keep going.

"And about how I want to make you mine for real, because nothing has ever been as real or true as you and me are together?"

Alex fumbles for words, every inch of her shivering right in front of me. "Noah, I -"

"And how I want to wake up smothering your body with mine in bed… *our* bed… every morning for the rest of our lives? And how I want to cook for you, while you sit there looking pretty because you can't cook for shit, but it's okay, because even your imperfections make you that much more perfect…"

Her lips quirk into a hesitant smile, but it's still covered in disorientation. I reach out to play with her silky hair and watch in amazement as tears fill her eyes. I think she notices how badly my hands are shaking, but it just makes her shake even more herself.

"Did you pick up on how hopelessly, madly, detrimentally in love with you I am, Alexandra? And how I've been this way since the day I saw you on that rooftop… When you read what I wrote, did it help you see that there will be no one else for me as long as I'm alive, and that I want to spend all of my days with the woman who changed my world when she smiled at me, and touched me, and melted my fucking heart with her beautiful green eyes?"

She's crying now, and it's about to break me.

She sniffles out my name, like she still has no idea what I'm doing. "Noah…"

I blink hard and press my forehead to hers. "Did you turn the page?"

"No," she whispers over my lips, quaking so hard I have to hold her face to calm her down.

I swipe at her tears with my thumb and a smile breaks through. "Do it."

She pulls back, eyeing me quizzically, though all of her worry from before has since been replaced with nerves and eagerness. I nod behind her and she turns back to the breakfast bar, flipping the page in my journal.

I take a deep breath and hold it while she gasps out loud, slapping a hand over her mouth.

She picks up the ring I bought her in Fiji, which was inside my journal, and turns back to me, gaping with wonder and shock blanketing her gorgeous face.

I sigh out hard. "Well, if you already *know*…" I grin teasingly as I take the ring from between her fingers and drop down to one knee.

"Oh, Jesus fucking Christ…" she pants, covering her face with her hands for a moment.

I laugh softly, and when she removes them, she's smiling. It's wild and enraptured and the most wondrous thing I've ever seen. I actually have to look away for a moment or I'll burst into tears myself.

"Alexandra Hope Mackenzie, I spent four years falling in love with you, which leads me to believe that I can go the rest of my life and never truly stop falling."

Alex weeps out a small laugh, smiling so big and bright for me.

"Somewhere in between having you, and not, I realized that that you'd had my heart the whole time. I thought I'd been seeking you, but really *you* found *me*. And baby, I've loved you since the beginning of our long-ass journey. So please... Please please please, fairy girl. *Please* marry me."

Alex squeals and jumps up and down, covering her mouth with her hands while she nods.

"Yes!" She whimpers and before she can do anything else I stand and grab her by the waist, lifting her into my arms and twirling her around in circles.

"God, I fucking love you," I croak, pressure building behind my eyes as I hold her butt tight and press my head up to her chest.

She weeps hysterically, gripping my shoulders and mewling the word *yes* over and over and fucking over. I'll be dreaming of the sound of her saying it for the rest of my nights.

Yes.

My heart is so full it's going to erupt out of me. I can't even comprehend this level of happiness.

I'm high. Love drunk. I'm stunned. In awe.

I'm fucking engaged.

I stalk to the breakfast bar and plop Alex down with a growl, wedging myself between her thighs. I gaze up at her with so much love in my eyes it could start seeping out in the form of tears. I think it already is a bit, but I'm okay with it.

Alex is still trembling all over as I take her small hand in mine and slip the one-of-a-kind diamond ring on her finger. We both take a moment to admire it...

Platinum setting, five-carat cushion cut surrounded by another carat of black diamonds. It's fucking stunning. And it looks a zillion times better on her finger than it did in that tiny luxury jeweler's in Fiji.

"Noah! My God, this ring..." Alex squeaks, abruptly taking my jaw in her hands and kissing my lips so hard and fast that I groan uncontrollably in her mouth. "You really bought it in Fiji?"

I nod, still kissing her, slowing it down a bit. "I knew I wanted to ask you...

And when I went wandering that day, while you and Fiona and Brandon were on the beach, I stumbled upon a family jeweler that specialized in unique rings. Apparently that family owns like half the shops in Fiji... Anyway, I saw it and I just knew..."

I stop to swallow and Alex gazes at me with wide, shimmering eyes.

"So you've had it for two months?" She smiles and I can't help but laugh, mildly embarrassed.

"I was waiting for the perfect moment... And sort of um... Working up the courage to ask you." My eyes drop and I chew on my lip.

Alex combs her fingers through my hair and I look up at her. "There is nothing on Earth like a shy Noah Richards, let me tell you." She giggles and I squint at her, pursing my lips to hide my unwavering smile. "But you took a chance with that proposal! What if I didn't read it?"

I laugh softly. "I have the whole thing memorized, anyway."

"So fucking cute," she sighs, tugging my lips to her once more.

"I promise I'll make you happy, Alexandra," I breathe to her in between heated kisses. "Forever and ever and fucking ever."

"I know you will," she murmurs, then presses her palm flat over my heart. "My prince... You already have."

Alex and I had sex on the breakfast bar.

It only lasted about twenty minutes, but we both came twice, which was pretty damn marvelous.

And now that we've cleaned up and redressed ourselves, my fiancée - *holy fuck, that's something I never thought I'd say* - is tugging me by my hand over to the foyer.

"I have a gift for you," she sings while skipping. I'm delirious over how happy she is right now. I can't even fathom that I'm responsible for her current state of bliss.

And that we're engaged.

We're. Fucking. Engaged.

Maybe I'd like to do a little singing myself. Or some dancing. I'll do the moonwalk while Alex films it at this point. I'm so beyond happy, I don't even know what to do with myself.

Seek Me

"A gift for me?" I croon, wrapping her up in my arms from behind while she wiggles her butt on my crotch. "You shouldn't have. *Fiancée*."

"Noah! Mmm... baby, you're making me all tingly," she giggles and I kiss the nape of her neck.

She stops us in front of a giant object covered in bubble wrap and waves her hand in front of it.

"Tada! Open it!" She starts jumping again.

"'Kay," I sigh and set out to do literally whatever she wants.

It takes a bit to unwrap the thing, but when I finally get through all the paper, I realize it's a painting. I'm over the moon before I even look at it.

"You painted me something, fairy love?" I lift her hand to my mouth and kiss her ring finger, which has now been claimed by yours truly.

She nods repeatedly. "Look."

When my eyes fall down to the painting in front of me, they widen and all the air sifts out of my lungs in a steady stream.

It's a painting of two people, and I know right away that it's me and Alex. There are no faces. It's more like a closeup of just our torsos, but I'm holding Alex to my chest, my hand resting over her heart, and she's doing the same to me.

It's so incredibly detailed, all of our tattoos are immaculately done. Our body shapes are perfectly depicted. It looks like a photograph, but it's not. It's oil paint.

It's so breathtaking, I literally can't breathe. A strangled noise erupts from my throat and Alex squeezes my hand. I pry my gaze away from the masterpiece she's made for me and I see that she's crying again. And I can't help it, but I am too.

"Baby... This is... Oh... Wow..."

"Do you like it?" She chirps at me through her tears, and I grab her again. I hold her the way I am in the painting, pressing my hand over her heart. And she does the same.

"I did this the day we started dating... Before I went to Maxwell's," she tells me.

"Really?" I'm blown away. *She's had this for eight months?*

"Yea... I mean, I've done a lot more work to it since then. But I never wanted to sell it. I knew it needed to be here. With us."

I whisper by her ear, "It's me and you, baby. Holding each other's hearts forever. From the night I met you, I knew I wanted that. When I saw you, sitting alone, looking so sad… I made it my mission to make you smile."

She huffs a soft laugh and kisses my neck. "Mission accomplished."

I dip my face into the crook of her neck and inhale her; the scent that has been my salvation for so many years. And I remember that night, on a rooftop, beneath twinkling lights.

"There she is."

And we stand like this, in my foyer, for minutes on end, feeling one another's heartbeats. Cherishing the love we've found in each other. A love that will last a lifetime.

A love that will never fade; discovered in trouble, grown in patience, and flourished in profundity.

I can't wait to marry this woman.

And the dark prince and his twisted fairy live happily ever after.

Epilogue

Alex

I do.

I can still hear the words echoing in my brain; that deep, raspy voice slated in smiles, agreeing to have me and hold me, in sickness and in health, for richer or poorer, in good times and in bad... As long as we both shall live.

I do.

I definitely do. That's an understatement, to be honest. I more than do. I fucking *need to* love and cherish this man, forever and eternity. It's in my bones. Etched in my soul.

I'll breathe my last breath loving Noah Richards with every fiber of myself, and in whatever afterlife there may be, I still *will*.

I do. Forever.

My husband steps out of the limousine first so he can help me with my dress, and when I'm out, he traps me against his tall, hard body, draped in a cashmere coat, because it's January in Long Island and it's freezing out, curling those long fingers around my jaw and kissing me, somehow rough and soft at the same time.

"My beautiful fairy bride," he whispers on my mouth, causing my knees to buckle.

Noah Richards can make a lot of things hot, but none more than *husband*.

I seriously can't believe I'm married to him. I must have been Mother Theresa in a past life. It's the only explanation.

"We're married!" I squeak at him and he laughs. "This is so cool."

"Isn't it?" He grins at me, lifting my left hand with his so we can admire our wedding bands together. "You're already my favorite wife. Hands down."

I giggle and lick my lips, ogling the hand that I can't wait to let run free all over my body.

Seriously, is there anything sexier than tattoos peeking out from the sleeves of a tux?

I swallow hard as my giddy smile falters.

Noah notices instantly and catches my chin. "Baby, don't do that. It doesn't matter that you were married before. The only thing that matters is that you're married to *me* now."

I laugh softly and he beams. It's such a wonderful thing to witness, I've been swooning all day.

I can't help the sting of this being my second marriage. It sucks just a little, even though Noah doesn't care at all, and I know I shouldn't either. This is my first actual wedding, surrounded by family and friends. And this is the one that will last eternity. *My last wedding.*

"Come on, sexy thing," he murmurs and pulls me with him. "Let's go dance and eat cake with our friends."

That has me excited. And we lace our fingers as we enter the private dining hall of a local restaurant where we're hosting our intimate reception.

The band announces us, and everyone cheers. My cheeks are flushed pink, mostly from all the eyes on me, but also partially from being so close to such a hot fucking dude. *My husband. My Noah.*

"Mr. and Mrs. Richards!" Andrew and Johnny yell at us, grabbing Noah and shoving him around like crazy, while I laugh alongside my Maid of Honor, Tessa, and my bridesmaids, Noah's sister, Haley, and our friend, Fiona.

Ask me if it's weird that one of my bridesmaids slept with my husband. It's okay, I'll answer truthfully.

It's not.

Sure when I found out about Noah and Fiona last year it threw me off a bit. But when we talked about it after, I realized that their time together did nothing more reaffirm Noah's feelings for me. After all, we spent many years hiding from our love for one another…

But he was always right there for me to find. I just needed to seek him out.

"Congratulations, gorgeous," Brandon and William croon, both coming in for hugs and kisses on the cheek.

"You look so beautiful," William smiles, playing with my veil.

"I almost cried," Brandon smirks and I laugh, play-punching him in the arm.

There are so many people around, it's sort of overwhelming. But just seeing Noah's prideful smile as he hugs his mom and dad makes all the stress fade away.

"I couldn't have dreamed up a better bride for my son," Gemma sniffles, hugging me so tight, it's as if she's squeezing the tears out of me. "Thank you so much for making him so happy."

"Oh my God, stop!" I whimper and she laughs, wiping her eyes. "I'll be blubbering all night if you keep that up."

"I can fix that," Tom steps in. "Thank you for transforming my son from a hooker to a husband." He winks at me and I burst out laughing.

"That did it!" I cheer and he pulls me into a chuckling hug.

"I can hear you talking shit about me, Father, and I don't appreciate it," Noah grumbles, wrapping his arm around my waist and planting a soft kiss on my temple. "Don't do anything to make her regret marrying me."

I peek up at him and bite my lip. "Never."

The best night ever goes on.

We drink, we eat, we laugh.

Noah and I dance our first dance as husband and wife to an acoustic *Everlong* by Foo Fighters, covered by our wonderful wedding band, who are friends of Noah's. Naturally.

Then Andrew and Johnny give toasts, which are most like roasts, that have us all in stitches.

Noah dances with Gemma and I dance with Tom, and it's just the sweetest thing I've ever been a part of. I love my new mom and dad beyond words.

My bridal party eventually steals me away for shots, which I'm more than happy to take with my girls.

"To Alex and Noah, the veteran couple of all of us!" Tessa raises her glass, and I slide one to Haley, who's not quite twenty-one yet, but it's a celebration.

"To my new sister," Haley grins and I pout, not wanting to cry again, but not really being able to stop it.

"Cheers!" Fiona squeals, and we all clink, taking them back and group hugging like a bunch of giggling fools.

"I am just so grateful to you guys," I tell them all, looking over their beautiful, expertly made-up faces, wearing the dresses I chose for them, and hair I had styled for them. "I wanted this day to be perfect, and it never would have happened if it weren't for all of you."

"Aww! Don't make me cry," Tessa hums, scrunching her nose.

"Oh my God, you're not pregnant again, are you?" Fiona gasps, teasing, and Tessa's eyes widen in horror.

"Please don't even speak that into the air right now," she mumbles. "Five-month-old twins, a seven-year-old *and* an eleven-year-old are enough."

We laugh and then all our eyes dart across the room at the kids. Michael,

Andrew's oldest, is dancing with his mom, Andrew's ex-wife, Vivian. And Tessa's youngest step-child, Lucy, is dancing with Andrew. It's one of the cutest things I've ever witnessed, and I momentarily wish I had my camera. But then I remember there's a professional photographer around here somewhere, and I see him snapping pictures of everyone on the dance floor.

Good. I want to cherish these memories forever.

Speaking of babies, Noah and William walk over, each carrying a twin in their arms. They're identical, especially since they're so young, so it always takes me a minute to remember which one's which.

I remember that Carter is wearing purple, and her sister, Madeline, is wearing pink.

Noah sidles up to me with an adorable little peanut in a pink dress in his arms, squealing and bopping around while he makes faces at her.

"I love this baby," Noah sighs, kissing her small head, the sight of which sends a jolt through my ovaries. *Hot damn...*

"She's pretty freaking cute," I hum, smiling at her because hers is contagious, as is the obvious baby fever happening in our little group.

I look over at Tessa tending to her other daughter while William rocks her, Carter being the much calmer of the two. Fiona and Haley and are also ensconced, tugging at Carter's little shoes and her purple dress.

"We should have one," Noah whispers, and my head snaps in his direction. I'm not sure if he meant to say that out loud, because he gives me a wide-eyed, nervous look while I gape at him. "I mean... some day... Soon...?"

My mouth drops open but nothing comes out. I'm speechless. And excited. My lips twist into a hesitant smile, which he returns.

"Really?" I rest my chin on his shoulder, admiring his beautiful face and deep coal eyes.

"Maybe..." he rumbles, running his fingers through Madeline's soft patch of dark brown hair while he stares at me. "Do you want one?"

"Maybe," I reply softly, tracing my name tattooed below his clavicle, which is exposed by his loosened bow tie and opened collar.

"For what it's worth, I know we could do it," he says, hugging Maddie to his chest as we both watch her, those eyes so damn blue, there would never be an ounce of doubt of whether she's Andrew's child.

"I think... I'd like being a parent with you," my voice shivers and he bites his lip.

"What do you say, baby girl? You want a cousin?" Noah asks Madeline then

Seek Me

lifts her up and swings her around until she does that adorable, full-bellied baby laugh that melts your heart into a puddle.

I feel eyes on us, and I glance up to see Noah's parents, Andrew and Tessa staring with raised brows. Tessa leans into Gemma and whispers something in her ear, and whatever she said makes Noah's mom immediately start crying.

"Oh dear God," Noah breathes through a concerned laugh.

"Yea, your parents want grandchildren. Like, yesterday," I giggle.

"Well, then I guess we'd better get started," he turns that sparkling dark gaze at me and that one look singes my panties.

Good thing I brought like four extra pairs. Gotta come prepared when my husband is around.

The night winds down, and most of the family leaves, but our group of friends stays. We fully intend on shutting this place down and partying all damn night. That was the plan, anyway.

Vivian and her boyfriend, Bill, get the four kids ready to leave, since they're watching them for the night to give Andrew and Tessa some much-needed alone time. But we can't let our flower girl and ring-bearer leave without the special gifts we bought them.

"Okay, so to thank you two for rocking the show today," Noah says to Michael and Lucy, "We wanted to give you these."

He hands them each a wrapped gift and we watch in giddy excitement as they tear open the paper.

Lucy gets to hers first. It's set of eleven-inch canvases and some of the best paintbrushes on the market. Luciana is a future artist from what I've been told by Andrew and Tessa, and she loves to draw and paint already. I figured I could pass on some of my wisdom to my niece

"Oh my gosh! Thank you, Alex!" She cheers and hugs me hard. "Art supplies from a real artist!"

I laugh and peek at Tessa who's beaming with pride.

"Daddy has your paintings all over his flat. You're my favorite artist," Lucy tells me with baby blue eyes aimed up at my face. It makes me want to fall down.

"Aww, thank you so much, sweetheart! That means the world to me," I hug her again. "Keep working at it every day. I'm always here to talk to you about art, whenever you want, okay?"

"Okay!" She bounces about, and it gives my soul some deep satisfaction that this seven-year-old girl is supported in wanting to pursue art by everyone in her life.

That's more than I could say for myself at her age, which makes me want to dedicate more time to teaching Lucy.

Meanwhile, Michael has opened his gift from Noah, and he's geeking out. It's his own pair of Classic Ray Bans. Just like his Uncle Noah.

"No way!" Michael shouts, taking them out of the box and immediately putting them on his face. Noah removes his Bans from his pants pocket and covers his eyes.

And now they look like twins. And it's fucking adorable.

"We're the two coolest dudes ever invented, my man," Noah grins, hugging Michael into his side while Tessa and Vivian snap pictures with their phones.

"We're so cool!" Michael high-fives Noah and all the adults laugh.

"Say thank you and congratulations to Auntie Alex and Uncle Noah," Andrew reminds his children, which they do, hugging us once more.

"Anything for you, kiddos," Noah tells them with a ruffle of Michael's hair.

We wave goodbye to them and watch as their parents grab their stuff and take them outside to get home to Brooklyn.

Noah pulls me into his chest and says, "I can't decide which two are my favorite of Andrew's kids... Them or the little ones."

I laugh out loud and he grins. "Andrew makes great kids."

"That he does."

"I think you'd make great kids," I whisper and his eyes dart to mine, his smile growing exponentially wider.

"You think?"

"I know. I bet you'd make beautiful babies." I realize that we're dancing, swaying to a steady rhythm.

"Only if they're half you," he lifts me and holds my body against his, so as not to step on my bare feet.

I rest my head on his chest and let out a sigh of contentment while he kisses my hair.

"Noah, I love you..." I tell him and he growls, "More than a friend."

He laughs out loud and I bite my lip because *damn* that sounds sexy. "We were never really *friends*, baby..."

"There better be more, because that hurts," I faux-pout, though I can't stop giggling.

I feel him pull back to look down at me, so I peek up at him. "We were always more."

"So much more," I blink, and he leans down to kiss me, soft and passionate

Seek Me

and eager, reminiscent of all our big kisses over the last six years…

Our first kiss, in his bed. The first time we slept together. The night I left Roger. When I left for Budapest. When I came back from Budapest. When I flew to him in Georgia, and when I left. Coming home from Tel Aviv and Barcelona to Noah, waiting patiently for me. The night we finally stopped hiding from our love for each other, to Noah's proposal and every kiss in between that led us to our first kiss as husband and wife, just a few hours ago.

The kiss that will lead us to each and every kiss, for the rest of our lives.

I hum on his lips, reveling in the feel of him, undone and exposed; bared to *me*. I'm the only person on Earth who gets this version of Noah Richards, and that right there is just one of the millions of things that make me proud to be Mrs. Alexandra Richards.

I rest my cheek back over his heart, where it belongs, and he strokes my hair through his long fingers.

"This was the best wedding ever, baby," I squeeze him tighter. "Thank you for marrying me."

A soft laugh rumbles from within his broad chest. "Thank you for existing. Thank you for being mine… Thank you for saying *yes*."

"As if I could ever say no to you," I smile, and I don't have to see his face to know he's smiling back.

I know that no matter what the future holds for us, Noah will always be right by my side, smiling and teasing me, making me laugh so hard I almost pee my pants, and swoon so hard I immediately drop them.

Marriage is never easy, and I'm sure there will be tough times for us. Life isn't perfect.

But the truth, *our* truth, is that we love each other deep, and raw, and with every single flawed and frayed bit of ourselves. The imperfect is perfect when we're together.

All the pain of my past led me to my true forever.

And that's pretty damn badass.

The End

Thank you for reading!

Looking for more Flipping Hot Fiction by Nyla K?
Check out the trilogy that started it all:

The Midnight City Series:

Midnight City

Never Let Me Go

Always Yours

Or would you like...

Standalone MMF/Taboo:

PUSH

Don't forget to leave a review! It's so very appreciated!

About the Author

Hi, guys! I'm Nyla K, otherwise known as Nylah Kourieh; an awkward sailor-mouthed lover of all things romance, existing in Brooklyn, New York with my fiance, who you can call PB, or Patty Banga, if you're nasty. When I'm not writing and reading, I'm exploring the city, working at my day job, eating lots of yummy food and fussing over my kitten (and no, that's not a euphemism). Did I mention I have a dirtier mind than probably everyone you know?

I like to admire hot guys (don't we all?) and book boyfriends, cake and ice cream are my kryptonite. I can recite every word that was ever uttered on Friends, Family Guy, and How I Met Your Mother, red Gatorade is my lifeblood, and I love to sing, although I've been told I do it in a Cher voice for some reason.

If you tell me you like my books, I'll give you whatever you want. My readers are my friends, and I welcome anyone to find me on social media any time you want to talk books or sexy dudes!

Get at me:
authorNylaK@gmail.com
Instagram: @authorNylaK
Facebook: Author Nyla K
Twitter: @MissNylah
Goodreads: Nyla K
BookBub: @AuthorNylaK

Flipping Hot Fiction

ACKNOWLEDGMENTS

There's so much I want to say to everyone who's supported me so far in my journey as an author, and I'm sure I could write another epically long book just about all these fabulous people. Though I've been writing for years, I haven't been publishing long, and already I've met so many people, both in real life and online, who have given me the guts and the inspiration to keep writing and producing books that mean something, to me and hopefully others. The fact that anyone in the world would read these stories, let alone love them, fills me with more joy than you can ever know.

To my family and friends, who have had to deal with my flakiness over the last year, my dodging plans and staying cooped up in my apartment, writing and editing my heart out... I love you guys for understanding what this means to me. You truly get that this is something I need to do, and you don't get upset or balk at my writer-hermit ass, which is so very appreciated.

To my fiancé, Patrick... you more than anyone have to put up with my crazy mood-swings when I'm hunched over my laptop, grunting one-word answers at you. I know I don't need to apologize for not giving you as much attention as you deserved when Noah and Alex were taking up every ounce of it. But I will anyway. I'm sorry for every night you went to bed alone with me typing furiously, and I love you so much for every second you listened to me writing this book. And for how much you loved Noah and Alex and their story, as someone who doesn't really read at all, let alone romance novels. You pumped me up when I was still unsure about what I was doing with these two. I hope you know how much you'll always be my real-life book boyfriend.

To Julia of Evenstar Books, my formatter extraordinaire, and my incredible author friend who always deals with my ranting. And also deals with how dreadfully unorganized I am when it comes to putting together a manuscript on-time... You are a real champion for working on my books, because they're long as hell, and you manage to format them like a rockstar. You make my books look like they belong on shelves all over the world. Thank you so much for your talent. I love you, Julesies.

To Jada D'Lee, my eternal cover designer… You are such a genius with your work, it's almost unfathomable. And I know with this one I was such a picky bitch. But like you always do, you got right away how much Noah and Alex mean to me, and how I needed their cover to do them justice. And what can I say? You knocked it out of the park, as always. I wasn't kidding when I said you're stuck with me. Buckle up, girlfriend!

To Anastasia King, Alessandra Vitale, April Savells, Julie Embleton, Peggy Spencer, Alicia Fontaine, Mary Dean, Tabitha Bishop, and all my other amazing writer friends who have been here to support me in many ways, from talking to me about books and writing, to buying, reading, reviewing and promoting *my* books… You guys are so fantastic you make my heart hurt. I never in a million years would be able to do any of this without you, and I feel so blessed to have you badass girls in my corner. You're all Alex. For sure.

And to the authors who inspire me, and who have taken time out of their busy author-lives to talk to me and give me advice: Staci Hart, Penelope Douglas, Karina Halle, K Webster, BB Easton, Sierra Simone, Helena Hunting, and so so so many more I can't even name right now. You guys are celebrities to *us*. You're Noah. Hands down.

To all the bloggers and bookstagrammers who took a chance on this new author, and became my friends in the process. Who made edits, took beautiful pictures, and wrote glowing reviews of *my* books, just to name a few: Chelsea, Xandria, Merci, Emily, Ally, Cassidy, Jay, Julie, Elizabeth, Brittany, Charlene, Kasey, Luz, Nadia, Mia and everyone else on Instagram and Facebook who shared and helped promote this book and my others before it. I literally could not do this without you guys. I honestly hope you know just how much your support means to me. And I promise there will always be more books for you to love!

To my Street Team, and everyone who helps with the Flipping Hot Readers group on Facebook… Oh my God, you guys are the best. Rose, Elizabeth, Cindy, Tauna… All of you! I love you guys beyond words.

To my editor, and my betas… You know who you are ;) None of my books would be anything without you guys. Thank you for taking the time to read the many, many, *many* pages I produce, and sharing my enthusiasm for love stories that are real, raw, long and significant. You help ensure the fiction is flipping hot, and flipping CORRECT, and I'll never stop appreciating you.

And lastly, but never leastly, my readers. Anyone who has ever picked up one of my books and read it, loved it, and written a review… You guys give me life. And more importantly, you give my *characters* life. You bring them to life when you read their stories, and it's all an author could ever dream of. I will forever keep writing lengthy, hot-as-hell, trying, emotional, and judgement-free works of flipping hot fiction for you guys. I love you all so much, and I really hope you loved Alex and Noah as much as I do.

Thank you to anyone and everyone who believes in me and supports me the way Noah supports Alex. You guys are the prince to my dark fairy. Stay tuned for more Nyla K. I promise I'll keep it big ;)

Made in the USA
Middletown, DE
06 October 2022